# THE DEFIANT
# AND
# THE DAMNED

## THE DRAGON QUEEN #2

# EC GARRETT

Paperback & Ebook Cover by EC Garrett/Midnight Pages LLC

Interior Formatting & Design by EC Garrett/Midnight Pages LLC

Copyediting by Yarn Wyvern

Proofreading by Yarn Wyvern and Ruthie Bowles

Map of Ur Daoine by Reina Diaz and EC Garrett/Midnight Pages LLC

Map of Elysium by Shepengul

Interior Character Illustrations by Reina Diaz

Act 1-4 Illustrations by Nomad Visuals from Creative Market

eBook ISBN: 979-8-9890690-4-0

Paperback ISBN: 978-1-965919-06-4

*For those who do not fear the dark,*

*but feel at home within its shadowed grasp.*


*And for my friends & family;*

*I would fight Dragons and cross oceans to save you.*

# THE DRAGON QUEEN

**Series Reading Order**

The Forgotten and The Feared

The Broken and The Brave

The Defiant and The Damned

TDQ3 – Coming 2026

# A WARNING

The Dragon Queen series is set in a Grimdark, medieval fantasy world, with a high amount of violence, gore, and danger. All incidents involving animals are inspired by the real-life cruelty animals in our world experience every second of every day. If The Dragon Queen series was a movie, it would be rated R or NC-17 due to graphic violence, graphic sex, language, and dire situations. Proceed with caution and review the trigger warning list below before you dive in. If it all sounds good? Then let the Game begin.

*Triggers that are frequent are in **BOLD** and triggers that are extremely frequent are in **<u>BOLD AND UNDERLINED.</u>***

## HATE, DISCRIMINATION, & OPRESSION

Bullying, Classism, Hate Crimes, Homelessness, **Poverty**, Racism, **<u>Religious Persecution, Religious Commentary,</u>** **Sexism & Misogyny,** and Slavery & Indentured Servitude.

## ALCOHOL & DRUGS

**Alcohol Consumption,** Drug Consumption, **[Magical] Drugging,** and Inhalation of Smoke

## SEXUAL & ROMANTIC

**Age Gap, Begging,** Blow Jobs, **Dirty Talk,** Exhibitionism, **Fingering, Graphic Sex,** Power Dynamic Play, Primal Sex, and **Sapphic Yearning.**

## MENTAL HEALTH & SUICIDE

**Anxiety & Anxiety Attacks, Depression,** Dissociation & Dissociative Episodes, Intrusive thoughts, **Nightmares, Post Traumatic Stress Disorder,** Self-harm (off-page), Sleep Disorders, and **Suicidal Ideation.**

## BLOOD, INJURY, & MEDICAL

**Amputation, Blood & Gore Depiction,** Body Horror, [Animal] Cannibalism, **Dead Bodies & Body Parts,** Decapitation, **Dismemberment,** Emesis, **Eyeball Trauma,** Loss of Autonomy, Loss of Limb, Physical Injuries, **Scars,** Starvation & Dehydration, Weight Gain

## DEATH & LOSS

**Death of a friend, Death of a Parent & Guardian,** Death of a Partner & Spouse, Death of a Child, **Death of a Sibling, Grief & Loss Depiction,** and **Murder.**

## VIOLENCE & CRIME

Asphyxia, Strangulation & Suffocation, **Blackmail, Building Collapse, Captivity & confinement, Cults,** Explosions, **Fire & Arson,** Imprisonment &

**Incarceration, Interrogation, <u>Knife, Sword & Axe violence, Murder & Attempted Murder,</u> and Torture.**

## WAR & GENOCIDE

<u>**Colonialism, Imperialism,**</u> Refugee Displacement, Massacres & mass murder, and War themes & Military violence

## ANIMAL DEATH & CRUELTY

Animal Attack, **Animal Consumption, <u>Animal Cruelty & Abuse, Animal Death, Animal Illness & Injury,</u> Animal Skinning/Butchering,** Animal Testing & Experimentation, and Animal Auctions.

## NATURAL DISASTERS

**Earthquakes,** flash flooding, storms, and tsunamis,

*Important: This book ends on a cliffhanger.*

TWYN FELLS
THE ULSTER WALD
REBEL CAMP
THE PASS OF BRÓN MÓR
THE CAVE
NORTHLANDS
GRIMHEIM
ÖSTERHAMN
ABHYANN GHEAL RIVER
EAHMOND
WESTLANDS
MATRICIA
SAVARRE
CASTRA BATAVORUMM
KHANANET
ANDACIA
INFINIUM SANDS
BARDAKER
SOUTHLANDS
SAVONA

THE KINGDOM OF UR DAOINE
PANORMUS
THE ANNAG FOREST
CASTAEL LARYN
SERVO BAVA
NOVIOMAGUS
EASTLANDS
THE PORT OF NADES
MIDHEYM SEA
EAST TO ELYSIUM
SUD AZYL

# THE REGIONS OF UR DAOINE

## THE NORTHLANDS:

Twyn Fells

Eahmond

Grimheim

Österhamn

Karski

Keave

Panormus - *Army Stronghold*

## THE WESTLANDS:

Savarre

Roanne

Stavorden

Matrica – *Army Stronghold*

## THE SOUTHLANDS:

Andacia

Savona

Castra Batavorumm – *Army Stronghold*

Khananet

Bardaker

## THE EASTLANDS:

Sud Azyl

The Port of Nades

Sevro Bava

Noviomagus – *Navy Base*

# THE LANGUAGE

## CHARACTERS

**Aanad:** *uh-NOD*

**Achan:** *AH-ki*

**Amalia:** *uh-MAH-lee-uh*

**Amari:** *uh-MAR-ee*

**Basa:** *BAH-sa*

**Beatrice:** *BEE-uh-triss*

**Constantus:** *con-STAN-tus*

**Constantyn:** *con-STAN-teen*

**Davyn:** *DA-vin*

**Drystan:** *DRIS-tin*

**Duke Haestan:** *duke HASTE-in*

**Drayven:** *Dray-ven*

**Dyana:** *die-AN-uh*

**Fi:** *FEE*

**Ignautius:** *IG-nauseous*

**Ireyna:** *eye-REY-nuh*

**Jhon:** *John*

**Kairos:** *CAIRO-s*

**Keres:** *CARE-is*

**Kydis:** *KAI-diss*

**Livyathin:** *luh-VIE-uh-thin*

**Mara:** *MAR-uh*

**Mireille:** *MEER-ee-el*

**Morrigyn:** *MORE-ih-ghin*

**Nyall:** *NY-uhl*

**Ophiya:** *oh-FEE-yuh*

**Os:** *oz*

**Remus:** *REE-mus*

**Ryu:** *REE-you*

**Soren:** *SORE-in*

**Syska:** *SIS-kuh*

**Vesimyr:** *VES-uh-meer*

**Vyktor:** *VIC-ter*

**Wytch:** *wich*

## PLACES

**Abhaynn Gheal:** *ah-VEEN geel*

**Andacia:** *ahn-DAH-see-uh*

**Annag:** *AHH-nug*

**Bardaker:** *Barduh-CUR*

**Brón Mór:** *BRON more*

**Castael Laryn:** *KAY-stil LAIR-in*

**Castra Batavorumm:** *Cahst-ruh Bahda-VORE-um*

**Eahmond:** *AYE-mend*

**Elysium:** *uh-LEE-see-um*

**Grimheim:** *grim-HIGH-m*

**Infinium:** *in-FIN-ee-um*

**Karski:** *CAR-ski*

**Keave:** *KEEV*

**Khananet:** *KAH-nah-net*

**Matricia:** *muh-TREE-see-uh*

**Midheym:** *MID-high-m*

**Nades:** *NAY-deez*

**Novomagus:** *NO-voh-MAHG-is*

**Österhamn:** *OO-ster-hahm*

**Panormus:** *puh-NOR-mus*

**Roanne:** *Rohn*

**Savarre:** *suh-VAR*

**Savona:** *suh-VOE-nuh*

**Servo Bava:** *SER-voh BAH-vah*

**Stavorden:** *stuh-VORE-din*

**Sud Azyl:** *sood a-ZEAL*

**Twyn Fells:** *twin fells*

**Ulster Wald:** *UHL-ster vahld*

**Ur Daoine:** *ur DANE-ya*


## OTHER TERMS

**A gahrá:** *ah GAH-ruh*

**Archidna:** *are-KID-nuh*

**Arkaydian:** *are-KAY-dee-in*

**Arkaydia:** *are-KAY-dee-uh*

**Ascidian:** *uh-SID-ee-in*

**Beastkyn:** *BEAST-kin*

**Bloodwyng:** *BLOOD-wing*

**Demis:** *DEM-ees*

**Dreamweavyr:** *DREAM-weev-er*

**Elysian:** *uh-LEE-see-in*

**Ethelen:** *ETHEL-en*

**Ether:** *EE-thur*

**Lir:** *leer*

**Macha:** *MAH-kuh*

**Magyka:** *MA-jik-uh*

**Magyk:** *MA-jik*

**Neiman:** *NEE-man*

**Oryx:** *OR-icks*

**Puggō:** *POO-gogh*

# THE DEFIANT
## AND
# THE DAMNED

THE DEFIANT AND THE DAMNED HAS A PLAYLIST CODE AT THE START OF EACH PART. HOWEVER, FOR CONVENIENCE, BELOW IS A CODE FOR A MASTER PLAYLIST.

SCAN FOR THE OFFICIAL TD&TD READING PLAYLIST

# PROLOGUE

*"Boys? I've asked you to blow out your candles and go to bed once already. I'm not asking again," Mara Ashcroft scolds her sons playfully, in the way mothers tend to do. Each of her sons climbs into their small twin bed on either side of the even smaller bedroom.*

*After the death of Mara's husband, the family moved into a small cottage. Small enough that Mara alone could afford its cost.*

*Cayden's bed is on the right and Baelor's is on the left. But it's far past bedtime, and their whispers have been getting louder and louder.*

*"Mum!" a voice calls, and Mara sighs. Work at the bakery has been exhausting, and all Mara wanted to do was sit by the fire and eat her dinner in peace. But being a mother came first, and Mara wouldn't have it any other way.*

*"Alright," she whispers, poking her head into their room. "What's wrong?*

*"We're scared, Mum," Cayden admits in a small voice that suits a child of four. Mara blinks, surprised.*

*Scared? Why is he scared?*

*Mara pads into their room, wrapping her thin robe around her skinny body. Food was expensive, especially in the North. The cold made it nearly impossible to grow anything at all. Mara takes a seat on her youngest boy's bed, wrapping her arms around Cayden as Baelor grabs his blanket and joins them. Both cling to her just as they did when they were babes.*

*"What happened? Why are you scared?" Mara asks gently, her concern growing.*

*Baelor, the elder of the two by a single year, looks away, his cheeks red with embarrassment. Cayden, not yet old enough to be embarrassed, responds. "We're scared to go to sleep."*

*Mara caresses Cayden's back, confused. "My love, nothing is going to happen to you while you sleep. There's no need to worry. If nothing happened, then sleep should come easily."*

*"Mum, you're not listening," Baelor turns and meet's Mara's gaze, his brown eyes scared. "It's not safe for us to go to sleep. The schoolteacher said so. If we sleep, the Gray Wytch will steal us from our beds and eat our hearts!" he protests.*

*Mara sighs, "Darling, there's no such thing as Wytches. There never has been. The Gray Wytch is a story and just that."*

*"But-but Wytches are real, Mum. It's not just a story. Greyson Farrow said so! He-he said that his mum's sister's friend knows someone who was taken by her. It's real mum! It's real and-and now she's going to kill us."*

*Mara wraps both boys in her arms, trying not to laugh. Even in the remote Northlands, gossip spares none, she thinks.*

*"It's just a story, darling," Mara repeats.*

*Her boys are safe. They're okay. Everything will be fine. Saying those words over and over in her head kept Mara calm.*

*It's the truth, after all. Nothing was coming for them.*

*"I think it's real, Mum," Baelor whispers. "Even our teacher thinks so!"*

*"And what exactly did your teacher tell you?" Mara says, suddenly furious that their schoolteacher is putting such fear into her children. There's enough fear and hurt in this world. Why make it worse?*

*"Sh-she told us the story of the Gray Wytch. Then we sang a rhyme about it. The teacher said if we sing the song before bed, the Gray Wytch will spare us."*

*Mara would strangle their teacher.*

*"Nobody is coming for you, darling. Please trust me," Mara says firmly. "Sing me this song and then we will all go to sleep, alright? I'll stay with you both tonight to show you that there's nothing to worry about."*

*The boys protest, but eventually settle down as they all squish together into the tiny bed. Something which only works since the boys are still quite small. Cayden and Baelor take deep breaths and then begin to sing, their small voices in sync.*

**Beware, beware the Gray Wytch of the Wood,**

**With her pack of beasts and bloody gray hood.**

**Beware, beware, and behave with all your might,**

**For if you don't, the Gray Wytch will come tonight.**

*Mara sighs. She's heard the song before. Damn that teacher.*

*"Well, you have sung the song so there will be no one coming tonight, or else they'll face my wrath!" She holds up her hands in make-believe claws and pretends to be scary, and the boys break out in giggles.*

*"I'll always protect you, okay? Nothing's going to happen."*

*"We did sing the song," the elder one reminds the younger.*

*"True," the younger one sighs. "Thanks, mum. We'll try to sleep."*

*"Of course, darling. I love you."*

*"Love you too," the boys repeat.*

*When Mara went to bed that night, nightmares plagued her dreams. The next morning, she went to wake both of her boys, but when she opened the room, she felt a cold breeze and noticed the windows were propped open. And their beds? Their beds were cold and empty.*

# PART ONE:
# THE DIVIDED

# CHAPTER 1
## AMALIA

They say the sky used to be full of Dragons—and for a brief moment two years ago, it was full of Dragons once more. But the Dragons left as quickly as their wings could carry them, for the land that once, long ago, was a safe haven had *changed.*

The Fae changed it. Turned it into a place of death and ruin.

The Dragons escaped Ur Daoine, digging their way out with bloody teeth and claws, each carrying fragile bundles in their jaws. Precious, precious bundles full of eggs and hatchlings too small to fly.

Once free from their prison far beneath the earth, the Dragons began the long journey East across the Midheym Sea, leaving the Fae and Ur Daoine behind for the first time in over five centuries.

Stories began arriving on Ur Daoine's shores in the weeks that followed. Stories of large, scaled bodies falling into the sea. Fishermen, who's boats were nearly overturned, spread tales of the winged beasts sowing a path of destruction along the east.

No one knows how many actually made it to Elysium, the legendary homeland of the Dragons.

Elysium. A supposed mystical island, full of Dragons in all sizes and colors. Many question if it's real, but those who live along the coastlines know the truth. It's impossible to ignore the accounts of fishermen getting lost or turned around when they head too far East, with no explanation of how or why.

Not all Dragons left Ur Daoine. The Dragonguard was left ravaged—most killed by the Beastkyn known as Remus Ostia. The ones that were left were young. Still dangerous, but not as battle hardened as the others.

If only we had known the truth of things.

With Achan Drayven dead and the High Council decimated, the Kingdom should have been plunged into chaos.

We thought the Fae were the ones who broke our world—we were wrong.

The Fae *lied*.

Immediately upon the destruction of the High Council, a new government began. It was formed not of a Council but of a singular, secular leader.

*The Archmage.*

He claims Constantyn spoke to him and chose *him* above all others as the rightful leader of our world. So, the Archmage took up the dropped mantle, and began his reign as Sovereign. His first act was to make it illegal to pray to any God other than Constantyn.

No symbols, no words, not even a thought of prayer. Sol Constantus is all. According to Him, at least. An Elf is running our Kingdom into the ground. The forests have started to shrink at a blinding pace. Some trees died from the inside out, rotten to the core. Storms are destroying the Coasts, with the Eastlands taking the brunt of it. Earthquakes shake the continent with a growing frequency. Sandstorms rage over the Infinium Desert at a higher rate.

We tried to help—*I* tried to help.

I thought we would make things better. That maybe it would finally be enough. Instead, I lost *everything* in the process, and all we did was make the situation worse.

Amalia Roth died in the Arena that day. That's what the world thinks, at least. A part of me *did* die that day.

Two years later, whispers of a new kind of monster begin to stir throughout the towns bordering the Ulster Wald. A monster in a dark gray cloak, and her pack of rabid Dyre wolves.

Fae soldiers following the Archmage have been stationed in every town within Ur Daoine. But turmoil is everywhere. The Dragonguard patrol our shores; though for what, I'm not sure. The Rulka Empire to the South has always left us alone. They once held treaties with the leaders of Arkaydia, so as soon as Arkaydia fell, they retreated, refusing any communication with the newly formed High Council.

Everyone is scared—and fear does strange things to people.

Strange, terrible things.

They *should* be afraid.

For there are many monsters in this world—

—and it's time to remind the world that *I* am one of them.

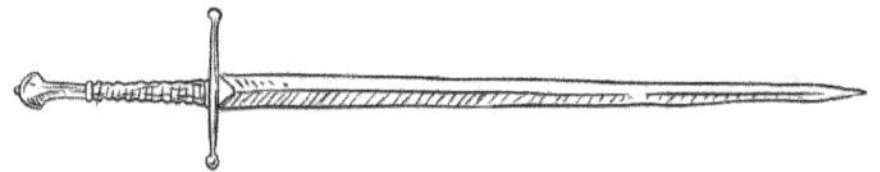

"Oy! Slag! What's taking you so long?"

The voice is slurred and belligerent, just on the cusp of violence. The type of volatile anger one only achieves when under the influence of wine and mead.

"Sorry about that." The door closes behind me as I fix a doe-eyed look on my face, forcing my jaw to unclench.

*Interested.* That's the look I'm going for.

"I was just freshening up," I continue as I smile, batting my eyelashes, "I have something to show you."

He doesn't notice how the smile doesn't match my eyes. He doesn't notice much of anything other than my tits, which are shoved up nearly to my chin thanks to the corset I have on, making them look twice as big as they already are.

"I've got something to show you too, sweetheart," the male growls, showing small fangs. Long white hair covers his pointed ears, and his armor is discarded at the end of the bed.

*Fae.* Imperial Fae, actually. Has some air magyk abilities, but the wine has taken care of that.

The room is small but comfortable. Nothing fancy. Just four wooden walls and a straw roof, both of which are strewn with the occasional mold spot—something common in the Northlands. The straw-filled mattress rustles as I crawl on top of the bed, straddling the male. He grabs my hips, yanking me down until his hard cock is throbbing against me.

"You have too many fuckin' clothes on," the male snarls, tearing my corset off, which sends buttons flying across the room with small *pings.* My tunic beneath follows as soon as it's freed.

*That was expensive.* I keep this thought to myself and let him continue to rip my clothes off, although he nearly sends me tumbling to the floor when he attempts to pull my pants down. Annoyance—tinged with something much darker—fills me. When my clothes are in tatters, the male makes his move.

"Fuckin' peasant clothes," he grunts. The smell of his alcohol-tinged breath mixed with sweat wafts around the room.

I click my tongue. "Careful."

I don't particularly care if he feels my sharp edges.

The male laughs, his already red eyes bloodshot and swollen, "You're not here for me to be *careful.* You're here to do whatever the fuck I want. Now show me that cunt I paid for."

His hand reaches down to cup me and my stomach fills with simmering rage. The male removes his hand and rubs his engorged cock across my entrance. There is nothing remotely sexy or smooth about his actions.

Just as he's about to slam his cock into me, just as I begin to feel the slight *stretch* of his presence, I put my hand on his shoulder.

"Wait," I whisper.

The male growls and pulls my hair, "Shut the fuck up."

"But I told you." I flash him a dark smile. "I have something to show you."

My heart does not race. My breath does not stutter.

Anxiety does not plague me as I slice my dagger through his member.

There is just anger, and within it, I drown.

Anger is easier than the gutting pain of grief. Anger I can *use.*

The drunk Imperial Fae beneath me never sees the dagger. Not until I slice it right through his sweaty cock. The severed member falls into my waiting hand.

"I would choke you with it, but it's so *small.*" I lift it up to inspect the cock, pursing my lips in disappointment. "There's really not much to choke on though, is there?"

I toss the bloody cock at his face and the Fae lets out a hysterical, high-pitched scream as the bed beneath us becomes soaked in his blood.

There was a time when I would loathe this. Despite the pains of my childhood, a part of me deep down would dislike this sort of torture. That part of me is dead.

I let the male go on for a few seconds as his body writhes in pain beneath me. But my patience is low, and he's been a fucking *cunt* all night long. I'm tired of playing nice, so I lean forward and plunge my dagger straight through the center of his throat.

"Ah, ah," I tsk, as the male begins choking on the blood gushing out of the wound. "Now, that won't do, will it?"

I pull out the blade and the blood flows harder. Slapping my hand over the wound, I lower the wall keeping my magyk in check. Deep within me, shadows and fire *roar* with need. I barely have to pull.

*Heal,* I order the flesh, and the flesh obeys, reattaching itself with wet, squelching sounds. Between his legs, I heal the wound just enough to stop him from bleeding out.

I *could* regrow his cock, but he doesn't deserve it. Not after what he *did.*

The male twitches as I reattach his spinal cord, flailing and slapping at my arms with wet grunts. I dismount his half-naked, blood-covered body and pull my torn pants up, using the Fae's belt to secure them. I throw the shredded tunic over my head and the white fabric quickly becomes stained with blood.

Without a word, I grab the male by his hair and yank him to the floor. He falls on the hard wood with a *thud,* moaning at the way his nose crunched when he went down face first.

"Whoops," I laugh. I drag the male's bleeding, naked body across the floor of the small room, streaks of blood following in our wake.

He fights me, struggling, but I only healed some of his wounds. The others are of no concern, and they're doing well to keep him malleable.

I open the door and pull him into the silent hallway. I drag his flailing, bloody body down the hall, navigating towards the stairs. The male is too busy whimpering like a pathetic worm to notice the lack of conversation from the tavern below.

The complete and utter silence. The male grabs my ankles, trying to push me over as the wound on his groin starts to clot, but I kick his hands away.

He grabs me again and my patience snaps further.

There is no time for him to react when I stomp on his right hand. Bones crunch beneath my boots and the male screams and the scent of urine floods the air as he wets himself, the liquid seeping out of the bloody hole between his legs.

"Pathetic," I sneer. The male keeps screaming as I step off his now-shattered hand.

**"YOU FUCKING BITCH! YOU'LL DIE FOR THIS, WHORE!"** he shouts at the top of his lungs, clutching his broken hand to his chest.

"How *adorable,*" I purr, looking down at him. "You think I'm going to let you live."

The male opens his blood-covered mouth as he pushes off the floor, trying to kneel. "I'LL KILL YO—"

His words are cut off before he can finish his sentence as I bend down and stab my dagger through his chest, puncturing his left lung. I push to grab his now bloodstained-red hair and shove him down the stairs, kicking his back so he picks up speed, bouncing down the hard wooden steps and crashing with a soft *thump.*

Soft, because something cushioned his fall.

Something...*sticky.*

I watch in amusement as the Imperial Fae male pushes up on shaky, scraped-up arms and takes in the scene before him.

There's a moment of silence. Then his breath hitches as he realizes that his hands aren't on the floor, but the dead bodies of his companions.

*All* of them.

Grabbing the jacket I discarded earlier, I slide my arms into the bloody sleeves. A high-pitched, panicked noise explodes out of him. He looks around the room and begins shaking.

"I told you," I say as I walk down the steps with a casual pace, "I had something to show you. You made my night, really. I thought it was only going to be *you* here. But look at what you *brought me?*" I motion to the dozens of bodies on the floor. "So many *gifts.*"

The male cranes his head, turning to look at me as I descend the wooden staircase and remove the bracelet containing the glamour on my left wrist.

I don't need a mirror to know what was once black hair is lightening into a dark, charcoal gray that flakes with ash as if it were made of burning embers. I don't need a mirror to know that what once were green eyes are now a pale blue, so light they're almost silver. And I most certainly don't need a mirror to know that a pink, faded scar now trails down my jaw.

"You," the male whispers in horror. "You're supposed to be dead. They said you died!"

I flash a cold smile. "I did."

*Heal,* I order his flesh again as I walk down the stairs. My magyk obeys, rushing into the male and commanding his lungs to reknit. The male screams, struggling to his feet as his wounds heal. The act of flesh and nerves knitting back together is quite painful, I've come to learn. He slips and falls to his knees, unable to catch his footing on the blood-slicked floor.

"Do you remember me?"

"Fuck you!" the male shouts.

I shake my head. "Wrong answer."

With a blur, I reappear by his side. I kick at the back of his legs, sending him to the blood-soaked floor.

Bending down, I bare my teeth in his face. "You were there that day, in the stables. You were stationed there the day they killed my horse."

"I don't remember!" He screams and I flip him over, smiling at the fear in his eyes.

"Then let me remind you," I purr, before slamming my raised fingers down on his eyes. I puncture them, pushing down until my thumbs meet his orbital sockets. They *squish* beneath my fingers as blood drips down his face.

I ignore the wails of pain lean down, whispering in his ear, "I did this to your friend, that day. Don't you remember? You scream just like he did."

The male starts sobbing openly and disgust fills me.

"It-it was just a horse," he cries, moaning in pain. "Just a stupid horse!"

I nod. "You do remember then."

I withdraw my hands, bloody and covered in pieces of flesh.

**Heal,** I order and the male screams again as I reform his eyes.

"I want you to see this last part," I whisper, as he moans in pain. "The ending is my favorite."

Sobbing and twitching in pain, the male's eyes eventually form and I nod again.

"Good."

With a sigh I let my magyk out. A circle of Hellfyre surrounds us and I pull hard enough on my magyk that I know my eyes glow silver and blue, matching the tips of the flames surrounding us.

"I want you to remember this," I smile, "I want you to see my face, because it's the last thing you're ever going to see."

Which is when I grab my swords—*Morrigyn's swords*—from where I left them by the bottom of the stairs and shove Neiman right through his motherfucking Imperial Fae skull as I unleash a scream from the depths of my shattered soul.

Pain and grief and a fury so great I fear I might never recover explodes in his face as my flames devour his body and the limp bodies of his *friends* around us.

I stare into his eyes as the light dims within and he goes limp.

Dead.

"That's for Taran, you disgusting piece of shit." I spit in his burnt face and pull the sword out, brain matter squishing against my blade, and with my other arm, I swing Macha hard, cutting his head off in one fell swoop. The head hits the floor, bouncing off another prone body.

I find a mug of ale, grabbing the wooden mug and bringing the room-temperature drink to my blood-covered lips. The taste of malt and iron mix on my tongue. It's disgusting, but the faint buzz I get after chugging the entire mug is worth it as my pain and anger softens, numbing into nothingness.

Around me, flames sizzle and burn, turning the bodies on the floor to *ash*.

I grab a second mug and chug again, nearly gagging at the taste. But it's gone in seconds and the buzz increases.

Like most immortals, I cannot get drunk. However, I'm only half-immortal. Arkaydians were the most human-like Magyka to exist. Easily able to pass for them. It's the Arkaydian side of me that allows me to feel the buzz of alcohol and windweed. I cannot get drunk or high, my metabolism is too fast for that, but I can get a small piece of it, allowing me to get a little tipsy.

There's a whimpering behind the counter and I realize I'm not alone. With a grunt, I turn and shove the dead body of one of the Fae soldiers to the floor, leaving it to my flames to eat up like a hungry inferno.

"Come on out," I call. There's more whimpering. Sighing, I step over the dead bodies and make my way behind the tavern bar, where two older women are quivering. I take a step towards them and they flinch.

Their fear stabs me in the heart.

*If I look down, will I see it? Pumping and bleeding on the dirty wood floor?*

I step back, giving them room to stand. They stay frozen, whimpering louder, and something in me snaps. I summon more Hellfyre into my fist. "Get out or die. Your choice."

I know I should be nice, but I no longer have it in me to care. They'll hate me anyways, regardless of what I do or say. One look at the carnage I wrought, and their minds will be made up.

Behind me, my flames swell towards the ceiling as it continues consuming the inn itself.

They shoot to their feet and scurry out the door, tripping on the dead bodies and nearly face planting a few times due to the blood-covered floor.

The door shuts behind me and I turn, walking through the center of town.

With a breath, I feed more magyk into my flames. There's a beat of silence and the tavern explodes. I walk towards the front, leaving the collapsing building with numb calmness. Screams echo from around the town as debris shoots into the air. A huge gust of wind hits, banking the flames briefly.

Then the screams get louder.

I glance over my shoulder, watching with a dark smile as a bright red Dragon lands on the inn, crushing the burning wood beneath her claws.

*Ryu.*

She roars, her copper and silver eyes bright against her bright red scales. With a dramatic flair, the red Dragon extends her wings, sending embers flying.

Ryu is completely and utterly perfect. Not a scar or a scrape on a single scale. Every time I look at her like this, I'm reminded why the Dragons have always been considered Gods. They should all have had her freedoms. To have never known a life behind bars.

*This* is what Dragons are meant to be.

In the quiet moments when my feelings rush back and the grief is so heavy I think I might crawl into a ball, something else returns too.

Anger—and a reminder of why I'm doing this. A reminder of what I *lost*.

Ryu is the anchor keeping my sanity afloat. Even in her beauty, Ryu is the most terrifying creature I've ever seen. There is no question who the apex predator is here. Who—or what—is the most dangerous being around.

I watch as she approaches, stomping through the crumbling, burning building. There's a pang of distant pain within me like the ringing of a gong. It clenches my heart and sends chills up my spine.

Two years ago, I saw a sight so similar to this.

Two years, and yet it was a different lifetime.

Their faces flash through my head.

*Dark hair. Gold eyes.* The pain is so great and the weight of the grief is so heavy, the moment I allow both of them to flood my body, it threatens to consume me and leave nothing left.

Ryu pounces on a falling ember, getting distracted. It's so childlike, I'm reminded that despite her huge size and rapid maturation that began six months ago, she's still a child.

All the knowledge in the world can't erase that.

I find the bright light of her mind and connect with her easily. The screams turn to shouts for help as buildings burn all around Keave, turning half the town into ash.

Not all of it, though. Just the Imperial Fae strongholds.

*"Time to go."*

*"Spoilsport."* Ryu stomps towards me with *sass* in every step. I can't help but consider just how wrong I was.

Ryu is about half the size of Bloodwyng, the Dragon who landed in Twyn Fells two years ago, but she's assured me she will continue growing for the next decade. According to her memories, the females of her line are Dragons of great size. I gasp silently at the pain stabbing into my chest at the thought of her mother—at the thought of my friend.

*"Come on, fuzz-butt is waiting,"* Ryu says gently, sensing my pain. She's been able to do that since the day we met. Somehow, she is minutely tuned to my emotions.

*"You know he hates when you call him that,"* I respond but she just snorts, uncaring as she stomps past me. For a Dragon of her size, you'd think the ground would be shaking. Instead, she moves silently, like a ghost in the wind. I've never seen anything like it. But I do know who taught her to move like this, and why.

*"Then perhaps he should be less grumpy—and fuzzy!"* she says indignantly, but her tone is teasing. *"Try getting fur up your nose and then see how it feels."*

*"Been there, done that,"* I chuckle lightly. *"Just don't come crying to me when he hears you call him that and bites you in the ass...again."*

Ryu rolls her eyes.

*"See you back at the den. I need to catch dinner."*

The red Dragon speeds up until walking becomes running. Something most Dragons aren't skilled in. But then again, Ryu does not fly. She...runs. And she can hover a little. But real flight? The thought *terrifies* her.

A year ago, when the growth spurts hit, Ryu also received the rest of her magic. Through it, she received the memories of her matriline.

She slept for two weeks as her body rapidly doubled in size. Her first words once she woke up will haunt me until the end of my days.

*"She fell."*

That's all she said. But it was all she *needed* to say. Two single words and I knew.

She saw Kydis' last memories. She saw her mother die.

Ryu stopped trying to fly after that. I asked her about it a few times, but she made it clear she doesn't want to talk about it. As much as I wish to see her soaring through the clouds, I cannot force her to do something she doesn't want to do. Nor should I.

I made so many mistakes with...*Dyana*. My empty heart shudders at her name.

I can't—I can't do it. I can't even think about her or it will send me to my knees.

So I don't think, and I don't feel. I don't feel anything at all. The windweed helps. It dulls the ache in my heart from the gaping void in my soul.

*"That won't work forever, cub,"* Virgyl's deep voice booms in my head as I approach him, Ryu disappearing silently into the forest. The only sign of her is the slight shaking to the trees.

"It works for now," I say aloud, my voice numb. Reaching into my pocket, I rip off a small piece of windweed and place it on my tongue.

Not actually a weed, the bark contains a mild poison that numbs pain and emotion. Northlanders have kept windweed a secret for decades. Most think it's impossible to find, but there are windweed trees near the cave, allowing me to stock up.

The bark tastes of clove and cinnamon. It's surprisingly nice. Instantly, the grief lessens and I can breathe again.

I grab a hold of Virgyl's thick neck scruff and hoist myself on his back. He smells like the forest. "Come on, let's go home, old fuzz-butt."

Virgyl sighs, *"Teenagers. You were worse."*

I blink and pinch him lightly.

His fur is so thick that he doesn't even feel it.

*"Did you get it done?"* he asks, head tilting.

"I did," I answer in a hollow voice.

*"One more name off your list."* He adds carefully, *"What will you do when it's done?"*

"Leave it," I snap and instantly regret it. With a deep breath I lean down and wrap my arms around his neck, whispering in his ear, "I'm sorry. I didn't mean to snap at you. I'll...figure it out when the time comes."

*"I know, cub. I know."*

Then we're off. Racing through the forest so fast I have to close my eyes. It's times like this I remember Virgyl is no normal wolf.

My nose is frozen by the time we get back to the cave. We spent hours racing through the forest, chasing the midnight hour—and making sure we weren't followed.

A few of Virgyl's younger cubs joined us halfway in. They ran alongside us, nipping at my ankles playfully. His mate Syska stayed behind with the pack Beta, Virgyl's daughter Beatrice, and the youngest cubs.

Ryu ambles out of the forest, her snout covered in bits of fur and blood, and burps loudly.

I sigh. My turn.

I quickly heat up yesterday's soup on the makeshift cave stove, which is really just a lowered fire pit with a metal grill on top. The smells of roasting vegetables and warm, herby broth fills the air, as the wolves play in the background.

Virgyl takes a seat next to me, leaning his huge head on my shoulder.

We stayed like that all evening. Together we watched as Ryu crawled into the cave, heading towards the back to rinse the blood off her scales in the hot springs.

I have Nyall Drayven to thank for that.

Nyall fucking Drayven.

I sigh, my peace ruined—as if it was ever there to begin with. Even thinking about his name makes me burn with anger.

Nyall made copious additions to the cave I call home; an expanded ceiling to fit Ryu's quickly growing Dragon body, an opening to the natural hot springs within the mountain, a larger eating area, side rooms, etc.

In our grief, I dove inward. I didn't speak for weeks.

But Nyall...dove into work, draining his magyk every single day with his carving spells. His only focus was making the cave more suitable for living and, more specifically, for hiding a giant Dragon.

The Prince was used to more modern means of living, so he *made* his surroundings modern too.

The wards around the cave are five times stronger than they used to be. No one will ever find us, thanks to the addition of Nyall's spells.

Then he did what everyone always does.

He *left*.

Virgyl licks my cheek, snapping me out of it. *"You're grinding your teeth, cub. It hurts my old ears."*

I cough a laugh. Genuine, but sad.

*"Sorry. I didn't realize."*

Virgyl licks my cheek again, *"You were thinking about them again, weren't you?"*

I sigh, feeling the weight and exhaustion of grief. *"Which 'them' do you mean? There are so many to choose from."*

*"Any of them. All of them. The ones no longer here."*

I nod. *"Yeah. I try not to. But it's just..."*

*"I understand."* My furry friend doesn't press for more information; he doesn't ask for more details.

I take a moment to ladle the hot soup into a wooden bowl and grab a spoon, tearing off some bits of stale bread from a few days old baguette I stole.

Virgyl lays at my feet, and I set my soup down briefly to take off my shoes so that his fur can warm my aching feet.

He's been in my life for almost eight decades. We've spent countless evenings like this, curled up together in some way, while his packmates and children play nearby.

The pack sleeps soundly that evening.

Dozens of generations of wolves lay around us. No one ventures this far into the Ulster Wald anymore, not since the first rumors of the Gray Wytch began making their way around northland towns.

Because they've been left alone, the Dyre Wolves should have flourished, and they did. Slowly.

When I met Virgyl, he had a pack of two dozen. Eight decades later and the pack has grown to be well over two hundred, but the past few pack births have...*failed*. I know Virgyl is concerned about his family.

The magyk is draining from the land, and all of Ur Daoine's inhabitants are affected—Dyre Wolves included. Goosebumps rise into existence on my arms at the thought of their morning song, the haunting howls echoing through the trees when a newborn wolf passes.

It's a sound I'll never forget.

The first time Ryu heard it was two moon cycles after we'd arrived on that horrible winter day. It was Nyall's first time hearing the song, too. The little red hatchling panicked, overwhelmed. She could *feel* the pain in their song. More so than Nyall or I could. We curled around her, trying to calm her down. Nyall whispered calming platitudes, which turned into stories of Aanad and how the Prince first met the Oryx. I stroked her soft, warm scales and we'd fall asleep there, the three of us cuddled together.

In those moments, it was almost enough to forget the pain. *Almost.*

Ryu is too big to curl up in bed with me now, so a few moons prior, I moved my mattress out into the open living area so that she can curl around me. *Her* request. Though I didn't mind when she asked; I had already been thinking about it. Even asleep, Ryu's scales are warm to the touch. There's no need for a heat source when you have a Dragon around.

The next morning, she kindly doesn't mention how I tossed and turned, or how I woke up screaming their names, the way I do every night.

Nor does she bring up the way I know I look exhausted.

I can feel it.

Every person I've lost...

I *feel* it. Like it's aging not just my mind but also my body.

I wear the trauma in my bones and bleed out the pain. Every step I take, they're there.

The pain is infinite.

Ryu rubs her nose against my body, trying not to shove me over in the process. I wrap my arms around her, reaching as far as I can—which isn't far—in a makeshift hug.

*"Love you,"* she whispers.

*"Love you back."*

I know what she wants to say. I can feel it. I don't know whether it's our long proximity to each other, or something new—I don't know enough about Dragons to know one way or the other—but I've started to be able to feel Ryu's emotions without having to reach with my magyk.

"I'm going to go pick some berries by the stream," I tell her and pat her on the snout. She huffs and follows behind me, like a giant, scaled protector. The wolves are gone, patrolling their territory of the woods, although I spy a couple females who stayed back with the youngest cubs. Many of them choose to stay away from me, untrusting of humans no matter how much Virgyl assures them I'm safe.

I get it.

People are capable of such evil, such cruelty.

I don't blame them for not trusting me—

—they shouldn't.

# CHAPTER 2
## MIRIELLE

It's so quiet beneath the surface.

Warm water caresses my skin as the surf crashes above me. Shadows constantly block the sun as Dragons fly far overhead. Small, colorful schools of fish swim past, darting through the tall kelp leaves floating around me.

*I wish I could stay here.*

Out there, I am lost. Adrift without a tether and caught in a raging current.

Dyana *hates* me.

The woman I loved, whose dead, cold body I carried in my arms for *days* on the journey to Elysium, the woman who I sat next to for *two years,* praying to Lir that she woke up—she hates me.

It's been four weeks since she woke up. Four weeks since she screamed at me. We haven't spoken since. I've tried and she ignored me.

For two years, I watched her. Tracing the lines of her face, trying to memorize them. Two years of hoping she would wake up.

Vesimyr wouldn't speak to me, but some of the others did.

*"The girl won't wake up. Vesimyr is old and his magic weakened. Do not trust him. Mourn her and move on."*

I cried myself to sleep that night, and the nights that followed.

This, though? Her miraculous survival, followed by her subsequent hatred? This feels worse than the pain of realization that Dyana might never wake up. My centuries of age scream, *"You're being dramatic! Suck it up!"* But my heart disagrees. My heart *hurts.*

On top of that, I am a prisoner in a foreign land. The rules as we know it no longer exist.

The Dragons are not at all like the legends said, and the Elysium Dragons are vastly different from those that spent centuries being tormented in Ur Daoine. To see a healthy Dragon was such a shock, I was rendered speechless. I knew the Ur Daoine Dragons were in bad shape, especially after the long journey. But *Gods,* to see them next to a healthy, wild Dragon broke me. The Elysium Dragons are dangerous. They think all other beings are lesser, treating us like evil pests. Something which I've never heard of a Dragon doing before. Not even in the scrolls.

If I am a prisoner, the Dragons of Elysium are the judges, the juries, and the executioners.

**"If you leave here,"** the Sene Skal said to me the day we arrived, **"we will eat you."**

All of the Ur Daoine Dragons were nearly unconscious when the huge blue Dragon descended upon us, its scales a resplendent navy that glimmered like the deep ocean. It was nearly as large as Kydis had been. How I had trembled as it opened its mouth and described the ways in which they would tear us apart and feast on our flesh if we left.

**"Ignautius,"** one of the other Dragons whispered.

The Sene Skal, Regent of Elysium.

The Dragonfear he wielded was so strong, I nearly lost control of my bladder after looking into his silver eyes for more than two seconds.

Vesimyr, who had only spoken to me once telepathically, turned to me when Ignautius left and whispered, *"This isn't right."* I'm not even sure if he meant to say it to me. He hasn't spoken since. He only talks to *her.*

My home, my friends, everything I had is gone. There is no rebellion here, no Prince with a plan to save us.

The Dragons told me to find a job within the palace so they could keep an eye on me. With my staff, Forsaken, broken and buried beneath the Arena stones, I decided I would teach myself blacksmithing and make a new one. Lucky for me, the head blacksmith is Demis, or at least I think that's what he is. I'm still not sure. He's definitely not human. That much I could tell. Kairos is his name.

For the past two years, I've worked at the forge as his pupil, learning how to make weapons so that eventually, I could make a new Forsaken. The only thing I will have from my past. In between shifts, I come out here to the beach beneath the castle and swim. Behind the castle, far in the distance, an active volcano spits lava and fire.

Apparently, some of the Dragons like to swim in it, and many make their nests near the lava fields. Yet the royal family lived in the castle, which now is occupied by the Sene Skal and his cohorts. After a year of pressing for answers, Kairos finally told me about what's going on in Elysium. When Kydis was captured, the regent took power. At first, he claimed to be keeping the throne safe for his queen. Then a century passed, and he stopped claiming anything but control and power.

If Kydis' hatchling is alive, the Dragons of Elysium would not welcome her and allow her to sit on the throne. A war would break out, and Elysium would win.

The royal castle—if it can even be called a castle—overlooks the beach from a tall hill. It's easily three times the size of the Black Citadel. It's bright where the Black Citadel was brooding. All white and ivory and brown. Everything was built to Dragon size, making those of us on two legs look so tiny we might as well be ants in their eyes.

My lungs begin to burn but I ignore it.

Now that I'm living near the water again, I've been building up my endurance and swimming every day. I can hold my breath for nearly half an hour now. It's going to take years to build up enough breath strength to be able to swim under the cloud border protecting Elysium.

The giant wall of white fluffy clouds circled the large island. The Dragons monitored the sky, but they ignored the ocean beneath.

That's how I'll get out of here.

I'll fucking swim all the way there if I have to. It might kill me, but I refuse to leave my life behind just because some power-hungry Dragon doesn't want his little island paradise being seen.

The burning in my lungs gets worse and I shout in anger, but the sound is swallowed up by the water.

I kick off the sand, swimming up towards the surface. I breach with a gasping breath, taking in the sweet salt air.

Above me, a large gray Dragon flies low, its tail dragging in the waves next to me. I'm splashed in the face and cough as water goes up my nose.

Atop the Dragon's back, Dyana's dark braid swings against her leather-covered back as Vesimyr heads towards the castle.

Dyana the Dragon Rider. They spend every day together, flying through the clouds as Dyana learns how to ride a Dragon. Vesimyr is one of the biggest Dragons here, next to Ignautius. It still gives me chills to see the world coated in shadows as he flies overhead.

I want to scream and cry for her forgiveness, but I don't.

Because she wouldn't want me to. She doesn't want me, not anymore. And I'm 384 years old—old enough to know better than to put effort into the impossible, despite how desperately I miss her. *Need* her.

It's a funny thing.

How little it takes for hurt to become anger.

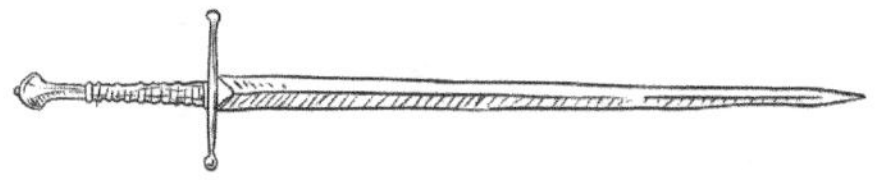

The Dragons are talented creatures, but certain things were simply outside of their abilities. Particularly things that require the use of *hands*. Which is why there is only one forge in the castle of Elysium.

It's mortal-sized but has the ability to make weapons even Dragons can wield. Which means the space is huge.

I found it by accident when we first got here. Whenever I go somewhere new, my first priority is to scope out the lay of the land. Figure out where everything is.

As I stand in the doorway of the forge, my mind wanders. Thinking back to when I first discovered it.

It never occurred to me that I could *build* a new Forsaken myself, and the moment I found the forge, I decided that was my task.

*Hissssss.*

I jump into the room, distracted from my straying thoughts as a Dragon walks past me, snapping at the air. The Dragon growls and tries to intimidate me.

I want to scream at it. But without Forsaken, I'll be Dragon food. So I take their pushy bullying and cruel behavior. I allow them to treat me like a worm. Even though I want to tell them that they're just as bad as the Fae.

With a deep sigh, I force my trembling hands to still and turn towards the small forge, where Kairos is carving another blade. His bare back is glistening with sweat from the heat, highlighting a muscular body. Thick black gloves cover his hands, and a thin, flimsy mask covers his face.

Kairos raises the mask and looks over his left shoulder at me, dropping the now sharpened sword in a bucket of cold water, all in one smooth movement.

There are no humans in Elysium.

Just mortals. Calling any Magyka or Demis an immortal in comparison to a Dragon just doesn't make sense. It would be like comparing an apple with a hawk.

"You look like you've seen a ghost." His low voice has an unplaceable accent. Something I've never heard before. It's almost Eastlander, but not.

"Suppose I did," I mutter. "I'll feel better when I remake this damn staff."

"You just made your first one." He gives me a knowing look. His obsidian eyes glow in the firelight. "Give it time. Think about what went wrong and try again."

"How many times am I going to have to fucking try before I can get it right?"

Kairos faces me fully and crosses his arms, his brow furrowing.

"You're being childish."

I stiffen. "Fuck off."

Gods—that's something Amalia would say.

I wince and scratch my head, digging my fingers through my damp hair. "Sorry, that was rude. You're right. I am being a fucking child. I'm just..."

Kairos waits patiently.

"I want out," I whisper. "I want to go *home.*"

Kairos sighs, his eyes going cold. "There is no going home." My eyes snap to his face as shock courses through me, and he nods. "I have...*witnessed* multiple escape attempts."

He leaves the rest unsaid.

"Ignautius meant what he said. He and his guards will tear you apart, should they catch you trying to leave. Not to mention, the wall would alert them of your proximity."

I want to tell him the rest of my plans, but I'm not sure I can trust him yet.

After the past two years, I'm not sure I can trust anyone at all.

"You're right," I grate out, picking up my drawing pad and getting to work sketching out a new staff. I also grab a book on the elements so I can study different metals that are stronger than the steel I tried last time.

Kairos *hmphs*, almost like he's disappointed, then returns to his work cleaning and polishing the now cool blade.

He dunks it once again in the water, rinsing the smooth metal.

If only I could rinse my past off just the same.

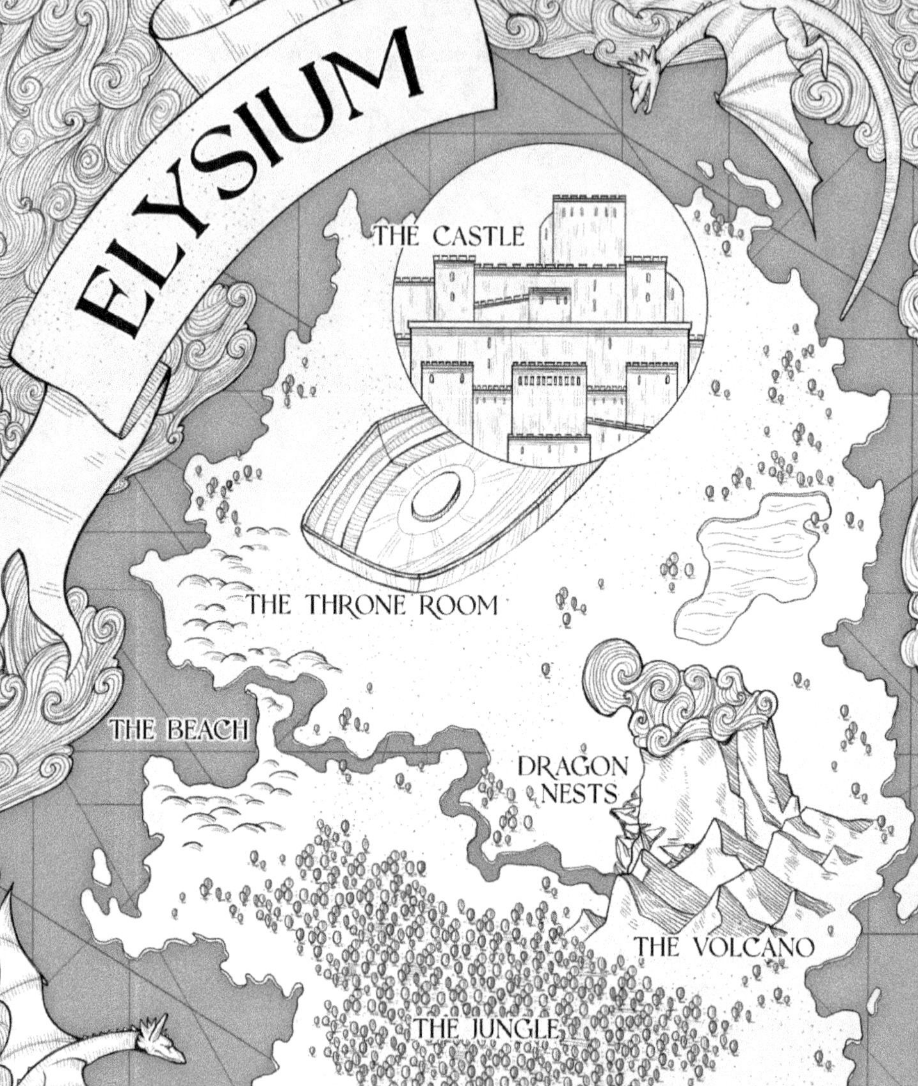

ELYSIUM
THE CASTLE
THE THRONE ROOM
THE BEACH
DRAGON NESTS
THE VOLCANO
THE JUNGLE

# CHAPTER 3
## DYANA

"Again!"

Vesimyr sighs. *"Dyana, I think that's enough for today—"*

I snarl against the cold ocean wind that batters my face, "No! We go again until I get it right."

The Dragon looks back at me, craning his giant, gray scaled neck, emerald eyes scowling.

I exhale loudly. "Please. I need to at least be able to *hold on.* Can we try once more, please?"

The beach below us is calm and serene. My seat vibrates and I'm shaken slightly as Vesimyr lifts each of his legs and shakes the sand off of his scales. He stills and suddenly the large body beneath me gives a full body twitch as he sneezes, spraying sand and fireballs across the picturesque beach.

"Excuse you," I tell him, as he sniffs and flaps his wings.

*"Fine. But this is the last one of the day. I'm old and it's tiring having to constantly catch you."*

My jaw drops and I slap his scales. "Such a rude Dragon!"

He snorts and smoke billows from his nostrils.

There is no Dragonfear anymore, at least with him. Since waking up, all the fear is gone. Vesimyr thinks it no longer affects me because of...well, *whatever* it is he did to me. He won't go into too many details other than that he healed me by giving me a drop of his magyk. *Dragon* magyk. Except, the magyk I've manifested since waking up—the...*light,* according to Vesimyr—doesn't resemble any Dragon magyk he's ever seen.

My magyk is Dragon, and yet not. That makes me a mystery. And to the Sene Skal, the Regent of Elysium, it makes me a huge fucking liability.

Tomorrow, I have to demonstrate my powers to the Sene Skal, a large blue Dragon named Ignautius, and the court.

Why? So they can determine if they want to *kill* me. Which is why since the minute I awoke from my two-year slumber, I've been practicing flying with Vesimyr and working on my strange new magyk.

Although, at this point I'm better at the former. I erase the thought from my mind and focus on holding onto Vesimyr's spinal spikes. They're hard and sharp, but the outer casing of the spikes is surprisingly warm and soft.

*"The ascent is the hardest. Hold on with your thighs and get as close to my scales as you can."*

I nod. "I remember."

He flaps his wings harder, and we begin to slowly lift into the air.

Vesimyr is still the only Dragon I've ever seen with two sets of wings, and since awaking on Elysium, I've seen many Dragons. It seems to give him more control in the air, based on my initial observations. Vesimyr flaps his wings harder and begins his ascent, picking up speed. The wind hits me with a force, and I hold on tighter, lowering my body against Vesimyr's scales, enjoying the warmth.

*"Move with me, keep your core tight and your hips loose."* Vesimyr orders. *"We move as one."*

I nod and his ascent becomes steeper, making it harder to hold on.

*"Put all of your weight in your seat bones. Don't rely on your hands."*

I try to follow his instructions, sinking my weight into my tailbone and squeezing my thighs so hard it burns. Vesimyr heads straight up into the clouds and I close my eyes, feeling his muscles move and trying to melt into every flap of his wings, leaning into the movements instead of resisting them. I focus on the spicy scent of his scales. On the way it calms my racing heart.

*"Yes! Just like that, Dyana. You can do this!"* His voice ripples through my head, encouraging me even though my thighs are burning.

*"I'm going to dive now. Don't lean back, lean into it!"*

*Fuck.* This is the hardest part. Vesimyr suddenly stops his ascent and hovers for a moment. I take a deep breath, centering myself the way Amalia taught me when I was a child.

We're above the clouds. It's so quiet up here. It makes me want to forget everything down on the ground.

Vesimyr opens his jaws and lets out a piercing call. I can hear them now, too. Vesimyr says I won't be able to understand the name of the Dragon's language, so I just call it Dragonsong. It's so layered, like many voices all at once, and the frequencies are so high, mortal ears are incapable of hearing them at all. I cannot sing the Dragonsong, but I can understand it.

With a mighty roar, Vesimyr dives straight towards the ground, and we go shooting through the clouds. I'm jerked back, but I hold on tight, forcing myself down on my stomach, though the wind pushes me back.

My thighs shake so hard I know Vesimyr can feel it, and in a single breath, my hand slips. The wind snatches me off the Dragon's back, sending me tumbling through the air. I scream into the wind. Not in fear but in pure frustration and agony.

*"Why don't you try landing on me?"* Vesimyr suggests. *"It will hurt a little, but you can do it."*

*"Okay. Let's do it."*

The beach beneath us appears through the clouds, growing closer and closer by the second. Vesimyr appears beneath me out of nowhere and I realize I need to turn my body, or else I'll be skewered by one of his spinal spikes. At the last second, I manage to get myself upright and land against his wings. He slows them and I slide down to his scaled back.

On aching, trembling legs, I carefully walk up his still moving body.

"I can't believe I did it—"

My words are interrupted by a scream as I slip and tumble off his back once again. There's no chance for him to catch me this time, and I plunge into the cool water. Saltwater rushes up my nose and I scramble to the surface, gasping for breath.

A giant claw dips into the water, gently picking me up between black talons so long and so sharp, they could rip me in half. Vesimyr lifts his claw and I surface, gasping for breath as he begins carefully flying us to shore.

He gently drops me on the sand before landing a few meters away, shaking the condensation off his scales. Vesimyr flicks his tongue and takes a deep breath, stretching his neck before walking over.

Vesimyr is the biggest Dragon here. I've heard the whispers.

*"Assassin."*

*"Butcher."*

*"Kinslayer."*

*"Traitor!"*

Mostly though, the whispers are about how Vesimyr is old and weak. How it should have been him that died, not Kydis.

He won't talk about it, and I've been careful not to push too much on the subject. But his presence in Elysium seems to be agitating the Dragons.

*"You should not worry about me, Dyana."*

My face snaps to his and I scowl.

"Are you reading my thoughts?"

The Dragon snorts. *"No. A vein on your forehead bulges when you're concerned. You are thinking too hard."*

I blink.

"It's creepy how observant you are, you know."

Vesimyr snorts and this time a wave of smoke wafts towards me. I cough, my eyes burning.

Vesimyr lays down and resting his chin on the sand so we're nearly eye to eye.

*"Long, long ago, there was a covenant between mortals and a small group of Dragons. The Dragons allowed these mortals to become their partners in battle."* The huge Dragon pauses.

*"These mortals were called Dragon Riders. Most of them were Arkaydian. Arkaydian magic was extremely compatible with Dragon magyk, but some Riders were humans without any drop of magic at all."*

I think about his words.

"Partners," I say slowly, testing the word. "I like the sound of that. I don't think I've ever had a partner like that before. Amalia was—" I stop and correct myself, "is, she *is* family. She's kind of obligated to help me."

*"And a partner isn't."* Vesimyr finishes my thought, and I nod.

We stare at each other for a while.

"Vesimyr?"

*"Yes, Dyana?"*

"Are you asking me to be your Rider?"

Vesimyr rolls his eyes and lets out a joyous note in Dragonsong, *"Yes I am. Be my Rider. Be my partner."*

My cheeks warm as a flush covers me.

"Yes," I whisper, and reach out to caress his soft scales. "Yes, Vesimyr."

The Dragon's body seems to relax, sinking further into the sand.

*Was he...worried? Aww!* I caress his scales.

**"Dyana Arkos,"** Vesimyr says aloud, **"I claim you as my Rider...and as my friend."**

I have the sudden urge to repeat the words back. I clear my throat and look at Vesimyr, my chin held high, **"Vesimyr, I claim you as my Dragon... and as my *friend.*"**

Magyk suddenly surges and I gasp as it explodes out of me, wrapping Vesimyr in bright light. I have to close my eyes and when I open them, my magyk has dimmed.

But Vesimyr's green pupils are now streaked with bright white light.

*"Interesting,"* he says, and I realize he's looking at me funny. *"There is a small ring of green around your pupils."*

"Like your eyes," I gasp.

*"Very interesting, indeed."* he murmurs, leaning close to inspect me. *"Well, there can be no doubting our claim now, partner."*

His breath is hot on my cheek and the scent of spiced ginger and burning woods increases. "This isn't a normal part of the Dragon Rider pact?"

Vesimyr waits a moment before finally responding.

*"I honestly can't remember—but I do not think so. However, there has never been another you. What you are, what I did to save you? It's never been done before. We are, as the mortals say, in uncharted territory."*

I sigh and the worry returns. He's right. None of this is normal.

"I'm not ready for tomorrow. I can barely control my magyk, V." I test out the nickname.

Vesimyr watches me for a moment. *"Do not worry about tomorrow. Worry only about this very moment. Do you know what I'm worried about?"*

I raise a brow.

*"Getting all of this damn sand off my scales. I itch in places I do not want to itch."*

Despite my worries, I can't help but smile.

"You're a funny Dragon," I laugh, patting the scales of his neck as he steps closer. We're both quiet for a moment, looking out at the ocean as the suns lower.

"I don't like the way the Dragons here treat you," I blurt, unable to hold it in any longer. "They're bullying you, Vesimyr! They're bullying all of the Ur Daoine Dragons. It's cruel and it makes me feel like our time here is running out. How long before they stop *playing* with us? Even if they kill me tomorrow, you and the others do not deserve to be treated like this."

Vesimyr nuzzles my cheek and I hug his snout.

"I don't know what to do, but I know we need to get the fuck out of here."

Vesimyr snorts. *"On that, we can agree. I have some ideas, but we need to tread carefully. Extremely carefully, or we both die."*

I side eye him. "Can you take them? If we have to fight our way out?"

He shakes his head. *"Maybe once, but not anymore. I'm bigger, but my magyk is still weak from being locked away so long. I'm not sure it will ever be the same."*

There's something off about his comment, but it must be my own worries clouding my judgment.

I get the nagging feeling that he just lied to me.

We sit there for a few minutes in silence, watching the waves.

*"You need to eat something,"* he murmurs. *"You get cranky when you're hungry."*

"So you're saying I take after you, then?"

Vesimyr stares pointedly when my stomach growls a second later.

"Fine. Food then more practice." Vesimyr lets out a displeased grunt and I laugh, "Not flying practice. *Magyk* practice."

*"As you say, fine. But do try not to blow up anything else this time, please."*

I snort, "I'll do my best."

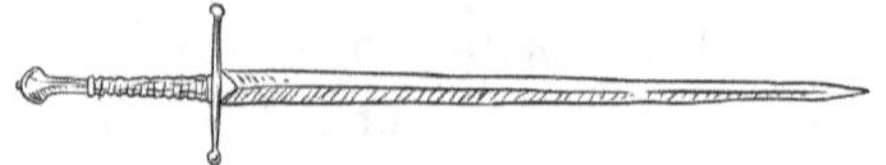

Bits of stone and debris fall from the ceiling, sending clouds of dust everywhere.

Vesimyr stares at me pointedly.

"I swear, I wasn't trying to take out that wall. I was *trying* to make a ball."

*"A ball?"* The Dragon coughs, swiping at the air with his claws. *"Are you sure you didn't accidentally mix up a letter and think 'wall'?"*

I glare at him, "Don't be an old grump. I'm sure I didn't mix up a letter..." I break off, sniffing.

*Maybe.* He might actually be right. But I'll never admit that.

"I was imagining a mini sun within my hands." I picture it and allow him to see it within my mind.

*"Ah. I see what happened. Your human words are so confusing. You need to practice making the ball, holding the magyk back, and then withdrawing it. You're just focusing on pushing your magyk out—it's not about the push; it's about the pull and the control."*

I glare at him and grind my teeth, "I am aware, thank you. That's what I've been trying to do all night!"

Vesimyr blows smoke at me and I cough.

When the air clears, so does my mind.

"I'm sorry. I didn't mean to snap at you. It's just so...foreign. Magyk feels like a language I do not know. I'm trying so hard, but it's...*confusing.*"

*"I know. You are doing very well. Look at how much you've learned in a short time."*

I sigh.

*"I think it's time to go to sleep, Dyana. You're exhausted from the magyk work. Don't drain yourself so much that you're unable to summon your light tomorrow."*

I want to scream and kick something. I push over a small empty wood table and run my hands through my hair, stressed and overwhelmed.

"We both know I'm going to fail tomorrow. Two months, and all I can do is blow things up *sometimes.*"

Vesimyr's tongue flicks out of his mouth and he looks around. Narrowing his eyes slightly, I jolt as the air becomes *alive* with magyk. I watch as the wall reforms before us.

"That's new." I glance to Vesimyr. "Have you always been able to do that?"

Vesimyr sniffs and looks towards me. *"I am a Dragon. I have many secrets. You will learn them all, in time, my Rider. Now go to sleep, Dyana. I'll watch over you from the rooftop."*

You would never know I knocked down a wall with little more than a single thought.

Vesimyr walks out of the room on surprisingly light claws. The sharp tips of his nails clink on the stone floor. I watch as the giant Dragon maneuvers himself through my large bedroom window so he can sleep on the tiled rooftop above.

"You still avoided my question!" I call.

There's a Dragon-y snort of amusement in return. I quickly undress and put on a clean cotton sleep shirt, crawling under the crisp covers of my small bed.

*"Goodnight, Dyana. Sleep well."*

*I'm standing at the base of a tall mountain.*

*No one else is around. I'm alone.*

*There is no birdsong, no shrieking wind. The world is silent as I look up the steep mountain in front of me.*

*The trees at the bottom are barren and burnt. But as my gaze travels further up the mountain, I watch as the trees become lush and green, the earth rich and vibrant. As if every step higher brought more life into the world.*

*I need to climb it.*

*Something I need is at the top. I don't know what that is, but I know all of my problems will be solved if I get to the top. All of the answers to my burning questions lay there.*

*Every night, I dream of this mountain.*

*Every night, I try and climb it.*

*Every night, I fail, unable to find my footing when the ground beneath me becomes too steep.*

*But this night would be different. It has to be.*

*I begin the arduous climb, a raw, frantic sort of anger fueling me. A desperate anger.*

*I need to reach the top.*

*I need answers.*

*"Courage, Dyana," a voice whispers in the back of my head.*

*The voice keeps my legs moving, even when my calves start to burn.*

*My fingers become bloody and torn as I climb up the mountainside.*

*Just as I'm about to make it to the end of the wasteland, a burning feeling in my chest stops me.*

*I look down at the red bloodstain rapidly expanding on my white nightgown.*

*Peering under it, I let out a scream as I take in the giant hole right through my chest.*

**"NO! No!"** I sit up in bed, screaming and flailing. My throat feels irritated, like I've been screaming for a while. The fabric of my nightgown is damp and sticking to my skin.

*"It's okay, Dyana, it was just a dream."* Vesimyr's voice is in my head instantly. But my heart won't stop racing.

I rub the aching spot on my chest, tracing the lines of the scar that was left there.

The grief hits me out of nowhere and suddenly I'm crying.

"Every fucking night. I have to relive the injury every night. I'm so..." my voice breaks. "I'm so tired of it, Ves."

*"Alright, that's it. Hold on and try not to scream."*

I blink, confused, when suddenly Vesimyr's large tail reaches into my room and scoops me up. He pulls me through the window and places me on the warm roof next to him.

When his tail lets me go, the appendage disappears and a few moments later, my entire mattress—blankets, pillows, and all—is dropped next to me.

*"Do you know why I sleep up here?"* he asks.

I climb onto the mattress and watch as the gray Dragon curls around me protectively, his head placed next to mine.

"Why?" I ask.

His tongue darts out and gently licks my cheek, making me squeak. *"It's because I—I do not like to be indoors anymore. After four centuries in the Pit, I have no desire to be beneath rock and stone ever again."*

My heart drops and I reach out to stroke his muzzle.

*"We are all the product of our traumas, Dyana. Do not feel embarrassed about being affected by them."*

"Do you feel safe up here?"

The large Dragon nods, the movement so small it doesn't jostle me.

*"You have nightmares almost every night,"* Vesimyr notes carefully. *"What do you dream of?"*

I glance at him. "Why do you ask?"

Vesimyr looks up at the brilliant night sky. Thousands of glimmering stars look down at us. *"I ask because I do not dream."*

"Oh." I blink, shocked. "Really? Dragons don't dream?"

Vesimyr looks down at me, and gives a shallow nod.

"That sounds...well, sometimes that would be nice. Right *now* that sounds nice. But dreaming isn't always bad. It can be nice."

*"I would very much like to hear about your dreams, if you do not mind sharing."*

I get the feeling that this question is hard for him to ask. The Dragon is being surprisingly vulnerable.

"Well, this dream starts off fine. I'm at the bottom of a strange mountain. It's barren near the ground, but as the mountain gets closer to the clouds, it becomes lush and beautiful. I try to climb it but can never make it to the top."

Vesimyr is quiet as he listens to my story.

"It always ends when I look down and see a hole in my chest, and the pain of death returns, waking me up."

*"Does the scar hurt?"* Vesimyr asks, nudging my chest.

I sigh, "Sometimes it...aches."

*"Hmm. That should get better with time."* Vesimyr pauses, *"I'm sorry you have to relive that moment over and over again, Dyana. That isn't a fate I'd wish on anyone."*

I nod and burrow under the covers, cold from the ocean breeze lifting my hair off my shoulders.

"Hey, I'm alive to tell the tale. That's thanks to you. I can deal with a little pain in return."

Vesimyr settles in and I can feel the way his body relaxes. He takes one of his large wings and drapes it over me, hiding me from any Dragons flying about.

*"You are safe up here, Dyana. I will protect you should any try and harm us."*

My body begins to relax at his words.

"Thank you," I whisper.

*"No matter what happens tomorrow, I do not regret it, Dyana. Know that, above all. Now sleep; nothing will happen to you while I'm here. Dragons protect their Riders."*

My eyelids grow heavy and before I can worry about why this could be a bad idea, I'm drifting to sleep in the safety of my Dragon's presence.

# CHAPTER 4
## AMALIA

The suns are setting, casting the sky in shades of red and orange as the air grows quiet.

Ryu ambles along behind me, following me to the berry patch. She knows I don't do well alone. Too much quiet, too much time left alone with my own thoughts, and I start to lose grip on my sanity. I start to question the entire point of living all together.

Everything reminds me of them. The slivers of golden light peeking out through the thick branches remind me of Os and his brilliant, golden eyes. The scent of fresh berries bursting on my fingers as I pick them reminds me of when Dyana was little.

We'd come out here and pick berries together. She insisted on using the juice as lip and cheek rouge, before parading around and pretending to be a princess from some faraway land.

She brought out the best in me—and now I am lost.

Birdsong echoes through the forest, bouncing off the trees. It *should* be peaceful. And yet I do not feel peace.

The Ulster Wald is relatively untouched from the evil of the South, but as I approach the berry bushes, I pass a giant tree with the bark peeling off.

*It's dying.* The Ulster Wald is *dying.* There is no escaping what's to come. The forest will not hide me anymore. It might keep me from sight, but it will not keep me safe. This is the new reality. No one in Ur Daoine is safe anymore. I've kept myself awake so many nights, tossing and turning, unable to stop thinking about how Achan's death was *supposed* to make everything better. But our situation only grew more dire in the wake of his demise, and that doesn't make any sense...not if Achan was truly in power. Which means Achan Drayven *wasn't* pulling the strings.  And what that means... The implications of such a reality are grim. It changes everything. Except it doesn't.If Achan was never in charge, then nothing has changed.

Lost in my own thoughts, I go through the motions of picking berries, although I'm barely paying attention, my fingers quickly stained dark pink from the juice.

I'm too distracted to be hungry.

*"I don't know why you like those,"* Ryu says with a huff as she rubs her scales against a large, still very much alive tree. *"They're disgusting."*

Her voice pulls me back into the present, "You like to eat live animals with the *fur* still attached. You swallow animals whole. Yet, I don't judge."

Ryu rolls her eyes at me and continues scratching her scales.

*"I do not always swallow them whole! Sometimes I roast them first."*

Ryu freezes and I feel the change in the air as Ryu cocks her head, her pupils dilating.

Raising a Dragon has given me endless amounts of new knowledge of their kind. Which is why I know that she's listening. Dragons have extremely good hearing and eyesight. It's part of what makes them so dangerous. Ryu's red body suddenly relaxes, and she continues itching her scales as her eyes go back to normal. What-ever it was, she doesn't deem it a threat.

I go back to berry picking, but in my head, I send her a question.

*"You heard something?"*

She huffs. *"An animal I didn't recognize. The sound threw me off for a moment."*

I *hmph,* not believing her for a second, but I go back to my berries, filling my cloth pouch with the ripe fruit. I'm just about to head back to the cave when a soft nose suddenly shoves under my armpit, sending me crashing into the berry bush. Tangy fruit juice gets everywhere, staining my face and hands. I quickly shove myself out of it and turn, dagger at the ready, but stop when I come face to face with an Oryx.

"Hello, Aanad," I say with a laugh as I put my dagger back in the holster on my thigh.

This is no danger.

This is a *friend*.

The Oryx mare shoves her face into my chest for cuddles. I avoid her red horn, not wanting to get impaled, but wrap my arms around her velvet-soft head.

We stay like that for a while as I caress her fur and scratch the inside of her ears.

Most horses dislike having their ears touched, but Aanad *loves* it. Her lower lip twitches and I press kisses against her forehead.

Happiness emanates from her, so strong that it teases my magyk and turns my cheeks pink with warmth as I flush.

She nickers lightly and then lifts her head, shoving me towards her chest so that she can curve her long neck around me, in a sort of horsey hug.

This is her way of saying, "I miss you."

"I missed you too," I whisper to her, kissing her velvet cheek.

As always, Aanad's black coat is shiny, but with the coming warm months, she's begun to shed.

Two small white spots now decorate her backside.

"I didn't know you had spots," I murmur. "You and Taran kind of matched then, huh?"

I feel her happiness shift, becoming colder, sadder.

"I know, I miss him too," I whisper. Saying it aloud *hurts*. Acknowledging just how much is even more painful. Her happiness returns as she lifts her head and licks my cheek.

I snort as she pulls back, giving me a look.

I sigh and rub my eyes. "You didn't by chance come alone, did you?"

Aanad looks at me, her happiness turning a little...guilty.

"Of course not."

*"You're in so much trouble."* I send the thought to Ryu, conveying my fury. *"I know you smelled him coming!"*

*"No idea what you're talking about!"* Ryu says cheerfully.

The red Dragon nudges Aanad. The two became friends in the early days of our time in the cave. A week after we arrived, I was shocked when Aanad casually walked into the cave with no warning and laid down next to Nyall and I, whickering gently at the baby Dragon.

Oryx, apparently, can find their riders anywhere. They're extremely hard creatures to bond with but once you do, they will always find you, no matter where you are or how long it takes.

Aanad slept for two days after the long journey, but her presence was much welcome. Even if she did remind me of Taran.

But Aanad left when Nyall Drayven did. Even thinking of it makes me angry. Not at her, but at *him.*

With a heavy sigh, I nudge past Aanad with a gentle pat on her silky shoulder.

Ryu looks at me suspiciously but they both follow along, playfully biting at each other like two naughty horses. We walk through the forest for a few minutes, and I pass the dying tree again. It pulls at me.

I force my gaze away and make my feet keep moving, taking me deeper into the forest as we approach the place I call home. The outside of the cave looks the same. Trees line the exterior of the large gray stone overhang, and light shines from within where the fire is going. Normally, I would be relieved and comforted by its sight. There is no relief and comfort in me now. Not when I know who is inside *waiting.*

I take a deep breath and walk towards the light, passing the edge of the cave.

No amount of preparation could steel me from this. From *him.*

The breath leaves my lungs and my chest becomes tight as my heart races as my eyes meet Nyall Draven's mismatched gaze.

He is sitting near the fire, his white-blonde hair now past his shoulders and half-pulled back in intricate braids. The tattoos covering his neck and arms, the way his eyes follow my every move...it sets me on edge. It makes my heart race and my blood boil. I'm angry and confused and terrified all at the same time.

I want to scream at him to leave and never return again, but I do not.

"What are you doing here?" I snap and instantly regret it as I watch his eyes darken and turn cold.

~~I don't mean it.~~ *Yes I do! Yes I do. He left, remember? He left.* Those words harden me.

Hurt is so easy to turn into anger.

Nyall says nothing as I deposit the berries into a large bowl in the makeshift kitchen area *he* carved for me.

We exist in silence as I take a long drink of water from my canteen, drops of it falling down my chin, dampening my shirt.

I set the canteen down with a loud bang, startling some of the wolves nearby.

"Why are you here, Nyall?" I snap again, annoyed by his lack of response. "I don't have anything to say to you."

He doesn't react but I turn and face him fully, meeting his gaze again. Seeing him is hard. He makes me *feel* things.

~~ANGER. DESPAIR. DESIRE.~~

And I don't particularly want to *feel* anything at all.

"Perhaps I simply wanted to see you," he says, staring at me with those luminous, mismatched eyes. But I see the sadness behind them and it hurts. "Is that so hard to believe, Amalia?"

I have to look away. But the memories assault me anyways.

*"Ask me, Amalia," he whispers against my lips. "Ask me to touch you. Ask me to make you feel good."*

*I gasp as his lips brush against mine. The honeysuckle scent of his magic is like a drug. The closer he gets, the less I can hold back.*

*Except...*

*"I can't." I pull away, feeling like someone had thrown cold water on me.*

I escape back into the present, unable to think about that night anymore. Despite how much I want to say those words.

"Yes, it is." I walk over to the small sitting area he wove into the floor. I sit on the pile of pillows in the corner of the floor divot.

Nyall sits across from me, his posture casual and confident. "You started ignoring my letters."

"I have nothing to say to you," I pointedly look anywhere but him, "but you know that. So why are you here, Nyall?"

He's quiet for a moment, "Tell me about Keave."

"Is that an order?"

"Yes."

I scoff, "I am not your subject. You are not owed a report of my movements."

"I'm well aware," he says. "But your actions are gaining attention, particularly with the sudden influx of refugees at the rebel camps. So yes, I'm owed a report, Amalia. My people are getting concerned."

I watch him below furrowed brows. "It sounds like you're losing your control, Drayven. Are your rebels being *rebellious?*"

Nyall takes a tight breath, clearly frustrated. "My people are *fine.* I have ensured it. But, the addition of so many people in such a short amount of time? We've been scrambling. Which caused my generals to...*question* your true intentions."

"I don't care about the opinions of strangers. Besides," I meet his gaze, infusing mine with steel, "I *want* the attention. Now, if that's all, you can leave. You're so good at that, after all."

~~Stop. You don't want to be mean to him.~~

~~Why are you saying this?~~

~~Please, don't go. Don't leave me alone again. I don't want to be alone. I don't want to be alone. I don't want to be alone~~

*SHUT UP!*

Now it's my turn to be watched. The Prince gives me a look that is full of disappointment and frustration.

Good. That's for the best.

~~I miss you.~~

Nyall's eyes flick to the side as he looks at something behind me, and I take a breath, feeling unsettled by his gaze.

A few of the wolves enter the cave and yip happily when they see Nyall. The Prince smiles softly, his anger receding, as they all come over, tails wagging, and lick his face.

"Ah, hello," he murmurs, running his hand down the wolves' backs. "It's good to see you too."

I glare at the furry little traitors.

They settle down around us. Virgyl joins and the wolves make room for their Alpha. He plops his large body next to mine, sensing that I need his presence and the weight of his touch to ground me.

*"What's this about?"* Virgyl asks me. He could project the thought to Nyall too, but I can tell my wolf friend speaks only to me. *"Ah. I thought I smelled Elf. Do you want me to bite him?"*

I fight a laugh. Virgyl misses nothing. *"He claims it's because of Keave, but he's lying. I can sense it—and not yet, but I will let you know if that changes."*

*"Of course, cub."*

Virgyl nuzzles me, leaning his big furry head onto my shoulder. I dig my hands into his thick black fur and take a deep breath.

"I've been hunting for an entire year. What's so different about Keave? Why does the Rebellion suddenly care?"

Nyall exhales hard, "For fuck's sake, Amalia. Maybe I'm just *concerned* that there won't be anything left in Ur Daoine to save if you're burning it all down!"

Anger is hot in my belly at his words.

I scoff and lean forward, grabbing a bottle of mead on the floor near the fire. Not bothering with a glass, I pop the cork and bring the rim to my mouth, taking a few good swallows.

I force myself not to wince at the burn of alcohol.

"You and your little *Rebels* are making an awful lot of assumptions."

Nyall sighs and shakes his head, frustrated.

"I'm not trying to get the Rebellion's attention," I admit. "My plans are bigger than you and your makeshift army."

Nyall stills, watching me closely.

I see when he realizes exactly what I mean.

"You can't be serious." He leans forward, his elbows on his knees.

I smile.

"No, *fuck* no. You aren't fighting the Archmage alone. That's what this is? You're fucking *baiting* him?"

I tilt my bottle towards him in a mock salute. "It *is* a bit concerning how small minded your generals are. I've been blatantly obvious about all of this and still...they couldn't see it." I make a faux wince, openly mocking him.

"Amalia, you can't face him alone!"

*"She's not alone."*

Ryu's voice rolls through our minds as she and Aanad enter the cave. Nyall flashes a wide, genuine smile at the sight of them.

Ryu walks over to Nyall and nuzzles him. He strokes her scales with familiarity and not an ounce of fear. The warmth in his eyes as he looks upon her great, bright red features makes my heart skip a beat—and makes me hate myself even more.

"So, it's the two of you against the world, hm?" he asks her, his tone gentle and playful, but I can feel the seriousness beneath the words. "The Gray Wytch and her Dragon."

"Ryu isn't *mine*," I snap at him, fury turning my vision red. "She belongs to no one but herself. Do not suggest otherwise."

I feel Ryu's happiness at the statement, as well as her amusement.

The corner of Nyall's mouth twitches and suddenly I'm staring at his lush lips. He's fighting a smile.

"Of course, I apologize."

*"If you think I am leaving my cub to face the Deceiver alone, you think wrong, Rebel Prince."* Nyall's eyes go wide as Virgyl speaks to both of us. The Dyre Wolf only spoke to him once, that first day.

*The Deceiver.*

That's what Virgyl calls the Archmage.

I've never asked why, but the name seems apt. The Archmage claims to speak to Sol Constantus, who is most likely made up. What greater deception than to pray to a False God?

Nyall nods at Virgyl. "I am glad to hear it. But that is still not enough. The Archmage has called back the Dragonguard and all infantry. He's gathering his armies. You cannot take on ten thousand soldiers and ten Dragons all by yourself."

I meet his gaze, furious at his doubt. "Watch me."

Nyall sighs, running his hands through his hair.

"Come on." He stands and puts his hand out, but I ignore it. Nyall raises a brow. "Your hands are covered in juneberry juice. If you don't wash it off now, they'll be stained pink for days."

"I don't care," I mutter.

"Too bad," is all Nyall says and then he's behind me, hoisting me over his shoulder. I shriek and the wolves let out barking laughs.

*"Are you going to do anything about this?"* I hiss at Virgyl and Ryu.

*"This seems like some weird, adult thing."* Ryu shrugs and lays down next to the fire, getting comfortable around the wolves. They love when she does this and cuddle against her warm belly.

*"Talk to the Rebel Prince, but if he tries anything, I'll bite his head off,"* Virgyl whispers in my head. I snort a laugh despite the perilous situation of hanging upside down. Then I punch the Prince in the kidney, *hard,* and he drops me on my head.

My ears ring and the wind gets knocked out of me. Nyall is already there, helping me up as he coughs, holding his side.

"Damn, that *hurt,*" he says, slightly breathless, but his eyes glow silver with lust. "You've been training."

It takes every fiber of my being to force myself to look away.

"Perhaps," is all I say, playing it off. He doesn't get to know every detail of my life. I don't owe him that.

But I *have* been training, and I'm secretly glad he can tell. When my grief turned to anger in the wake of his departure, I decided to take it out on my own body. So I trained every single day. Harder than I trained for the Gauntlet.

My muscles grew thick and strong as I practiced with my swords every single day. Ryu and the wolves even sparred with me, although I didn't use my swords for that, just hand-to-hand.

I've done everything Remus taught me and then some, going back to the early lessons my father gave me about magyk.

I've been practicing that as well.

We walk in silence for a few minutes, navigating the tunnels lit only by the occasional sconce. Until finally the air turns humid and warm. We make a right turn and go down a small slope into a large atrium.

Nyall discovered hot springs as he was carving into the mountain. A series of small tubs connect to a small lake. Ryu loves to swim in the warm water, and she's promised there's nothing at the bottom of the lake that would hurt us. Dragons, it seems, are adept swimmers. Although I almost had a heart attack when she didn't surface for ten minutes. I forgot Dragons can go for hours without breathing.

Ryu once mentioned something about how she has memories of her ancestors being scared of the ocean, but when I asked her for more details, she shut down, lost in the memories.

Nyall passes me, walking over to one of the smaller tubs. It's shallow enough that I don't need to swim—barely. But it's the hottest tub out of all of them.

I follow Nyall, ignoring the goose bumps pebbling on my arm as I remember the last time we were down here.

He picked this tub then, too.

I know that asshole is doing this on purpose.

~~I DON'T WANT HIM TO STOP.~~

He begins undressing and I turn, refusing to look at his sculpted, ink-covered body.

"What the fuck are you doing?" I ask, my voice embarrassingly high-pitched. "I was just going to wash my hands, not get in!"

I hear the sound of his clothes hitting the damn hot springs floor and my body turns molten.

"When is the last time you brushed your hair, horse girl?" he calls. Light splashes follow as he slides into the water. "You can turn now, unless you've become too much of a prude."

I'm going to punch him in his stupidly handsome face.

"Why does my hair matter?"

"Because you look like you've been rolling around with wolves. No wonder these towns you're visiting are so terrified. You have a bramble on your head. Now stop being a baby and get in the springs, Amalia. Or do you need me to undress you myself like a damn nursemaid?"

I snarl at him but begin stripping too, letting my shirt fall to the ground and gingerly pushing my leather pants off. Looking at the opposite wall, I quickly wade into the water and submerge myself as far from Nyall as I possibly can.

"You're such an asshole," I hiss, but the bastard just sinks beneath the surface until only his eyes remain above the water. "I will kill you in your fucking sleep, I swear to Gods."

My threat falls flat as he takes in my body with wide eyes.

Eyes that are locked on me and my extremely visible naked breasts.

*"Wash your hands and your hair, or I will do it for you."*

My eye twitches and I magykly shove him out of my mind. The last time I did this, he went flying into the air.

This time, he only rocks back slightly.

*"You're not the only one who's been practicing."* His voice is an arrogant purr in my head.

*Fuck.* I can't get him out.

He...he can't see my thoughts.

*He can't know how much pain I'm in.*

My heart suddenly races, and my hands begin to tremble as sweat beads on my forehead.

*"Get OUT!"* I scream at him and pull even more magyk from that deep pool within me, forcing him out.

He winces, surfacing to take a deep breath. The Prince lifts a hand to his temples as he grimaces.

But it's the concern in his eyes that makes me want to sink beneath the surface and never come back up for air.

"You win...for now." It's a clear warning, and one I don't like.

I match the casualty in his tone, "Good. Now I'll wash my hair."

Nyall rolls his eyes.

"But touch me, and I'll sear off your fingers. Have you seen cauterization up close, Prince? Smelled the scent of burnt flesh in the air?" I taunt, but it doesn't faze him, which only annoys me further.

He makes a pleased sound, eyes still closed. "Such a romantic."

In silence, I grab a pumice stone and a bar of soap and get to work on my berry-juice-stained hands.

"They've stopped keeping track of how many Fae you killed. The numbers got so high that they all just...stopped," he says neutrally. "*Will* you ever stop?"

The question isn't in judgment, for there is none in his voice.

I shrug. "It will be enough when it's enough."

"You mean when all Imperial Fae are dead? Does that include me, Amalia?"

I snap my head up, looking at him, "No. Of course not. But the fact that you think that..." I shake my head and look away. "It doesn't matter. Think what you want. But fuck you for always assuming the godsdamn worst of me."

He goes quiet for a long time as I finish up on my hands and soap up my hair. It tangles immediately and my fingers get caught in the long gray strands.

The water makes it look black.

"Let me help," Nyall says, suddenly behind me. I nearly jump out of the water, but before I can say no, his hands are in my hair, gently untangling it.

"Don't touch me," I snarl, trying to wiggle out of his hold.

But my fight quickly drains as he starts brushing my hair with a comb he manifested out of thin air. He can only do that with objects already nearby, so it must be my own comb he's using.

"Fuck, Amalia. I'm not going to hurt you." He pauses and I feel him consider stopping before his hands start moving again as he brushes my hair.

"You think the worst of me, too, you know," he whispers.

Guilt floods me and I shove it all away.

Nyall doesn't touch me anywhere else. He stands enough behind me that there's still space between us.

But Gods.

*Gods.*

Even having him this close makes my heart skip a beat.

Knowing there's not a scrap of clothing between us makes my skin tingle.

There's a squelching sound as Nyall pours my hair oil into his hands, massaging my scalp and running it through my now smooth strands.

My mouth falls open and I lean back without thinking, melting under his touch.

At the feeling of his hard cock against my lower back, I jerk forward, yanking my hair out of his hands. I dive beneath the surface, rinsing the excess oil, and head straight for the edge of the springs.

I quickly get out of the hot water, immediately missing the relaxing warmth. But the cold wind of the cave assaults me as I grab my soiled clothes and hold them to my chest, turning to face him.

Nyall Drayven is watching me with such need that I stop breathing for a moment.

"You're scared of me," he comments.

I go to respond but Nyall stands fully and he's so tall that his erect cock is completely visible. The Prince Without a Throne wades through the water towards me.

No.

Wades isn't the right word.

He moves with feline grace, like a cat, prowling as if I'm his prey.

"I'm not scared of you," I sneer, hoping he buys my lies.

The Prince smirks.

That's a no to buying my lies, then.

Perfect.

"You're lying. You *are* scared of me."

I look away, terror making my chest hurt again.

"You're scared of what I might find in the deep dark corners of your mind, Blue." Nyall whispers.

*That nickname.*

*That stupid fucking nickname.*

"You don't get to call me that," I snarl.

Nyall discovered that some of the wolves call me Blue and latched onto the nickname like an urchin to a rock. In those days, he stayed close. Nyall realized that in moments of silence, my thoughts spiraled. So, he'd tell me stories until I fell asleep. Sometimes the stories were told aloud, so the wolves could enjoy. Sometimes the stories were more intimate, and he'd whisper them in my head.

Then he would ask me questions. Suddenly I was telling my own stories.

Dyana...she was the only one who knew anything about me.

A little prodding and my secrets flowed like burning lava. My grief wore down my walls, in the days when Nyall was still here.

After he left, my walls hardened, becoming impenetrable.

I wish I could take it all back.

~~No you don't.~~

Fingers snap in front of my face and I jump.

"Don't get lost, Blue," Nyall says gently, his voice low.

"Put your damn clothes on," I snap, turning and getting dressed myself. I'm willing to wear dirty clothes if it means I can have some sort of barrier between us. "And I said don't...don't call me that *name.*"

Because hearing him use that name makes me so dangerously close to shattering all together.

But I can't get myself to say that last part.

Because then he would know just how badly his leaving broke me.

And I was already so broken to begin with...

Which is why there's nothing left.

"I'm here for another reason, Amalia," Nyall says, his breath near my cheek.

I nearly jump out of my own skin but force my hands to keep moving as I finish getting dressed. I pull the shirt over my head and turn, taking in the shirtless Imperial Fae in front of me.

Nyall pulled on pants, but his abdomen is bare. His tattooed chest glistens, still damp from the hot springs. He's bulkier than he used to be, which means Nyall was telling the truth. He *has* been training. But the Prince is still leaner than Os was.

The name sends a bolt of pain straight to my heart and I have to close my eyes for a second, remembering to breathe under the crushing strain of grief.

Nyall exhales, "We debated over this, but I have an invitation for you. The Rebellion has need of your... particular set of skills."

"No," I shake my head.

Nyall glares. "I'm not finished."

"I don't care."

I expect him to fight back but the Prince just shrugs and goes to walk past me. Just as his shoulder is near mine, he pauses and meets my gaze with a wicked smile, "That's too bad. I guess we'll just raid this year's Mercatus alone then."

Everything goes still as my heart thuds and the cave goes dark, the shadows reacting to my fury. It takes a moment to realize I'm also on fire. Nyall doesn't step away though. I watch as the midnight blue flame tipped in orange reflects against his eyes. My thoughts race, calculating how this might change things.

"If you're lying, I'll—"

Nyall stops me with a raised hand. "It's the truth. We found it, Amalia. We have the location. If we stop Mercatus, it will deliver a major blow to the Archmage."

Ever since the Dragons left, Castael Laryn has doubled down on the capture of all magykal creatures, collecting them for its army. But some are...purchased privately. For *fun*. Which to the Imperial Fae, translates to various methods of torture.

"I must admit, it's been a while since I've been surprised. I never thought I'd be helping the Rebellion make their dreams come true.

Nyall raises a brow. "And what dream is that?"

I smile, and it's a thing of nightmares. "I'll join your Rebellion, Prince. But I have a few...*conditions.*"

Nyall blinks, and it gives me great joy to see, within the tumultuous emotions playing behind his eyes, a brief shiver of *fear.*

He should be afraid. They all should.

# CHAPTER 5
## IREYNA

"It's been two years!" the Archmage roars. "Two whole years and what do you have to show for it?"

He slams His hand down on the table before swiping the glass dishes to the floor. They explode into broken shards, peppering the dirt beneath me.

*I am a failure.*

"NOTHING! YOU HAVE NOTHING!"

*I am a failure.*

I repeat the words over and over in my head, begging Sol Constantus for mercy. I don't *want* to be a failure. I never set out to fail. In fact, I do everything in my power so that I don't. But still, I always end up here. On my knees, folded onto the floor, my forehead against the cold ground as I prostrate myself, begging for His forgiveness.

"I'm sorry, Father. You are right, I have failed you. No matter how badly I hurt Him, the *prisoner* will not speak." My voice trembles as the fear overwhelms me. "He gives me nothing. Pain doesn't work on Him."

*I'm a failure.*

The Archmage sighs, "Get up. You're embarrassing yourself."

My cheeks heat with shame as I get back up and brush off my knees.

*Worthless,* my inner voice whispers. *You are a worthless, embarrassing, failure.*

"It doesn't matter that the beast won't speak. I have plenty of...*other* uses for Him."

I raise my gaze, meeting His. The Archmage's eyes glow a luminescent purple. I've always found them to be so beautiful that it's difficult to look away. He claims that the color of His eyes happened when He was touched by Sol Constantus and chosen by Him as His representative on earth. These are the eyes of someone who has looked upon Sol Constantus. It's why no one else has purple eyes. None but the Archmage have spoken with Him.

I always feel so unworthy in His presence. He is everything I could ever dream of being.

*Sol Constantus...please choose me.*

"What would you have me do?" I stand tall, with my arms at my side; a soldier ready for orders. "Let me prove my loyalty to you. Let me show Sol Constantus that I am His servant."

The Archmage smiles, His long white robes pious and pristine.

"Of course you would, my dear. Which is why I've decided that you will be joining the Dragonguard. One of the left behind hatchlings has finally matured and reached full-size. It needs a strong Rider to tame it and keep it in check."

The Archmage stands to the side and I gasp as I take in the white Dragon behind Him.

From my angle on the floor, His figure blocked it from my view. I kneel in the old Dragon Pit. It's truly a miracle that the Archmage was able to save it. Sol Constantus has blessed the Holy Father with such power. The white Dragon is led out of its stall. It trembles, looking around with fear in its golden eyes.

"It's been getting snappy with the handlers, so make sure to use your switch whip and remind it who is in charge."

"What is the Dragon's name?" I breathe, looking at the creature in complete awe.

It's still quite a bit smaller than other mature Dragons I've seen. Maybe the size of four horses combined.

But its white scales are resplendent.

"Name?" The Archmage scoffs and I blink, looking at Him in surprise. "It is not worthy of one. These beasts are evil, Ireyna. Do not forget yourself."

"But—"

The Archmage slaps me across the face and pain explodes in my cheek. I blink away tears and force myself to stand, not reacting or crying out.

"Do not question me! To question me is to question *Him.*"

*I can't do anything right.*

*I'm so stupid!*

"I apologize, Your Holiness," I intone with reverence. "You are correct, as always."

I want to be good. I don't want to be a failure or deserving of violence. But I just can't stop sinning.

"Do not disappoint me again," the Archmage says, His voice so dark that I shiver.

"I won't, I swear," I promise. "Thank you so much for tHis opportunity, Your Holiness. I will make you and Ur Daoine proud."

"You better," he says. "Learn to fly, and we'll discuss your first assignment."

I nod. "Yes, sir."

The Archmage turns to leave but glances over His shoulder. "We no longer need to break Remus Ostia, but continue with His punishment in between your training. There will be no peace for the beast. We need Him to get to her."

"Of course, Your Holiness." I nod, my heart racing.

I ignore the way my heart screams at me in guilt.

*I have to keep torturing Os.*

*I know it's for the greater good but...*

Shaking my head, I ignore my thoughts and put them somewhere that turns my head quiet. I look again towards the Dragon and fight a smile. The first genuine smile I've had in so long. I've long dreamed of joining the Dragonguard. The fact that this Dragon in front of me is *mine* seems like something out of a dream.

Maybe He sees how hard I'm trying. Because this...this *feels* like a reward.

*THis is a gift from Sol Constantus. It has to be.*

All of my hard work is finally paying off.

Which means it's time to learn to *fly*.

# CHAPTER 6
## DYANA

Nervous energy runs through me, resulting in a sweaty brow and even sweatier palms. Vesimyr is silent as he walks next to me, moving slowly so that I can keep up. For a being so large, he's surprisingly quiet. I still expect a loud *thunk* with each of his steps, but it's like he soaks in all of the noise, dampening it.

He moves like a *shadow*.

*I need to ask him about that sometime.*

The Dragons ahead watch us, suspicion and anger in their eyes. The hearing room is huge. It's like the Arena but brighter and more open. Colorful flag-like tapestries hang on the walls in between rows of individual atriums suitable for Dragons of various sizes.

*"They call this the Throne Room."*

I fight the urge to roll my eyes. *"How human of them."*

Vesimyr snorts and a small cloud of black smoke bursts from his nostrils. Despite myself, despite the terror within me, I flash him a wide smile over my shoulder.

The crowd of waiting Dragons parts for us, their eyes either fearful or suspicious.

*"Liar, liar, scales on fire!"* I hiss at Vesimyr in our minds.

*"I do not understand this saying,"* he responds, confused. *"My scales are most certainly not on fire."*

*"It means you're a dirty liar! I asked if you could take Ignautius and the court, should we have to fight our way out and you said, 'probably not.'"* I mimic his tone. *"They're scared of you, Vesimyr. Terrified, even. That means something."*

Vesimyr nudges me with his snout. *"I did not lie to you, nor did I claim to be stronger than the Sene Skal. I could take Ignautius, but he's had centuries of time to build up magyk and strength, meanwhile my own has been steadily drained. I'm only just starting to get back to my former strength. It will be years before I'm back at full-strength."*

*"Damnit,"* I curse. *"Do the others know that, though? Or do they think you're just as powerful as you once were? Because it clearly isn't keeping them from fearing you."*

*"I was kept separate from the others...back in the Pit."* He says the word as if it's venomous. For a single moment, I feel the depths of his searing rage. It could burn the world down twice over.

Taking a deep breath, I lift my chin and let his rage fuel me.

*"Perhaps it's a blessing in disguise. Leave them guessing. Nothing is scarier than a mystery."*

He *hmphs* in agreement.

Closest to the ground are the mortals. Mirielle is among them, as is the tall man she spends her time with.

Kairos. That's what Vesimyr said the blacksmith's name was.

There is a small part of me that misses her. But the hurt is bigger. It overshadows any warm feelings we once shared.

Mirielle's pale green eyes meet mine, but I quickly look away. Despite how hard I try not to think about it, Mirielle remains a reoccurrence in my thoughts.

I don't want to see her or talk to her. Not after what she did. She lied to me every step of the fucking way, but even worse? Mirielle stole *my* choices from me. She treated me the same way Amalia did—like a child.

I'm not a kid anymore. I get that they have centuries on me, but I refuse to stay in the shadows. The only one who gets to decide my fate is *me*.

Instead of letting my thoughts linger on Mirielle, I turn my focus to the huge blue Dragon in front of me.

The Sene Skal is almost as big as Vesimyr.

Unlike my companion, the Sene Skal only has two legs. His neck is longer than many of the other Dragon's here, giving Ignautius a more serpentine appearance. Giant dark blue wings with sharp, black talons at each tip flare, showing off a wingspan that almost touches the walls.

Ignautius and the rest of the Skal—which is essentially a court of loyal followers—all wear decorations around their neck and legs, almost like a mix between jewelry and armor. Ignautius turns and I notice the golden plates that go down his spine, providing increased protection.

*"That is why I doubt. They've had the damn smiths forge custom armor. Most of it is just for show, but Ignautius has plating over all areas of vulnerability, making it nearly impossible to injure him,"* Vesimyr whispers.

I glance down and see that Ignautius also has gold plating covering his entire belly, the area where Dragon's scales grow thin and soft.

*"Shit. I didn't even notice last time he spoke to us."*

*"Many dragons have some sort of magyk affinity—but Ignautius doesn't. He won this seat by killing every challenger."*

Ignautius suddenly swivels his head around with a high-pitched shriek. Bright yellow eyes stare into mine.

Even though Dragonfear can't affect me anymore, my stomach still knots and I begin to tremble under the weight of his gaze.

His court chuffs and snorts, making fun of my reaction.

Vesimyr bows, going down to his knees, and I follow suit.

**"Honored Sene Skal, thank you for seeing us,"** Vesimyr says aloud.

Ignautius sneers. *"What's this? Have you suddenly discovered manners, Vesimyr?"*

Vesimyr takes a deep breath but doesn't respond.

*"I see. Has your little worm proved itself useful?"*

The Sene Skal suddenly lunges forward and snaps his jaws down right in front of me, coming so close I can smell his breath. A low growl sounds as he inhales my scent. A large, forked tongue emerges as Ignautius licks his teeth.

*"I will dine on your flesh tonight, worm,"* he says to me. *"You're an abomination, and I will wipe your stain from this world, returning our island to peace."*

I watch out of the corner of my eye as Vesimyr goes still, his green eyes flicking to watch Ignautius.

"I am ready for the demonstration." I meet his gaze, refusing to back down, exactly the way Amalia would have.

Ignautius hisses at me and his court joins him, sounding like a viper pit.

*"Very well, get on with it then."*

The Dragons suddenly take to the air as they find spots around the large auditorium. Ledges and holes are carved into the walls, showing the setting sun in the distance.

Hundreds of Dragons watch me as the room goes silent. I walk into the center of the room as Ignautius takes a seat in a large metal throne. It's made of some sort of steel, but it shines almost like a diamond. I've never seen anything like it.

*"It's called Elysian. It's the strongest ore in the world, and can only be created from a Dragon,"* Vesimyr answers. *"But don't think about that. Focus, Dyana."*

I crack my neck and wiggle my hands, trying to get out the nervous energy coursing through me. With a deep breath, I picture a giant ball of sun between my hands. I reach deep within myself. I'm not sure what to look for, but suddenly something warms my skin, covering my arm in goosebumps.

I dive into that feeling.

Then I'm there, and it feels amazing, but I don't know what to do with it, so I just pull, pull, pull—and *imagine.* I picture the shape and imagine the feel of the ball within my hands, all while yanking on my magyk.

There's a crackling sound and something bright burns against my eyelids. I open my eyes to see a giant ball of light floating between my hands. My palms tingle and my fingers warm as it caresses my skin.

*"Yes, Dyana!"* Vesimyr shouts happily in my head.

But my hands tremble and exhaustion suddenly sends me to my knees with a cry.

"Oh Gods, I can't—I can't pull it back." I gasp.

Several Dragons hear. They begin to scatter, flying into the air to get out of the path of my magyk.

But it's not quick enough.

I lose my hold on the ball of light. It shoots out of my hands and hits the floor, causing a huge explosion of stone and rock. My ears ring and the air turns dusty as debris goes everywhere. Something dark covers me and I realize it's Vesimyr crouching on top of me. I reach a hand up and place it on his warm belly scales.

Tears begin to stream down my cheeks at the realization that, despite my initial success, I failed.

Ignautius is going to kill me.

*"I've asked much of your trust so far, Dyana. But I need you to trust me once more, I promised I wouldn't let him kill you, and that's a promise I intend to keep."*

I cough, waving the dust away as everything goes quiet, settling.

**"ABOMINATION!"** Ignautius screams, moving the conversation out into the open. His voice is so loud that I have to cover my ears. **"YOUR LIFE IS MINE!"**

I hear Vesimyr sigh as he stands fully, allowing me to stand as well. On wobbly knees, I get to my feet, staying close to Vesimyr and leaning against his leg.

**"Article Twelve,"** Vesimyr says. His voice is quiet but it doesn't matter.

The auditorium quickly fills again. Whispers break out and the Dragons look confused as they glance around wildly.

**"What did you just say?"** Ignautius snarls.

Vesimyr raises his chin and meets Ignautius' gaze.

Although it was already quiet, there's a sudden weight to the air as the two Dragons look at each other. It's the weight of a challenge.

**"Article Twelve of the Law of Elysium. All Claimed Dragon Riders may claim refuge and be welcome."**

More gasps.

**"You dare to cite the codex? At me?"** Ignautius bends, looking like he's about to launch forward to charge. I step out from behind Vesimyr's legs and look at the Sene Skal, terror in every breath but fuck it.

*"I trust you,"* I whisper in Vesimyr's mind before clearing my throat. "He does not lie. I am the Dragon Vesimyr's bonded Rider."

Ignautius' eyes go wide before they fill with fury. **"You bonded the abomination? Without my permission?"**

**"Do you know what is not in the codex, honorable Sene Skal?"** Vesimyr asks calmly, but I do not miss the hint of bite in his tone. **"The requirement of any permission. The Dragon Rider bond is one of our most sacred tenents."**

Ignautius roars, looking like he wants to charge Vesimyr and tear him to shreds. But Vesimyr stands tall, refusing to look away.

The air turns hot and tense.

**"Dyana Arkos is my Rider,"** he says loudly. **"She is now in possession of a kernel of my magyk, of Dragon Magyk. The bond is true."**

There's a sort of tugging sensation and I let go of my magyk. It bursts out of my hands, but instead of a ball, light in the shape of a small Dragon forms.

But...I'm not doing this.

*"You're...using my magyk?"* I ask the Dragon, sending the thought to him.

Vesimyr *hmms* in my head, *"Yes. I wasn't sure if it would work. I can't hold it long though."*

**"Abomination!"** Ignautius hisses. But the big blue Dragon backs down, hesitation in his yellow eyes.

Holy shit.

*"Did you claim me as your Rider just in case I failed?"*

Vesimyr snorts, *"Of course. But Dyana, you were already my Rider regardless of any vow. That was a formality. You are mine, and I am yours; vow or not."*

*"Oh."*

*"Yes, 'oh'. Now, play along."*

Vesimyr clears his throat and looks at Ignautius, **"Dyana needs training from someone versed in similar magyk."**

**"What, the mighty Vesimyr isn't up to the task?"** Ignautius taunts.

Vesimyr glares but doesn't rise to the bait. **"I can use her magyk, but Dyana needs to know how to wield it on her own. We need Embyrne."**

**"No."** Ignautius snaps.

**"You call Dyana an abomination, so an abomination is what she needs,"** Vesimyr says.

My jaw drops. I watch as Ignautius leans his head back and lets out a mighty laugh.

*What the fuck is happening?*

**"So, you wish for one worm to train another? Fine. It's useless anyways."** The blue Dragon pauses and lets out a high-pitched stream of song, followed by a mighty roar. *"And when the three of you fail, I will finally be able to kill you."*

The last part, Ignautius hisses in our heads.

*Hmm.* He doesn't want his followers to hear how evil his true goals are.

The sound of loud thumps suddenly approaches. With a loud creaking sound, the auditorium doors burst open and I turn around, trying to get a look.

The racing thoughts in my head go quiet at the sight of the person being led into the room.

It's a woman.

Pale blonde hair that gleams like white gold is what I notice first. Then smooth, umber skin and bright, yellow eyes that survey the room with clear disdain. The kohl lining her eyes only intensifies the bright yellow of her pupils.

The mystery woman is tall, her figure lean and muscular. Her movements are smooth and precise, almost like she's gliding instead of walking. She's clothed in a floor-length black silk dress; plain and simple yet wholly devastating. The fit is loose, but it does nothing to hide her body beneath. Bare feet poke out from beneath the trailing skirt. She wears no other adornment, other than the gleam of a gold ring piercing between her nostrils and several gold hoops of various sizes decorating her ears.

The Dragons leading the woman into the room tug on chains that connect to silver cuffs around her wrists. The woman snarls, baring her teeth, but the Dragons just laugh in response.

**"Pathetic,"** Ignautius tsks, before turning to face me. I freeze under his attention. **"You will train daily with the Beastkyn, or you die."**

The woman comes to a stop before Ignautius. She's shoved to her knees, forced to bow by the Dragons beside her, and the answering glare she gives them turns my blood to ice.

I cough and nod, "I will train with the—"

*Wait.*

Wait.

*"She's Beastkyn? Like…Os was?"* I burst into Vesimyr's head.

*"Do you not see the resemblance?"*

*Resemblance?*

I stare at the woman, only to find her staring back, still on her knees before the Sene Skal.

*"Good. It's settled. You have three months to train with Embyrne, and if you haven't shown adequate progress with getting this new magyk of yours under control, I'll eat you for dinner."*

I blink, rocked by the casual threat and by the sight in front of me.

Yellow-gold eyes.

Dark umber skin.

Tall and muscular.

*Holy fucking shit.*

Still, nothing could have prepared me for Vesimyr in my head saying, *"This is Remus Ostia's sister."*

The woman cocks her head, interest and suspicion filling her gaze in equal parts.

**"No."**

The word bounces throughout the auditorium.

Ignautius growls and the Dragons gasp.

**"What did you just say?"** The Sene Skal's voice is merely a whisper, but the fury it holds makes my stomach turn into knots as nausea makes my mouth fill with hot saliva.

"I am not training some human child."

My jaw drops. "I'm no *child.*"

The Beastkyn—*Embyrne*—scoffs. "You can't be more than what, two and twenty?"

"I'm twenty-six, *actually.*"

Embyrne rolls her eyes, completely unimpressed. She turns to Ignautius and motions to me, her chains clanging. "She's a child. You cannot possibly expect me to be able to teach her anything."

Ignautius snaps at the air in front of Embyrne, but she doesn't even flinch. **"You forget yourself, abomination. You have no choice in this matter. Or would you like to spend the next century in the dungeon? That can certainly be arranged."**

Embyrne raises a brow, "And if I say that I prefer the dungeons? What happens to the mortal then?"

Ignautius bares his teeth, **"Then I kill her."**

*"Gee, I wonder whether or not he wants to kill me..."* I joke to Vesimyr.

*"You are human,"* he responds. *"Or you were. Many of the Dragons here hate humans. They think them no better than animals. What you're seeing is centuries of unchecked prejudice."*

*"And also, he's a murder-hungry psychopath,"* I add.

Vesimyr snorts, *"Yes. That too."*

Embyrne sighs and it brings me back into the moment.

"So, either I train this...*thing,*" she motions to me and my jaw drops again, "or she dies and you throw me back in the Dungeons."

That *bitch.* I am not a *thing!*

**"Yes."** Ignautius nods.

"But if I fail in training her, she also dies?" Embyrne asks dryly.

Ignautius lets out a low clicking sound, **"And you still end up back in the Dungeon."**

Embyrne sighs, "Fine. I will do what I can, but I make no guarantees it will work. Her grasp on magyk is terrible at best."

*"Scale from 1 to 10, how much trouble will I get in if I punch that bitch in the face right now?"* I snarl into Vesimyr's thoughts.

He holds back a snort of laughter. *"A lot. However, you will soon get the chance to do so. Be patient, my young friend."*

*"Fine,"* I grit out.

The Beastkyn turns to the Dragons who shoved her to the ground. She gracefully stands up and brushes her hands off before holding them out to one of the Dragons.

"I can't train her with these on. Drop the cuffs," Embyrne orders.

There's a moment of silence as Ignautius breaks out in dark laughter. The sound of it echoes throughout the room.

**"Just the left,"** the Sene Skal orders and Embyrne's eyes flash with fury, but she says nothing as one of the Dragons leans forward, waving a hand over the cuff. It unlocks and drops to the floor with a loud *clank*.

Vesimyr must sense my confusion.

*"Look at the cuffs."*

I scoff, *"What do you think I'm doing? I am looking!"*

*"Not with your eyes. Look with your magyk."*

Oh. *Right.*

I keep forgetting I have that. Concentrating, I focus my magyk on the cuff on the ground. The second I do, it stings so bad I nearly black out.

*"Fucking hell, what is that?"* I gasp.

*"Elysian cuffs. Elysian is not just the strongest metal in the known world and what our island is named after, it's also conductive and easily paired with spells. Those cuffs are made out of Elysian and there's a binding spell carved into the edge. It blocks all magyk from whoever wears the cuff."*

I glance up to the cuff Embyrne still wears. *"And the right one?"*

*"Look closer."*

This time, when I focus my magyk on the cuff, there's no sharp sting. But I suddenly feel...trapped.

*"What is this?"* I ask. *"It feels strange."*

*"That, my young friend, is a spell that suppresses her Beast."*

Oh my Gods.

*"It's...killing her Dragon side."*

Vesimyr sighs and it's a weary sound. *"Yes. Before the Great War, Kydis was considering making the spell illegal. If worn long enough, it will suffocate the Dragon so thoroughly that it will die and leave them, for lack of a better term, mortal."*

*"That's cruelty,"* I gasp.

*"Yes it is, Dyana. It's terrible. But Embyrne's Dragon is strong, even after all of these years. I can feel it."*

*"Why her?"* I ask. *"Why did you want her to train me?"*

*"Because Embyrne has a very unique type of magyk. Most Dragons don't have elemental powers. They usually lean more towards mental powers. But Embyrne can mimic, using the powers of anyone close to her, Dragon or otherwise."*

*"A mimic? I've never even heard of that."*

*"It's extremely rare; it's why Ignautius has kept her alive. Even though they disagree with her choice to change forms, the Skal needs her."*

Interesting.

Still.

I can't believe she's Os' sister.

It feels purposeful, her presence.

This can't be a coincidence. It can't be.

I won't *let* it be.

# CHAPTER 7
## RYU

*It's always the same dream.*

*I watch through my Mother's eyes as we plunge towards the ground, Achan Drayven magykly pinned to my back. I feel the way he stabs and attacks her. Her pain is mine. Her wounds are mine.*

*"I never wanted this to be how we meet," she whispers in my mind. "I'm so sorry, Ryu."*

*"You're dead," I reply. "This isn't real. This is just a dream."*

*I feel rather than see her sigh. "You can deny your birthright, but don't deny your magyk."*

*"What do you mean?" I cry. "I don't know what you mean!"*

*"My darling"—the ground quickly approaches—"I wish we had more time."*

*"I do too," I'm sobbing in her head, unable to stop any of this.*

*"Dreams are never just dreams," she whispers, before we hit the ground and I—*

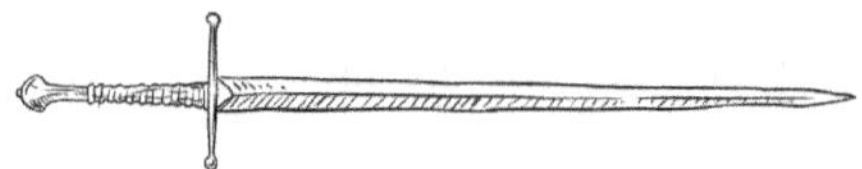

I gasp, waking up as my wings flail.

"Shh, it's okay," Amalia whispers. "I'm here. It was just a dream."

I pant and fall back against the ground, where Amalia is crouched next to me.

I do not like how quickly my body and mind are aging. It's...it's helpful, but I was just looking up at her a year ago, and now I have to crane my neck down just to meet her blue gaze.

I feel like we have no time, and that scares me. But there is much I do not tell her, my fear included.

*"I'm okay,"* I reassure her.

She caresses my snout. "No, you're not. And that's okay. But you never have to talk about it. Just know that I'm here. You're not alone, Ryu."

I nod and Amalia curls up against my belly.

A glance to the left shows Nyall is awake and watching us.

I wish I was still young. I wish I didn't understand her heartbreak. It was all so much easier when I didn't understand.

Nyall raises his hand and makes the number one.

I'm much closer to Nyall than Amalia realizes.

She doesn't know that I've been visiting him in secret for the past year, and I'm not sure I'll ever tell her.

We developed a code.

One finger—or in my case, talon—means, "Are you okay?"

Two fingers or talons means Yes.

Three means No.

I raise two talons without alerting Amalia and Nyall smiles softly.

He makes a closed fist, which means, "Liar."

I raise two talons again and his smile drops.

He raises his hand, pointing towards his eye, before lowering it and pointing to his heart, and then pointing to me.

*"I love you."*

I swish my tail back and forth subtly, telling him that I agree.

*I do love him too.*

Nyall smiles and I can tell he's missed me. I'm thrilled we're joining him, but I'm also scared. I don't want it to create more division between him and Amalia. It's not my place to comment on her...romantic endeavors.

But *Gods.* When will Amalia realize Nyall is in love with her?

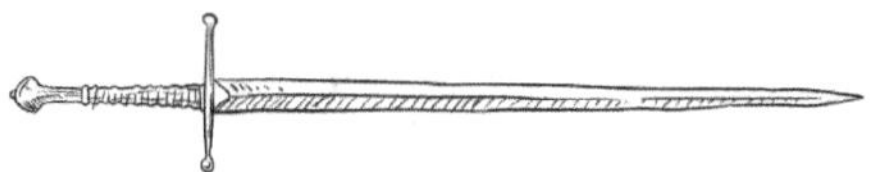

"Virgyl is going to escort us to the camp," Amalia announces.

She packed with startling speed, choosing to leave most of her things in the cave. I have nothing to pack, but I did eat two extra deer this morning in case I can't spare time to hunt the next few days.

A full stomach is all I'm packing.

I watch as Amalia mounts the fuzzy wolf instead of riding with Nyall and Aanad.

I am not the only one watching, though. A quick glance at Nyall shows his eyes are also trained on Amalia. I don't miss the flash of disappointment in his mismatched gaze as Amalia chooses Virgyl over riding with him.

Aanad stomps her sharp hooves with frustration.

*"They're taking too long,"* she hisses in my head. *"Tell them to hurry up. I want to run!"*

I haven't told Amalia or Nyall that I can speak to animals. There are some things that do not need to be shared.

I've never asked Aanad why she hasn't spoken like this to Amalia.

*"Mortals are slow,"* I remind her and she hisses again.

*"Too slow! I want to run!"*

Aanad always sounds like she's on the verge of a violent outburst. Her voice was old and scratchy, not at all fitting her exterior.

*"Rude,"* she hisses, hearing my stray thought. *"I will kick you in the shin, Dragon."*

*"Try it and I'll finally decide to try roasted Oryx!"*

Aanad laughs in my head as she nickers and tosses her head.

A few bags are attached to my back, and the weight of it feels strange. Not unwelcome, but strange.

Nyall gives me a knowing look and I turn away. I don't want to fly, and neither of them have ever given me a hard time about it.

But the guilt. The guilt eats away at me.

I feel like I'm failing them. I feel like a *disappointment.* What kind of Dragon is scared of flying?

As Nyall mounts Aanad, a few of Virgyl's wolves join us. The pack barks happily at me and I swish my tail, playing with them.

It distracts from the guilt and fear.

*"It's a three-day journey,"* Virgyl announces, and I watch Nyall's mismatched eyes go wide. *"Speed is not the answer, endurance is. We go slow and stop when it gets dark."*

I send him a feeling of understanding and we head out.

I don't miss the way Amalia glances over her shoulder, her eyes sad and empty as she says goodbye to her cave.

It's our home.

The only one I've ever really known.

But we can help. I might not be able to fly, but that doesn't make me useless. Together, we can help. I know it. Or at least that's what I force myself to believe.

Rain begins to fall as soon as we set off.

Amalia and Nyall wear waterproof clothes, but their strange mortal hair gets damp instantly.

Several of the wolves walk underneath me, taking advantage of the heat of my belly and the shelter of my body.

A year ago, I was the one walking beneath the wolves' bellies.

It's a grueling day. We stop once at a stream for water, and the wolves catch some rabbits. I'm still full of deer, so I stay behind to watch the mortals, much to Amalia's eternal annoyance.

"I can defend myself, Ryu," she always tells me, but I never listen.

The mortals are shivering by the time we make camp that evening. The sky has just turned dark as Nyall dismounts and raises his hands, using his strange magyk to create a large, invisible shield over us.

We're in the open, but at least we would be dry.

The wolves and I head out to catch dinner, but I glance back at the two people who have ended up becoming my family.

*Please work this out,* I want to say.

Instead, when Amalia isn't looking, I use one talon to open her bag and casually slice a hole into her sleeping sack.

Virgyl watches me with yellow eyes, and I motion for him to look away.

*"She will be cranky about that,"* Virgyl warns.

*"She's cranky about everything."*

He huffs a laugh and disappears into the forest. I quickly follow, not wanting to get caught.

# CHAPTER 8
## AMALIA

A ripped and broken sleep sack sits in my bag.

*"You are not as sneaky as you think you are,"* I call to Ryu, but she doesn't respond.

*Meddling child!*

"Something wrong?" Nyall asks. The question is innocent enough, but it enrages me so much that I kick my bag, sending it flying.

Nyall blurs and catches it.

"What's got your panties in a twist, Blue?"

I glare at him, "I told you not to call me that."

He smirks, "I don't really care. Now, why are you kicking things like an angry child?"

In my head, I'm stabbing him. Over and over again. "My fucking sleep sack is ruined."

Nyall raises a brow. "You packed a ruined sleep sack?"

"No, it just...*ripped.* Somehow."

I look pointedly at Ryu, but she turns around so that I face her butt and tail. Nyall hides a smirk.

"I see," he says, playing along. "You can have mine then."

Nyall abandons the small fire he just made and grabs his sleep sack, walking over. He hands me the luxuriously soft fabric. It's so much nicer than mine that I feel embarrassed instantly.

"It's fine—" I try to turn it away, but he shoves it into my hands.

"Stop being obstinate and just *take* it, Amalia. I can sleep on the ground. I'm sure one of the wolves will volunteer as a pillow for the night. They're fuzzy enough as it is."

Deep down, a part of me wants to *smile.* The Prince of Ur Daoine, the son of Achan Drayven, wants to *snuggle* with my wolves.

Then I remember him leaving. I remember the barbed words we hurled at each other.

I remember the *pain.*

We stare at each other, the silent tension so thick I could cut it with one of my daggers.

"Fine," I respond hurriedly. "Thank you."

Nyall nods and lets go of the sleep sack, which I cradle in my arms.

Turning away from him, I get the sack set up and strip out of my pants, letting my tunic fall to my knees and crawling in, exhausted.

"You need to eat something before you fall asleep," Nyall calls over, but I shake my head.

"I'm not hungry."

Then I get a strong whiff of Nyall's honeysuckle magyk.

Oh *Gods,* the sleep sack smells like him.

I need to...I need to get away from it.

I nearly jump out of the sack, "Never mind, you're right. I *should* eat something."

"Good girl," Nyall says, and my knees nearly go out.

I hate the way those words make me feel.

*Proud. Happy. Delicious.* NO. NO. NO. NO! I smother my emotions as I walk over to Nyall, who silently hands me a small container full of dried fruit, nuts, and cubes of hard cheese. There's a lid that fits over it, keeping the mixture fresh.

Fancy Fae bullshit. Despite my annoyance, the food is great, and soon, my stomach becomes full. A heavy, contented feeling washes over me and I head back to the sleep sack as Nyall finishes starting the fire.

My eyelids grow heavy as the fire begins to warm the space.

I slide into the sleep sack, getting comfortable. The ground is hard, but the sleep sack is so plush I barely feel it.

Before I know it, my eyes fall closed as I relax fully.

Eventually I fall asleep to the scent of honeysuckle and fresh air.

A scent uniquely, and perfectly, Nyall's.

A scent that, unfortunately, brings me great comfort, and I hate him for it.

*LIAR.*

During the night, I distantly feel someone caressing my hair and tucking another blanket over me, which is when I realize I'm shivering and cold.

A soft kiss is pressed against my forehead. *"Sleep. I'll look after you."*

I'm so out of it, I don't think anything of the low voice, and fall back asleep, none the wiser.

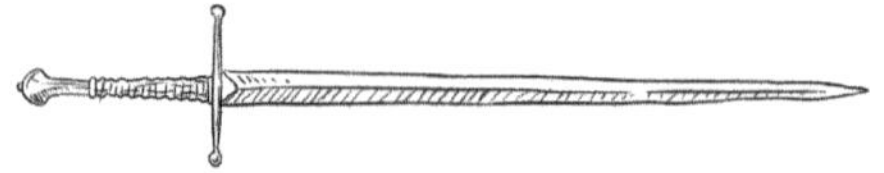

The next two nights are the same.

Nyall continues to let me use his sleep sack, and every night, I grow more and more restless. It feels like something is crawling beneath my skin and I can't stay still.

I feel frantic and hurried, but there's nothing chasing us.

All of this close contact with Nyall...it has me on edge.

*I have to keep him out of my mind.*

*He cannot know.*

*I don't—I don't want him to know.*

~~*LET HIM IN. LET HIM IN.*~~

But every time I think about him, I can't help but think about Os too. It feels like I'm betraying him. Betraying the incredible sacrifice he made.

My eyes are still closed, and our campsite is quiet, but beneath my heavy lids, gold eyes watch me.

*I'm so sorry.*

*I miss you.*

Emotions broil within. A deadly mixture of self-hatred, regret, and debilitating guilt.

Sleep and relaxation evade me, so I open my eyes and shove the emotions down.

My chest tightens to the point of pain, but I ignore it. I've become so good at that.

I roll out of the sleep sack, each muscle protesting. Three days of riding from dawn until dusk has turned my body painful and stiff.

"We'll get to camp by nightfall, and I'll have a hot bath drawn up for you," Nyall says casually as he hands me some mystery piece of dried meat.

I grimace, not wanting to eat it, but...I need the energy.

I can't afford to not eat.

I chew on the dried jerky and try not to think about what animal it came from as Nyall gets us packed up.

Ryu is practically glowing with all of the attention Nyall is giving her—that *traitor*.

But I will never truly begrudge her for it. She deserves to have a relationship with those who raised her.

*Regardless* of my feelings about them.

I watch as Nyall wakes up and stands, stretching his arms over his head. Sometime in the night, he shed his shirt, so the movement shows off his muscular back.

I can't look away. I should. I *want* to look away but...

Something catches my eye.

Nyall has new tattoos, ones that don't look Fae at all. I can't quite make out the shape along his left shoulder, but it almost looks like...*wings*.

He drops his arms and I blink, trying to shake off the hypnotism of his physique. Nyall walks over to Ryu, whose eyes are cracking open. She's been sleeping curled up around him and the wolves, which also puts her large body in between us.

Something I'm most grateful for.

~~LIAR!~~

Nyall squats down and caresses Ryu's snout, whispering something to her. The Dragon's silver and copper eyes are luminous and sleepy, and full of so much love that it nearly shreds me in two. His tattooed arms and hands are so harsh next to her gleaming red scales.

Pride and resentment go to war in my heart. I don't want to keep Ryu from Nyall.

I don't want to keep her from love. But...what does that mean for me?

Ryu looks at Virgyl and the wolf coughs before looking at me. *"We're going to scout ahead. I want to make sure the camp is safe to approach. Catch up with us."*

Then they turn to leave.

My jaw drops as I realize Virgyl is in on this too.

*"You told him?"* I snap at Ryu.

She glares and I take a deep breath, quieting the anger.

*"I'm sorry. I'm just...tired. I'm not mad at you and shouldn't have snapped like that."*

Ryu stands and ambles over to me, leaning down to brush her snout against my cheek.

*"Firstly, he already knew. Second, of course. Fuzz-butt and I talk all the time. Third, I will always forgive you."*

I rub my eyes, already tired of this day.

*"I know you're doing this on purpose,"* I accuse, but she just brushes it off. *"Pushing Nyall and I together."*

*"Yep,"* Ryu chirps happily.

I look at her with sad resignation, "Why? There is no point."

She pulls back, meeting my gaze with a curious look in her eyes.

*"Because you deserve to be happy, Ama. You've sacrificed so much for everyone else...you deserve happiness you can keep."*

I blink away the tears that threaten to fall. "I don't think that's true, Ryu. I'm not a good person. I don't deserve anything at all."

Ryu is quiet and I can feel her sadness, so I add, "*You* make me happy, Ryu. You and the pack. You keep me going."

Ryu licks my cheek. *"That doesn't mean you are undeserving of love."*

*"I can't, Ryu,"* I admit, sending her the thought. *"I just can't."*

*"Just try,"* she suggests before licking me again and turning to walk away. *"Tell Aanad I say hi."*

"Looks like you'll be riding with me today," Nyall muses and I nearly jump out of my own skin.

"Eavesdropping isn't cute," I snarl.

Nyall shrugs, his mismatched eyes sparkling with mirth. "Who said I was eavesdropping?"

"Well don't do it, it's rude," I finish and Nyall just raises a brow.

I pack my stuff up as Aanad enters the small clearing while Nyall takes down the spell that kept us safe and dry.

She nickers and nibbles at my fingers as I caress her forehead. "Hello, sweet girl."

Her head pushes harder against me, asking for scratches.

It's such a small moment.

But it makes my heart ache.

I miss this. I miss *them.*

"Let me give you a leg up," Nyall says casually, and I don't think much of it until his hands are around my calf muscle.

His hands are cool and deft as he bends down and places my foot upon his raised leg.

I use it to lift myself onto the saddle, but...it's been a while.

Two years, to be exact.

I falter and Nyall's other hand lands on my ass as he shoves me up onto Aanad's back. He easily mounts behind me, landing in a single, smooth jump.

"Show off," I mutter, but my words fall silent as he winds his arms around my waist and grabs the reins.

"I can do it," I snap, but he doesn't listen.

"You're my guest." His breath is hot against my ear as Aanad picks up a walk. The movement shoves me against him so that Nyall's front is pressed against my back, our hips aligned. As our bodies become synced with Aanad's floaty gait, we're pressed even closer together, hips swaying as if in a dance.

It knocks the wind out of me, feeling him this close.

"How long is the ride today?" I ask.

Gods, I can't do this all day.

"We'll be there by dusk."

Great. Just fucking *great.*

"Something wrong, Amalia?" Nyall asks.

I grit my teeth. "I'm *fine.*"

Then Nyall's warm breath tickles my ear. "Is that why you tense up the second I touch you?"

I inhale so hard, I nearly choke.

"Perhaps I dislike your proximity," I force the words to leave the tip of my tongue.

They taste bitter.

Nyall laughs and I feel every movement.

"For someone who is such an accomplished *liar,* you aren't very good at it. At least not with me."

"I'm not lying," I snap.

"Suit yourself," he sighs. "You're the one making this difficult."

My jaw *does* drop then, and I glance behind me, but the angle is awkward.

"I'm really starting to hate you," I mutter, but the words lack the fury I intended them to have. Instead, my words sound sad.

*Regretful.*

"No, no," Nyall *tsks* and grabs my waist. I screech as he lifts me off the saddle and twists me in the air. I land, riding backwards, with my legs over his.

"If you're going to tell me you hate me," he purrs, our noses nearly touching, "then the least you could do is look me in the eyes when you say it."

My heart races and I force my mouth to form the words.

"Say it," Nyall bares his teeth at me, but his eyes are *smiling*.

"No."

"SAY IT!" he snarls, snapping his fangs near my neck. It's playful—but it's also the realest he's been with me since...since the cave.

Nyall Drayven unleashed is my biggest weakness.

Not the *Prince*. Not the *leader*.

But the monster beneath.

"I hate you," I breathe.

Saying it feels wrong.

"No, you don't," Nyall sighs, sounding as tired as I look. He looks at me with sad eyes, that ironclad control of his firmly back in place. "You only wish you hated me. But you don't, Amalia." His lips are nearly against mine when Aanad jumps over a log, and I'm almost launched off her back.

"Put me back," I snarl, getting in his face, "or I'll fucking *walk.*"

Nyall sighs and twists me so that I'm facing forward again.

"For what it's worth," he says near my ear, so quietly I strain to catch the words, "I will never hate you."

"Duly noted," I respond, hoping he can't hear the way my voice is trembling, or how my heart is beating so hard within my chest, I can feel the vibration rattling my bones.

His words *hurt*...because I feel their naked truth.

"When we get there," Nyall starts, "if you could refrain from acting like you hate me, at least in public, that would be best."

I scoff, "Worried about your reputation, Prince?"

His tone is low and serious when he answers, "No, Amalia. I'm worried that my armies won't trust me if I'm putting all of our resources behind the girl who haunts their nightmares. If they see us fighting, it will only cause more distrust."

I hate that he's right.

"Fine," I mutter.

We both fall silent, lost in our own thoughts.

I don't know when it happens, but eventually, I grow tired and lean against him. My eyes fall shut and sleep wraps me in its dark clutches.

*"Amalia, save me!" Os cries out.*

*"I'm coming!" I scream.*

*I'm in a long hallway that looks like our Gauntlet training quarters.*

*Os is somewhere at the end of the hall.*

*I can't see him, but I can hear him.*

*"HELP!" His cries echo until I can't even hear my own thoughts, just his pain. I sprint faster, pushing my legs as fast as they can go.*

*"HANG ON!"*

*Then his voice changes.*

*"You left me."*

*It's him.*

*And it's Dyana.*

*Both of their voices at once.*

*"You LEFT ME!" they scream, and I scream back, crying out in horror as I sprint faster. Trying to get to them.*

*"I'm going to save you. I'm going to save you," I sob.*

*"You're never going to save anyone," they hiss at me.*

*Then the floor opens up beneath me and I'm falling, plunging into a dark pit of the Earth.*

*I blink and look over as Dyana and Os fall next to me.*

*But their bodies are mangled and bloody. A huge hole is in Dyana's chest where there should be a heart.*

*"You did this," they whisper. "This is your fault."*

*"NO!" I scream and reach out for them.*

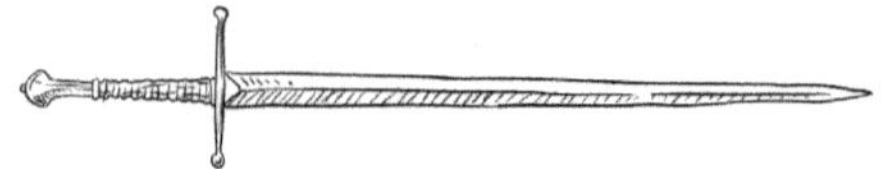

With a gasp, I jerk awake, hands outstretched.

"Hey, it's okay," Nyall whispers, his arms around me as his hand rubs my forearms. "You're okay. You're safe."

Adrenaline floods my body as my heart races. Too panicked to remember all of the reasons why I *shouldn't*, I lean back again Nyall.

But reality hits hard and I blink, shaking it off as I pull away from his touch.

Nyall sighs and I hear the disappointment in his tone. It threatens to break me.

"We're almost there," Nyall clears his throat. "You've slept all day."

"Right," I say, my voice dry and scratchy. "Sorry."

He shakes his head. "Don't be. I'm glad you could get some rest."

Nyall hands me a small jug of water and I gulp it down quickly. I turn in the saddle, handing it back to him but pause, watching as his eyes trace the spilled drops of water down my neck.

He shakes his head, like he's shaking off the sight of me. "Virgyl and Ryu are just ahead."

I turn forward, trying to forget the look in his eyes.

"Good," is all I can muster as a response.

Sure enough, a huge black Dyre Wolf and a bright red Dragon wait for us in a small clearing atop a hill.

*"Have a nice day?"* Ryu asks pleasantly.

I glare at her as she laughs in my head.

*"The camp is secure. The pack and I will wait in the forest until we know it's safe."* Virgyl's voice drowns out her laugh.

I nod and give him a soft smile, "Thank you."

Virgyl turns his gaze to the male behind me, *"If Amalia or Ryu are hurt, I will hold you responsible."*

"They won't be," Nyall promises. "I swear on my life."

Virgyl holds his gaze for a few moments longer, and Nyall's face goes slack before he nods at the wolf.

Virgyl said something else to him.

Something not meant for me to hear.

Jealousy flares within me but I tamp it down.

Virgyl probably just threatened him again. He would never betray me.

Nyall makes a clicking noise and Aanad picks up a slow trot as we make our way up the hill. At the top I nearly fall off Aanad's back.

A sprawling valley sits beneath us, nestled between the dense trees of the Ulster Wald and clusters of steep, snow-tipped mountains. The valley is decorated with hundreds if not thousands of pale blue tents of varying sizes. All bearing the sigil of a bright red Dragon.

"You..." I break off. Unable to even finish my sentence.

"Is something wrong?" Nyall asks in an innocent voice. "Do you like my sigil, Amalia?"

"It's Ryu," I realize, looking at Nyall with wide eyes. "You made...Ryu your symbol?"

*"Don't be mad,"* Ryu says in my head. *"He asked me if it was okay."*

"I'm not mad," I say aloud, and admit the truth. "I like it."

"Good," Nyall whispers. "I hoped you would." He makes another clicking noise and Aanad descends down a winding narrow path to the camp.

I'm suddenly overcome with the overwhelming, all-consuming feeling that there's no going back from this. Every part of it. Every day, every *minute* I spend with Nyall breaks down more and more of my walls.

Shouts sound throughout the valley as Nyall is spotted. Then several screams follow as they take in the huge red Dragon following us.

Nyall raises a hand, and the screams stop as a group of armed guards monitoring the entrance stands aside.

"My lord," they all whisper and bow as we pass.

I roll my eyes at the deference.

"Remember what I said," Nyall whispers. "I know you're mad, and I accept that. But we have to show a united front if this is going to work...*please.*"

"Yeah, yeah," I sigh and put on a polite smile. "I'll just imagine I'm stabbing you."

"Yummy," Nyall brushes his lips against my ear and my jaw drops a little. "My favorite kind of foreplay."

Then he's leaping off Aanad's back and I'm left there, wide-eyed and shocked. Nyall holds his hand out, offering to help me down. He merely laughs when I ignore the offer and slide off of Aanad's back myself. My legs are stiff and painful from so many days in the saddle.

Hundreds of people mill about. Magyka and human, coexisting in peace.

All stop and stare as we pass.

They flash smiles at Nyall but look at me with a mixture of fear and hatred.

Most have to look away from Ryu, unable to handle the Dragonfear her presence incites.

"If they are cruel to her, I will—"

Nyall cuts me off as we come to a halt, "They wouldn't dare, and if they do dare, I'll kill them."

I blink at the blatant threat.

"You really mean that," I realize and Nyall looks at me like he's annoyed it took me this long to notice.

"Yes I do."

I nod, pleased. "Good."

*"Have a little faith,"* Ryu whispers to me.

I snort, *"I have no faith."*

I feel her sadness and look back, sending her a soft smile.

*"I have faith in you, and old fuzz-butt,"* I whisper to her. *"Just not people."*

Ryu laughs but I feel a wave of happiness and sadness drifting back to me. Nyall watches us carefully, affection clear enough in his gaze that it makes me breathless. and hit the ground, instantly regretting it when my legs nearly give out.

"My lord!" someone calls, and I reach for my dagger. "Back already?"

Nyall's hand on mine stops me as he leans down to whisper in my ear, "No stabbing...*yet.*"

I glare at him but leave it as a tall, muscular male with deep umber skin, warm brown eyes, and silver hair approaches.

"You made it back safe," the male says with a smile, before looking down at me. His smile widens as he takes me in, before glancing at Ryu behind us. "Oh good, here I was worrying that things were getting boring."

The male reaches a hand out. "I'm Davyn, Nyall's second. I'm in charge of the camp when he's away."

I force my own hand to meet his, shaking it gently. "Amalia."

"Oh, I know," he winks at me. "I'm just glad you're here so that this one," Davyn looks at Nyall, "won't be such a pain in the ass anymore."

Davyn is clearly Demis, but they're not known for having senses of humor.

Nyall glares at him and Davyn laughs. "Can you have two hot baths drawn, please? And ensure Ryu's nest is ready."

"Already done. I saw you up on the hill." Davyn smiles again, his teeth white and blinding. "Better hurry though or the water will get cold."

Nyall groans happily and pulls Davyn in for a hug. "I could kiss you!"

"Gods, please don't." Davyn cringes, "We've discussed this before, you're not my type."

Nyall laughs and slaps Davyn on the back a few times before letting go.

I blink.

Nyall has...*friends.* This is his *friend.*

The only real friend I ever had is dead. Dyana was the only one who was ever excited for me to come home, the wolves not included.

To have a person *trust* you; to have a person *miss you.*

It was a beautiful feeling. One I'm not sure I'll ever feel again.

Sadness fills me and I stand there awkwardly, unsure what to do, when Ryu's snout nudges me.

"You said Ryu's nest," I process this aloud. "What kind of nest?"

Nyall turns to me with a smirk, "I'll show you."

Davyn takes Aanad and I follow behind Nyall, Ryu not far behind me.

It's a short walk before we come to an extremely large blue tent being held up by wooden planks embossed with glowing white symbols.

"This is yours," Nyall looks at Ryu. "It's enchanted to be bigger on the inside, so you don't have to sleep out in the open anymore."

Ryu makes a trilling noise that I know means she's extremely pleased, and dashes into the tent.

I peek my head in and blink at the size of it, and at the large pile of pillows on the floor, which Ryu is already burrowing into.

I sniff, "My tent is close to hers, I presume?"

"About that," Nyall says, and anxiety fills me instantly. "I told you we've recently taken in more refugees...which means there are no more unused tents. We'll have to share."

You've got to be kidding me.

My eye twitches and I slap a hand over it.

Nyall flashes a pleased smile at me and turns, walking away. "This way."

I grit my teeth and stomp after him, fuming.

Nyall enters a large tent just next to Ryu's, and I follow.

Warmth greets me and my skin tingles as I pass through the door.

It's enchanted too.

The tent is luxurious but small. Furs and rich velvets decorate the space, and two steaming baths sit near a crackling fire in the middle of the space. There's a table with papers strewn about, and two chairs.

As my gaze travels over the rest of the tent, I come to a crashing halt.

"Absolutely not." I shake my head. "There's only one bed. *Clearly* this won't work."

Nyall shrugs and begins stripping, leaving me standing there like an idiot. "This is the only option. We've shared a bed plenty of times. Once more won't kill you."

I sneer at him, "I'll go sleep with Ryu then."

Nyall sighs. "Get in the fucking bath, Amalia. You're being ridiculous."

"I hate you," I repeat as he drops his pants.

~~I don't hate you at all.~~

"Keep telling yourself that," he says pleasantly. "Now, get in the goddamned bath. You smell terrible."

Part of me wants to be a petulant child about this and throw a tantrum.

The pragmatic side of me knows that making a fuss won't actually help anything. So I grit my teeth and strip off my own clothes, disregarding my human notions of nakedness.

Nyall's back is to me as he lounges in the bath, but I do not watch to see if he glances at my naked body as I slide into the foamy water.

The warmth is divine, and I sigh, melting into the metal tub.

"Told you," he says smugly.

I splash him with water, and he flicks his fingers as his white magyk blasts water at my face. I sputter, half-choking, as Nyall snickers in the background.

"You're such an ass," I hiss, ignoring the fact that I'm hiding a smile.

"Perhaps," Nyall shrugs, and we fall silent.

The water is opaque and milky, the scent of lavender in the air. Whatever they put in the bath strips the dirt and grime of the past few days away, leaving me feeling clean and sleepy.

I'm not sure how long we lay there in the tubs near the crackling fire. Long enough that the water begins to turn cold, and I realize I'm shivering.

Without speaking, Nyall reaches an arm over to my tub and dips his pointer finger in the water.

Glowing white bands encircle his finger as he swirls it through the water.

Soon, the tub water is steaming and deliciously hot.

"Thanks," I sigh, blaming my sudden manners on the warm water.

"Tell me when it gets cold, and I'll do it again."

I nod and sink down until the water covers me neck to toe.

My eyes have just begun to close when Nyall clears his throat, waking me.

"If you don't wish to share the bed," Nyall says carefully, interrupting my relaxation. "Then I will take the floor again. I do not wish for you to be uncomfortable. We used to have spare cots, but with the sudden increase in bodies..."

I glance down at my quickly pruning fingers.

*Don't be a fucking child, Amalia.*

I can keep my walls up while staying civil.

Or something like that.

I sniff and spare a glance at him.

His blonde hair is damp and free from the braids. Drops of water trail down his chest, making his tattoos sparkle.

Dark circles have grown beneath his eyes.

"No," I say slowly. "You need to get some sleep too. You look exhausted, and you're no good to your rebels if you're so tired you can barely keep your eyes open."

Nyall blinks, surprised.

"So," I take a deep breath. "We can *share.*"

He rubs his hand over his face with a sigh. "Thank you."

"Just stay on your side," I mutter, forcing myself to stand. I ignore the way his eyes follow my movements, but I can *feel* his gaze on my body and it's almost too much to take.

In this small, enclosed space, I *feel* his closeness.

The entire tent smells of his honeysuckle magyk.

*I hate it.*

~~*LIAR.*~~

I rifle through my bag, arguing with my own thoughts. Somehow Davyn had already gotten our stuff in the tent when we entered.

Throwing on a clean tunic over my head, I sigh at the delicious feeling of clean fabric. The shirt clings to my damp skin but I ignore it as I climb into the small bed, scooting as far to one side as I possibly can, and face away from Nyall.

As I lay in bed, listening to him puttering around, I force my eyes to close.

But I don't relax.

I trace his movements, picturing where he is in the space.

Every *step.*

Every *breath.*

I don't even do it on purpose, I simply can't help but be *aware* of him. The bed dips under his weight as he slides under the covers next to me.

He's facing me. I can tell.

It's also the easiest way we will both fit. I grab a spare pillow and shove it behind me without looking.

He snorts, "What's this for?"

"Put it between us. I don't want a hard cock against my ass in the morning," I grumble.

"As you wish," he says with a laugh, and I feel the pillow go between us. The bed is so small that the simple movement of placing the pillow causes his fingers to brush against my lower back.

Thank fuck he can't see my face.

My jaw drops open at the feeling of his hands on me.

Then they're gone.

~~Come back.~~

*Good. This is good. The less contact, the better.*

~~*LIAR. LIAR. LIAR!*~~

I can feel the heat of Nyall's body next to mine, and a small part of me wants to wrap myself around him and never let go.

Instead, I do nothing.

I lay there pretending to fall asleep, while inside, my head and my heart go to war.

Remus's face appears in my head, his gold eyes full of pain and disappointment, and I have to hold my breath to keep from sobbing.

"Goodnight, Amalia," Nyall whispers as the room goes dark.

I open my eyes, finding only darkness.

He can't see me, so I stop hiding the pain on my face.

I hold in the sobs.

Hold in the tears.

But the pain...I let it free, let it crease my brow and purse my lips.

~~Please, see me.~~

~~Save me.~~

I suffocate my thoughts, ignoring them, as I whisper into the darkness, "Good-night, Nyall."

# CHAPTER 9
## MIRIELLE

"FUCK!" I kick the bucket of water next to me, spilling it everywhere as water coats the forge floor.

My latest attempt at rebuilding Forsaken is a bust. *Again.* The shattered pieces of the would-be staff lie on the floor in front of me.

"It's not strong enough," I curse, sliding down onto the damp floor. "Why is it never strong enough?"

My head falls into my hands as I breathe deeply, trying not to lose my patience completely.

"Godsdamnit," I breathe. "Why isn't this working?"

"You're testing the weapons on a Dragon scale?"

I jump at Kairos' voice. My eyes meet his.

He's holding the undamaged scale. He knows what this means.

The question is: what is he going to do about it, and do I play dumb?

*"Trust him,"* a distant voice whispers.

*Fine.*

I cross my arms. "Yes."

Kairos doesn't move. He just continues to look at me with those obsidian eyes.

Then he reaches a hand out.

I blink, taken aback, before I place my hand in his.

He helps me up and gives me the scale with a nod.

Sweat drips down my brows and all over my body, and I grab the scale with wet hands.

It's cool beneath my touch, but Kairos's hands are cooler as his fingers brush against mine.

It's so surprising, I have to swallow my gasp to keep it from coming out.

I lay the scale on the table and turn, wiping my sweaty hands on my apron and drying them as much as possible.

The forge is so hot that I'm always coated in sweat, my curls damp against my forehead.

I can only wear a thin sleeveless top beneath my apron, and it's always soaking wet at the end of a shift.

I've...gotten used to it.

Two years of this. Two years of learning how to create weapons to rebuild the staff I once had. Two years of trying to build something strong enough to kill a Dragon, should I have to fight my way out.

The sweat of the forge isn't all bad, though.

Sweat is, after all, *water*.

As I wait for Kairos to respond I subtly use my magyk to grab hold of spilled water on the ground and the sweat droplets gathered on our skin.

The magyk tingles against my senses as I quietly form the water into the shape of a dagger.

Kairos turns and glances at the dagger, completely unimpressed.

I blink and let go of the magyk. The water crashes back to the ground, and my skin becomes damp once again.

"You're not surprised," I note.

Kairos gives me an amused look, "Do you think you are the only one with magyk?"

With a raised hand, he takes hold of the water in the room and mimics my dagger.

Only, it's 10x bigger.

"You're Demis," I gasp.

The corner of Kairos's mouth twitches.

"Not quite," he says, twisting his hand to make the dagger spin in the air.

After a moment he releases it, and the water returns to the floor once again.

Not Demis.

"Magyka?" I ask, curious.

Water and fire are the most difficult elements to master, too wild to be controlled.

Only the strongest magyk users can wield them.

Kairos ignores my questions, neither confirming nor denying the accusation.

"I can hear your mind racing. I am not going to tell you what I am, so you can stop guessing."

I blink and realize I'm being incredibly rude.

"It's just been so long since I've met anyone else like us and been able to...be myself. But I'm being rude. I apologize."

Kairos's eyes soften. "You are forgiven."

His eyes flick down to the shattered staff on the ground.

"The metals you're using...they're too weak," he says, shocking me. "You need something stronger. Something like Elysian."

"Tell me about it," I order and he raises a brow. "How exactly does one get ahold of Elysian?"

Kairos sighs, "That's the problem. It is impossible. No one but the Dragons know where it is, and none but a Dragon are strong enough to retrieve it."

*Fuck.*

"Perhaps you could ask your friend," Kairos suggests gently. "Dyana."

*That name.*

"No," I snap and immediately wince at the anger in my voice. "That—I don't want to do that. Besides she doesn't want anything to do with me. The more space between us, the better. For *everyone*."

I sigh and walk over to a set of chairs at the side of the room.

Kairos follows, joining me. The tall male takes a seat in the chair to my left. He's so tall, he makes his chair look tiny in comparison.

"You were lovers," he surmises. "You and Dyana."

The sigh that leaves me is one that betrays my age.

"Before we got here," I look up to the ceiling, my voice hollow. "Then I ruined it."

"How?" Kairos asks.

I glance at him with a raised brow. "You're prying."

The very same thing I just did to him.

He smirks. "True. I apologize."

The both of us fall silent.

"We were together," I tell him. "I...*courted* her, you could say. But it was during the Gauntlet. The timing was terrible. The Gauntlet—it's only won with great sacrifice."

Kairos looks at me, "And what was your sacrifice, Mirielle Zenyth?"

I let my head fall back as I move my gaze back to the ceiling.

"Her. My sacrifice was her."

Kairos doesn't react. I suppose he must have guessed that would be my answer. The male stays quiet, not pushing for further detail.

"Your idea, it's a good one. We do need to find a Dragon to help us. But I don't want to go through Dyana to do it."

"You spent days flying with them," Kairos notes. "I think if they were going to eat you, they would have. You need to find one of those Dragons and see if you can befriend it. Get it to talk to you."

I roll my eyes, "They're not going to talk to me. No matter how hard I try. None of them said a fucking *word* when I had to spend nearly a week carrying Dyana's dead body in my arms."

Suddenly I'm right back in that moment. Her dead body in my arms, the smell of rotting, decomposing flesh beginning to reach my nose.

Her skin was so cold.

The anger, the desolation I felt; it all comes roaring back.

I jump to my feet and whirl, pointing at Kairos. "Do you know what they did? For three days, they flew next to me while I held her dead body in my arms. I know well enough now that they can talk. But not one of them said *anything*."

Kairos's eyes are full of pity and I have to fight the tears that suddenly want to explode from my eyes. "I was right next to them," I whisper. "And they. Did. *Nothing.*"

I pause, panting.

"There is no love between us. I will try to ask for their help, but you need to know that they will likely ignore me. To them, I am *nothing!*"

I didn't mean to shout.

"You're angry," Kairos says gently.

I sigh and drop my head into my hands, massaging my damp scalp.

Raising my head, I meet his eyes, "Yes. I am angry. So angry that sometimes there is nothing else. Just this void within me."

He nods. "You've been spending lots of time at the beach."

Kairos misses nothing.

I wring my hands together, fiddling with my fingers. "The water...it helps. It quiets the screams inside my head. How ironic is it that only when I am holding my breath beneath the surface, do I feel like I can finally *breathe?*"

Kairos stares at me like he can't figure me out.

"Why are you asking me all of this? Why do you care?" I ask plainly.

He stills, but his eyes continue to rove over me.

"Just because I didn't get a chance to escape," he says quietly, "doesn't mean I hope you befall the same fate."

Now it's my turn to still.

Is he saying what I think he's saying?

We stare at each other, not saying a word, and yet, I realize he *is* saying something.

"Kairos, this isn't your battle," I say slowly.

He raises a hand and stops me. "I'm going to help you, Mirielle Zenyth," Kairos pauses and his mouth twitches in a ghost of a smile. "For I too am *angry.*"

# CHAPTER 10
## DYANA

"Get up," a voice sounds in the distance.

"Get UP!" it shouts again.

I groan and swat the air. Except my hand hits something—and that something hits back.

My eyes burst open as a palm cracks against my cheek. Embyrne stands above me, arms crossed. The sky is just beginning to lighten behind her, giving the Beastkyn a halo effect.

"Good. I was debating pushing you off the roof. Now we can avoid that." She nods as I shove to my feet, wobbling slightly on the tiles of the roof. I've taken to sleeping up there with Vesimyr nightly.

The nightmares have gotten better thanks to his presence, which is why I was in such a deep sleep.

Until this crazy bitch showed up and hit me! My cheek still burns and I cup it, mouth hanging open.

"You slapped me awake?" I say, my voice embarrassingly high. "What the fuck?!"

"Tough shit. Now let's go."

My jaw drops at her general unfriendliness. Embyrne looks me up and down, her gold eyes unsettling. "We have a lot of work to do. Don't be a lazy human."

I meet her unimpressed yellow gaze. Streaks of pink and orange light start to appear on her cheeks and collarbone as the sun rises behind us.

"You know, I can see why they don't like having you around," I say, expecting her to be surprised. But the Beastkyn doesn't even blink.

Then a huge silver tail slaps down just behind her, rattling the roof and destroying a good amount of tile.

Embyrne just bares her teeth at my Dragon companion, who had been silently watching all of this from a meter away.

*"You're being loud and I'm hungry,"* Vesimyr says, and I can feel that it's to the both of us. Then a large grumbling sound emits from his stomach area. *"I need to eat or else I'll get cranky. Would you like me to get cranky, Embyrne?"*

Embyrne and I both blink. Then the Beastkyn rolls her eyes. "You don't scare me, old one."

A long-suffering sigh layered with a growl is the only response.

"I will give you ten minutes to get dressed and meet me in the hall, Rider."

Then she looks at Vesimyr and lifts a brow, cocking her head in that distinctly animal way, "You're deluded if you think anyone here is buying the old and weak act, *Executioner.*"

Vesimyr's eyes flare at the name, but Embyrne turns and jumps right off the roof. I inch over to the edge and look to see where she landed, but Embyrne is nowhere to be seen.

"Why did she call you that?" I turn and ask aloud.

The big silver Dragon sighs, looking weary. He scratches his head with a large talon for a few moments, and then turns to me.

*"Go get dressed, Dyana. It is a name that belongs to someone I used to be. That is not my name anymore."*

"I won't make you tell me," I start, "but Vesimyr, you're my only friend. That makes you the only person here that I trust. I hope you know that you can trust me in return, and if you're ever ready to tell me the story, I would be happy to listen."

Vesimyr watches me carefully. Then the Dragon lifts, stretching slowly as his bones crack and pop. He groans, flapping his wings and lifting his silver snout to the sky. Vesimyr takes a deep breath before craning his neck down until we're face to face.

*"I have never had a friend,"* he confesses quietly, *"but I would be honored to call you my friend, Dyana."*

I have to look down to hide my giddy smile, and the blush on my cheeks. A snout nudges my cheek, and I wrap my arms around him as far as they can go.

*"Also, the Beastkyn was annoying me. I do not approve of these slapping tactics."*

I snort, looking up at him. "I *knew* you were listening! Aren't you supposed to be protecting your Rider?"

He huffs, laughing. *"Perhaps I was curious about what she was doing. Now, you only have six minutes left, so go get dressed before she hits you again."*

Oh shit, he's right.

"Can you do the thing?" I ask and his tail wraps around me, depositing me down into the room that I originally slept in. Now I just bathe and change there.

I rifle through the dresser drawers and find a green short-sleeved top and matching pants, but the pants are a little too short and the shirt shows off a good portion of my midriff.

Vesimyr's magyk...it changed me. I didn't just wake up with magyk.

I woke up with *tits!* Big, round, *gorgeous* breasts. I used to be fairly flat, but when I woke up from the coma, I had breasts. It's *amazing.*

The rest of it though? The added 8 centimeters of height? The hair that grows back no matter how much I cut off?

The first thing I did when I woke up was try to cut my hair. It reminded me of everything that happened.

But the next day, it was long again. Long*er,* even.

My skin is smoother and clearer than it was before, too, and my cheekbones are sharp. If you didn't know otherwise, you'd think I was a Demis.

I look like a Fae. Minus my dark skin and dark hair. All of the Fae are pale. My ears remain human and I'll occasionally find myself running my fingers along the edge, just to make sure there's no point.

*"I did not turn you into a Fae, Dyana,"* Vesimyr says. We've had this conversation at least once a week since I woke up.

"Okay, but are you *sure?*"

In my mind, he sighs, *"Yes, it is quite literally impossible for you to suddenly become a Fae. I promise, you are not Fae or Demis."*

I believe him.

But the similarity is strange. I look more Demis than Mirielle does now.

As I brush my hair and weave it into a two-strand braid down my back, Mirielle's face is in my mind.

I don't want to think about her, but she's changed too. Her red curly hair used to touch her shoulders, but now it's halfway down her back.

Not because of some magykal reason, but because of how much time passed.

Sometimes I forget when and where I am, still thrown off from being in a magykal coma for two years.

I try not to think of it, because my thoughts always drift to *her*.

Amalia.

She's out there, somewhere. I know it. She cannot be dead. But...if she's alive, it's been two *years* of her believing that *I'm* dead.

Impatience hits me hard and suddenly I'm rushing into the hall, ready to train.

I need to find Amalia.

Before it's too late.

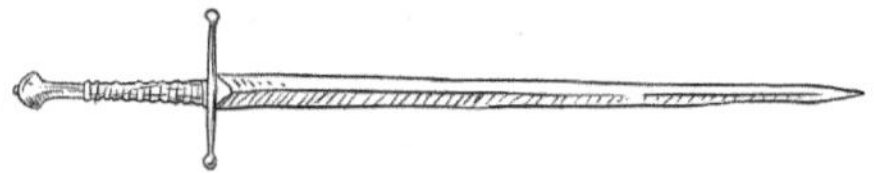

The sun is high in the sky above me as I lie on the ground, panting.

My stomach turns again and I roll over quickly, getting on my knees to bend over and empty it once again.

Vesimyr winces at the gagging noises. I gasp for breath and wipe my mouth.

"Nobody told me your magyk feels like shit!" I groan, getting up on my feet.

I feel disgusting. I'm so sweaty that my clothes are sticking to every inch of my skin.

Embyrne laughs, "Look at that. Only two months with magyk and the human is already greedy for it. How terribly predictable."

*Bitch.*

"Hmn, I heard that too—and that's *Beast Bitch*, to you."

I nearly choke on my own spit.

"Now, go again. Mental blocks are easy."

I wipe my mouth with my arm, wincing at the feeling, "Oh good, I'm so glad it's easy for you. I, however, am not *you*!"

"Figure it out," is all she says with a shrug.

*Figure it out?*

"Some teacher," I mutter.

I close my eyes and take a deep breath, trying to focus.

At first, I'm alone. It's just me and the small, distant spark of magyk deep within me.

*"Use your magyk and fight back. Keep me from taking it,"* Embyrne's voice thunders in my head, whereas Amalia's presence in my head was so quiet.

Embyrne is fucking *loud.*

*"Do you have to shout?"*

She makes a sound of frustration.

*"Fight back or die."* Then Embyrne is there, in my head, pulling on the magyk at my core.

I try to shove her out, try anything to keep her away.

I imagine a giant wall of light encompassing me and pull hard on my magyk, not knowing what the fuck I'm doing.

But Embyrne doesn't stop. She grabs hold of my magyk and *yanks.* My eyes burst open as light explodes from me, jumping into her waiting hands.

A yawning emptiness grows inside of me. A void of who I once was. The scar on my chest burns and my limbs go numb, as if my body starts to die without the presence of my magyk. I gasp, trying to take a breath, but it hurts.

Everything hurts.

"You failed," Embyrne notes unhelpfully. *"Again."*

Then she's tossing the ball of light straight at me. It bursts through my being and the feeling sends me straight to my knees as I empty the contents of my stomach once more. It feels so good to have the magyk back, but the process of removal and return fucking sucks.

*"That's enough for today."* Vesimyr interrupts. *"It won't do any good if Dyana is so tired she can barely walk. We have three months. Don't burn out in the first week."*

"Fine," Embyrne snaps, the glow of her golden eyes flaring for a moment. "We meet here tomorrow at sunrise. The sooner you get a hold of your magyk, the sooner you'll be able to keep me *out."*

I try to come up with a flippant response but she's already walking away. Today, instead of a loose dress, she's in tight pants made of some sort of shiny material, and a matching top that leaves her arms bare. The shirt rides up as she walks away, showing off a hint of Embyrne's lower back.

Sparkling gold tattoos peek out and I immediately squint, trying to get a closer look. But she turns the corner, leaving me with more questions than answers.

I huff and walk over to where Vesimyr lays on the dirt floor, sitting down on his front claws. He kindly shapes them into a chair-like position and I groan, everything in my body hurting.

"This is so much worse than Gauntlet training."

*"Magyk use is much harder. It's what most magykless people simply can't understand. They yearn for power, but don't realize how difficult it is to manage."*

"When she takes my magyk, it...it feels like my body starts to die," I admit to the giant Dragon.

He's quiet for a moment.

*"You are alive, Dyana. That is all that matters. It might feel like that, but Embyrne can only hold your magyk for a short amount of time. I could feel it overwhelming her."*

"Really?" I ask, surprised.

Vesimyr nods. *"I suppose you could say that it's one of my powers to see magyk, although I am not the only Dragon on record to be able to do so. Magyk glows, and I can get a sense for how powerful someone is based on how brightly they shine."*

"And Embyrne?"

Vesimyr looks at me slowly, *"Embyrne is true to her name. She glows like a roaring fire. But when she absorbs your magyk, she doesn't glow...she burns."*

"Do I uh, glow?" I ask tentatively. I'm unsure why the question is embarrassing, but I feel my cheeks heat nonetheless.

Vesimyr doesn't answer. Instead he adjusts, using his claw to place me onto his back. I drop onto his scales. The action used to startle me, but now it seems as normal as breathing to be tossed around by a Dragon.

"How is this normal?" I ask aloud. Vesimyr chuffs and takes a running start, leaping off the outdoor training arena Embyrne took us too. She said no one uses it anymore. It was once for mortals who lived here, but since the island closed off, the mortals—even magykal ones—have begun to die off, leaving many of the human settlements abandoned.

**"Magyk?"** Vesimyr asks.

I shake my head and clarify as he flaps his wings and takes us airborne. The angle is sharp and I grip hard with my thighs. It burns, but I know that eventually I'll get used to the feeling.

The wind hits my face and forces air into my lungs as we soar through the clouds, passing other Dragons on the way.

Most scatter at the sight of Vesimyr, but some call out to us.

*"He should have died in The Arena."*

*"You don't belong here, Executioner."*

*"Your Queen is dead."*

*"I'll tear your head off, silver."*

That last one makes something in me snap.

All of the sudden, my magyk surges to the surface.

*"Dyana, don't!"* Vesimyr warns. But it's too late.

I point with one hand at the purple Dragon who threatened my Dragon, ready to unleash all of my supposed magyk on it, but we suddenly dive, heading straight to the ground.

"Oh come *on!*" I growl. "Dragons fight all the time!"

*"Now is not the time to be getting in trouble, Dyana."*

"I don't care. I'm done with them bullying you!"

*"I would rather be bullied than killed. If we are to get out of here, we need to be careful."*

I glare at the back of his scaled head as we flee the scene quickly. The other Dragons hang back but I don't miss the way the purple Dragon's eyes burn with barely leashed fury.

Vesimyr increases his speed until we're shooting towards the sand. This time, I stay on. I want to whoop and scream, celebrating the win. But Vesimyr banks, taking a tight turn around the castle before making a hasty landing into the large window near my room.

"I won't let them treat you like shit. I know you miss her, I know she was your friend, but Kydis isn't here. Kydis didn't save the Dragons and lead them home. *You* did. I won't stand by and watch as they treat you like this, Vesimyr. You don't deserve it, and I won't apologize for it either." I finish with a huff and begin the slow process of sliding down Vesimyr's side, while trying not to break my legs upon landing.

Vesimyr, however, suddenly dips and I'm falling towards the floor.

My thoughts freeze and I brace for pain, but my body reacts as I suddenly somersault, landing on my feet, with one knee down and the opposite hand on the floor.

"What the fuck was that?" I ask, panting. My hand goes to my chest, not because it hurts but because I feel like I'm about to have a fucking heart attack.

"You...you threw me off, you ass!" I turn, pointing a finger at my menace of a Dragon.

*"Dyana,"* Vesimyr starts with a sigh. *"You hold onto your humanity so tightly. You have to stop thinking like a human and start thinking like a Dragon."*

I scoff, "Forgive me if it's a bit hard to let go of 26 years of humanity. It's not going to happen overnight."

He's quiet for a while and I lean forward, pressing a palm against his snout and gazing into his green eyes. The ring of white around his slanted pupils glows brightly at my touch, as if the bond recognizes my proximity.

"Throwing me off your back aside, you said you'd protect me. So you need to let me do the same for *you*, Ves. That's what friends do, you know," I remind him with a raised brow, crossing my arms.

Vesimyr sighs and lays down, although it means his body is half shoved against the wall. *"Kydis wasn't my friend, Dyana."*

I blink, "But I thought…"

If a Dragon could smile, that is what I would call Vesimyr's toothy grin. *"She was my queen and the rightful ruler of Elysium. Reina Kydis had my loyalty, as does her hatchling, should the hatchling be found alive. But you, Dyana Arkos? You are the only person in my long life who I have been able to call friend."*

"I'm really the only one?" I ask, changing out of my sweaty clothes.

At first, I was uncomfortable changing in front of the Dragon. Until he reminded me that *"Dragons are always naked. I do not care about your human body, Dyana Arkos. Cease this silly human embarrassment at once."*

After that, any worry vanished, and I began changing comfortably in front of my Dragon companion.

*"Yes, Dyana. You are. I have never been very liked among Dragon kind. Maybe in the early days, but I've always stood alone. Even in the Great War, I never took a Rider, despite a large cohort of Dragons partnering with the Arkaydians."*

"Tell me about the War." I throw on my nightshirt just as a Demis with green skin and leaves in her hair drops off my dinner on a platter. It's plain, mostly fruits and raw vegetables, but the meat is always well seasoned and generously portioned. It melts in my mouth as I dig in, taking a seat on the floor and leaning back against Vesimyr's warm scales.

*"It's a long story, but I will tell you the short of it."*

Vesimyr looks up, as if trying to remember the details. *"The day the Fae arrived, I felt it. At the time, I had a nest in the area near some sea cliffs off the north-eastern coast of the forest you call the Ulster Wald"*—I blink at the mention of my home—*"I had taken a mate, after centuries of debating it. We weren't in love, but we both wished for hatchlings. Arkaydia was safe, and our forest untouched. But the day the Fae arrived, the sky grew dark, and a storm appeared out of nowhere. I felt the shift in the land when the portal appeared. Even hundreds of kilometers away, I felt it."*

I'm barely paying attention to my food as I listen eagerly.

*"I went to investigate. The Fae were welcomed, and everyone assumed they were peaceful, but I knew something was off. After a few months, I got word that a few Dragon nests were raided and their eggs stolen. The Fae denied it and the Arkaydians believed them, but I did not. So I said goodbye to Kora, who had just laid a clutch of three eggs and was nesting around them, and flew to Elysium to warn the Crown."* He pauses, taking a deep breath.

The food sours on my tongue as I realize the destination of this story. I set down my plate and put both of my hands on Vesimyr's leg, leaning my chin against his scales. Whatever his story, I will not reject him.

*"I was on my way back when I heard Kora's screams in my head and knew something was wrong. By the time I got there, all that was left was her bloody, dead body and an empty nest. She fought to the death to protect our hatchlings, and they cut her throat for it. After that, I flew back to Elysium and joined the Crown as we prepared to go to war. It was a short time later that the Fae finally admitted their actions, as well as their desire to take power over Arkaydia and claim it for themselves. We fought them for 100 years, Dyana. An entire century of warfare and bloodshed, for nothing."*

"Gods," I whisper, a tear falling down my cheek. "Vesimyr, I'm so sorr—"

*"Do not apologize, my young friend. It was over five hundred years ago."*

I look up at him. "So? No matter how long it's been, trauma never goes away, Vesimyr. I might be young, but even I know that. We simply grow around it, but it doesn't lessen."

We sit in silence like that, he and I. Dragon and Rider.

*"I do not dream, but if I could, I think I'd dream of them. Kora was never my love, but she was kind and gentle. She would have made a wonderful mother to our children."* His voice is low and for a moment, I wonder if he might cry.

Wait, can Dragons cry?

The sun sets in front of us and we watch it from my window, each contemplating our own grief.

"Wherever they are," I start, "we will make our families proud. In this life or the next. I vow it."

Vesimyr lowers his head to nuzzle against my cheek. *"Don't ever change, Dyana. As the centuries pass and kingdoms fall, never lose your joy. It is a rare thing to find in this world."*

I smile against his scales.

Later, I take a much-needed shower in the bathroom while Vesimyr catches his own dinner. Dirt and sweat drip down my body, coloring the warm water brown.

Drying off, I slip my nightshirt back over my head and braid my wet hair, tying it off with a spare piece of fabric.

Vesimyr waits for me, hovering outside the window when I emerge. With his tail, he gently lifts me into the air and deposits me on the roof. I climb into bed as he wraps his body around me, expanding his wings to cover me from wandering Dragon eyes.

I'm almost asleep when I hear his rich voice in my head, *"You do not glow, Dyana. You **sparkle**."*

# CHAPTER 11
## AMALIA

**THEN:**

*"Son of Shadow, did you think you could really escape? Did you think we wouldn't find out about the child?" Achan Drayven's voice projects past the walls, sounding like he's standing right next to me.*

*Father laughs, dark and emotionless, as he faces Achan outside. I watch from a small hole in the wall as Puff, my small mousey companion, hides in my hair.*

*"Did you really think I would let you anywhere near my child, Achan?" he taunts. "There has never been a reality where you ended up with my daughter."*

*"Hand her over and I won't tie you to a pole in the Pit," Achan responds, his black horns so scary I can barely look.*

*"Never." Mother's voice is violent and angry as her and Father walk out, meeting the Fae males.*

*"You can't escape me, Asteroth. There's nowhere to run," Achan calls.*

*"I love you, my darling," Mother whispers into my mind.*

*"You and your mother are the best things to ever happen to me. Never forget that little spark."*

*"I love you too. But what's going on, Daddy? You're coming back, right?" I ask, but they don't respond. There is only silence and darkness. "Daddy?"*

*The cabin begins to rumble and the floor wobbles. A tiny hole of light opens up from a can falling over.*

*My parents stand together, hands clasped, facing the horned Fae.*

*"What the fuck do you think you're doing?" Achan snarls as they begin to glow.*

*One with shadow and one with light.*

*Apart, they weren't strong enough to stop him.*

*But when they combined their magyk...they were unstoppable.*

*"Stop them!" Achan shouts, and the wind picks back up, blasting them, but my parents stand still.*

*They glow brighter, until I can barely watch.*

*Then a huge BOOM sounds as a wave of energy explodes outward, and everything goes dark.*

*The scene shifts. Now, my mother is on her knees, clutching her throat as Achan Drayven stands over her and laughs while she chokes on her own blood thanks to the dagger he has stabbed through the middle of her throat. He doesn't remove the dagger, he just stands there, smiling as she drowns, coughing up the blood now filling her lungs.*

*My father screams, tackling Achan to the ground, roaring like one of the mighty Dragons in my stories.*

*Then the scene...changes.*

*Everything blurs. I blink, and it's Father standing over mother.*

*It's him who cuts her throat.*

*I scream and the scene changes again, going back to the way it used to be.*

*I watch the life fade from Mother's body, her bright eyes turning dull and empty. Father screams bloody murder next to her seizing body.*

*One blink, and he's screaming at Achan.*

*Another blink, and he's on the ground, writhing in pain.*

*The wind picks up, this time at my back, like a cosmic nudge. My legs move before I make the decision to walk. I gingerly make my way through the broken boards as Father holds his hands out in front of him, using his shadow magyk to attack Achan.*

*Nothing works.*

*The dream shifts again, and now it's the Archmage standing in front of Father.*

*Except now my Father is on his knees, his magyk gone.*

*I try to go faster but trip, cutting open my shin.*

*I need to save him.*

*I need to save my Father.*

*"Daddy!" I scream to him in my thoughts, but he doesn't respond.*

*The scene shifts and my Father hits the forest floor.*

*"Get up," I say. **"Daddy get UP!"** I shout hysterically.*

*But he doesn't move.*

*His body remains still as his chest stops moving and his violet eyes go dark.*

*Achan Drayven sniffs and clenches Father's heart, squishing it until it pops.*

*"Such a rare little girl. Come here, girl. Let us leave." Achan Drayven stands there, waiting. One blink, and it's not Achan beckoning to me.*

*It's the Archmage.*

*I continue climbing out of the broken boards of the cabin until I meet unmarred ground. Then I pause, looking around again.*

*"Don't think of running. It's no use." Achan/the Archmage holds out his hand, a sinister smile on his face. "You belong to me, little girl."*

*I look at his hand for a moment, then back to my parents.*

*Mother takes her final breath, gasping as her body finally goes still.*

*Father is already dead, so I turn to Achan/the Archmage and stare into his horrible eyes and say, "No."*

*Then I let that feeling, that something newly awoken, explode as I let my head fall back and scream.*

*Everything goes black yet again as magyk surges out of me.*

*When I can see again, Achan Drayven is gone.*

*He fled.*

*He actually ran.*

*Beneath my brow, I watch as my hair burns like a coal ember, all of the white fading away.*

*Charred, half-frozen bodies lay around the entire clearing along with the broken trunks of ancient trees.*

*Shadows wrap around my hands as if to comfort me, but I ignore it.*

*"Daddy?" I ask, voice trembling as I walk over to where my parents lay, now covered in flakes of ash. "Daddy? Please." I cry, falling to my knees at the sight of his cloudy eyes. "Wake up, Daddy. Please, you have to wake up."*

*I sniff, curling into a ball and tucking my legs against his still, cold side. "You're reading to me later, remember? The story of the Wytch and the Prince. You need to stay awake so we can read."*

*But there is no response.*

*The tears come, then. Sobs so loud, so violent that my entire body shakes. "Daddy, wake up."*

*But he doesn't answer. His eyes don't open and his chest doesn't move. Air no longer fills his lungs.*

*"Mom? Please." I look over at the body of my mother, but there's no answer.*

*They're gone.*

*"Please don't leave me alone," I whisper, tears streaming down my face. The fire bursts from me again, surrounding me with a flame that is both hot and cold.*

*"Please don't leave me alone. Please come back," I beg. "Come back, Daddy. Please come back."*

*I blink and their bodies disappear.*

*What? This...is strange.*

*I'm alone in the clearing, the destroyed cabin strewn across the ground.*

*"MOM?" I scream, looking for her body.*

*"DADDY? WHERE ARE YOU?"*

*My cries go unanswered, and I fall to the forest floor, sobbing, and completely and utterly alone.*

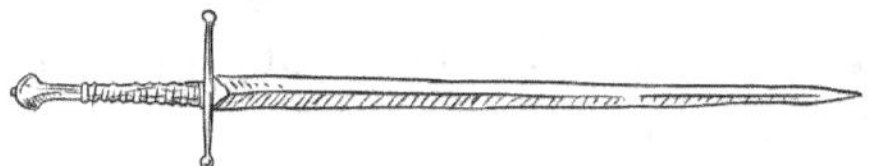

**NOW:**

I wake with a gasp, heart racing and sweat dripping down my back. The dream is already fading, but this one was different.

*Why* was it different?

It slips further and further from my grasp until I can't recall why I feel anxious and unsettled in the first place. I also don't recall the bed being this *warm*. The blankets are suffocating and something hot lays across my stomach, while heat blasts me from behind.

Groaning, I try to flip off the covers, which is when the bed *moves*. I freeze, becoming hyper aware of the fact that it isn't the bed that's gotten warm, it's my bedmate.

Sometime in the night, Nyall's arm found its way around my waist and my legs found their way between his.

We're completely tangled together. Which is when he moves, making a sleepy sound, and I become even *more* aware of the fact that his hand is splayed across my stomach. Beneath. My. Nightshirt.

His palm isn't hot, but it still *burns* against my skin as his touch sets my nerve endings alight.

The pillow is nowhere to be found. Instead, his hard chest presses tightly against my back. I don't know whether I should stay still or try and remove myself from his arms. Instead, I freeze; unable to move, while internally, I panic.

I don't even know if I *can* get out.

His hand moves again, and I have to swallow the moan threatening to make its way out of my lips.

With a shaky breath, I wiggle to the side, hoping his arm will fall. I try to extract myself, sliding my leg out from between his, but Nyall makes a sleepy sound and grabs me again, pulling me closer.

I make a small squeak at the feeling of his hard length pressing against my ass.

Then his hand is beneath my shirt again. This time he lets it travel higher, hugging me until his palm is against my sternum, right between my breasts. Nyall's fingers brush against the swell of my left breast and I see stars.

A small moan *does* escape me.

Gods. It feels so good to be *touched.* So good that if I don't stop this now…I won't be able to later.

"So soft," Nyall mutters in a sleepy voice.

"Nyall," I say, voice trembling. "Wake up."

But Nyall doesn't respond. I try to wake him up again when his fingers begin to move. In a single breath, his hand cups my breast, massaging it slowly.

My jaw drops and my back arches, pressing harder against him.

I didn't even mean to do it but. My body reacted before my mind could even process what to do.

A part of me resents Nyall for it. For the...*effect* he has on me.

"So fucking soft," Nyall repeats in a sleepy voice as his hand continues to knead and tease at my breast.

My heart races, thumping in my chest so hard I'm surprised it doesn't break my ribs.

"Nyall," I plead, voice hoarse. "Pl-please wake up."

"Nope. Too comfortable," he whispers. "And you're so *warm.*"

*Ohmygods.*

His other hand is suddenly on my waist, and I nearly jump.

Heart pounding, Nyall drags his fingers down to the waistband of my underwear, trailing the tips through the hair atop my pubic bone.

"So *soft,*" he breathes.

I'm on fire. Not literally but it feels like my skin is burning at his touch.

~~Don't stop. Please.~~

Gold eyes flash through my mind and my heart skips a beat. I yank on my shredded self-control and hold Os' face in my thoughts as I slam my elbow back into Nyall's chest, hitting him so hard it shoves him off the bed.

Nyall shouts as his body hits the floor with a hard thump.

"Goddamn, that fucking hurt," he groans, but I'm already vaulting off the bed and putting as much space between us as possible.

"What the fuck, Blue?" He groans again, sitting up and wincing.

I—I can't.

*I can't.*

I feel like crying, so I keep my back to Nyall as I get changed. My heart races as my skin heats and panic sets in. Controlling my breathing becomes difficult but I force the whirling sea of emotion within me to *drown.*

"Hello? Are you going to just fucking hit me and then ignore me?" Nyall's voice is bewildered.

I take a final deep breath and turn, meeting his confused gaze.

"So, you don't remember feeling me up in your sleep, then? How *convenient* for you." My voice practically drips with venom.

I hear Nyall give his own sigh before he runs his hand through his hair.

"No, actually. I don't remember that. Do you always remember what you do in your sleep, Amalia? Is that some new power you've suddenly discovered?"

I glare at him, "I would have remembered *that.*"

"Well, I apologize. I didn't mean to do that," Nyall says carefully.

"Didn't you?" I challenge. "You seemed rather awake for it, actually."

Nyall crosses his arms, mirroring my displeasure. "Whether you believe me or not, I can't help what I do in my sleep, Amalia. But my apology remains true. It was not my intention to do anything other than *sleep*. I will keep my distance going forward."

~~*NO. NO. NO. NO. NO!*~~

I nod sharply. "Thank you."

We stand there, staring at each other for a few moments.

It's tense. It's awkward. I want to scream until my throat *bleeds*.

It feels like there's so much going unsaid, but before either of us can say anything, Ryu pokes her big head into the tent entrance, a large, half mauled deer carcass in between her jaws.

Gods.

The sight is shocking, not just because of the dead animal in her mouth, but because of the fact that she's even bigger than the last time I saw her.

*"You grew again,"* I whisper.

*"I will continue to have growth spurts for the next 48 years. We finish maturing at 50. They'll slow down soon."*

Right.

*"Does it hurt?"* I ask, and I feel her hesitate.

*"Breakfast?"* she asks, changing the topic.

"You cannot fling your prey around among the humans. We've discussed this before, Ryu."

If I didn't know before that Dragons can roll their eyes, I do now.

I make my tone gentle as I remind her, "Not everyone here is human, and I can hear your stomach growling from almost a kilometer away."

As if on cue, my stomach growls so loud that Nyall turns to look at me with surprise.

"We do have meatless options, if deer carcass doesn't sound appetizing," Nyall notes.

"Thanks," I mutter, trying not to show how fucking relieved I am.

The dead deer seems to be staring at me.

Right as I look at it, Ryu crunches on it a bit. The sound of flesh and bones crushing between her teeth makes me nauseous.

Ryu grunts and leaves, removing the dead animal from my sight.

"Children," Nyall sighs. "Try not to let that ruin your appetite. We have a meeting to get to after breakfast."

I glance over at him, "A meeting?"

"Yes," Nyall says, throwing a clean shirt over his head. I look away as he changes his pants, pretending to be somewhere else. "The generals want to meet you."

*Lovely.*

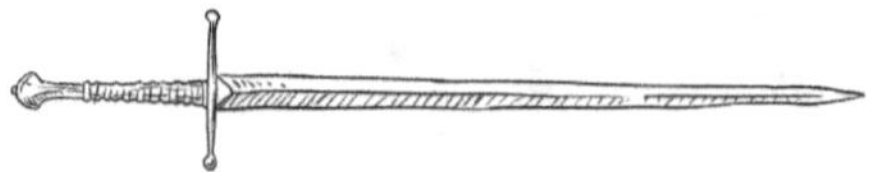

The walk over to what appears to be the war room—a giant tent full of maps with a large table surrounded by chairs—was misery.

In the midnight dark, it's easier.

Ignoring their looks.

Fear. Anger. Wariness. Distrust.

In the light of day, it was plain. As Nyall and I walked over here, rebels stopped in their tracks, frantically shuffling out of the way. As I passed them, their whispers cut me, over and over. By the time we reached the privacy of the tent, the hollow feeling in my belly has expanded, taking over my whole being, until I feel nothing at *all*.

Nyall pulls out the chair at the head of the table and sits, gesturing for me to sit on his right. The symbolism of that choice isn't lost on me.

I'm to be presented as the weapon.

It always comes back to this. The question of how I can be *used*. I don't particularly mind anymore. The part of me that feels ashamed, that doesn't want to be a weapon, died alongside Dyana. Any emotions leftover live locked so deep within me, I sometimes wonder if one day they might get lost.

"Nyall! You're back!"

My dagger is out and at the ready at the shout, but Nyall places a hot hand on my arm.

I flinch away from him and glare, annoyed that I was caught off guard.

My eyes flick forward as I look at the woman entering the tent. Her smile is bright and blinding as she walks towards Nyall.

The woman has straight blonde hair that goes to her chin and hazel eyes. Then those eyes move past Nyall and settle on me.

She's around Dyana's age. There's something familiar about her, but I can't place it. Her smile drops and her face goes cold as she takes in his hand on my arm.

I almost laugh but instead, I shake off Nyall's hand and inspect my dagger, tuning everything out.

Distantly, I hear the sound of more people entering the tent.

But I keep my gaze plastered on the intricate silver dagger in my hands. I inspect the hilt, pretending not to hear the way the people in the tent are whispering about me.

Seats are taken and the conversation continues for a few minutes before dying down.

There is not enough room for Ryu to join us, so she's out hunting for food. But I can feel the presence of her magyk lingering in the back of my mind.

She's listening in, and not too far away, should this turn sour.

"How fares the North?" Nyall asks the blonde woman.

Anger is red-hot in my veins as I observe the blonde woman with a new curiosity.

*She* speaks for the North?

*"As if it would be you,"* my thoughts whisper and in a blink, my anger dies, turning into something colder and heavier.

~~*THEY HATE ME.*~~

No, I cannot speak for the North. I cannot speak for anyone.

My eyes narrow as I listen in on their conversation while pretending to be lost in my own thoughts.

"It's fine," she says. "Although the villagers are nervous. Between the Archmage and the recent attacks from the Gray Wytch"—my gaze flicks to the side as I meet her angry blue eyes—"they're terrified, and unsure of who is the true enemy. A sentiment I happen to share."

Nyall clears his throat and tries to introduce us, "Mara, this is—"

Mara holds up a hand, "I know who she is. Everyone does."

I lean back in my chair, spinning my dagger in my hand.

"Oh good," I purr. "And here I thought we'd have to waste time on introductions."

Nyall shoots me a glance, but I ignore it and smile at Mara, who nearly flinches back at the sight.

*Is my smile that terrifying?*

*"Yes,"* Ryu responds instantly, and I mentally roll my eyes at her. *"If any of them mess with you, I'll eat them."*

*"That will definitely win them over to our cause,"* I snort. *"Now back to my smile. Is it really that scary?"*

*"It's not your smile, exactly. It's the fact that you never smile, Ama. So, when you do...it usually means something bad is about to happen."*

I sigh as a dark sadness takes me over.

I know that some of this is my fault.

I chose this fate.

And yet...I had no choice.

I am both the victim and the villain, born into life on the run, raised by grief and anger. The violence and cruelty of this world has molded me, shaping me in its image, and now...I'm not sure I can turn back.

I'm not sure I can *be* anything other than a blade—particularly when grief keeps sharpening my edges.

"Amalia?" someone asks, and I realize I was tuning them out.

I glance over to Nyall.

"She's bored, clearly. I knew this was a bad idea," Mara sneers.

My gaze snaps to her and I flash a manic smile, "Sorry, I was just talking to my Dragon. She was saying that if you keep being an uptight bitch, she'll eat you."

I hear Ryu sigh in my head and can practically see her shaking her head in disappointment.

Nyall looks at me with wide eyes. "Metaphorically, you mean."

I smile as I look at him, "Not in the least." Then I wink at Mara who silently fumes. The others at the table go pale, balking at my casual threat.

Nyall looks around the table, "Right. Well, I think introductions are in order."

Mara frowns, "We know who she is."

I smile at her again and Mara has to look away.

"That might be true," I note in a bored tone, "But I don't know any of you. Why should I help *strangers?*"

"We don't need *your* help." Mara snarls. "Nor do we want you here. You *or* your Dragon."

I was willing to drop her rude behavior but hearing the hate in her voice when referencing Ryu has my attention piqued. Which is rather unfortunate for her, because it has also piqued my anger.

Nyall clears his throat, "Yes, we do actually, and I want *both* of them here." He pauses and I watch as the relaxed Rebel hardens into the flippant, cold Prince once again. "Do you doubt me, Mara? Do you hold my opinion to such little value?"

Mara's cheeks turn red, and she goes quiet. "Of course not."

Nyall nods, "Good. Then believe me when I say that I trust Amalia Asteroth. That's all you need to know."

The air is thick with tension.

"Now, why don't we have some introductions. Mara?" Nyall looks at the blonde woman, his face relaxing as the Prince disappears. Now it's just Nyall.

I prefer this version.

The blonde woman takes a deep breath and looks at me with a cold gaze. "Fine. Mara Bryer, General of the Northlands."

*Hmm.*

Davyn is next, "We're familiar already, right, lass?"

The corner of my mouth twitches.

I like Davyn.

He reminds me so much of...*Dyana.*

~~*SHE'S DEAD. SHE'S DEAD. SHE'S DEAD.*~~

~~*SHE'S DEAD. OH MY GOD. I MISS YOU SO MUCH.*~~

Saying her name hurts.

I have to hold my breath to keep from screaming.

The rebels go around the table, introducing themselves.

There's Keres, who is second to Davyn, and in charge of training the new recruits. With a sharp jawline, glowing porcelain skin, and dark blonde hair cut in a shorter, more masculine style, Keres is undeniably gorgeous.

They speak gently, but there's an aura of authority about them.

Then comes Soren, with her long woven locs decorated with gold rings and beads.

Soren is General of the Southlands, the second largest territory in Ur Daoine.

After Soren is Amari, the General of the Westlands, with short black hair and hard brown eyes that watch me with open dislike.

Lastly, I meet Drystan.

A short male with wide shoulders and a permanent frown, he shared the same red locks as another Eastlander I once knew.

"He took over for Mirielle after..." Nyall breaks off and clears his throat, clearly not over Mirielle's disappearance with the Dragons.

No one knows whether we will ever see her again, or if she even survived the journey.

We know nothing.

I don't fault Nyall for replacing her, especially as they go over their newest numbers.

10,000 souls now make this valley their home. Many of them women and children. Less than *half* are soldiers.

The Eastlands and the Southlands brought the largest contingent of volunteers, but many of them are untrained.

Keres walks through their progress, but many have never learned how to fight.

Nyall listens intently, adding information where he can, but as I watch them talk, I realize something.

They might call Nyall Drayven "Lord," but here, they are equals.

No one treats Nyall like a Prince.

Instead, he's treated with respect, with *love*.

My gaze moves from the generals to the Prince at my side.

*"Surprised?"* His voice suddenly rolls through my thoughts and my instinct is to kick him out, but I pause.

*"Perhaps,"* I respond nonchalantly.

*"What did you expect, Blue? Bowing and reverence?"*

I look away, focusing instead on the plain clothes all of the generals wear.

*"Maybe,"* I admit.

*"There's none of that here."*

I ignore him and focus back on the conversation.

"Let's cut the bullshit," Mara interrupts, and the table goes quiet.

Then her blue gaze lands on me.

"By all means," I purr, letting my Hellfyre flare in my eyes, making them glow.

A weapon raised.

"Many of us at this table believe your presence will only make things worse."

I wait for Mara to continue.

"I will speak plainly." Mara nods to some of the others, and I note that Soren and Amari sit a bit straighter, as does Drystan. "We do not want you here. If it were up to me, you'd be leaving tonight."

"Mara," Nyall's voice is low and harsh, "we've discussed this. We need Amalia and Ryu."

"Bullshit!" Mara slams her hand on the table. "She's only going to make things worse and you know it! She's the Gray Wytch, Nyall. She's just as bad as them."

Hearing that word brings a rush of memories.

I feel the brush of Nyall's magyk against my mind, but I ignore it, keeping my attention on the angry blonde woman in front of me.

"Ah," I tsk as the memory becomes clear. The table goes still. "Eahmond. You danced with my...friend." I swallow the pain I feel at referring to her so vaguely.

Mara's eyes turn murderous.

"I am, and *you* are the evil whore who KILLED MY SONS!"

# CHAPTER 12
## IREYNA

The Dragon flinches as I reach to pet her snout.

"It's okay," I reassure her, trying not to get annoyed.

We've been at this for weeks.

I don't want to rush her, but the beautiful white beast is still terrified of me. Still, she's learning...*slowly.* There have been moments where I've caught her yawning and leaning her leg against me.

"How about this," I tell her, trying to get creative. "We have to get past this, because if we take much longer, they're going to force you into it, and I think we both know that won't be fun for anyone."

The Dragon blinks, looking at me with her big blue eyes. She leans forward, her snout nearing my face. Her neck was slender, and her scales were smaller—shinier, even—than the other Dragons I had seen before.

"So, you don't like when I raise my hands. What about if I try not to lift them up above my shoulders?"

I slowly lift my hands, and she watches me with keen eyes.

The name hits me so suddenly I nearly stumble.

"Anonyme," I whisper to the white Dragon. "It means Nameless. That's what I'll call you. Anonyme."

The Dragon huffs and bumps her snout against my cheek softly.

"I'm going to lift my arms now, but not above my shoulders, okay?"

Anonyme takes a deep breath as I slowly lift my hands, stopping before they go above my head. Laying them against her white, scaled neck, I marvel at the texture.

She doesn't flinch. Not once.

"Good girl," I whisper. "Now, you know what comes next. I'm going to climb on. We don't need to go anywhere today, but we need to show that we're close to flight ready."

I swear the Dragon understands me and nods.

"Right, I'm going to go slow but please try not to kill me."

Moving to her side, I grab hold of the black rope around her neck and belly. Using it for leverage, I climb up her shoulder as slowly as possible, not wanting to scare her. Despite the fact that she's not a large Dragon, I feel like I'm in the clouds as I get to the top of her back. The ground seems so far away.

I get to the top and crawl in between her shoulders, using the rope to hold onto. Her muscles tense beneath me as my legs drape along the top of her belly.

"You'll be fitted for a saddle tomorrow," I tell her. "Come on, let's try walking around."

She snorts as I squeeze with my legs, moving her forward.

The movement is so different from that of a horse.

Anonyme crawls, using the clawed tips of her iridescent white wings as extra limbs to hold her aloft.

From this angle, her neck seems so much longer. Small white spikes dot around her head, but the spikes along her spine remain small, unlike other Dragons. My seat jostles beneath me as she moves around the courtyard.

*I'm on a Dragon.*

*I'm on a fucking Dragon.*

We walk around for another few minutes before the heaviness of reality settles on my shoulders.

"That's good for today," I tell her, and the Dragon comes to a halt. I pat her scales and slide off her back, legs wobbly.

"I'll see you tomorrow," I rub the scales of her arm before walking away. Fae attendants surround her and I ignore her alarmed cries.

*I'm sorry.* The thought is far away. It almost *hurts* to think the words. A headache starts in my temples, making me wince.

I ignore the shrieks of pain. The more I *care* the more it hurts my head.

I ignore everything as I walk to the dungeons and think of how to torture someone I once loved.

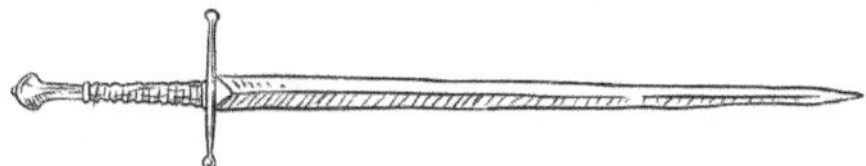

Remus Ostia struggles against the metal table, but Elysian straps hold him in place.

There is nowhere he can go. He knows this. Two years later, and still he fights.

"Os, this would all be so much easier if you would stop fighting. I *promise.* We could find a place for you in the Archmage's court."

My pleas fall on unhearing ears. Os ignores me, turning his gold eyes away.

I miss his hair. I miss running my hands through it. Resentment of that gray haired *bitch* fuels my anger and I grab hold of it.

*Let's try something new, then.*

"Stop fighting, or I'll kill her."

Os goes still and I smile. "I'll hunt your little girlfriend down and kill her. Shall I bring you her head, perhaps?"

The snarl that escapes Os is so loud it shakes the walls. I don't allow him to see how much it shook me as well.

The Beast quiets, panting silently as he glares at me.

*So. That's his weakness.* The Holy Father was right—as always. Os won't tell us anything about the Dragons.

But to protect his precious *Amalia?* That just might get him to talk.

"Where is she, Os? Tell me. I can go get her and bring her to you. Does a reunion sound nice?"

The Beast trembles.

"Don't you miss *Amalia?*"

He roars, jerking against his restraints. "Harm her, and I'll kill *everything* you love."

"No," I tsk. "I don't think so. You won't be harming anything for a long time."

I lift the scalpel and smile at him, "This next bit is going to hurt."

I tune out his screams and the throbbing ache in my head, and begin to *cut.*

# CHAPTER 13
## MIRIELLE

"Any luck?" Kairos asks as he takes in the scene before him.

I'm sitting in a puddle on the floor with shards of broken metal around me.

"Clearly not," I snap and catch myself. Taking a deep breath, I crack my neck. "I'm sorry...I'm just pissed off. I didn't mean to snap at you."

"I know, but I appreciate the apology." He nods. "The wisdom that comes with age."

I glance up at him. Kairos holds out a hand and I reach for it, grateful for the help. He easily pulls me onto my feet.

"I stopped counting, but I'm around 350. You?"

He nods and drops my hand. I blink, shocked at the loss of his touch...and at the way I miss it. I want him to pick up my hand again.

I'm so distracted, I almost miss his answer.

"A little over five centuries."

I smile. "There are those who would consider us young."

Kairos laughs and the sound makes the frustration of another failed blade dissipate.

I've felt so alone these past two years, and even more so the few months following Dyana's awakening.

Perhaps I'm not as alone as I thought, though.

"I don't know what else to do." I motion to the broken shards on the floor.

"Come," Kairos beckons for me to follow, "you've been working day and night on these blades. Exhausting yourself will solve nothing. Let's take a swim."

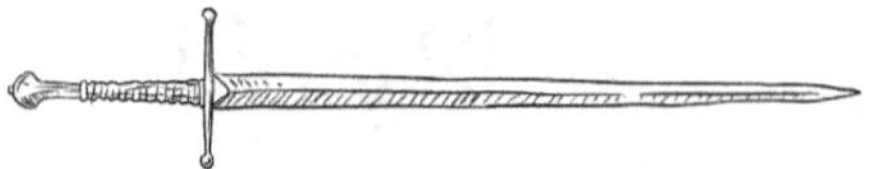

Despite the darkness of night, the brilliant glow of the moon illuminates the shallow water. Glowing fish and rays dart around us, covered in bioluminescent algae.

"Better?" Kairos asks, and I nearly jump.

Blinking, I look at him in confusion.

"Ah, you cannot talk under water?" Kairos tsks. "Forgive me, Mirielle. I assumed otherwise."

My jaw drops.

To be able to speak underwater...that's unheard of.

Shaking my head, I grab his hand and smile, showing him it's not a problem. If only I had Amalia's skill of mind speaking. As if he heard my thoughts, I suddenly feel Kairos's magyk brush against my mind.

*"There,"* he says. *"We can speak in here."*

*"You can hear me?"* I ask.

Kairos nods.

*"How?"*

*"You wanted to know what I am,"* he smiles, his locs streaming behind him in the water like a crown. *"It isn't safe to discuss up there."* Kairos glances up at the world above.

We're sitting on a bed of sand next to a vibrant coral reef just off the edge of the beach.

Despite the silence, the reef is teeming with life.

*Wait.*

I glance at Kairos, blinking rapidly as I finally connect the pieces.

*"There it is,"* he smiles softly. *"Now you understand."*

Then he shifts.

*Holy shit.*

"You're Ascidian?!" I forget myself and scream the words into the water. Sea water floods into my mouth and I begin to choke. Frantic, I kick my legs, swimming towards the surface.

*"Yes,"* he laughs. *"I am."*

Gasping for breath, I break the surface. Kairos follows in his Ascidian form. Black eyes lift from the water as he hovers at the surface next to me, watching.

Ascidians are often called something else. Something more easily understandable. *Sea Wyverns.* Smaller than Dragons, and without their large wings. Instead, Ascidians have fins. Where Dragons have claws, Ascidians have webbed feet.

They were only ever stories, though. Never the real thing. Until now.

Instead of scales, Kairos has thick skin, almost like a seal. His body is dark blue with white stripes along his webbed wings. Soft teal horns accent his face.

His eyes are black like a shark's. Kairos swims around me and I marvel at his size.

He's huge, bigger than many Dragons here, but he glides through the water with the nimble grace of a much smaller creature.

A long teal and blue fin lines his mid-back all the way down to his tail. It bobs in the current, almost like soft feathers. The tip of his tail flicks back and forth as he hovers beside me. Two webbed feet stick out behind him, each tipped with razor sharp claws.

But his fangs. They're huge. Bigger than any of the sharks I've seen. They're meant for tearing through flesh and bone with ease.

*"You're beautiful,"* I whisper, in awe.

Taking a deep breath now that my lungs are clear, we dip back below the surface.

"Thank you," the creature responds and my jaw drops. "You've heard a Dragon speak aloud. Did you think they were the only ones with the ability?" Kairos scoffs.

The resentment in his voice is plain.

In my thoughts, Kairos replies *"Beastkyn are not the only ones treated as lesser beings."*

I reach out, grabbing a hold of Kairos's fins, marveling at how soft they are. He swims us down to the sandbar, easily navigating through the water.

Mesmerizing. That's the only word that properly describes it.

He's absolutely mesmerizing.

*"The only God I believe in is the one I've seen with my own eyes. Lir."*

I nod, *"I pray to Lir as well."*

*"Trust him,"* the whispered words suddenly return to the front of my mind. Lir was guiding me towards Kairos.

"The Dragons aren't better than us, despite the fact that they think that. Are they Gods?" Kairos asks, switching to speaking aloud. His words are pushed into the water. I can hear him as if he was speaking in mortal form. It's incredible.

"I don't know, Mirielle. I hope they aren't, because if they are, it would mean there is no one left to stop them.

I *hmph*, bubbles leaving my nose.

"There must always be a balance, even with Gods." Kairos notes, and I nod in agreement.

We lay against the sand for hours, talking about life. Eventually, we both fall silent and my lungs start to burn.

"I can fix that," Kairos glances at my chest. "Should you decide you want it."

I blink and push off the sandbar, paddling towards the surface. Even after we make it to the beach and begin to walk out of the water, Kairos's promise remains in the back of my mind.

# CHAPTER 14
## DYANA

"Get up," a voice interrupts my dreams just before cold water splashes on my face, waking me up painfully fast.

"What the fuck is wrong with you?" I screech into the still dark sky.

Every morning for the past week has been like this. Embyrne wakes me up in some sadistic, horrible way at the ass crack of dawn, and we train until sundown, leaving me exhausted and barely able to walk every evening.

Vesimyr, however, has grown grumpier and grumpier every time. Particularly since Embyrne made sure some of that freezing cold water got tossed onto his scales too, which I confirm with a glance behind me.

The big silver Dragon growls, his green eyes with white around the slanted draconian pupils glow against the rising sun behind us. In the half-shade of the morning, Vesimyr's scar looks even more menacing than usual.

Or that could be the way he's baring his insanely large teeth at my new trainer.

"What, didn't get enough beauty sleep, old man?" Embyrne taunts.

That's all it takes. So fast I can't track it, Vesimyr lashes his tail at Embyrne, landing the spiked tip against her chest. She lets out a choked sound as she's shot into the air and off the roof.

My jaw drops. Then I'm laughing so hard I have to grip my sides.

*"Vesimyr!"* I gasp.

*"What? She has become an annoying pest,"* Vesimyr snarls to me. *"If she wakes me this way again, I will have no other choice but to eat her. I greatly dislike these rude awakenings!"*

I glance back at him, "Damn. Would you really eat her?"

He rolls his eyes. *"No, but I would think about it. I will not become the next Ignautius."*

"Well, if she does it again, I'll just stab her or something."

"That wouldn't work," a voice calls and I spin, gasping at the sight of Embyrne hovering in the air with her arms crossed. She gently lands on the roof, looking no worse for wear. "I would steal your magyk and choke you with it before you had even grabbed your dagger, little human."

I snarl, sounding just as draconian as the Dragon next to me. "You could try."

"Look at you," she tsks. "So protective over something that was never yours."

I stand, facing her with my shoulders back. "You're right. But it's mine now, and no one is taking it from me. Least of all, you."

Embyrne raises a dark brow, her yellow-gold eyes blazing. "Good, then you can prove it. You have 10 minutes to meet me in the arena."

She jumps off the roof and disappears in a flash. I let out a growl and turn to Vesimyr.

"Okay, *maybe* you can eat her."

My companion laughs and stands, stretching his gigantic body beneath the now risen suns.

The light makes his scales practically glow. He flares his double set of wings, completely blocking the light and covering me in shadow.

*"I have some things I must do today. Will you be alright on your own?"*

I nod, "Yeah. As mean as Embyrne is, I don't get the feeling that she's going to kill me. Bruise and batter? Most certainly. But she would have killed me already if she had the chance, considering she can steal my magyk."

Vesimyr nods, *"I agree. That's why I picked her. That, and her general dislike of Ignautius."*

I let out a laugh.

"What are you going to do today?" I ask as he lowers me down into the room. The tip of Vesimyr's tail is covered in sharp black barbs, but he wraps the mid-part of his tail around me instead. I've never gotten so much as a scratch from him.

How something so large can be so gentle will forever evade me.

Vesimyr looks at me with a strange glint in his eye.

Caution, almost.

*"Dragons and mortals are not allowed to leave Elysium once granted refuge,"* he says slowly. *"But that doesn't mean all creatures are barred from leaving...just the large ones."*

I blink, "Wait, what?"

But he turns his large body and maneuvers back out of the window.

"Come on, you're just going to leave me hanging?" I screech, and he takes off, flapping his giant wings. "What does that even mean?"

*"Have a good day at training, Dyana."*

"You're such a dick!" I call, knowing he won't understand the reference. But he doesn't respond.

Oh. Maybe he...doesn't know what that means?

However, something warm and loving brushes against my magyk and I instantly recognize it as Vesimyr.

No words are needed as our magyk mingles, making my skin tingle. I'm going to figure out what my secretive Dragon is up to. *Someday.* But for now, I have to go get my ass kicked.

*Again.*

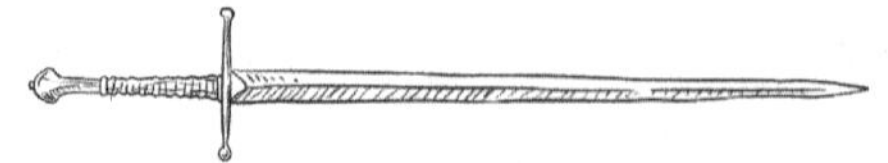

"Try harder!" Embyrne growls. "You're pathetic!"

We're fighting hand to hand, but she's clearly going easy on me, which only makes me angrier.

"Imagine I'm in your mind. Fight me and keep me out!"

Embyrne thinks that physically fighting will help activate my magyk and trigger my mental walls.

"Fight, Dyana! You're not even trying!"

So far, all this little exercise has done is leave me with a welt on my right arm and a skinned left knee.

"You've said that. But it's not working!" I hiss as she goes on the attack again. "And I AM trying! I'm trying harder than I've ever tried at *anything* in my godsdamn life."

"Good. Now try *harder.*"

"Fuck you! I AM trying harder!"

"No, you're trying hard for a *human,*" she snarls. "Try like a *Dragon!*"

Embyrne sneers at me, unleashing a high kick against my cheek.

Pain flares but then, the uncomfortable new sensation of my flesh knitting back together follows. It's a horrible feeling and I'm instantly nauseous.

A double punch to my stomach follows. I try and block her, but she's too fast.

"You're acting like a human, Dyana!"

"I'm *trying* not to."

"No you're not, stop lying to yourself. You're acting like a *coward.*"

That word echoes throughout the arena. It worms its way into my bones, passing the hurt and embarrassment until it settles somewhere deeper.

Somewhere so deep, I'm scared to follow.

"I am not a coward," I pant.

Embyrne tsks, looking disappointed. Then she slaps me across the face, shattering my cheekbone.

I scream and then scream again at the feeling of the bones reattaching. Crackling sounds in my ears and my entire face turns numb.

"I know your story, you know. We all do. I heard the whispers. The girl who saved the Dragons," she puts on a voice of fake awe, mocking me as she walks over and stands above me. Her leg jerks out to kick me in the side, but I roll away, dirt coating my tongue in the process. I cough and gag but get back on my feet.

I'm covered in sweat, dirt, and blood. I feel disgusting, and every muscle in my body groans in exhaustion.

"I didn't save anyone," I wipe my mouth on the back of my dirty hand.

"No, you didn't."

Jab. Her fist blurs towards my face and I weave out of the way, faster than a human is able to move.

Blinking at my own speed, I pause, and that hesitation costs me as her foot meets my liver, sending me to my knees in pain.

Then her fist uppercuts me, hitting below my jaw.

More bones break and I spit, spraying blood everywhere as the bones reknit. But the pain is all encompassing.

"All you did is put those Dragons in more danger," she hisses, her eyes glowing with fury. "You didn't save them, because there is no such thing as *safe* anymore."

I push to stand just as she yanks on my magyk and steals it, sending a bolt of light right at my chest.

Exactly where my scar is.

It hits me and I scream, feeling like I'm right back atop Vesimyr's back, watching as Amalia fades into the distance.

"You doomed them, Dyana." Embyrne whispers in my ear, before punching me in the back. I groan but stay standing. I slap out in front of me, unseeing. It hits something soft and Embyrne snarls.

"You aren't the hero, Dyana," she says, slapping me again. I fall to the ground, exhausted and in pain from both her assaults and the lack of magyk as my body starts to shut down. "But you could be."

I pause as my magyk is sent back. The nausea returns, but I don't throw up.

"You could be the hero we've been waiting for," Embyrne whispers. "If you'd stop being such a fucking coward, you could save us all."

I pant as my vision returns. Everything is blurry at first, but then Embyrne's face above me becomes clear. Her face is the picture of fury.

"Maybe your friend really is dead," she adds, and I go still.

"What?" I ask quietly.

"Amalia, wasn't it? Have you thought of what you'll do if you get back to Ur Daoine and realize she's dead?"

"Don't you *dare,*" I snarl.

Embyrne shrugs, going to walk away, "She sounds like kind of a bitch, anyways. Maybe it's for the best that she's dead. Buried beneath the Arena rubble, broken and burned—"

Magyk explodes out of me and I scream, sending it directly at Embyrne. It sends her flying through the air as the arena around us begins to shake. Stones fall and without thinking, I picture them flying through the air at Embyrne.

She lands just as the stones go flying.

Instead of hitting her, she steps aside calmly, a dark smile on her face.

"What?" Embyrne taunts, her golden eyes burning. "Don't like hearing about your dead friend? Does that make you *angry,* Dyana?"

I scream again and send another bolt of magyk at her, but she steps aside again.

Which makes me even angrier.

"You won't even be able to bury her and prepare her for the afterlife. There will be nothing left of her, Dyana. Nothing at all."

I'm so angry, there are no thoughts in my head.

All I can think of is Amalia's broken body.

A ball of light appears between my raised hands, perfectly round and smooth.

*"She'd be so disappointed in you,"* a voice whispers in my head as Embyrne breaks into my thoughts. I can feel her reach for my magyk. I gather all of that anger, that pain, that fury, and with it, I sever the connection, shoving her out of my mind with so much force, she flinches as if cut.

That's what I pictured.

My light, stabbing and cutting away at the connection between us.

I imagined it hurting her.

Embyrne meets my gaze, and what she does next surprises me more than anything she's said or done before.

Embyrne Ostia, the Abomination of Elysium, looks at me and *smiles.*

"Good. Very good. Now we might actually have a chance at getting out of here alive."

I blink and look down at the ball of light still between my hands.

"Oh," I whisper.

"It's about time you used that anger, girl."

I look up at my teacher, who is now standing beside me, observing the ball of light.

"You...you said all of that to make me mad," I realize aloud.

Embyrne looks at me like I'm the slowest person who ever lived. "No shit."

Amalia might still be alive.

Embyrne was just saying all of that.

But still.

That fear...that stupid thread of fear doesn't leave me.

Instead of avoiding it. I grasp it tightly, letting it fuel me.

Amalia has to be alive.

She has to be.

A thought hits me with the force of a lightning bolt and I look at Embyrne with surprise.

"Hold on, what exactly do you mean by 'we'?"

Embyrne crosses her arms, her deep umber skin glowing against her short, white-gold curls.

"When you leave here," she starts, "I'm coming with you. I need to find my brother."

*Oh God.*

*She doesn't know.*

For a split second, I consider telling her the truth. I consider all the ways I was lied to, and how it made me feel, and then I remember that if Amalia might still be alive...it's possible Os is too.

Unlikely, but not impossible.

So instead of telling Embyrne her brother is probably dead, I stay quiet...but deep inside, a seed of guilt begins to sprout.

# CHAPTER 15
## AMALIA

**"YOU KILLED MY SONS!"** The words echo in my head as Mara unsheathes her dagger and leaps across the table.

She stops when her blade is hovering just above my heart.

A tattooed hand is all that stands between me and death.

A hand that belongs to Nyall Drayven.

"No."

Nyall Drayven says a single word, and Mara drops her dagger, slinking back in her chair. She bares her teeth at him, clearly unhappy about the decision. But she takes his orders anyway.

*What has the Prince done to ensure such unyielding loyalty?*

I watch her carefully. Memorizing her features and searching through my memories. The timing isn't right—and she's too *young*. I stopped hunting after I found Dyana.

I can't picture her sons, because I've never seen them before.

Mara trembles with barely leashed anger. "Fuck you."

I look her up and down, deciding how to play this.

The truth is both the easiest and the hardest route.

"I did not kill your sons," I say. "You won't believe me, but I did not kill them."

"LIAR!" Mara shouts, slamming her dagger into the table. "They had just learned the tale of the Gray Wytch in school and then you came along and stole them away in the night."

I wish I was angry.

I want to be.

Instead, all I feel is *sad.*

"I can assure you; I didn't kill them. I did not take them from their beds. I have never met your children before."

I don't know why I try.

Even before I began speaking, I knew it wouldn't matter. The people of this land made their mind up about me long ago.

I let myself become their monster.

Mara sneers, "Pretend all you want. But ten years ago, you took my babies. You killed them!"

"I didn't kill them," I repeat, but it's no use. Even if their blood isn't on my hands, the blood of so many others *is.*

"Lying bitch," she hisses.

**"Don't."** The deadly calm in Nyall's voice makes me shiver. **"Don't speak to her like that.** Ever. Do you understand me?"

"Yes, my *lord.*" Mara quiets, but that fury doesn't leave her eyes.

"I am many things, Mara Bryer," I say carefully. "But I am not lying, nor am I the killer of *children.*"

"Fuck you," she sneers, and I smile.

"Don't get me wrong. I kill *plenty* of adults. I like the ones with attitude problems," I lean forward, suddenly *craving* the violence and bloodshed. "They're so fun to *play* with."

"Careful—" Nyall murmurs.

"I agree with Mara," Soren speaks up. Unsurprisingly, Drystan nods in agreement. "Why should we trust you, Gray Wytch? You've amassed quite the reputation, one that rivals the Archmage and Achan Drayven himself."

Nyall glares at them. "Amalia is here as my *guest.*"

"We don't want her here, Nyall. You brought us in because you trust our opinions, yet you balk in the face of them now. Does our loyalty mean so little?"

*We don't want her here.* How many times have I heard that?

"If your loyalty is so easily lost and your trust is broken, then by all means, there's the door." He motions outside.

*We don't want you here.*

"Prove we can trust her, then." My gaze flicks to Davyn, surprised that he's the one who spoke up. He meets my eyes. "Prove we can trust *you.*"

I consider this for a moment before looking at Mara. "Your leader trusts me. Is that not enough for you?"

Nyall doesn't say anything on the contrary, proving the truth in my words.

"I don't have to prove *anything* to you, to *any* of you."

I look around, meeting the gazes of all who sit around the table. Some look away, uncomfortable at the eye contact, while others glare back.

"I'm here because you need someone who lacks your pithy human morals. I'm here because you need someone who can do your dirty work, isn't that right, Nyall?"

The Prince meets my gaze with an undefinable look.

Pride, maybe? Or regret. It's hard to tell.

"Mara," I start, and the woman freezes. "You hesitated instead of stabbing me with your dagger." Mara blinks. "*That* is why you need me. The time for hesitation is over. If I were in your shoes, I would have stabbed the dagger through my heart without a second thought or moment of hesitation."

The generals look at me with fear now.

*Good.*

"Good. Now you're getting it. You don't need to trust me. This has never been about trust. This is about getting the job *done.* So stand aside while I do the dirty work. Nyall asked me here to *spare* you because, Mara, I *never* hesitate."

One flick of my hand sends my own dagger through the air. It hits Mara's dagger right in the center, knocking it off the table and sending it ricocheting into the wall next to her head.

Mara shrieks, and I smile.

Davyn meets my grin with one of his own, while the others go pale with terror.

"So easily scared," I purr. "I will not pretend to be anything less than a monster, but if you think I'm the worst thing you'll find when you look into the dark, you've got another thing coming."

I pause, their attention wholly on me. "Achan Drayven was evil, but the Archmage is worse, and based on what we've seen...he's even more powerful."

"*Good* won't beat him," Nyall speaks up, supporting my claims. "The time for hesitation is over. I do not wish to scare you, but Amalia is right. This is war, and wars are not won with good deeds and kind words. Wars are won in blood. Wars are won through *sacrifice.*"

Nyall looks around the room, meeting their eyes. "I know you don't trust her, and I'm not asking you to trust her, but I am asking you to trust me, and I trust the Gray Wytch. I trust that when it comes down to the line, she will make the hard decisions, especially if it means winning this war."

"You doubt us," Soren notes, and I watch as that seed of resentment within her grows, spreading to the others.

"It's not about you," I speak up. "Look at the bigger picture. Have you not seen the way the land is dying? Have you not seen the rotting trees?"

They regard me in silence.

"Our kingdom is dying." There's a thread of hysteria in my voice, but I keep going, "Our kingdom is dying and the Archmage is *killing it*. Achan Drayven started this, but the Archmage is finishing it. This only ends when he is dead."

"We can kill him," Mara adds, and I laugh, making her flinch.

"No, you can't." I summon my magyk and it springs to life, eager to be used.

Shadows unfurl from my palms and a wall of Hellfyre wraps around the table, trapping the generals.

The scent of cool, smokey lavender fills the air, tinged with warm cinnamon.

"There is no power as strong as Hellfyre," I say, twirling the shadows and flames through my hand as I fill the tent with darkness. "The only thing that rivals it is the power of a Dragon. We fought Achan with Dragons, Hellfyre, and all of the magyk we possessed. The most powerful magyk users in the Kingdom, united and focused, and do you know what happened?"

My voice trembles and I clench my fist, the flames rising until they nearly coat the tent ceiling, yet it remains unburnt.

"Nothing. *Nothing* happened. We killed Achan for nothing, and it nearly took out all of Castael Laryn in the process. Two Dragons died that day, along with countless others in the Arena. Do you know who walked away unharmed, out of all of us? The Archmage."

I take a deep breath for this last part.

"Going after the Archmage is very likely going to kill me. Nyall as well."

Mara looks at Nyall in shock.

"Is this true?" she says, her tone cutting. "Is this your plan?"

I glance at Nyall, who watches me back. Our eyes meet and time goes still.

*"I'm sorry,"* Nyall whispers.

*"I know."*

His dual-colored eyes are conflicted. One blink, and he's back to the strong, unshakeable leader. Nyall looks at Mara and answers aloud. "Yes. There's a very good chance that those of us who go against the Archmage directly will die in the process. The sheer amount of magyk it's going to take to take him down will drain us dry."

Everyone is quiet, processing what this means, before Drystan speaks up.

"Do you think we stand a chance?"

I meet the Eastlander's gaze and nod. "I do. But power has a price. Someone has to bear the cost."

"You and Nyall," Soren surmises. "You're going to bear the cost."

I sigh, leaning back in my chair as exhaustion hits.

"Yes. We will. But we're not going after the Archmage right away. We need time to plan, and in the meantime, we're going to do everything we can to weaken his hold on the land. Starting with the Mercatus."

Keres nods. "The Archmage is draining magykal creatures for power. That's why they imprisoned the Dragons."

"Taking away one of his power sources will be a heavy blow."

Mara turns serious. "What about the repercussions? Will they attack us back if we dismantle the Mercatus?"

I shrug. "Maybe. But I'll deal with that. Besides, you've picked a good location. The Ulster Wald is dangerous as it is. By putting your camp so deep into the mountains, it protects you."

"What about the Dragonguard?"

I meet Mara's gaze. "What about them?"

"Will you kill them? The Dragons?" Soren asks.

"If we cannot free them from their compulsion?" I ask, with sadness in my heart. "Yes. If they're too far gone to be saved, we will kill them."

Mara goes quiet, glancing at the other generals.

They all turn to look at me, their gazes harsh.

Soren speaks up, "You weave a pretty tale, and you might be right. Trust might not matter to you, but for us, it's everything."

I grind my teeth, frustrated. "I don't care."

"And *we* require a demonstration. *Proof* that we can trust you," Mara snaps. "Don't think we've forgotten."

*Gods this human is fucking annoying.*

"This is ridiculous," Nyall protests, but I raise a hand, silencing him.

"What sort of demonstration?" I ask, curious.

Mara's eyes flick to Nyall, and I pause at the anger within them.

Ah. I'm not the only one being punished.

"A fight. Just swords and magyk, no Dragons. If you can beat us, *maybe* we will consider letting you stay. But if we win? You leave."

They want the chance to take their anger out on me.

"Absolutely not," Nyall says, his voice hard.

But I'm already standing. "I accept."

Already my blood *sings* and my magyk writhes in anticipation. Ever since I started practicing and using it on a regular basis, it's been harder and harder to hold it *back.*

My flames want to *burn.*

Mara and the three other generals stand, bloodlust in their eyes.

*"Amalia, are you sure?"* Nyall bursts into my head. *"I don't like this."*

I smirk, "Don't worry, Prince. I won't kill them."

I promise nothing, though, about making them *hurt.*

Rain soaks through my clothing as the ground beneath my feet turns muddy. The sky is dark and murky with overcast clouds, and a cold wind batters us as it comes down from the icy mountaintops.

We're in a small field at the southeast end of the valley. This is clearly where they run drills and train recruits, based on the torn-up ground.

I stand across the field, facing the four generals.

With a thought, I summon Neiman and Macha. Morrigyn's blades appear in my hands in an instant.

I learned they could do this on accident one day. I summoned them as a joke, thinking nothing would happen, and nearly fainted when they actually *listened.*

The crowd gasps at the sight of the black blades.

At the knowledge that Morrigyn chose *me* to wield them.

Mara growls, unsheathing her own longsword, while Soren withdraws two daggers and Amari carries two swords that curve inward, creating an almost circular type of blade.

Drystan holds no weapons. He only wields a strange looking walking stick.

*He's the magyk user, then.*

Ryu is still away hunting, so I have no one standing on my side.

The entire camp stands behind the generals, while Nyall stands at the center, with Keres and Davyn by this side.

"For the record, I think you're all idiots for doing this," he says loudly. "First team to be disarmed, wins."

*Disarmed.* I huff a laugh.

This wasn't going to be a nice fight.

This was going to be a bloodbath, regardless of the Prince's desires.

Nyall, Keres, and Davyn walk to the outer edge of the field, leaving me and the generals facing each other.

"I'm going to enjoy this," Mara sneers.

"As am I." I blur, going on the attack so fast they don't have time to react. I bring the flat side of Neiman down on the back of Mara's legs, sending her sprawling in the mud.

The air behind me whooshes and I weave to the left, avoiding Soren's blade. Whirling, I meet her parry with Macha and twist Neiman around, bringing the sharp side of the blade down on Soren's hip.

She screams and I kick her to the ground. Mara gets up with a growl and faces me again.

I motion with my fingers for her to come and get it.

With a scream, she charges, swinging her blade quickly.

But not quickly enough.

I spin out of the way, "How are you a general when you're so slow?"

Mara roars and attacks me again. I meet her blow for blow, getting lost in the heat of combat. My blood is screaming for more, when Drystan slams his staff down on the ground and a force field explodes into existence around the field...locking Nyall out, and locking me *in*.

Mara swings her blade, ready to slice into my arm, but I veer to the left and easily sidestep.

*Tsk,* I click, and kick the back of her legs, sending her into the mud yet again.

I hear a whoosh of air behind me and turn just as Soren brings her blades down. I try to avoid it, but one catches me in the shoulder, burrowing into my flesh and sending bolts of pain down my arm.

I glance down at the blade and laugh. "You're going to have to do better than that."

With a grunt, I yank the blade out. Blood drips down my shirt from the now open wound.

"I didn't need to do better than that," Soren says and I pause. "I just needed to distract you."

Wait. What? My thought dissipates as something slams into the center of my back, sending me to the ground.

I blink, trying to push up to my knees, but the ground beneath me flares to life in a circle of green light. It encircles me and the generals, but keeps everyone else out.

They fucking *warded* me? That means Drystan is Demis. A *powerful* Demis, because this is advanced magyk. *Really* advanced. Wards like these meant to trap and subdue violent criminals.

I look down at the circle, searching for a weakness, before I come across a strange symbol.

"AMALIA!" Nyall's shout penetrates the magyk barrier. I glance to the side and meet his mismatched eyes, watching as he slams his own swords against the barrier.

That doesn't work, and he quickly turns to magyk. Bands of white light surround him, Davyn, and Keres as they start to pummel the barrier, trying to break it.

Cracks form, but not fast enough.

Another dagger hits me in the back and I gasp, watching as my blood hits the ward in a dark splatter. The pain grounds me.

A glance over my shoulder reveals Amari appearing out of thin air.

They can cloak? Drystan isn't the only magyk user then after all.

The green light snaps, rushing into me, as all thought empties from my head, until there is only fear left in its wake.

*Fuck.* I knew I missed something. The strange symbol. They're trying to get into my head.

They're trying to get into my fucking head!

All at once, the reality of what will happen if their attempt works hits me. Panic is a tight cord thrumming through me as my heart races. I fight the magyk, but it's too strong.

The green light shatters my walls, making my insides feel like they're *burning.* I scream in pain as every single ward I've ever built around my own mind is ripped to pieces.

I feel naked. *Exposed.*

"Now everyone will see your true intentions. You can't hide, Gray Wytch, not anymore." Amari's voice is poison in my ear.

Which is when I start to laugh, despite the fact that tears are already falling down my cheeks. "Oh, you're such an idiot."

I feel the moment the last of my walls collapses. A wave of emotion explodes out of me, so strong, I see stars.

Screams sound in the distance.

Then those screams turn to wails.

I look up and meet Nyall's tearstained gaze. He's on his knees in the mud, watching me with wide eyes and a slack jaw.

Oh Gods.

Nothing is hidden.

He can see it all. *Feel* it all.

My pain. My *feelings* for him.

*"Amalia,"* he mouths.

Birds shriek from the clouds above, and the pained howls of Dyre Wolves cry out. But it's not enough. The pain keeps coming as the grief overtakes me.

The generals conveniently *forgot* something rather important.

Nothing is more dangerous than a woman with *nothing* left to lose.

My head falls back, and I let out a soul-deep scream that shakes the trees. The screams continue as I send a blast of Hellfyre into the ward, breaking it.

Drystan, Soren, Amari, and Mara scramble through the mud. Drystan breaks the shield trapping us in here as he slams his staff against the shield border. Keres and Davyn shift their magyk, encircling the generals and holding them in place. The high-pitched warble of a Dragon sounds in the back of my mind.

Ryu. I drop to my knees as my screams die out, turning into hoarse panting.

*I'm so lonely. I should have died with them. I deserve to be hated. It should have been me. It should have been me. I should have died.*

The thoughts grab hold of me, pulling against my consciousness until all I can think about is how unfair it is that I have to go on when they're not here.

Everyone in this valley can feel what I'm feeling. I glance up, rain soaking me to the bone. Through the misty weather, I watch as Keres and Davyn hold the generals in place. Nyall is walking over to them, but my grief quickly turns to anger.

"No," I call, my voice scratchy and hoarse from screaming. On trembling legs, I walk over towards them.

They hurt me, and now I'm going to hurt them back.

With a single thought, shadows burst from my hands, wrapping around their bodies and pulling them closer like bugs caught in spiderweb.

Drystan and Keres notice that it's my magyk and drop their own, allowing me to decide the generals' fates.

A brave choice.

I yank the generals onto their knees and release my shadows.

They look up at me, their eyes wide in fear as I form my shadows into a blade, slicing it across Mara's throat.

"You thought I killed your sons, so you decided you'd kill me too, hmm?" I taunt as blood sprays my face, dribbling down her chest. She sputters, choking.

*Heal,* I order her flesh, and it knits back together. There's a wet *slurping* sound as the flesh reattaches and the bleeding stops.

"Was this your idea?" I ask, but Mara gasps, feeling her neck.

I turn to Soren and slice my shadows across her neck, repeating the act.

None of them talk.

So I kill them all.

Over and over again.

For *hours.*

I torture them, there in the middle of the field where all can watch, until the mud is no longer brown but a dark, murky red.

All the while, the valley of the rebels are feeling my every emotion.

I haven't put my walls back.

"Maybe you're not worth saving after all," I sneer and wipe the blood from my face.

With my shadows, I yank them onto their knees so they're all looking at me.

"If I ever hear that you do this to anyone else again, if I hear so much of a *whisper* that you're doing these spells?" I ask and lean forward, baring my teeth. "That you're mentally *raping* people?"

They collectively wince at that word.

"That's right, you fucking *raped* me. If I hear so much of *any* of this ever again, not even my magyk will be strong enough to heal the destruction I will wreak upon you. Understand?"

They all nod, trembling in terror.

The scent of urine washes away as the rain continues to fall.

"I'll let you in on one last secret," I say, furious and hurt and *horrified*. I lean forward and let my magyk *flare* to life within me until I know my eyes are glowing with the icy *burn* of Hellfyre. "I can kill the Archmage and *any* monster that dares threaten this world, because I'm a monster too. Just. Like. Them."

Ryu suddenly bursts into the clearing with a loud roar and the rebels scream, running away as Ryu gallops over to me. Hovering above me, she extends her wings, tenting them around us, as if to give me a place to hide.

I pull my magyk away from the generals and let them slump into the mud, finally free of my torture.

Their sobs are music to my fucking ears.

Nyall tries to touch Ryu's scaled arm, but Ryu snarls at him.

I glance up just in time to see the look of devastation upon his face at Ryu's reaction.

*"You let her get HURT,"* Ryu roars in our heads, and even I flinch. *"How could you do that, Nyall? How could you stand by and let this happen?"*

The tears come fast and fall hard.

Hearing her anger...her hurt.

It brings it all back.

"I hurt them back, Ryu." I whisper, and she nods, proud that I got some semblance of retribution.

*"Good. Still—I recommend you let me eat them."*

"I might take you up on that," I say, my voice hollow. "But not now. Not yet."

*"Fine."*

Grief is a weight, and right now, it's too heavy to bear. My legs give out as the pain from my multiple dagger wounds kicks in. As does the horror.

Oh Gods. They all know. Embarrassment floods me. Embarrassment and shame.

Ryu catches me with her paw before I hit the ground. Her silver and copper eyes meet mine as she lifts me into the air, gently placing me on her back.

If I wasn't in so much pain, I would be in awe.

I've never sat on her back.

I just wish this wasn't what it took to happen.

"Let's go," I whisper to her. "I...I need to get out of here. *Please,* Ryu."

I lean against her neck, trying to hide myself from the world, and buy myself time to build my walls back up.

"Wait, wait, just hold on," Nyall begs, but Ryu growls at him again and takes off, galloping through the camp.

*"AMALIA!"* Nyall's voice projects into my head and I wince. *"STOP!"*

Ryu's almost to the edge of the camp when she comes to a sudden halt. I nearly fell off, unused to her movements. The spikes along her spine act as handholds, and I grip them tightly.

Nyall holds his hands up in the air, blocking the way.

Bands of glowing white light decorate his arms.

"Please," he pants, his miscolored eyes wide. *"Please* don't go. I didn't know they were going to do that. I would *never* allow that."

*"You still let it happen,"* Ryu snarls.

"By the time I realized it was a ward, the spell had started. I tried—I *tried* to get to you," he breathes heavily. "Please believe me. I swear on my fucking *life,* do you hear me? I. Swear."

Fine.

"Do you hate me for what I did to them?" I ask plainly.

"I think you went easy on them compared to what I have in store," Nyall snarls.

"No. Don't do anything more. Let them live with this. I just humiliated them in front of their subordinates. No one will ever respect them the same way again. They will have to work *hard* to earn it, and you should let them."

"You just tortured them for hours and now you're arguing on behalf of them?" Nyall asks, clearly confused. "I would have killed them if I were you," Nyall frowns. "Your restraint is...remarkable."

Restraint.

Is that what we're calling it now?

"I want to be alone, Nyall," I tell him. "I was also just humiliated in front of your entire camp. I need to be alone."

"Amalia, I..." he stops, his eyes softening.

I don't know how I know, but that look on his face...that look of absolute devastation. I know that's not just from the weight of my grief.

It's from the shocking realization of just how lonely I've been since he left. Since all of them left.

He felt it.

He felt it *all*.

I lean up and pat Ryu as I slide off her back. My legs are still wobbly, and tears still drip down my cheeks as I look Nyall Drayven in the eyes.

"What they just did," I breathe, "is rape. It's magyk *rape,* Nyall. They entered my mind without permission and destroyed my wards. They *violated* me, and you *watched.*"

I don't want to be mean.

But I can't help it. It comes so easily.

"You saw me trying to break the barrier, Blue. You know that's not true," Nyall says softly, and I hate the fact that he can see right through my snide comments now. "There is no reality in any world, in *any* lifetime, which would have me sit by in silence while you're being hurt. It *killed* me. What just happened fucking *killed* me."

Want and loneliness war within me.

So I put the final piece on the board.

"The thing is, you did sit by in silence while I was hurt. You *did* the hurting. When you left. When you didn't even have the guts to say goodbye," I tell him, and his face falls as the realization hits. "I...I *trusted* you. I—I don't know what I thought. But don't forget that you've hurt me plenty *too.*"

His mouth opens, but no words come out at first. "Amalia," he breathes, and I watch the grief hit his eyes. "I'm so fucking sorry."

"I don't belong here," I say. "I don't belong *anywhere.*"

"You do," Nyall snarls. "You belong with me. You belong at my side. You belong with Ryu and with the wolves. You do belong. Just—Gods, let me fix this. Please."

I can't look him in the eyes any longer. Looking away, I wipe the tears from my wet cheeks.

"I will return in four weeks when it's time to leave for the Mercatus. Not for you, but for *them.* After that, you're on your own. I will not fight the Rebellion's war."

"Blue, please. I need—*we* need you."

I watch as Davyn and Keres approach, coming to stand behind Nyall.

"Let it be known, I think what the generals did is vile," Davyn growls. "Good on you for what happened after, lass. Good on you."

Keres nods. "Not everyone here ascribes to their hate. They deserved every second of what you gave them."

"Be that as it may," I say hoarsely. "I'm still leaving. They don't deserve my help. Not yet.

"Forgive my impunity, lass, but even if they don't, *we* do." Davyn says carefully.

I pause, leaning against Ryu for strength. She moves her wing to cover me partially, leaving me tucked against her arm.

Nyall watches with a look of devastation.

I hate myself for putting that look there.

I hate myself for making him feel this way.

But it's for the best. It has to be.

"Fuck the other generals," Keres says. "Let His Highness deal with their bullshit. I saw you fight in the Gauntlet. We need your knowledge."

The forest in front of us suddenly shakes as the sound of paws hitting the ground reaches my ears.

Dozens of Dyre Wolves stream through the trees, led by the biggest one of them all.

Virgyl.

All strength leaves me as the giant black wolf approaches.

*"Oh, cub."* His voice is heartbroken as he takes me in. I fall to my knees and wrap my arms around him.

I don't respond to Davyn's speech, which is when Keres speaks up.

"Train the recruits with me."

I gasp, my breath hiccupping on a silent sob that I hide as I press my face into Virgyl's fur.

They want me to be a trainer? Fate is a cruel bitch.

"Please, Amalia. I swear on my life, you will not be harmed here ever again," Nyall begs, the desperation in his voice plain.

Ryu lowers her neck and nuzzles my hair, all while keeping her eyes pinned on the males in front of us.

I pull away from Virgyl and look him in his yellow eyes.

"Fine," I say, that hollow feeling returning as my walls begin to rebuild. "But I'm staying with Ryu."

**"And we're staying with *you*,"** Virgyl says aloud. Nyall flinches, while Keres and Davyn hold their hands over their ears as they cry out in pain.

Virgyl rarely speaks aloud, not just because a talking wolf is rather alarming, but because his voice holds much of his magyk.

His voice is pure power.

Nyall's face falls further but he hides it quickly and nods, "Of course. You are all welcome here. You are *always* welcome here."

I pull my face from Virgyl's thick fur, which is now damp from my tears. Without looking at him, I say to Nyall, "I want our tent moved to the farthest edge of the camp, too."

"Of course," Davyn pants, removing his hands from his ears.

They're covered in blood.

I nod and look up at the cloudy sky. The rain had let up and the suns are peeking out from behind the clouds.

"I will return when the suns drop below the horizon," I say, and climb back on Ryu's back carefully. It takes a few tries to heave myself up to her shoulder blades, but I finally make it, panting at the effort it took.

"Of course," Nyall whispers, but his eyes never leave mine. His mismatched gaze is pleading, desperate for me to let him in.

~~*Please don't leave me. Don't let me walk away alone. I hate this.*~~

But I say nothing. I hold the thoughts in, trying as hard as possible to block him from my mind.

*"Is this okay?"* I ask Ryu, placing my hand on her scales.

*"Yes, Ama. It's okay."*

Tears fall harder as Ryu picks up a walk and we walk out of the camp, leaving Nyall and the rebellion behind, the pieces of my exposed heart torn apart and strewn across the valley floor.

"JUSTICE DOES NOT
DESCEND FROM ITS
OWN PINNACLE."

— DANTE ALIGHIERI, 1265-1321.
THE DIVINE COMEDY: PURGATORY

SCAN FOR THE PT. 2
READING PLAYLIST

# PART TWO:
# THE DEFIANT

# CHAPTER 16
## AMALIA

**TWO WEEKS LATER:**

My days have fallen into a tense new pattern. Every morning, I wake up in pain from another night of fitful sleep on the hard ground. I try to lay on Ryu's scales, but it's hard to sleep partially sitting up.

My body is paying the price of my defiance.

After getting dressed, I walk to the breakfast tent.

Porridge. *Again.*

Thankfully the Rebellion has made good use of their surroundings, because every morning there is freshly made, warm berry jam. It turned the porridge purple and sweet.

I've come to look forward to it.

What I don't look forward to is the way the rebels go quiet when they see me. They scatter, getting out of the path and avoiding my wrath.

Virgyl always accompanies me, along with a couple of other wolves from his pack. Ryu follows behind them, hovering her wings over tents and carefully navigating through the narrow walkways.

The cook, Fischer, always goes pale at the sight of me. Somedays, I'm numb to it. But the days when I wake up after a night of endless nightmares... those days, a small part of me *shatters* in the wake of their fear and their *pity.*

Fear I can take. Fear I'm used to. But pity? Pity *cuts* me.

Every morning, I find a seat at the very edge of the breakfast tent. Tables of all sizes are strewn about.

No one sits near me. The mere sight of me sends multiple people to their feet as they abandon their breakfasts all together. But this morning is different. A few seconds after I sit down, one of the wolves sitting next to Virgyl lets out an excited whimper as its tail wags.

"Is this seat taken?"

I would know that voice in a crowded room.

*Nyall.*

~~I miss you so much.~~ I nod my head towards the wolves, signaling that it's full, and busy myself with the bowl of porridge in front of me.

"How is training going?" Nyall's voice is still scratchy from sleep. The question is innocent enough that I have no choice but to answer.

I swallow my porridge and wipe the back of my hand across my mouth.

"Which part?"

Nyall shrugs, busy eating his own porridge. "Both."

"Alright," I sigh. "Most of the Magyka and Demis are fairly low, power wise. But you have a good amount of elementals, which is rather rare these days. That sets you apart. Not to mention the other Mages."

*Mages.* That's apparently what they call themselves, those who use Nyall's particular type of magyk.

"A glowing review," Nyall retorts, his tone laden with sarcasm.

I scoff. "It could be a lot worse. Many of them are extremely proficient fighters. Especially the humans. They push twice as hard as any Magyka or Demis. Their weakness is their strength. But all of them need to stop being so damn afraid of defending themselves."

*"Sound familiar?"* Ryu asks and I glare at her mentally.

*"Shush."*

"Alright, so they need better motivation. What do you suggest?"

I glance at him, surprised.

"I'm not sure. Maybe it's just...me," I look away. "The second I go on the attack they start blubbering. There's been lots of crying. If I'm too scary for them to fight? Then they might as well give up now."

Nyall props his chin on his hand, looking at me in contemplation. It drives me insane how handsome he is without even *trying*.

"Sounds like we need to remind them what they're fighting for."

I take another bite of my porridge, chewing it and swallowing before finally responding. "Sounds like you have an idea about just how to do that."

Nyall smiles, which concerns me greatly.

"As it happens...I do."

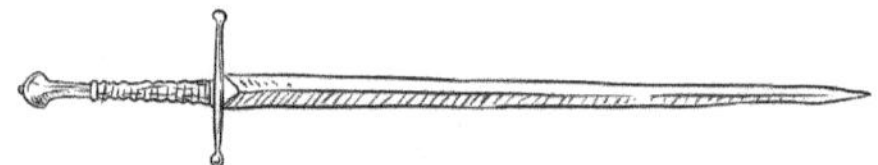

"We have five weeks until the Mercatus." Nyall looks around the table.

The generals who trapped me have joined us, Drystan not included.

A male with a gorgeous sepia complexion and curly black hair peppered with streaks of gray replaced him. Fion, though he prefers to be called Fi, flashes a polite smile, his warm amber eyes honest and relaxed. I quickly learned Fi was the stoic type. He said little, but when he did speak, everyone listened. He was the oldest general here by a few decades—or centuries, depending on his species. Fi isn't human, that much I can tell. But the rest remains a secret.

Mara has gone quiet to the point where I'm not sure she's up to the task of leading any longer. But that's not my job to decide or share.

Soren and Amari still tremble when they see me.

The latter two can be afraid of me all they want. With them, I enjoy it.

But the others? They need to get the fuck over it.

Reluctantly, I reach out with my magyk, searching for Nyall's mind. We connect instantly.

*"As much as all of this terror warms my cold, dead heart, everyone needs to get over their godsdamned fear of me."*

Nyall snorts, *"You do remember that you've spent the past—what, eight or nine decades ensuring that they reacted in this very manner?"*

I bare my teeth at him.

*"Do you ever talk to them? Socialize with them?"*

I roll my eyes. *"Socialize? That's your solution?"*

*"No, but a...celebration after a successful mission is."*

*"Excuse me?"* I ask, but Nyall locks me out.

"We need to practice," he announces, and the table goes quiet. "*All* of us. The recruits need more real-world experience. Training can only go so far. We also need to practice working together, as a *team*. Being afraid of each other, being *angry* with one another...that will get us killed."

Nyall Drayven.

*The peacekeeper.*

"He's right," I sigh, making several people at the table jump. "I recognize that regardless of how we all feel about each other, working together is required. Some practice runs would be good for the recruits, too."

"Have I died?" Davyn elbows me. "Are you actually getting along?"

I glare at the male to my left and elbow him back, hard enough that he groans. At the same time, Nyall slaps him on the back of the head.

"Clearly you're perfect for each other," Davyn hisses, cupping his ribs. "Fucking sadists."

Nyall cracks a small smile.

Mara clears her throat, surprising me. "I might have...something we could use as a training exercise. I've just gotten word that the Fae soldiers from Panormus are heading towards Karski. They'll be at the base there for three days."

"Do you know which regiment?" I ask. Mara's eyes widen.

"The 15th and 31st."

*Perfect.*

"Good." I glance at Nyall. "We need to leave tomorrow. Can you portal us there?"

He nods, an excited glint in his mismatched eyes.

Gods.

He's so gorgeous like this. Black Fae glyphs decorate every bit of exposed skin, all the way up to his sharp jawline.

Nyall Drayven is stunning. And I'm absolutely terrified of him.

As the rebellion leaders around the table begin to walk through how this practice run will work, I fall into my thoughts.

Nyall hasn't said anything about that day in the field with the generals. We've barely spoken until today.

Just polite words said in passing.

I didn't realize how much I missed him until now.

*Stop it. I can't miss him. Don't be stupid.*

But...if he knows, what's the point in playing pretend?

"Find me four more towns like this," I hear Nyall say to Davyn and Keres. "Work with Mara and the others. Nothing past Savarre. We'll do four practice runs and take different recruits with us each time. The best ones can be moved up in rank and join us with the Mercatus mission."

The logistics of running an army. I'm just glad I don't have to do it. That's one job I've *never* wanted.

Keres nods and Nyall leans back in his chair.

"It's settled then. Tomorrow night, we go to Karski."

"On second thought, this seems like a bad idea," Davyn whispers.

"No shit," I murmur. "But His Highness decided this was the best way to teach them, and you only *really* learn from fucking up."

"You knew this would go wrong?" Davyn's jaw drops. "Tricky lass!"

The new recruits to the Rebellion follow behind us. Nyall created a large portal to Karski, a town and trading outpost in the Northlands.

The generals came too. I've been paired with Mara. Both of us were rather vocal when asking for a different partner, but Nyall didn't budge. He just winked at me and sent me a single thought.

*"Practice."*

I keep imagining punching him in his pretty face.

We're part of the insertion team, dressed in disguises so that we can fit in when we enter the tavern. The cotton dress I have on is itchy, but it fits well enough.

The light blue shift was difficult to get over the white tunic, but the contrast of the two colors is pretty. Thin sleeves billow in the chilly spring wind as we walk towards the tavern.

The plan is to scout out the Fae soldiers and distract them enough that we can grab them.

Nyall wants to...ask them some questions. Which is code for torture the information out of them. Not that I mind.

Still, I'm frustrated and cranky. Teamwork isn't exactly my strong suit.

*What would Dyana do?*

I almost laugh, but I swallow it, along with the tears threatening to fall down my cheeks.

*I miss you. I miss you so much.*

Channeling my beloved younger sister, I throw a bawdy smile on my face and let my hips swing. I rather enjoy the sound of Nyall *choking* at the sight. I throw a flirty wink at him over my shoulder and his jaw drops.

Despite this silly little mission, I do actually want to accomplish something here. They can fear me, but they don't respect me.

I need to change that.

I *want* to change that, which is another thing that terrifies me.

With my foot, I push the tavern door open, laughing in a high-pitched girly tone. The glamour hidden in a small silver bracelet that Nyall handed me turned my hair inky black and my eyes a warm brown. Mara didn't need any disguise. The peach dress she wears was so striking with her blonde hair, the tavern denizens all stop and stare.

She blushes and flashes an innocent smile.

Looks like I'm not the only one more experienced than they claim.

She giggles and skips over to me, wrapping her arms around my waist.

"I'll never like you," she whispers. "But I...I'm sorry, for what we did."

The air whooshes out of my lungs and I nod numbly, the flirty smile never leaving my face.

A mix of gratitude and embarrassment makes my cheeks flush.

Luckily that only sells the tipsy image further.

We mingle for a while, playing cards and flirting with the Fae soldiers.

It's very rare to see Imperial Fae out of their signature uniform of armor, good hair, and narcissism. But they're dressed in plain clothes. The fabrics and designs are more modern than anything a true peasant would wear, but they're good enough disguises.

Why do they wish to remain incognito?

*Hmm.*

A glance to my right and my heart skips a beat as I lock eyes with one of the Fae who was there that day in Twyn Fells.

*The Imperial Fae rips off his helmet, pointed ears emerging with pure silver hair, so light it's almost white, contrasting against glowing, unnatural blood-red eyes.*

Those same blood-red eyes look back at me. Although the red has faded into a pale orange.

"You're a pretty one," he says looking me up and down. "You are...unattached?"

I nod, all the while in my head I'm imagining all of the different ways I can kill him.

"Perfect." The Fae pats his lap and it takes everything within me not to gag as I walk over to his chair and sit down on his legs, fighting the urge to throw up all over his shirt. *He deserves it.* The Fae's skin is uncomfortably hot and immediately it makes me sweaty.

"That's a good girl. Sit there and be pretty for me."

I nod, passive and agreeable on the outside but internally, I'm screaming.

*There's no time to react as the green Dragon suddenly snaps his head to the side and jumps forward, his long neck reaching right into the crowd of people and grabbing Mrs. Hunton, snapping her in two as her legs dangle out of his mouth. A shocked noise falls from me but it's drowned out by the sudden wails and screams of the crowd. The Dragon chews, crunching down and silencing her screams. Organs fall from her chest cavity as blood sprays from the Dragon's mouth. That's when the screaming starts.*

The male eventually gets bored of the conversation and pats my thigh, signaling I'm to stand.

I diligently obey, batting my eyelashes at him.

"Let's go upstairs," he breathes, the stench of hard liquor on his breath. "Daddy needs a ride."

Not trusting myself to say anything nice, I wordlessly nod.

The Imperial Fae looks behind me and smirks. "Bring your pretty little friend, too. It's been a while since I've had a blonde."

I want to stab him in the fucking throat.

Instead, I stand there and smile.

"You two will put up an entertaining fight, won't you, little puggōs?"

I motion to Mara and she walks over, winding her arm through mine as we follow the Fae upstairs. The plan was to get him outside. But the thing about plans is they usually go astray.

"What do we do?" Mara murmurs.

"I need you to trust me. I know this one."

Mara looks at me with wide eyes. "You know him?"

I nod. "Trust me. *Please.*"

I watch the wariness in her eyes, but she nods eventually. "Fine."

"Follow my lead and play along."

"You're changing the plan, aren't you?" Mara asks quietly as we ascend the staircase, following the Imperial Fae. "You keep getting this...I don't know, this *look* in your eyes."

I glance at her and flash a bloodthirsty smile, "You might not like this next part."

Mara curses and the Imperial Fae looks over his shoulder. We pause and I lick my lips, willing my eyes into something resembling lust.

It works. The Imperial Fae growls and walks faster.

Soon, we're at his door.

The Fae lets us in, and I blur, moving faster than he expects. Within seconds, I've sliced my dagger through his clavicle, pinning him to the wall. It won't kill him thanks to his healing powers, but he can't call for help. Shadows rip out of my hands, wrapping around the Imperial Fae until they cover his mouth and his wrists are bound behind his back.

"There, that's better," I smile. "Now, my friend and I have a few questions for you. You will answer them."

His words are muffled by my shadows. Carefully, I lift the shadow on his mouth.

"You fucking bitch—"

I muffle his words again. "For every question you don't answer, I'm going to cut off a limb until all that's left is your useless cock. Then I'm going to cut that off too. Do you understand?"

The Fae's eyes widen as it dawns on him that I'm serious.

Mara makes a noise, and I glance back at her. "Lesson one. Imperial Fae can heal reattached limbs unless the removed one is too far away or fully destroyed. They can't grow a new limb, so if something happens to the original…"

"They're left that way," Mara breathes. "Gods."

"There are no Gods here right now." I let a manic smile appear on my face and turn back to our captive. "Now, ask him what the Rebellion wants to know first."

Mara pauses, not answering for a moment. I hear her take a shaky breath. "How many of your troops are stationed in Matrica?"

The army stronghold in the Westlands.

Why do they need information about the Westlands?

I let my shadows lift from the Fae's mouth.

"I'll never tell you," he spits.

I purse my lips in disappointment. "That's rather unfortunate for you."

With a flick of my wrist, I draw my flames across his skin. It severs muscle and bone quickly, cauterizing the flesh around it. His left leg falls to the floor and I kick it away. The hot scent of blood permeates the air.

The Imperial Fae is writhing in pain and screaming behind the shadow gag. I loosen it again and the begging begins.

"Please, please no. I'll-I'll tell you whatever you want."

"Much better," I slap him playfully on the cheek. "Was that so hard?"

"Matricia," Mara reminds him. "How many troops are stationed in Matricia?"

"F-five thousand."

"There should be ten," Mara's eyes narrow. "Why are the numbers so low?"

"They were dispatched North. The Archmage thinks an attack on Panormus is what you'll do next."

"He moved them to Panormus?" Mara curses. "How many are in Panormus now?"

The Imperial Fae trembles. "Fifteen thousand."

Gods.

None of the regional strongholds in Ur Daoine have more than ten thousand troops. Never.

Why is the Archmage so sure the Rebellion is attacking Panormus?

"How many troops are stationed in Castra Batavorumm?" Mara asks, stepping closer to the Fae.

The stronghold in the Southlands, in the middle of the Infinium Sands.

"Five thousand," the Fae pants.

Interesting.

Less than usual. It means we need to keep the majority of Ur Daoine's troops focused on the North.

Mara glances at me and nods.

She's finished.

I look back at the Fae. "Now it's my turn."

*"This is the part you won't like,"* I whisper in Mara's mind, easily entering her thoughts. *"You will want to look away. Don't. The Archmage can and will do far worse, should our plan fail."*

I hear her nervous inhale as I crouch down in front of the Imperial Fae and remove the bracelet around my wrist.

"Now, I don't actually have a question. It's more of a...declaration, you could say."

The glamour falls and I watch him take in my features. The realization is slow, but I can tell the moment it hits him because his pupils dilate, fear completely overtaking his system.

Perfect.

"Good, you remember me. That makes this easier."

The Fae doesn't have time to blink as I reach down his pants and rip his cock off with a hard pull.

My shadows silence his screams, but I pull them away for just a brief moment as I lean down and kiss his cheek.

"That's for Mrs. Hunton, you evil piece of shit."

Then I shove his bloody cock down his own throat.

The Fae chokes on it, unable to breathe. With his hands still bound, I grab him by the hair and drag him over to the window.

"Open the window!" I call to Mara.

She scrambles and opens it wide.

I would ask for help lifting him but to be honest, I don't need it.

Flexing the strength that runs through my blood, I lift the Imperial Fae and hurl his body out the window, into a thick Ulster Wald spruce next to the tavern.

Mara and I lean out and watch as his partially legless, bound body bounces between branches on a torturously slow descent to the ground. His body hits every branch possible, until finally the Fae hits the ground with a hard thump and a pained groan.

I finally release my shadows and he curls into a ball, sobbing.

Nyall approaches from the side and looks up.

"I know that look. You're definitely in trouble," Mara mutters.

Oh dear. Did I upset the Rebel Prince? How *terrible*.

*"Exactly how many times did you throw him out of the window, Amalia?"* His voice brushes against my thoughts.

*"Just once."*

*"Right. Shall I remove the cock from his throat, or was Mara able to get the intel we needed?"*

I glance down, resting my chin on my hands, *"By the tone in your voice, I'm assuming this means the rest of you failed in your own tasks, leaving it down to the ladies to save everyone's asses. Is that right?"*

*"Brat,"* he growls.

*"That's a yes. And we did get the intel, thanks to me."*

*"Good. Then he can stay like this."* Nyall walks past the body and trips over it, accidentally kicking the Fae in the head.

*"He bragged...about the people he killed that day in Twyn Fells. Kick him again, will you?"*

Nyall coughs and his leg flicks back, kicking the Imperial Fae in the liver.

"Time to go," Nyall calls, and I nod, turning to Mara.

"We have to jump, don't we?" she asks. I nod and she curses. "Of course we do."

"Climb on my back," I motion and Mara dismisses me at first, but I blur and toss her over my shoulder, accessing my full strength. "This way is fine too. Now, don't scream."

I blur and jump out of the window, avoiding the branches as much as I'm able.

I land on my feet but the impact is so great, it still knocks me to my knees as the wind *whooshes* from my lungs. Mara pants as I slide her off my shoulder.

"Never do that again," she spits. "Ever."

I shrug. "We survived. You're welcome."

"Let's go," Nyall calls again, and we jog over as the rebels quickly exit the town.

Immediately upon returning through Nyall's portal, the arguing begins.

"Shut up!" I shout and they quiet down as we walk to the war room and take our seats. "Before everyone shares what went *wrong*, Mara needs to share what we found out."

"You were successful?" Davyn sits up straighter when I nod.

Mara quickly fills them in and everyone's attention piques. The generals get busy moving around wooden pieces on a large, carved map of Ur Daoine. The wooden pieces represent amounts of troops, and the numbers Mara received tonight are vastly different from what they had listed before.

"You're sure he wasn't lying?" Soren asks and my gaze flicks to her.

"Positive," Mara answers, surprising me. "I saw the look on his face. He was terrified."

"This is...very helpful. We now have accurate numbers on the entire Ur Daoinan army."

Mara nods and glances at me. "It was her."

Now it's my turn to be surprised. The table quiets, ready to listen to our conversation.

"I do not like to admit when I'm wrong. I'm still not sure I like you, or that I'll ever believe you about my sons, but I saw tonight, what you meant. There *are* some decisions that we aren't prepared to make. I thought that wasn't the case, but when I hesitated, you didn't."

~~I wish I didn't have this experience.~~

~~I wish dealing pain and death weren't my fate.~~

"You were right. We, the rebellion, do need your help."

"And we haven't even used the Dragon," Amari speaks up.

"Ryu is not a thing to be used," I snap. "Should Ryu ever decline to help, that response will be respected, or you will find yourselves at the end of a very short stick."

"Noted," Mara says quickly. "Thank you for explaining."

The table returns to the conversation of troop size as plans are laid out for the next practice run.

We have to keep the Archmage's attention on the Northlands, so next time, we're going to run a fake raid and destroy the Armory at the Ur Daoinan Army Base in Panormus

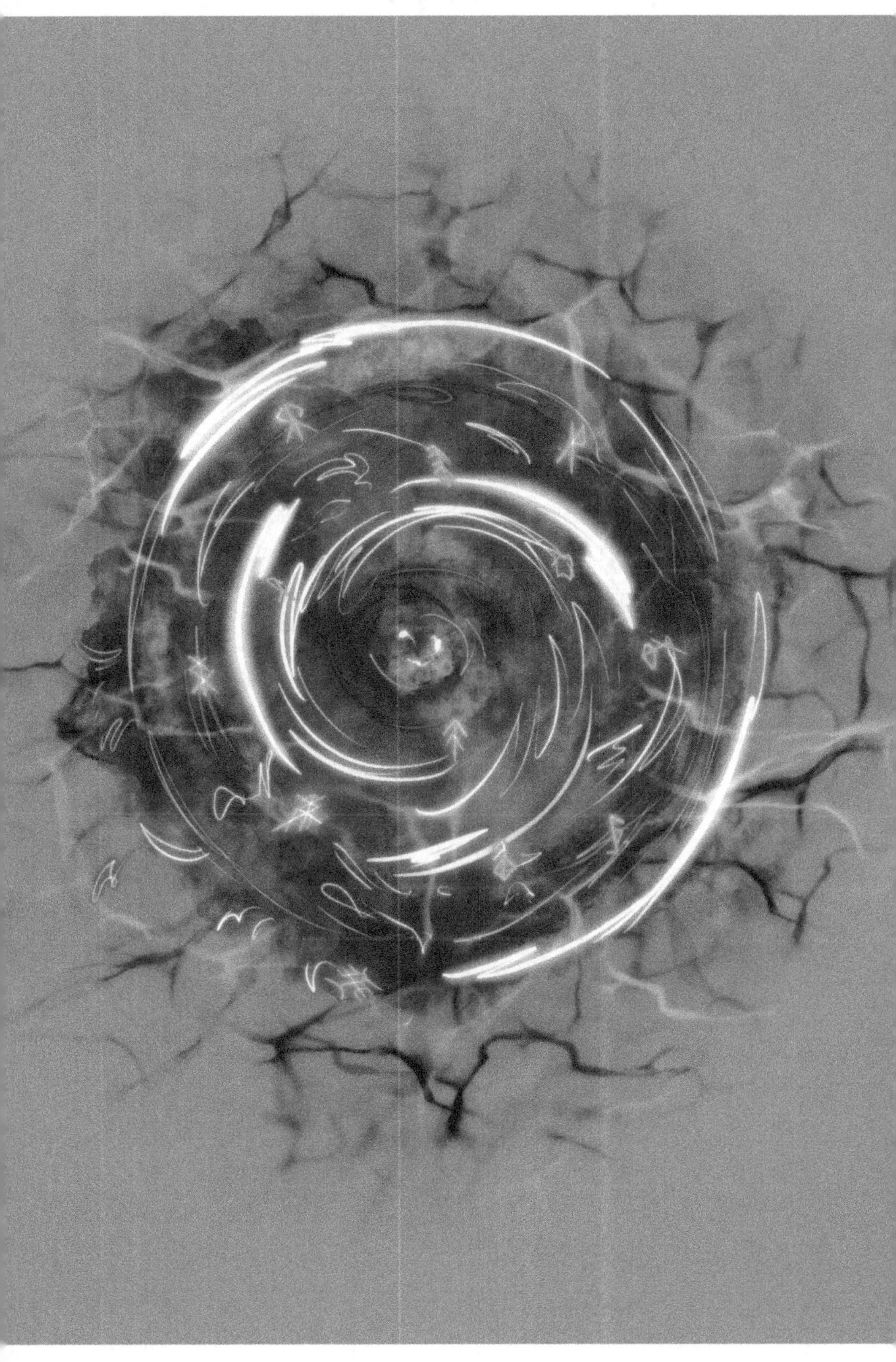

# CHAPTER 17
## DYANA

"Come on! Give in already!"

Sweat drips from my brow as I fight against Embyrne's magyk while she assaults my mind.

"In your dreams," I grit out between tight lips, panting.

"Are you thinking about me at night, Dyana? How interesting." Embyrne smirks and launches forward, kicking out with her right leg to trip me. I see it but not soon enough and end up falling face first against the dirt floor.

I've become so familiar with it lately, I might as well be a worm.

"The only time I think of you is when I want to punch something."

"Do you often throw tantrums? How childish." She tsks.

I push up to my hands and knees but her foot lands on my back, kicking me back down. The air rushes out of my lungs and I gasp for breath, inhaling more dirt, causing me to cough so hard I almost pull a muscle.

"Fuck you," I snarl, unable to think of anything better to say.

"Is that a statement or a question?" the Beastkyn purrs before flipping me on my back. Her face hovers above mine, golden eyes blazing and a wicked smirk on her angular face.

Embyrne's moods shift faster than the tides. One second, she's flirting, and the next, she's beating me to a pulp or complaining about my lack of skill.

I lift my legs and hook them through hers, tossing her to the side. She snarls and her nails turn to sharp black points as she lashes out at me. I feel her slice the skin on my cheek and a burning sensation follows, making me hiss in pain.

"If I were in your bed"—she leans down and presses a kiss against my cheek. Her tongue darts out and she licks up the blood, letting out a pleased, draconian growl. I still, my heart skipping a beat. Then her fist meets my stomach. I gasp in pain—"the last thing you would be doing is sleeping."

The pain fades fast as my upgraded body heals my injuries.

Embyrne stands, brushing her hands off and leaving me physically and emotionally reeling.

"You kept me out of your mind the whole time. Well done."

I'm shocked my neck isn't broken from the fucking whiplash of this...creature. Woman. ~~Beautiful person.~~

I level a mental punch to that last thought.

No. Absolutely not.

Not Embyrne. I cannot be attracted to the person who beats me up on a daily basis.

I also can't afford to fall for anyone.

Nothing can distract me from getting to Amalia.

Nothing.

A weird feeling of Déjà vu hits and my vision blurs for a moment. I get up to stand, ignoring it, but stumble as I disappear into a memory.

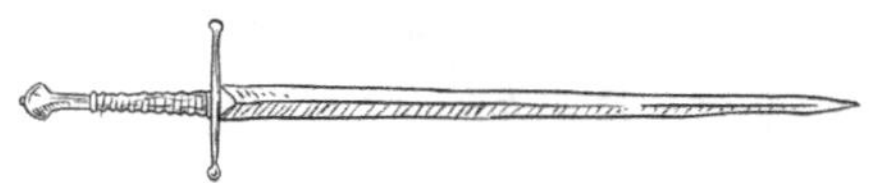

*"I always knew you were into some weird stuff. You like challenging people. For example, take me," I flop back and cross my legs, "I was a challenge because you had*

to take care of another person. Although I helped." Amalia raises both brows in a look of knowing disbelief. "No, no, don't even act like I didn't! You were an unhinged feral woodland creature. My knowledge of the outside world was key in preparing you for life in public. But you still had to take care of me, and we're the opposite. You love being quiet and hiding away with your animals. I like talking and dancing."

I gesture to myself, "Social," and then gesture to Amalia, "Unsocial."

Ama never lasts long when I start off on this. I learned early on that I could win our disagreements if I annoyed her enough that her patience snapped.

"Fine. Fine! Os is attractive, and the eye contact thing was hot. But it doesn't matter for one huge reason: we have to figure out how to survive the next five weeks and then the Gauntlet. That is damn plenty to focus on, and you know it. There's no time for little crushes and frivolity."

I cough, "Boring."

Ama makes a faux shocked face and shoves my shoulder and slapping a pillow at my face.

We both break out into raucous laughter, despite the direness of our situation.

These moments.

These are the ones that keep me going every day.

My friend.

My family.

"I'm being serious, Dy." Ama says after we quiet down. There's a gentleness in her voice that makes me cave immediately.

She's right.

"We have to train, and we have to train hard. If we want any chance of getting out of this, it's going to be because we're winning. I've thought it over for the past ten days and there's no other way out. We have to win, Dy. That's the only option."

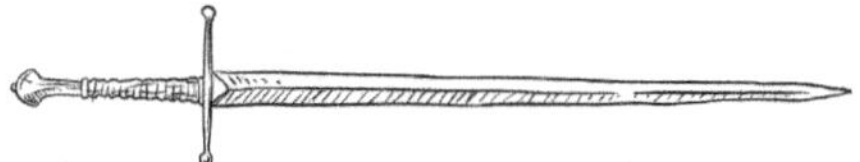

"Dyana? Dyana? Don't make me slap you again," a concerned voice breaks into the memory, shattering it. I gasp and reach my arms out, confused as to why I'm lying on the ground.

A soft hand against my cheek stops me.

"You're okay," Embyrne says, and then she repeats it again, turning it into an order. "You are okay. Take a deep breath and let whatever it was go."

"Sorry," I whisper.

Embyrne shakes her head. "Do not apologize. Bad memory?"

I nod.

Embyrne flashes a sad, hollow smile. "It happens to me too."

I blink in surprise, and she laughs.

"Nothing is what it seems. Perhaps what looks like a paradise is, in truth, just another prison."

The pain in her voice tells me everything I need to know.

"Embyrne," I breathe. "Do they...*hurt* you?"

Embyrne sniffs and wraps one arm around my waist, lifting me onto my feet with insane ease.

"I do not wish to discuss it." she says carefully. "Like I said before: when you leave here, I'm coming with you."

Something goes unsaid. The rest of her sentence lies quietly in the air between us.

"I push you," Embyrne starts, "not to hurt you, but because whatever your plan is, every way out of here will involve a fight. If you want to survive, you need to say farewell to your humanity and spread your wings. Let go of the human Dyana. Embrace the Dragon."

I sigh, cracking my neck and looking around the abandoned arena.

"I know. It's...harder than I anticipated. So much harder."

Embyrne stares at me. "Then try even harder. Every fucking day, try harder than you did the day before. Until there is nothing left but success. Failure isn't an option here."

I whip my head towards her, suddenly furious. "You know what? Fuck you. Do you not see how hard I'm trying? I pass out every night because I'm so exhausted I can barely stand. I haven't given myself a single minute to grieve despite the fact that the only family I have left might be dead," I pant, tears welling. "Since the moment I woke up, I haven't stopped trying. So fuck you for saying that and fuck you for judging me."

"Grief can wait. Ever since you arrived, your life has been at risk. So put the sadness aside and try *harder.*"

I shake my head at her, disappointed. "You don't get it. I'm not like you. You're full Dragon. I only have a small piece of that. Stop expecting me to be like you."

Embyrne shrugs, but her eyes gleam with challenge, and a thread of fear grows within me.

"I expect you to be yourself. But if you continue to hold back, we will either be stuck here forever, or we'll die trying to escape."

"Show me how to survive, then," I plead.

Embyrne's smile is hollow. "You have everything you need already, Dyana. Apparently you just...aren't ready for it."

I snarl but she takes a running start and jumps off the cliffside at the edge of the arena. I race to follow but stop.

What if I fall? The ground looms 90 meters below.

Embyrne is gone, but through the thick, tropical forest, a gleam of gold flashes in the corner of my eyes.

*Stop being such a godsdamn human!*

I stop thinking, and my body takes over as I suddenly leap into the air and plummet towards the ground. A high-pitched scream explodes from my lips, and I feel Vesimyr panicking in the back of my mind.

I crash through the trees, bouncing between the thick branches and leaves, leaving welts and scratches all over my body. My clothes tear, exposing my skin to even more branches.

I hit the forest floor on my back and for a moment, I'm unable to breathe.

Embyrne stands above me, arms crossed, and a single brow raised.

"We need to work on your landing, apparently."

I gasp and stand up, immediately going to punch her.

But the lack of pain makes me pause. I look down and two things become clear immediately.

One, I'm topless and my pants are almost hanging off.

Two, I'm...*fine.* The scratches have already healed, leaving only some light blood smears. The bruises are gone, and all that's left is *me.*

I just jumped into the air and off a fucking *cliff* and I'm *fine.*

"What the fuck?" I gasp. "I just fell over 90 meters. My legs should be broken. My entire body should be broken."

Embyrne scoffs, "Do you have too much wax in your ears?" I blink and she shakes her head in frustration, speaking in a mockingly slow voice. "You. Are. Not. Human. Anymore!"

"Well, yes but—"

"No buts, Dyana. That's the thing. All of your human weaknesses are gone. Well, physically at least. You cannot think like a human anymore. You have to think like a *Dragon.*"

I'm struck silent as the truth of her words sinks in.

My fear.

My hesitation.

"I hate you," I mutter, wiping my eyes.

A cool breeze brushes against my chest and my nipples harden, making me hyper aware of my nakedness.

I open my eyes to see Embyrne staring at my breasts, a hungry look in her eyes. Then her gaze travels down the rest of my body. My left leg is almost fully exposed, leaving my ass half-hanging out of my pants and exposing my hip bone.

Her eyes shutter closed and she takes a deep breath, as if the sight of me has shaken her to her scaled core.

When they open, any lust I thought I saw is gone. The forest suddenly shakes as Vesimyr descends, crushing many trees beneath his huge bulk.

His belly is red, his fire at the ready, as he bares his teeth at Embyrne.

**"What happened? What did you DO?"**

I jump in front of her as he gets ready to unleash his flames.

"Ves! I'm fine. The only thing wounded is my dignity." I pant, my arms out to the sides, as I protect Embyrne.

A glance over my shoulder shows her golden eyes are now wide with shock.

Then the Beastkyn turns around and runs into the forest, leaving me standing there, blinking in confusion.

"Uh, okay. Bye!" I call. I whirl on my Dragon and lift my pointer finger, poking him on his soft snout. "You scared her away, you big oaf!"

His eyes roll and he sighs, his fire dissipating as his silver belly goes back to normal. *"I see you're just fine, then. I felt your panic and thought Embyrne had…"*

"Had what?" I ask, crossing my arms. "Go on!"

*"Well, hurt you,"* he admits. I try hard not to smile.

"Don't be such a mother hen. I can hold my own."

He's quiet and I scoff.

"I'm serious! I kept her out of my mind all day this time."

Vesimyr blinks, *"You did?"* I nod and he flashes his fangs in a draconian smile. *"That's wonderful, Dyana. Well done."*

Then he looks around and stares back at my naked chest. *"Care to share why you're all the way down here half naked instead of up in the training arena?"*

I cough, "Well. She jumped, and without thinking I just...jumped after her."

*"Ah, I see."*

"My landings need a bit of work," I mutter. "The trees, uh, ripped off all of my clothes."

But my Dragon doesn't laugh at me, instead he lowers his body to the ground so I can mount his back.

"I can't ride back naked!" I whisper-yell.

Vesimyr sighs and I hear Embyrne's voice in my head, telling me to stop being such a human.

Embarrassment warms my cheeks and I lift my chin. "Okay. Fine. But no dilly-dallying. It's a little chilly this evening anyways. And I do not feel like giving the entire island a peep show!"

*"What is this 'peep show'?"* Vesimyr asks in a confused voice, and I can't help but laugh. A flash of warmth and pride brushes against my magyk. I fight a smile and climb up Vesimyr's leg, using the edges of his scales as handholds. Wedging myself between the spikes on his back, I hold on tight as he takes off.

Amalia and Os pop into my head as we ascend into the sky, and it immediately makes me want to cry.

But the way they looked at each other in those last few weeks...with such raw hunger and emotion I often had to turn away, feeling like I was interrupting an intimate moment...

For a moment, for a brief, single moment, I could have sworn that Embyrne looked at me like that too.

And I don't have a fucking clue what to do about it. That terrifies me more than any Dragon ever could.

# CHAPTER 18
## IREYNA

"Fly, or I'll pick someone else for the Dragonguard."

The Archmage's voice echoes in my head as I mount Anonyme.

A shallow metal and leather saddle now sits in between her shoulder blades. The straps weave through her brilliant white scales, securing around her belly and between her wing joints.

I get comfortable in the seat and attach my leather vest to the saddle for extra security.

"Alright, girl. We need to fly. You heard him."

She trembles and I pat her scales.

"Sometimes, we have to be brave."

Still, she doesn't move.

Anger flares and I shout, "FLY, ANONYME!"

The white Dragon beneath me is startled as I kick her sides. She quickly flaps her wings and runs forward. The wind picks up, hitting my face as she leaps into the air.

As we ascend into the clouds, reality hits me.

*I'm flying.*

My head falls back and I let out a joyful shout as Anonyme circles around Castael Laryn.

The air is cold and crisp up here. Already, condensation gathers on my cheeks and forehead. Little droplets of water decorate Anonyme's white scales.

She twirls through the air, and I'm almost thrown from the saddle. Thankful for the foresight to attach my vest to the saddle, I grab the reins and try to steer Anonyme back to the courtyard.

"Let's circle the city five times and then head back!"

Anonyme snorts and completes her task.

Five times we circle the city.

Five times, I feel like I'm dreaming.

But sooner than I'd like, I'm guiding Anonyme back to the courtyard. She lands awkwardly and I'm jostled about. As she stills, stopping, I unlock myself from the saddle and slide off her back on wobbly legs.

I lean against her side, laughing, as her serpentine neck angles to the side so she can look at me.

"Good job," I whisper. "We'll do this again tomorrow, okay?"

A clapping noise interrupts me and I turn around, falling to my knees in a single move.

"Your Holiness," I breathe. "You honor me with your presence."

"So," he starts. "You got that wretched beast to fly. Good. I didn't want to replace you, you know. It's just the nature of these times. War is on the horizon, Ireyna. We must be ready."

"We will be," I lift my gaze finally, looking upon him as I issue the promise.

"Good. That is what I like to hear," he nods. "You are blessed, child. He sees your loyalty and this is His reward."

"Blessed Sol," I intone in a low voice.

"Blessed Sol," the Archmage repeats before walking away, dozens of attendants following in his wake.

"Oh yes," he calls, and I freeze, startled. "Has the other beast given you anything of use, yet?"

I shake my head and the Archmage sighs. "Yes, as I suspected. His only use to us is his blood. We only need to keep him alive enough to harvest it."

I nod.

I wish Os would see the truth of things. I wish he'd actually *listen* when I speak to him about Sol Constantus.

Constantyn is our savior. He will lift us from evil and bless our kingdom, ending drought and erasing the plague from the pages of history.

I know this to be true with every fiber of my being.

It has to be.

It *must* be.

Anonyme nudges my shoulder, and I gently caress her snout, never lifting my arms above my shoulders.

"I'll see you tomorrow. I need to go take care of something," I tell her with a pat. I turn and walk away, never once looking back, as I head to the dungeons once more.

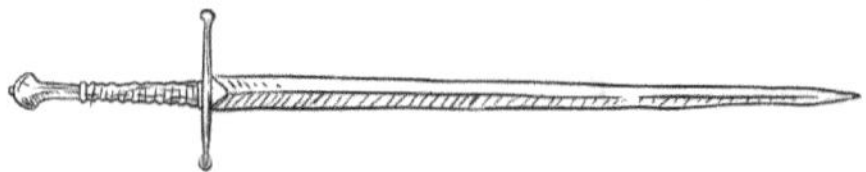

"What, no plea to convert to your side? No blessing from Sol Constantus?" Os taunts.

I shrug. "No. You clearly will not change, despite how much I want you to. There is no reason to keep trying."

"What does that mean for me?" he asks.

I motion to the instruments around me, "This is your future, Os. This is what you've chosen. Remember that when you haven't seen the sun for centuries. Remember you chose this fate."

Os is quiet as I attach the needle to a vial, stabbing into his femoral artery. Blood quickly fills the vial. Attached to it are hollow tubes that drain into big, decorated metal pots.

"It's such a shame, really. If you had only accepted Constantyn as Savior and the Archmage as your Lord, we wouldn't have set a trap for your gray-haired girlfriend."

Os snarls, fighting his restraints.

"You wouldn't dare," he threatens, and I snicker.

"Like you could do anything about it if I did. You're trapped here, Os. I could go find Amalia today and flay the skin from her muscles, and there's nothing you could do about it."

"I'll fucking kill you," he swears. "I swear to whatever Gods are listening, if you harm a hair on her head, I'll burn this place to the fucking ground."

"Empty threats and hollow promises," I retort. "Your words mean nothing."

I look down at the blood-filled tubes.

"Now, be a good beast and give me all of that Dragon blood. I have things to do."

Things like kidnapping Amalia Asteroth.

# CHAPTER 19
## RYU

*It is a common misconception that Dragons do not dream. The reality is quite the opposite. We do not merely dream when we close our eyes at night. We also live the lives of our ancestors.*

*Ever since I matured and the memories began to assault me every waking moment, my dreams have been full of my mother. I can't control the dreams, but I'm aware that what I'm seeing isn't real.*

*But something about this dream is different.*

*I'm standing in front of a steep mountain. The bottom half is barren, with charred, bald trees, sharp boulders, and steep terrain.*

*Halfway up the mountain, the landscape turns lush. Barren trees turn green and verdant. The path becomes gentle, and the way to the top is clear.*

*I don't know why, but I feel the need to climb the mountain.*

*Looking around, I see no other Dragons.*

*Is this a memory, or something else?*

*"You shouldn't be here," my mother's voice calls. She's next to me, hovering in the air as I crawl up the steep mountain.*

*"You'll never make it to the top. You can't even fly."*

*The disappointment in her voice hurts so bad, I nearly trip over my claws.*

*I bare my teeth at her. "You're not real."*

*"I'm as real asthis Mountain," she snarls, baring her large fangs in my face.*

*Her scales are a deep red that shines beneath the bright sun.*

*Every time I see her in my dreams, I'm in awe of her size.*

*She really was the biggest Dragon that ever lived.*

*Well, besides Great Livyathin.*

*I'm almost to the lush part of the forest but something grabs me from behind.*

*I look down to see claws around my belly but it's too late. My mother pulls me off the mountain and hurls me into the air, scratching my belly as I pass her claws.*

*I watch in pain and horror as my blood falls to the earth, organs and intestines following behind.*

*I plummet towards the ground, flailing. Mother falls beside me, watching with a disappointed look on her scaled face.*

*The last thing I see before I hit the ground are her claws reaching for my face as she scratches out my eyes.*

*"You're no heir of mine."*

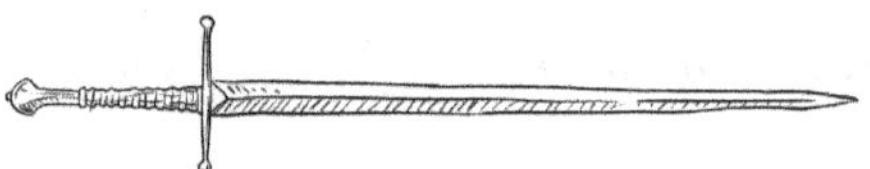

"Shh, shh. It's alright, love. It was just a nightmare," Ama whispers, her hands petting my snout. I blink away the dream, surprised to find myself panting.

"Take a breath, Ry." Amalia caresses my scales slowly and the feeling grounds me. "You're alright," Amalia murmurs, climbing onto my front legs. I close them, creating a little nook for her to lay in. She makes a pleased sound and gets comfortable, motioning for me to lay my head next to her body.

"Would you like me to tell you a story?" she asks as I lay my head down.

I nod.

After my nightmares, I…I don't always like to talk. Luckily Amalia can feel my emotions, helping her understand what I'm feeling without requiring words.

"Alright. Let's see…" She pretends to think for a second and I lick her cheek, making her giggle.

I wish she'd laugh more.

"How about the story of when my horse Taran broke into the feed room and ate a week's worth of grain?"

I can feel the hurt in her voice when she says his name.

She's spoken about him before.

*Taran.*

All I know is she loved this creature very much. Aanad said Taran was Amalia's friend.

So I listen closely as she tells me the story of his hungry antics. I try to ignore the dream, but the image of that mountain remains fresh in my mind.

Eventually, my eyes fall shut and I return to sleep, but I don't forget the mountain.

Nor do I forget my mother's words.

"HngGGggh-Ppbhww- zZZzzzZZ." Ryu's snoring is so loud that it nearly shakes the tent. I *try* to ignore it but when her wing suddenly smacks me in the face, nearly breaking my nose, my patience snaps.

Even the wolves left. They couldn't take the loud sound of the bright red Dragon's snores, or the way her tail sometimes wags in its sleep, which would be rather cute except for the fact that her tail is covered in spiked barbs sharp enough to puncture straight through my leg.

I love Ryu, but I believe we've officially moved into the annoying 'teenage' Dragon years.

It takes a lot to wear me down enough to go crawling back to Nyall Drayven, yet here I am. Trudging through the muddy camp in the middle of the night. My few belongings gathered in my arms.

*Fuck. Fuck. Fuck.* I curse with every step, annoyed at myself.

I don't *want* to see him.

*Yes, you do.*

The thought sits with me as I finally make it to his tent. I steel myself and enter Nyall's room. The air smells delicious, like warm pears and cinnamon. My mouth waters instantly.

Until I look across Nyall's tent and see Mara's hand on his arm.

Then she smiles, and Nyall smiles back.

He *smiles* with her.

I'm relatively certain if I looked down, there would be blood dripping out of a wound in my chest.

Mara leans forward, her eyes twinkling, and—

I'm back outside before I can see anything else. I know where this leads.

*It's fine. I don't care.* ~~*LIAR.*~~

I walk off in a daze and no direction. My chest is tight to the point of pain and my heart is heavy as a bone-deep feeling of loneliness settles over me.

*I shouldn't care. I shouldn't care.* ~~*BUT I DO.*~~

The lie echoes through my thoughts.

"Goodnight, Amalia," a voice suddenly whispers, startling me.

I have my dagger at their throat before they can take a breath. Panting heavily, my brows furrow as I take in the woman in front of me.

Mara.

"Don't scare me," I snarl.

Mara blinks, "Noted. Now do you mind? I'm exhausted." She motions to the dagger at her throat.

Oh. *Right.*

My hand falls and I step back, clearing my throat. "I was lost in my thoughts and didn't hear you. I apologize."

Mara's eyes widen in surprise. "Thank you...I, uh, think. Night."

With a nod, she keeps walking, leaving me behind.

Looking around, I realize that I've gone the wrong way and turn around, going back the way I came. I retrace my steps and am just passing Nyall's tent again when his magyk brushes against mine.

*"What do you want?"*

He snorts. *"Hello to you too. Can't sleep?"*

I grind my teeth together and cross my arms, glaring at the closed drapes on the door of his tent.

*"Ryu has started snoring with this latest growth spurt."*

*"Ah,"* Nyall's voice is amused. *"Well, the invite to share still counts. I even promise to behave."*

~~MAYBE I DON'T WANT YOU TO BEHAVE.~~ I grimace with the effort it takes to hide that thought from him.

*"Fine,"* I bite out. *"Just for the night, though."*

*"Just for the night,"* he repeats. *"Shall I conjure hot water for your tub?"*

*Oh Gods.* The idea of languishing in a hot tub nearly makes my knees go out.

*"I'll take that as a yes,"* he laughs. *"Now, are you going to stand out there all night, or will you stop being a stubborn ass and come inside?"*

*"You're the ass,"* I snap and immediately want to die of embarrassment.

*What kind of response was that, Amalia?*

*"Always the poet,"* Nyall chuckles.

With a deep breath, I walk into Nyall's tent, the drapes brushing against my back. The air still smells of pear and cinnamon.

"What is that smell?" I ask.

"My homemade cider. Want some?"

I shrug and strip, joining him.

"Close your eyes," I demand, glaring daggers into his head before hearing his sigh of acquiescence and his hand lifts to cover his eyes.

Only then do I pad over and plop down in the tub, making the water splash so hard it spills onto the floor. I sink beneath the surface until the milky water reaches the bottom of my chin.

"Okay," I whisper, and his tattooed arm stretches over the gap between our two tubs, handing me a steaming mug. "You can open your eyes."

"Careful, it's hot."

I snort and bring the warm mug to my lips anyways.

Flavors of juicy pear, vanilla, and spices dance on my tongue.

"Oh *wow*. You made this?" I ask in shock.

"Mhm," he murmurs, sipping on his own mug. I take another sip and nearly moan at the rich flavor.

"I'm impressed, Drayven. You've come a long way from that *awful* wine you made last year."

I make the mistake of glancing at his face the moment I call him by that awful name. Watching him flinch makes me instantly regret my words.

"I would prefer it if you don't call me that name," he says carefully. "But thank you."

I nod, jostling my mug. "If you prefer."

Then the warmth hits me as my chest flushes and my cheeks turn pink. I feel *drunk*.

"Uh, Nyall? What exactly did you put in this?"

Nyall laughs and it's a louder, *freer* sound than usual. I find myself smiling wide and letting out a girlish *giggle* at the sight of him.

*Dear Gods. What's happening to me?*

"It's spelled to hide the taste of alcohol, but it's strong enough for Magyka and Demis to feel its effects. It's the same spell as the wine, actually. I just figured out how to mask the flavor."

Oh shit. I'm *drunk?*

Nyall snickers again and I realize I said that out loud.

"Yes, you did."

*Fuck!*

He laughs even harder and soon, I'm laughing with him. Nyall's joy is contagious.

"This was a bad idea," he mutters, mostly to himself, but I shrug.

"Do you care?"

We pause and look at each other before cracking up again.

"Gods, you're so fucking beautiful when you laugh."

The alcohol numbs the pain. But it also numbs my guilt and grief.

I blame the cider as I turn to Nyall and smile widely, a hot pink flush on my cheeks.

"Doesn't sound like such a bad idea to me. Do continue," I wave my cup at him.

Nyall bows, making me giggle. Despite the water in the tub beginning to cool, Nyall's cider has me feeling warm and toasty.

I lift the mug to my mouth again to take another sip but nothing happens.

"Huh?" I wonder, looking at the mug. "Oh, oops."

The mug is empty.

Nyall laughs and grabs a jug of cider from the other side of his tub. He lifts it over him and carefully angles it above my mug to pour me another cup.

I quickly bring it to my lips. Some spills into the bath.

"Whoops." I cringe, slurring my words slightly, "Wow. I don't know the last time I really got drunk. Or if I ever even have been. I thought I had been drunk before, but now I really think I wasn't."

I keep rambling, voicing my thoughts aloud for quite some time. Thanks to the liquor, I'm not aware of how much time has passed but once I began talking, I couldn't stop.

Nyall sighs, leaning back in the tub as his head falls back and he closes his eyes.

"Am I boring you, Pretty Prince?"

Nyall's eyes open and he slowly turns his head, meeting my gaze. Then a wide smile appears on his face.

"Pretty *Prince?* Is that my new nickname."

"Mhm," I nod. "It is. Now answer my question!"

I swat at his arm and he splashes me, making me squeal.

"You could never bore me, Amalia," Nyall admits in a strangely serious tone. "I was enjoying listening to you talk, actually. The sound of your voice is…relaxing."

Warmth runs through me but not because of the alcohol. My cheeks heat and Nyall smirks at the sight.

Slowly the burn of the alcohol fades as our systems metabolize.

Eventually, Nyall sighs. "I could stay here all night. I wish I could."

"I can't believe how strong that cider is!"

"Me neither. You can see why I don't make it that often. Is your water warm enough?"

I trail a finger across the surface of the bath water. "It's gone cold."

"I can fix that," Nyall reaches his arm over, but I lift my hand out of the water, clasping his.

"No need," I say, unleashing my Hellfyre. It surrounds both tubs at the bottom.

"Your flames can heat…but they are not hot."

I laugh at Nyall's explanation of it.

"You're not entirely wrong? It's more that I can control whether they freeze or burn."

"Interesting," Nyall nods. The water in our tubs quickly heats up and steam begins wafting off the surface.

I let the Hellfyre die down until it fades completely.

"Your control has improved," Nyall notes, pouring us fresh mugs of cider.

Normally, a comment like that would enrage me. But sincerity is plain in his face and voice.

"Yeah," I nod. "This is dangerously good, Nyall."

He snickers. "I am glad the lady enjoys it."

I snort at the word 'lady'.

"I am and will never be any sort of lady." I cringe at the thought. "Manners? Behaving? Bah! It's so…"

"Human?" Nyall asks in a sleepy voice.

"Yeah," I breathe into my mug of hot cider. "Yeah it is. I could never live like that."

"In society, you mean?"

The alcohol slows my thoughts but at the same time, I have clarity.

"Yeah. I don't think I'm built for that kind of life."

"I thought I was," Nyall sighs. "But I…do not hate being hidden away from the world, living life in this tent. I would take anything over that hideous black castle."

The Black Citadel. I shiver thinking about it. I can't believe Nyall lived there for centuries.

This must be so different.

We go quiet for a few minutes, the crackling fire and occasional slosh of water the only noises in the tent.

The burn from the liquor grows quieter once more, barely lasting half an hour.

"Amalia?" Nyall breaks the silence, startling me.

"Yeah?"

"I'm...worried about you," he says, his voice low and full of concern.

Fuck. Not now. Please, not *this* conversation *now.*

"I'm fine," I lie, but the words taste awful in my mouth.

"I can feel the lie, Amalia. I know you're not fine."

My cheeks heat from shame instead of the cider and the sudden need to *escape* him takes over.

*I do not like how clearly he sees me.*

"This was a mistake." I turn to get out of the tub and slip, my reflexes slow from the liquor.

Nyall blurs and is by my side, catching me in an instant.

"I'm fine! I'm fine," I snarl, so embarrassed I feel like I might burst into flames.

"Why do you do that? Why do you keep pushing me away when I can *feel* what you want? You're not fine, Amalia. You're not fine at all. No one would be after what you've gone through!"

I look up and exhale, deflating slightly. "I can't do this tonight, Nyall. I'm not ready for this conversation."

*I'm not sure I ever will be.*

"Okay," he pauses. "That's fine. But I would like to talk about it soon."

*Fuck.*

"Fine. That's...fine." I respond. "Now please turn around."

Nyall sighs and turns, giving me privacy to change.

*Shit. I didn't bring clothes!*

"You can borrow mine," Nyall says, sensing what I'm worried about.

"Thanks," I mutter, making my way to his set of drawers. I grab a long sleeve black shirt that is thin and soft. It sticks to my damp skin and I turn to face Nyall.

"You can look now."

Nyall glances over his shoulder, watching as I try to look anywhere *but* his very naked *butt.*

"Perhaps I want privacy *too.*"

I roll my eyes and turn, giving him privacy to get dressed as well.

But I forgot that I'm standing where his clothes are.

I squeeze my eyes shut as his arms brush against mine as he reaches around me.

"You're a little in the way," he whispers. "Apologies."

"It's fine!" I snap, heart racing. "Just, hurry up. Please."

The plea does it. I hear his shaky exhale as he pulls a shirt over his head and slides on loose cotton pants.

We both look at the small bed, the air tense with nerves.

"Get in first, and I'll put the pillow between us," Nyall adds, though he says the word 'pillow' like it morally offends him.

I nod and climb in, scooting to the furthest edge, trying to make myself as small as possible.

When I'm settled, I feel the bed dip as Nyall climbs in behind me.

The air warms from the proximity of his body, but he never touches me.

Not even a little.

Instead, he slides a pillow between us and mirrors my position.

Nyall snaps his fingers and the fire dims, turning the room dark.

Shadows play across the tent ceiling, like ghosts haunting my every move.

I lift a finger and the shadow detaches off the ceiling, twirling around my fingers like it's saying 'hello' to an old friend.

"Useful trick," Nyall murmurs.

I don't respond.

This magyk is all that I have left of my father. It's my legacy, but for so long, it's felt like a curse.

"You should let your magyk out more often," Nyall whispers. "It's nice to see you like this."

I sigh and let the shadow return to the ceiling. Tucking the covers tight against me, I curl my arms beneath my chin and take a deep breath.

"Thank you."

*That's my response? Gods, Amalia. You're an idiot!*

"Goodnight, Amalia."

Mentally slapping myself, I force the words out of my mouth. "Goodnight, Nyall."

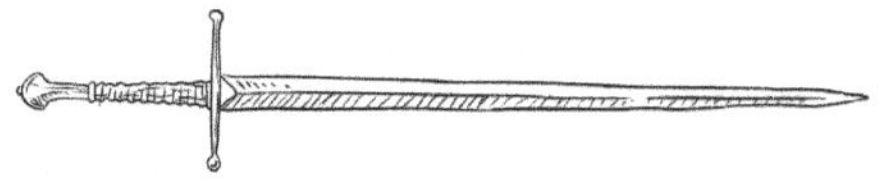

"Alright, tonight, our practice run is going to be to hit the Panormus Armory. We'll also be taking Ryu with us because once we spring our trap at the Mercatus, I'll portal her in to assist with the attack." Nyall stands at the head of the table, addressing the room.

I glare at him.

"Amalia also reminded me that the animals we're freeing will be terrified, so seeing one of their own kind might help. For that reason, a dozen of the Dyre Wolf pack will be accompanying Ryu in the portal."

"Can you hold a portal that long?" Mara asks, and I get the sense that it's genuine curiosity, not a lack of belief.

Nyall's face goes hard. "Yes. But it will take me out of the fight. Amalia will need to cover me. As it so happens, I'm the only one who can unlock the armory in Panormus, so we're going to practice this exact plan tonight."

I nod. We discussed the plan this morning.

I appreciate that he gave me a heads up. I do not like surprises.

"Mara, you and Amari will distract the soldiers while Fi and Soren cover us." They all nod.

"We'll bring two dozen recruits who will stay hidden in the trees nearby. Their presence tonight is simply a contingency, should we have to fight our way out."

None of the rebels around the table look excited about the prospect of this ending in bloodshed.

They're still so unseasoned.

So *young*. So *human*.

Most of them have Magyka and Demis blood, but so far, none that I can tell have an extended lifespan. Regardless of the magyk in their blood, most of the rebels around this table are human—or close enough.

Their reactions remind me of Dyana. Of that shock and shame at witnessing such violence. I don't think Dyana ever got used to it. Not until the Gauntlet.

It's times like this when I feel my age. While I look like I could be anywhere from my late 20's to my early 30's, in reality, I'm 92 years old.

I was 10 when I met Virgyl, and 72 when I met Dyana. The century mark nears, but sometimes I feel like I've lived a thousand lifetimes.

The weight of trauma is a heavy one.

As Nyall talks through the plan, I watch him, studying the calm confidence he projects.

"I've been preparing an unlocking spell for the armory, but it takes a few minutes to draw and charge the symbols. While I charge the spell, Amalia will cover me."

"And once it's unlocked?" Mara asks.

"Then we steal the weapons. I'll cast a small portal into the armory here in the valley. Once the weapons are gone, Amalia will light the armory on fire, drawing the attention of the army away from our escape. We will meet you in the trees and portal out from there."

The rebels are quiet as they process his words. Some look nervous, but after practicing, I'm mollified to see that some look confident.

We'll get them over their human fears...*somehow.*

But I do have one concern.

"That's a lot of magyk," I say to Nyall aloud. He glares and I raise my hands, feigning that I won't bring it up again. In my head, I brush my magyk against him and he lets me in.

*"I shouldn't have said that aloud, but you know I'm right,"* I whisper. *"Can you handle casting those three spells in such a short time frame?"*

*"Do you doubt me that easily?"* he asks in a joking tone, but I can also hear the pain behind it.

*"I don't,"* I start. *"But I know everyone has a limit. Perhaps I simply do not wish to watch you burn out."*

*"I will be fine, Blue. Don't worry about me."*

I furrow my brows.

*"I'm not worried about you,"* I snap, but the words are hollow.

I *am* worried about him, but I shouldn't be.

Not because he's capable, which he *is,* but because I...shouldn't care. And yet here we are, with my heart clenched in worry at the thought of something happening to Nyall Drayven.

"Something wrong?" Davyn whispers. He's seated to my left, while Nyall is at my right.

I shake my head.

"You look upset, lass." He gives me a knowing look.

"It will be *fine,*" I force out, and he nods, backing off. My emotions are getting harder and harder to hide, and that scares me.

"Is the Dragon okay with this?" Mara asks me and I blink at her in surprise.

"Yes," I nod. "She has consented to help us. After we're through, Nyall and I will be going over the plan with her as well."

"And it understands you?" Soren asks.

"*She,*" Nyall's voice travels through the tent, making the hair on my arms stand up on end. "Ryu is not an *it*. Ryu is a *she*. A living, feeling, thinking being. Not an *animal.*"

I cough and glare at Nyall, "Animals are *living, feeling, thinking* beings *too*. Just because they cannot communicate with us, doesn't make them less than." Re-membering the original question, I turn to Soren and force a soft smile on my face. Her eyes widen at the sight of it. "Yes. Dragons can understand us. They can also speak to anyone they wish, they simply chose not to."

"Why?" Amari asks.

I want to slam my head onto the table.

How has this planning meeting turned into 'Dragon Education with Amalia'?

Nyall's laughter echoes in my thoughts, *"They are simply curious. I promise, their questions mean no harm. After all, there has been much misinformation spread about Dragons in the centuries of my Father's rule."*

I sigh.

He's right. Of course he's right.

So I swallow my frustration and impatience down and lift my chin. "I am," I clear my throat, *"sorry* for not explaining more about Dragons beforehand. It is...new to me as well."

Partially true.

Everyone looks at me with wide eyes, ready to hear what I have to say. I ignore the look of pride from Nyall.

"Most of what you have been told about Dragons isn't true. My mother's people, the Arkaydians, believed Dragons were Gods," I pause, taking another breath. "I do not know if I truly believe in any God, but I believe in animals. I believe in Dragons. I think if any being in this world *was* to be a God, it would be a Dragon."

They take this in with varying looks of fear and wonder.

"All Dragons *can* communicate. They used to do so more openly, but when the Fae started to turn on them, their trust was broken."

Fear and wonder turn to looks of sadness.

"Even if she doesn't choose to speak with you, Ryu can understand you perfectly. I know I am in no place to offer advice," I snort. "But I would offer you this: treat Ryu and all Dragons, all *animals,* with respect. There are many ways to communicate; words are simply one option. Never presume someone or some*thing* cannot understand just because they cannot *reply* the same way you can."

Several rebels nod.

"Can you speak with more than just Dragons?" Amari asks quietly.

Everyone stares at me with wide eyes, curious.

"Um, that's complicated. I can *communicate* with them, but Dragons are the only animal I've ever communicated with using words."

"What do you use, then?" Mara asks gently.

In many magykal cultures, this amount of prying would be considered very rude. But Nyall was right.

If I want them to get over their fear of me, I need to be patient and answer their questions.

They are like curious, unsure little children.

I have to be patient.

Which fucking *sucks* because patience isn't my strong suit.

"For me, it's feelings. For my mother it was similar."

"Interesting." Davyn rubs his chin. "That must come in handy."

The corner of my mouth lifts in a small smile, "Yes it does. My mother could even swap vision with the animals she'd bonded to."

"Explain?" Keres asks, clearly not understanding.

"She could swap sight with any animal that she had a magykal connection with, seeing through their eyes. It's how we were able to stay on the run for so long when I was a child."

I feel Nyall's surprise. *"You never told me that."*

*"It never came up,"* I reply cooly, hiding the fact that it feels...it feels painful to talk about, but it also feels good.

Relieving, almost.

Like for a moment, I'm not alone.

I feel rather than see his pleased smile. He brushes his magyk against mine again, the taste of honeysuckle on my tongue.

Then I feel warmth and pride, and it makes me want to cry.

"We should go talk to Ryu," I say, looking down at the table.

I need out. I need air. Emotions are bearing down on me that I'm not strong enough for and it's making me *panic*.

"Of course." Nyall nods and stands. Everyone else stands for him in a show of deference. He might not be a Prince here, but I have a funny feeling I'm watching as he becomes something *more*.

Something worthy of *respect*.

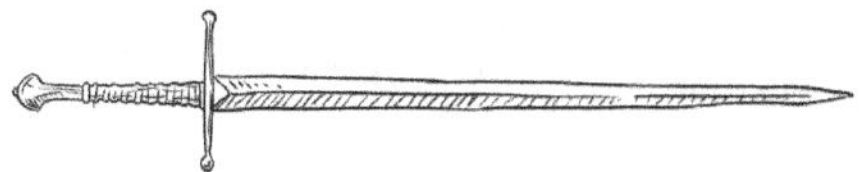

Ryu stares at us with her copper and silver eyes.

She meandered out to the forest, wanting space to roam and spread her wings without worrying about hitting someone in the face.

*"Gods, she's gotten bigger,"* Nyall whispers to me.

*"I know."*

*"I can hear you,"* she says, not blinking. Her huge, red body is lying on the ground. She's been rolling around, itching her scales and there's dirt everywhere, along with huge marks in the ground.

"We've talked about eavesdropping," I tell her, crossing my arms.

Ryu rolls her eyes, and she leans her large neck back and shakes her head, sending dirt flying.

The spikes around her head have gotten bigger too, giving her the appearance of wearing a crown. Her front legs are crossed politely as she lowers her neck again and rests her head on her claws.

*"So, let me get this straight. You want me to babysit some mortals in the safety of the trees and wait while you two get to be heroes."*

Nyall's smile falls. "Well, yes."

Ryu sighs and the force of her exhale is so hard, it nearly blows us over.

*"Fine, it's better than sitting around doing nothing. At least Ama was always up to stuff. I miss burning down buildings."*

I choke. "Ryu!"

Nyall looks at me with a knowing look, like this is all my fault for teaching her bad behaviors.

"Don't you dare. This is not my fault!"

*"It is, actually,"* Ryu says, her eyes closing. *"Now, I need a nap before all of this excitement later."*

I glare. "Are you going to be dreaming of burning down buildings and eating people?"

*"Perhaps."*

I roll my eyes. Meanwhile, Nyall snickers. The wolves run around Ryu, playing beneath her lowered wings in a game of hide and seek.

*"I promise not to eat anyone,"* Ryu says sleepily. *"Now, let me sleep."*

I blink. My small Dragon has grown pushy and independent.

*When did this happen?*

A different sort of sadness falls heavy on my shoulders.

"Sleep well," I whisper, petting her snout and placing a kiss against her scales. She sighs happily and I breathe in her sweet scent.

She still smells like a little hatchling to me. Even at this size.

*"I know she's bored,"* I send my thoughts to Nyall. *"But I can't stand the thought of her getting hurt."*

*"I know, Blue. Me neither. But just as you said earlier, this is her choice."*

I sigh as we walk away together, a comfortable silence descending. The wolves follow us into camp and I'm grateful for their presence.

I do not know their names as they haven't told me, but one of them, a large, copper-colored wolf with white markings, walks beside me and I let my hand drift through its fur. The Dyre Wolf's tail wags and it looks back at me with a silly, wolfy grin.

Connecting my magyk to the wolf, I express my desire for them to tell Virgyl we'll be leaving with Ryu for the night.

It's a complicated thought to express in just feelings, so it takes a few minutes until I feel like the message is appropriately understood, but the Dyre Wolf eventually nods before asking for more scratches.

The rest of the day remains tense, but eventually, night falls and darkness descends over the valley.

That's our cue. We all meet in the training yard, which means walking with Ryu all the way through the camp.

They *watch* me.

Every fucking step and someone is watching me.

You would think I was used to it.

The truth is, I've never gotten used to it. Feeling dozens of eyes watching me.

It makes me wish I could disappear.

*"Do you know of an animal called a chameleon?"* Ryu asks suddenly. She walks behind me, purposefully slowing her steps to not overtake us.

I try to picture it. *"I think so? It's a lizard, right?"*

*"Yes, they can change their colors. Octopuses can too."*

I blink. *"Octo-what? What the hell is that?"*

*"It's something that lives in the ocean. I've never seen one, but many of my ancestors have memories of eating them. I remember they're quite tasty."*

I glance behind me and raise my brows.

*"Never mind. The point is, whatever gene that gave chameleons the ability to change color is also a gene that some Dragons have."*

I try to process this. *"They can change the color of their scales?"*

Ryu nods. *"It allows them to blend in with their environment. My grandmother was one. Kydis wished it had passed to her."*

*"Have you ever tried changing color?"*

Ryu snorts, *"Of course. It skipped me, too. It's a shame that we can't simply disappear."*

*"Yes, it is,"* I sigh, and her snout brushes against my back, shoving me lightly. I can't help but laugh.

Forced to lift her head, Ryu grumbles in my mind as she steps over more tents, unable to fit through the narrow pathways anymore.

"Does it hurt?" I ask softly. "The growth spurts? You've had a lot, lately."

Ryu is quiet and that is an answer in itself.

"I know you said they would slow down, Ryu, but...they don't seem to be."

*"My ancestors agree,"* Ryu says, and I nearly stumble face first into the mud.

"Wait," it suddenly hits me. "Do you mean that the memories *speak* to you, Ryu?"

*"Yes. It's almost as if they're alive but only within my mind."*

*Holy shit.*

Curiosity eats at me until Ryu sighs, *"Go ahead. Ask it, Ama."*

"Do you talk to your mother?"

Ryu is quiet for a few moments. She only says one word before falling silent again.

*"Sometimes."*

Shock renders me silent. We walk the rest of the way to the field side by side, each lost in their own thoughts. The generals and the few dozen recruits chosen to join us are already there when we arrive. All go still and fall silent as they lay eyes upon Ryu.

I glance back and watch as she lifts her head and bares her fangs, flaring her wings slightly in the act.

"Show off," I whisper.

*"They needed a reminder to fear me."*

My eyes roll so hard I'm surprised they don't roll right out of my head.

*"I fear you've learned far too much from Amalia,"* Nyall's voice suddenly drifts through my thoughts.

*"No, no. That was definitely you who taught her that. You love peacocking."*

A choking sound to my right alerts me to Nyall's presence. I glance at him as he finishes drawing symbols in the sand.

Clapping his hands together his magyk activates and the symbols start to glow.

"You didn't need this...that day," I say carefully. "Why?"

"I was only able to do that because I siphoned, and still, as you recall, it was a rather bumpy ride."

"Ugh, yeah."

Nyall continues explaining, "I've been testing ways to smooth the portal process, as well as to hold it for longer periods of time. The symbols on the ground create a spell that increases my magyk, and I've augmented it to include enhanced strength and control."

Interesting.

"How long do the spells last?"

Nyall's answer is immediate. "Not long. A few hours, perhaps."

"Then we'd better hurry," I say, summoning Neiman and Macha into existence and letting my magyk out.

It bursts out of me, thrilled to be used.

Shadows dance around me as my Hellfyre coats the black titanium blades.

The field falls silent as everyone falls into place, lining up behind each general.

Nyall faces them with a hard look in his mismatched eyes. "You know the plan. Stick to it and meet in the trees if all else fails."

They nod.

"If you are caught, you know what to do."

Everyone smiles but it's odd.

Until I realize that I can see their back teeth, and one of them is black.

*Oh.*

I glance at Nyall, shocked, but he doesn't look back.

*It's their decision. Not mine.*

~~*HE CANNOT DIE. HE CANNOT DIE.*~~

*"It will be alright,"* Ryu whispers and the mere knowledge that she was *listening* is enough to help me put my emotions away.

*"Yes, it will be,"* I respond.

*I will make sure of it.*

Nyall cracks his neck and closes his eyes, lifting one hand out in front of him

At first, there is nothing. Just the silence of nighttime.

Rings of light appear along Nyall's forearms, illuminating his muscular build hidden beneath the white fabric.

Nyall takes a deep breath and snaps his fingers.

Magyk explodes from his hand. Purple, blue, and green smoke whirl around each other on the ground until a huge, swirling portal waits for us.

We can't see the other side. It's just smoke.

I glance behind me and see the terrified gazes of all who wait with us. Davyn and Keres wave from a distance. I bet *they* wouldn't be afraid of the portals.

With a sigh, I glance at the swirling smoke. "Alright, I'll go first and make sure the coast is clear."

Everyone murmurs in agreement, and I want to roll my eyes.

But I stay serious and walk forward until I'm face to face with the portal. Lifting a finger, I push my hand through the smoke. It's cooling and tickles.

With another deep breath, I step through the portal, ready for the worst.

It's only dark for a second. A single second. Then in front of me, the smoke begins to reveal a different sight.

A forest, but the trees are smaller and thinner. The weather is a bit warmer and more humid. As I step out and look around, I realize Nyall really did improve his portal.

That was almost too easy.

I pop back through the portal and assure everyone that it's fine.

Ryu goes first, grimacing at the portal smoke on her way out.

She shivers, shaking her great body. *"It tickles!"*

*"I agree,"* I snicker.

Then Ryu sneezes, covering me in Dragon snot.

"Lovely," I mutter.

The rebels make it through safely, looking no worse for wear. Nyall is last and he shuts the portal down behind him by tracing a symbol in the middle of the whirlpool of smoke.

It dissipates, leaving us in a new forest, hundreds of kilometers away.

The army base sits just beyond the trees.

Panormus itself was a small town. The forest we're in is just south of the base, and the town sits on the north side.

The armory is also on the north side. They use the townsfolk as their protection. It was insane, and very, very cruel. I brush out with my magyk, getting a lay of the land.

Dozens of lights glimmer in the dark void of my mind. They keep appearing until it's not just dozens—it's hundreds, *thousands*. My head throbs and I have to pull away.

"Fuck," I curse. "The town is busy. There are *thousands* of them."

"Then we keep them out of it. As much as we can."

Mara, who is just behind me, whispers, "Worried about the innocent, Wytch?"

I don't move a muscle, but my heart hurts as if she stabbed a dagger into it.

"This can't turn into a fight. It will be a bloodbath."

"How full is the barracks? Can you tell?"

I take a deep breath and disappear into my mind once again. The lights repeat and I get a count for the general number of minds in the vicinity. My head throbs but I push past it. "Twice as many as the town. Maybe eight thousand?"

I pull away with a gasp, panting.

Nyall looks concerned but I wave him off, straightening my back and forcing my breathing to calm.

I need to practice that more.

I've only ever tried with a few hundred. But thousands?

Seeing, *feeling* the presence of so many all at once is overwhelming, and I cannot show it.

Right now, I need to be strong.

I glance back at the others. Faces full of worry, anger, dread, and amusement greet me, the latter from Nyall.

"You know what to do," Nyall says, and everyone nods as Mara and Amari step forward, passing us as they walk into town. They're in cotton dresses, with harvest baskets full of food as their cover. If anyone asks, they were harvesting and became lost. That will distract the soldiers, allowing Nyall and I to slip past unnoticed. Fi and Soren will cover us, following from a distance and taking cover in the trees.

Both equipped with arrows tipped in poison as well as offensive magyk. Fi has some minor water magyk, and Soren is one of the best defensive fighters we have.

As we wait for Mara and Amari to make it into the barracks, looking like damsels in need of saving, Nyall sidles up to me.

"You ready for this?" His voice is quiet, meant to go unheard by the others.

I glance at him, letting my Hellfyre burn just enough that I know my eyes are glowing with it.

Whenever someone sees me like this, they balk and back away, terrified.

Nyall Drayven isn't terrified.

Instead, he looks *hungry,* and I know it's not for food.

Forcing my gaze away, I push aside the Hellfyre. Cracking my neck, I allow my emotions to fall even farther away.

This wasn't the time.

Mara and Amari finally pass into the barracks, which is our cue.

Nyall lifts his hand in a fist, signaling that we're off.

In sync, we walk out of the forest without looking back.

With a lazy *flick* of my hand, I summon shadows to cover us. Not thick enough to be too obvious, just enough to obscure us from sight.

"My star pupil." His eyes twinkle, even in the dark.

He helped me learn this particular trick. Thinning the shadows enough to create a smoke-like cover.

The comment annoys me. More than usual. Maybe it's the scent of his honeysuckle magyk in the air, even among my shadows. Maybe it's the fact that ever since I started sharing a bed with Nyall again...the nightmares have stopped.

A part of me wishes they hadn't.

It would give me a better reason to hate him.

Still, anger is *easier*, so I turn to him and snap, "The only thing you taught me was that I can't rely on you."

NO. I DON'T MEAN THAT. I'M SO SORRY. PLEASE.

I want to rip my own skin off at the way Nyall flinches at the words. His face hardens and we both fall silent.

In this moment, some of the anger swirling inside of me redirects, pointing back at me. But Os' golden eyes glow brightly in my mind. Every single time I start to cave, start to allow myself to *feel* something, I see his face.

It feels like desecration. I knew Remus Ostia for only a few months, and yet the hot burn of our connection still simmers within me.

Two years without him, and it's still fresh in my mind. Though, it's started to get hard to remember the heat of his skin, or the feel of his hands.

The details have begun to blur ever so slightly, and that breaks my heart even further. Because they will continue to blur, until I can barely remember his face.

No. I *refuse* to let that happen. I will never forget him, or those golden eyes.

But...

The male beside me. A *Drayven*. The last person I ever expected to *feel* something for, yet here I am. *Feeling*.

A noise in the distance snaps me back into reality and out of my thoughts. Nyall and I flatten ourselves against the large metal building that houses the barracks.

The layout was simple. The barracks were centered around a large metal building that housed their war room, bunk beds, showers, the kitchen and mess hall, and a training area.

Another, larger training area was outside the base along with a landing spot for the Dragonguard, should they show up.

Gods, I hope they don't show up. I'm not sure I'll ever be ready for another Dragon fight.

The noise quiets down and Nyall taps my shoulder, signaling I should proceed.

We walk forward, silent in our movements, until the building ends. The armory is across from the large, empty training field. This is where Mara and Amari come in.

*"Find out if they're in position,"* Nyall's voice sounds in my head.

I nod and easily connect with the two rebels. *"Status?"*

*"Yep. We'll go into view now."* Mara says, her inner voice quiet.

*"Good luck."* I shut off the connection.

From the shadows, we watch as they walk into view of the open barracks. Shouting quickly follows and they panic, as we planned.

Regular people panic.

Rebels don't.

Amari starts crying and tosses her basket to the floor, raising her hands above her head.

Mara falls to the ground and puts her wrists in front of her through silent sobs.

Good *Gods.*

I glance to the side to see Nyall smirking.

*"This does seem like your particular kind of drama,"* I murmur.

*"No idea what you're talking about, Amalia."*

I roll my eyes.

Soon, the soldiers are ushering them inside, apologizing for the mishap. Clearly, they are nothing more than lost harvesters.

Rebels would never be so *weepy.* The soldier's attention remains firmly on the two women now in their company.

*"Let's go,"* Nyall says, and we take off in a jog.

The armory is a small building across the barracks field. We were going to do this on the side facing the town, but with so many souls there…

*"We need to do this on the west side, not the north. I don't want to face the town."*

*"What? Amalia we—"*

*"If we get caught,"* I interrupt him. *"I would rather fight Fae soldiers than innocents who simply don't know any better."*

I feel his eventual agreement.

*"Alright. My magyk is going to be bright, so it means you'll need to maintain thick shadow cover to block it out regardless of any fight."*

Now it's my turn to smirk.

*"I do enjoy a challenge."*

Nyall laughs as we arrive at the east side of the armory.

*"Make sure Soren and Fi are in position,"* he whispers.

I quickly find Soren and Fi's glowing minds and connect with them.

*"Are you in place to cover us?"*

*"Yeah, but what the fuck? You're supposed to be on the north side. It's going to be harder to cover you from here."*

*"Deal with it. Do your job and I'll do mine."* I disconnect and take a deep breath, focusing on my shadows.

They thicken, covering us until it's almost complete darkness.

Nyall's whispers fill the space and the scent of his honeysuckle magyk grows stronger as bands of light encompass his arms. He begins moving his hands together, rotating and bending them in a sort of dance. The lock on the armory door in front of us begins to glow as white symbols appear on its metallic surface.

There's a high-pitched, very quiet snapping sound, followed by a large thump.

*Shit.*

"Someone saw us. That was Soren and Fi," I whisper aloud. "Hurry it up, Prince."

"Don't call me that," he huffs back in an equally quiet voice. "Let me concentrate."

Rolling my eyes, I detach myself from the shadows. "I'm going to take a look, the shadows will stay with you."

"Don't—"

Nyall tried to protest but I was already gone, stepping through the smoke and peeking out into the world.

*Fuck.*

A group of ten soldiers is running towards us. They saw the shadows.

Soren and Fi take out as many as they can, but more soldiers join, running across the field to join the others.

With a deep breath, I summon my Hellfyre, letting it rise to the surface until my veins are full of freezing, raging fire.

A single flick of my hand and it explodes out of me like a giant wave.

They don't even get the chance to scream before they're reduced to *ash*.

There's a distant tug deep within me, a sort of heaviness, followed by a jolt of pain in my head.

*I'm using too much magyk.*

Frustrated by my own limitations, I growl and send a wave of Hellfyre barreling at the remaining soldiers.

But they keep coming. Dozens steam out from the barracks. It's never-ending.

With a growl, I send one more wave of Hellfyre, ignoring the pain in my head.

Piles of ash and charred bones begin to form all over the ground as I take more and more soldiers down.

Those who are left stagger around, confused and in shock.

Then the screaming starts from whoever is left.

I pull back into the smoke fully and face Nyall just as the armory unlocks.

"We need to go."

"How many?" he asks casually, making more hand motions as symbols light up the inside walls of the armory.

"Don't worry about it. But we have to do this my way." I pull him away, ignoring his angry growl.

"Amalia!"

I drop the smoke and Nyall takes in the ash falling from the sky. The world is quiet in the wake of my rage.

I steel myself, ready for the judgement and hate.

Nyall finally looks at me and nods. "Let's go. I can still hear survivors. Someone will see us."

I blink.

Nyall reaches out and grabs my hand. Dark streams begin to fall down his face as ash mixes with sweat. I watch in a shocked daze as Nyall clasps my hand, interlaces our fingers, and begins pulling me towards the forest.

The judgement will come later. It always does.

We quickly race back towards the forest as I send a wave of Hellfyre at the armory, setting it on fire.

It doesn't take long.

Soon, every weapon is going off in an explosion that nearly sends Nyall and me off our feet. He has to put a hand on my arm to keep me from tripping.

We sprint towards the trees, Soren and Fi joining in from the side, followed by Mara and Amari behind us.

"Make the portal!" I scream.

The sound of shouting gets louder behind us as the remaining soldiers left alive chase after us.

Nyall grunts, lifting his hand as black and purple smoke stream from his fingers, making a big portal.

But not big enough for Ryu.

"Nyall!" I curse. "Make it BIGGER!"

"I'm trying," he grits.

I don't know why I do it, but suddenly I'm grabbing his arm and releasing my magyk. It flows into Nyall with an ease that terrifies me. But he's able to increase the size of the portal enough that Ryu and the other recruits can get through.

Just as I'm about to walk through, I hear it.

The sound of something piercing *flesh*. The groan that follows nearly sends me to my knees.

I look back to see an arrow poking out of Nyall's chest. There is a wet *thunk* as another arrow hits him.

Then another.

I'm frozen in horror, unable to move as Nyall falls to his knees with a groan. A high-pitched ringing sound fills my ears. As he kneels there, bleeding and in pain, the world comes crashing down around me.

Looking up, his mismatched eyes meet mine with a look of such regret it takes my breath away. "Fucking GO, Amalia!"

With a snarl, I turn back and grab onto him, yanking him to his feet. He moans in pain but follows anyway.

I lean close and get in his face.

*"No,"* I snarl, so furious I could punch him. "And you are not *my* commander. You don't get to tell me what to do. So shut the fuck up and get on your feet."

He laughs and immediately regrets it, moaning again at the pain.

*Shit.*

There's another thunk and he groans again.

Pain suddenly sears through my ribs, and I look down at the arrow poking out of my ribcage. A groan falls from my lips.

With a deep breath, I yank the arrow out and break it in half. Shoving Nyall through the portal, I turn and unleash a wave of Hellfyre to incinerate the soldiers shooting at us.

They scream, trying to run away as soon as they see it coming. It's too late. There is nowhere they can run.

They *hurt* him.

So, I don't stop burning until there's nothing left, save the town. My head starts to throb at the rush of so much magyk. A rush of warmth coats my nose and suddenly something wet and hot drips down from it. When the liquid coats my lips, I get confirmation that my nose is bleeding.

But I can't stop.

No. That's a lie.

I won't stop. I don't want to.

The faces of my loved one's flash in my mind. Dyana. Os. Kydis, even. Lastly, I see Nyall. Beautiful, foolish Nyall. His groan of pain So I keep going, keep *burning* until the only thing that's left of the thousands of Fae soldiers are piles of ash.

# CHAPTER 21
## DYANA

My trainings with Embyrne changed after that day in the forest. In the weeks that followed, I finally started to grasp my magyk.

She didn't have to wake me up in the morning, anymore. I found myself waking up naturally just as the suns began to rise. Vesimyr was quite grouchy about the fact, preferring to sleep in.

"Channel your magyk into a ball," Embyrne calls. She circles me, her bare feet sinking into the dirt. Sweat beads at my hairline, but the magyk flows easily when I call to it, pulling on the center of my being like I'm unrolling a ball of yarn. The magyk obeys, flowing down my arm to the tips of my fingers, until it forms a round ball between my two raised hands. It's as if I'm holding one of the suns within my grasp.

"Good. Now make it circle around you."

Straining, I concentrate on Embyrne's order and picture the intended result. Previously, I had been focusing on the action versus the result. It seems my magyk responds better to the latter. I picture the ball having just completed a circle around me and it makes a slow, slightly wobbly circle as I keep it aloft.

"Steady," Embyrne calls, a warning in her voice. "Trust yourself and calm your breathing."

I'm trying but my body *hurts.* It's like the magyk is pulling on every muscle.

*For Amalia. Do it for Amalia.*

I keep Amalia's face in my head as I force my thoughts to move past the pain. Resolve and determination fills me with strength, even as my muscles tremble.

I do as Embyrne says, calming my breathing and making the ball circle me in a steady, constant motion.

Now I understand why Os and Nyall were so muscular. You had to be to control magyk. The effort was staggering.

The ball finishes its eclipse around me and Embyrne nods, stopping to stand in front of me.

My legs threaten to give out but I won't show it.

I won't give in.

"Now expand it around you. Make it a dome."

I take a deep breath, my hands shaking, and imagine being encased under a large, golden dome.

The ball explodes as my magyk surges, raining down on me until a dome surrounds me. There are some holes in it, but it's the first successful shield I've ever made.

I'll take it.

"Good enough. Now I'm going to attack you, and your only goal is to hold onto that dome. It's now your shield."

Vesimyr—who is lying outside of the Arena, sunning his scales and taking a nap—grunts as Embyrne pulls on his magyk.

Her hands become encased in a green glow as she uses my own Dragon's magyk to pummel my dome.

She tosses green fireball after green fireball at me and each hit burns, like it's stinging beneath my skin. More holes start to show up in my shield. With a loud grunt I shove more of my magyk into it, healing the patches.

We keep this up for nearly an hour. Embyrne is barely winded, meanwhile I'm panting and on my knees.

"We're done for today." She nods and I drop the shield, falling forward and catching myself with my hands.

"What's next?" I'm breathless and wobbly as I push back to standing. Vesimyr's tail sneaks in to catch me when I stumble.

Embyrne, however, is already there to catch me.

She glares at Vesimyr's tail like it's an evil, unwanted appendage. A loud growl from the outside follows as Vesimyr senses Embyrne's disdain.

Then it occurs to me.

*Are they...fighting over me?*

Embyrne yanks me away from Vesimyr's tail with a hiss and I blink.

Holy shit.

They *are* fighting over me. Am I the prize or the prey, though?

"What's next," Embyrne says, "is turning that light of yours into a sword."

"Pardon?" I ask, eyes wide. "Did you just say a sword?"

"I did." She nods. "You kept me out today. That means you can make your light *solid,* Dyana. So what's next is you figure out how to take your light and turn it into a sword."

My jaw drops.

I did make the light solid...I just didn't think of it that way.

*Holy shit.* Vesimyr's head pops up as he takes an interest in Embyrne's words, listening in on our conversation.

"I have a theory," she says. "I think your light, when solidified, might be able to cut through hard metals."

Vesimyr draws closer, his eyes wide with interest.

**"And if it could do that,"** he finishes aloud. **"It could cut through scales, too...or Elysian armor."**

*Oh shit.*

"You think that this…light sword might be able to kill Ignautius, don't you?" I ask and Vesimyr trips me with his tail, sending me to the ground as Embyrne tackles me.

*"Don't say that aloud, Dyana. Not ever."* Vesimyr whispers, looking outside and glancing up at the sky.

*"You think the Sene Skal is listening?"* I ask.

But it's Embyrne who answers. *"He has spies everywhere. There is nowhere safe on this island, Dyana. Not even here."*

"Fuck. I'm sorry. I forgot—"

"It's alright, Dyana. Next time, send us a thought instead of saying it aloud."

I nod and that's when it occurs to me that Embyrne is still straddling my waist.

*"I'll, uh, be outside,"* Vesimyr mutters in my thoughts, shuffling his large body out of the Arena once again.

Embyrne's pale gold eyes never leave mine and my breath hitches at the intensity in her gaze. Her gaze drops to my lips and before I can react, she's surging forward, and her lips meet mine with a ferocity that leaves me gasping.

She growls into my mouth and I'm so overwhelmed that all logical thought leaves my head.

Embyrne tastes like *fire*. One taste and I'm *craving* more.

Our mouths duel for control as we get lost in each other, our movements angry and frantic. Her hands sink into my hair, undoing my braid with her movements. The Beastkyn pulls tightly, and I realize that I can't move. Embyrne laughs and the wicked promise in that sound…holy *fuck*.

I'm at her mercy. Instinctively, I roll my hips and her core grinds against mine. She makes a pleased groan before pulling my hair tighter and bending me backwards, so that my back is arched and my neck is bared to her.

Need courses through me so fast and hard. Embyrne grinds her hips against mine. She has nothing under her dress today. When she showed up in that loose, floor length dress again, I almost lost my goddamn mind. The semi-sheer fabric shows off her gorgeous body beneath, and it's been driving me insane all fucking day.

Her teeth bite down on my lip, *hard.* I squeak but when Embyrne fixes her lips over the wound and sucks, drinking my blood as her tongue flicks against the cut, encouraging more blood to flow, I do lose my mind. I moan and she swallows the sound with a greedy laugh.

"Enough," Embyrne whispers, suddenly pulling away. I immediately miss the warmth of her mouth and the feeling of her body pressed against mine. I miss it so much I almost let out a loud whine, but clamp my lips together so it dies on the tip of my tongue.

Embyrne stands and holds out a hand, helping me up. I look down and grimace at the dirt all over my shift. My hands lift to brush it off, when her hand lands beneath my chin, making me freeze. Embyrne tilts my head back, so she can look into my eyes.

I can't move. I can't push away.

I don't know if I even want to.

*"You appear flustered. Did something happen?"* Vesimyr interrupts and I jump, shocked by his sudden presence. He leans into the Arena, using his long neck to navigate until his head is just beside me. He looks me up and down with concern in his eyes. *"Is that blood on your lips?"*

*Kill me.*

I blush, "I'm fine."

*"Good. I'm hungry and based on the strange sounds coming from your stomach, you are too."*

My cheeks turn an even brighter red and I cough, "Right. Yes. That sounds good."

"Sleep well, Dyana." Embyrne says, smirking at me. My embarrassment isn't lost on her, that's for sure. "Don't oversleep or I'll have to come wake you up myself, and according to you, my methods are rather sadistic. You wouldn't like that, would you?"

Oh my *God.*

My heart is beating so fast that I stammer and turn, getting a running start and jumping into the air. I leap onto Vesimyr's back easily. I can't do much more than this, but I've been trying to practice using all of my new gifts, not just my magyk.

I'm not human anymore, and I need to stop acting like it.

But the more I stop acting human, the farther away I feel from my old life.

From Amalia.

"Light sword tomorrow. Got it." I nod at Embyrne who watches me with crossed arms and an amused look on her face.

"Goodnight, Dyana," she says. A glance down and a brief flash of fang is her way of saying goodbye to Vesimyr. My Dragon growls at her and pulls his neck out of the cave.

I sit just above his shoulder blades. We discovered that if I sit further up his neck than I previously had been doing, it helps my balance.

I haven't fallen off in ten whole days. Except for the fact that Vesimyr now claims we need to practice our air mounts, in case another Dragon throws me off mid-battle.

Just the thought of an airborne battle had me emptying my stomach. But I left my fear in the sand alongside my puke.

*"May I ask you something?"* Vesimyr suddenly enters my mind as his wings flap and we make a steep vertical assent.

It doesn't hurt my thighs as much anymore to hold on. It's starting to become second nature. But the wind against my back will never get old.

"Of course."

*"You...like Embyrne."*

I squeak. "Um, no. Definitely not. She's a fucking sadistic asshole."

*"Dyana?"*

I furrow my brow, concerned, "Yes?"

*"I can smell that you're lying. I can, uh, scent how much you like her."*

My screech echoes through the clouds.

"Okay, that is too far. Don't just stand there smelling me. Ignore it!"

Vesimyr snorts. *"As you wish. It's nothing to be ashamed of, Dyana. Dragons mate all the time."*

I cringe. "Okay, that gives me a mental picture I'll unfortunately never forget."

*"But I thought when we arrived, that you were mated to the redhead."*

I look down at the bright blue ocean beneath us and consider how to answer.

"Mated? Gods no. But during the Gauntlet we...we were together, I suppose. I thought that she was right for me, but sometimes, there is too much to forgive."

*"Forgive?"*

I nod, knowing that though he cannot see me, he can feel it.

"She lied to me, as did...Amalia." I force the words out of my mouth.

The first time I've said it.

*"Lies can hurt. But they can also protect,"* Vesimyr says gently. *"What did they lie about?"*

"They took away my choice," I whisper, leaning down to brush my hands against Vesimyr's scales. "I think...to them, I was always a child. They saw me as incapable of making my own choices. They're both older, sure. But they forget that for a human, I am...or I was, an adult."

*"You still are,"* Vesimyr adds. *"It sounds like they care a lot about you."*

"Yeah. Amalia's lie...it hurts more. But at the same time, I understand it more. She's not just my friend, she's my big sister. When she made that decision, she was acting as family..."

*"But Mirielle isn't family,"* Vesimyr finishes for me. I nod again.

"If anyone should have been honest with me, it's her. She had no loyalties to Amalia and honestly wasn't her biggest fan. But she also lied about her identity."

Vesimyr cranes his head back to look at me briefly, *"What do you mean?"*

I sigh, "It's a long story."

*"Well, as you are my only friend and I have nowhere else to be, it seems like I have plenty of time to listen."*

Smiling, I take a deep breath and launch into the story.

"Her first lie was pretending to be human to get into the Gauntlet. Her second was that she was spy and a member of Prince Drayven's Rebellion."

Vesimyr is silent as he listens.

"But then I learned that she...orchestrated all of it. Our meeting, getting close enough to Amalia and I that there was trust between the three of us. It was all with the goal of getting Amalia to join the Prince. None of it was real."

*"I am sorry, Dyana."*

I nod. "I am too. After that, the Gauntlet began, and Mirielle and Amalia got together in secret to plan how to disqualify me. They knocked me out and took me out of the games. They didn't think I could handle it."

*"You are angry about that,"* Vesimyr notes.

I grind my teeth. "Yeah. Yeah I fucking am. But I...I'm more angry about the fact that Mirielle promised Amalia that if things went south...we'd leave Amalia behind."

*"Ah,"* Vesimyr says, seeing the full picture. *"You blame Mirielle for Amalia being left behind."*

I sneer, "Yes, I do."

*"And yet, your lover saved your life. Held onto your dead body for days atop my back, never once letting go even when exhaustion made her pass out."*

Guilt is a horrible thing. Once the seed is planted, the flower is impossible to prune. It will grow back every time.

"I know," I say quietly. "Even if I can forgive her someday, I can't forgive the way she didn't give me a choice in the matter."

*"Neither can I,"* Vesimyr agrees. I blink in surprise and suddenly tears stream down my cheeks.

I blame the wind instead of the boiling emotions inside of me.

*"What she—what they—did to you is wrong. I'm very sorry that happened, Dyana."*

I wrap my arms around his neck.

"I know," I whisper. "I see Mirielle's face and instantly, I'm furious."

*"You have a long life ahead of you,"* Vesimyr says, reminding me of the fact that I'm now immortal. *"It's only been a few months that you've been awake. You don't have to forgive anyone yet."*

I bite my lip. "You...don't think less of me for being angry at her?"

Vesimyr snorts. *"Of course not. I let anger consume me for many centuries, Dyana. I would never think less of you for something I did too."* The silver Dragon pauses for a moment. *"But what I don't want is for your anger to change you. Use it, but don't become it. Look at where my anger got me."*

We pass a group of Dragons near the castle and they all growl at Vesimyr's figure. Elysium Dragons, Ur Daoine Dragons, all of them. Many of the Ur Daoine Dragons are unable to fly again. The long journey damaged their already weak wings so permanently that some of them are forever stuck on the ground.

"I'm not ready to face her," I tell him with a sigh. The Dragon nods, accepting my words and not pushing me any further.

But later that night, when sleep finally consumes me, I once again dream of the mountain.

*The terrain is steep, and I struggle to find a rock to hold onto as I climb up the steep mountain.*

*I have to get to the top.*

*"You shouldn't be here," Mirielle's voice calls. She's next to me, easily holding on while I'm panting, each muscle quivering with effort.*

*"You'll never make it to the top."*

*I bare my teeth at her. "Shut up! You're not real."*

*"I'm as real as this mountain." She shrugs and blurs forward, moving so fast I can barely track her. When she stops, her curvy figure is perched on a large boulder just beneath where the forest turns lush.*

*She crosses her legs, emphasizing generous curves.*

*Want and hate war within me. Both in equal amounts, leaving me confused and frustrated.*

*I force myself to keep climbing until I reach her.*

*This is the closest I've ever gotten to the lush part of the forest. But as I pass Mirielle, she sighs and blurs again, appearing in front of me.*

*I jump, shocked, and Mirielle rolls her eyes.*

*"It would have been easier if you had just stayed dead," she says. Before I can process Mirielle's words, her palm lands on my sternum, exactly where I was injured, and she shoves me off the mountain.*

*I plummet into the air, flailing, as the ground quickly gets closer. Mirielle's smile is the last thing I see before I crash into the Earth.*

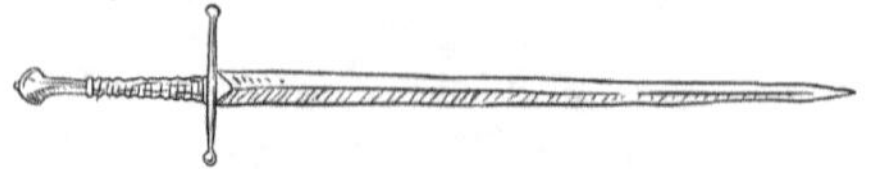

I gasp, sitting up so quickly that Vesimyr's whole body twitches. He wakes instantly, his head swiveling around to look at me.

*"Dyana? Are you alright?"* he asks, following the trails of sweat making their way down my neck.

"It-it was just a nightmare," I stammer, panting like I really had been climbing.

*"The same one you've been having?"* He settles back down now that the possible threat has been sorted out.

"This one was different. Mirielle was there," I tell him, trying to slow my racing heart as I lay back down on the mattress. I scoot closer to Vesimyr, wrapping my arms around one of the claws on his smaller set of wings. I pet the sharp claw, soothing myself with the motion. Thankfully, he lets me.

*"Talking about her earlier brought back the trauma,"* he says, and I nod. *"What did she do in this dream?"*

I bite my lip. "She...pushed me off the mountain."

Vesimyr stills.

"She killed me," I breathe, "and then she smiled."

*"Hmm,"* my Dragon friend murmurs, contemplating what this means. *"Get some sleep. I promise, no one is killing you while I'm around. And, you're no longer quite so easy to hurt."*

"I know" is all I can think of to reply as I try to relax, closing my eyes and hugging my blanket tight.

If it wasn't real, if I'm not so easily hurt, then why does the scar between my breasts *ache?*

# CHAPTER 22
## IREYNA

When I get to the courtyard, I come to a stop, heart pounding.

Anonyme should have been brought here. She should be waiting for me. But all that waits for me today is the Archmage.

I don't understand why, but some days the Archmage makes me nervous. Perhaps it's the power He wields. Knowing he's seen Sol Constantus, *spoken* to Him. It is intimidating.

His robes today are covered in tiny silver beads that jingle with every movement.

I reach His side and bow, as customary. "Your Holiness. Blessed Sol."

"Blessed Sol, Ireyna. How is your training going? I require an update."

I know Dragons are just animals, but I've come to enjoy my time with Anonyme. With every passing day, I always look forward to my training sessions with her. Particularly now that we've moved onto flying.

The feeling of soaring through the clouds on Dragon back is like nothing I've ever experienced before.

It's perfect. Truly a gift from Constantus. Blessed Sol.

Which is why I must listen to the Archmage, for He is the chosen representative of Constantus on this earthly plane.

"Training is going well, Your Holiness," I finally answer. "I feel confident that we will be ready for battle soon."

The Archmage nods, face and eyes void of all emotion.

"And our little blood bag?"

The image of Os pops up in my head.

I wish things were different. I wish it didn't have to be this way. But Os just...refuses to see the truth. No matter how hard I try.

"I am keeping him alive enough to keep reproducing blood, but broken enough that He can't fight back," I say.

*Lie.* There is nothing I will ever be able to do to stop Remus Ostia from fighting back. But that's not my fault.

The Archmage nods, hands hidden in His robes. "Good. Keep training and make sure your scaled bitch is beaten into submission as well. You're going to need a well tamed Dragon for your first mission."

"My first mission?" I ask.

But the Archmage simply nods and walks away.

"When will that be?" I call after Him.

There is not an answer.

*Fuck.*

What kind of mission is this going to be? I look around and find one of the attendants, telling them to fetch Anonyme for me.

If we're being assigned to a mission already, I'll be damned if it's a failed one.

I will make Castael Laryn and the Father proud.

# CHAPTER 23
## RYU

*"Where is Amalia?"*

Nyall falls to his knees in pain. "She was right behind me. She should *be* right behind me."

But she's not.

*Come on, Ama. Come on.*

Healers swarmed as the Fae Prince fell to his knees, but Nyall swats them away, more concerned about our missing Wytch.

"Goddamnit, come on, Amalia!" Nyall's snarl makes me proud. He almost sounds like a Dragon. Healers rush him, concerned about the various arrows poking out of his chest.

I can sense his flesh already beginning to heal, but several of the arrows cut into his organs.

Those wouldn't heal so easily.

Nyall bats away the healers, yanking the arrows out himself without so much as a wince.

We wait in restless agony, for what feels like a lifetime until finally, *finally* Amalia steps through. Relief floods me.

Amalia's eyes are wide and hollow, still alight with the glow of her Hellfyre. Streaks of gray and black ash cover her clothes and face, and blood coats her abdomen—wait, *blood?*

*"You're hurt?"* I burst into her head, easily cutting through her mortal magyk.

*"It's fine."* Amalia says in a voice as hollow as her eyes.

"Why do you not heal it the way you heal others?"

The question isn't mine. The human, Mara, approaches Amalia with a concerned furrow to her brow.

This is the one who claims Amalia slayed her kin.

There is so much they do not know about her, my Ama. I watch as Mara reaches for Amalia's wound, and all of the human's previous hate and distrust cycles through my memories.

Mara's hand is almost touching the arrow poking out of Amalia's side, but I'm there in the blink of an eye, snarling in her face as I hover over my mortal companion.

**"NO ONE TOUCHES MY WYTCH."**

I open my jaws and allow all to hear my voice. Several people scream and I watch as many of the little mortals cover their ears, wincing in pain. Mara screams and falls into the mud, scrambling away from me.

**"TOUCH HER AND DIE."**

Others start to cry. The scent of urine becomes prominent in the air.

"S-sorry," Mara gasps.

*"You spoke to them,"* Amalia whispers. It's not a question, but her tone leaves room for an explanation.

*"You are hurt. They could hurt you further."*

I glance back to see her fighting a smile, her pale, freckle and ash covered cheeks flushed pink.

*"You are my family. Dragons protect their families."*

*"You are my family,"* Amalia repeats, her hand lifting to rest on the scales of my leg.

Her palm is so tiny. Still, I feel the touch, and I feel the emotions behind it. While Amalia is closed off with others, she's always been open with me. Love and warmth swirl around her as she rubs my scales.

*"Perhaps, my not-so-little hatchling, Mara was just trying to see if I had already healed, or if the wound was still open."*

I scoff, sending a cloud of smoke from my nostrils.

*"Perhaps,"* I repeat, frustrated at the way she's always right.

Healers shout in the background, getting Amalia's attention. Her brow furrows as she watches them help Nyall to the healing tent.

*"Now comes the hard part. If they cannot heal his organs..."* I break off.

*"Right,"* Amalia whispers. *"Will you...stand watch for a second while I heal these?"* She motions to her own injuries.

I nod and lift my head, scanning the surrounding area for any potential threat.

Amalia lets out a quiet groan as I listen to the sound of her flesh knitting back together.

"It was easier when they could knock me out and do it for me," she mutters, pulling her hands away from the wound.

I would respond, but Amalia's attention is already on the direction the healers took Nyall. She starts off, still covered in blood and shirt torn to bits, but though she would never admit it, nothing else matters to Amalia right now other than Nyall.

"Would you like to follow?" She glances back at me, her blue eyes blazing in the dark. The suns are rising in the east. The mission took most of the night.

I nod and begin to follow, turning my great body and lifting my tail so that I do not destroy the mortal's tents.

What I've told Amalia is true. The growing should stop soon but that's just a hope.

It *should* stop soon.

It *should.*

But I have a feeling it won't, not unless I want it to.

Dragons...cannot choose how big they get. Not really. We can however, decide to stop growing if we're getting too big.

Small Dragons cannot get bigger. Once growing stops, it stops. But for some of us—especially Dragons with blood ties to the Royal matriline —our growing can be so out of control, we have to stop it ourselves.

But that is a problem for another day.

Today, what I'm concerned about is the Half-Fae, Half-Elven male in the healing tent in front of me.

Nyall shouts in pain at something and Amalia meets my eyes.

*"Make sure they heal him right,"* I growl, and her protests quiet.

*"Do you want to watch and make sure I do it okay?"* Amalia jokes, but I pause.

*"Try it."*

I feel her shock. *"What? You-you want to see if I can swap sight with you?"*

*"Yes. Are you surprised at this?"*

*"I...I am, I guess. It's an honor. But Ryu, I don't know if I can."*

I snort again. *"Amalia Asteroth, your power is will. There is nothing you cannot do once you set your mind to it. Just try."*

*"Fine,"* she huffs, and I feel her concentrate, then the dark, fruity scent of her magyk brushes against mine.

I feel the moment it works. One second, I'm looking down at the healing tent beneath me, surrounded by similar looking tents in the rebel-controlled valley.

Then the world shifts and I'm *inside* the tent, looking through Amalia's eyes.

*"Holy shit!"* She gasps in my head. *"It worked."*

*"Told you so,"* I laugh. *"Can you see what I see?"*

*"It feels like tugging a string. One string and I can watch through my eyes with you...tug the other string and I can see what you see instead,"* she explains.

*"Ama, this is incredible. This gives us a whole new advantage."*

*"I really didn't think I could do it."*

I hate the way she doubts herself. *"Maybe you just needed to find the right partner to do it with."*

I feel her smile. *"Perhaps."*

One of the healers in front of us groans in frustration.

"Let me see," Amalia says, and I watch as we get closer. Nyall is laying half-conscious and shirtless on a table, bloody towels everywhere.

"The arrows punctured his liver and one of his kidneys. He's lost too much blood, so the organs have started to become septic. The tissue cannot heal what's not there. We can knit flesh and bone, but we cannot replace organs."

"Fuck off then," Amalia orders. "If you can't help him, then get the hell out."

*"Bitch,"* the healers mutter that and various other insults under their breath as they leave.

When they're finally gone, Amalia relaxes and we look back at Nyall. I watch as her hands remove the gauze on his wounds until the skin is gaping open.

### *HEAL. REMAKE. REPAIR. HEAL. REMAKE. REPAIR.*

Distantly, as if in my own mind, I hear her will Nyall's flesh back together.

She cannot control the mind. Amalia will never have power over the mind, but the body is different.

Nyall's flesh knits together with loud squelching sounds. Puss and blood drip out of the closing holes until there is nothing left.

"The one's inside, now," Amalia mutters. "I need to..." She lays a hand down on his abdomen. "I need to *feel* it."

Then everything goes dark as Amalia closes her eyes.

"Where are you?" she whispers to herself, brow furrowed in concentration.

"There!" Amalia gasps and I feel the way her magyk jumps to attention. She orders his organs to repair.

**_HEAL. REMAKE. REPAIR. HEAL. REMAKE. REPAIR._**

They're slower, but it works.

I watch in awe as she coaxes his body into making fresh blood cells, fresh tissue, until his organs are healed.

Nyall stirs below her hands, waking up. I suddenly feel like I'm intruding.

Something tugs at my attention. *"I will leave you two alone now that I know he's healed."*

Amalia hisses, *"You did this on purpose, Ryu!"*

*"Perhaps,"* I say happily before disconnecting our minds.

Sometime soon, she's going to see the truth.

But mortals are so scared of love.

They do not see the truth of things; that love is the most powerful force in the world.

That tugging at the corner of my mind increases as I leave Amalia and trudge over to the edge of camp.

"Did you see what she did?" The voice is far away, but I hear it perfectly.

The human, the one I scared earlier. Mara.

"Thousands, Amari. Thousands! She turned them all to ash." Mara's voice is frantic.

I focus on the conversation, trying to pick up on the other person she is with.

Mara is in a group.

"I saw it. I understand that she saved us...but what she's capable of? *No one* should have that kind of power. Ever. That's exactly how we ended up where we are now." Amari's voice is low and hushed. "Do you know some of them have started praying to her? Nyall won't tell her. Even *he's* afraid of her reaction. Praying!"

"She's one step away from being just like the Archmage," Mara agrees. "I tried to ignore it. I tried to look past it and be the better person. I *thought* I could do it, but after today. She didn't even blink when her Dragon almost ate me."

I snort at the idea.

"I saw that. I was so scared for you," Amari whispers. "I don't know what to do. We can't exactly abandon the rebellion."

"No, absolutely not. We brought people here. We asked for their trust in exchange for their *lives*. We can't abandon them."

"But..." Amari starts. "We need Amalia to leave."

"What if that means Nyall leaves too?" a new voice asks.

Soren.

She and Fi covered Amalia and Nyall earlier.

Her voice is less convinced.

"What then?" Soren asks again. "We cannot function without a leader."

"Yes, we can," Mara says. "He loves her, but he won't leave us to follow her."

"Are you sure?" Soren questions, still not believing.

"Positive."

*No you're not.* I want to say. But I stay quiet, listening from far away.

"What about her Dragon? How can we get her to leave if that beast is always hovering around?" Amari asks.

"Gods, hearing it speak will haunt me in my dreams until the day I die." Mara's voice is hollow as she recalls the sound of my voice.

Good.

*I hope it does haunt you, small mortal.*

"I don't know how we will get her to leave, but should the opportune moment arise, do I have your support?"

"Yes." Amari's answer is first.

"Soren?"

Soren doesn't answer Mara for a few moments.

"As long as you have the rebellion's best interest in mind, you have my support."

*Smart mortal.*

The caveat ensures the vow is flexible.

So. They are going to go after Amalia.

Not today.

Not tomorrow.

But soon.

I have never eaten a person. Not yet. I prefer a much richer, fattier meat.

Sheep, plump off grass are a particular favorite. Griffyns too, though the wolves and I keep that particular fact from Amalia. Hiding all of the feathers takes ages.

She thinks they're cute. I think they're *tasty.*

With my size, when I need to kill a mortal, stomping on them or burning them to death works much better. But after hearing Mara conspire against the person I love the most in this world?

I might just reconsider my stance.

If there's one thing Amalia has taught me, it's that the most important thing in this world is family.

# CHAPTER 24
## DYANA

*"KINSLAYER!"*

*"YOU'D BE BETTER OFF DEAD."*

*"Nobody's going to miss you, Executioner."*

*"DIE ALREADY, YOU OLD BASTARD!"*

*"I hope the Sene Skal slits your throats."*

Insult after insult is hurled at us as Vesimyr flies past a large group of Elysium Dragons near the castle.

It's been like this every single day since the demonstration, but the threats have gotten more *passionate* as of late.

The longer we're here, the more volatile the situation has become.

A few times, Dragons have tried to dive at us, pretending to attack. Vesimyr said they're just posturing, but thanks to my time with Amalia, I know better.

It's not posturing. It's a warning.

Someday soon, the threats will be followed by actual attacks as the Dragons of Elysium challenge Vesimyr in an effort to kill us both.

My Dragon might be in denial of that, or perhaps he just doesn't want to scare me, but I know that a time of reckoning is upon us.

The fear it sparks within me has been pushing me hard. I mastered the light sword and have moved onto other shapes of weapons, as well as using two at once.

Next is throwing them and summoning them back. How to maintain their shape and solidity from a distance has proven to be extremely difficult.

But hearing the Dragons hurl insults at us, threaten us? It fuels me.

I cannot lose another friend.

Nor will I stand by quietly and watch as it happens.

*"Are you alive?"*

I'm on my back, lying on the dirt floor, as Vesimyr hovers above me.

*"What did she do to you this time? Embyrne!"* Vesimyr turns his head, looking at my trainer as he unleashes a mighty roar. *"What did you do to her?"*

"Calm down," I sigh, still breathless. "I'm fine. I'm just not sure I can move."

*"Did you break my human?"* Vesimyr hisses, stalking towards Embyrne. I sit up and glare at him.

He freezes in his tracks, green eyes widening.

"One: I'm not human anymore, thanks to you. Two: I'm just fucking tired," I tell him. "Nothing is wrong."

*"Right,"* he sniffs and looks at Embyrne who has been watching us with her arms crossed. *"That's good."*

"Were you going to try to kill me, Kinslayer?" Embyrne purrs. "How predictable." Vesimyr growls at the nickname.

*"Hurt my Rider, break her in any way,"* he says in a low voice, *"and there will be no trying. I will simply tear your head from your shoulders."*

Embyrne chuckles in our heads, her gold eyes gleaming with the possibility of challenging the old Dragon, *"You could try."*

Vesimyr bares his teeth at her in a draconic smile, *"Tell me, have you had any luck with my magyk yet, Embyrne?"*

Embyrne goes still.

*Wait.*

*"What do you mean?"* I stand with a loud groan.

Embyrne grits her teeth and looks pointedly at Vesimyr. *"You know damn well I can't use your magyk."*

Vesimyr lifts his chin, *"Then keep that nickname out of your mouth, because you know damn well that without any magyk, you cannot beat me."*

Embyrne's golden eyes are cold as ice, but she shrugs. *"So you say. Perhaps I'll steal Dyana's magyk and use it against you. Are your scales thick enough to withstand her light, I wonder?"*

Vesimyr growls and Embyrne growls back. The sight is insane. In this form, Embyrne is so much smaller than Vesimyr's huge, looming figure.

But she looks upon my Dragon without an ounce of fear or hesitation.

There is no doubt in my mind that she would challenge Vesimyr to a fight, if the opportunity arose.

"Are we done with the posturing?" I ask aloud, stretching my sore shoulders. The bones pop and crackle as I twist, the sound echoing through the arena chamber.

"For now," Embyrne replies. She glares at Vesimyr before looking back to me with a small nod. "I'll see you tomorrow. You'll get the dual wielding down soon, Dyana. You're progressing fast."

Then she turns and leaves, her muscular figure disappearing into a dark hallway leading underground.

Tunnels connect the main castle to the rest of Elysium. Vesimyr told me they're too dangerous for humans to use, but Embyrne walked off without a care in the world.

Sometimes it's easy to forget she's a Dragon.

Her situation is so similar to Os'.

Both trapped in their mortal forms as punishment for choosing to shift. Both looking for a way out.

Os found his, but...Vesimyr told me it was likely he died too. Buried beneath the destroyed Arena.

Something occurs to me then.

It's so obvious, I can't believe I haven't brought it up.

"Where are you getting your information about Ur Daoine?"

Vesimyr nearly jumps out of his scales at my sudden question. I whirl, walking up to his nose and looking him in his big green eyes.

*"Um,"* he starts.

I raise a brow. "Um? Is that your answer?"

He quickly coughs. *"No. It's not."*

He's silent for a while, long enough that I take a seat on his front legs.

With a large sigh, Vesimyr answers my question, *"My magyk is...different. It's part of why I've never been well liked among the Dragon court. But it's also because of the advantage it gives me."*

He clears his throat, *"You weren't entirely wrong when you said the other Dragons are afraid of me. Most of my magyk is a bit...strange, to them. For example, I can communicate with all animals. Very much like the way your friend Amalia could."*

Hearing her name makes my chest tighten to the point of pain. But my mind races at the Dragon's words.

"You're getting your information from the birds," I gasp. "That's where you disappear to!"

Vesimyr nods.

"And other Dragons can't do this?"

He shakes his head, *"They cannot. Not truly. They can speak to animals the way I speak to you now, but the animals cannot understand their full meaning, nor can they respond. It's a weakness few know about."*

I raise a brow. "I'm guessing you've also ensured it stays a secret."

Vesimyr nods, *"The other Dragons are none the wiser. Which is ironic, considering most Dragons think themselves to be fountains of knowledge."*

"If they don't know you can talk to animals, how come they're still scared of you?"

Vesimyr tilts his head to look me in the eyes, leaning forward and pressing his snout against my cheek. *"Because, they don't know a single thing about my magyk. They know I have it, and they know that I can use it to kill other Dragons."*

"Kinslayer," I whisper. Sadness wafts off him and his green eyes shutter closed.

*"Yes. After Kora, I went back to Elysium and joined Kydis. I was her executioner, going after and killing Dragons who broke rank and sided with the Fae."*

I freeze. *"Some Dragons sided with the Fae?"*

Vesimyr snorts, *"Oh, yes. Can you not see how similar Elysium is to Ur Daoine?"*

I sigh, "I can. I was just...trying not to make that comparison. It's hard to feel hopeful when everywhere ends up being ruled by psychotic idiots."

*"I couldn't have said it better myself."*

"Let's head back." I climb up Vesimyr's leg scale onto his back, sitting between the spikes of his spine.

As soon as I'm seated, Vesimyr lifts into the air.

I want to enjoy the breeze. I want to wonder at the view before us.

But my heart is suddenly so heavy, and a wave of sadness hits.

"Do you regret it?" I ask. "The lives you took?"

Vesimyr is quiet for some time. The breeze is chilly on my face as the sun begins to set in the distance.

Time has been moving so fast. There's only one month left of training and I...I'm scared I'll still fail.

I'm trying so hard to be brave.

To be strong.

But the pressure is a heavy burden to carry.

*"Yes,"* Vesimyr answers finally. *"I regret it very much. I regret every life I've had to take in this forsaken world."*

I caress his scales with one hand, feeling his muscles shifting underneath me.

*"I've never once regretted protecting my people, though."*

"You shouldn't," I tell him. "You thought you were doing what was right."

*"Achan thought he was doing what was right. Ignautius thinks he's doing what was right. A supposed moral high ground doesn't excuse anything."*

I'm silent, processing his words.

*"The Dragons I killed were actively working with the Fae to target our nests. That's how they found Kora,"* he says her name with such pain, it makes tears well in the corners of my eyes. *"I regret killing them, but it was necessary."*

"Vesimyr," I breathe. "I'm so sorry."

*"I am too. I wish there had been another option, truly. Kydis and I spent days arguing about the best solution, but when I learned it was they who led the Fae to our hatchlings, our mates?"* He pauses for a moment. *"I knew then what had to be done."*

"I think you're brave," I say. "Brave and kind and honorable—"

***"KINSLAYER!"*** A Dragon shouts at us.

*"Ignore it,"* Vesimyr says in a calm voice.

I try to. Until it goes too far.

***"I hope Ignautius rips you limb from limb."*** That same Dragon—a great beast with dark orange scales, yellowish wings, and two legs—shouts at us again.

The image of Vesimyr's body being torn into pieces plays in my head, and in that moment, something inside me snaps.

"Nope," I whisper. "I won't do it. I will not sit here and be quiet!"

*"Dyana,"* Vesimyr warns, but I'm already turning to the orange Dragon, one arm in the air, as I summon my magyk and shoot a thick beam of light directly at it.

The Dragons hovering next to it scatter.

But the orange Dragon is fast. It swerves to the side, avoiding my blast.

**"Attacking a Dragon unprovoked?"** it growls aloud. Its voice is rough and terrible. Goosebumps cover my arms at the sound. **"That's grounds for execution, filthy worm."**

Faster than I can track, the orange Dragon dives at us. Vesimyr drops down, spinning upside down as he curves over and around it in an impressively agile maneuver.

There was a moment, when he went upside down, that I thought I was going to fall off, but the months of practice have paid off. I don't leave his back, not even once.

I do have to hold on for dear fucking life though.

When Vesimyr pauses, the orange Dragon is nowhere to be seen.

The clouds are still as we hover there, both on edge and panting.

*"I think it's gon—"*

I'm cut off as Vesimyr suddenly rolls to the left, avoiding the jaws of the orange Dragon as it flies at us from below.

Vesimyr isn't fast enough to avoid the Dragon's claws, though. My silver companion lets out a groan of pain as the orange Dragon slices open Vesimyr's belly. Steaming black blood falls towards the earth, streaming from the wound.

"Vesimyr!" I scream.

*"Use it. Use the anger,"* Embyrne's voice echoes in my head.

I focus on Vesimyr's pain until it morphs into a fury so great, I'm trembling. I locate the orange Dragon as it hovers above us, getting ready to attack.

"Just hold on," even in my thoughts, my voice is frantic.

*"Don't do it,"* Vesimyr says, his voice shaky.

"Too late."

The orange Dragon launches at us, and I lift both hands off Vesimyr's scales, lifting them into the air and summoning a giant ball of light. Bigger than anything I've summoned before. When the orange Dragon is just about to hit us, the ball explodes, singeing the Dragon's wings.

Vesimyr, however, is completely untouched.

The orange Dragon cries out in pain as it falls, struggling to fly with injured wings.

We watch as it aims for the beach, landing in the sand with a hard thump.

"Go!" I scream to Vesimyr, who quickly flies towards the castle, despite his wounds.

*"Do you have healers here?"* I jump into his thoughts, my magyk brushing against his.

*"No,"* he groans. *"It will heal on its own. But I doubt we have time for that. Ignautius will hear about this."*

I take a deep breath. *"Okay. Then we need to heal you a different way."*

*"That sounds like you have an idea,"* he says, and I sense the worry in his tone.

*"Take us to the forge—the mortal one. We need Mirielle."*

# CHAPTER 25
## MIRIELLE

Nothing could have prepared me for seeing Dyana and her Dragon walking through the door of the forge.

Seeing her makes my heart hurt. I've *tried* not to miss her. But it's easier said than done.

Dyana's black hair is longer and full of wind-swept waves, but it's currently pulled back in an intricate braid. It reminds me of Amalia.

Her warm brown eyes are full of worry. We haven't been this close in a while, and it's the first time I notice a new ring of bright green around the perimeter of her irises.

*That's new.*

"I need your help."

My hackles raise. She doesn't speak to me for *months* and ignores me, and now Dyana needs my *help?*

I'm about to tell her exactly what she can do with her request when Kairos' warm hand lands on my arm.

Right.

We...need their help too. Which means I can't be rude—no matter how badly I want to be.

I force my face to turn blank. "What kind of help are you talking about?"

Dyana clasps her hands together, concern making her eyes water. "Vesimyr is injured. I need you to cauterize his wounds. We don't have time for him to heal naturally."

She looks back at the large silver Dragon for a moment and then frowns. "Well, do you have any other ideas? You said it yourself, we don't have time!"

I suspect Vesimyr says something back along the lines of, *"Absolutely not"* because Dyana scoffs and looks back at me.

"It's happening," she says with a nod. "If...you can help us."

Then her eyes flick to the right as she looks at Kairos.

He looks at the silver Dragon with cautious eyes and steps forward.

Vesimyr growls and Dyana slaps his leg. "Stop it."

Kairos gets closer to the Dragon and Vesimyr gingerly raises one leg, shifting enough to show the deep gashes along his belly.

Blood drips onto the stone floor, quickly creating a pool of it beneath him.

Kairos turns back to me, watching the emotions play across my face with that all-knowing gaze. With a shallow nod, he steps away and the Dragon lowers its leg. Dyana watches it with such concern.

She watches the Dragon in the same way that she used to watch Amalia.

Kairos approaches my side and crosses his arms, his biceps bulging.

"Why should we help a Dragon?" he asks in a deep voice.

Vesimyr bares his teeth.

"Shh," Dyana says, responding to something he said. Then she takes a deep breath and looks at Kairos.

"I don't know you, but I do know you have *her* trust," Dyana pauses, her warm brown eyes flicking to me, making my heart somersault. "I cannot answer your question fully, but I will say this: your quarrel isn't with either of us. On that, I swear."

Kairos doesn't move a muscle. I glance back and forth between them.

"Still—why would a prisoner help their jailer? Why shouldn't we let your Dragon bleed to death?"

*Oh shit.*

Dyana glares at him and Vesimyr lets out a hissing sound. Then the anger leaves her, leaving only concern. Dyana looks around at the space casually and whispers to Vesimyr, "Are we alone?"

Vesimyr nods and she *tsks.*

"Right, what you're about to learn—and *see*—doesn't leave the room. This is me trusting you, *both* of you. Okay?"

In a single breath, something appears in her hand, and I nearly fall to my knees.

A sword made of pure, pale gold light sits in Dyana Arkos's lovely hands.

I nearly stumble.

"You didn't do that at the demonstration," I mutter, stepping forward to get a closer look at the sword. It's *beautiful.* Like pure magyk. The sword almost appears to be made of glass, but the edges shimmer lightly, reflecting prisms all over the room.

Dyana lets out a hollow laugh. "I'm a quick learner, apparently. At least with the right teacher."

Oh yes. *Embyrne.* The mimic.

"Impressive."

Dyana's eyes widen in shock at the genuine compliment. Sadness quickly replaces my awe.

How quickly things change.

"This isn't…the *only* thing I can do with light," Dyana says quietly. "I've discovered I can do quite a bit more than just make a sword."

Dyana pauses, swallowing, perhaps from nerves.

"I can also use it to cut through hard metals."

I blink, confused.

"Okay?" I say, not sure what she means.

Dyana rolls her eyes. "I can cut through Dragon scales, Mirielle. Any weapon that I make out of this new magyk? We're fairly certain it can cut through Dragon scales."

Damn. That's impressive.

She stares at me as if I'm supposed to be reacting differently.

Sighing, Dyana looks away for a moment. "Fucking hell, do I have to spell it out?"

Vesimyr nudges her and Dyana nods. "Right."

Something brushes against my mind and I let it in.

*"I'm going to kill Ignautius. My weapons can pierce his scales."*

My jaw drops.

I go to respond but she cuts the connection. I stand there, in shock. But Kairos springs into action.

"Red will fix the Dragon," he murmurs. "We will help you—with both goals."

"Me?" I blurt. "Wait, hold on—"

He glances at me and raises a brow. I've never once hesitated.

But Dyana is throwing me off.

Fuck.

I cough and put my shoulders back, "Okay. Yes. We'll help."

On the outside, I will my face into calm composure, tapping into centuries of practice. My muscles still and I show no emotion other than professionality.

On the inside, my thoughts race.

How the fuck did she learn so fast? The last time I saw her, she had zero to nil control abilities over her magyk.

Now, she can wield fucking light swords.

She can *make* weapons strong enough to cut through Dragon scales.

This changes things. New motivation thrums in my bones as Kairos and I begin preparing the cauterization instruments.

Dyana Arkos is planning to kill the Sene Skal.

Dyana Arkos is planning to *escape Elysium*—and I need to escape with her.

I have to get back to Ur Daoine.

I have to finish this.

"Don't move," I tell the silver Dragon, shoving the stem of the iron poker against his gash. The smell of burnt flesh makes me want to vomit, but I hold my breath as the raw muscle sizzles, closing up. The fear around the Dragons is still there. My stomach is in knots and my sweat isn't just from the heat. But after the first few burns, I realized the Dragon really wasn't planning on hurting me.

At least not right now.

Normally, his wound would heal fully in time, but the cauterization might have permanently damaged his scales. At least it's better than an open wound.

"You said you don't have much time. Why?" I ask, passing the used iron back to Kairos as he hands me a fresh one.

I press the length against the last bit of open wounds again and Vesimyr grunts. Dyana watches me carefully, inspecting everything I'm doing as if she's worried I'm going to hurt her new friend.

I have no reason to hurt him. Even if she thinks otherwise.

"A Dragon attacked us," Dyana says in a hushed, careful tone. "And I...fought back. A little too well, perhaps."

**"It's either dead, or unable to ever fly again,"** Vesimyr says aloud. His voice is low and full of power. It makes the hairs on my arm stand on end as my stomach turns.

"Got it," I finish the last wound, "so, you're running from Ignautius because he's going to be looking for you."

Dyana glares at me. "We are not *running*. But I'm not facing him without Vesimyr at full strength."

My iron rod drops to the floor with a loud clang.

I was right.

But she's not just planning on escaping, she's planning on fighting her way out.

"Tell me you're not serious, Dyana!"

She flinches as if I had hit her.

Vesimyr growls, moving gingerly. He pushes onto all four legs, moving to stand behind Dyana protectively.

"Holy shit, you *are* serious." I gasp.

Dyana doesn't respond. She just nods and thanks me for my help.

As she turns to leave, I jog to catch up with her. My hand lands on her shoulder and in a single blink, Dyana has me pinned against a wall, a dagger made of light pointed right at my throat.

I knew she's been training, but Gods above.

She's fast.

Faster than me.

And she can make more than just a sword. The dagger shimmers, blurring for a moment as it reforms into a spiked knuckle. It blurs again and a scythe appears.

Dyana sees me floundering, rendered speechless, and smiles.

"I am not the helpless girl you once knew," she says in a hardened voice. "Worry about yourself, Mirielle. Don't worry about me."

She lets me go and I take a deep breath.

Vesimyr pauses in the doorway, looking down at Dyana.

She shrugs and continues on, but the Dragon looks back at us with a strange look in his eyes.

Then his magyk is spearing into me, barreling through all of my mental walls as Vesimyr's voice sounds in my thoughts.

*"The volcano holds what you seek,"* he says. Kairos inhales sharply, grasping his head.

Vesimyr is speaking to both of us.

*"It will be empty when the sun sets. Go then."*

Then his magyk retreats, leaving me and Kairos gasping for breath.

"What did he mean?" I wonder aloud.

"Elysian," Kairos says, shock coating the deep tenor of his voice. "He *means* Elysian, Red."

I gasp.

"Why would he help us?"

Kairos shrugs, but his eyes remain hard. "I have heard Dragons do not like uneven exchanges."

He raises both hands, weighing them.

"We saved his life," he lifts his left hand, lowering the right, "he gives us information we've been looking for." The hands reverse, and I understand what he's saying.

"Interesting," I wipe a dirty rag across my sweaty forehead. "Sounds like I'm going to a volcano."

Kairos snorts, "*We're* going to a volcano, Red."

"No," I shake my head, but Kairos is already taking off his apron.

"I'm not asking for permission," he says, walking off. "Pack enough for a few days. We meet here first thing in the morning. It's a two-day journey and we need to hurry. It doesn't sound like we have much time."

I blink.

"Have much time for what?"

Kairos turns to me. "You've connected the dots. I saw it. Your mind is always strategizing."

He approaches me, until we're nearly chest to chest and I have to tilt my head back to look into his onyx eyes.

"Dyana Arkos is escaping, and we're escaping with her," he says.

My jaw nearly drops, but I keep it locked in place.

"Now go get packed. We need to get the Elysian."

# CHAPTER 26
## IREYNA

"Blessed Sol."

"Blessed Sol," the audience responds.

The Cult of Sol Constantus meets regularly at temples throughout the Kingdom. Twice a mooncycle, we gather together and pray to Sol Constantus for guidance.

"It's so lovely to see all of your shining faces with us today!" the Archmage announces, spreading His arms wide.

He's dressed in His High Ceremony robes. Similar to the robes He typically wears, these are white. But that's where the similarity ends.

These robes are embellished with fine silver and purple gems, and accented with metallic silver embroidery.

The High Ceremony robes are my favorite.

Someday, it's going to be *me* wearing them—if I'm blessed. There has never been another Archmage. Sol Constantus has never blessed another with the gift of seeing Him.

"Isn't it a beautiful day out? Blessed Sol!"

I blink.

Last I checked it was cloudy out.

I suppose clouds are better than a storm though.

The Elves and Fae that serve the Archmage walk up and down the long aisles in between rows of wooden pews where the citizens of Castael Laryn huddle together.

My pew is empty. It always is.

I sit in the very front, an area reserved for those closest to the Archmage.

The High Council used to sit Here, but they're long gone.

As the Archmage begins His sermon, my mind wanders.

I try to pay attention whenever I'm at the temple, but instead, my mind goes to the white Dragon.

Anonyme.

"Those who sin will be forgiven; but turning from Him? That is the gravest of sins. For He is all."

"Blessed Sol," we return. The words fall from my mouth automatically.

"Yes—He *is* all. Which is why it is divine right to rule. What He says and what He wants is the truest law."

I hear murmured ascent.

"My friends, my *neighbors,*" the Archmage pontificates. "It is our divine *purpose* on this plane to show the people the truth; that there is no other God but the one True God. Constantyn."

"Blessed Sol," we return again.

Boredom overtakes me. I typically enjoy these, but this...apathetic feeling takes over me.

"Give thanks to Him and He will bless you! Show the Kingdom the path forward is through Him, and our Kingdom will be blessed indeed."

"Blessed Sol," we return a final time.

The last part of the ceremonies involves the Archmage's servants to walk through the aisles, burning incense.

A deep violet smoke fills the air. It smells of spices and shadows.

Suddenly I can't remember what was bothering me, or why I felt bored.

Happiness overtakes me and I watch the Archmage finish His sermon with renewed interest. It's as if every word from His lips is from Constantyn Himself.

All feels right in the world.

*I am on the right path.*

He is right. It *is* a beautiful day, isn't it?

# CHAPTER 27
## AMALIA

A bolt of pain shooting up my neck wakes me. With a groan I slowly turn my head side to side, pushing past the painful cramp.

I must have slept in a bad position. Reality crashes into me a second later.

My neck hurts because I fell asleep in a chair by the fire in Nyall's tent. Eventually, some of the healers and their assistants had returned, offering to help carry Nyall back to his room.

I thanked them and apologized for earlier. One of the healer's jaws nearly dropped at the gesture.

When the healers took Nyall back to his tent, I had followed along. I was staying with him after all, but with him unconscious, it felt wrong to share a bed. I took to the chair, and now, hours later, my body is screaming at me for it.

That's it, surely.

As I gently stretch my neck out, the pain lessens. I take a deep breath and open my eyes.

It's dark out—the suns are well and truly gone. I slept for an entire day.

Exhaustion still sits heavy in my bones. I have a feeling I could easily sleep another few days, escaping the weight of reality. Shadows play along the tent ceiling in between beams of moonlight.

Leaning up onto my elbows, I get disoriented. Someone *moved* me. I should be in the chair, but instead I'm staring at it from across the room.

Nyall must have woken up and moved me to the bed. Sleepy and confused, I go to roll off but run into a hard pillow.

Sleepy and confused quickly turns to grumpy and aggravated, so I kick the pillows, not liking being trapped.

"Fucking hell," a rich voice groans in the dark and I go still. "Is there a reason you're attacking me?"

Nyall is in bed with me, and I just kicked him where he had been injured.

"You scared the shit out of me, you fucking idiot!" I hiss at him, startled and concerned.

Nyall puts his arms behind his head, not even wincing at the pain I know the movement caused. The position makes his biceps and abdomen flex, which is when I realize the sheets have fallen down his body.

His very *naked* body.

~~Get out before it's too late.~~

**SHUT UP!** *Shut up.*

~~*Don't let him in. Letting him in means getting hurt.*~~

*Just stop.* **Please.**

Maybe it's the way I feel safer in the dark. I don't need any magyk to be covered in shadows.

Something about this hour makes me feel more like myself. Sleep has relaxed my walls, allowing my brain to slow.

As I look at Nyall Drayven, cast in shadows and moonlight, my thoughts don't race, nor do I feel riddled with the grief of surviving while my loved ones do not. The darkness and sleep have stolen my grief for the time being.

It will come back with the light of the day. It always does.

But right now? Right now I...feel safe.

"Looked your fill?" Nyall teases, and his white teeth flash in the darkness as he smiles.

I zoom in on the points of his fangs.

They're small, so small they're only *just* longer than human canine teeth. They don't always poke out past his upper lip but right now they do and it makes me *need.*

I have the sudden urge to see how sharp they are.

I realize I haven't answered his question, so for the first time in over two years, I am honest.

"No."

My voice is quiet, but I feel like the answer bounces off the tent walls, echoing through the room.

Nyall blinks and in that brief second, I catch a glimpse of surprise.

"By all means, do continue," Nyall smiles, his mismatched eyes beginning to glow. He lays there, still and unmoving, allowing me to look as long as I please.

But I am not the only one *watching.*

I smirk, "Have *you* looked your fill?"

Nyall's smile fades as his mouth opens just slightly as his gaze travels over my body. I feel his eyes on me, as if his hands were tracing patterns on my skin.

I glance down and my cheeks flush as I realize I'm in a similar state of undress.

Not naked, but I'm only in one of Nyall's short sleeved shirts. It comes to my upper thighs, but every movement reminds me there's nothing underneath.

Nyall's eyes flick back up to mine. "No," he finally answers my question, "I will never have enough of you."

*Oh—*

"But, we both need our sleep. You look exhausted and I feel like I've been trampled by a fucking Dragon. Come here," he interrupts my thoughts and grabs my hand, pulling me into his arms.

"You do not get to tell me what to do," I protest, trying to wiggle out of his grasp.

"Just this once," he whispers. "Just this once, stop thinking and let yourself *relax.*"

Part of me wonders if his words are a spell, because the second I hear *"relax"* my body stills.

Taking a deep breath and letting it out slowly, I allow my muscles to ease one by one, until I'm melting into Nyall's arms. Exhaustion immediately follows and my eyelids grow heavy.

"Behave," I warn in a sleepy voice.

His arms tighten around me, hands warm even through the thin cotton of my shirt.

"Amalia Asteroth, when have you *ever* known me to behave?"

I snort, and suddenly I can't stop laughing.

It's that kind of laughter that comes when you're exhausted and burnt out. A cynical, cathartic kind of humor.

I can't remember the last time I laughed this hard.

"I'm glad you survived," I breathe, trying to catch my breath.

"A compliment?" Nyall snorts. "I need to check with the healers because I most certainly have a concussion. Amalia Asteroth would never give *me* a compliment." I elbow him hard enough to make him gasp and he curses. "Fuck, now I really do need a healer."

"Just go to sleep! Stop being such a pussy," I hiss.

Nyall snickers. "Your bedside manner is world-class."

Nyall's breath brushes against my cheek. He pulls me harder against him and adjusts us until my head is tucked under his chin, and our legs are intertwined.

I start to protest but he just shushes me.

"Sleep, Amalia. You're safe."

The sound of his words makes me melt even further, and the world fades. I wake, hours later, and the sky is still dark. The suns would be dragging light across the sky soon.

The bed beneath me is so warm and I try to move, but I can't.

Blinking away sleep, I lift my head up and realize Nyall has hauled me on top of him. I'm wrapped around him like a vine, my head tucked into the crook of his neck as we share his pillow. My lips are pressed into the soft skin of his clavicle.

Nyall's right hand is fisted in my hair, while his left is on my hip, which puts my core just inches from Nyall's hard length.

I need to move but sleep still pulls at me, and the warmth of Nyall's body compared to the chilly spring breeze drifting through the tent is delicious. Sometime in the night, my top must have ridden up, because my naked chest is pressed against his abdomen.

*Oh.*

I move slightly and nearly cry out at the feeling of my bare pussy against the warm skin of Nyall's leg. His cock is hard, even in his sleep, its warm length against my ass.

We're wrapped so tightly together, where he ends, I begin.

I missed this feeling. I missed it so much.

Nyall's hand on my hip tightens and my mouth falls open as he lowers his palm until he grabs my ass cheek and kneads it.

The movement tugs softly against the lips between my legs. My breath hitches. Nyall makes a sleepy, pleased sound before he slides me down, so that his thigh is between my legs and my pussy pressed into his skin.

*Oh Gods.*

I can't help the small whimper that leaves my lips as he adjusts his leg, pressing it harder against me. The position puts pressure directly on my clit and I'm trembling with need.

I need more. It's—it's not enough. Not even *close* to enough. The longer he presses against me the more my will *fails.*

"Ride me, horse girl," Nyall whispers, his voice low and sleepy. "Rub that pretty pussy against my leg."

*Holyfuckingshit.*

I don't even *mean* to, but my hips move of their own accord, grinding against him.

*"Mhmm,"* Nyall murmurs. "That's it, just like that. Get yourself off. *Use* me."

A moan falls from my lips and Nyall fists my hair harder, pressing a kiss against my neck before hovering his lips near my ear.

There is no pretending anymore.

We aren't asleep.

I couldn't stop my hips even if I wanted to.

But I don't.

I can't lie anymore. Not about this.

Because in this moment, there is nothing I want more than to get off with Nyall Drayven.

I grind against his leg, shivering and panting against his neck. Nyall wraps one arm around me while his other continues to fist my hair.

"I don't believe in the Gods," Nyall breathes. "But *fucking hell,* Blue. You're *divine."*

I whimper, "I need to—"

"Shh," he whispers, his lips pressing into the side of my cheek. "I've got you. But we have to be quiet. The Suns rise soon."

I go still at the idea of a new day. Of the return of my grief.

"Not yet," Nyall says, his voice firm, clearly feeling me tense up. "Just close your eyes, Blue. The world is still asleep. This?" Nyall moves his leg against me, and I have to press my lips against Nyall's neck to silence my own moan. "This...can be just a dream."

"Just a dream," I repeat, panting.

"Yes." Nyall's voice is a wicked purr. "So be a good girl and make yourself come."

*"Help me."* I send the thought his way, so turned on I can no longer form real words.

Nyall goes still, so I go for the kill. Turning my head and lifting up on my arms, I brush my lips against Nyall's smooth cheek before dragging my lips against his.

It's so slight, I'm not sure it can count as a kiss.

But it's close.

So, so fucking close.

My tongue darts out of its own volition. I simply can't help but taste him. Honeysuckle blasts my senses.

*"You taste like magyk,"* I moan in his head.

Nyall's hand in my hair tightens and he pulls me against him as our lips crash together. His tongue flicks at the seam of my mouth and I open for him.

Nyall Drayven doesn't give. He *takes.*

The Prince Without a Throne devours me, swallowing my moans. His hand traces down my body until he's between my legs.

"Give me *everything,*" Nyall snarls just as his thumb reaches between his leg and my body to press against my clit.

It's like a shockwave hits me and all of my senses stray as the pleasure overwhelms until it's all I feel. I jerk in his arms and moan into his lips, but he takes it all.

Then the pleasure becomes too much. Too big.

I grind harder against Nyall's hand and suddenly it's not his leg I'm riding, but his fingers.

"Please."

I'm not one to beg, but this male has me in *shreds.* Nyall curses before dragging his thumb through my wet outer lips and slowly, so slowly, inserting two fingers inside of me.

I go still, my jaw dropping as Nyall Drayven eases inside of me.

He pulls back, studying my expression with concern.

*"Your eyes are glowing,"* he whispers in my mind. *"Are you okay?"*

It's been two years.

Two fingers might as well be a cock with how tight it feels.

"Fucking *move.*" I try to make it sound like an order, but my words end in a reedy moan as Nyall begins to move his fingers. "Gods, please. I need—"

"I know what you need, sweetheart," Nyall murmurs.

"More," I whisper. "Give me *more.*"

The wicked smile upon his face makes my core flood with pleasure, coating his fingers.

Nyall's spare hand finally leaves my hair. He traces down my neck, leaning in to kiss me. But just as his lips meet mine, so does his hand meet my throat.

Tattooed fingers wrap around my neck, holding me in place. Nyall doesn't squeeze hard enough to hurt, but that *slight* lick of pressure nearly sends me into the clouds. I gasp but Nyall swallows it with his mouth.

Our lips dance as his fingers begin to thrust faster, until I'm a sweaty, panting mess in his arms. The wet sound of his ministrations echoes through the room. Normally I would be embarrassed but it only turns me on more.

"So wet," Nyall purrs, then his fingers disappear. I let out a mewling whine and Nyall chuckles. Then his fingers are back.

But there's a *third.*

"Nyall, I don't know if I ca—" I stumble over my words.

"You can." He smiles against my lips. "Relax, Blue. Relax your muscles. I've got you—remember?"

I still, focusing on relaxing my inner abdominal muscles.

*He's got me.*

*He's got me.*

The tension melts away and that third finger slides in easily. My back bows.

"That's it," Nyall praises me, and I want to moan at his words. "Just like that."

He thrusts his fingers in and out, curving them slightly to hit my most sensitive inner walls. I feel so *full.* I didn't even know I was empty until right now, and I need *more.*

"You're magnificent," Nyall whispers and I melt into his arms, panting and sweaty. Our kisses slow, turning lazy and sensual.

Noise eventually sounds in the distance.

I let out a quiet whine.

*I'm not ready. Not yet.*

But the noise is enough.

My concentration snaps and the pleasure fades from me.

It's like jumping in a freezing cold lake. All of a sudden, reality is *there.*

I pull back from Nyall and we stare at each other as the tent brightens and the day finally arrives with the rising suns.

He watches me with a sad sort of knowing.

Then he smirks as he pulls his fingers out of me, watching my reaction and the way my jaw drops. I know he can *feel* the way I want to plead for more.

My heart stops beating as I watch him raise his arm, bring his fingers to his mouth, and *lick.*

A moan does leave me, then.

I simply cannot help it. I am only so strong and the sight of Nyall Drayven cleaning my pleasure off his hand will be my undoing.

The way his eyes shutter and he groans at my taste.

The way he licks with more ferocity after tasting me, needing more.

"Gods, you taste so fucking good," Nyall sighs. "Fuck, Amalia. You're going to *ruin* me."

My will nearly crumbles. But as he finishes, and as the suns continue to rise, so does the heavy weight of reality.

I pull away and Nyall drops his hand. He sits up, following my movement but I shake my head.

His brows furrow and he takes a deep breath. "Was this okay? Are you alright?"

"I'm fine," I snap, voice trembling.

I'm not mad. I don't know why I snapped.

*Anger is so easy.*

The gentle, caring tone in his voice makes me want to cry. I want him to keep going. I want to crawl into his arms and never leave, but Os' golden eyes flash brightly in my mind.

The guilt *chokes* me. As if I'm betraying his memory.

"Do you want to talk about it?" Nyall asks gently and I shake my head.

*Not right now.*

"Talk to me. You *know* me." Nyall says, following as I get off the bed and begin to dress.

My patience snaps at his incessant pushing.

"No, Nyall! I don't want to fucking talk about it. *We* can't happen, okay? I can't do this."

Nyall says nothing, but I feel him close in on me. "It didn't seem like that a few minutes ago, Blue."

"That was a mistake," I nearly choke on the word. Saying it is painful. My hand strays to my abdomen, checking for some phantom wound and finding none.

"Is this about that day in the training field? About...what you know godsdamn well I *felt?*"

I yank on some worn in leather pants, taking out my fury on the laces. "I don't know what you're talking about."

"Bullshit. You're *lying* but I don't understand why. Why do you keep pushing me away when I know you—"

Pants on, I spin and shove at his chest with a snarl. "Don't say it."

Nyall steps forward until we're chest to chest. "You can't make me stay quiet. Why are you so afraid of *liking* me?"

"I don't *like* you," I protest immediately, but even the words feel hollow on my tongue.

"Blue," Nyall says gently. "I felt it. But I also felt your pain. Talk to me. I *want* to be there for you, but I can't do that if you keep hiding."

"I'm not hiding," I respond numbly, and he scoffs.

"You are, because you're afraid to like me. I know why, of course."

I go still, looking up at him with surprise.

Nyall nods and runs a hand through his hair. "It's because I'm a Drayven. I'm *Fae,* right?"

I should nod. Grab hold of this opportunity and use it to cover my tracks.

But pleasure still runs through my body and it's scrambling my brain.

"It's not that," I sigh. "Just, leave it. Please."

Nyall looks up at the tent ceiling and takes a deep breath before looking me in the eyes. The intensity of his gaze makes me shiver.

"You're not the only one who *loved* and *lost,* Amalia."

I blink, taken aback. "But you *hated* your father."

Nyall shakes his head with a sad smile. "For someone so intelligent, your ignorance is astounding."

"Fuck you," I snarl.

"No, fuck *you* for thinking *you're* the only one grieving him, Amalia."

I take a step back, shocked. "I—what?"

Nyall steps forward, following me. "I'm well aware that every time you look at me, I enter a battle against Os' ghost. I know why you keep hesitating. I *felt* your pain. We all did. But you aren't the only one who's grieving him."

I'm frozen, unable to move. "You were...*friends?*"

Nyall smiles and his hand lifts to cup my cheek. I can't help the way my body leans into him.

"Once," he answers finally. "A very, very long time ago."

I wish I had known...but it also changes nothing.

"It doesn't matter," I respond. "Os is...*burned* into my soul. It—it must be the familiar bond. I cannot betray him—even his ghost."

It's the first time I've said it aloud.

The words *hurt* in their sharp truth.

I pull away from Nyall, but his hand moves to my shoulder and he stops me.

"Amalia," he laughs gently. "Look at me."

I meet his gaze, confused and hurt.

"It's never been *or.* It's always been *and.*"

My heart skips a beat. "What?"

Nyall smiles sadly and leans down to press a kiss against my cheek. I sigh at the delicious feeling of closeness as Nyall whispers in my ear, his breath against my cheek. "I am not asking you to choose between us, Blue. It's never been one or the other."

My mind stops.

"What do you mean?" I ask, confused and unsure what Nyall is saying.

The smile he gives me is a sad one, full of regret and unanswered promises.

"Ask me the name of my first love, Amalia."

For some reason, the question terrifies me.

I swallow my fear and force the words to leave the tip of my tongue. "Who was your first love, Nyall?"

I feel Nyall's smile against my cheek as his lips drag back to meet mine. He presses a soft kiss against my mouth, and I have to strangle the urge to beg for more. Until Nyall opens his mouth and says the last thing I would ever expect, and the world disappears beneath my feet.

"The name of my first love...is Remus Ostia."

# CHAPTER 28
## AMALIA

"The name of my first love is Remus Ostia."

I step back, eyes wide. "What?"

I couldn't be more shocked if a tornado made of unicorn dust appeared in the middle of Nyall's tent.

He *loved* Os?

I take another step back, wrapping my arms around myself. "You... were together? Why didn't he tell me this? I don't understand."

Nyall smiles again but this time it's sad and full of regret. "No, we weren't together, but there was a moment I thought that *maybe* he felt the same. Then it was too late. I never told him how I felt. I think he knew, but I never got the courage to ask."

I blink, shocked.

I knew Nyall had been with males before. Gossip spread like wildfire about the Heretic Prince. That gossip eventually made its way up north.

But...Nyall loved Os.

Nyall *knew* Os.

"What happened?" I need answers.

Nyall shrugs. "It was just after the war ended and the original rebellion lost. Os pushed me away, not wanting to get hurt again after so much hurt."

I have no words.

"Sound familiar?" Nyall raises a brow and I frown, not liking the comparison. "You both are so alike. It's easy to see why you ended up as Familiars. You and Os are like two sides of the same coin.

I don't have a clever retort or a barbed quip. I have no words at all.

"I can't answer why he didn't tell you; I can only tell you that I know Os cared about you—a lot. I have never seen him care about another person that much before." Nyall sees the shock on my face and nods. "Right. I'll give you space to process this. I'm sorry if this was...too much."

He turns and finishes dressing before leaving the tent and leaving me alone with my thoughts. Just before he pushes through the tent door, Nyall glances over his shoulder and I feel his magyk brush against my mind.

*"Just so you know though, Blue? I'll be craving the taste of your pretty little pussy all day."*

Then he's gone. Out of the tent and out of my mind. His words knocked the wind out of me, and I'm left gasping for breath as silence descends and our connection fades.

Nyall...loved Remus?

For a few minutes I just...stand there. Shocked into stupidity.

Then the shock turns to a frenetic need to do something. Anything but just *stand* here. I throw clothes on and put my hair in a loose braid, but the strands are tangled, and frustration sets a fire in my belly.

Spying a pair of scissors on Nyall's dressing table, I grab them and feel a twinge of inspiration. With a deep breath, I begin cutting.

I don't think.

I don't consider the consequences. I just *cut,* and with it...I think some of my pain is excised.

As the strands fall to the floor in a gray pile, a lightness overcomes me, as if a weight has been lifted.

Looking in the small hand mirror, I trim until the hair is just above my shoulders. Still long enough to tuck behind my ears, but shorter than it's ever been before.

I barely recognize myself.

Something about that gives me a rush of adrenaline. I summon Neiman and Macha and holster them across my back.

No more hiding.

Nyall is brave enough not to hide. I want the strength to do the same.

Amalia Roth is well and truly gone as I make my way out of the tent and head to get breakfast.

I'd be lying if I said the whispers didn't bring me joy.

I don't pay attention to whether they whisper about my hair or my swords, instead I focus on my porridge.

It's always porridge.

"Spar with us?" Keres, calls and I freeze.

I look down at my food and back at them, unsure it's me they're speaking to.

Keres smiles and nods. "Yes, you. Come spar, Amalia. Show us what you've got."

What is this feeling? This...*inclusion*. I do not recognize it. Warmth blossoms in my middle.

I'm used to everyone wanting me far away, but Keres wants me to join them.

They want me around.

I nod and abandon the half-eaten food. Too much is on my mind to be hungry.

Nyall and Os. Os and Nyall.

I feel like the wind has been knocked out of me after that revelation. But why does it also feel...*right.*

So strangely right, it feels divinely wrought.

Did Morrigyn do this? Arrange our fates so that I would meet them *both* in my lifetime?

Glancing back at her swords, I grab Neiman, pulling it out of the holster and examining the dark blade.

Distant whispers sound as I run the soft pads of my fingers along the smooth metal blade.

These whispers aren't from the camp. They're different.

I can't make out any words, but when I pull my hand away, it stops.

"Did you do this?" I ask it. The swords, unsurprisingly, don't respond.

"I wish you'd talk to me, Mother. I wish you would give me guidance."

There is nothing. Morrigyn, as per usual, doesn't respond.

My ideas of fate fade and I'm left confused, overwhelmed, and intrigued. The latter of which scares me, but I keep replaying the way Nyall touched me last night. The memory is so strong, I can still feel his hands on me, *in* me.

Thinking about it makes drool flood my mouth and my hands tremble. It's a visceral feeling, being able to trace the pounding rush of my blood as it surges to my core, making my clit throb.

My pants feel tighter as I stand and head to the training yard, following Keres. When they turn to greet me, the mischievous glint in their eyes puts me instantly on edge.

"What are you so pleased about then?" I ask, prodding them.

Keres snorts. "Nothing. Nothing at all."

"Liar," I glare, suspicious. But we fall into comfortable silence.

"We're sparring today," Keres says with a smile. "I know the recruits would love to try and beat you."

"They won't," I retort, meeting their smirk with one of my own.

"Oh, I'm aware. But the Prince is no longer the top fighter here. You have become the one to beat."

"How many?"

Keres's brows furrow. "How many what?"

"How many want to spar with me?"

"A dozen."

I rub my eyes. "Right. Then let's get on with it."

Keres nearly trips in shock. "You'll spar with *all* of them? Uh, okay. Wow. That's great. They're going to lose their shit when they see you."

Sparring ends up being more fun than I anticipated. Keres was right, the recruits did freak out when they broke the news that I'd be sparring with them.

Except, a dozen quickly turned into three dozen. Lucky for them, the bouts were quick.

"Dead." I slap the flat of Neiman's blade across the recruit's chest. Katryn is her name. She winces in pain, grabbing her breasts as she falls chest first to the ground.

I dust myself off, looking out at the crowd. Katryn was last.

I reach a hand out and help her up. Her wide brown eyes are surprised at the gesture.

"You did well," I nod. "Keep practicing and it will get easier. It's always a struggle at first."

"Was it a struggle for you?" she pants, getting to her feet and shaking the dust off. Katryn wears a simple tunic with matching cotton pants tucked into boots.

"Yes," I admit. "I suspect it's a struggle for everyone, and if they suggest otherwise, they're lying."

She huffs. "I just wish I could figure all of this out *faster.*"

I flash a ghost of a smile. "Don't we all? Work on the basics, repeat them over and over again until you don't even think about it. It will get easier, Katryn. Just keep at it."

Katryn flashes a grateful nod and walks away. It took me two hours to beat three dozen of them.

Humbled. They all look humbled.

But exhausted smiles sit on all of their faces.

"Enough time for one more?" Nyall's voice is suddenly whispering in my ear, and I nearly jump.

"You?" I laugh and the recruits go still, their eyes widening as they watch our every move. Keres and Davyn suddenly push their way to the front, watching too. "You want me to *fight* you?"

"Well, unless you're *scared.*"

I turn to Nyall and pat his arm, "Scared? I am not scared of you, Prince. The only thing I'm concerned about is wounding your precious ego and embarrassing you in front of your entire army when you get your ass beat by a *girl.*"

The crowd *"oooohs"* at my barb but Nyall just smirks.

"You're not the only one who has been training, Blue. Unless you're scared of losing."

The crowd snickers and I glare at Nyall, knowing exactly what he's doing.

"I won't lose," I hiss at him. "Take your position. I'm going to wipe the floor with you, Drayven."

Nyall's eyes go hard at the use of his surname.

"Alright, Prince." I call, "Show me what you've got."

Nyall traces a symbol in his palm and bands of white light suddenly encircle his arms.

"You sure you want to go full magyk?" I ask, but the bastard just smirks. "Fine. Don't say I didn't warn you."

With a single thought, I unsheathe Macha and allow my magyk to explode. Hellfyre unleashes from within, coating the two onyx blades.

I pull harder at the magyk at my core and shadows explode, covering the training yard and drowning out the sun, turning the world dark and eerie.

Nyall's light is easily seen, glowing through the darkness, while I remain hidden.

Just as I'm about to attack Nyall from behind, he blurs, moving so fast I can't track him. By the time I get reoriented, a bolt of white light hits me from behind, blasting me into the air.

Shadows burst from my chest, and I solidify them enough that they take the impact of my fall.

Rolling onto my back, I flip up onto my feet and send a ball of Hellfyre directly at Nyall's stupidly handsome face.

He easily avoids it, but barely.

The smell of singed fabric wafts through the air.

"Not fast enough," I tease, my voice echoing through the shadows.

"Neither are you," Nyall whispers in my ear again and I jump.

How did he get there so fast?

"I always know where you are."

Then he hits me with another blast of white light, but I stop it with a shield of shadows.

At the very moment of his pause, I drop the shield and jump at him with a roar, blades raised. He blocks my attack, which I planned for. While he's busy with my blades, I surround us in Hellfyre tightening the circle until we're barely able to move.

"You cannot escape," I smile. "And you're going easy on me."

"I don't want to mess up that pretty face," he purrs, and I nearly drop my blades.

Which is when he hits me with another blast of light.

I'm sent flying and the shadows support my fall yet again. But my head slaps against the ground hard enough, despite the shadows, that lights flash behind my eyes. Blood fills my mouth as I accidentally bite down on my tongue.

I blink away the stars and stand up, cracking my neck and grabbing hold of my blades once again.

"Playtime's over," I announce coldly and unleash on him. Not with magyk but with my blades. Hellfyre bursts to life around us as I create another circle, blocking him in, while I attack with Neiman and Macha.

Daggers are suddenly in his hands, embedded with illuminated runes along the sharp blades. He parries every fucking shot I take.

Every single one.

We go on like this for minutes, *hours* even. I have no idea how long we remain there, in that fire circle, but he won't give.

Exhaustion begins to wear on me. We both pant heavily, but the fight isn't done.

"Stop fighting me," he whispers, blocking a weak attack with Neiman I was making at his ribs. "Or don't. Either way, I'm not giving up, Blue. Not ever. I will never stop fighting for you."

Nyall smirks at the shocked look on my face and unleashes a wicked kick at my head, using my moment of hesitation to his advantage. I try to avoid the kick, but he still catches me in the jaw. More blood coats my tongue as it floods my mouth, the taste hot and metallic.

As the Prince leans in, I spit the blood right on his face.

The crowd gasps loud enough that I can hear it.

But Nyall just laughs. Then he drops one of the daggers, reaches his hand up, and smears my blood across his face, using it to *mark* himself.

Oh. My. Gods.

Just when I think I can't get anymore shocked and horny, that fucking *bastard* brings his bloody hand to his mouth and *licks* it, tasting my blood. In front of the ENTIRE camp.

I'm fairly certain I'm having a heart attack. My chest is so tight I can't even breathe and all of the blood is rushing to my *aching* core.

Someone clears their throat, and it knocks me back into reality. I attack again, unleashing a wave of Hellfyre so big Nyall can't escape.

He throws his other dagger on the ground as I surround him in flames.

"Yield," I demand.

Nyall smirks. "No."

Then he walks. Through. The flames.

I'm so shocked I nearly forget how to breathe.

"How?"

"How?" Nyall asks as I drop the Hellfyre and allow him to approach. "Do you still not know?"

"I—" I can't even form words. I sit there, gaping like a fish out of water, shocked to the core.

Nyall laughs and tucks my hair behind my chin, "I like this, by the way. It suits you. Brings out your eyes."

Heat surges to my cheeks as I flush. "Thanks."

Then the Prince leans forward and kisses me.

In front of the entire crowd.

"Your flames cannot hurt me, you silly, hardheaded female, because I *love* you."

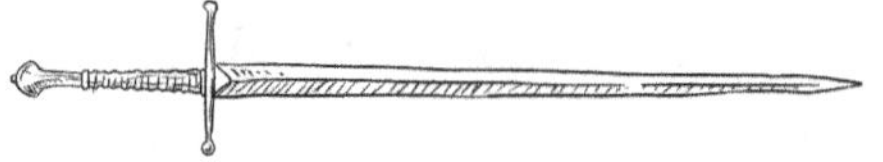

Ryu finds me there. Sitting in the mud. Shocked and numb.

The recruits and everyone else eventually left. Nyall included. I think he knew I wanted time alone.

"Did you know?" I ask her, but I already know the answer.

*"I think you were the last person in the entire camp to figure it out."*

I groan and look up at the sky.

The stars are so bright tonight. Clouds normally cover them, but it's surprisingly clear.

"I don't know what to do, Ryu. I always have a plan—or some semblance of one. But I don't have a fucking clue what the right path is."

*"Love them both. Love the memory, and love the Prince."*

She makes it sound so simple.

*"It is,"* she answers.

You're reading my thoughts.

*"Not really, I can just sense your thoughts through your smell and the sound of your heart."*

Oh. Okay then.

*"This ability is one of the reasons why Dragons are the ultimate apex predator. We can predict our prey quite well."*

Lovely.

*"Think of it this way,"* Ryu says gently. *"Would Os want you to be happy? Would Dyana? Isn't the best way to honor them to live while you can?"*

Hearing their names shatters my heart.

"Yeah," I say in a hollow voice. "I know that you're right, but it's so hard. I miss them so much. I miss her."

*"I know you do,"* Ryu says gently. She lays her big red body down around me, blocking me from sight of the camp and giving me some privacy. Her scales are warm and I snuggle in closer, ignoring the mud soaking through my pants. Wrapping my arms around her as much as I can, I lean into her warmth and try to block out reality.

*"That won't work, you know."*

I hush her. "Let me pretend, at least."

She huffs and a cloud of smoke follows.

*"I know that in your mind, you feel like you need to choose between them,"* Ryu says carefully. *"But you don't. You've never had to."*

"So you did know, then," I sigh.

*"You raised me, as did he. I am closer to Nyall than it might seem."*

"Why didn't you tell me?"

Ryu shakes her head and licks her lips, making a smacking noise. *"It was not my truth to tell. Besides, there is a time when this truth would have made you run away."*

"I would not *run away,"* I grumble, but the words ring hollow.

*"Yes, you would. That's how you protect yourself. Nyall understands, but no amount of running is going to change how he feels."*

Fuck.

"So what do I do?" I ask.

*"I'm a Dragon, and you want my advice on mortal mating relations?"*

I cringe and shove her lightly, "Oh my Gods, *no.* But I just... I don't know, Ry. I feel frozen."

*"I know. You don't need to decide anything right now. But you cannot live your life trying to please a ghost."*

Tears suddenly trace a path down my cheek.

"I know," I whisper to the scarlet Dragon. "I know I can't. But I don't know that I can ever truly move on."

*"You don't need to move on from them. You only need to continue with your life. They will be with you forever, Ama. They will live eternal with every beat of your heart."*

The tears fall harder and I lean against Ryu. Her scales are so warm. Wrapping my arms around her neck, we embrace. The low growls and grumbles of her stomach, the sound of her deep breaths; it calms me. Eventually the tears dry up and I feel like I can breathe without falling apart.

"How is a two-year old so wise?" I mutter, pulling away from her and wiping my cheeks.

Ryu snorts.

*"I'm a Dragon, silly."*

Eventually, we part ways so she can hunt for dinner.

Ryu sleeps in the forest, now. She's grown too big even for the special tent Nyall made.

I make my way to the large mess tent where dinner would be served as the suns begin to set. Laughter sounds from inside and I hesitate, instead glancing through gaps in the tent walls to see who's inside.

Nyall is there, sitting next to Davyn, Keres, Mara and Soren. They look so happy.

Then I spot an empty seat to Nyall's right, along with a bowl of today's soup.

Warmth rushes through me at the realization.

*"Come eat,"* his voice is a low purr through my mind.

*"I will make them uncomfortable,"* I protest, but it's weak.

*"Just shut up and get in here, Blue."*

*"Fine,"* I snarl and push through the tent doorway, entering the light of the room.

The conversation dims as the tent goes quiet, but I try to ignore it as I take a seat next to Nyall.

Everyone watches me with looks varying from fear to unabashed curiosity.

"Hi," Nyall looks up at me with a silly smile and I smell his pear cider.

"More cider?"

Nyall smirks and I flush remembering the last time we had cider together.

Davyn passes me a full mug. "Here. You deserve it after that beat down you dealt earlier today."

"Here, here!" Keres laughs and Nyall pretends to look affronted. To my surprise, the entire tent cheers along and I blink, unsure what's happening.

"They are cheering for *you*," Nyall whispers.

*Oh.*

Out of the corner of my eye, I watch Mara's smile drop. For a brief second, her eyes are full of fear. Then it's gone and her beatific smile returns.

With a thought, I send my swords back to Nyall's tent and stretch my neck, rolling my shoulders in relief at the lack of weight upon my back.

"Here," Nyall puts his mug down and wipes his hand over the back of his mouth. I follow the movement and suddenly I'm staring at his lips. "Let me help."

Before I can protest, his hand is creeping up my back until his bare palm is at the base of my neck.

Everyone pretends not to watch as Nyall starts kneading the tight muscles of my neck and shoulders. It's a struggle not to let out a loud moan at the feeling.

At first, I sit ramrod straight. But the more Nyall works on my muscles, the more I melt into his touch, until I'm almost leaning over.

"Eat," he whispers. "Before you fall asleep at the table."

"Fine." I dig in, enjoying the soup while Nyall rubs my neck and shoulders.

It's divine.

"That was fucking impressive earlier," Davyn says, sipping on his own cider.

"Thank you," I smile softly. "I had a good teacher."

"You trained under the Beast, right? Os?"

The name makes my heart skip a beat, but Nyall's hands squeeze my shoulders lightly, reminding me that I'm not alone.

With a deep breath, I take in the grief and let it fade.

"I did," I answer finally, meeting Davyn's gaze. "I never learned much about my magyk. Os taught me not only how to fight, but how to actually defend myself."

"I saw one of his fights," Soren pipes up. "It was terrifying."

"All of the fights were awful," Nyall says, his voice full of venom. "But Os was the best fighter there."

"They were horrible," Davyn nods and Keres adds in their agreement. "But watching the Beast fight is something I'll never forget."

I smile, "You should have seen him as a Dragon."

Davyn nearly chokes. "Wait, he's a Dragon? A real Dragon?"

"Ah," I laugh, warm and fuzzy from the cider. "You didn't know? It was so obvious."

Nyall chuckles. "I agree."

"He was a Dragon?" Soren asks.

I nod. "His nickname came from the fact that he was Dragon Beastkyn."

*Was.*

The sadness returns and Nyall clears his throat.

"Beastkyn?" Keres asks. "I've heard of the term but I'm unsure of what it means."

Nyall is the one who answers, surprisingly. "It is extremely rare. You're aware of shifters, obviously." Keres nods and Nyall continues, "Well, shifters are mortals, beings that look like us, who *will* their body to shift into an animal. But at their core, they are mortal."

Everyone watches him, like students listening to a teacher.

"Beastkyn are the opposite. They are magykal beings that shift into the shape of mortals, but at their core, they are all animal."

"Wow, so he chose to shift into a man?" Davyn asks.

"It wasn't a choice," Nyall says, his voice going cold. I glance over at him and see shadows within his eyes. "Well, it used to be his choice. But my father used magyk to bind Os within his body, preventing him from shifting for almost 500 years."

The table goes quiet.

It's Keres who speaks up, finally. "He was kept from his true form all that time?"

"Yes," I answer. "Until I burned through his bindings and freed him."

"Only for him to die," Keres shakes their head. "That's terrible. But at least he got to shift again...before the end."

This conversation is taking a dangerous turn. Emotion clogs my throat and makes my tongue heavy in my mouth.

Davyn takes a sip from his own mug of cider. "Well, you're a damn good fighter, Amalia. I hope we can spar too someday, although I better have a fucking ice bath ready after cause, damn, you pull no punches."

My laughter echoes through the tent and I watch several people stop and stare.

"I like the short hair," Soren adds, and I don't miss the way Mara's eye twitches.

"I agree, it suits you," Mara pipes up, clearing her throat.

So why do I feel like the smile on her face is forced?

"Thank you," I whisper. "It...was time for a change."

The heaviness of their stares makes the joy hard, but I try to ignore it.

Nyall leans in and presses a kiss to my temple and my eyes shutter, closing at the feeling of his touch.

When I open them, Davyn is smirking and Keres winks at me.

Oh my *God*. I *am* the last person to know.

*"Everyone knows?"* I ask Nyall.

He snorts. *"Amalia, why do you think I put the rebel base in the godsdamn Ulster Wald?"*

I look at him with wide eyes, and the bastard just smiles at me before taking another sip of cider.

*"Yes, everyone knows. I will never be quiet about my feelings, as if you are some secret."*

Oh.

The emotions well up too fast and I stand quickly. "It was a long day, I'm going to retire."

Everyone nods, slightly alarmed but not suspicious, as I quickly take my leave. The cold night air greets me and I take in a deep breath, but it doesn't work. My chest is tight, and panic makes my thoughts whirl.

I look around at the camp and realize I've been so focused on holding myself together, I didn't see what was right in front of me.

As the panic crests, I take refuge in the shadows, allowing my worries to take over for a moment.

The shadows hold me, keeping me safe from sight and prying eyes.

I don't know what to do next, and that fucking terrifies me.

But I do know that when Nyall touches me, it feels like everything is right in the world. The chaos in my mind stills and everything goes away.

# CHAPTER 29
## MIRIELLE

"What do you mean, 'I need to go speak with the Dragons'?"

Kairos stands before me, arms crossed. A large bag sits on his back, as does mine. I told him I could carry both, but he refuses to let me.

"We need to find a Dragon we can ally with, at least for now. Vesimyr, perhaps?" Kairos suggests and I wince at the thought. "He did tell us where to go."

He sees my hesitation and nods, "Another one, then."

"Why do we need the help of a Dragon? I thought you knew where to go."

"I do, but the volcano is heavily guarded. We need a distraction. A *Dragon*-sized distraction."

Fuck. He's right.

With a sigh, I nod. "Alright. Shit. It has to be one of the Ur Daoinan Dragons I arrived with. The others are insane."

"I agree."

We take off, leaving the castle and venturing into the jungle to the north, heading in the direction of the great volcano that sits in the middle of the island of Elysium.

"The Ur Daoinan Dragons like to gather near here. There's a lake they bathe in."

"Good," I say aloud, but inside, I'm terrified.

Approaching any Dragon is dangerous.

There is no guarantee they will listen. They might just try to eat me.

The jungle is thick and lush, but eventually Kairos stops. I nearly run into his hard back.

"Through here," he whispers. "But we must be quiet."

I nod and follow, crouching down when he does. We crawl through the trees until we approach an opening. I peek through the tall leaves and find dozens of Dragons splashing and swimming in the water.

"Oh wow," I breathe. "I didn't know Dragons could swim."

"They do," Kairos whispers. "But only in lakes."

I look to the side to see him smirk.

Ah.

They *can* swim, but choose not to do so in the ocean for fear of running into an Ascidian.

*Him.*

"Good to know," I murmur, refocusing on the Dragons in front of us. I vaguely recognize some of them. My eyes land on a small Dragon with rich green scales that shine in the light of the two suns.

"That one," I say suddenly. I don't know why.

The green Dragon has one normal wing and one with a broken, out-of-place wing joint.

Kairos glances at me with a raised brow and I nod.

"Alright. That one, then. Are you sure though? It looks like it can't fly."

But...maybe it *could*.

"Can we fix its wing?" I ask him suddenly. Kairos blinks, looking at me before looking back at the green Dragon, accessing it. "With the Elysian? Can we rebuild it?"

Kairos's eyes narrow and he looks at the green Dragon in contemplation. "Yes," he answers finally. "I believe so."

"Good," I say, standing and pushing through the grass. "Then we have something to bargain with."

"Mirielle!" Kairos hisses, but I ignore him.

"Hey!" I shout and the Dragons freeze, all turning to look at me. "Yeah, hi there. I'm the one who rode with you from Ur Daoine. My name is Mirielle."

The Dragons watch me with wary eyes. Some flash their fangs while others back away.

But I'm not looking at all of the Dragons. I'm only looking at *one* Dragon.

The green Dragon watches me with keen eyes. Dragonfear makes my muscles tremble and my heart race, but I ignore it.

"I need the help of a Dragon," I call. "All of you know I'm trustworthy. I flew next to you for days. I helped you escape."

The green Dragon steps forward and my heart skips a beat. The other Dragons meander away, while the green approaches me, bending down until its head is next to mine.

Horns curl up from the Dragon's head, framing it within a delicate crown.

Pale silver eyes, like the color of the moon, watch me with unnerving intelligence.

The membranes of the green Dragon's wings are pale yellow, but the horns on its head are the same green as its scales.

It's gorgeous.

The Dragon approaches, getting closer until its nose is nearly shoving me.

Then it *does* shove me. I almost fall back but catch myself. The Dragon shoves me again, lighter this time, and I shove it back.

"Will you help me or not?" I ask, panting. "Please."

Something brushes against my senses, so strong it nearly sends me to my knees.

*"Why should I help you?"* a feminine sounding voice asks.

The Dragon sounds young. Not a child, but not an adult either.

*"I am the same age as you, mortal."*

I blink. The Dragon is reading my thoughts. "Stop that."

*"Hmm, no,"* she decides and my frustration spikes. *"I am a Dragon. We know much, mortal. Now, why should I help you?"*

The green Dragon bares her teeth, fangs bigger than my head, and growls. The sound vibrates my bones and I have to lock myself in place to keep from crumbling in fear.

"If you help me, I will fix your wing."

*Lir, please let that be true. I do not wish to lie to this creature.*

The green Dragon stills and backs up, looking at me with curious gray eyes.

*"You can fix it?"* she asks quietly.

"Yes. With Elysian. My mentor and I work at the forge—we can use the Elysian to rebuild your broken wing. But I just need help getting it."

*"I see. The answer is no, then."*

My heart sinks. "Please, we can't make it to the volcano without a Dragon."

*"I cannot help you, mortal."*

I look the Dragon in the eyes and shake my head, disappointed.

"I never knew Dragons could be such *cowards,*" I snarl before turning and walking away.

Kairos stands, greeting me, but when he sees the look on my face, he stops.

"We won't get any help." My voice is full of poison. "We have to go it alone."

"Then we go alone," Kairos nods, "and we will figure it out."

Right.

We will figure it out.

*Hopefully.*

We've been walking for hours, hiking through the humid jungle, but the volcano still seems so far away.

So far, we haven't come across any other Dragons aside from the ones flying overhead.

Sweat drips down my back, but after two years of working in a forge, this is nothing.

I've grown used to being *sticky.*

We make camp for the night and sleep beneath the stars, using leaves and rolled up clothes for pillows. I barely slept a wink, mostly tossing and turning, unable to get comfortable.

The next day, we get started at dawn.

"We'll make it to the volcano today," Kairos says as he cuts through more heavy foliage in our path.

Bugs sing their *buzzing* songs on repeat, filling the forest with ever-present noise. It would be nice if they weren't also *biting* us.

I slap my arm, smashing a bug that was sucking blood from my skin. "Fucker."

Kairos slaps his chest, doing the same. "I really hate this place."

"What, they don't avoid Ascidian?" I snort.

Kairos rolls his eyes. "I wish."

I huff a laugh and slap another bug off my other arm. Swollen welts cover my bare skin. The itching is enough to drive me mad.

"Let's hurry up before the bugs drain us dry."

Eventually the ground turns rockier and the foliage thins. Emerging into an opening, we approach a small spring connected to a waterfall. I crouch down and dip my fingers beneath the surface of the water.

With a happy groan at the refreshingly cool temperature, I splash the water on my face and Kairos quickly follows suit. I cup my hands and gulp some down, unable to get enough.

Taking a deep breath, I splash water on sweaty arms.

"I guess this place isn't *all* bad," I huff.

Kairos suddenly jerks his head up, but it's too late.

Something hard hits me from behind, knocking the wind out of me. I'm shot across the spring, landing face first in the water.

Luckily the spring isn't as shallow as it looked. I sink beneath the surface and for a moment, peace returns.

The moment ends, and I kick my legs as I fight my way back to the surface. Something dark and long suddenly darts through the water, and I jerk to avoid it but it's too fast. The object wraps around my waist and *yanks*. I'm lifted from the water and tossed onto the bank. I gasp for breath.

"What the fuck?" I pant.

A loud shout follows, and I look up in horror to see Kairos fighting off a long, wormlike creature with small centipede legs and the tentacles of a squid. The creature clacks its sharp beak, charging at Kairos, but something large and green tackles the creature.

I'm stunned as I watch the green Dragon who turned us down place its jaws around the worm's neck and *bite.*

The worm's neck is crushed instantly, and it dies, slumping to the ground.

Kairos pants, and the Dragon spits the worm out of its mouth.

"Thank you," Kairos says, nodding his head in a small show of reverence.

*"Fix my wing and no thanks is needed,"* the Dragon says, and I can tell the words are said to us both.

"You'll help us?" I gasp. "You changed your mind?"

*"Yes. Now, hurry up. We have a lot of ground to cover and your legs are very short."*

"What do we call you?" Kairos asks as I stand up and wring out my wet clothes.

The green Dragon glances at me, *"My name isn't able to be pronounced in your tongue...but you may call me Basa."*

"Okay, Basa. Lead the way," I nod at her, fighting a smile.

I knew she was the one to ask. As we follow Basa towards the volcano, I send a quick prayer to Lir for guiding me to her.

# CHAPTER 30
## DYANA

No sign of Ignautius.

*"We'll stay indoors."* Vesimyr's voice drifts through my thoughts as we make it back to my room.

He ambles over to the window and spins so that his back is to it. Gingerly, Vesimyr lifts his tail and grabs my mattress, bringing it back. I told him to leave it on the roof. I slept better up there—next to him—than I've slept in ages.

Well, years, technically. The last time I had slept so well was before the Gauntlet—which was well over two years ago.

I don't miss the slight wince of pain Vesimyr makes as he sets the mattress down on my bed frame.

"You need to lay down and rest," I chide.

*"I'm fine."*

I roll my eyes. "Just lay down already. We might as well get some sleep while we can."

He lets out a large huff as I begin making the bed.

Another groan sounds behind me and I sigh.

"Here," I toss the mattress onto the floor, the blankets on top of it. "Lay down and I'll watch over you, okay?"

*"I do not need to be looked after like some helpless **hatchling**."*

Vesimyr continues to complain, but I can tell I'm wearing him down because he curls around me, belly first, despite his protests.

I struggle to swallow at the incredible display of trust.

For such a proud, mighty animal to willingly be at its most vulnerable in the presence of another—it robs me of speech.

"Maybe you don't, but I want to," I say softly. "You watched over me, just like Mirielle. More even, I'd wager."

Vesimyr says nothing, which confirms the thought.

"So, cool your scales and let me take care of you this time, okay? I want to, Ves."

Vesimyr lets out a deep breath and nuzzles against my cheek. *Just this once, I will allow it.*

I snort, "Thank you, oh mighty one."

His snout shoves me lightly and I can't help but let out a loud laugh.

*"I would dearly enjoy hearing some of your stories, Dyana."* Vesimyr says it with a hesitancy that tells me he's not used to being vulnerable with another creature.

I lay back against his neck and get settled. "I always asked Ama to tell me stories when I couldn't sleep. It's only right that I continue the tradition. What story would you like to hear?"

*"Tell me of Amalia and how you met. You've called her both your sister and your friend. Which is she?"*

Though talking about her makes my heart hurt, it also motivates me. I *will* see her again. I vow it.

"Amalia began as a friend, but neither of us have any living family, and neither of us had many friends," I say quietly. "So eventually, friendship turned into family. She and Virgyl raised me."

Vesimyr's tail smacks the floor, startling me.

*"Sorry,"* he murmurs. *"Who is this Virgyl?"*

"He's the Alpha of the Dyre Wolves. He found Amalia, alone and abandoned, when she was a child and took her in. When she found me, she and Virgyl did the same."

*"Interesting,"* Vesimyr replies. *"Tell me about this Wolf."*

I laugh. "He can be a grump, but Virgyl was always kind. He would let me climb on his back and pretend he was a pony."

Vesimyr snorts.

"The best part though was most of his packed lived with us and there were always wolf pups around."

*"Pups?"*

"Yep. Having puppies around constantly was *amazing.* They're so clumsy, with giant paws and no coordination. Many nights I'd fall asleep in a pile of wolf pups, all of us cuddled together." I chuckle. "But it wasn't always fun. Getting so close to the wolves also meant it was hard to see them get hurt. Many creatures reside within the Ulster Wald and the wolves would often return with bloody wounds. Amalia would use her flames to cauterize them, and taught herself to sew so that she could sew closed large gashes."

*"Ah—that's how you knew to cauterize my wound. I was wondering where you thought of that. It was very smart thinking, Dyana."*

I smile. "Thanks. Now close your eyes and let your mind rest. I'll keep talking, but stop fighting sleep with all of these questions and comments!"

*"I don't know what you're talking about,"* he says, but his voice is teasing. *"How about a different story? What about your first romance? I'm not sure what humans call it."*

I blink. "Interesting choice." I nod. "Alright. How about the story of my first kiss?"

*"Scandalous."*

"Shh. Just be quiet and listen," I poke his side.

*"Bossy,"* he murmurs, falling silent.

"Right. Now, where to begin…let's start with the look on Amalia's face when I announced out of the blue one day that I was ready for my first kiss. I thought her eyes were going to fall out of her head. Even her black wolf looked surprised!"

Vesimyr's breathing deepens and I watch as he falls asleep to my story.

I continue on for a few minutes, telling the tale of the girl I danced with, and how her lips tasted like vanilla and cinnamon.

When the story is over, I take advantage of my Dragon's slumber and inspect his wounds more closely. The gashes look better, but they're still red and puffy. The cauterization job wasn't pretty, but he's not bleeding. His body will heal the rest.

I try to shut my eyes, but my mind keeps racing, so instead, I count his scales until I eventually fall asleep.

I don't fall far.

I stay in that half-asleep, half-awake state all night, unable to relax. Because it's only a matter of time before Ignautius shows up.

In the morning, when the sky begins to lighten, I'm woken up by the distant birdsong.

My eyes are so heavy, but I force them to open.

*I won't be meeting Embyrne this morning.* The thought blasts through my head so fast, I nearly get whiplash. Her name wakes me up.

The thought of missing our training used to fill me with joy, but…I do not feel joyous, now.

Vesimyr groans, stretching slightly as his eyes open.

The Dragon's scales are a little paler than normal, but his green eyes are brighter, and not full of pain.

*"I haven't slept that hard in a long time,"* he says in my head.

I'm just about to respond when my bedroom door explodes, sending shards of wood everywhere. Several splinters hit my arms and I scream.

Vesimyr pushes up onto his feet but he's slower than usual and a small Dragon darts forward, slapping a silver band around his ankle.

Vesimyr slaps the Dragon away with his thick tail, snarling.

The silver band flares blue and Vesimyr shrieks in pain.

"Stop!" I shout. "Stop, please!"

I'm already on my feet and running towards him.

Multiple large Dragons appear in the doorway. A mortal looking servant steps forward, walking beneath their stomachs.

"You are summoned," the person says. They wear blue robes with gold embroidery. It's the same shade of blue as Ignautius' scales.

One of his followers, then.

"We did nothing wrong," I say calmly. "Let Vesimyr go!"

"When the Sene Skal summons," the mortal says, "you must answer."

The small Dragon is in front of me, lashing out with razor sharp claws pointed at my face. I bend backwards so far, I should have fallen. Instead, I watch in slow motion as the claws miss me.

The small Dragon growls in frustration and I straighten up, panting.

*"Vesimyr?"* I ask in my thoughts. But there's nothing.

I look around with my magyk, frantic.

Oh Gods.

The cuff.

It cut off his magyk...which means we can only speak aloud.

Shit. *Shit!*

I stop what I was doing and raise both hands in a clear sign of surrender.

Vesimyr glares at me as I address the mortal.

"Fine. We will surrender to the Sene Skal," I say, my voice sounding calmer than I feel. "But hurt my Dragon, and I will hurt you worse. That's a promise."

The Dragons snort, not taking me seriously, but the mortal simply nods and turns.

I take the lead, walking in between the Dragons waiting for us in the hallway, and Vesimyr follows.

As soon as he fully emerges into the hall, we're surrounded. Dragons are on all sides, watching us with bared teeth and sharp armor decorating their scales.

The Dragons shuffle along beside us like dogs herding sheep.

Vesimyr limps slightly, and because of the damn cuff, I'm unable to ask him if he's being serious or faking them out.

Which leads to instant worry about how he's feeling. I try to sneak glances below his belly, but the angle isn't right and I can't get a good look at the gashes, nor do I want to give the guards any reason to be suspicious.

But thanks to Amalia, I know how animals behave.

You cannot show weakness, or else they will cull the herd.

Vesimyr is either making himself into a giant target or convincing them he's not even worth their time.

Unfortunately, I'm unsure of which it is.

Since the castle is Dragon-sized, the walk takes almost an hour.

The halls are empty. I take advantage of the walk to examine the castle. The ceilings are so tall that I can't make out any of the details above my head.

Half of the castle is indoors, but the rest is outdoors. We walk into the morning sun as we cross a large courtyard.

By the time we make it to the auditorium where Ignautius waits, I'm covered in sweat. The open atrium is in the shade, but the ceiling and sides are mostly open, allowing the Dragons to easily fly in and out.

Rows near the highest points are packed with Dragons, with some smaller Dragons down on the ground alongside the mortals.

I say a prayer of thanks that I had the foresight to sleep in leggings, but my night shirt is a thin, white cotton that leaves nothing to the imagination, particularly against my damp, sweat-soaked skin.

The auditorium is packed with Dragons and a small group of mortals.

Part of me is concerned when I don't see Mirielle among them, but my attention quickly shifts to the big blue Dragon in the center of the room...

And the orange Dragon right next to him.

I force myself not to react as I get a full look at the damage I did to the Dragon's wing.

The bones are broken and the membranes between the wing joints are full of singed holes. The orange Dragon holds it awkwardly against its side, glaring at me with murder in its gaze.

**"DYANA ARKOS,"** the Sene Skal booms. **"YOU HAVE BROKEN THE CODE."**

*Fucking hell,* how does he know my full name?

Vesimyr said the Sene Skal had spies all over the island, and he was right. They've been listening to us.

Rage begins to grow deep within me, turning my blood into fire as I burn with anger.

I will not exchange one dictator for another.

"That code only applies to Dragons," I note. "And just as you've told me many times before, I am not a Dragon."

Vesimyr has shared much about Elysium, and my questions weren't merely due to interest.

**"You possess our magyk,"** Ignautius sneers. **"Therefore, I declare you are subject to the same code as the rest of us."**

The Dragons of the auditorium whisper.

I want to smile. Ignautius doesn't realize the gift he's just given me. Vesimyr knows something is up based on the way his green eyes are boring holes into my back.

"Are you saying that I am a Dragon, my lord?" I ask sweetly.

More whispers explode behind me. Vesimyr nudges my shoulder, coming to stand beside me. I lean against his leg, using the touch to ground me.

*I'm not alone*, I tell myself.

**"You make a mockery of our kind,"** Ignautius bellows, speaking not just to me, but to all Dragons watching. **"For your insolence and your actions against one of our own, you are going to die."**

I cross my arms, "What about the three months? There's five weeks left before our deal is through."

Ignautius snarls, making the orange Dragon next to it jump in fear.

**"The deal is through,"** Ignautius hisses, more snake than Dragon in that moment. **"It was over the second you unleashed that awful magyk."**

"I thought the Sene Skal was a Dragon of honor," I note in a bored voice. "I guess that was a lie, too."

Gasps from the audience.

**"I tire of you."**

Ignautius makes a motion and the Dragons who escorted us here suddenly rush us.

I take a deep breath and pull hard on the magyk at my core. It explodes, covering us in light as a giant dome sparks into existence, protecting us from harm. I stretch it as far as it can go, making sure Vesimyr is within its confines.

Loud thumps sound, followed by pained shrieks.

I peel open my eyes and look at the fully formed shield.

It worked. *Yes!*

The Dragons that tried to rush us are getting up from where they fell to the ground. Some clutch their arms, protecting raw burns.

It can penetrate scales.

It can damage them.

Smirking, I look at the Sene Skal, who rages furiously outside of the protective shield.

"If I am subject to the laws of your kind," I say, taking a deep breath. "IGNAUTIUS, SENE SKAL OF ELYSIUM, I CHALLENGE YOU!"

**"You *what?*"** Ignautius snarls. **"You have no right to Challenge!"**

"On the contrary," I smile. "I have *all* the right."

I clear my throat and raise my voice, "YOU HAVE BROKEN THE REFUGE PACT. WHAT KIND OF LEADER CAN'T FOLLOW THEIR OWN CODE?"

The Dragons gasp.

"YOU DECLARED ME A DRAGON. BY RIGHT AND BY YOUR FAILURE TO UPHOLD THE CODE, I CHALLENGE YOU, IGNAUTIUS, TO A FIGHT TO THE DEATH!"

The scream dies on my tongue as my words reverberate throughout the auditorium.

"Take *that,* you fucker."

I see a few of the mortals' jaws drop.

I caught him off guard.

*Good.*

The blue Dragon begins to laugh, and now it's my turn to be caught off guard.

**"You cannot Challenge me,"** he snorts. **"If you knew anything of our code, you would know that Challenges are held in the air. You are physically incapable of such a task, stupid worm."**

The Dragons around us laugh and my cheeks go warm in embarrassment.

I take a deep breath, focusing on the warmth of Vesimyr's scales, and drop the gold shield.

The Dragons who were going to swarm us don't move, wondering if it's a trap.

I look Ignautius in the eyes and lift my chin, "I NAME VESIMYR THE KINSLAYER AS MY CHAMPION!"

Vesimyr looks down at me and nuzzles my cheek. I wish we could speak to each other, but I just hope he knows what he's doing.

Ignautius stills. **"What did you say?"**

A few weeks ago, he finally told me his plan.

I would challenge Ignautius—although we were supposed to have five more weeks to prepare for it—and then I would name Vesimyr as my champion.

**"Are you going to leave your Dragon to fight alone on your behalf? What a selfish little bitch."** Ignautius snorts, his eyes turning to Vesimyr.

I snap my fingers and draw his attention back to me. "I am Vesimyr's Rider. That means we fight together."

Ignautius snarls.

"Well? What say you? Are you going to meet the call, or are you a failure *and* a coward?"

I take a few steps forward, looking up at him. "WHAT SAY YOU?"

The room is so quiet, the only sound I can hear is my own racing heart.

**"I accept,"** Ignautius says finally. Then he looks at one of the Dragons that waits near us.

The Dragon nods and disappears.

A few seconds later and it returns, this time with a snarling Embyrne at its feet.

They have a Dragon who can teleport.

*Fuck.*

The sight of Embyrne makes my stomach drop as a feeling of dread rises.

*Why did he bring her here?*

She stands, glaring at the Dragon who brought her here, and walks towards Ignautius, not even sparing a glance at me.

That's okay. He cannot know how close we've become.

She gives a shallow bow to the Sene Skal, her golden eyes remain downcast in a sign of respect. Which would be believable if it weren't for the thick cuffs around her wrists.

How anyone can look at her and not see a prisoner is beyond me.

**"Ah, Embyrne Ostia,"** Ignautius says slowly. **"The Abomination. You cast your back on your own kind, choosing the form of a mortal over one of divine making."**

Embyrne remains silent, her head bowed.

**"When your brother left us,"** he says, **"I was glad. One less Beastkyn, one less scourge on Dragonkind. I've heard whispers that he perished in Ur Daoine, you know."**

Embyrne says nothing. Her chest barely rises with each breath. She's stiller than the stone holding up this room.

Ignautius sighs and waves his claw, signaling for her to get up. **"I have a gift for you."**

"How generous," Embyrne says in a saccharine voice as she stands. Her head, though, remains bowed.

**"That gift is your freedom."**

Embyrne's head snaps up, her golden eyes wide with shock. "What?"

**"Your little trainee has issued a formal Challenge,"** he says, and Embyrne's flinches. **"She has named her own Champion, but that's a bit unfair, don't you think?"**

No one says anything.

No one moves.

Ignautius looks down at Embyrne with a dark smile, **"Embyrne Ostia, I name you as my Champion. If we win, I will grant you your freedom."**

My heart drops and I stop breathing.

~~No.~~

~~Not her.~~

~~This wasn't supposed to happen.~~

~~Not like this.~~

*This is fine. This will be fine.*

"But—" Embyrne protests, but Ignautius silences her with a raised claw.

**"I am not asking. You will do this, or I will kill you."**

Embyrne's face is pale and cold as she nods.

Then she looks at me, emotionless.

*I didn't think this is how this would go,* I want to tell her.

*I'm so sorry,* I want to scream in her face.

Instead, we each say nothing.

Yesterday, we were colleagues. Perhaps even friends.

Today, she becomes my enemy.

Embyrne shakes her head and looks at Ignautius. "Of course, my lord. I would be honored."

**"Of course you would,"** Ignautius chuckles and looks at me. **"Challenges happen under the light of the full moon. You have 10 days to prepare."**

10 days. 10 days?!

*Fuck!*

Ignautius leans forward until his face hovers in front of me.

He exhales hard and a wave of smoke hits me, making me cough.

His breath smells like rotten carrion, and I struggle not to gag.

**"You will not win this, Dyana Arkos. Enjoy the next few days, as they are to be your last."**

"Embyrne is powerful," I blurt, taking a chance on the big blue motherfucker not seeing right through me. "It's only fair if you remove Vesimyr's cuff. Make this a fair fight. Show the people the true honor of the Sene Skal."

He growls in my face, but the Dragons around him look around, whispering.

And within those whispers, is a tiny seed of doubt.

That's all it takes, and I breathe a sigh of relief. He had to cave. There was no other choice. I forced him into a corner.

A God is nothing without a believer. Ignautius thinks he can play God because he has Dragons to blow smoke up his scaled ass day in and day out.

Remove that, and it's checkmate.

Ignautius senses their wavering and grinds his teeth. **"Fine. Remove the cuff. It makes no difference. You both will lose."**

The Dragons come forward; their movements hesitant as they unlock the cuff from Vesimyr's leg. They scramble away the moment he's free.

*"I'm so sorry,"* I burst into his thoughts with my magyk.

*"Do not apologize. You did well."*

*"But it's so soon—"*

*"Focus on today,"* Vesimyr orders. *"That's all you can do. Focus on what's in front of you, and nothing else. We'll be ready."*

I nod. *"Okay. But, what about Embyrne?"*

Vesimyr looks at me sadly and I feel his magyk brush against mine. It feels almost like...a hug.

*"I'm sorry, Dyana. There is nothing we can do now. Embyrne's fate is sealed."*

I don't accept that.

I won't.

I stay quiet, but within the confines of my mind, I scramble to think of a way to save her.

~~*Please don't make me kill her. Please.*~~

*I have to get home. Whatever it takes, I'm going to get home.*

*I will not abandon my family.*

*"Okay. Okay,"* I say to my Dragon as we're led out of the room. *"10 days. We have 10 days to figure out how to kill them."*

Vesimyr sniffs and flashes a small smile.

*"I have a few ideas."*

I force a smile onto my face. *"As do I."*

“Haste denies all
acts their dignity.”


— Dante Alighieri, 1265–1321.
The Divine Comedy: Purgatory

scan for the pt. 3
reading playlist

PART THREE:
THE DARK

# CHAPTER 31
## MIRIELLE

"I hate this fucking jungle," I pant, swinging one of Kairos' machetes and slicing the giant slug in half.

Kairos grunts in agreement as he brings his own machete down on another slug. Basa stomps on them, shredding their gooey bodies. We came upon the nest of giant slugs randomly. I thought nothing would happen, but when the slugs started to attack us, moving faster than any slug ever should be able to do? That's when I decided I really do hate this place.

"This place is cursed!" I shout, stabbing the last slug and chopping its head off.

A mixture of goo, slime, dirt, and bug bites covers all of my exposed skin and my clothes.

"Basa, how much further?" I ask the green Dragon as she kicks around the slug carcasses.

I've learned Basa does not enjoy being questioned. The more I ask, the more she shuts down. Which is why I'm so surprised when she actually answers.

*"A few hours."* Her voice is suddenly in my head.

Thanks to Amalia doing the same thing two years ago, I can school my shock. But the sudden ancient voice and the presence of the Dragon's magyk makes me tremble, even despite my centuries of experience.

*"Some older Dragons think the magyk of the island causes the creatures here to...change, growing larger than they otherwise would."*

Even Kairos blinks at Basa's words. She said this to us both, then.

"Interesting. That does make sense." I nod. As we continue forward, I find myself getting lost in her scales.

They bear are so many scars.

*"I do not want your pity,"* Basa says suddenly. Kairos doesn't react, which is the only way I can tell this thought is private.

By the time I can make my brain form a response, her presence in my mind is gone.

I've always liked animals. But is this...*guilt,* what Amalia felt? It's so different when you can *hear* them speak.

Lost in my thoughts, Kairos and I follow Basa through the verdant jungle. I nearly trip over Basa's tail as she stops.

The suns are low in the sky.

*"There is a large tree to your left. Shelter there for the night,"* she says before walking off.

True to her word, a large tree full of knots sits just to our left. Below it lies a small, covered hole, surrounded by raised roots. We will be safe here. After walking all day, I'm too tired for dinner. Kairos clearly feels the same. We crawl under the tree and lay out our sleep sacks.

He tosses me some dried fruit and I munch on it before climbing into mine, dirty clothes and all.

Sleep is fitful.

I feel like the moment I close my eyes, it's already morning.

My entire body hurts. I don't think I moved all night based on the muscle cramps I get as I stretch out.

Sometime in the night, Kairos ended up pressed against me. We're not tangled. Each of us lies within our own sleep sack. But his warmth is nice.

Not being *alone* for once is nice. It's the first time I've felt really comforted by another person's presence since we left Ur Daoine.

Kairos is a very attractive male.

I am attracted *to* him, but I don't want love right now. Dyana's memory is too near, and I don't know what the future holds. All I want is to rebuild Forsaken and get back to Ur Daoine.

To get back to the *plan.*

Lir be damned would I fail now.

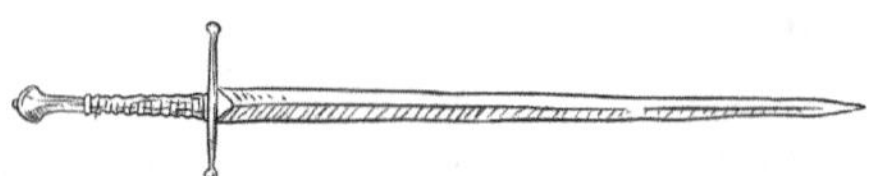

We set off that day and walk for *hours.* Eventually the jungle starts to thin and the ground changes. Moss and greenery turns to volcanic rock as the forest thins. My calf muscles strain as I balance on the rocky terrain. Dirt is smoother, easier to balance on.

*"It will get difficult from here,"* Basa says in our heads suddenly. With her talons, she easily crawls over the rocks.

Kairos nods and glances at her. "We'll be ready."

*"Good."*

"Where will we find the Elysian?" I ask her.

Basa is quiet for a few minutes, then finally answers. *"No one knows why, but Elysian comes from volcanic rock. Something about the rock changes when a Dragon has nested nearby."*

"Fuck," I breathe. "We have to go into a nest, don't we?"

*"Yes. But I will take you to one that is not being used."*

I glance over at Kairos, whose eyes are contemplative.

He understands as well as I do what Basa means.

The nest *might* be empty, but we need to be prepared to face off against angry mother Dragons.

Dragons are dangerous, but none more so than a nesting female.

I might not know *much* about Dragons, but I do know that.

*Lir, guide and protect us.*

A noise calls from above and we glance up to the clouds.

*"Walk beneath my wing. You must not be seen here, or we will all die,"* Basa says, her voice tense.

Kairos and I hurry closer, until we're nearly leaning against Basa's legs. She lifts her good wing slightly so that it's just above our heads.

*"I can feel a nest nearby. Stay on your guard."*

We quietly unsheathe our weapons as we approach the volcano.

Part of me cannot believe we got a Dragon to agree to this.

Basa is putting herself at great risk doing this.

I lay a hand on her leg, but she flinches, leaning away from me. I drop my hand immediately.

*"Thank you,"* I try to send the thought towards her, but I don't know if she hears it. *"Thank you for helping us."*

A few minutes pass, and the air turns even hotter as we climb towards the top of the volcano.

*"Here,"* Basa says quietly. *"There is a small cave just ahead. The nest there is empty."*

Kairos and I struggle up the steep volcano, trying to stay under Basa's wing.

When she stops and goes *into* the volcano, entering a small cave, I breathe a sigh of relief.

Until I see what's inside.

"Oh my god," I breathe, looking past the piles of broken Dragon eggs to the giant Dragon skeleton in the back.

It's curled around a nest of broken eggs, as if to protect its young, even in death.

Kairos places a hand on my shoulder as we leave the comfort of Basa's wing and walk into the space.

"It's ok," I whisper. "Just...sad."

He nods, before pointing towards something in the dark.

It's so hard to see, but there's something shiny in the cave wall.

I walk over to it and squat, pulling a piece of volcanic rock away.

"Kairos," I gasp. "Look."

Behind the black, volcanic rock is pure Elysian.

"Holy shit."

Kairos's eyes are wide as he removes more of the rocks, revealing even more Elysian.

"How much do we take?" I ask him.

Kairos glances around. "As much as we can fit."

There's only so much we can carry between the two of us.

I take a deep breath and turn to find Basa watching us closely.

*"Yes, I will carry some."*

I blink in surprise at her statement. "Are you sure?"

*"My wing might not work,"* she glances back at the broken wing on her left side, *"but I am still strong. Use some of your mortal fabric to create some way to hold the rocks, and you can tie them to my back."*

"Thank you," I bow my head, fighting tears. "We do not deserve your help."

*"You helped us escape,"* Basa says, and this I think is said only to me. *"We owe you our lives."*

"I swear to you, we will fix your wing," I tell her. "You will fly again, Basa."

*"Maybe,"* she says, looking around. *"Hurry and gather your rocks. This is no place to linger."*

Kairos and I get out our axes and get to work breaking open the rocks.

We have to ditch some of our supplies to make room in our packs for the Elysian, and when those are full, we use our sleep sacks, tying them around Basa's neck.

"Is that comfortable?" Kairos asks as he secures one of the bundles.

*"It's fine,"* Basa's words are short, and I feel her nervousness.

"We need to hurry," I tell him, and Kairos nods, securing the second bundle.

"This is all we can fit," he says. "Any more, and we won't make it back."

"Will it be enough?" I ask him and his silence sets me on edge.

"It has to be."

His response doesn't soothe my nerves, but he's right.

We have no other option.

Putting on our heavy packs, we get ready to head back down the volcano when a loud, layered screech interrupts us.

"Fuck," I say.

*"Hide,"* Basa hisses at us.

I look at her, at the way she trembles, and in this moment...I realize my earlier thought was right.

I know why Amalia did what she did.

The thought of Basa protecting us, of getting hurt in the attempt...I refuse it.

I will not stand by while this creature who has risked so much in helping us is injured on our behalf.

**"No."**

My words echo through the cave and Basa growls, but I grab my sword and push past her until I'm standing just near her head.

"I will not hide while you protect us," I tell her firmly. "Whatever it is, we face it together."

*"Stupid mortal,"* Basa snarls, but now I recognize her anger as a front for her fear.

She steps back, hesitating as the Dragon approaches.

We wait in tense silence as it crawls into the cave.

Blue scales, so dark they're nearly black, and eyes of green greet us.

For a moment, I wonder if it will be friendly. That moment is over as soon as the Dragon sees us and bares its teeth, letting out a roar so loud, I nearly wet myself.

*Not friendly, then.*

The Dragon charges and I sprint forward with a scream, but Basa is faster.

I watch in horror as she attacks the bigger Dragon, biting at it and swiping with her claws. The blue Dragon snarls and fights back, scratching at Basa's back.

"The Elysian!" I shout. "Don't let it break the bundles!"

Basa turns, protecting her back, but this leaves her belly exposed.

The blue Dragon lashes out, kicking her into the wall. Basa screams in pain as the blue Dragon claws her belly.

All of the anger stewing within me explodes, as if it was waiting for permission to be felt fully. Mirielle disappears until all that's left is hurt and rage. I charge the bigger Dragon and bring my sword down on its tail, severing a large portion of it.

"LEAVE HER ALONE!" My shout shakes the cave.

The Dragon screams and abandons Basa. Hot, steaming blood spills onto the ground as the Dragon cries out in pain.

It snaps at me and I bend back, avoiding it, but the Dragon's claws catch me in the side, shredding my abdomen. I gasp and drop my sword, clutching my stomach in pain.

Kairos is in front of me a second later as he unleashes on the Dragon.

I blink, watching him fight. I've seen him test some of his weapons, swinging them around lightly, but this is *nothing* like that. His movements are so smooth, it's like he's gliding on air, moving through a graceful dance as he slices at the Dragon.

Eventually, it retreats, bleeding and injured. The blue Dragon flies away from the volcano, leaving us panting and exhausted in its wake.

As the rage fades, fear replaces it.

"It's going to Ignautius," I realize. "We can't let it escape. The Dragon will go straight to Ignautius!"

"It's already in the air," Kairos adds. "There isn't anything we can do."

Basa looks at me and there's a strange sort of *knowing* in her yellow gaze.

*Yes there is.*

*"Do it,"* she says, as she gets up on all fours, not even groaning at the pain I know it caused. Blood drips down her legs, but the green Dragon never complains.

Not once. With a shaky breath, I step outside of the volcano and set eyes on the injured blue Dragon. It hasn't gotten far, flying slowly as blood falls from its wounds.

Smothering any guilt, I grab hold of my magyk, searching for nearby water. There's a stream nearby. I can feel it.

*Lir, help me.* I send out the frantic prayer and *yank* on the water in the stream. It rushes towards me with playful eagerness.

The water levitates, traveling towards me, but I reach my hands out, fingers shaking, and shape it into a rope. Setting my sight on the Dragon once again, I strain beneath the weight of the water as I toss the rope around the Dragon's neck.

For a second, nothing happens.

Then the water obeys my call. It floats into the sky in a thick, moving rope, as the water wraps around the Dragon.

I *pull* with all of my might, channeling centuries of anger and resentment.

Blood begins to fall from my ears and stars burst behind my vision, but I cannot stop now.

I *won't.*

Hands suddenly press against my shoulders, anchoring me.

"Do it," Kairos says, his voice resolute.

The injured Dragon slams into the ground, whimpering and shrieking. With a final breath and a prayer to Lir for forgiveness, I smother it, covering the Dragon with water. The Dragon panics, writhing and fighting, but it's no use. Seconds later, its panic rises, thrashing harder as water fills its lungs. Tears fall from my eyes as I drown the blue Dragon, suffocating it until only an empty, scaled husk is left. I can't let go of the water either.

With a groan, I take it back to the stream, finally dropping my hold on it. Panting, I step away from Kairos. I don't want his comforting touch.

*"Do not feel bad; you did what you needed to,"* Basa says quietly, and I'm surprised when I feel her snout nudging beneath my arm.

I look to my right as she slides up next to me, her golden eyes sincere.

*"Thank you,"* she whispers, and my jaw drops.

She did hear me earlier.

I nod and caress her smooth scales gently.

Basa still trembles beneath my touch, clearly fighting her own demons, but she accepts it.

"Are you okay?" I ask.

*"Are you?"*

I sigh and look down. My abdomen is shredded, but it's just in the top layer of muscle. I will survive and the wounds will close slowly. *Too* slowly.

I glance at Kairos, "Any chance you have a needle and thread?"

Turns out, he does.

He and Basa watch as I sew myself up. Kairos offers to do it for me, but I decline. The pain centers me, reminding me of my path and why I set off on it in the first place. It stings and burns, but soon enough, I've closed the wounds. Movement is uncomfortable as I stand. I can feel the way my flesh pulls against the thread, wanting to separate. It will hold, but the scars will remain forever.

Basa lays down on the volcanic rock. We moved back into the cave to stay out of sight. Showing me her belly, her voice drifts into my thoughts.

*"Please,"* she asks.

"Okay," I breathe, getting more thread. Basa's shallower wounds have already scabbed over, but there's a large open gash in her lower belly. "But I don't think a needle and thread will work. The needle isn't strong enough to pierce your skin, Basa."

The Dragon starts to get up, but I stop her.

"I have another idea. Can you use your Dragonfire on some of the Elysian rocks to heat them?"

"You want to cauterize it," Kairos says, realizing my plan. "Like with Vesimyr."

"It should work just the same, even with the ore solidified."

I nod and Basa relents, unleashing her flame on a pile of Elysian rocks we place in front of her. Even from a distance, her flames heat the air so much it's almost unbearable. Her flames stop, and the Elysian rocks glow. Any longer and they would begin to melt.

"Okay, I'm going to direct you on top of them. We can't pick the rocks up or it would burn us to the bone. But I arranged the pile in the shape of your wound. If you lay on it just right, it will cauterize it for you."

*"Fine,"* Basa says, crawling forward. I direct her carefully over the pile. When it's perfectly lined up, I nod and she lowers herself.

The sound of her flesh sizzling and bubbling against the rocks echoes through the room.

But Basa doesn't cry out. She lays there in silent misery. Watching her does something to my heart. Some of my own misery dissipates. What are matters of the heart, when there is so much *more* at stake? It's a reminder. Love is fleeting. Dyana was...a moment. A part of me will always miss her, but that part grows smaller in the wake of the bigger task ahead.

Basa's bravery, even after all she's endured, makes me feel focused in a way I haven't since leaving Ur Daoine.

After a few more seconds, I have Basa stand up, and sure thing, her wound is cauterized, fully sealing it.

"Good," I say. "It worked. Can you make the walk back?"

Basa nods.

Kairos and I get our packs on again and resecure the bundles around Basa's neck, then we set off back to the keep.

A Demis, a Magyka, a Dragon, and dozens of pounds of raw Elysian.

# CHAPTER 32
## AMALIA

*The terrain is steep, and I struggle to find a rock to hold onto as I climb up the steep mountain.*

*I have to get to the top.*

*"Help," Remus calls. "Help me, Amalia."*

*Oh gods. I have to save him.*

*I climb as fast as I can, straining my muscles to the brink.*

*"You'll never make it." I hear Remus as if he's next to me, but he waits ahead. I can see the glow of his gold eyes, smell his smoked vanilla and leather scent in the air.*

*"I will! I will save you!" I scream at him.*

*Remus laughs, and it's a cold, dark sound. "No you won't. You're too weak."*

*Just as I'm about to reach him, right where the Mountain goes from barren to lush, I trip.*

*"You will lose everyone," Remus mocks. "You're a failure, Amalia. We died for nothing."*

*I try to get back up, but I slip again. The mountain is too steep.*

*"It should have been you," a voice says.*

*It's not Remus.*

*It's Dyana.*

*I gasp as she appears just before me, crouching down with a mocking look in her eyes.*

*"It should have been you who died," she says. Before I can process Dyana's words, her palm lands on my sternum, exactly where the bolt of magyk pierced her chest.*

*Exactly where it killed her.*

*I go to place my hand over hers when she shoves me. Hard. I stumble, losing my balance.*

*Then I'm plummeting through the air as the mountain disappears.*

*She pushed me off the mountain.*

*Dyana's smile is the last thing I see before I close my eyes, just as my body breaks upon the ground.*

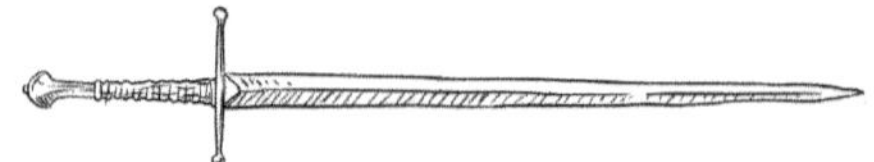

I wake up, panting and covered in sweat. A glance to my left confirms that Nyall is gone. I'm alone.

Outside, the camp is full of activity. I can hear dozens of distant conversations.

We leave for the Mercatus today. Nyall will create a portal for us to the southwestern Ulster Wald. From there, it's a two-day ride to Matricia and the Westlands.

We can't portal any closer, lest we risk being seen.

I take a brief bath, scrubbing off the sweat and trying to shake off the nightmare. Donning leather leggings that easily tuck into my boots and a sleeveless tunic, I go to braid my hair, forgetting it's now too short to do so.

Dropping my hands, I get busy packing my stuff. Once I'm done, I toss on my old gray cloak.

At the feel of it against my skin, my heart steadies and the nerves from my nightmare dissipate.

A large, scaled head pushes into the tent and I meet Ryu's copper and silver eyes.

*"Ready?"* Ryu asks.

Nodding at the red Dragon, I lace up my boots, shrug my pack over my shoulder and leave the tent as we walk together to the training yard.

Despite the fact that we're now in the warmer months, the Ulster Wald remains cold.

Rain falls lightly from gray clouds. A low fog hangs over the mountaintops, making the air heavy.

I watch as the Dyre Wolves play in the tree line, running in and out of sight.

*"We will come with you through the portal, but remain within the Ulster Wald,"* Virgyl had said.

It surprised me that he would use the portal, but the southern Ulster Wald is days away, even for one as fast as a Dyre Wolf.

As we approach the training yard, I feel a wet snout against my hand and look down to find Virgyl at my side.

Instantly, I lean into his thick fur.

*"Climb on,"* he says. *"I will carry you through."*

I'm surprised but nod and climb on, sinking into his black coat.

"I missed you too," I lean down and whisper in his ear before placing a kiss against his neck. He makes a happy, canine sound that warms my heart.

A few members of his pack follow us into the yard.

Everyone stares at the Gray Wytch and her Dyre Wolves.

But I do not mind their stares.

For once, I welcome it; that uncanny feeling of hundreds of eyes set upon you.

*Let them look.*

Chin raised, I continue into the center of the yard where Nyall has his portal ready.

The generals and recruits are there as well, all sporting their own packs and weapons.

Nyall turns and blinks, his mouth opening in shock as he takes in the sight of us.

I blush under his gaze but raise my chin.

"Something wrong, Prince?" I ask.

The use of his old nickname snaps him out of it.

"Not at all," he purrs. With a clap of his hands, his magyk bursts to life as light bands envelop his arms and the portal takes shape behind him.

"Lead the way, Wytch." Nyall bows.

The air shifts, and everyone watches as the wayward Prince Drayven *bows*.

He's deferring to the Gray Wytch.

He's deferring to *me*.

Part of me wants to slap his stupidly handsome face. Nyall just changed the dynamic of our entire mission—of everything, actually.

Those who dislike me will whisper that I've snared their leader, putting him in my grasp to take over leadership.

Those who support me will be emboldened. And the combination of the two will be volatile.

"I hate you," I whisper as I pass him.

*"I call that foreplay,"* he purrs in my mind, and I nearly fall off Virgyl at the words.

The wolf walks through the portal with ease. Ryu and the pack follow close behind.

We emerge through the dark fog of the portal into the southern Ulster Wald.

Virgyl stops in his tracks, horrified by the sight before us.

Trees, rotten and withered, decorate the forest around us.

No animals chitter. No birds call from above.

There's nothing.

It's empty and desolate.

It feels like the forest *died.* There is no life here. Not anymore.

The sight of it crushes me. It feels so wrong.

*"This has to stop,"* Virgyl says to me. *"Before our home is gone for good."*

I hear rather than see the others arrive behind us.

Their gasps of horror make me want to burn Castael Laryn to the ground, starting with the Black Citadel.

"Then we stop it," I say aloud, sliding off Virgyl's back and looking him in the eyes. I caress his snout, holding it in my hands as I touch his mind and make him a promise.

*"I will not let our home disappear."*

Virgyl pulls his face away, tilts his head back, and lets out a mournful howl. The rest of the pack does the same.

The sound is so mournful, many of the rebels start crying.

I have no more tears to shed.

No room for more grief.

Instead, I sear this image into my memories, so that I never forget what I'm fighting for. The air becomes lush with the scent of honeysuckle as Nyall approaches.

He looks out at the dying land like a male haunted.

"We stop this," I tell him. "Whatever it takes."

Nyall meets my gaze and I want to cower in the wake of the pain I see reflected there. I know my own gaze is similar; a mixture of pain, numb emptiness, and rage so great it could destroy a continent, destroy a *world.*

Nyall turns and faces the group behind us, and I do the same. The movement puts me at his right.

*I always end up at his right.* I tuck the thought away for later.

"We stop the Mercatus and free the creatures, dealing a blow to the Archmage. But this?" Nyall gestures to us all. "This is just the beginning. Which is why it's crucial we get this right. We will isolate the Archmage from all of his sources of power until there's nothing left. Then we destroy him and take back our Kingdom."

Everyone nods, wiping their tears away as devastation becomes determination.

"What we do now, we do for the innocent. The ones who have no choice. The ones who have been taken *advantage* of."

I watch him speak, completely hypnotized.

This is the Prince. The Leader of the Rebellion.

This is the person who has earned the loyalty of so many.

We set off, heading South. The wolves will accompany us to the edge of the forest before heading home.

We'll be in the forest for one day, and out in the open for another. Something shoves me and I whirl, ready to slap someone, but my hand stops as I see Aanad.

"Aanad! You scared me," I tell her, leaning forward to wrap my arms around her big Oryx head. "Hi, sweet girl."

Her coat is warm velvet beneath my hands.

"It's good to see you. I've missed you."

Aanad nickers, clearly agreeing with the sentiment.

"I think she likes you more than me," Nyall chuckles, approaching us.

I blink as more horses walk through the portal before Nyall closes it.

*"We need to be quick tomorrow. Quicker than mortal legs can run,"* he says in my mind. *"The less we're in the open, the better."*

*"You're worried about being spotted by the Dragonguard,"* I realize.

He nods. *"Do not let the others know. I don't want to scare them without reason. We might not see them."*

*"But...it doesn't hurt to be prepared."*

*"Exactly,"* he says.

I look around and realize something is missing.

"What will I ride?" I ask.

Nyall smiles, "Well, you can either ride with me, or you can ride Ryu."

The memory of being on her back is still so vibrant in my mind.

*"Do you want that?"* I ask Ryu, finding her mind easily.

I know she was listening.

*"I..."* She hesitates, and it's all I need to hear. *"Not today, Ama. I'm sorry."*

My head snaps to the side. *"Don't you dare apologize. You are in control of your life, Ryu. I will never make you do something you don't want to do. It will always be your choice. No one else's."*

Emotion briefly threatens to overtake me.

I took Dyana's choice away...and it killed her.

I won't make the same mistake again.

"Thank you," Ryu whispers.

I smile at her and she leans her thick neck down to nudge me with her snout.

*"I'm glad it was you, that day in the Arena. I'm glad my mother trusted me with you."*

I inhale so fast, I nearly choke. She nudges me once more and then ambles ahead.

*"Love you, Ama Mama."*

Tears threaten to fall from my eyes at the Dragon's quiet words.

*"I love you too, sweet Ryu."*

As Ryu passes Nyall, who is mounting Aanad, she leans down and nuzzles him with her snout before continuing on by.

Suspicion forms but I keep it to myself, not wanting to offend her.

I walk over to Aanad, the forest floor crunching beneath my feet. Nyall holds out a hand and I accept it, letting him haul me up onto Aanad's back.

I'm in front and I grab the reins on instinct, but he stops me.

"I've got it. Just relax. You don't do nearly enough of that."

I roll my eyes so hard I'm surprised they don't fall out of my head and yank the reins back out of his hand.

"This *is* relaxing, you oaf. How about you sit back and let someone else be in charge for once?"

Nyall blinks, surprised, and his cheeks turn pink. He smiles and wraps an arm around me.

"Fine, lead the way then, Blue." His words are a purr in my ear and I get so tense, it startles Aanad beneath me. I feel her tense up too and force my body to relax despite Nyall's touch.

Clicking Aanad forward, she breaks into a brisk walk. Her gait is so smooth.

It hits me like a brick to the chest.

This is the first time I've held reins in my hands since... *Taran.*

The warm leather turns cold in my palms, and nerves make my stomach turn. Aanad senses my unrest and I feel a warmth of love sent my way.

I send it right back, along with my gratitude. He would be happy I'm with her. Taran adored Aanad. In another life, they would have been the cutest pair. I've always wanted to raise a foal.

"What are you thinking about?" Nyall asks gently. I blame Aanad's hypnotic gait and the way it's relaxing my soul for my honest answer.

"Taran. I miss him," I admit in a quiet voice. "He and Aanad would have made such cute babies."

Aanad's ears flick back, listening closely.

I feel her agreement, and sadness.

"It can exist, you know. In dreams." Nyall's words are gentle, meant to soothe.

I sigh, "My dreams are rather unhappy as of late."

Nyall's hand suddenly is flat on my stomach. He grasps me tightly, pressing our bodies together.

"I could...fix that, if you wanted."

I almost forget to breathe.

"What do you mean?"

Nyall smirks at my back. I can *hear* it in his voice. "I'm a Dreamweavyr, remember? If there is something you wish to dream of, I can make it happen."

Holy shit.

Holy *shit.*

"I would like to help, Amalia, if you would let me."

Gods. I shudder at his words. "How?"

"I can communicate in dreams, but I can also control them. Turn them into nightmares, *or* turn them happy."

*Wow.*

"What about your own dreams?" I ask, curious.

He laughs, but it's hollow. "I can only do it with others. Dreamweavyrs cannot control our own dreams, *unfortunately.*"

"I'm sorry," I say, before I can think better. "That you can't...stop your own nightmares."

I nearly jump when Nyall's lips press a soft kiss against my neck. His touch is warm and a part of me is *screaming* for him to never stop.

"It's alright," he murmurs. "I've been sleeping so *well* as of late."

My hands tremble as he presses another kiss against my neck.

Then someone shouts in the background. Just a roll call, but it's enough to snap us out of it.

I gasp and lurch forward. Nyall lets out a frustrated sound.

"Could your father do it?" I try to think of anything but his lips on my skin. I continue prodding him with questions as I steer us through the woods. Honestly, Aanad is steering herself. If I need to guide her at all, I use my legs anyway. The reins are just there for show at this point.

"No, our magyk was always very different," Nyall says with a tone of frustration.

"Was your mother a Dreamweavyr?" I ask, and he goes quiet for a moment.

"I do not know. I don't think so. But it's a power that one can easily hide. She, or someone in her family, must have had it. That's all I can guess."

"Seems likely," I agree.

Aanad steps over a log and it makes me lean back harder. Nyall's arms keep me steady, but it makes our bodies even closer.

"You're avoiding my question again," he whispers, leaning his chest against my back. The feel of his hard muscles *flexing* against me sets my heart racing.

Forcing my mouth to move, I manage a response. "I'm caught between the desire to *never* let anyone control my dreams, and the fact that my nightmares regularly leave me exhausted."

"Two valid points," he says. "You don't need to answer now, I was just being a dick."

A laugh escapes me and I glance over my shoulder to meet Nyall's wide, amazed eyes.

"You said it, not me," I wink at him. "Though I do agree."

Nyall laughs too. "Thank you, Lady Sunshine. Lady *Kindness.*"

I snort, and soon, we're giggling like children. As our laughter dies, so does the joyous adrenaline.

I'm left with the hollow realization that I never laugh like that anymore.

Not since Dyana left, and even then...it was rare.

Joy is so unfamiliar, it leaves me frozen. Unsure what to do in the face of it.

But it also makes me sad.

As a child, I had so much of it. When my parents died, a part of me died with them.

The part of me that *lived,* and loved to do so.

"Come back," Nyall whispers in my ear. "Come back to me."

"I haven't gone anywhere."

Nyall huffs. "You disappear all the time, Blue. Into your own mind. You'll get this look on your face and go quiet," he explains, and a mixture of shame and embarrassment fills me. "It's like the memories *steal* you away from me."

"I didn't...I didn't know it was noticeable," my voice trembles.

"It's not," Nyall reassures me. "I just notice everything about you, Amalia. Every-thing."

My heart warms. Shame and embarrassment turns into surprise and something I don't have a name for. Something hot and potent.

We ride until nightfall, mostly quiet, sans a few conversations here and there. The mood is tense and serious.

*This has to go well.*

As we all lay out our sleep sacks, Ryu curls around us, tucking me close to her body. Nyall too.

Between her and the wolves on the other side of us, we're surrounded by warmth.

*"Goodnight, Amalia,"* Nyall whispers across my mind.

I hesitate.

*"Nyall?"*

The Rebel Prince turns to me, his mismatched eyes clear and true.

*"Can you...fix my dreams tonight?"*

Nyall's eyes widen before he schools himself.

*"I would be honored, Blue."* His voice is full of awe. Like he never thought I'd actually agree to let him into my mind willingly.

*"I'm trusting you,"* I say, quiet even in the silence of our minds.

I want to sleep and have it be *restful.* I also know I need it for what's to come.

We have to stay at an inn in Martricia tomorrow night, and I doubt I'll get much sleep there.

"Rest," Nyall says aloud, and something about the tone of his voice makes my eyelids heavy. I feel his warm lips press against my temple. He stays there for a moment, *inhaling* me like a drug. "I've got you, baby."

Sleep takes me and I fade away, curled against Nyall Drayven.

*I sit in a field of flowers, horses grazing around me. A soft nose nuzzles my shoulder.*

*Expecting Aanad, I turn, and my jaw drops as I see the horse it belongs to.*

*"Taran?"*

*He nickers, and I can't help but cry.*

*They're happy tears for once.*

*I throw my arms around him and he licks my cheek happily.*

*There's someone in the distance, but their figure is blurry. A male, I think. I smile and wave, happy and without fear for the first time in so long.*

*Even though it's blurry, I can tell the male waves back.*

*We stay like that for hours, Taran and I. Or at least that's how it feels.*

*Eventually, he bows, letting me climb onto his back. Taran breaks into an easy trot before building to a soft, rolling canter.*

*Tears stream down my cheeks and I let my head fall back as laughter explodes from me.*

*I know this isn't real, but Gods, do I wish it was.*

*This is more than a mere dream.*

*This is Paradise; a piece of it, and I never, ever want to let it go.*

# CHAPTER 33
## IREYNA

"I want you to find out the location of the Asteroth girl. She's been a problem for long enough; it's time to get rid of her."

I nod at the Archmage's orders.

I agree. There's just a tiny problem.

"He's not going to tell us where she is," I sigh. "Os is a stubborn motherfucker."

"Then we trick him into it. Start with questions about her. Then mention the incident in Panormus. Bait him into giving us intel on her. If pain isn't working, then we go after his motivation."

"Good idea, Father. I will do my best."

The Archmage looks at me, His purple eyes eerie and glowing. I shiver beneath the weight of His stare.

"Don't do your best, *succeed*. Or else I will find someone else who can."

I grind my teeth together and nod.

The Archmage sighs and leans back in His wooden chair. Made out of black wood and carved into an elaborate filigree along the edges, it resembles more of a throne than anything else.

"Your feelings for that beast. They're getting in your way."

Biting my tongue until blood fills my mouth, I grimace.

"Leave your feelings in the past, child. They will not help you now. Do you think, even if he gave us what we needed, I would let you *fuck* Remus Ostia?"

I jerk back as if slapped. My face flushes hot and red with embarrassment and horror.

"N-no."

The Archmage slams His palm down on the stone table. "No! Exactly. There is *no* future for you and that miserable beast. None. He's going to die, and I'm going to kill him. Right now, it's just a matter of what we can find out first. But mark my words, child, he *will* die. As will the Asteroth girl. That is the wish of Sol Constantus."

I gasp at the name.

The Archmage's face turns serene and he leans back in his chair.

"He sent you a vision?" I breathe.

The Archmage nods. "He did. I know our path forward. The Asteroth girl, the beast, the prince; they all need to die. The rebellion must be put down for good."

*Why is it always her?* Amalia Asteroth has been a pain in my side for the last two and a half years.

"I will see it done."

"Good," the Archmage nods before lifting his hand and waving me off. "Now get out."

I stand and bend over in a deep bow, before turning and leaving the room.

Anonyme can wait.

Today, I have a prisoner to torture.

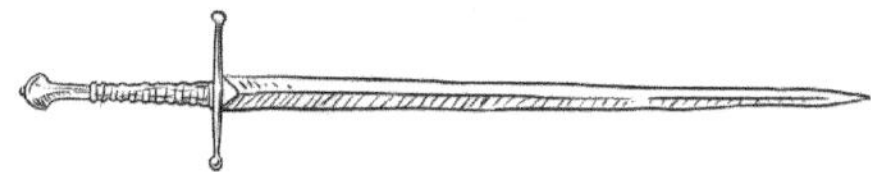

"Oh good, and here I was getting *bored.*"

Os' snarky voice hits me the moment I walk into his cell.

He's strapped to a metal table in the middle of the room, unable to move.

It's still a shock to see all of that wavy black hair gone. We have servants shave his scalp once a week.

The first thing I learned about torturing someone is to remove their identity. Give them nothing to hold onto. Nothing to *hope* for, and just when they finally give up, you offer something shiny. Something *tantalizing*.

Then they're in. Mentally fucked and roped into helping their own jailer.

"There was an attack in Panormus around a week ago. Do you know who was behind it?"

Os scoffs.

"Your little girlfriend."

The Beast goes still, his bright gold eyes *burning* with rage.

"It's such a shame though, about the explosives we rigged. Nobody knows whether or not she survived, but...let's just say, the piles of ash and bones were quite telling. Sorry to be the bearer of bad tidings."

Os snarls and lunges, trying to break his restraints. But they don't budge.

I smile and laugh. "I, for one, am a little relieved! She's mortal after all."

"I'll rip your fucking throat out!"

I shrug. "That would make it hard to tell you what else we learned. Amalia wasn't alone." I note the way Os goes still, his muscles tensing up as a wild look takes over his face.

"The *Prince* was with her." I smirk. "And I don't know about you? But I'm really hoping he's one of those piles of ash."

"LIAR!" Os roars.

"Oh calm down," I roll my eyes. "I'm sure they made it out just fine. I mean, they're what...invincible? What even *are* their powers?"

Os doesn't reply, he just growls and tries to wiggle out of the restraints.

"We have scouts that gathered the piles of ash, and the Holy Father is going to run some tests on it. We'll know soon whether or not your girlfriend and the Drayven bastard are dead."

Os pauses and looks at me, his head cocking. Then a wicked smile breaks out on his bruised face. Even beaten, even jailed, even broken down and tortured; Remus Ostia is still gorgeous.

"They're not dead," he says calmly. "You are lying."

*Come on. Come on. Tell me something!"*

"Shall I bring the results to you myself? We can read them together."

Os bares his fangs. "Fire won't hurt her. Not now. Do you really think they're both so easily killed?"

*Yes. There we go. Keep talking.*

"I watched her get burned in the Gauntlet. Now who's the liar?"

Os scoffs. "Dragonflame is different. Nothing is immune from that."

*Okay. Good.*

"And the Prince?"

"Do you think Nyall Drayven survived almost 500 years under Achan's claws to end up being taken out by an *explosive?*" Os laughs. "You're a fucking idiot if you believe that. His magyk rivals the Archmage himself."

My fist meets Os' face with a *crunch* of blood and bone.

I lean forward and spit. "No one is as strong as the Archmage. That's blasphemy!"

Os just smiles, blood and all. "What's wrong, mad I insulted your little priest?"

I punch him again and unleash my full strength. So rarely do I allow myself to use all of the tools at my disposal.

Os' face *cracks* again as I shatter his bones. He moans, but not once in the last two years has he screamed in pain.

Not *once.*

Father said no violence.

Just this once, I think Father is wrong. Walking over to the laid-out tools, I grab a long, sharp scalpel.

"Tell me more about their powers, and I'll leave."

Os looks away.

"Or, I will slice the skin off of your back, piece by piece. Your choice."

Remus Ostia turns his head and meets my gaze in a direct challenge.

"I see," I sigh. "Very well."

I walk over to the table and motion for Fae attendants to enter the room. They bustle in, electric prongs at the ready. Os is turned without being fully unbuckled from the restraints. Now his back is to me, and he's face down on the table.

I lean down until we're eye to eye. "Tell me about Amalia's magyk. Can she talk to animals? Can she make plants grow? What's her Arkaydian affinity?"

Os spits in my face. I wipe it off with the back of my hand. Then I lift my scalpel and flash Os a smile, showing him just how much I enjoy this.

"I'm going to make you *scream.*"

Then I start slicing.

# CHAPTER 34
## DYANA

I jump onto Vesimyr's tail, avoiding impalement on the spikes at the very end, and run up his back. It's still a struggle to balance, but I've gotten better, and luckily Vesimyr is standing still on the *ground* instead of airborne. Thankfully that means I'm not also being slapped around by his wings.

We first tried this as he was lying down.

Then he stood up and had me do it.

I fell on my face so many times, I think I have a permanent bruise.

Now we've moved onto doing it while Vesimyr is walking.

It's not a complete straight shot up his spine due to the spikes protruding every third meter. I have to weave in and out while maintaining my balance and speed.

Doing it while he's moving beneath me is near impossible.

"And I'm supposed to be able to do this while you're flying?!" I scream as a tree branch smacks me on the face, scratching my cheek. I dip down and get poked in the side by one of his spinal spikes. "Ouch," I hiss.

*"You alright back there? I'm hearing a lot of complaining."*

"Shut up!"

*"We have four days left. You need to be able to mount and dismount in any situation, and we still need to practice falling, my young friend."*

"I don't particularly want to learn how to fall, Vesimyr!"

*"Hatchlings are taught to fly by being tossed off the side of a cliff—or a volcano."*

*Good Gods.*

*"Oh, and you need to practice keeping out Embyrne,"* he adds unhelpfully. *"You have to prevent her from taking your magyk."*

"What about you?" I pant, making it to between his shoulders and sitting down with a huff. He stops and sits, making me tilt backwards. I tumble right off his back with a loud shriek. "Am I the only one practicing things over here? Can't you practice, I dunno, not being *grumpy?*"

*"I am not grumpy,"* he objects. *"I am old!"*

"Grumpy *and* old," I shout back as he starts walking again. He trips and I go sailing off his back, falling face first into a mud puddle.

"You did that on purpose!" I hiss at him as I lift my face, wiping it out of my eyes.

*"You need to be able to stay on in any situation, at any moment."*

I roll my eyes.

"Fine."

*"Summon your swords and let's do that again. Tomorrow, we're doing this in the air."*

I sigh and pull on my exhausted magyk, summoning the light and shaping it into a sword.

"Let's do this."

"One of your spikes stabbed me," I tell Vesimyr over dinner.

Vesimyr sighs. *"Yes, that's what they're supposed to do. Although I'd much rather you not impale yourself on me, please."*

He insisted we eat outside of the castle, no longer trusting their food. When I asked if he thought they were going to poison us, he just looked at me.

I don't know what sort of animal he caught, but I was shocked when he had me build a fire pit so he could roast it.

"Thanks for not making me eat this raw. That would be really gross," I say to him. "It's surprisingly good."

The meat was tender and flavorful despite the lack of seasoning.

*"Want to know what it is?"* he asks.

"Nope."

Vesimyr snorts, *"Very human of you."*

"Oh hush."

We both fall silent, finishing our dinner. Afterwards, I grab a hollow coconut shell and go to the stream nearby for some fresh water.

Vesimyr follows me, leaning down and gulping down water directly from the stream.

"I want to talk to her," I say, and he pauses, looking at me. "Embyrne. I want to...talk to her, before the fight."

*"I don't know that it's possible, Dyana,"* Vesimyr says carefully, regret in his tone.

I look at him and train my face into the picture of innocence. "What if you...use your magyk? Use an animal to get her a message, or something?"

*"And expose what will be one of our greatest advantages over them? Absolutely not."*

I wipe the water from my lips before tossing the coconut on the ground.

"You're right. I'll find her myself."

Vesimyr sputters, following after me as I walk back to the fire to grab my stuff.

*"Where do you think you're going?"* he asks.

I crack my neck and pocket the spare meat I snuck into my pockets.

"I'm going into the tunnels."

Vesimyr blinks.

*"You can't go alone!"*

I cross my arms, "And you are too big to go unseen, my scaled friend."

Vesimyr, I swear to the Gods above, *pouts*.

"Don't give me that look, you know I'm right. But you don't need to worry. There is, uh, one thing I figured out about my magyk that I haven't told you about."

Suddenly I'm nervous.

I take a deep breath and pull on my light. It coats my skin until it covers me completely—which is exactly when I disappear.

It shocks Vesimyr so much that he jumps back, crashing into a few trees. They fall with a huge thud as the Dragon blinks rapidly.

I release the light, letting it dissipate, and pop back into view.

*"How?"* he asks, immediately coming over to inspect me.

"It occurred to me after I realized I could shape and solidify the light. If I can shape something, I can also bend it."

*"A refraction,"* Vesimyr nods. *"Or a glare, even."*

I nod. "Rendering me invisible. Well, not fully. If you look closely enough, you can see the air shimmer. I did it in front of the bathroom mirror, once. But if you don't know what to look for..."

Vesimyr bares his fangs in a toothy grin. *"You continue to surprise me, my young friend. This gives us a new advantage."*

I take a deep breath, "And...it allows me to navigate the tunnels unseen. Theoretically."

*"You're serious about this, then?"* he asks.

I nod.

Vesimyr sighs, standing. *"Then go tomorrow during the day. Do not go tonight."*

I blink. "Okay. Tomorrow then."

*"Dyana…"* Vesimyr hesitates and then shakes his head. *"Never mind. Let's get to the den and get some sleep. You look like you're about to keel over."*

I roll my eyes but nod, knowing he's right. We pass the fire and Vesimyr stomps on it, dousing the flames in a single move.

The moment we got back from the summons, we left the castle, moving into the forest.

Vesimyr and I built a makeshift tent out of woven logs and leaves, using the tree coverage for protection.

They know where we are, but now we have some privacy. Most of the other Dragons are inland near the volcanos. The only things that inhabit this forest are the—

SQUEEE! A piercing shriek explodes from my left and I nearly jump out of my skin as a wild boar comes racing at us.

This isn't like a normal boar, either.

It's as big as a fucking *horse*. I haul ass to scramble up Vesimyr's scales. The Dragon jumps, avoiding the boar's large tusks, before he lunges at it, impaling the beast with his claws.

The boar squeals in pain as Vesimyr pulls his claws out, slicing open the beast's belly. Steaming organs fall to the ground as the boar topples over and dies.

Vesimyr sighs. *"Well, we can save him for breakfast?"*

I slap his scales and climb back down. "That's disgusting."

Vesimyr rolls his eyes. *"If we don't, other boars will come eat him and then we'll have a whole pack of them on our hands."*

I wince. "They're cannibals?"

Vesimyr picks up the boar with his tail as we walk back to our tent.

I fall onto the bed that Vesimyr insisted he carry with us, making me feel rather spoiled by the big guy.

For such a large creature, he was really quite the softie.

Vesimyr dumps the boar and wraps it tightly in some leaves before placing it up in the trees, away from prying noses. He curls his long body around to lay down next to me, his head resting on his legs.

*"Dragons are cannibals."*

I blink. "Explain."

*"When a Dragon kills another, consumption is usually part of the process."*

"Yeah, but that's...that's not the goal, right?" I ask, nervous.

Vesimyr sighs, *"Let go of the human, Dyana."*

Rolling my eyes, I groan aloud because I know he's right.

"Okay, so...you've eaten another Dragon?"

Vesimyr just looks at me. *"I'm proud of you for asking, but I can feel the way you're uncomfortable about the question. We do not need to talk about it, Dyana."*

"But you said stop being human," I protest.

*"I know,"* he nods. *"But that can also take time. You do not need to do it tonight. Focus on getting some rest, because I can also feel how tired you are. Magyk drains, Dyana. You have to refuel it with food and rest."*

I stick my tongue out at him, and he chuckles. "I hate it when you're all wise."

*"Yes well, as you like to remind me, I'm old as dirt,"* he says in a dry voice. *"That means I've seen some things."*

I snicker and lie down, still in my clothes just in case we have to run. My muscles are exhausted and the moment I relax, I begin to fall asleep.

I was going to ask for a story, but I don't need to, apparently.

For once, I do not dream.

Not even of the mountain.

The next day is here, and my eyes are opening with the rise of the suns, despite the fact that it feels like I just fell asleep.

*"You didn't move once,"* Vesimyr says. *"I almost thought you died, at one point. Then your chest moved."*

"That's kinda creepy." I look over at him. "Were you just watching me sleep?"

Vesimyr ignores me. *"How do you feel?"*

"Much better. How long was I out?"

*"Almost 10 hours."*

"Wow, I can't remember the last time I slept that long."

The Dragon reaches up and grabs the boar from the tree. *"I'll get breakfast going. Grab some water while I start the fire and get this roasted for you."*

"Oh God, we really are going to eat it?" I ask.

Vesimyr blinks at me and I force the guilt and icky feelings down.

"Thank you for cooking it," I whisper, sincerely grateful because I know he's trying and it's the best he can do with the situation we're in.

Vesimyr blinks again and nods before stalking off into the forest, the trees swishing with every movement.

I quickly strip off yesterday's clothes and put on a fresh, nearly identical blue cotton tunic and pants. I stuffed as many clothes as I could into a large sack-bag that Vesimyr found. He said it's Dragon-sized, which is why it's nearly the size of me. I cannot carry it myself, but with four large claws, *he* can.

I'll take the forest.

I'll take the wild boars.

I'll even take humidity that makes me constantly sweaty.

But if I had to pick one vice, it would be that of clean clothes.

I follow for a bit before turning right and heading to the stream. I grab two hollow coconuts and fill them. I chug the first before I even leave the stream, gasping for breath as I come up for air.

I didn't realize I was so thirsty. Damn.

I refill it and head back to camp, coconuts full of water in my arms sloshing with each step. Any water I don't drink can be used to douse the fire.

The boar is perfectly roasted and sizzling when I return. Vesimyr pulls it off the flames and uses a single nail to slice sections of crisped-up flesh.

I force my thoughts to empty. Refusing to think about the animal's death.

It tried to attack us, after all.

The meat is lean and juicy, and the skin is perfectly crisp. Vesimyr hands me a few more slices and I devour it all.

"Take the rest," I tell him, and he nods.

I watch as he tosses the roasted boar into the air, snapping his jaws around it. The crunch of meat and bone makes me want to wince, but I fight it.

I don't want him to think I'm disgusted when he's done so much to keep us alive.

He swallows it and licks his lips, his split tongue like that of a snake.

*"Good. Now, we practice."*

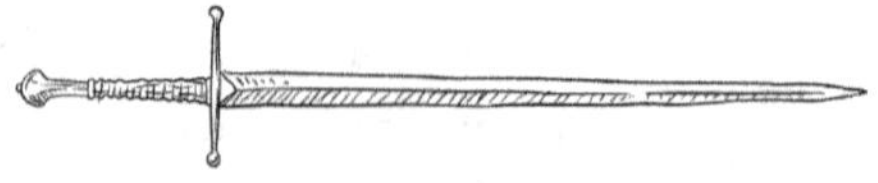

The suns are high in the noon sky above our heads, turning the tropical forest into an inferno.

"Gods, it's hot today." I groan.

Vesimyr nods. *"We're done for now. You need to get to the tunnels. This is the perfect time to do it."*

The lethargy from the heat disappears in an instant.

"Okay. Right. Let's go."

He nods and marches off into the forest. I remain on his back for the ride, and considering how long it takes, I'm glad for it.

We reach the abandoned arena Embyrne used for training an hour later.

"It was so much faster to fly," I mutter, and Vesimyr snorts.

*"This is the safest tunnel to use, as it's the farthest away from the castle. I will give you directions in your head while you walk."* Vesimyr brushes his magyk against mine, *"I can get a basic sense of your location when our magyk is connected. That, and I can smell you."*

I frown. "Gross."

*"You need to hurry and get back before the suns set."*

"Nighttime in the tunnels isn't fun?" I ask sarcastically.

But Vesimyr looks back at me with a serious look in his eyes. *"It is not, and if they go for you in there, I won't be able to get to you in time. Be fast, Dyana. Do not linger. Say what you need to and leave."*

I nod, "Got it."

He climbs up into the partially enclosed arena and I slide off his shoulders, landing in the dirt with a thud.

Walking up to the large tunnel doors, I force my heart to calm, refusing to be nervous.

I can't be.

With a deep sigh, I pull at my magyk, coating my skin in light until there's no visible cracks. Then I *bend* it, angling the light.

*"There, I can't see you at all."* Vesimyr nods. *"I'll wait for you here."*

"Okay, I'm going in," I tell him.

With a deep breath, I step into the darkness.

The light disappears as I descend into the earth, the ground sloping beneath my feet.

I feel like an ant trying to sneak up on a bear.

The tunnel is quiet.

The only sound to be heard is the soft squishing noise of my footsteps sinking into the dirt floor. I try as hard as I can to make no sound, but I also need to hurry.

Eventually, the tunnel becomes so dark that I can barely see.

I take a deep breath and hold onto the light covering me, while I push more light through it, creating a small floating orb to guide the way.

I test it, pulling and pushing my magyk as the ball expands and contracts.

With another quiet breath, I continue on, alone in the darkness.

Eventually, the tunnel begins to change. It breaks off into other tunnels, going in different directions throughout the island.

I float the orb higher, examining each tunnel option. Giant scratches and gouges mark the walls of most of them.

*"Take the tunnel on the left."* Vesimyr's voice sounds in my head, and I nearly scream.

*"You scared me!"*

*"Sorry,"* he says in an unapologetic tone.

I turn left and gingerly head down the new tunnel.

More scratches and gouges appear, decorating the ceiling and the walls above me.

Small, glowing bugs appear in the dirt. They crawl along the ceiling and the walls, allowing me to let the orb diffuse. The bugs provide enough light that I can see without it.

*"It's empty, like you said,"* I tell Vesimyr.

*"Good. Still, you need to hurry."*

*"Shh, I'm concentrating,"* I chide, mostly because I'm nervous. *"The glowing bugs are cool though. As long as they don't start dropping on my head."*

*"They're pests, actually,"* Vesimyr sighs. *"They like to attach to the skin between our scales and burrow into our muscles to lay their larva."*

I wince. *"Ew. That's disgusting—and noted."*

I can feel the big Dragon nodding.

*"Do me a favor and step on a few of them,"* he mutters in an annoyed voice. *"Last time I went in the tunnels, I had dozens of them in my skin. I still get itchy in the spot."*

*"I see. So you decided to stay back not because you were afraid of being seen, but because you have beef with some glowing bugs."*

*"That's not true!"* he hisses, and I can't help but smile. *"I just really hate them, is all."*

*"Uh huh."*

We go quiet as I continue my progress through the tunnels.

A noise sounds ahead, and I freeze.

*"Something is coming,"* I whisper to Vesimyr.

*"Let me see,"* he responds, sounding concerned.

*"What do you mea—"* I nearly choke on my words as his magyk suddenly encases me and my vision turns shimmery.

*"What are you doing?"*

He chuffs. *"It's called Dragonsight. We can see through each other's eyes. Centuries ago, it was a common trait between Dragons and their sworn Riders. It was one of the reasons Dragon Riders were so powerful."*

Oh wow.

*"You're seeing what I'm seeing."*

I hear him make a noise of confirmation. *"Now, hush while I figure out what's coming."*

He's quiet for a moment and we both listen to the shuffling sounds. *"You should be fine. It's not a Dragon, it's a millipede."*

I blink. *"That sounds a lot bigger than a millipede, Vesimyr."*

*"Elysium creatures are...different."*

*"Oh my Gods, Vesimyr, tell me it's not a giant fucking WORM."*

*"Technically they're not worms,"* he starts, but my shrieking thoughts cut him off.

He sighs at my cursing and blubbering, *"Plaster yourself against the wall to your left and when it approaches, hold your breath. It can't see anything, so as long as you stay out of the way and don't make any sound, you'll be fine."*

*"Great,"* I mutter, doing as he says.

The moist smell of dirt is overpowering as I flatten my body against the wall, crouching down slightly to make myself as small as possible.

I force myself to take slow, quiet breaths and slow my heart, despite the fact that I'm sweating profusely as a millipede the size of a fucking horse comes into view.

My mouth floods with saliva as my stomach threatens to turn.

Giant antennae flick and wiggle around, testing the air. Thick boney plates cover the creature's body. But the hundreds of black legs moving beneath it is so gross, I have to look away.

*Don't scream, Don't scream.*

I repeat the thought over and over to myself, feeling as the millipede's legs skuttle over my feet. A stray antennae hits me in the face, caressing my cheek slightly.

I force myself to complete stillness, despite the way I'm screaming internally.

My light shield holds strong, and the millipede continues on the way I just came.

*"I fucking hate it here,"* I curse to Vesimyr. *"I hate it so much."*

*"Not to worry, I shall eat the bug when it emerges from the tunnel. You won't see it again."*

I wince, *"Gross. So fucking gross."*

*"They're quite tasty actually."*

*"Great, more for you then."*

He snorts, *"Now hurry up. Your time is dwindling."*

*"How much longer?"* I ask, stepping away from the wall and continuing on down the tunnel. I try to increase my pace while not making much noise, but it's a hard balance to strike.

*"A few minutes and you'll be near the castle. Embyrne's, uh, den is near there."*

*"Why did you say 'den' so weird?"*

He's quiet for a moment, *"I'm afraid you'll have to see for yourself."*

Nerves kick in and my heart races.

*"Don't scare me,"* I chide him jokingly. But he doesn't laugh.

Gods.

What am I going to find?

After a few minutes of walking, the tunnel changes, breaking off into multiple different smaller tunnels.

*"Fifth tunnel to the left, and then the third on the right."* Vesimyr directs me and I follow.

Fifth tunnel on the left, and then third on the right.

The dirt beneath my feet turns muddy and suddenly the ground begins to slant.

I'm going deeper into the earth. The dank scent of moist dirt turns cloying, invading my senses until I'm nearly choking on it. The only light down here comes from me.

A weight settles on me as my magyk begins to tire. This is the longest I've held any light form without a break, and I can feel it. Like a tired muscle, with every second it becomes harder to hold it together as the weight becomes heavier.

*"You're getting tired. Do not drop your light, Dyana. Pain and exhaustion...they are things we create in our minds. You are strong. Do not let it win."* Vesimyr sounds in my head, feeling my near-exhausted magyk.

A dull throb begins behind my eyes. I'm nearly sliding when the ground beneath my feet turns flat once again. I take a deep breath and pause for a second, forcing the exhaustion and pain away, pretending I can shut it off.

It fades slightly but doesn't go away. It's a struggle not to pant as I nod and continue.

I can't turn back.

I've come too far.

The tunnel opens up into a large cave with stalactites hanging from the ceiling. The only sound is the rhythmic dripping of water far above my head.

As the cave ground slopes down again, I follow it with my eyes, watching as it creates a bowl-like shape in the middle of the floor. I peak over the edge, curious as to what's at the bottom of it, and nearly fall to my knees.

*No.*

*Oh Gods. Please, no.*

*"Once, Elysium was a haven for anyone with rare magyk,"* Vesimyr's voice is sad and full of regret. *"Now, anyone different is punished, none more so than the Beastkyn."*

I can't bring myself to respond.

Not as I look at Embyrne. Not as I examine her bruised, naked body chained to the bottom of the dirt pit.

Not as I jump down that slope and land next to her, my feet splashing in a puddle.

She doesn't even move. Doesn't make a single sound.

"Embyrne?" I whisper.

Her head lifts slightly, her short, white-blonde curls mussed and caked in dried blood and mud.

The sight of her purple, swollen face, of those gold eyes dulled with pain...

*Fuck.*

I drop the light, realizing that she can't see me. "Embyrne? It's me, Dyana."

She flinches back as I lay a hand on her shoulder. I pull back, unsure what to do.

"Leave." Her voice is low and scratchy. So different from the lilting, sarcastic tone I've become so used to. "Go, now. Forget what you've seen."

I blink.

"No."

Embyrne looks away, her chains jangling as she wraps her arms around her legs.

Despite the fact that she's taller than me, down here, Embyrne Ostia is a shell of her true self.

Diminished and beat down.

"You're an idiot for entering the tunnels," she says in a cold, numb voice. "If they catch you, they'll kill you."

I kneel on the ground, the wet, cold mud soaking into my pants.

"I know. I just...I don't know, I guess I wanted to see you before the challenge." I breathe, trembling with fury and dread. "I'm sorry you got dragged into this. However this all turns out...I'm sorry, Embyrne. I'm so sorry."

Embyrne's face is emotionless. "This isn't new. Your presence has changed nothing. Don't be so selfish to assume everything is your fault."

That stings.

But I know this trick. I know it from all of the years in dealing with Amalia and her moods.

"Pushing me away won't work." I state plainly. "I will leave, but have you ever considered that it's okay to let someone *help?*"

There is no response.

She refuses to look at me, continuing to gaze down at the floor.

Gods.

What have they done to her?

"There is nothing you can do to help me now," she responds finally. "There is only the challenge, and if you ever want to leave here, you have to win."

"I know. But I don't want to fight you," I admit, my voice wavering. "Isn't there something else that can be done?"

Embyrne shakes her head, "No. There is not. It doesn't matter what either of us want. The challenge is happening, and we will fight to the death."

She looks up, meeting my gaze, her golden eyes hollow. "Ignautius will know if I'm going easy on you."

My breath is shaky as I exhale. "I know."

Embyrne stares into my eyes as she says, "I'm going to kill you, Dyana."

My heart feels like someone is stabbing a dagger into the center of it.

"I won't let you," I reply finally.

"Then I'll be glad to meet my death at your blade. Do not hesitate. Do not let your emotions sway your judgment. You falter, you die."

I hold my breath to keep from screaming but on the inside, I'm roaring at the heavens.

*THIS ISN'T FAIR!*

I must have said it aloud because Embyrne lets out a dry laugh, but it turns into a painful sounding cough. "Don't you see? Nothing is fair on Elysium, Dyana."

I can't even bring myself to respond.

I'm frozen, unable to help but unable to walk away.

"Leave. Turn around and go back the way you came," she says, sounding tired. Embyrne looks away and it breaks my heart.

"Right." I breathe. Without thinking, I dart forward and throw my arms around Embyrne. I do not squeeze, in fact I barely touch her, afraid that I might hurt her further. It's more of holding my arms in the air around her. I gently lower my arms until they're touching hers, moving slowly as to not startle her.

"I'm sorry," I whisper, which is when something strange happens.

Despite the exhaustion tugging on my magyk, it suddenly acts of its own accord, bubbling up to the surface and shooting out of my fingertips as light blasts into Embyrne. Her back arches and her mouth opens in a pained gasp as her veins begin to glow, light traveling beneath the surface of her skin.

Bruises fade.

The dullness in her eyes dissipates.

And I watch in shock as my light *heals* Embyrne Ostia.

I step back and stand, hands shaking.

I can *heal.*

*How the fuck can I heal? What was that?*

Embyrne looks up at me, the swelling around her eyes gone, with a look of astonishment...

And fear.

"What was that?" she asks. "You shouldn't be able to do that."

I hesitate. "I don't know. I didn't do anything. It just...happened."

She goes to say something else, but a large thud sounds in the distance, as dust falls from the ceiling far above us.

*"GET OUT NOW! IGNAUTIUS IS COMING!"* Vesimyr suddenly shouts in my head.

"Fuck!" I breathe. "Ignautius is here."

"Go! Whatever you do, do NOT get caught."

I nod and quickly crawl back up the bowl, sparing one last glance over my shoulder at Embyrne.

She watches me intently, an unreadable emotion upon her face.

*"Thank you,"* her voice brushes against my mind. *"For what it's worth, I wish things were different too. But remember what I said, Dyana. This changes nothing."*

Anger is quick to rise. Before I can respond, Embyrne's magyk is gone and I turn, running up the ramp to the main tunnel system.

*"Quick, you only have a few seconds before he's to you."* Vesimyr's voice is frantic.

Which is when I remember that I dropped my light. I'm completely visible.

I yank on my magyk with every ounce of strength I have. It begins to coat my skin, but not fast enough.

I will it to move faster.

Just as it finishes covering my toes and I make it up the steep ramp, Ignautius turns the corner.

Gods.

Despite being quite used to Vesimyr's large size...something about Ignautius terrifies me to the core.

The sharp spikes around the crown of his head are a darker blue than his scales—so dark they're nearly black—matching the dark shade of his talons.

The Sene Skal is followed by dozens of smaller Dragons.

**"Let us pay a visit to my Champion,"** he calls. **"I will beat her until she submits."**

Oh *Gods.*

They're going to hurt her.

I want to run back and protect her, but I can't.

I can't and I know it.

The pain of having to leave her behind is tangible. It's a knife to the chest, without any bleeding.

The Dragons in front of me respond with excited calls, as Ignautius walks right past me, descending down to Embyrne.

As his tail passes, it flicks out, and I duck, pressing myself against the wall again, but not fast enough.

A spike on the end of his scaled appendage hits me across the cheek.

I bite my tongue and swallow a scream as blood begins to pool in my mouth, the taste hot and metallic.

Not even as blood begins to drip down my neck beneath the shield of light.

*"Don't just stand there, MOVE!"* Vesimyr shouts in my head and my legs begin to move of their own accord. I quickly retrace my steps, silently going back the way I came.

No Dragon sees me and no bug descends on me.

All I can think about is the Beastkyn I just left behind.

It's the second time I've done so, technically.

That knowledge makes my blood burn with anger.

Eventually I emerge back in the training square, where Vesimyr is curled up on the ground waiting for me.

The sadness in his eyes tells me everything I need to know.

"You knew," I breathe.

The great silver Dragon nods his head, his scales scraping together in the creases of his neck.

*"I'm sorry, Dyana."*

I blink. "It's not like it's your fault."

Vesimyr looks away and doesn't respond.

Something in the back of my head marks this moment.

I don't know why, but something about his response seems odd.

"It's...not your fault, right?" I ask.

*"No, it's not. But I feel responsible regardless."*

I walk over to him and lay a hand on his leg. The cold, smooth surface of his scales calms my anger and soothes the regret. Or perhaps that's just the presence of my friend.

"This sucks," I whisper, leaning against him.

*"I am not quite familiar with that word, but I can feel what you mean, and I agree. Perhaps that is what I'm sorry for. That I can't...protect you from all of this."*

"You can't save me all the time, Ves. No one can do that. It's...an impossible task."

*"That is certainly true. Yet despite the logic, I will always feel responsible for the wellbeing of my kind. Perhaps it is my age."*

I snort, "Always blaming it on the age."

We fall quiet for a few moments, when I confess the worry that has been carving a hole in me for days.

"I'm...not sure I can kill her."

Vesimyr doesn't respond for a few seconds.

*"And if it's her that stands in between you and freedom? Between finding Amalia?"*

Fuck.

I knew this is what he'd say. But hearing him say it makes it feel all the more real. I swallow my whirling emotions and look up, meeting his green gaze.

"If that is what it takes…then we have no other choice."

*"That's where you're wrong, my young friend. There is always another choice. In this case, the other choice is death. You are choosing to live, and that is nothing to feel ashamed for…regardless of the consequences."*

I let out a trembling breath.

"I hate Ignautius for putting us in this situation."

Vesimyr stands and turns his large body, so that we're face to face, his giant head hovering above me. He lowers it so that we're nose to nose, and I lift a palm, placing it on his cheek.

*"As do I. So, my Rider, let us prepare. We have a Dragon to kill."*

I nod, allowing my fear to bleed out until all that's left is anger.

So much anger.

"Yes," I agree, my voice laden with steel. *"Let's."*

# CHAPTER 35
## MIRIELLE

The walk back to the castle was grueling. But the moment we returned, we got to work. Our first attempt with the Elysian was a failure.

We couldn't figure out *why* it didn't work, until Kairos realized that we have to dilute the ore.

"It's too concentrated," Kairos said.

He knew better than I, so I didn't stop him when we experimented with diluting the Elysian ore with silver. When it worked, *we* got to work.

I've been at the forge from sunset to sundown every day, working the Elysian ore into a staff.

I drop it in cold water and there's a loud *sizzling* sound as it rapidly cools.

Panting and covered in sweat, I pull the staff out with a glove, testing the temperature.

It's warm, but not uncomfortably so.

I peel off my gloves, nervous for some strange reason, as I hold my new staff for the first time.

But would it work?

Basa kindly donated one of her scales that was about to shed. Apparently it's a monthly occurrence, similar to how a snake regularly sheds its skin.

With a deep breath, I line up on top of the faded green Dragon scale.

Kairos watches from a meter away, and Basa does the same from the hallway.

*Work. Please.*

I send up a quick prayer to Lir and bring the sharp blade of the metal staff down on the scale.

It's so fast, I barely see it. There is no resistance.

None.

One second, I'm coming down on the scale, the next? It's sliced in half.

"Oh my gods," I gasp, looking up at Kairos and Basa in shock. "It worked. It fucking worked."

*"Good,"* Basa says, ambling into the room. She spreads her good wing, and her bad wing trembles. *"Now you can fix this."*

Kairos and I spent the walk back to the castle discussing exactly how we would fix the wing joint and what it would entail.

With a nervous gulp, I look at Basa as she approaches.

"This is going to hurt."

She snorts. *"Do you think me naive? I'm well aware. I am used to pain, mortal."*

"Okay," I breathe. "Then here's what's going to happen."

I walk her through the plan, and she agrees, so we begin enacting it.

Basa lays down at our feet and we begin the process of taking off her bad wing.

We would keep it, filling the bad spots with metal, but first, we need to build her a new wing joint.

Which means exposing the old one.

Basa pants, trembling as we cut into her hard tissue.

Forsaken slices through her body with terrifying ease.

Basa starts to whine. Not a scream, not a cry, but a small, scared whine.

So, I tell her a story.

I tell them both a story.

A story I've only ever told one person: Nyall Drayven.

The story of my life. Basa quiets, listening as she tunes out the pain while we begin creating the wing joint structure with a plaster-like substance Kairos made from the root of a plant that grows here.

When the wing joint is finished, we pour the melted Elysian ore mixture into it. Basa groans deeply as the metal hits her body, melding with it.

"Move quickly," I tell Kairos. "Precisely, but quickly."

He nods.

Once the wing joint is poured, we move onto her wing while that cools. Basa's eyes close as she passes out from the pain. I was hoping this would happen. That she'd fall unconscious.

Her wing is mostly useable, but the membranes between the wing joints are shredded.

Luckily Kairos has chainmail molds. He pours them while I get to work cutting into the part of her wing bone that is twisted and deformed.

I build the new bone with plaster, before letting Kairos pour more of the ore into it.

It sizzles, cooling as we attach the chainmail. It's so fine, it barely weighs as much as a feather.

We attach it to the bones, before peeling off the plaster around the new metal bones.

Basa's still out as we drag her wing over and start to attach it to the metal wing joint.

It can't just attach. It has to be functional too, so Kairos created molds for a series of hinges that will make the wing flap and flex the way a normal one would.

I've never seen anything like it.

He's a master, truly.

I watch in awe as he places the hinges, attaching them with Elysian screws.

It feels like it's over in minutes, but I know we've been at it for hours because my legs feel like they could give out any second.

But we're done.

Kairos and I slide to the floor as Basa begins to wake.

*"Is it done?"* She groans.

"Yes. It's done." I tell her. "Now...you just need to test it."

Basa groans, shaking as she pushes up on her legs to stand.

Lifting her head, she takes a deep breath and stretches her wings.

The metal one groans for a moment before snapping into place. It throws Basa off and she stumbles, unaccustomed to the weight of the full wing after so long without it.

*"You did it,"* she says.

Kairos walks over and I follow as we inspect it. He orders Basa though a series of stretches and flexes, testing the hinges.

To all of our shock, after a few minutes, something strange begins to happen.

The wing joints start to melt, merging into one.

In a few seconds, the metal is one solid piece.

"Are you doing that?" I look at Basa in shock.

*"No. But I am not surprised. Dragons...we are made of magyk, Mirielle."* It's the first time she's said my name.

Basa flexes her wing more and it moves like real muscle and bone.

The chainmail membranes sparkles in the light.

It's beautiful.

*"It would follow that Elysian is magyk too."*

We all pause for a moment and turn in unison, looking at my staff.

"It doesn't seem magykal," I note.

Kairos agrees with a *hmph.*

Basa scoffs, shaking her head at us. *"Small-minded mortals! It simply hasn't revealed its magyk to you yet. All magyk is sentient to a degree. It will show you when the time is right."*

"Or it won't," I shrug. "We did dilute it, Basa. Perhaps the presence of another weaker, magykless metal means it's just a *powerful* weapon, not a *magykal* one."

*"Perhaps,"* Basa admits, and I let go of the idea of Forsaken being a weapon of magykal destruction.

It's destructive enough already.

I turn, surprised to see Basa bowing.

Kairos does the same, blinking in surprise.

**"Thank you,"** she says aloud. I tremble at the sound, but not just with fear, with *honor.*

"You honor us," I tell her, bowing back. "We are even."

Basa shakes her head. *"You are wrong, mortal. You saved my life a second time back at the volcano. I still owe you."*

I try to protest but she won't have it.

Honor seems to be something Dragons take very seriously.

At least, the Dragons of Ur Daoine do.

"Come with us," I say suddenly. "If Dyana wins the challenge, come with us. To Ur Daoine."

Basa is quiet for a while, watching me with those keen silver eyes.

*"And if she doesn't win?"* Basa asks. *"What then?"*

I take a shaky breath and reply in her mind, not wanting to say the words aloud. *"Then I kill Ignautius. Or at least injure him enough that he cannot pursue us when we leave."*

*"You mean to fight your way out,"* she realizes.

I nod.

Basa is goes quiet again, cocking her head and smacking her teeth as she contemplates.

*"I will hunt and consider your request. I must confer with my kin."*

Then she's turning and walking out of the forge.

Kairos puts a hand on my shoulder as the shock fully hits me.

"It worked. It all fucking worked."

He chuckles and picks me up, twirling me around. I let out a joyful shout. "It fucking WORKED!"

Kairos laughs and I laugh along with him.

"I'm exhausted, but I'd kill to go for a swim right now," I admit to him and Kairos nods.

We head to the beach, stripping down into our underwear and diving into the dark waves.

Glowing fish trail by in bright schools.

It's perfect.

We stay there for a while, sitting in the shallows. Kairos shifts and I lay against his cool scales.

Eventually I surface for air and swim back to shore. Kairos follows, shifting into mortal form as we walk up the beach and dry off.

"I forgot something at the forge," I say to him. "I'm gonna grab it before bed."

He nods. "Goodnight then, Mirielle."

"Goodnight," I smile and turn, heading down to the forge and leaving Kairos. We're both housed in the mortal wing in the lower level of the castle, so the forge is only one level below us.

It's warm, but quiet since there are so few mortals here. Each of us gets our own room. It was small but comfortable, with soft beds and clean sheets.

Lost in my thoughts, I nearly run right into Basa who stands in the center of the forge.

"Basa, what are you—"

*"I will come with you,"* she interrupts me. *"But I would like to tell my kin to join us too. There are... Many of us know Elysium is no longer a haven for Dragonkind. It's just a prettier prison."*

Holy shit.

*"Okay,"* I respond in her thoughts. *"Okay. Yes. But we can't let any of the Dragons who follow Ignautius know."*

*"I will ensure it,"* she growls, and I have no doubt that Basa will do whatever is necessary to make that a reality.

A new ferocity was in her eyes.

A burning sort of rage, laced with the tantalizing grip of hope.

Because escape might actually be possible...unless Dyana loses.

# CHAPTER 36
## AMALIA

I wake up to wet cheeks and an equally wetter pillow. Turning over, I'm taken aback to see Nyall's mismatched amber and green gaze watching me.

*"You've been crying."* His voice is a whisper in my thoughts.

Words and cohesive thoughts escape me, so for once, I stop thinking.

Through our sleep sacks, I snuggle up to his chest and wrap my arms around him, pressing my cheek into his clavicle.

"Nyall...thank you," I breathe shakily. Emotion is heavy in my throat.

I pull back and clasp his face within my hands, letting my tears fall in earnest.

Then I *smile.* Nyall blinks, as if the sight has stunned him.

*"Thank you,"* I repeat the words in his head.

"I take it you slept well?" he asks with a shy smirk.

The tears fall harder, but my smile doesn't fall as I nod. "I did. I had *wonderful* dreams. I can't—I can't recall the last time that happened."

The raw sincerity in Nyall's gaze strips me bare.

"I'm very glad to hear," he whispers back. "Do it again."

I cock my head, confused. "Do what?"

*"You know what,"* Nyall purrs in my thoughts. *"Smile, Blue."*

I snort and roll my eyes.

Nyall copies my earlier actions and clasps my face in his hands, caressing my cheeks with his thumbs.

"Please," he breathes, the words barely louder than the quietest whisper. Hearing that makes my heart thump harder, beating against my chest like a drum.

I gaze into Nyall Drayven's eyes and think of my dreams. Of being on Taran's back, of nuzzling his soft nose.

Of being *free.*

And so, I smile, watching as such a simple thing makes the Fae Prince *tremble.*

*"I could live for a millennium, Amalia Asteroth, and you will remain the most beautiful thing I've ever seen,"* he pauses.

*"Is this the famous Prince Drayven charm I've heard so much about?"* I tease with a playful smile.

*"Honestly, I don't give a fuck what it is, just keep smiling. Want me to get naked and dance around the forest?"*

I raise my brows. *"I wouldn't complain, but I do fear your Rebellion would be forever traumatized."*

Nyall cringes and shrugs, *"True, but I don't care. I'll do anything to make you smile."*

I take a deep breath, feeling his words hit me like bricks.

Fuck.

*Fuck.*

My heart feels like it's bursting.

What *is* this?

*"Nyall, I—"* I start, but words fail me.

Nyall's smile is so warm, I nearly melt. *"Why are you constantly surprised by how I feel about you?"*

~~*Because I hate myself and everyone else hates me too.*~~

My mind is still asleep, leaving my mental walls soft.

I can see the moment Nyall hears my words. He flinches as if hit and shame floods me.

*"Don't you dare feel ashamed, Blue. Don't you dare. You've been through hell and back. You're allowed to feel whatever the fuck you want to feel, you hear me?"*

I sigh and bury my head in his shirt. "Trying to."

"Well then, hear me better. No shame. Never."

*"Easy to say for a Prince,"* I remind him, and immediately feel bad. *"Sorry, I—fuck. This is all just...hard for me."*

*"I know. So take your time. I'm quite nearly immortal. I have nothing but time, and I would like nothing more than to spend that time with you. In whatever capacity you're comfortable with."*

Tears begin to trail down my cheeks, getting Nyall's shirt wet, but he just rubs his hands along my back. It's not sexy or suggestive.

It's *grounding.*

The movement calms my breathing and slows my mind.

*"Thank you,"* I say, because right now... that *is* all I have to say. I just hope it's enough for him.

Nyall leans back and grabs my face, tilting my chin up so he can press a soft kiss at the corner of my mouth.

*"Stop thanking me, Blue. You are not some broken project I'm trying to fix. I like you exactly as you are."*

*"Always the flirt,"* I tease, before dropping my smile and growing serious. *"But you're right...I'm not your project. I'll never be anyone's project ever again."*

Nyall nods, his eyes hard. *"Never again."*

The suns finally begin to peak out through the trees. The end of the forest is visible, and the thought of saying goodbye to my wolfy friends hurts.

A wet nose suddenly presses against my ear, and I start to shriek when Nyall slaps a hand over my mouth.

*"Virgyl! That was not a nice way to wake up!"* I growl in my head, sounding particularly wolfy.

*"You need to head out soon if you're going to make it to Matricia tonight."*

*"Ugh,"* I roll my eyes. *"Fine."*

*"And you were not asleep, cub. Your thoughts are louder than Ryu's snores."*

Ryu's head lifts and her eyelids blast open. She glares at Virgyl with the hatred of a thousand suns.

*"What was that I heard about my snores, fuzz-butt?"* she asks.

*"You do not scare me, my scaled cub. But it is cute that you want to try."*

Ryu glares and smoke begins to stream from her nostrils.

Nyall sighs and stands, stretching and groaning loudly enough to be obvious. The rest of the camp quickly wakes and follows suit.

*"I blame you,"* I tell Virgyl. *"You raised me, and I raised her. We have generational trauma from your nightmarish wake up calls."*

*"Yeah,"* Ryu agrees with a snort.

*"I'm too damn old for this,"* Virgyl sighs and walks away. One look into Ryu's eyes and we break into raucous laughter. For Ryu, this involves rolling onto her back and kicking her legs in the air as she makes strange snorting, grunting sounds.

The rest of the camp watches with wide eyes, but Nyall quickly gets them busy packing up.

When we finish, we're both panting hard.

*"That was nice,"* Happiness emanates off Ryu so strongly it makes me feel intox-icated.

*"It was,"* I chuckle. *"We need to team up on him more often."*

*"My thought exactly."*

*"You do know I can still hear you,"* Virgyl adds in our heads. I find the large black Dyre Wolf in the forest and stick my tongue out at him. He does the same and I blow him a kiss.

*"Children,"* he sighs wearily. *"Get packed up or else you two will be left behind!"*

It only takes a few minutes to get ready for the day. I didn't pack much, which helps.

Nyall did, but I didn't want to embarrass him by asking about it.

Soon, it's time to say goodbye.

Virgyl and the Dyre Wolves line up, watching me with mournful eyes.

*"Do not be sad. We will see you again soon."* His voice is a poultice on my wounded heart.

I wrap my arms around him and bury my head in his thick black fur.

"I miss you already," I breathe.

*"And I you, cub."*

Oh Gods, the tears threaten to fall again, and it takes everything in my power to hold them in.

*"No matter where you go,"* he says, *"you will always be part of my pack. Always."*

"Thank you, Virgyl."

I let go and press a kiss against his wet nose before Virgyl makes me shriek as he licks my cheek.

Soon, the other wolves are surrounding me, rubbing their fuzzy heads against me and licking my face. Happy *awoowoo's* fill the forest.

"I'll see you soon," I tell them, petting their backs and foreheads.

Pressing one last kiss against Virgyl's head, I turn and head over to Nyall.

Mounting Aanad, I go to slide behind the saddle, but Nyall places his hand on my leg, stopping me.

"You lead. You prefer that, right?" His question is genuine and my jaw nearly drops.

"Yes," I answer carefully, as if it's a trick.

Nyall smirks, "Then after you."

Nyall waits until I've slid into the saddle to leap onto Aanad's back in a single, easy movement. His arms come around my waist, pulling us flush together and lighting my body on fire.

"Comfortable?" His breath is hot against my ear, and I shiver, nodding.

Clicking Aanad into an easy walk, we leave the forest, entering wide open plains. If we went east, the plains would continue. Stray west, and the plains turn into dense marshlands.

I only glance back to look at the forest line once.

Glowing yellow eyes within the darkness watch me.

I wave and they blink before disappearing.

The day passes quickly since we have to move fast, but the ride is hard with only very short breaks.

Everyone is panting and covered in sweat by the time we reach the marshes. Tall grasses that reach above our heads sway in the wind. The ground is only halfway dry with paths through the marsh; the rest is submerged.

Matricia is in the center.

Luckily there's a way through the swamp. The air smells slightly of sulfur. It's not bad but different.

We approach a lake within the marsh, a result of flooding from the rainy season.

To my surprise, Soren steps forward and lifts her hands. A few recruits—those with Earth magyk—line up behind her mimicking her pose.

*"Soren has Magyk?"* I slide into Nyall's mind.

*"Mhm. She dislikes using it though. As a child, she was tortured for using earth magyk. Soren sees it as a curse and would rather be human."*

I exhale, sadness filling me. *"I don't blame her."*

For a few seconds, there's nothing. Then the water begins to bubble. Dozens of logs lift out of the water, hovering just above the marsh lake surface.

"Hold it," Nyall orders before igniting his magyk.

I watch as he carves bright white symbols into the air, moving his hands about in a way that is almost a dance. Matching symbols begin to appear on the logs and then they *change.*

It's almost like the wood melts together. One moment there are dozens of logs, the next, it's one giant piece of wood.

"Grab it with your minds and think of flattening its shape," Nyall shouts at the Earth mages.

The wood groans but eventually, it goes flat, dropping to the surface with a quiet plop.

"Good," Nyall nods, extinguishing his magyk, "very good. Now, everybody on."

As we approach the newly made ferry, the horses begin to grow restless.

I glance back, meeting Nyall's gaze. He nods and I sink into my mind, grabbing hold of the horses.

I send love, calm, and comfort down to their minds.

**"It's safe. Don't be afraid,"** I try to convey.

In seconds, all of the horses grow quiet, calming down and licking their lips happily. They meander forward towards the ferry.

The rebels look at me with awe and fear.

"Dismount for this part," I tell them, and everyone slides out of their saddles.

Somehow, I end up next to Mara and her mount, a pretty Chestnut gelding with a white star on his head and four white socks.

"He's gorgeous," I tell her.

She blinks and looks to her horse, "Thanks."

"What's his name?" I ask, reaching out a hand to let him sniff me. He shoves his velvet nose into my hands, and I happily oblige him by caressing his forehead.

"Hope."

I glance at her and she rolls her eyes. "I thought he was a mare when I first got him. I knew nothing about horses. By the time I figured it out? It felt so cruel to change his name."

"I like it. It fits," I smile at the horse. "Hello, Hope."

Hope nickers, rubbing his head against me.

"Don't be rude," Mara says to him.

I run my hand down his soft brown face and lean in, pressing a kiss against the sweet gelding's warm cheek.

"He's just saying hello," I murmur. A part of my heart feels healed being this close to a horse—the other part *aches* at the fact that Taran is gone.

With a sigh, I pull away. We fall silent as the rest of the rebels make it onto the ferry. Once everyone is on, Fi and a few others whose names I haven't yet learned step forward.

Hands raised, they manipulate the water around us and the ferry jerks into motion.

The horses panic for a moment, but I lock onto their emotions again.

**"Calm. Be Calm. You're Safe."** I repeat the words over and over again until they relax.

"What happens if they resist you?" Mara asks and I'm yanked out of my thoughts.

I frown. "What do you mean?"

"You're compelling them," Mara points out, not aggressively, but I can feel the derision pouring from her.

Surprisingly, her continued lack of trust *hurts*.

"I'm not compelling them," I tell her. "They never lose agency."

"It looks an awful lot like compulsion to me," Mara says, leading Hope away.

*I'm not compelling them...am I?*

I'm left standing there, looking silly. Snapping out of it, I quickly find Ryu. She's too big for the ferry, but the water isn't all that deep, so she follows behind us, wading through the marsh.

If she were still a small hatchling, this would be impossible. But here, out in the open, Ryu looks huge.

*Gods, she's growing so fast.*

There are benefits to being the biggest predator around. She doesn't need to worry about anything in the water biting her. Animals are smarter than we give them credit for, but most importantly, they value survival above all else. Fucking with a Dragon doesn't end in survival.

I walk to the back of the Ferry and sit at the edge, facing Ryu.

*"I do not like this,"* Ryu says quietly.

Concern shoots through me.

*"What's wrong?"* I ask. *"Do you sense something?"*

Ryu snorts, *"No. It's not anything specific. Just a feeling that I don't like."*

*"Keep an eye on that feeling and tell me if it does get more specific, okay?"*

*"I promise,"* she replies.

*"Good. How's the water?"* I ask, trying to distract her.

*"Disgusting. I prefer the hot springs."*

*"I blame Nyall for this,"* I mutter.

*"I heard my name,"* Nyall whispers in our heads.

*"Yes, Ryu misses the hot springs. You've spoiled her!"* I chide him in an unserious tone.

*"And how many times have you fallen asleep in there and woken up all wrinkled and pruny?"* Nyall asks tartly.

*"I have no idea what you're talking about,"* I sniff.

Ryu snickers.

*"Uh-huh, I'm sure,"* Nyall purrs. *"You love my hot springs, admit it."*

*"I, for one, am not too proud to admit that I do love them,"* Ryu says happily.

I roll my eyes and grind my teeth, annoyed that he won.

*"Fine,"* I admit begrudgingly. *"I...love the hot springs too, **you ass.**"*

*"Your compliments are so special,"* Nyall sighs.

The connection fades away as Nyall focuses on navigating.

The ferry grows quiet as the marsh becomes denser. The tall grass is over our heads, hiding our movements.

"We're close," Nyall announces.

Crickets sing in the background, but no birdsong sounds from above.

As we float along the lake, I spot fish and toads floating upside down on the surface.

Dead.

A serious pallor falls over the group.

Eventually the ferry stops, and we disembark, wading through the tall grass for a few minutes before coming to a denser forest area. The trees are lighter, not like the dark spruce trees of the Ulster Wald.

The forest is our cover and would be our base for the mission.

Matricia is half an hour east, and we can't just waltz into town with a Dragon, so Mara and Amari will stay back with Ryu and several recruits until we need them.

When I send the signal, they'll join us.

Nyall, Fi, Soren, and I begin stripping.

The four of us would go into down disguised as couples.

*Couples* for fucks sake.

Not even looking at the clothes, I slide on what looks to be blue leather riding pants and a white, off-the-shoulder blouse. Pulling on the final layer, an embroidered blue silk dress with slits on both sides to allow for riding, I finish by lacing up my boots.

Until a hand touches my arm.

I glance up to see Nyall handing something to me. Hands out, I look back down to find a pair of gorgeous, knee high black leather boots.

*"They're not real leather, nor are your pants,"* Nyall's voice wafts through my thoughts. *"They're made of mushrooms."*

*"Really?"* I ask in disbelief.

*"I didn't like the thought of you wearing some dead animal."*

I look at him in shock.

*"Thank you,"* I nod, and crouch down to put them on.

"Let me," he offers, grabbing my leg. He kneels and places my foot upon his thigh.

The rebels pretend not to watch, but I can feel their attention.

It doesn't stop him, though.

Nyall places my foot in the boot and laces it up with expert precision, making sure it's not too tight, and not too loose.

He does the same with the other foot.

I've never worn clothing this fine in my entire life.

It's all so soft and silky. The mushroom leather feels and looks like the real thing.

"You're magnificent," Nyall breathes in my ear before helping me stand.

*"You're not so bad yourself,"* I say in his head.

He's dressed in a long, black and silver embroidered brocade jacket. Snakes decorate the jacket, the silver shining against the black background. The eyes of the snakes are embellished with large, opulent rubies, as are the buttons.

Nyall wears a fine black tunic beneath the jacket, tucked into suede riding pants and similar looking boots in black leather with silver accents.

Then I look up and see his *hair*.

Braids decorated with silver beads are strewn artfully throughout his white hair, pulling it back enough to see his ears.

Silver and black rings decorate the points.

I swear his tattoos look darker, more prominent too. They line his neck perfectly.

"Are you ready?" he asks, holding out a hand.

Hesitation, fear, confusion, anger, grief, regret, need; my emotions are a whirlwind inside of me.

But I step *through* the storm.

I don't avoid it.

I embrace it, and I let it go.

Placing my hand in Nyall's, I look into his mismatched eyes.

"I'm ready."

Fi coughs and gives Nyall a pointed look.

"Ah, one more thing," Nyall reaches into his jacket pocket and pulls out two gold rings. He smirks as he grabs my hand and slides one of the rings on.

It's brief.

Just the slight taste of cherry blossom on my tongue, mixed with Nyall's honey-suckle magic.

Something tickles my chest and I watch as my hair turns long and inky. My waves disappear, going straight, and more tickling against my brows tells me I have bangs. But I wonder what my eyes look like.

"Hazel," Nyall whispers. "Your eyes are hazel."

"I—how did you know I was thinking that? Are you reading my mind, Nyall Drayven?" I hiss.

"Oooh, using the full name, are we?" he purrs. "You know I like when you get all bossy."

I roll my eyes and watch as he puts on his own ring.

His blonde hair darkens to a light brown, and his eyes a cool amber.

The tattoos disappear, but the aura of danger does not.

*"Silly Blue."* His magyk is a caress against my soul and it steals the breath right out of my lungs. *"You are not the only one who hides who they really are."*

I blink and there's a pull on my mind. I follow it, allowing him to guide me.

It's so brief, but one second, it's simply his mind, and the next, I *feel* his walls fall.

Walls so like my own.

The torrent of power chokes me. It's thick and heavy, the taste of honeysuckle so strong that I'm drowning in it.

Then the walls return, and I'm left in silence.

Gradually I return to my body, aware of the chatter of those around us.

I glance back at him over my shoulder, shocked to my core and absolutely terrified.

Nyall goes stiff and I touch his arm, grabbing it tightly. "No, not you. Of *Him.*" Nyall's stiffness dissipates and in his eyes is an emotion I cannot describe. Words fail me.

"When it's time," his voice is low and full of so much emotion I nearly cry, "don't hold anything back. Our best chance is if we do this together. Both of our magyks at full force?" He smirks. "I pity the fool who would take that on."

But I feel his doubt. My smile is a sad one, hollow and forced. "It won't be enough, will it?"

"Stop it," he says, his voice firm and full of anger. "If we go in thinking we'll fail? We will. Hope will be our power. All that miserable fucker knows is resentment and pain," he pauses, taking a breath. "That's all I knew for a long time too. But now," Nyall glances at me before turning and finding Ryu, "Now it's not just the future of my subjects, I fight for. It's for my own future as well."

Oh Gods.

My heart feels like it's going to explode.

"Nyall," I whisper, but he just presses a kiss against my cheek and turns my face forward.

"I like when you say my name," he whispers back.

Fi coughs again and I step back, having *completely* forgotten about our audience.

Embarrassment runs through me, but I use it to fuel my anger.

"You fucker," I snarl, poking him in the chest.

"Ah ah." He catches my finger with a smirk. "That's no way to treat your husband, dearest."

The choking sound that comes out of my mouth echoes through the forest.

I fix him with a smile so dangerous I watch as his pupils narrow. It's the only visible sign, but his eyes betray him.

"Explain. Now." I demand.

Nyall takes a deep breath and points to my hand, "Why exactly did you think I picked a ring?"

"I knew we were going to play a couple," I say begrudgingly, "but married?"

"It was Davyn's idea," he shrugs.

I glare at the Prince, not believing that excuse for one second. "Uh huh, I'm sure."

Then an idea strikes me and I smile, but this time it's prim and proper. The venom is gone.

Nyall is instantly suspicious. "What are you planning?"

"Nothing," I reply sweetly. "Nothing at all, *husband.*"

Nyall looks at me in disbelief before schooling his face and turning to remind the rebels of our plan.

*"Well, Prince,"* I purr in his head, sex dripping from my words. His pupils go wide as he continues talking. So I decide to make it a little harder. *"I propose...a little game."*

*"I'm listening,"* he responds instantly.

*"Whoever gets the most intel today, wins."*

*"And when I win?"* he asks. *"What will you give me?"*

I scoff, *"Already so confident you'll win? Typical male"*

*"Tell me of my prize,"* he demands.

*"Fine. If you win, I'll give you a massage...**naked**."*

Nyall stumbles over his words for a moment before catching himself with a cough.

*"You wicked thing,"* he humms. *"Do you like torturing me in public like this?"*

*"Just paying it back, dear,"* I say tartly. Then it's time to set off.

Ryu stays behind and I hug her snout.

Pressing a kiss, I turn and follow Soren and Fi. Neither of which needed a glamour.

"And if you win?" Nyall whispers at my side, surprising me.

*"I get the massage."* I send him the thought.

*"Then it appears we have a problem,"* Nyall responds. *"Because I would equally enjoy both results."*

Soren and Fi chose to walk, since they're dressed in less fine clothing. Nyall easily hauls me onto Aanad before mounting behind me.

I allow him to take the reins and we quickly make it past Soren and Fi. I nod at them beneath my brow.

We all need luck right now.

Me, most especially.

I take a deep breath as we continue down a wide path through the tall grasses, deeper into the marsh.

Turning to look at Nyall, I meet his amber gaze and *smirk.*

*"I'm aware."*

Nyall's jaw drops and his eyes grow wide.

*"Amalia..."*

*"I said, Prince,"* I let the heat burning within me infuse into every syllable. *"I'm well aware. So let the best spy win."*

His voice is a dark promise in my mind. *"Wicked woman."*

# CHAPTER 37
## AMALIA

"We need a room for the evening. Your *best,* ideally," Nyall orders the second we walk into the high-end inn. The wood is brand new and it's on stilts, keeping it safe from flooding. The inn is only three stories, so the rooms must be small.

But with Nyall's glamour and his pointed ears, they just *handed* us the key.

Fae privilege, apparently.

They lead us to the room. Nyall scoffs at the sight of it.

"This is your best?"

The worker hesitates before sighing and leading us on.

"I thought so," Nyall tsks.

We're brought to a larger room with a big, fluffy bed covered in white blankets. A fireplace sits in the corner, though it's too warm to need it. A large window looks out at the marshes and the rest of the town, and two plush chairs are placed near it, a small table between them. It would be a lovely spot to read.

"Much better," Nyall nods and hands the worker some coins. The worker smiles, flushing with excitement.

"Of course, Lord and Lady Nevyard."

I nearly choke at the name.

When the worker leaves, I break out in laughter.

"What?" Nyall asks with a shrug.

Then he's in my head. *"Ask it in here, I'm sure they've placed spy stones in each room."*

I blink. *"Fine. Your name spelled backwards? Really?"*

*"In over four centuries, no one has figured it out. So yes, really."*

*"Wow,"* I wince. *"That's just sad."*

There's a knock on the door a few moments later. Our heads snap to look, instantly suspicious.

Nyall unsheathes a dagger and opens the door, keeping it hidden but at the ready.

A Fae dressed in equally fine clothing hands Nyall a letter sealed with wax.

Bowing, the Fae leaves and Nyall closes the door.

"Darling, did you get a letter?" I ask in a sweet voice, looking at the note.

"It's for auction guests," he says aloud, but in my head, his voice is a hard whisper. *"I wondered if we'd need to find them or if they would find us."*

*"They watched us arrive."*

Nyall nods, confirming my thought, tearing open the card.

"It's an invitation. We're to dine with the auction owner and the other Fae clients tonight."

I clap my hands in faux cheer. "Oh how lovely. "

*"This has only been sent to the rich,"* Nyall says. *"I can tell by the quality of the paper. There will be more than just Fae there. This is the auction scoping out their highest bidders."*

"Let us get dressed, then! Sounds like we have plans tonight."

Nyall smirks at me.

"Let's."

Nyall begins unpacking our bags and he tosses a bright red dress my way.

It's never a color I wear, but it will do well to hide any blood stains.

*"I picked it for that reason,"* Nyall whispers.

We quickly change, each sneaking glances at the other.

The dress is silky and cool against my skin, but it leaves nothing to the imagination.

My nipples poke out against the fabric, and it hugs my waist, falling in a pool near my feet.

Two thin straps hold it all up. Nyall hands me a red, sparkly sash and I grab the fabric gratefully.

"Did you have to pick this dress?" I ask, annoyed.

"Nope," he says happily. "I did not."

I turn, ready to glare at him but he's there, pulling the dress down to expose my breasts. Nyall leans down and sucks my hard nipple into his mouth. I gasp as he bites it, then pulls back to blow cool air right where it hurt. A whine leaves my mouth as the pleasure makes me burn.

*"Nyall,"* I beg.

He just chuckles and switches his attention to my other breast, cradling the one he just left.

I grasp his head, holding him to my chest and holding myself up. My knees grow weaker with every lap of his tongue.

Nyall moans and I nearly see stars at the mere sound. His lips begin a trail up my neck.

*"I need to bite you, Blue,"* he says in my mind, and I shiver. *"It's typical for Imperial Fae to mark their partners."*

*"Fine,"* I gasp as he licks a line up my neck. *"Do it."*

*"It will make you come,"* he murmurs.

*"Then let me come on your hand, please, husband."*

Nyall's groan is loud and pleased. Then his hand is trailing up my leg, pulling the dress with him. It doesn't allow for undergarments. Even something with thin fabric would show through.

His fingers play with my upper thigh, teasing me.

I grasp his chest and pull us close as he begins to kiss my neck harder.

*"It will only hurt for a moment,"* he soothes.

I laugh. *"That's a shame. I enjoy when you make it hurt."*

My words unleash the beast within as Nyall bites down on my neck with a rough snarl.

His fangs pierce my skin, but he has to bite hard to do so. The pain is fierce but gone as soon as he begins to *suck.*

It quickly changes into a heavy feeling that makes my core throb as the blood rushes between my legs.

"Oh," I gasp, my head falling back. Nyall repositions us, so my back is to him, my weight leaning against his.

My breasts are still exposed as he teases my folds.

Another pull at my neck and the pleasure increases tenfold.

Then Nyall's fingers are there, opening me as he teases up and down, paying extra attention to my aching clit. I twitch at the feeling, unable to stay still.

He swirls his pointer finger through my pleasure, coating himself with it.

Then he thrusts his fingers inside of me, using my own pleasure for lubrication.

I can't help the loud moan that explodes from me as he begins to fuck me. Soon, I'm riding his hand, hips thrusting as I grind into him, desperate for more.

He pulls back from my neck, withdrawing his fangs with a wet gushing sound. Licking up the dripping blood, Nyall guides me closer and closer to the edge of the abyss.

*"Be a good girl and come on my hand,"* the Prince covered in my blood orders.

*Ohmyfuckinggod.*

With another loud cry, stars burst behind my vision and I come, writhing and shaking in Nyall Drayven's arms.

He withdraws his hand slowly, as if savoring the feel of me.

I watch through the pleasure-numb haze as he brings his hand to my mouth. He brings his hand forward and traces my lips, coating them in my own desire.

My tongue flicks out and I moan at the warm, salty taste. Then Nyall is there as he devours my mouth with his own in a kiss so burning hot, I'm surprised I don't combust into pure Hellfyre.

He cleans every last drop from my lips as I lose myself in his kiss.

Eventually, Nyall pulls back, but I want to whine again, already missing his touch. It takes all of my might to hold back and say nothing.

Then Nyall raises his hand, cleaning his fingers off with a hot look in his gaze.

*"And they say I'm the dangerous one,"* I murmur in his head.

*"You are. Tasting you again only makes me want you more. I crave it, Amalia. You're fucking intoxicating."*

Gasping, I step forward, needing a little bit of space to breathe. My dress falls and I righten it as Nyall does the same with his jacket.

We both turn and look at each other. His face is covered in my blood. I walk over to the bathroom, which is around the corner and blocked by a wooden room divider. Grabbing a spare washcloth, I wet it under the waterspout and wring it out so it's not dripping.

Walking back over to Nyall, I lift the washcloth to his face and begin to clean him off.

He grabs the cloth from me when I'm done and does the same to my neck.

*"Leave some blood,"* I say. *"Let them see it."*

His eyes shutter closed and Nyall takes a deep breath, composing himself. He drops the cloth to the ground, leaving my neck a little bloody.

"Ready?" he asks, eyeing my neck like he's hungry for more.

I nod. "I am."

Nyall winds my arm through his and we make our way downstairs, pretending I didn't just ride his hand to a mind-blowing orgasm.

We leave the inn and head into the town.

All of the buildings are so close together, it's almost as if it's one giant structure.

The wooden buildings have woven grass roofs. Some sit on stilts, others aren't. The ones that aren't bear water damage and smell rotten.

I'm sure the leaders of Matricia won't be fixing the rotten houses anytime soon.

When we get to the middle of town, we pass a large square. In the middle is a raised platform, with stairs leading up to it.

Next to the platform is a post, and attached to that post, are six nooses.

Dried blood decorates the platform and the ropes.

It takes effort to school my face into a neutral expression.

I draw an X across my chest in the way those who follow Sol Constantus do when they pray.

Let them think I'm another ignorant disciple.

Nyall follows suit as we pass into the north side of town.

Eventually, we walk up to a large, windowless building in the northern most part of town.

Guards line the doorway, and we flash our invitation. They pat us both down, checking for weapons, before letting us inside.

The Guards are Magyka, I'm sure of it. As they patted me down, I caught the taste of cherry and chocolate.

Anything sweet and fruity is Magyka.

Rotten tastes usually belong to Imperial Fae.

Honeysuckle, with Elves.

And Demis are hit or miss. Some barely have any taste or scent to their magyk at all.

I have yet to see other Fae, but that changes the second we enter the building.

Fae, Demis, and Elves roam around the room with fancy drinks. It's like we stepped into another world.

Red velvet curtains frame regal paintings and mirrors etched in gold and silver.

Plants from all over the continent decorate the corners of the room. The furniture is equally as lavish, with decorative beading and embroidery, rare leathers, and precious metals.

The show of wealth is disgusting.

As we walk further into the room, everyone stares at my neck. Some with interest, some with annoyance.

*"Mostly interest,"* Nyall purrs. *"Not that I blame them. You look good enough to eat."*

Heat floods my belly, shooting down to my core.

*"Now is not the time,"* I tell him.

*"On the contrary, we are a newly married couple. This is the perfect time. I want you flushed and horny all night. No one will suspect a thing."*

I nearly trip at his words.

*"Fine. No guarantees though."*

*"I shall endeavor to change that, then,"* he whispers.

Our conversation goes quiet as we look around the room, walking through the crowd.

It's so over the top that it's cruel.

We passed several homeless people on our way here. I ignored it; afraid that if I looked, I would break. But I felt their eyes watching me.

If only they knew I was here to kill their overlords.

They will have a roof to cover their heads by the time I'm through here. I vow it.

Humans with thick metal cuffs attached to their wrists and ankles walk around with trays of fancy food and drink.

Nyall grabs two glasses of something red and sparkling.

I raise a brow subtly, but take a deep breath and bring the glass to my lips.

The liquid is sweet and tastes of apples and cinnamon. The bubbles burst on my tongue.

It's delicious.

And it's also poisoned.

There was a bitterness to the cinnamon. Clearly, they need to hire a better poisoner. I'm no poison expert, but this is from the Ulster Wald.

There is a tree very similar to the one windweed is harvested from.

They look similar, and if you were unfamiliar, could easily mix the two up.

Whether they meant to get windweed, I'm not sure. But this is from a Craven Tree.

The poison wouldn't kill anyone, but given in low doses over time, would weaken the consumer until they die.

Consumed for one night? It meant a hangover with a side of extreme fatigue.

*"The drink is poisoned,"* I tell Nyall. *"Craven bark. They want the buyers tired and out of sorts tomorrow so they don't pay attention to their bids."*

*"Very good."* Nyall nods, taking a sip of the drink. *"Subtle, but it's there."*

*"That's one point to me,"* I remind him.

He smiles and releases my arm to wrap his around my waist, bringing me closer.

"The night is young, dear wife."

I roll my eyes, but excitement turns my stomach into knots. Energy bursts through me until it's hard to stand still.

"Shall we?" I ask.

He nods and we separate, moving around the room and socializing.

The game has just begun.

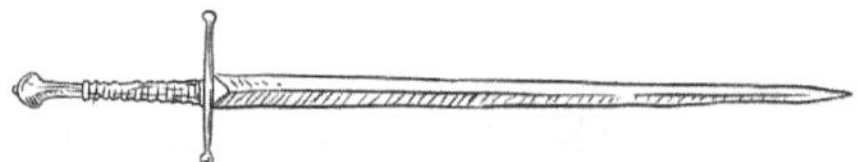

In approximately two hours and fifteen minutes, I've heard jack shit for intel.

Nothing.

*"How's it going?"* Nyall asks. I'm listening to an Imperial Fae talk about their plans for their game.

That's all I've heard all night.

How they are going to kill the creature they win, or some other horrific form of torture.

Confinement, too. What cage will suit the creature best.

How much its meat will go for in their town.

To say I'm angry would be like calling the sky blue.

Obvious is an understatement. The depths of my anger could reach the heavens. Although right now, I very much doubt there is such a thing waiting after our lives end.

This feels an awful lot like hell.

*"It does, but unfortunately it's real,"* Nyall says, reading my thoughts. *"You're doing great. It's going to be over soon."*

Trying to hold it together, I make a graceful exit, claiming to need the restroom and find my husband.

*"Found anything?"* I ask as I locate the restroom and escape the crowd. Confining myself in the small stall, I lean against the door and take a deep breath, trying to stay calm.

*"Nothing except plans for their prizes,"* Nyall sighs. *"You?"*

*"Same."*

Nyall goes quiet for a few moments as I use the restroom and rinse my hands with water.

Drying them, I make my way out and nearly shriek when I run straight into Nyall's hard chest.

"Hello, wife." He winks.

"Husband," I say back, grinding my teeth. I hate being surprised.

*"I propose we up the stakes of our game."* His voice is dark and full of wicked promises.

*"How so?"* I ask, curious.

Nyall leans down and presses a soft kiss against my lips, flicking at the seam of my mouth with his tongue. I open for him and his tongue gently tangles with my own. I melt in his arms, and he holds me tight, one hand buried in my hair.

*"How about the first one to find any intel wins?"* he asks.

*"Fine, and the prize?"*

*"Mmm..."* He presses another scorching kiss against my lips, and I nearly moan. His hand around my waist lifts to my breast, clasping it and rolling my nipple between his fingers. Unable to hold it back, I moan aloud, and several people passing us stop and glance, caught off guard at the casual display.

Nyall does nothing to hide his actions.

He allows them all to watch as he kneads my breast, pulling it out of the dress and bending down to suck on my nipple again. My head falls back and I groan, unable to handle it.

With a pop, he lets my nipple go and rights my dress.

Panting, I watch as he turns and winks at the onlookers. "It's our honeymoon," he says to them, and the ladies swoon while the males chuckle and salute Nyall.

*"You're the wicked one, Prince. Not me."* I pant, sounding out of breath even in my thoughts. *"Now what's the prize?"*

"The prize is you," Nyall surprises me and answers aloud. "Naked and sitting on my face."

I stop breathing.

"Yes, that's much better," Nyall murmurs, tracing my flushed cheek. "This is my favorite look. *Needy.*"

He makes no move to quiet his words, and those nearby hear. I whine as he grabs my arm and we walk back into the crowd, but more people watch us, curious about the couple that can't keep their hands off one another. My heart races. My skin is hot and flushed.

If Nyall wanted me to look horny and glazed over with lust, I do believe he has achieved his goal. *That fucker.*

*"You are an evil male,"* I snarl in his head. The only response is the pleased sound of his laughter.

"I don't believe we've been introduced," a deep voice says. Nyall and I turn to find a tall male with a heavy-set belly and a red beard behind us. His head is bald on top but the sides contain luscious crimson curls a few shades darker than the beard.

"I am Duke Haestan, your humble auction manager. I run the Mercatus. My father is the one who founded it, actually..." The male continues, going on and on with various boasts about his history.

So, we've been deemed important enough to impress.

Nyall and I play the part well, *ooh*-ing and *ahh*-ing over the story in the right places, eager to hear more.

Nyall is so charming in fact, that I catch myself getting lost in his performance. It's seamless. I cannot tell where his character starts and the real Nyall begins.

"Lady Nevyard, how did you and your husband meet?" someone asks.

I flash a Dyana-worthy smile, "On horseback, actually. I was out for a ride near the capital and ran into Lord Nevyard while riding."

"It was love at first sight, right, pet?" Nyall asks, snuggling up to my side. I want to stick my tongue out at him and flash him a rude symbol, but I hold back.

*"Call me 'pet' again, see what happens."* I warn him.

"It was indeed. We're so lucky." I try to make my eyes look lovesick as I look up at Nyall and bat my eyelashes. He laughs in his head, but caresses my cheek lovingly.

Duke Haestan smiles, buying every second of our act. "And what are you looking forward to most, tomorrow? We have a lovely selection this time of year."

I bite my lip flirtatiously and put my arm on Duke Haestan's arm. He flushes, blushing at my touch. I lean in and whisper, "I want the most powerful, rare creature you have."

"Ah, the griffyn, then. Unfortunately, the Crown has put forward their interest on the beast."

"Oh, darn." I frown, trying to look sad. "Well, what's the most powerful after that?"

Duke Haestan smirks. "That would be the unicorn."

"Oh my, you'd enjoy one of those, wouldn't you darling?" Nyall asks me.

I nod enthusiastically and clap my hands, like a vapid, silly child.

Internally, I'm screaming.

"The Crown has put ahead interest on him as well," Duke Haestan says with a smile.

"No!" I gasp. "Really? Oh, how dreadful. What in the world do they want a griffyn *and* a unicorn for anyways?"

Duke Haestan looks around and leans in, giving me a conspiratorial smile.

"Word is, they need more recruits. Building an army, they are. Creatures make powerful weapons."

"Too true," Nyall nods, taking a sip of his wine.

"But a unicorn?" I ask with a pouting frown.

Duke Haestan pats me on the shoulder, "Don't worry dear, we have plenty more creatures to choose from."

*"The Archmage is scared of something,"* Nyall whispers in my head.

*"Agree. And if they need more recruits, the Rebellion is finally making headway."*

*"The recruits are coming to us instead,"* Nyall agrees.

*"Exactly, which is hurting their numbers."*

*"They're panicking."*

I murmur my agreement.

Nyall grabs my hand and kisses the top of it, flashing me a hot look. "My darling," he says aloud. "What do you say we turn in for the night?" Nyall leans down and presses a kiss against my cheek. "I have other plans for you this evening."

I let out a giggle and allow him to lead me out. We wave goodbye to the auctioneers and Duke Haestan, passing by human servants on the way out.

Their gazes are seared into my memory. So hopeless and withdrawn.

*"We will free them too, then,"* Nyall interrupts my thoughts. *"All of them. No being should be enslaved to another, animal, mortal, or immortal alike."*

I smile, feeling the sincerity in his words. Squeezing his hand, our fingers lace together as we walk back to the Inn.

It's quiet out, with guards on patrol.

There's a tense feeling in the air as if they're waiting for something.

It's a struggle not to look over my shoulder.

*"We already knew they'd follow us,"* Nyall reminds me.

Whoever follows us does so all the way until we enter the inn.

Nyall stops at the bar to grab two more cups of wine. Laughing at something someone said, he makes his way over to me and hands me a cup. Pressing a sloppy kiss to my cheek, I let out a laugh as we make our way upstairs. Nyall's hands land on my ass and he squeezes, making me squeal.

*"Perfect,"* he murmurs. *"The squeal was a good touch."*

*"You're not the only one good at spying."*

Nyall unlocks our room and lets me enter first. Closing it behind us, the *click* of the lock echoes, making me shiver in anticipation.

He holds up a hand and I pause.

Someone knocks on the door and Nyall opens it. Inn attendants carry in buckets of hot water, filling the large, empty copper tub behind the wooden room divider. They stream in, filling the tub until the entire room is full of steam.

Finally, they finish, leaving us in peace.

Nyall sighs and closes the door, before making a graceful motion with his hands.

Light bands burst into existence around his arm as Nyall uses his magyk.

He draws a symbol on the door, etching it as if his finger was a pen.

There's a loud popping sound and Nyall nods, stepping back.

His magyk goes dark.

"We're safe to speak aloud." he nods to me, taking off his ring and putting it on the table by the window. Nyall's features return to normal. It's a relief to see that white-blonde hair and his mismatched eyes.

I prefer him this way.

I pull my ring off and do the same. My hair shortens. It's like a blanket has been taken off my body. I feel lighter, freer.

We each breathe easier as ourselves.

"Well, neither of us won."

"Or," Nyall says carefully as he walks towards me. He takes the ring from me and sets it on the counter. "*Both* of us won."

"True." I flick my tongue.

I stare at the bath and the room seems to grow smaller. My heart thuds against my chest so hard, I wonder if he can hear it.

"Care for a bath?" Nyall asks with a wicked smile.

"I would." I nod.

Then I slide the straps of my dress off my shoulders. Slowly, the dress falls to the ground, exposing my naked body beneath.

I stand before him, allowing him to look his fill.

Nyall Drayven devours me with his eyes.

The room and the outside world fade.

It's just us.

I know the rebels wait in the forest, Ryu watching over them.

I know Soren and Fi are somewhere in Matricia, hopefully about to get some sleep as well.

But I do not care about *any* of it.

I only care about the male in front of me.

"You're magnificent," Nyall says, his voice low and reverent. He looks at me the way a pilgrim looks at a God.

With worship in his gaze.

I walk past him, shoulder brushing his, and step into the steaming hot tub.

Positioning myself on the end of the tub facing Nyall, I sink beneath the water until it touches my chin. The water is fully transparent—no bubbles blocking the view.

I am exposed, well and truly.

Nyall takes a shaky breath and begins to strip. His eyes never leave mine.

His jacket drops to the floor, followed by his tunic and pants.

I look with unabashed abandon.

His cock is hard, the tip shiny with precum.

Then I spy the metal barbell through the skin just below the tip.

I gasp.

"I thought that was just a dream," I mutter, reminiscing on the dream I had during the Gauntlet. We'd been in the shower and his cock was pierced.

"I remembered how much you liked it, and had it done a few days ago," he smirks. "Do you like it, Blue?"

"A few days?" My jaw drops. "Nyall! Doesn't that need to heal?"

Nyall laughs and walks over to the tub. "First off, I'm an Elf—and I'm Imperial Fae. You could say that I'm *special.*"

I roll my eyes and stick my tongue out at him.

Nyall smirks. "Secondly, I used a spell to speed up the healing."

*Oh.*

My tongue is heavy and drool coats it as Nyall approaches the tub. His cock is gorgeous. I swallow, shaking slightly.

"Did it hurt?" I ask. He steps into the water and I scoot over, making room. The tub is large, but our legs are pressed together.

Nyall leans back his eyes never once leaving me. "Not at all. Do feel free to kiss it better though."

I fight a smile and sink down into the water. Grabbing a bar of soap at the edge of the tub, I begin lathering my arms when a hand stops me.

Looking up, I find Nyall's eyes full of lust. "Let me," he breathes. *"Please,"* he whispers in my head. *"Let me take care of you, dear wife."*

I'm fucked. I am well and truly fucked, because hearing Nyall Drayven *beg* to touch me, *beg* to take care of me? I will never recover.

I manage a nod and Nyall pries the soap from my hand. He tugs me close so that I'm almost sitting in his lap, as he begins lathering my body.

It feels so intimate. Almost more so than sex.

I thought the dream was good, but *fucking hell.*

As Nyall's hands massage soap into my wet skin, I can't help but melt into him with a sigh.

"When is the last time you really relaxed, Amalia?" Nyall asks softly as he soaps my hands and massages in between my fingers.

All of the weapon work has turned my hands into calloused, worn appendages. But apparently, it also made my muscles hard as a rock. Pain shoots through me as he works the knots out of the fleshy part of my palm.

"Too much?" he asks quietly.

"No," I gasp. "Not at all. It's a good pain. Please don't stop."

He nods and continues. My eyes close as I lean into his shoulder, putting my head against his neck.

"To answer your question," I finally respond, my voice low and sleepy. "I... don't know the last time I relaxed. I did not get many days off with my job in Twyn Fells, and before that, I was living in the cave. I worked so much, any time off was spent resting and just...surviving."

"You've been running your entire life," Nyall notes. "It's hard to relax when there's always something dangerous around the next corner."

Nyall's hands move up my arms, massaging the tissue of my shoulders. I groan as he finds more knots.

"I relaxed a little bit with Os," I say quietly. Nyall's hands pause for a moment before he continues.

"He had that effect on me too."

My heart bursts.

"For a being so dangerous," Nyall continued, "Os was very good at making you feel safe."

I nod, unable to form words.

We fall silent for a few minutes as Nyall moves onto my back, turning me so I'm facing away from him.

"Nyall?" I whisper. "I'm...I'm not sure I know how to relax anymore. I'm not sure I know how to be anything other than vengeance, grief, and fear. I don't even know if I even know how to be happy."

Nyall is quiet as he takes in my words, but it also allows me the space to think.

"There was this one day, back in Twyn Fells," I begin quietly. "Food poisoning hit the Birdcage, the brothel Dyana danced at. They were all given the day off, and most of the horses in the stable were out on journeys and wouldn't be home for weeks."

I chuckle. "We grabbed our bags and ran into the forest. Not to run away, but to hide, just for the day. Away from prying eyes. We brought food from Mrs. Hunton and made a picnic. Twyn Fells was still in sight in the distance, but it felt like...freedom. We read our books, talked about them, and snacked on fresh bread and stew. That day, I felt happy and relaxed."

"Sounds wonderful." Nyall presses a kiss against my cheek.

I nod, a tear falling. "It was."

The hands massaging my body stop. Then Nyall's fingers are below my chin, gently turning so I'm looking over my shoulder at him.

I hug my knees, embarrassed and feeling incredibly vulnerable.

"Don't cry, Blue," he whispers.

I smile, my voice shaky, "These are good tears. It's a memory I'll always cherish."

*Just a memory. That's what Dyana is now: a memory.*

"Turn back around," Nyall whispers. "It's my turn to tell you a story. If you can, try and relax and just...listen."

I nod and let out a big exhale, trying to do as he asked.

"I was born just before the end of the war," Nyall says softly. "It had been raging for nearly a century when I came into this world. Elves mature quickly, so within a decade, I looked to be in my twenties. By 15, I was fully mature and had stopped aging."

Nyall continues washing me, his hands moving down my back. I lean forward, allowing him to reach my lower back. His touch is so delicious, my bones feel soft and mushy.

"I thought the world of my father. At first, he tried to keep my Mother's death a secret. Tried to get me to love him like a child would love a parent," he pauses. "Then I saw the Dragons. That...was the first time I began to question."

"When I was young, my Father made me work in the Dragon Pits. Said it would build character. One night, I heard a strange noise and went to investigate, even though I was supposed to head back to the Citadel. What I found...it changed me."

I wait, curious.

"I found Dragon eggs, a half-dozen or so, guarded by a large black Dragon who had somehow escaped. A Dragon who was not happy I had discovered them."

I glance back in surprise and Nyall takes it as an opportunity to turn me.

"I came face to face with the Dragon that was Remus Ostia. Gods, I was terrified. Not just because I feared him, but because he was so utterly glorious that I was frozen. I couldn't move, couldn't run away, couldn't do anything."

I wait for him to continue, desperate to hear more.

"I thought he would kill me. But he didn't. He just stood there; protecting the eggs."

"He just wanted to protect them," I breathe, proud and utterly heartbroken all at once.

"Yes, he did. Something about that moment, about seeing the hesitation on his Dragon face when I stopped threatening the egg...it pierced through Achan's manipulation."

"What happened next?" I ask.

Nyall's smile is soft, "I visited him nightly. I'd bring milk from a local farm down, transporting it with a spell. I'd either bring a live animal for Os, or steal some already killed game from the farmer too." Nyall pauses, lowering his voice. "The farmer eventually got suspicious. He was the first person I ever killed."

Nyall pulls me backwards until my back is pressed against his chest, my head resting in the crook of his neck.

"I'm sorry," I whisper. "It's never easy. Never."

Nyall leans down and presses a kiss against my forehead. I take a deep breath as Nyall lowers his hands and moves onto my breasts.

"I fell in love with him, during those nights. Seeing this giant, awesome creature go to such lengths to protect its young was one thing, but realizing the depths of their power and intelligence changed me."

"Dragons seem to have that effect," I breathe. "Even if they let you live, you are forever changed."

Nyall nods, focusing on my nipples as he kneads my breasts, lathering them with soap.

"You have changed me too, Amalia Asteroth. I never expected you either. Both of you crashed into my life like lightning bolts to the heart. You are burned into my *soul.*"

"Nyall..." My voice is a desperate plea. "Kiss me. *Please.*"

He leans forward, his hands still on my breasts. Nyall's lips hover just in front of my own, so close I can feel his breath.

"Is that all you yearn for, Blue? A kiss?" He chuckles as I moan in frustration.

"No, it's not," my voice trembles. I grab his face and force him to look me in the eyes.

I want to remember this moment.

"I have been lying, Nyall. For two years, I have lied." I swallow my fear and press on. "I have *always* wanted you, you silly male."

Nyall's smile could rival both suns.

"I want you, Nyall Drayven. I want you so badly I feel like I can't breathe—"

My words are cut off as Nyall's lips crash against mine. I gasp and he swallows the sound as I'm hauled into his lap. He wraps my legs around his body and lifts us, carrying me out of the water. I'm wrapped around him like a parasite, but it's still not close enough.

Nyall never breaks the kiss.

*"The damn inn could be burning down and I wouldn't fucking stop."* His voice is a dark purr in my head.

I chuckle, but the sound turns into a moan as he fists my hair, kissing me harder.

Nyall tosses me onto the bed and I bounce, water droplets flying everywhere.

He grabs my ankles and yanks me to the edge of the bed, so that he's standing between my legs.

A snap of his fingers and a pillow appears beneath my hips, lifting my core into the air.

Nyall pries my legs open, revealing my wet, aching pussy.

"Fucking hell," he curses, falling to his knees with a gobsmacked look on his face. "You're perfect."

"Then stop staring and do something about it," I growl.

Nyall smiles. "Oh, sweet Blue. You are not in charge here. *I* am."

He snaps his fingers and light encircles my wrists, pulling them together and locking.

Nyall's smirk as I struggle against the restraints is annoying, and all too sexy.

"You're at my mercy, Blue."

With a snarl, I unleash my Hellfyre and snap through the restraints. He laughs as I sit up and get on my knees before him. Grabbing him, I use my strength and haul his body onto the bed, crawling on top of him as I use my shadows to bind his hands.

His smile is so delicious, I have to lean down and kiss it off.

"No, Prince, you're at *mine.*"

I crawl down his body until his cock is bobbing just before my mouth.

Eyes on his, my tongue flicks out and I lick the precum off the tip, teasing the metal barbell.

Nyall's entire body twitches and his mouth opens in shock. "Oh *fuck.*"

I chuckle before taking the tip of his cock in my mouth and *sucking.* With my other hand, I reach down and cup his heavy sack. The skin is soft and smooth as I massage his balls. Nyall moans my name and a rush of energy fills me.

I suck harder, moving down on his cock until my nose hits the soft white curls atop his pubic bone.

"Holy fucking shit," Nyall cries out. "Blue, you—*oh my gods.*"

His cries only become more obscene and out of control as I deep-throat him. The barbell touching the back of my throat is an interesting feeling.

But his taste?

It's sweet honeysuckle nectar on my tongue, and I want *more.* I suck harder and his hips bow off the bed, hands fisting my hair.

"Amalia, fuck. If you keep doing that I'm going to come in your throat."

I make a pleased noise and suck harder, bobbing faster and faster. The noise is equally as obscene as Nyall's cries.

With a deep groan, Nyall comes down my throat. The flavor of honeysuckle increases, and I moan, needing more of the taste.

Then I'm pulled off his cock as Nyall throws me to the bed with a feral snarl.

"My turn," his voice is so unhinged and raw, I nearly come there and then.

But he shoves my legs open until I'm once again bared to him.

He dives into my pussy like a male starved, licking and sucking until I'm panting and crying.

Nyall runs his tongue all the way from my clit, through my folds, to the crease between my cheeks. He circles the rim of my tight bud and I cry out, thrashing as pleasure rocks through me.

"Please," I beg. "I need to come."

"Let me help with that," Nyall whispers against my pussy.

Then his mouth is gone and he's hovering above me, lips covered in my shiny pleasure.

His pierced cock drags through my wet pussy lips and I moan, hips already reaching for him.

"Please." I pant. "Gods, *please,* Nyall."

Nyall leans down and kisses me. "This time, I'll fuck you, but next time?" One of his hands clasps my chin as he pulls back, looking me in the eyes. "Next time, I'm taking my fucking time."

Right as the words hit me, he thrusts inside. My back arches and I reach out for him. Nyall wraps his arm around my neck, holding me in place as his hips begin to move, thrusting slowly.

After two years, he feels huge. The feeling of being stretched around him, of him being *inside* of me; it's perfect.

"Nyall," I cry out, as his thrusts get harder. "

"Come for me, Blue. Come all over my cock."

His words send me over the edge. light bursts behind my eyes as pleasure overwhelms me. I soar over that cliff's edge, plunging into the orgasm. My muscles pulse around Nyall's length, coating him with cum.

"Fucking perfect," he mutters as he pulls out and thrusts again. I'm so wet it can be heard with each thrust, the noise echoing through the room. It only enhances my pleasure.

Nyall changes positions, flipping me on my stomach and pulling me up onto my knees so that he can fist my hair with one hand, and wrap the other around my rib cage.

That hand around my ribs lifts, cupping my breast and pinching my nipple. I gasp in pain and Nyall takes that moment to thrust inside of me again.

The new angle makes him hit the perfect spot, and I'm instantly moaning.

"Such a good girl," Nyall purrs. "Come for me again."

His thrusts get faster, deeper, harder.

Soon, I'm falling apart, drenching his cock with my pleasure and shattering in his arms.

He holds me up, swallowing my moans with a scorching kiss.

Turning us again, he leans back and brings me down on top of him so that I'm straddling his waist.

"Ride me, Blue."

I smirk at the pun.

Sinking down on his cock, I sigh at the feeling. Even those few seconds without him and I missed it.

Then I smile at Nyall and tense my muscles.

His eyes widen and his mouth drops, "Holy *fuck,* do that again."

I repeat the movement, and he groans, "Fuck, Blue. Oh my *God.* "

I snicker and repeat it once more before beginning to grind my hips. I ride him with ease.

He moans beneath me, hands on my hips, eyes watching me like I'm some goddess.

It's powerful, that look. It makes me feel like I could conquer the world.

Nyall pulls me down to lean against his chest as he begins driving into me from below, his hands holding my body still.

Moaning in my ear, he falls apart and I feel as his hot cum coats my inner walls.

Panting, we cling to each other. Neither wanting to move.

"That was..." Nyall's voice is shaky as he looks at me. He reaches a hand up to caress my cheek. "Perfect."

I blush and press my face into his chest.

"No, no. No hiding." Nyall pulls my face towards his so that I have nowhere to hide.

"It wasn't that," I tell him.

"Then what embarrassed you?"

"Oh, it's just that my first thought after we finished was, 'when can we do this again?'"

Nyall lets out a loud, boisterous laugh.

"Wicked girl," he purrs, leaning in to kiss me. He withdraws, cock pulling out of me as cum follows, leaking out of my lips. As soon as he's gone, I already miss him.

So I let my walls down and let him in.

I allow him to feel my need, to feel how much I enjoyed that.

His jaw goes slack, and his eyes fall to my lips.

"You're not going to get much sleep tonight," he says finally, his eyes flicking up to mine. He wraps me in his arms, and I laugh.

"Do that again," he whispers, kissing me lightly. I giggle against his lips and Nyall smiles.

"Perfect," he breathes. "You are perfect."

"Then give me more to smile about, Prince."

He does.

# CHAPTER 38
## IREYNA

"So Dragonfire can hurt her." The Archmage reclines in his chair. "Good. Do you think you can get more from him?"

I shake my head. "No. He caught on to what I was doing. I won't be able to do it again."

The Archmage shrugs, his face unemotional. "Have him moved to one of the new cages and remove his cuffs. I want to harvest some of his scales before I kill him."

"Yes, Father." I nod.

There's a knock on the large black doors and a guard enters. "Your Holiness, we've received a letter."

The Archmage sighs, waving his hand in the air. "By all means. What is this letter?"

The guard stammers. "A-An anonymous *tip,* Your Holiness. About the Asteroth girl."

One second, the Archmage is seated at the table, a few chairs away from me. The next, he's at the guard's shoulder, looming over him.

**"Give me the letter,"** the Archmage commands.

There's a layered tone to his voice.

He's compelling them.

~~I WONDER IF HE'S EVER COMPELLED ME?~~ I smother the thought and it disappears, falling into my subconscious. The guard hands the Archmage the letter before running away, terrified.

"Take care of him," he says, meeting my gaze. The weight of his stare has always felt so heavy. Like someone staring into my soul.

Nothing is hidden from the Archmage.

I can feel him worming around in my head. Whatever he finds, pleases him.

"Yes, Father." I bow before leaving the room. As the doors close behind me, I unsheathe the dagger hidden beneath my tunic.

The guard doesn't hear me. He doesn't even have time to react.

I'm too fast.

I speed up until I'm at his back. With one hand, I reach around and slice my dagger across his throat. With the other hand I cover his mouth, silencing his oncoming screams.

He writhes in my arms and eventually, his legs give out.

The guard crashes to the ground and I step away, letting his body hit the floor with a hard *thunk.*

As I right myself, the guard begins to thrash harder, choking on his own blood.

Something clanks behind me. The sound of metal armor rubbing together.

I glance over my shoulder at the group of Fae guards. Their eyes are wide, and several of them reach for their swords.

"I am on orders from the Archmage," I smirk. "Hands off your weapons, or lose them."

Their hands fall to their sides, and they nod before turning and walking away.

Leaving their dying compatriot behind with little thought.

The guard on the ground takes one last, shuddering breath before he succumbs to blood loss.

Sheathing my dagger, I leave his body for the others to see.

Perhaps it will remind them of their place.

For the Fae are not in charge here anymore.

*We* are.

And I'm done playing mortal.

Not hiding the blood covering my hands, I walk back into the Archmage's council room.

"Ah, good," His Holiness nods at me, "well done. Now you can learn about your assignment."

"My assignment?" I ask, taking a seat.

"Yes," the Archmage's voice is rich and melodic. "The tip about the Asteroth girl. I want you to check it out. Take your Dragon."

Adrenaline and excitement rushes through me.

"Yes, Father." I bow my head. "What are your wishes if I do find her?"

The Archmage leans back in his chair, pondering. A wicked smile appears on his face, one that leaves my arms covered in goosebumps.

"Bring me her body," He purrs. "Bring me her body *and* her Dragon."

God.

"I will send you with spells, of course."

Adrenaline turns into nervousness. But I cannot show it. I cannot show Him any weakness.

"Yes, Father. I will see it done."

"I will contact the army and have them meet you there, should it turn into a fight. 5,000 soldiers ought to do it. You'll leave tonight."

I bow and stand. "I must prepare."

The Archmage is next to me a moment later. He grabs my hand, pulling me close. I step away from my chair and fall to my knees, the picture of piety.

"Such a dutiful servant. You serve Sol Constantus well. Find the Asteroth girl, and He will be pleased."

I nod. The Archmage pulls me onto my feet before turning away. But His voice whispers into my thoughts.

*"Good luck, my child."*

# CHAPTER 39
## AMALIA

Two years of need. Built up and ignored.

The hunger within me is so immense, I wonder if it will swallow me whole and leave nothing but crumbs behind. Nyall makes a contented noise in his sleep and pulls me closer against him.

Our naked bodies are tangled so closely, I'm not sure where he ends, and I begin. Light has just begun to enter the world as the suns rise above the horizon. The small window in our room glows. The world would be waking up soon, but I do not want to move.

Nyall sighs and tucks me closer. "Neither do I."

"Reading my thoughts, Prince?"

He chuckles and it's a sleepy, contented sound. Nyall leans down and presses a kiss against my bare shoulder, and I sigh at the simple pleasure of it.

"You were projecting," he murmurs. "I've never actually had to try to read your thoughts, Blue. You practically shove them at me."

I turn in his arms and poke him in the chest. "I do not *shove* them at you. That's so dramatic."

Nyall smiles and it makes my heart melt. Any anger leaves me.

"Perhaps it's just...fate."

I try to look annoyed, but the way my heart *thuds* at his words, he very well might be right.

"What's this? The Heretic Prince *believing* in a higher power? I never thought I'd see the day."

Nyall rolls his eyes, and I lean against him, wrapping my arms around his torso.

It's so natural—being like this. The feeling of our bodies pressed together is a kind of perfection I didn't think possible. How many nights have I spent tossing and turning, imagining moments like this? Imagining him touching me this way.

Nyall's arms tighten around me, and he makes a pleased sound. Gently he turns me again, so my back is to his chest. His hand descends between my legs, teasing the seam of my lips.

"So wet already," Nyall mutters with the reverence of a prayer. "Fucking hell, you feel so good. How do you *always* feel so good?"

His fingers dip inside me and my walls clench around him. Nyall curses and lifts my leg, hooking it up and back on top of his own, leaving my core open and bared. Thrusting two fingers inside of me, my back bows and my mouth opens on a gasp.

"Just like that, baby." Nyall purrs, "Ride my hand just like that."

*Oh gods. That nickname.* Something about it sends me over the edge.

**THEN:**

*"Blue, I—"*

*My patience snaps. "No, Nyall. Just stop. You don't get to call me that."*

*"Does the fact that I've kept you safe for the past year mean fuck all to you?"*

*Nyall's words are like knives, cutting through the sinew of my patience.*

*"I can keep myself safe." My voice is cold and cutting.*

*Nyall sighs. "I know you care about me, Amalia. What we've gone through...well, it changes you."*

*My breath shudders. "I do not care about you."*

*Nyall sees through it. "How long are you going to keep lying to yourself?"*

*"Excuse me?" I whirl, anger hot in my belly. "Fuck you, Nyall. You want to talk about lying to yourself? What's the rebel leader doing hiding out in a cave with a wanted fugitive and some wolves? What kind of leader abandons his people."*

*~~I'M SORRY. I'M SO SORRY. PLEASE DON'T LEAVE ME. PLEASE DON'T GO ANYWHERE. I DON'T MEAN IT I'M JUST HURT.~~*

*I shoved the emotions down, ignoring the way that voice in the back of my head was screaming at me that this was a horrible mistake.*

*Watching the way his face turned hard at my words was like a stab to the chest. I wanted to scream that I didn't mean it.*

*But I did.*

*"You're right," Nyall says tightly, looking off to the side.*

*The next morning, long after we finally went to sleep, he was gone.*

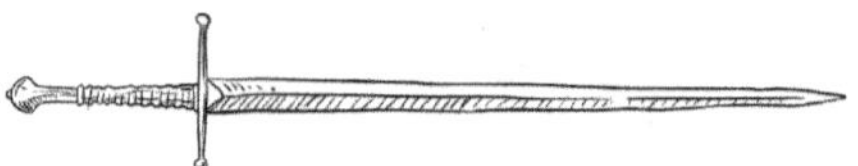

**NOW:**

Enough lying.

Enough *hiding.*

*"You once asked me a question."* I whisper in the safety of Nyall's thoughts. *"You asked me if I...cared."*

Nyall grinds against me, thrusting his fingers in and out so fast it makes it nearly impossible to form a coherent thought.

*"And?"* he whispers, one hand landing beneath my jaw as he cranes my head back. The angle allowing him to press a searing kiss against my lips.

"I lied, Nyall." I whisper against his lips. "I lied."

Nyall pulls back and looks at me with such vulnerability it makes me shiver.

"I care," I repeat quietly. "I care so much that it *kills* me."

He slows his thrusts as his movements inside of me turn wanton and lazy. It's the hottest thing I've ever experienced.

"Say it again," Nyall orders in a soft voice. He watches me, shock and pleasure warring equally in his mismatched gaze.

I lean forward and kiss him *hard.* Pulling back, I clasp his face between my hands and look him in the eyes.

"I care about you, Nyall. So fucking much. When you left…it killed me. It hurt just as bad as—" The words turn into rocks on my tongue. I can't say it.

Nyall's fingers withdraw from my core and then his hard cock replaces it. The new piercing at the tip makes the pleasure increase tenfold as he slides into me.

"I would wait a lifetime to hear those words," he whispers, dragging his lips up my neck. "It killed me to leave you. I didn't want to. I could have stayed in that cave with you *forever,* Amalia."

The angle is so vulnerable, so bare. He lifts his hand, grasping my face to turn and face him. Nyall's lips meet mine and I moan, melting into him.

"Please don't leave again," I whisper, so quietly I'm not sure if he can hear it.

Nyall pauses, pulling back enough to meet my gaze.

"I'm not going anywhere, Blue. I'm staying right here, with *you.*"

I let out a hoarse cry and dive back into his lips. Nyall meets me halfway, just as frantic.

The world stops turning and we are the only ones to exist.

I am the dust between the stars as Nyall Drayven claims my body.

"Come with me, Blue," he whispers against my lips. "I want to watch you."

"I can't—" I cry but Nyall just chuckles, his breath warm against my cheek.

*"You can. Reach down and rub that swollen clit. Touch yourself for me, Blue. Get there."*

I shudder and my hand slips between my legs. I can feel his cock sliding in and out of me and, gods, what a decadent sensation. I push my thumb hard against my clit, rubbing in small circles.

*"I used to imagine it was you,"* I confess, the pleasure absolutely destroying any last amount of control I possess. *"That it was your fingers against my pussy, not my own."*

*"Fucking hell, Amalia."* Nyall curses and I swear he grows even harder inside of me. His hips jerk faster and his breath comes harder.

*"I'd whisper your name as I'd come all over my own hand."*

His hand reaches down to hold my hip in place so he can pound into me so hard that I can barely even breathe.

*"Come with me, Blue. I can feel it. You're almost there."*

We turn into a maelstrom of sighs and whispered curses as we swallow each other's moans. We fall together as I come so hard I black out. I never stop feeling him, though.

Nyall goes to pull out, but I stop him.

"Stay," I whisper against his lips. "Don't go yet."

Nyall smiles and kisses me. That sleepy languidness has returned. Or perhaps we're both just well fucked.

I would be embarrassed, but I just feel relaxed.

Truly relaxed, and it's been a long time since I last felt like that.

I remember this feeling.

It's been so long, but I remember now. I was so scared of this because I think a part of me knew that it would feel so fucking right.

This is what it feels like to be *loved*.

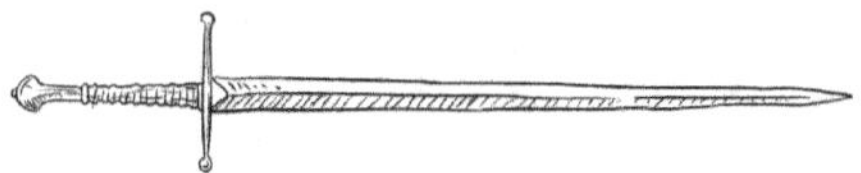

Eventually, we make our way out of bed and get dressed.

I balked when I saw the outfit Nyall picked for me, but as we walk into the Mercatus, I'm suddenly very glad he went over the top.

My dress is a mix of dark gray fabric and chainmail. It's all artfully intermixed and clearly for show, not function.

It's slightly reminiscent of what I wore to the Welcome Ball two years ago.

*"I loved that dress,"* Nyall purrs in my head. *"Particularly the way your nipples were visible through the fabric. You looked fucking delicious."*

Heat rushes through me at his words and my cheeks flush.

*"I'm trying to focus,"* I hiss at him.

*"As am I."* Nyall flashes me a saucy wink. *"On you. And your nipples. And your warm cun—"*

I smack his arm. *Hard.* Last night was the time for being horny and distracted. Today is not.

All of the auction attendees are here in equally fancy outfits.

Two large doors at the other side of the room open, and we're ushered in by human servants to a large auditorium. Silken chairs with feather pillows and beaded throws line an oval stage.

Velvet curtains cover the stage entrance.

They'll display the animals here, then.

I don't know what I expected, but this isn't it.

Humans lead us to our seats.

I squeeze Nyall's arm as we approach the front. Duke Haestan gave us front row seats.

The auditorium fills up quickly. The lights dim and Duke Haestan appears from behind the curtain.

*"So, now is when we decide. Do we strike during, or after?"*

I take note of the exits...or lack thereof.

It's only the doors behind us. That's the only way out besides going through the stage.

And because of our new front row seats, over a hundred Fae lords and ladies now stand between us and those doors.

Not to mention the guards stationed outside the doors.

I'm sure there are more backstage, too.

*"After."* I glance at Nyall. *"We need to follow them back to wherever they put the animals for staging."*

*"I agree."*

**"MY LORDS AND LADIES!"** Duke Haestan's voice is projected, but I get the sense that it's not his magyk. It's some sort of spell. **"WELCOME...TO THE MERCATUS."**

Duke Haestan smiles, and then all of the lights go out as we're plunged into darkness.

But I'm not afraid.

I *am* the dark.

# CHAPTER 40
## DYANA

*The terrain is steep, and I struggle to find a rock to hold onto as I climb up the steep mountain.*

*I have to get to the top.*

*"Need any help?" Embyrne calls. She's next to me, easily holding on while I'm panting, each muscle quivering with effort.*

*I bare my teeth at her. "Shut up! You're not real."*

*"I'm as real as this mountain," she shrugs and blurs forward, moving so fast I can barely track her.*

*Want and hate war within me as Embyrne glances at me over her shoulder.*

*Embyrne shouldn't be here. I don't know why, but I know she shouldn't be here.*

*I must say it aloud because she laughs. "Why not? It's your dream, Sunshine."*

*The nickname makes me stumble.*

*"A mountain is a strange choice for a dream. In fact, this whole dream feels a bit...strange."*

*I force myself to keep climbing until I reach her.*

*This is the closest I've ever gotten to the lush part of the forest. But as I pass Embyrne, unable to stop until I reach the top, she sighs and blurs again, appearing in front of me.*

*I jump, shocked and Embyrne rolls her eyes. Her golden eyes are bright and glowing, and her lips are pursed in a quizzical manner.*

*"Are you able to stop climbing?"*

*I scoff. "Of course."*

*But I don't.*

*I can't.*

*I lied.*

*Suddenly Embyrne is beside me, climbing alongside me. The lush part of the mountain is so close that I can smell honeysuckle in the air, and hear the cool babbling brooks that line the comfortable looking terrain laden with thick green grass.*

*"Now I feel it. The need to just...keep climbing." Embyrne says. "I don't like this, Dyana. I think we need to wake up."*

*"It's not like I can just wake up—"*

*My words fall short as Embyrne suddenly tackles me. She cradles my body against hers as we fall through the air.*

*Just as we're about to hit the ground, I hear a wet ripping sound as blood begins to drip on my arms.*

*Wings.*

*Giant, pale gold wings explode out of Embyrne's back, covered in specks of red blood.*

*Embyrne flaps her wings and groans as if in pain.*

*"I can't hold us up," she gasps. "It's been so long since I flew."*

*We crash towards the earth so fast, I don't even have time to say goodbye.*

*I hit the dirt with a hard thump and Embyrne screams—*

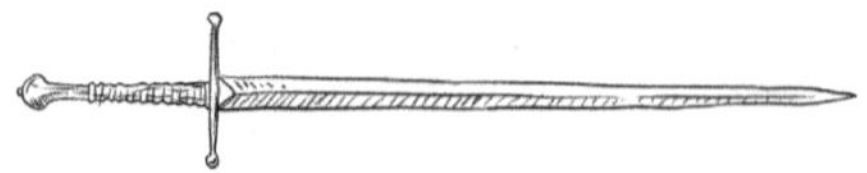

I wake up screaming, my voice nearly hoarse.

Vesimyr's face hovers over mine and something wet hits my cheek.

"I'm fine," I groan as Vesimyr swipes his wet tongue across my cheek.

*"Oh, you're awake."* Vesimyr says with relief. *"You were making these strange whimpering noises, and then you started flailing. It was rather alarming."*

I sigh and run my hands through my hair, pulling lightly as if to pull myself back into reality.

"I'm fine, just...a weird dream."

Vesimyr lays down next to me and lays his big head on his front arms.

*"Was it the mountain again?"*

"Yeah. Except it was...different. The mountain itself was the same. But the dream was different. Embyrne showed up."

Vesimyr blinks. *"She was there?"*

"Yeah, and she kept saying, 'this dream feels weird'. Why would she say that?"

Vesimyr's eyes narrow. *"It was a dream, but Embyrne's presence was real. Which means she was dreamweavyng."*

Now it's my turn to blink.

"I think Amalia told me about that once. Os did it to her when she got hurt, right before the Gauntlet began."

*"Yes, it's a very rare power. The fact that she can so easily wield it is...slightly unsettling."*

"Can you do it?" I ask, turning on my side to face him.

Vesimyr hesitates before nodding. *"Yes, I can."*

"But you didn't feel her enter my dreams?"

I swear, the Dragon pouts. *"No, I didn't. Which means it's my magyk she borrowed to do it. That's the only way I wouldn't feel her presence."*

"What does that mean? That she used your magyk?"

Vesimyr growls, *"It means she's figured out how to borrow my magyk, or at least part of it. Which gives her and Ignautius the upper hand."*

Fuck.

Fuck!

*"We have one day left to train,"* Vesimyr reminds me. *"We need to make it count."*

We both look up at the still dark sky above.

"But maybe just..."

He finishes the sentence for me. *"Another hour of sleep won't hurt."*

I nod heartily. "My thoughts exactly."

Some sleep, and then we train.

And we train *hard*.

The moon is bright as it illuminates the packed square.

It's almost midnight and despite the fact that I would normally be asleep right now, my body is trembling from the adrenaline.

I've been on edge all day, even after training.

My body aches but it doesn't stop me.

We've come too far to turn back now.

Vesimyr and I land in the crowded courtyard in front of the castle and the Dragons beneath us scatter like ants.

Hundreds of Dragons are waiting to watch the Challenge. Their scaled bodies decorate the roof of the castle and the sandy beach beneath us. Some already wait in the air, content to watch from afar.

Others practically vibrate with anticipation.

Mirielle and the other Magyka stay near the castle.

I ignore the concern in her pale green eyes as my gaze meets hers. Mirielle gives me a tight nod and small smile. I send one back before quickly turning away. I wish her gesture of encouragement hadn't made a difference. I don't want to admit that it helped. But knowing she has my back despite how everything ended?

It fills me with steel.

Without using my hands, I run up Vesimyr's spine and land between the spikes on his shoulders. A thick piece of black leather is wrapped around his neck, giving me something else to hold onto.

He warned me there would be some...rather evasive maneuvers.

At first, I was quite offended.

"Why have we just spent months training if I could have used reins?" I asked, arms crossed.

My Dragon looked at me with disappointment. *"Because you still need to know how to fly. Most flying doesn't require what we're about to do."*

Then I demanded a demonstration.

He made me eat my words when I almost splattered on the beach sand, having fallen off.

We never trained for upside down flying.

"Okay, okay. FINE. I will use the reins," I gasped as the air returned to my lungs.

Vesimyr nodded, looking rather full of himself, so I flipped him a rude hand signal when he turned his back and stuck my tongue out at him.

Just because.

Despite all of our training, Vesimyr was right. A vertical ascent is a different beast from the type of flying we're about to do.

I'm trying to stay alive, not give myself even more possible ways to die, and I will not fall off during the Challenge.

If Vesimyr goes down, I go down with him.

Or so I was planning, until Embyrne Ostia appears next to Ignautius in the blink of an eye.

One second, she wasn't there. Next, she was standing next to him.

She has no armor, unlike Ignautius whose scales are covered with thick black Elysian plates. Instead, she's in head-to-toe black leather that hugs her slender figure.

Black kohl lines her gold eyes, making them even brighter thanks to her dark skin and pale white hair.

Embyrne practically glows in the moonlight, looking like something straight out of some epic fantasy story.

I flip my gaze to Ignautius, surveying his own armor.

*"Go for the neck, that's where the armor is weakest,"* that's what Vesimyr said. I focus on it, trying to *will* my eyes to see the armor in microscopic detail.

Then I see it. Right where the breastplate meets the pauldron, the armor isn't actually connected. It's just overlapping. Which means I can slide a blade into that opening.

Vesimyr doesn't have any armor. His scales are his only protection.

The silver sheen on his body seems almost enhanced under the light of the moon. His green eyes are brighter and that ring of light, the same color as my magyk, glows around his pupils like they're bleeding light.

Everyone watches us as we walk into the middle of the square, approaching Ignautius.

*"Kinslayer,"* someone whispers, and the insults begin.

*"Murderer."*

*"You're going to lose."*

But not quite as many as I expected.

Instead, I see more looks of fear as we pass.

What I don't expect, though, are the looks of respect.

Of admiration.

It's few and far between as I gaze along the crowd of waiting Dragons.

But those looks of admiration all come from Dragons who were in Ur Daoine with us. Who flew alongside Vesimyr as Mirielle held my dead body atop his back.

Embyrne mounts Ignautius carefully, sitting in a similar spot in between his shoulder blades.

The image of her bloody, resplendent golden wings enters my mind.

As Embyrne finishes righting herself, her gaze lifts, and our eyes meet.

It's one second.

One single second—

—and yet it feels like a lifetime.

*"I'm sorry,"* I try to say with my eyes. *"I'm so fucking sorry."*

Her face mirrors mine as her eyes fill with regret. It's so fast, I almost miss it.

But I saw it.

I saw the pain in her eyes.

The loneliness, and seeing it makes me crack.

Something deep inside of myself that broke that day in the Arena, that I've been so desperately trying to hold together, shatters.

In its place is a righteous determination that I've never felt before.

*This can't be it.*

Vesimyr keeps saying there is no way to save her. Hell, Embyrne even thinks it. But I don't accept that.

They all think that there is no other way out of this. They simply accept their fates and expect me to do the same.

And I've had it.

I've fucking had it.

I refuse to believe that this is the only end.

It's not that I can't kill her.

I do not doubt my ability to finish the job. Not after being in the Gauntlet.

But...I don't want to.

I don't know why, but I do not want to kill my cranky, sometimes annoying trainer.

A trainer I've become...a little too attached to.

I don't know what that means, and I don't know what I want.

But I know I do not want this.

One flash of regret through those golden eyes, and I'm scrapping our old plans as an idea forms in my mind.

An insane, batshit crazy idea.

Amalia's face pops into my head.

This is something she'd do, and she'd absolutely hate that I'm following in her footsteps.

But she always taught me that sometimes, rules are meant to be broken.

I will find Ama. I promise.

I will find her, and I will save Embyrne; damn the rules and this fucking island to Hell.

Although, I'm starting to wonder if Hell is already here.

**"THE CHALLENGE RULES ARE AS FOLLOWS,"** a Dragon beside Ignautius bellows. It's a rotund brown Dragon with yellow wings and pale ivory spikes around the crown of its head.

The square falls quiet as we listen as the Challenge rules are read off.

**"RULE NUMBER ONE: THE LAST DRAGON RIDER TEAM LEFT ALIVE, WINS."**

I roll my eyes.

*"Yeah, we know."* I mutter to Vesimyr, who snorts quietly.

*"Just wait for the next rule."*

**"RULE NUMBER TWO,"** the Dragon bellows again and I flinch at the grating sound of his voice, **"THERE ARE NO OTHER RULES. ANYTHING GOES."**

*"Creative,"* I say dryly.

*"Isn't it just?"*

**"RULE NUMBER THREE,"** the Dragon suddenly bellows yet again and I scoff.

*"What happened to there are no other rules?"* I ask.

Vesimyr shakes beneath me, holding in his laughter.

**"ONCE THE CHALLENGE BEGINS, NO ONE MAY INTERFERE."**

*Lovely.*

The square goes quiet again as Ignautius releases his wings, stretching them until we all get a view of his impressive wingspan. His blue scales look nearly black in the moonlight.

Then everyone looks to us.

I meet Ignautius's silver gaze, lift my hand, and *smirk*.

*Snap.*

At the sound of my fingers, light explodes out of me, coating both myself and the Dragon beneath me.

In seconds, we're both dressed in translucent, glimmering armor made of pure light.

"Try getting through this, you ugly fuck." I snarl aloud, sounding rather draconian.

Ignautius snarls back, baring his teeth, and I think, in this moment, something else inside me clicks.

I didn't just get magyk.

Well, perhaps I did, but it also changed me.

I am not a human, nor am I Magyka.

I'm a fucking *Dragon*.

*"That's my girl,"* Vesimyr growls in my head as he cracks his neck and unleashes his wings.

*Both* sets.

The Dragons around us gasp.

Ignautius lets out a horrible roar before he takes to the skies, ready to begin the challenge.

Which is when I say to Vesimyr, *"There's been a change of plans."*

My Dragon is quiet for a moment as he lifts into the air.

*"Tell me,"* he demands.

*"You...might not like it,"* I hesitate. *"But just like you've asked me to trust you, I'm asking you to trust me now."*

He's quiet as we ascend into the clouds under the light of the moon.

*"I trust you, Dyana. I trust you more than any other creature on this planet. Tell me the plan."*

I nod and begin explaining my idea, my *theory,* and my Dragon agrees.

# CHAPTER 41
## MIRIELLE

As Dyana and Vesimyr rise into the air, fear begins to choke me.

I wasn't even aware I was trembling until Kairos grabbed my hand.

"She can do this," Kairos nods.

I glance at him and let my emotions bleed into my eyes. "Can she?"

He watches me carefully, as if he's not sure what to make of me in this moment. Kairos looks at Dyana more closely, considering the situation.

"She isn't human. Not anymore," he notes.

I scoff. *Am I that easy to read?*

"I'm aware."

Kairos glances at me again. "Are you?"

*No.*

The answer must flash on my face, because Kairos nods. "You knew her before. It is hard to let go of the past."

Anger is hot in my belly at his words.

"I've let it go. Let *her* go," I pause, watching as Dyana and Vesimyr ascend into the clouds. "The problem is, I know what she has to lose. Desperation leads to mistakes."

"It can also lead to victories," Kairos chides. "No one fights harder than someone with *everything* to lose."

"We'll see."

The trembling has stopped.

Fear has faded into something different.

Something harder.

It's so easy to let the emotions dissipate. To latch onto that anger, that resentment, and let it *burn*.

Kairos squeezes my hand and lets go.

I'm well aware that he did this on purpose.

Triggering my anger just enough that I can use it as a blanket to suffocate my fears.

We've both lived far too long to be naive about it.

"Thanks," I nod at him, sending him a grateful look.

His smile is soft. A mere twitch of the lips.

But it's enough.

Our attention turns to the sky as the group around us goes quiet. The Dragons who can fly scatter. But the Ur Daoine Dragons, many of which still bear injuries, wait alongside us.

Something hard suddenly hits my back, sending me to the ground.

I groan but turn quickly, pointing my new staff upward at whoever is attacking me.

Basa watches me with amusement in her eyes.

"You should still be resting," I remind her.

She snorts a cloud of smoke, making me cough. *"I do not wish to rest. I wish to fly."*

I blink.

"Now? Right now? Have you tried to fly at all since waking up?"

*"No."*

Then her wings snap out, fully flexed. Basa lifts her head to the sky and roars with triumph.

Flapping them, she easily lifts into the air.

If Dragons could smile, then Basa would be smiling. Her eyes twinkle and I watch a lightness wash over her. She roars again before lifting into the clouds.

It worked.

It *worked.*

The metal wing works perfectly. It must hurt like hell, but Basa clearly doesn't care.

A look to the side tells me Kairos feels the same joy.

It worked. Thank Lir it fucking *worked.*

A screech from one of the Dragons above steals our attention.

Dyana and Vesimyr hover in the sky across from Ignautius and the Beastkyn Embyrne.

"Come on, Dyana," I whisper, while in my head, I send out a frantic prayer to Lir.

It all comes down to this.

# CHAPTER 42
## AMALIA

**"THE FIRST ITEM UP FOR BID!"**

I thought I would be able to do this. I thought I was strong enough.

**"A UNICORN FOAL, LADIES AND GENTLEMEN!"**

But I am not.

I'm not strong enough for this.

The foal is tiny. Only a few days old but already underweight. Its hooves are still soft. The foal cries out, clacking its mouth. It's crying for its *mother*. It's crying for *food*. Each cry from the foal's mouth makes my anger burn hotter and hotter.

The noise is like claws raking open gashes in my soul. I can feel my sanity shredding apart, along with any patience I managed to gather.

*"Breathe,"* Nyall's voice whispers through my thoughts but I can feel it starting.

The panic. The *fury*.

*"I know. Save it. Hold onto it, and when the time is right, show them every fucking ounce of it."*

The unicorn foal is hauled around the stage. It whinnies and shrieks, terrified as it watches us with wide eyes. Its body trembles and the whites of its eyes show as it looks around, desperate for safety.

*Mother, please. Please do something.*

Nyall grabs my hand and squeezes it. I haven't moved a centimeter since the foal came on stage.

Then the bidding starts in earnest. I follow the auction with violent agony. But I remember every hand, every *bid,* every *laugh.* I memorize their faces, *burning* them into my mind. The audience enjoys it. They clap and cheer and *enjoy* the creature's misery. Every single one of them.

The bidding for the foal goes quickly. It's led backstage and I take a breath.

I glance to the back, making note of the closed doors.

*"You have an idea."* Nyall's voice is serious. There is no hint of humor or flirtation. This is affecting him too. I meet his gaze and for a moment, for just a brief moment, I let my fire out, let it *flash* in the dark.

It's gone before anyone can think twice about it.

But Nyall saw.

*"Yes I do."*

*"Tell me."* There's an edge to his voice in my thoughts. A *violent* edge.

I lean forward and press my lips against his.

*"No one leaves."*

I pull back, expecting disgust, anger, perhaps even fear. *Definitely* judgment. But as Nyall watches me, there is only acceptance.

*"I'm with you, Blue. But the consequences—"*

*Ah.*

Worse than judgement. *Logic.*

*"I don't care."* It's true. "Damn the consequences."

These people *cheer* and encourage the torture of magykal creatures. Of beings unable to speak up for themselves. They do not deserve to leave here alive.

None of them do.

*"Alright."* Nyall growls. *"Damn the consequences. No one leaves."*

His words, his *confidence,* steel me, hardening me as the other bids are brought onto the stage.

A grown unicorn, then two baby griffyns, their feathers still soft and pillowy. There is no shield strong enough to protect me from this. Each animal, each *creature,* kills me. I can *feel* a part of me wither away with everyone. Every time they scream with terror, it cuts into me so hard, it should draw blood.

But my dress remains clean. On the inside, though, I am a bloody wreck.

*"It's almost done,"* Nyall consoles. He pulls me onto his lap, smirking as he presses a kiss against my shoulder.

The heat of his body grounds me.

Holds me together.

His arms wrap around my waist, caressing my stomach with his fingers as he tucks me against him.

*"It's almost done, sweetheart. It's almost done. You're doing so well."*

*"Fuck you,"* I hiss.

*"Wicked, vicious girl."*

I roll my eyes, but the moment does the trick. Until *it's* brought out.

Nyall's arms around me tense and I feel him freeze.

It's...an Oryx. A *pregnant* Oryx.

*Oh my Gods.*

It's so young...far too young to become a mother. The whites of her eyes show and the mare shrieks, trembling so hard she can barely walk.

The crowd *laughs.*

I was already planning on killing them. But now I'm going to make it slow. I'm going to make them *hurt.*

It's not enough. My anger wants more. I want to put them on this stage, strip them naked and shove them around as they scream in fear. Let's see how they like it. My hand is up before they even announce the starting bid.

**"100,000 gold coins for her,"** Nyall's voice rings out, echoing throughout the room.

My head snaps to the side as I look at Nyall's raised hand. He beat me to it. Nyall winks at me, but I feel the underlying anger.

The bidding war begins, but as it reaches 1,000,000 gold coins, the other bidders back out.

No Oryx was worth 1,000,000 gold coins. But it was to Nyall Drayven.

Pride fills me. I watch as he bids on every single remaining creature. Shame fills me too. Shame and sadness. Because I know why he's bidding. I see the same pain in his eyes that rips pieces out of my heart.

Shouts start to sound from the crowd. Bidders angry that Nyall had just taken the last 10 creatures of the Mercatus. Duke Haestan tries to calm the crowd, but I can tell he's nervous. Nyall has thrown him off; not just for the exorbitant amount of money he's just spent, but because of the *pleasure* Nyall clearly takes in their anger.

"This is unfair! He stole our bids!"

Nobody notices as I stand up. They're too busy shouting.

Nobody notices as I walk onto the stage, covered in shadows.

Nobody notices anything at all, until my sword is shoving through Duke Haestan's throat, sending him choking to his knees.

The crowd goes quiet before someone screams.

Which is exactly when I drop the glamour.

**"That's Amalia Roth! That's the girl who killed the High Council!"**

**"RUN!"**

**"KILL HER!"**

They try to run. Some away from me, some towards me.

Nyall is at my side a second later, his own glamour dropping.

The bidders running towards us stop, frozen in horror at the sight before them.

At the sight of the Rebel Prince and the Gray Wytch.

This wasn't the plan, but there is a reason I am not a leader. Nyall is most likely filling the rest of the team in on the situation and telling them to get their asses *here.*

I am not a leader. I'm a *weapon.*

Weapons are unsheathed as the bidders prepare to take us on. What an unfortunate *mistake.*

"You think you can take me?" I ask quietly. I know they hear me, because several start trembling as I let my Hellfyre flare. The shadows begin to whirl and bubble, moving on my command.

Hellfyre erupts in my hands, trailing up my arms.

I meet their terrified, angry eyes and *smile.* "You should never have come here."

I burn them from the inside out.

They didn't even have time to scream.

One second, they're standing before us.

The next?

They're *ash.* Every. Single. One.

My shadows swirl around us as the Hellfyre burns brighter on my arms, the color of the flames darkening to a deep navy tipped in light blue and orange.

As I let go of the power, dizziness takes over and I stumble.

Nyall catches me the moment I begin to fall, cradling me in his arms.

"I'm alright," I say, breath shaky. "I'm alright."

Then I realize. I never let go of the flames.

Horrified, I look down, expecting that the Hellfyre would be burning through his skin.

Nyall's eyes twinkle with mirth. "Your flames don't burn me, remember?"

My jaw drops and he laughs, setting me on my feet but not withdrawing his arms. Instead, his thumbs caress my sides. The feeling of his warm hands against the thin fabric of my dress makes me *burn* for an entirely different reason.

"Sorry...it's a habit."

"It's alright," he murmurs. "But I'm going to break that habit, Blue."

Something warm trickles from my nose and Nyall wipes it away with his hand.

"You pushed yourself too hard."

"I know, but right now? I really don't care."

Then I stop thinking for once and *act*. Leaning in, I run my hands through his white hair and *pull*, bringing the Prince close so I can kiss him.

For a moment, I get lost.

The feel of him is so comforting, my body instantly relaxes. But the scent of burnt flesh in the air is...*grounding*.

With a mournful sigh, Nyall pulls away from my lips as the guards start pounding on the door.

Nyall doesn't even look behind him. He doesn't need to.

Instead, he watches me, as a wicked smirk appears on his face.

His magyk erupts around us. Bands of white light encircle his biceps as some of his tattoos begin to glow.

The doors burst open and Nyall glances over his shoulder, raises a single hand, and *snaps*.

Arrows of white light shoot into their bodies.

It's a massacre.

When he's done, all that's left are piles of blood and flesh amongst the ash.

Are we as bad as Achan? As the Archmage?

As I look out onto the carnage, a part of me wonders if I even care.

Cruelty begets cruelty.

But someone has to stop this.

We cannot go on living this way. None of us can.

"You are Morrigyn's right hand. Her blade. Her justice. Her *punishment.*" Nyall clasps my chin, tilting my head up to face him as he holds a hand out, helping me to stand. "You are not like him."

My eyes close as it hits me.

"Why?" I ask, my voice hoarse. "Why are you so sure of me? That I'm *good?*"

Nyall smiles so warmly I want to cry.

"I'm not."

I blink, startled.

"I don't *care* about good and bad, Amalia. I care about *you.* All of you. Every fucking piece."

The tears begin to fall in earnest, coating my cheeks.

"You think I don't see it, don't see you, but I see all of you, *including* your heart. I see how you try not to care because you care too much. You love so hard that it *hurts* you."

*You see me.*

I bow my head as the sobs explode out of me in silent grief.

Nyall gently lifts his hand, tilting my chin so he can look me in the eyes.

"There is *nothing* you could do that would drive me away. Would make me *fear* you. *Nothing.*"

I wish I believed it. I want to.

I want to believe it so badly.

I know *he* feels truthful. I don't think he's lying. But everyone fears me eventually.

But I nod, I pretend that I accept his words as truth. Maybe if I pretend long enough, one day I'll actually believe it.

Nyall wraps his arms around me. I inhale the scent of his honeysuckle magyk and it calms me.

He pulls back and cups my face with both of his hands. His eyes are so earnest, so honest, it strips me bare. I let him see my self-hate, let it all show on my face. Let my sadness free and let my grief run wild. I show him my anger and how hot it burns. So hot I sometimes wonder if it *will* burn me up.

Nyall never looks away.

"Amalia...Blue, I—"

There's a sound beyond the now open doors, interrupting whatever Nyall was about to say and we turn in unison as the rebels round the corner.

Soren and Fi aren't with them, but everyone else is here.

They balk at the scene before them.

"Justice has been delivered," I tell them, summoning my other blade and sheathing them both—*Morrigyn's* blades—in two holsters I summoned onto my back. "Now let's free the animals and get the fuck out of here."

# CHAPTER 43
## DYANA

Ignautius and Vesimyr hover in the air, eye to eye. Only a few dozen meters are between us.

"Almost midnight," the blue Dragon sneers at us before licking his lips. "I'm going to dine on your flesh before the day is through."

"You can try," I taunt back.

*Come on, you fucker. Get angry.*

Usually Vesimyr would chide me for making comments like this, but tonight is different. I want Ignautius angry, *too* angry to think.

The moon is nearly directly above us, signaling midnight.

The brown Dragon ascends, hovering between us as it brings a giant horn to its lips. The shape of the horn is rather strange so that it can fit a Dragon snout. For a few moments, there is only silence. Then the brown Dragon takes a deep breath and blows into the horn.

*"Together,"* I whisper in Vesimyr's head.

*"Together."*

Then he charges. One second, we're hovering, nearly still. The next, Vesimyr is racing straight at the blue Dragon. Ignautius holds his ground, rearing his neck back while the scales around his belly turn bright orange and red. Vesimyr rolls to the left just as the Sene Skal unleashes his flame. It's so hot, sweat instantly coats my skin. The air is fuzzy with heat, and I hold on tightly to the reins as Vesimyr stops rolling only to curve into a beautiful swan dive towards the ground.

There's a sizzling sound and a sudden roar as Ignautius unleashes his flames at us yet again, but they turn to smoke as my light armor douses them.

The Dragonfire doesn't penetrate my magyk. I laugh loud enough that Ignautius can hear me, "You'll have to do better than that, you sick fuck."

A roar of anger and Ignautius charges again as we do a vertical ascent before Vesimyr flips upside down suddenly, using the momentum to put us above Embyrne and Ignautius. I hold onto the reins with one hand and with the other, pulling on my magyk and shove a giant ball of light at Ignautius's backside, behind where Embyrne is sitting. She notices and screams. Not in pain, but in fury that I avoided her on purpose.

Ignautius lets out a roar of pain as my light burns through his scales.

Embyrne looks back and waves her hand, healing the wound as something pulls on my magyk, making me nauseous. She...she's using my magyk to heal Ignautius. The magyk *I* revealed to her when I visited her in the tunnels.

"FIGHT ME!" she shouts into the night sky.

I don't answer, and my plan doesn't change.

But fuck that.

"FIGHT ME, YOU FUCKING TRAITOR!" I scream back.

Her past words echo in my mind.

*"Use the anger."*

She wants me to be angry?

*Alright, Embyrne. I can show you angry.*

Ignautius flips, following us, but Vesimyr is already right-side up and darting into the distance as we fly over the ocean, away from the island.

Rain begins to pour as we get further and further out to sea. It doesn't penetrate our armor, but I'm not wearing a helmet, which means my hair is soaking wet. Thunder and lightning sound from overhead as Vesimyr takes a vertical ascent into the clouds.

Ignautius catches up and tries to bite Vesimyr's tail. Vesimyr smacks Ignautius in the face instead, but the blue Dragon reaches his clawed wings up and rakes them against Vesimyr's backside where there is no light armor, and it draws blood.

Vesimyr screams in pain and I scream alongside him, watching in horror as his lifeblood drains into the air, falling through the clouds. My magyk blasts into Vesimyr as I try to recreate the moment with Embyrne.

It works, and Vesimyr's wounds quickly heal.

*It worked.*

*Oh my God.*

*I can heal.*

The how and the why evade me because frankly, they do not matter. Nothing matters more than the challenge.

Embyrne shouts and suddenly birds are attacking us from all angles. They peck at my head and I shriek, batting them away with my arms.

*"She's using my magyk,"* Vesimyr groans. *"Dyana, she's draining me."*

No.

*No!* I refuse this fate.

It's like I detach from my body, watching everything from a distance as I turn in slow motion and lift my hands.

A bow made of pure light appears in them. I don't know why I picked a bow, but I don't pause to question it. Pulling back the arrow, I nock it. There's a high pitched sound as the arrow shoots forward.

The arrow hits true.

I blink, coming back to myself to the sound of Embyrne's screams and watch as she pulls out an arrow made of pure light from her left shoulder.

Just next to her heart. I...almost killed her. I don't know whether to be angry or relieved.

Ignautius and Vesimyr twirl around each other, claws reaching and jaws snapping, as we ascend higher into the storm.

Lighting goes off next to my ear and I shriek. The claps of thunder mixed with the Dragon's roars makes my ears bleed. Rain eventually makes its way through my armor, drenching me.

Vesimyr suddenly drops a few meters, roaring in pain. I glance to the right and watch as Ignautius finishes tearing a large hole in one of Vesimyr's wings.

His larger one. The primary set.

*Fuck.*

I send magyk into his wings, but the armor covering our bodies falters, flickering in and out of existence.

A groan explodes from my mouth as my head starts to throb at such a large pull on my magyk.

"Drop the armor," Vesimyr orders.

"No!"

"Trust me!" he growls as his wings finish healing.

I'm sobbing openly now and toss a scream into the air as I let go of my hold on our armor. It dissipates completely, revealing us to the elements. And making us vulnerable.

"We need to head back to shore," I shout.

Vesimyr nods and dives into a storm cloud so dark, it's nearly black.

I can't see anything. Just darkness.

Vesimyr is quiet beneath me as he twists and twirls, never flying in a straight line. Ignautius suddenly snaps his jaws next to me and I scream, surprised at the close proximity. I shove him away but pain flares in my right arm and I cry out.

There's a dagger in my forearm.

*Oh fuck.*

Without letting go of the reins, I let out a shout of pain and pull the dagger out. I almost pass out. For a second, the world blurs. But already, my flesh is knitting back together.

It's not fast enough though. I can only hold onto the reins with one hand.

Vesimyr emerges from the storm, heading straight for the beach.

My magyk is almost depleted, I can feel it.

*"We need to weaken him!"* I shout in his thoughts.

Vesimyr nods.

*"Get me closer,"* I say.

I feel his agreement and he dives down, drawing Ignautius closer to the surface. Just as we're about to hit, Vesimyr banks. Ignautius isn't quite so nimble, so he hits the surface, sinking down until his wings are nearly out of sight. Embyrne scrambles up his head as Ignautius flaps his wings and tries to get out of the water.

That single moment of pause is all I need.

I aim at Embyrne again, light growing in my palm as I form another arrow in my bow.

There's a pull on my magyk but I keep that shield of light strong, and the pulling stops.

I kept her out.

At that moment, I unleash my arrow.

Yet again, it aims true. I've never used a bow and arrow in my entire life, but suddenly I can shoot *impossible* targets.

Ignautius is hit just behind the neck. Embyrne screams as Ignautius roars in pain, writhing in the air.

There's a shout and Embyrne's magyk comes barreling towards me. I expect physical pain, but instead, her magyk *rips* into my head. It attacks the walls I've worked so hard to build, tearing them down with terrifying ease.

I cry out, falling against Vesimyr as I clutch my head in pain, blood from my earlier wound dripping down my face.

"No!" I croak, trying to shove her out.

But it's too late. By the time I build my magyk enough to shove her out of my head, she's used my healing magyk to heal Ignautius.

I blink my eyes open as they make it out of the water and Ignautius hovers in the air.

My stomach turns and I shut my lips, refusing to gag at the feeling of her stealing my magyk.

Before they can react, I lift my hands and summon my bow, releasing my arrow with a high-pitched zing.

I watch as it hits Embyrne in her abdomen, just below the heart.

She groans and Ignautius snarls.

**_"ENOUGH OF THIS! IT IS TIME FOR YOU BOTH TO DIE."_**

"You'll have to catch us first," I scream back. "NOW, VES!"

Vesimyr charges towards the beach before making another vertical ascent just as we meet the sandy beach.

The entire castle watches as Ignautius follows, both Dragons ascending into the air at unfathomable speeds.

Wind batters me, drying my hair and freezing my cheeks.

_"Okay,"_ his voice sounds in my head. _"When I give the signal."_

I nod, holding on tight.

There, at the peak of the clouds, high above Elysium, Vesimyr flips backwards, putting us just above Ignautius and Embyrne.

Vesimyr takes a deep breath and unleashes a torrent of hot flame at Ignautius.

Which is when I let go.

The world pauses as I drop into the sky.

For a moment, it seems like I hover there along with the Dragons.

One blink, and I'm plummeting, not towards the ground, but towards the blue Dragon.

I angle my body and prepare for the shock of landing as I hit his back.

Ignautius has sharper spikes than Vesimyr, so my already painful hands become slick with fresh blood as I crawl up his spine, one spike at a time.

My arms tremble so hard they feel like they're going to fall off, but I make it, using the larger spikes as footholds.

When I reach Embyrne, she's ready for me.

Just as she starts to stand, Vesimyr blurs, moving so fast I can't track it, as he opens his mouth and bites down on Ignautius's neck.

The blue Dragon screams in pain, thrashing so hard it tosses Embyrne into the air.

I watch in horror as she falls towards the ground.

Before I think otherwise, I'm diving through the air towards her.

Vesimyr lets out a scream of pain and I glance over my shoulder, watching as Ignautius bites off most of Vesimyr's tail, the muscles and thin scales completely shredded.

Both Dragons fall through the air, each losing gallons of blood from their wounds.

Neither stops fighting.

They twist together, snapping and scratching at each other.

I turn and watch as Embyrne gets closer to the sand.

I angle my body straight towards the ground to get to her as fast as I can.

I'm on her in seconds. I grab onto her and shakily form a light dagger in my hand.

*"DO IT! KILL ME!"* She screams.

I huff a laugh, "No."

She watches with wide eyes as I reach down and try to slice off her cuffs.

But my daggers meet resistance.

*Fuck.*

*FUCK.*

Embyrne lets out a dry laugh. "That was your plan? Nothing can cut through Elysian."

The sandy beach approaches so fast and I realize that this is it. This is when we die.

"I'm sorry," I breathe.

Then I repeat the words in my head to the great silver Dragon plunging to the Earth behind us.

*"DYANA!"* Vesimyr screams in my head. *"I'M COMING!"*

*"Kill Ignautius!"*

*"HOLD ON!"* Vesimyr's roar is so great, both Embyrne and I flinch at the sound.

There's no time to react as we plunge towards the ground.

I close my eyes and hug Embyrne tight, ready for the pain.

*"I'm sorry, Ama,"* I send the thought out, imagining it meets whatever frayed, old bond we used to have. I imagine she hears it.

Just as we're about to hit, just as I expect to die, a huge, scaled body hits us from the side. We're sent tumbling into the air, unable to slow down but no longer about to shatter on the sand. I'm ripped away from Embyrne.

Something big grabs me and we hit the water. Everything goes black as pain explodes through every bone in my body.

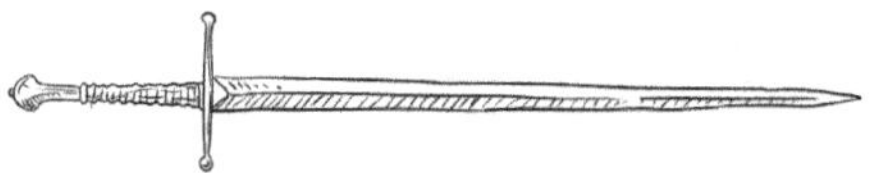

I wake with a gasp. It's pitch black.

I'm not on the sand, I'm on something warm.

Something...moving.

Light suddenly penetrates the darkness as the creature below me moves, revealing wings.

But there's something wrong with the way they're moving.

Which is when I see the broken bones poking through silver Dragon skin.

"Ves?" I pant, my voice hoarse, as if I've been screaming for hours.

*"Can't talk,"* his voice sounds in my head. *"My wings...they're broken. I think my back is broken too."*

"No," I breathe. "Don't—don't move. It's going to be okay."

I try to stay calm but adrenaline courses through me as I begin to panic. Forcing my body to move, I roll over to my stomach and push up to my hands and knees, sliding off of what I now realize was his belly.

He landed back first.

Oh Gods.

His lower half is in the water, but his upper half is on the sand. Water floods my boots but I could care less.

Vesimyr lowers his wings further, letting out a groan of pain. There's so much exposed bone.

I cover my mouth in horror as I take in the shredded membranes between his wing joints. The exposed, fractured bones breaking through his skin. The steaming red blood coating his silver scales.

There's a loud groan next to me, and we're a few meters away from Embyrne, who is on her back in the sand. Blood pools next to her, but she's alive. Her chest moves up and down, albeit slowly.

Which is when I hear that groan of pain again. Which means it wasn't Embyrne making the sound.

I force my legs to move, wincing at what feels like a badly sprained ankle. Pain bolts up my leg with each step, but I don't stop until I fully emerge from the safety of Vesimyr's broken wings.

Ignautius survived.

The big blue Dragon pushes up to stand.

"Vesimyr, can you walk?" I snarl.

*"Yes, but Dyana, I'll be too slow. You need to run."*

"I'm not leaving you," I bare my teeth. "Partners don't *leave*. So, you need to get up."

Vesimyr groans next to me as he tries to roll onto his back. I force my own legs to stand. I'm shaky, but I get up off my knees.

I take a few steps, nearly tripping in the sand, and face Ignautius. His wings are broken in a few places, other pieces nearly ripped off. Blood drips from his snout where a few of his large fangs have shattered.

But he's *alive.* He's alive.

My head falls back as I take a deep breath, forcing the air into my lungs.

*I'm not a human. The pain isn't real. It's a brief moment. It's inconsequential.*

*You need to finish this.*

*You need to finish this.*

Vesimyr and Embyrne's voices echo in my memories as I force the pain away, locking it away.

For the first time since waking up, I feel the full loss of my humanity.

The world around me turns sharp and I take another breath, lowering my head, as I meet Ignautius's silver gaze.

He lets out a mighty roar before charging towards me, mouth open.

I'm so tired.

*I'm so tired.* But I ignore all of it and let out a hoarse scream as I yank on my magyk. A huge longsword materializes in my hands. It refracts rainbows in the air around us.

"Vesimyr, GO!" I shout.

But he slumps back down in the sand, giving up trying to get up.

*"I cannot. Not until I heal."*

"GET UP!"

Vesimyr nudges me lightly with one of his claws.

*"Partners don't leave. I'm staying, Dyana. Whatever happens, we will face it together."*

"Damnit! You stubborn Dragon."

Ignautius is almost on top of me, so close that I can smell his breath, when I roll to the side, swiping out with my sword.

His roar of pain has me back on my feet. A few meters away, a large portion of his wing twitches in a pool of blood.

Ignautius is screeching in agony as he charges me again. But he's off balance.

I draw my sword up and sprint towards him. He snaps his jaws so close, I nearly lose my head, but I swerve to the left and narrowly avoid it. Raising my sword, I slide it through the softer scales of his belly.

Hot blood sprays me, nearly burning my skin on contact.

Ignautius falls to the ground as he curls his remaining wing around his belly, trying to hold his organs in.

Which is when my magyk falters.

One second it's there, the next, a pounding headache explodes behind my eyes.

There's nothing left to pull on.

"DYANA!" a scream behind me sounds and I turn, watching in slow motion as Mirielle sprints down the beach, a large double-sided staff in her hands.

It looks just like her old one.

"CATCH!" she shouts and then she's throwing it through the air like a javelin. Without thinking, I take off and squat before jumping into the air to catch it.

**"She in-interfered!"** Ignautius's voice is all garbled.

The staff is cold in my hands as I land in the sand. My ankle is screaming at me, but already I can hear the sound of Ignautius's flesh healing itself.

**"She ch-ch-cheated!"**

I limp over to his twitching body. He snaps at me, trying to bite my legs, but I kick out, hitting one of his teeth so hard it breaks off.

Ignautius trips, falling into the sand and I see my moment.

With a scream, I raise Mirielle's staff and bring it down on the Sene Skal's neck. The sharp edge slices through his scales, through muscle and bone. It gets halfway through his neck as Ignautius writhes and shrieks in pain beneath me. I yank the staff out and bring it down on his neck once more. I lose myself in the bloodbath, chopping away until Ignautius's head detaches.

I let out one more roar and kick the head, sending it rolling down towards the water, where it begins to turn the surf red.

It's like everything goes perfectly, completely quiet. For a few minutes, no one reacts, as we all stare at the red surf in shock.

Eventually the whispers begin.

*"He's dead."*

*"Ignautius is dead."*

I distantly hear the whispers begin to travel through the air as the Dragons watching realize what's happened.

*"They won. The old bastard and the abominations won."*

*"They cheated!"*

*"What do we do now?"*

Someone is shouting at me, but it's so far away. As the adrenaline drains, the pain hits. Then the beach turns sideways as I hit the sand and pass out.

# CHAPTER 44
## AMALIA

The second I step through those curtains, emerging into the back area, I freeze. My muscles won't move. I can't think, can't breathe, can't even feel my heartbeat; I think that stopped too.

The smell of urine and feces hit me in the face as the others stream in around me.

But I can't move.

I can only look on in horror as my screams die on my tongue. My heart begins to race so hard, it might break my rib cage open and fall to the ground.

All around me are magykal creatures shoved into tiny, painful cages. Soren and Fi appear, having already started freeing some of the animals. How they managed to get in here before us, I have no idea. There are so many *more* than what were shown to us. We saw the ones with no visible wounds or injuries.

The others...they are dying. There is no other word for it. Tortured to death in a cage, their paws never touching the ground. The air is thick with the scent of blood and infection as the rebels begin to open the cages and grab the animals.

I...I thought I'd be spurred into action. But I can't move.

I'm frozen in horror. I can't do anything but stare at the animals.

"We'll have to make a portal right outside. We can't get them all out of here in one trip."

There. I can move. My head snaps to the side as I look at Fi. He's right. Which means...I have to break a promise.

*For Os,* I whisper to myself as I lower my walls. I haven't done this since...the Gauntlet.

I let myself into their heads. I take their pain. Even though it might just kill me in return.

A loud roar sounds from outside as Ryu blasts through a wall, sending stone and dust flying. Her copper and silver eyes are furious.

*"Amalia, you know you shouldn't do that!"*

The weight of their pain is *crushing* but I merely grit my teeth and keep going.

*"You're as stubborn as the wolf,"* Ryu sighs.

The animals are happy now. Relaxed enough to let the rebels handle them. The smallest ones are wrapped up in blankets we brought in. The bigger animals get harnessed, if possible. Ryu somehow convinces the baby griffyns to climb onto her back.

I watch it all, frozen in place. No one notices how I'm suffocating under the weight of their pain.

No one sees the panic in my eyes. No one except for Ryu.

As the animals are carried out and as Nyall begins to create a portal, I remain still. Ryu nudges me gently, forcing my body to move. My feet step but I do not feel it. Still, she guides me out of the building, her nose beneath my arm.

*"Thank you,"* I whisper in her head. *"There are things in this life that I simply have to do."*

*"I know, I just wish it didn't hurt you in the process."*

*Me too.* I don't share that thought with her.

Something hits me in the back and I blink, forcing my head to look down. One of the baby griffyns fell. It squawks at me, terrified. I open myself to it, reaching out to its bright mind and grabbing hold.

*"I am a friend,"* I whisper to it, as I send feelings of love and safety. *"Trust me."*

Carefully, I reach down and pick it up. It's much heavier than it looks, and much softer. The griffyn chick's feathers are silky soft. It flares its wings, wrapping them around me as I hold it against my chest. Luckily, its nails aren't very long, otherwise my hands would be in bloody shreds.

It squeaks in my ear as I transfer the griffyn's back paws to one hand and wrap my arm around it, tucking it around the griffyn's body beneath its fluffy wings. Until a sound reaches my ears.

A sound that sets my hair on end—the roar of a *Dragon.*

**"IT'S A TRAP!"** I shout, projecting my voice so that all the rebels hear me.

"I know," a voice whispers to my left and I glance to the side just in time to avoid the blade. Looking up the long blade, I find the blade wielder.

"Ireyna," I hiss. "I had rather hoped I would never have to see you again."

The tall woman smiles. Her black hair shorter, ending just below her chin. A thick black tattoo now marks her neck; some symbol I've never seen before. It makes her look even more severe.

"Yes." Ireyna nods, her onyx eyes cold. "I had hoped I would never have to see you again as well. You should have died that day. That's a mistake I'm here to remedy."

All at once, everyone *moves.*

Ryu roars but something hits her from the side. I turn and watch in horror as a white Dragon tackles her. It's smaller, but no less deadly. Particularly because Ryu has never met another Dragon before.

Before I can react, Nyall is shooting white magyk at Ireyna as soldiers emerge behind us, encircling our group. Everyone drops the animals, many of which can't walk by themselves.

I rip into Nyall's mind. *"Build the portal and get them out of here."*

*"I'm not leaving you!"* he snarls, sounding more draconian than Ryu.

*"Then come back for me, but if we don't get them out, they'll be killed in the crossfire! Fucking MOVE!"*

Nyall growls aloud and it becomes a shout as he redirects his magyk into the portal. The large tunnel of smoke appears.

"Take the griffyn," I shout at Nyall. "I'll cover you."

The Prince nods, but I can see the pain in his eyes. I know he doesn't want to do this, but he has to. Nyall grabs the griffyn and steps through, many of the rebels following behind.

The Dragons wrestle in the marsh as Ryu lets out a shriek of pain.

With a thought, I summon Morrigyn's blades into my hands and drench them in Hellfyre.

"Leave now, and I won't kill you," I nod to Ireyna.

She smirks, and it's that moment, that *reaction*, which causes my stomach to drop. She's too confident. Which means there's something I don't know.

I hear the sharp whistle of a blade moving quickly through the air and jump to the side. Whirling, I come face to face with…

"Hello, *Wytch*," Amari hisses. "You deserve everything they're going to give you."

With a shout, I charge, jumping into the air and bringing my blades down in an X position.

*Cut the head off the snake.*

Ireyna disappears just as I'm about to slice my blades through her neck.

I land hard, disoriented, and roll back to my feet. But she's already there, parrying with a sharp silver longsword.

I'm fast, but she's faster. I force my body to move as fast as it can but she's still faster.

What the *fuck?*

Then I stumble and her blade meets my shoulder. The sharp bite of pain makes me gasp and I clutch my arm.

*"HEAL,"* I order the flesh.

But my flesh doesn't respond.

Ireyna's laugh makes my tongue turn heavy. I glance over as she approaches me with a wide smile on her face.

The woman crouches and I scoot away, but her foot meets my side, sending me face first into the mud.

"You stupid little girl, did you think I was human just because my ears were round?" Ireyna taunts. "You're so naïve."

*Oh shit.*

"Did you really think you were stronger than me? I'm 300 years old, *girl*. You are *nothing.*"

I push myself off the ground and lift my swords, ignoring the blood streaming down my arm, making it hard to keep my grip. Shooting bolts of pain go up my arm, making my vision blurry.

But that won't stop me.

"I am the right hand of the Morrigyn." I spit a wad of blood at her feet and flash her a bloody smile.

Ireyna scoffs and flashes me an equally manic smile. "I do not care about the false idol."

Soldiers charge but Ireyna holds up a hand, stopping them. "No, she's *mine.*"

Ryu screams again in the background, this time not of pain but of rage.

Ireyna's attention diverts for a moment.

Good thing I only *need* a moment.

I yank on my magyk, ready to rain Hellfyre down upon her and all with her.

But...nothing happens.

There is...nothing.

I reach deep within me, clawing for my magyk, but it's *gone.*

Ireyna watches me panic with a smirk on her face.

"Your wytchcraft won't work on me," Ireyna laughs and leans to the side. "Null spell, courtesy of the Holy Father."

*Oh gods. That's the tattoo on her neck.*

I panic, charging with my swords but she parries easily, meeting my every effort. She's so strong, I quickly move to losing ground as I defend myself.

Before I can react, her foot lands on my chest, sending me to the ground. She swings her blade down towards my head and I quickly roll out of the way. If I still had long hair, her blade would have sheared it right off.

I try to get up, but Ireyna swings her blade down once more, aiming for my shoulders. I fall out of the way, but I land right on my already bleeding wound.

Pain explodes through me. Something hard smashes into my hands, making me drop my blades.

Ireyna stands on my left hand, crushing the fingers. I refuse to scream. I won't give her the satisfaction.

She squats down, ready to say something to me, which is when I strike. Kicking out with my leg, I send her to the ground and crawl on top of her. Grabbing her head, I smash it back into the dust, trying to crack open her skull.

Ireyna struggles against me, punching and hitting me, but I don't let up. My hands reach around her throat, squeezing so tightly her face turns blue. I lean down, ready to scream in her face, when I hear the words leave her mouth.

"H-he's alive."

Everything in my head goes quiet and I loosen my hold on her instantly.

"Who is alive?"

A portal suddenly whirls into existence next to where we lay on the ground. *Thank the Gods.*

"Os," Ireyna whispers. "He's *alive.*"

# CHAPTER 45
## AMALIA

"Os," Ireyna whispers. "He's *alive.*"

I roll off her and scramble to my feet, but someone pushes me to the ground. I glance back and find Amari pointing a blade at my neck.

Trembling, I look back at Ireyna.

"You're lying," I breathe. "You fucking *bitch,* that is a LIE. I saw him die. I was *there.*"

Ireyna laughs. "You think Remus Ostia is so easy to kill? His body can break, but he is a Dragon. He will always heal."

For a moment, my head is silent. I'm frozen as she looks at me in mocking pity.

Ireyna smiles. "Not a lie. Os is *alive.*"

I'm leaping on top of her and pummeling my fist into her face so hard that I can feel her nose shatter beneath my fist.

"I am not lying," she laughs, choking on the blood streaming from her nose and mouth. It splatters my face, but I don't even feel it. "I should know, considering I've spent the last two years torturing him."

Then Ireyna is gone.

I fall, off balance at her sudden disappearance. Whirling, I try to find her, only to notice the soldiers retreating.

There's no sign of her. She's gone.

"GET BACK HERE, YOU FUCKING COWARD!" I scream.

Her laughter bounces off the buildings and I jump to my feet, looking around for any sight of her.

Wait...I don't hear Ryu.

The shrieks of pain and anger stopped.

*Where is my Dragon?* The moment I think it is the moment I know something is very, very wrong.

Nyall steps out of the portal right as I spot Ireyna in the distance.

"No..." My voice is hoarse. Horror turns my blood to ice.

*No, no, NO, NO, NO.*

~~*Please, no. Please don't do this to me. I won't survive it.*~~

The white Dragon has Ryu's neck between her jaws.

It bites down and Ryu cries out in pain. Her eyes are wide and full of fear as steaming crimson blood runs over her scales.

*"RYU, DON'T MOVE!"* I try to scream into her head, but my magyk doesn't respond.

"RYU!" I scream aloud, running towards her.

A shout behind me tells me Nyall has seen it too. His footsteps trail behind me.

"IREYNA!" Nyall's scream is full of so much anger it nearly drowns me. "DROP THE DRAGON AND FACE ME!"

Ireyna laughs at the panic on our faces.

We sprint faster but it's not enough.

Ireyna disappears, and with her, she takes the two Dragons.

*No.*

*No.*

*No. No. No. NO.*

Distantly, I hear someone screaming.

It takes a few moments to realize that person is me.

Ryu is gone. Ryu is gone and Ireyna *took* her.

My magyk returns but all it does is fuel my anger. Leaning my head back, I let it explode, blasting flames into the sky. I'm destroying their homes, and *I don't care.* There is nothing left, nothing but pain and rage as I burn within my own inferno.

A hand touches my cheek.

Nyall pushes through my flames, unhurt and unburned. He kneels before me, tears streaming down his cheeks.

"We will get her back," he swears. "We will get Ryu back, Amalia."

"Amari," I breathe.

Nyall goes still. "What?"

"She told them we would be here."

I watch from a place of cold numbness as the rage upon Nyall's face grows.

I let my flames die out, but anger still burns hot within my chest.

Nyall grabs my hand and pulls me back to the portal still swirling behind us.

The rebels follow us, Amari included.

Nyall says nothing until we get back to the safety of the Ulster Wald. The entire group is silent and tense.

The moment we're all safe and the portal disappears, white magyk explodes out of Nyall, caging Amari within it. Nyall's white hair floats on a phantom wind, and his eyes begin to glow silver.

Creatures mill about, many wrapped up in blankets and held by the rebels.

"You betrayed me." Nyall's voice is so cold, I'm surprised it doesn't bring the snow. "You betrayed *her.*"

Amari trembles and points a finger at me.

"She is EVIL, and you are blind to it! How can you not see what she is?"

Nyall flashes his fangs, fury burning bright within his eyes.

"No," I whisper, and meet Nyall's gaze. "She's mine."

I am breaking apart, splintering into shards of glass on the ground.

Amari told them where we would be.

Amari helped them steal my Dragon. My *child!*

Nyall meets my gaze for a moment.

*"Our child,"* he corrects.

With a nod, Keres and Davyn appear, grabbing each of Amari's arms and dragging her to the training field. The entire camp is gathered. They watch in complete silence.

I tune out their whispers, tune out their suspicion and their fear.

Distantly, I hear them ask where the Dragon is, before others tell them the answer.

~~They took her. They took her. They took her. THEY TOOK HER.~~

My thoughts are single-minded.

There is only one thing that matters right now.

I don't believe for one second that Os is really alive. I would know. I would *feel it*...wouldn't I?

~~But what if she's right?~~

The thought etches itself on skull, worming its way into my brain until it's all I can think about.

*What if?*

*What if Os is alive?*

It only fuels my already uncontrollable rage.

Amari is brought into the middle of the field. Still in my dress, I reach down and rip the bottom half off, giving myself freedom of movement.

"Just kill me and be done with it." She spits in my face.

"No," I tsk. "No...I don't think so."

I face her, tossing my swords to the ground instead of letting them disappear into the ether.

"No magyk. No weapons."

Nyall nods at my proclamation before turning to walk away to join the others at the edge of the field. Davyn and Keres drop Amari's arms and join Nyall.

*"Make it hurt."* His voice is that of a vengeful God.

Amari watches him with disgust. "You're supposed to be our leader, and you will let *her* decide the fate of your people?"

Nyall ignores her. His eyes are only on me.

"The kill is yours."

The words are quiet, but the field falls silent in their wake.

I take a deep breath and I'm in Amari's face a second later, fists flying. She evades me, but I'm faster.

Ireyna's face appears in my mind.

I leap onto Amari so hard that I send her crashing to the ground.

Ever since Ryu disappeared before my eyes, a red haze has tinted my vision, painting the world in crimson.

Amari fights me off, punching me in the side as I wrap my hands around her throat.

Leaning forward, I exhale Hellfyre into her open mouth, watching as she writhes beneath me, burning to death.

***"HEAL,"*** I command her flesh, and her flesh obeys.

I heal her just enough that the fire continues to burn, killing her without letting her fully die.

I lean down until we're nose to nose and let my fire abate.

"You're the reason she's gone," I whisper. "You're the reason they took her."

The cycle repeats as I let my Hellfyre fill her once more.

The crowd remains silent. Everything else disappears as I picture Ryu, terrified and chained as she's tortured by the Elves.

I stop healing her. Standing above her, I watch as her skin turns red and begins to bubble.

Then I stop the flames again.

On the brink of death, I order her flesh to heal. Something equally as painful. Amari's screams turn hoarse, and she begins to cry, her tears trailing a path down her raw cheek.

"You-you're not j-just as b-bad," she hiccups. "You're *worse.*"

I flash her bloodthirsty smile. "I know."

Then I let my head fall back and *howl.*

# CHAPTER 46
## MARA

My heart is torn into pieces as I watch someone I once called a friend get tortured by Amalia Asteroth.

The Gray Wytch's scream echoes through the forest. Her battle cry. More terrifying than the Dyre Wolf's howl.

I *warned* them. I told them not to do anything. That *this* is what awaited us if we did. It's not worth it. Because this is just *her* punishment. I dread what happens when it's Nyall Drayven's turn.

That's the problem. Nyall Drayven loves Amalia Asteroth. The Rebel Prince and his Gray Wytch.

Which means any insult to her, is henceforth, an insult to *him* too.

The Wytch's howl fades, breaking off as her voice grows hoarse. But then, something *else* happens. Something howls *back*. At first, it's a single note. One voice. Then more join in. Dozens of other howls harmonizing together, both a eulogy and a declaration. The howls die down, leaving us in heavy silence.

The silence, however, doesn't last long. Not a howl, this time, but a deep, thumping drum.

No, not drums...*Paws.* The sound speeds up, getting closer and closer as the forest begins to shake. It sounds like the mountain is going to come down around us. Louder than rolling thunder and more terrifying than a summer monsoon.

The Dyre Wolves are here. From the tree line, hundreds of glowing eyes emerge as a great, black Dyre Wolf appears beneath the bright of the moon. Wolves stream around the Alpha before sprinting towards us. They run into the field, circling

Amalia and Amari. The black wolf approaches Amalia, its snout pressing against her cheek.

*This.*

*This* is why I hesitate. I don't like her. I never will. She's a murdering psychopath, but apparently she's a murdering psychopath with a *heart.* Or some small part of one, at least. I can officially say I've seen it.

That is what our enemy doesn't have. Will *never* have. That is why Nyall loves her.

It will have to be enough; it's our only option.

The black wolf licks Amalia's cheek before sitting down next to her. He's so large, though Amalia is standing, they're the same height. And then the Wytch sets her wolves upon Amari.

The large black Dyre Wolf goes first.

I look away as others join it.

They don't just kill her. They *consume* her. Tearing her apart. Limbs fly. A wolf runs by with a piece of her hand in its mouth. Amalia watches it all. Her blue eyes nearly gray, leeched of all color. A hollow, terrifying look on her face. Blood coats her clothes and hair, the splatter decorating her bare skin. The dress she arrived in is destroyed, covered in mud and bodily fluids.

This...is our savior. This...*being.*

I have never been a religious person, but something strikes me, then. The Cult of Sol Constantus preaches that following Him will save you. For otherwise, you are doomed to Hell. One of them, depending on which God you believe in.

I believe now that they are wrong. We are already doomed to Hell. Hell is *here,* *because* Amalia Asteroth is no Wytch. She is a demon. She has to be.

No matter who wins this war, we are all *damned.*

"DO NOT WEEP YET:
YOU'LL NEED YOUR
TEARS FOR WHAT
ANOTHER SWORD
MUST YET INFLICT."

— DANTE ALIGHIERI, 1265–1321.
THE DIVINE COMEDY: PURGATORY

SCAN FOR THE PT. 4
READING PLAYLIST

# PART FOUR:
# THE DAMNED

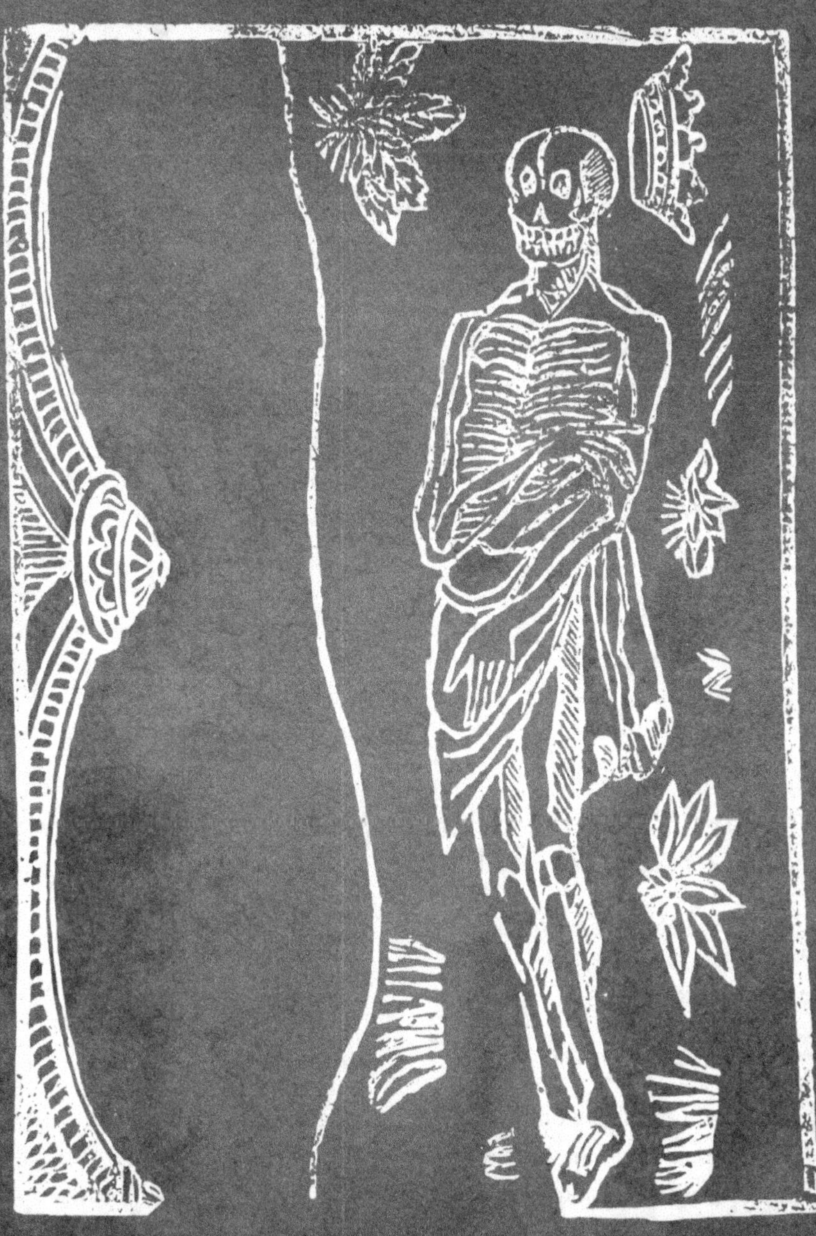

# CHAPTER 47
## RYU

It's so *cold*.

Even when winter hit the Ulster Wald, my fire never dimmed, and my scales never cooled. But my fire feels so far away. I keep reaching for it, but it slips out of my grasp.

Consciousness comes slowly, as if my brain is stuck in quicksand. There's a pull on my mind, nudging me into the dark.

***"Wake up."***

***"Wake up."***

***"Wake up."***

The voice echoes in my head, bouncing off my skull.

I know that voice.

I...need to wake up.

With a groan, I *will* my spirit to my body. I imagine the feeling of my closed eyelids until I *can* feel my closed eyelids.

It takes all of my strength to open my eyes.

Everything is blurry.

*Where am I? What happened?*

Drops of water bead on my scales, making me shiver. Pain wrecks my jaw along the left side where the white Dragon hit me in the teeth. My tongue trembles as I brush it over the broken, cracked fangs.

I move my legs but bolts of pain shoot through my bones, bleeding into my muscles and nerves. I try to roar but something holds my jaw mostly shut. Blinking, I look down at the metal muzzle around my snout. I can open my mouth a little, but not enough to do much of anything other than drink water.

Blinking, I try to make sense of my surroundings.

*"You know where you are,"* my mother's voice whispers through my memories. *"You know why you are here."*

Pain shoots through my skull as I try and remember the details.

*"Shh,"* she whispers in my thoughts. *"Relax your mind and remember where you are. Remember, Ryu."*

*Remember.*

*Remember...*

Flashes of Amalia's face run through my head. Her screaming at me, looking on from a distance with horror. The world around us turns upside down as something hits me from the side.

Something *large.*

I...I was fighting a *Dragon.* The memory becomes clear.

I fought the white Dragon, and I lost. The white Dragon's rider used magyk like Nyall's and portaled us out of there.

The memory turns dark where I lost consciousness. Whatever they hit me with was strong *and* loaded with magyk. Dragon's do not easily *weaken.* Even one as young as me.

As the memory fades, the full realization of where I am hits me.

*"Yes."* My mother's voice is ancient and weary as she confirms my suspicion.

I'm in the Pit. It's...it's been rebuilt. But how?

How is this possible?

For a moment, my mind exists in two places. I see through the eyes of the Crimson Queen, surveying her cage.

Her *prison*.

At the same time, I look around at my own.

*"I never wanted this for you. I'm so sorry."*

Her voice fades, leaving me alone.

The cave I'm in is dark. Gray stone surrounds me, with no light in sight. A large tunnel leads out off to the right, but it's currently blocked by a tightly woven iron gate.

Setting aside the pain, I force myself up, standing on my two front legs while my back two remain laying down—there isn't enough room to fully stand.

I've managed to remain calm, but as my head hits the top of the cage bars, panic suddenly descends.

*"Amalia?"* I ask in my mind, but it's like the connection is gone.

Like *she* is gone.

*No. No. No!* I push up on all fours and my body bangs against the metal bars. The walls begin to close in and my heart races, blood pumping so fast I'm surprised it doesn't burst right out of me.

*"AMALIA!"* I cry out. *"AMALIA!"*

There is no response.

*"Ama—please."* My voice is small and scared. Stars burst behind my eyes as my panic grows. *"Ama—Mom. MOM. Please...I'm scared."*

I need my family.

None of us have ever said it. But I know it and so do they.

Kydis hatched me, but Amalia and Nyall *raised* me. They are not only my friends, but they are also my parents. My *family*.

And now they're gone.

My legs give out as my breath comes faster. Hot, steaming tears drip from my eyes.

*"Breathe,"* a voice runs through my head suddenly. *"Breathe, little one."*

"I-I can't—"

A large black claw slides through my cage and grabs hold of my leg. *"Yes you can. Close your eyes."*

I scoff.

*"Do it."* The Dragon's voice is firm but scratchy, as if his throat is slightly charred. I do not know if all Dragons have this ability, but I've always been able to tell the true nature, true *magyk* of a creature, just from their voice or scent. Even behind a glamour. I just know.

Which is why I know the voice in my head belongs to a Dragon. An old Dragon. A powerful one, though that doesn't matter right now. What matters is that if he's here, he's a prisoner. Just like me.

I close my eyes and focus on the feeling of his talon, of those black sharp claws, the feeling of his scales against mine.

*"You're not alone,"* he whispers, as I force myself to take deep breaths. *"I remember the first time they put me in here. I woke up and the sky was gone."*

I concentrate on his words as I cling to his claw.

*"You've been here before?"* I manage to ask.

*"Yes."* His voice turns sad. *"I have."*

*"I'm sorry."*

His claw squeezes mine gently.

"It is not your fault."

The panic slips away, leaving exhaustion in its wake.

*"We're in the Dragon Pit, aren't we?"* I ask quietly.

*"Yes."*

*"Wasn't it destroyed?"*

For a moment, the Dragon is silent. Then, his charred, scratchy voice answers. Not in my head, but out loud.

**"It was remade."**

I let out a trembling breath and move my body, turning so I can look at whoever this old Dragon is, but the moment I catch sight of him, I freeze.

Golden eyes—pure, molten, brilliant gold—*watch* me. He's a black Dragon, with scales so dark, no light reflects off them. It's as if he's almost made of shadows.

But his eyes glow like a lit furnace. He's also the biggest Dragon I've ever seen. I thought my cage was cramped but he...he's *shoved* inside of it.

*"What is your name?"* he asks.

*"Ryu."* I nod my head, bowing to him, but the Dragon waves a claw in the air.

*"I suspect it is I who should bow to you."*

I blink. *"How—"*

*"You look like her. The Crimson Queen."* He says this in my head, not wanting to let prying ears hear. *"And your magyk...it sings.*

*"I don't have magyk, though. Not really."*

*"You do; you just haven't found it yet."*

Hmm.

*"What's your name?"* I ask.

The Dragon takes a deep breath and there's a bright flash of light. In a moment, the great Dragon disappears and in its place is...

*A man.*

*"Beastkyn."* My mother's voice rings in my memories. That's what they call a Dragon that can shift into mortal form. Beastkyn.

The Beastkyn kneels next to me, placing his warm hand on my cold scales.

*"My name,"* he says softly, *"is Remus Ostia. But you may call me Os."*

My heart stops. I *know* that name. I've heard it so many times before.

*"You're supposed to be dead,"* I breathe. *"You died. They saw you die."*

Os takes a deep breath.

*"I very nearly did."* He meets my eyes. *"Now, tell me, Ryu…why were you calling my familiar's name?"*

If it weren't for the muzzle around my snout, my jaw would drop.

Those molten eyes turn pleading and desperate.

*"How do you know Amalia?"* Os asks. *"How do you know my familiar?"*

# CHAPTER 48
## AMALIA

Nothing else exists outside of saving Ryu.

*Nothing.*

Voices call after me as I leave the pack to their *consumption*. A long time ago, I might have felt guilty for how easily I can be cruel.

Right now, I *relish* the blood on my hands. The rebels look at me with a mix of fear, horror, and disgust.

*Good.* Satisfaction worms through me.

*Be afraid. This is what happens when you take what is mine!*

I will always choose her. Choose my *family.*

Nothing, *nothing,* will stop me. There is no risk I will not take to save Ryu, and that's their mistake. They haven't seen me untethered. They think they have. But it's been a long two years since that day in the Arena.

I don't even notice as Nyall sidles up next to me. I'm already back inside of his tent, throwing stuff in a bag. I don't need much, so I pack light, just a spare set of clothes and weapons.

He does not ask where I'm going or why. He simply takes in my packing with a nod.

"Do you want me to portal you there?"

I shake my head. "Can't risk it that close to the city. They'll be monitoring *everything.*"

Nyall frowns at the truth in my words.

"It's a two-day ride from the edge of the forest to Castael Laryn if I don't stop. Can you make me a portal to the edge of the Ulster Wald at least?"

His hand reaches mine and he grabs it, squeezing gently.

Nyall nods. "We're going to get her back. I swear it."

For a moment, we just stand there, staring into each other's eyes. Everything is about to change. He and I *both* know the consequences of what's about to happen.

The war we've been talking about and preparing for is *here.*

They started this war, and *I'm* going to finish it.

"I have to meet with the generals and then I'm going to meet you there."

"How?"

Nyall's eyes narrow. "I'll portal into the Annag and meet you at the city gates."

"They'll be able to feel the magyk, Nyall."

The Prince turned Rebel snarls, allowing the fury simmering within him to flare to the surface as silver threads burst in his eyes. "I don't give a *fuck* if they feel me. I'm not letting you walk in there alone."

"I'm fine—"

Nyall clasps my face. "Stop. This isn't about your capabilities. This is about the fact that Ryu is *ours.* She's *ours,* Amalia. Our family. I will rip Castael Laryn to the fucking ground if need be, but I'm coming with you. You are not alone anymore, Blue.

A very real part of me understands. This is the reality of being a leader. This is why I can't be one.

I want him to come with me, but I also know he can't just leave.

"Amalia, look at me." He cups my face and the tears finally escape me as I sob silently within his hands. He presses a kiss to either side of my face before pressing his forehead against mine.

"We're going to get her back. We're going to get *our daughter* back. I will tear the Black Citadel down with my goddamn bare hands if I have to."

I crumble fully and he wraps me in his arms as we stand there, united in grief for the hatchling we raised.

I eventually pull away, despite how difficult it is, and look up into Nyall's mismatched gaze.

"Come on," he says. "I'll walk you to the stables. You're taking Aanad."

I would protest, but the Oryx is faster than a normal horse. I need Aanad, despite wanting to leave her out of this.

"Thank you," I breathe as we make it to the stable and Nyall quickly tacks her up. He traces white, glowing symbols up and down her legs before doing the same across my saddle bag.

I connect with Aanad and sense Nyall's magyk. He infused her legs with strength, protecting her muscles and bones from injury. One peek into the saddle bag shows me it's now full of food.

"Ride hard," he whispers into my ear as he grabs one leg and hoists me into the saddle. Nyall grabs my hand.

"It's a two-day ride, but even on Aanad, that's a near impossible feat. In three days, meet me at the eastern side of the wall of Castael Laryn at sundown."

I nod.

"You know that this is a trap?" he asks in my mind.

"Of course I know this is a trap. They will regret baiting me."

"Yes, they will," he growls, reaching his other hand up. Nyall fists my hair and yanks me down for a hard kiss. "We'll get her back, Blue."

I feel him slip something around my wrist, but I don't need to glance down as the magyk hits me.

A glamour. My hair is longer and dark brown. I have no idea what color my eyes are, but I don't care.

"Thank you," I breathe.

We *will* get her back. Even if it means we die in the process. That's what this is—admitting she's not just our friend, but our *child*. It means we will die for her. Both of us.

"Go," Nyall nods and steps back. He makes a movement with his hands, activating a small portal, one just big enough for Aanad and I to pass through. Beyond the smoke, I can make out the edge of the Ulster Wald. Now we won't have to waste days trying to make it out of the forest.

We share one final look before I whistle to Aanad, who breaks into a floaty canter as we dash into the smoky portal.

I never once look back.

# CHAPTER 49
## MARA

"Where is she?" I ask as Nyall enters the war tent. "Where's Amalia?"

Nyall lifts his chin and surveys us, "Amalia went after Ryu."

Holy *shit*. I mean, I'm not surprised, but *fuck*. She's going after the Archmage now? She's not waiting until the morning?

There's no way to go to Castael Laryn and avoid that confrontation.

"What are you going to do?" Soren asks. Everyone is gathered around the table, solemn, hollow looks on their faces.

"I'm going to follow her."

Several around the table go still. Someone gasps, "You can't leave us!"

"I'm not leaving you," Nyall crosses his arms. "You all are coming with me."

My heart stops.

"The war we've been waiting for? It's here. This is it. All of our training comes down to this. I want every single rebel of fighting ability prepared and armored."

"We can't mobilize the entire rebellion in two days, Nyall." Soren's eyes are wide.

"We can and we will. I'm not letting Amalia face this alone. She *deserves* our help, as does Ryu."

We're all silent as the reality hangs heavy over our heads.

"I'm going to Castael Laryn," Nyall says simply. "If you don't want the Rebellion to do so, then you lead it."

I blink in shock.

"You would leave the Rebellion?" Soren asks quietly.

"Yes, I would." Nyall nods, no remorse in his gaze.

"You've spent centuries working on this, Nyall," Soren protests, standing. "You can't just abandon it for some *girl*—"

Soren's words cut off a second later.

We all watch in horror as a band of white light wraps around her neck, *choking* her.

"I'm going after Ryu. *And* Amalia. The only discussion to be had is whether or not the rebellion is going to war." The white light dissipates and Soren gasps, panting and clasping her chest as fear makes her eyes go wide.

"Decide," Nyall leans against the wall, watching us. "Now."

***"I am going after Amalia as well,"*** a loud, growling voice slams into our minds in unison and we all flinch. A huge, black wolf head appears as Amalia's Dyre Wolf enters the tent. ***"Because Amalia is walking into a trap."***

Others flock behind him, wolves of smaller build but no less terrifying. Their eyes all glow with an eerie light.

"I know," Nyall looks to the Wolf with a respectful nod. "I told her the same."

***"That is not the trap I speak of, young Prince."***

"Can someone please explain?" I ask, trying not to sound frantic or hysterical.

***"Sit down."*** The command hits us at once and everyone around the table, with the exception of Nyall, sits down. For a moment, the wolf *commanded* my muscles.

How the fuck can he do that? Fear rises within me as the wolf looks around at us.

It's his next words though, that freezes my blood and robs the breath from my lungs.

***"For over 500 years, you have been told a very carefully crafted lie."***

The wolf takes a deep breath and begins to speak. We all listen carefully, taking in every word.

But what he says shocks me to my core. He explains the trap, the *true* trap, and several people in the tent whimper aloud, horrified by the truth. Spit floods my mouth as my stomach turns and nausea rises.

Oh Gods.

Oh *Gods.*

We were so wrong. So, so wrong.

When the wolf is done explaining things, he pauses, letting it sink in.

***"That is not the only lie you've been told,"*** the wolf begins once more. ***"Amalia—the Gray Wytch—never killed any children."***

The words sink in and I look around at the others, equally confused.

The Wolf sighs, seeing more explanation is needed. ***"Amalia Asteroth has spent the better part of 60 years listening as everyone around her thought the worst, and she said nothing. Because she never killed any children; she saved them. We both did."***

"What do you mean?" I ask, my voice trembling. "My sons are dead. Not saved."

***"No, Mara Ashcroft, your sons are not dead."***

My heart skips a beat.

"W-what?"

***"When Amalia and I learned that the High Council, the Archmage, was stealing children for inscription into their dread armies, we decided to stop it."***

No one makes a sound. Nyall doesn't look surprised. He knows this truth.

***"The only way to stop them truly was to make the Ulster Wald so terrify-ing, they'd hesitate to even step a single foot in the forest. So we hunted,***

*and we killed, but the children...they survived.*" The wolf cranks his neck and meets my eyes. *"All of them survived."*

"They're alive?" I breathe. "Where...where are they?"

*"Cayden and Baelor Ashcroft reside in Grimheim."*

A strangled sound leaves me, and I slap a hand over my mouth as tears spill out of my eyes.

"They're alive?" My voice trembles. "My-my boys are truly alive?"

*"They are."*

"Oh." I bow my head and sob, letting out almost two decades of grief.

"Why didn't she ever say anything?" It's Fi who speaks up. "Amalia...let us hate her."

*"Yes,"* the wolf nods, *"she did."*

His yellow eyes look around the room. *"Her reasons are her own, but the Gray Wytch plays an important role. The fear she brings has kept the Ulster Wald safe."*

"She has?" I ask.

The growl the wolf responds with sets my hair on end. *"Yes, she has. The kidnappings finally stopped, and they haven't begun since, because they know what will happen if they steal from the Gray Wytch's domain."*

"She claimed the North." Fi nods. "And in turn...the Fae left it alone."

*"The Fae are, for lack of a better word, idiots."* The wolf looks at Nyall, bowing his head in an apology. Nyall waves a hand, understanding that the wolf doesn't include the Prince in this. *"But all beings, no matter how smart, respond to fear. The only reason you all are safe here is because of her actions, her sacrifices."* His voice gets deeper. *"I do not ask you to give your lives for this war, but I will ask you now: will you help her?"*

"You have two days to decide if the Rebellion will go to war," Nyall says finally.

I push to stand. "We don't need two days."

Everyone looks at me, but I don't need to meet their gazes. I know what my heart wants.

"The Rebellion stands with Amalia Asteroth and Ryu the Red." The words roll off the tip of my tongue, coming easily, *truly*. "The Rebellion stands with the Shepherd of the Forest."

The wolf lifts his chin, standing tall and proud at the words. **"Then we go to war."**

Several others stand and bow to the wolf before leaving the tent. We're all momentarily struck sightless by the bright light of the suns streaming in.

"It's day? Already?" I gasp.

"Midday, actually," someone calls, poking their head back in. "Late afternoon based on the suns."

*"Ah—apologies. That is a side effect of my magyk."*

"Shit," Nyall curses. "We need to move."

# CHAPTER 50
## DYANA

"God," I groan. "Every muscle hurts."

*"Yes, well we did battle a giant Dragon and a powerful magyk user before plunging to the ground,"* Vesimyr's voice says casually.

I blink my eyes open. I'm in the same bed I woke up in two years ago. Vesimyr is curled up at my side, healed from the Challenge.

*"Yes, you are healed as well. Sore is the only thing you'll feel, and that will go away quickly."*

I sit up and look at him, brushing back my tangled black hair. "He's dead."

*"Yes."* Vesimyr nods his gray, scaled head. *"He is, which means we can leave."*

We can leave.

We can LEAVE.

I let out a loud laugh, smiling so wide, it nearly hurts my face. "We did it. Holy shit. We did it!"

*"No, Dyana. You did it. This is your victory."*

I leap off the bed and jump on him, wrapping my arms around the huge Dragon's snout. He lets out a laugh and smoke wafts from his nose.

"I wouldn't have been able to do it if it weren't for you," I remind him. "This is *our* victory."

Vesimyr's tongue darts out as he licks my cheek, making me squeal. *"As you wish."*

I step back and look around the room. A glance outside tells me it's the next day. The suns have just risen, painting the world in a wash of red and orange.

A glance back at Vesimyr shows that he watches me carefully, a knowing look in his green gaze.

"We leave tomorrow," I tell him. "It's what, a four-day flight from here?"

Vesimyr shakes his head, *"Five, and that's without stopping."*

"Then we can't wait any longer."

Vesimyr nods. *"No, we can't."*

"Congratulations," a voice calls. I look over to see Embyrne. She's unable to react as I race over and throw my arms around her lean body.

"I'm so sorry," I whisper. "I'm so glad you're okay."

"Me too," she whispers in my ear, her arms tentatively rising to pat my back. I can tell she craves the touch, but it's been so long since anyone touched her kindly, she's not sure how to react to this.

I pull back and meet her golden gaze.

"I'm coming with you, Dyana," she says. "I want to get off this godsforsaken island and never return. I don't know what waits out there but...I want to see it for myself."

I look down at her wrists and the cuffs that still sit there.

*"Ves?"* I ask in my head.

*"Yes?"* my Dragon responds.

*"Can she—"*

*"Of course."*

I clear my throat and lift my chin. "You can ride with us," I tell Embyrne, who blinks in surprise.

"I—thank you." Embyrne nods. She surprises me by leaning in and giving me another hug.

Something brushes against my mind and I let it in, feeling Embyrne's magyk. There's a snapping feeling, like a wall settles into place, before her voice whispers.

*"Do not react,"* Embyrne's voice is frantic. *"I've blocked Vesimyr from hearing this but...Dyana I'm not sure you can trust him. He's not what he seems."*

I nearly step back in shock, but her arms suddenly lock me in place.

*"Please listen,"* she begs. *"When I finally connected with Vesimyr's magyk, it felt wrong."*

*"What are you talking about?"* I ask. *"He's the only one here I truly* **can** *trust."*

*"Maybe...but Dyana he—"* Embyrne struggles to find the words. *"I don't think that Vesimyr is a Dragon."*

Shock floods through me.

*"His magyk isn't like anything I've ever seen before, but it's different. Very different."*

I have no words suitable for a response as the shock renders me silent.

*"Be careful with him,"* she whispers. *"I do not wish to see you hurt."*

She clears her throat and steps back. "I'll get my things. I assume you wish to leave as soon as possible?"

"Yes," I nod, trying to ignore her previous words but the suspicion she just planted within me *throbs* in my heart.

Vesimyr lets out a large sigh. *"I will speak with the Dragons."*

I turn and look at Vesimyr, confusion flowing within me. "What will you say?"

He takes a deep breath, *"That all are free to join us. But death very well might be what awaits us."*

We go silent, processing his words.

"It's better than being stuck here," Embyrne says finally. "I suspect the Ur Daoine Dragons will join you, but the Elysium Dragons...they will be very frightened."

Vesimyr nods. *"They will. They can stay here if they wish. No one is forced into this fight."*

Embyrne nods. "Then I'll leave you both and gather my things. Let me know when it's time to go."

She meets my eyes once more and nods, her face stern and pleading all at once, before turning and walking out of the door.

*"I will go speak with the Dragons."* Vesimyr nods. *"Get your things and meet me down on the beach. It's time to leave Elysium."*

The big silver Dragon lifts his two sets of wings and takes off, leaving me behind, all the while my head swirls with questions.

*Is Vesimyr truly a Dragon?*

*Or is he something else?*

# CHAPTER 51
## MIRIELLE

*"Will you swim or fly?"*

I abandon my packing and turn to find Basa walking into my room. Her metal wing is tucked tightly against her back alongside the scaled one.

"Swim. It will be faster."

She blinks, her silver eyes missing nothing.

*"You want to get there first."*

I freeze, every muscle in my body going tense.

*"I hold allegiance to none,"* Basa notes. *"Except for the two who fixed me."*

My jaw nearly hits the floor. "Basa—"

She raises a claw. *"I do not need to know. Whatever your secrets may be, Mirielle Zenyth, know that they are safe with me."*

Speechless. I am struck speechless.

"Thank you," I whisper.

Basa nods. *"I will fly above. They are leaving soon, so I will leave now to get a head start."*

"Don't strain your wing!" I remind her.

Basa scoffs. *"I've been locked in a prison beneath the earth for centuries. A little pain is not going to stop me from taking back the skies."*

With that, she turns around and leaves, stomping out of the room.

*"I will meet you in Ur Daoine, Mirielle Zenyth."*

Comfort and dread war within me.

While I am endlessly thankful to have Basa on my side, a part of me wants her to be as far away as possible from the events to come.

"Almost ready?" Kairos peeks his head into the room.

*And him. I am not ready to disappoint him.*

"Yeah." I force a smile onto my face. "I am. What about the forge?"

Kairos shrugs. "There will be other forges."

"But your weapons. So many of them are here."

"Oh, I'm taking those," he smirks. It's the most emotion he's shown the entire time I've known him.

It's nice to see him so jovial.

"I also built something new, something I haven't shown you."

I blink, concerned.

Then he pulls out a saddle.

A *waterproof* saddle. One made out of Elysian.

"That's not for a Dragon..."

*"The saddle is for me,"* Kairos's voice rolls through my head. *"If we're going to get there first, we need to leave soon. "Finish packing and gather your things. Lir has calmed the currents for us. "*

My heart sinks to the bottom of the ocean but I hide it all, flashing a believable smile.

As Kairos leaves, the smile falls.

Yet again, I am left overwhelmed with comfort and dread, both pulsing through me in equal measure.

A part of me is glad someone else knows.

But *I* did not tell him...and that means I can't trust him. Not fully, at least. Not yet.

# CHAPTER 52
## RYU

"Grab it!"

They stab me with metal prods. I scramble away from them, shoving my body against the cage bars, but it's no use.

There is nowhere I can go.

The metal pierces the delicate skin between my scales, sending jolts of pain through me. With their prods, they clamp a large metal collar around my neck. It rubs uncomfortably against the muzzle.

Os snarls at them, reaching through the bars with his claws and slashing at the guards. He manages to cut one of them before other guards run in, their armor clinking and clanking together. They jab at Os with their prods, electrocuting the great black Dragon. But he never backs down. He never stops fighting them, even as chains are attached to my collar, and I'm led away. There's a flash of bright light as the Dragon shifts, leaving a tall male in its place.

"Where are you TAKING HER?" he bellows.

The Fae ignore him and Os snarls. Another flash of light and he's back in Dragon form, roaring and hitting the cage so hard, it *should* bend the bars.

The metal does not budge.

*"Survive!"* Os bursts into my head and his magyk stings, instantly giving me a headache. The fact that Os can get into my head despite the way our magyk is being suppressed shows just how powerful he is.

Blood begins to trickle from the holes of my ears.

*"Survive, Ryu!"* Os shouts. *"Do whatever you must. Whatever it takes. Don't hesitate, not for a second. Not if you want to see Amalia again."*

Then the connection between us goes flat. The pain ebbs slightly and I sigh in relief.

I think pain is something I'm going to quickly become familiar with.

Os' words ground me, anchoring me to the earth. That last part though, the idea of never seeing Amalia again—that lights a *fire* in my core.

I fight the Fae every step of the way, kicking out with my feet, so they put chains around my ankles, making it near impossible to walk.

*Clank.*

*Clank.*

*Clank.*

The chains drag behind me *clanking* with every step as I'm led out of the newly made Dragon Pit, up towards the surface. The path is steep and winding. I slip, losing traction as the dirt shifts beneath me.

There is no way to fight them. It's like there's a weight on my mind, an all-consuming, crushing weight. It's pushing not just my magyk away, but my *will* to fight back.

After countless minutes treading through the dark, we emerge through a large passageway. Light hits my eyes and for a moment, I can't see anything.

Then the breeze hits my nose.

*Oh, I missed this.*

"Move it!" one of the guards screams at me. I flinch and he punches me in the nose. Pain ricochets through my face as I'm yanked forward, the muzzle cutting into me.

The moment of peace ends as I'm dragged into a half-built colosseum full of people.

Rows of seats are carved into the Earth around an in-ground arena of sorts.

The muzzle makes it hard to look up; it forces my head to arch downwards. Which is why I did not see her right away.

*The white Dragon.*

# CHAPTER 53
## IREYNA

When I get to the square, I come up short.

It's *empty.*

No Dragon is waiting for me.

The moons glow brightly above my head, illuminating the empty square. I look around, confused.

We're supposed to be working on flying at night. Matricia was the first time we've been out at night, and already there are things I want to work on.

But Anonyme is nowhere to be seen.

A stray guard walks by and I shout at him, "You. Come over here."

The guard pales and marches over. "Yes, ma'am?"

"Where is my Dragon?"

"I—I don't know, ma'am," the Fae says, fear in his glowing orange eyes.

"What do you mean, you *don't know?*"

"I have heard nothing of a Dragon being in the courtyard this morning, ma'am."

I'm at his throat a second later, my dagger pressing into his skin.

"Did you take her?" I snarl. "Are you lying to me?"

The Fae trembles. "N-No."

"Good. Now go *find* her." He nods and I let him go with a shove. The Fae soldier falls to his knees, his armor clanking together.

"Now!"

The Fae scrambles to his feet and runs towards the Black Citadel.

A shout far in the distance catches my attention. The Archmage rebuilt part of the Dragon Pit, but He also rebuilt the Arena.

What used to be an above-ground, multi-story coliseum is now an in-ground, open air arena.

Today is the first fight. The Crimson Queen's daughter—the Dragon we caught—is going to be part of the first bout.

To be honest, it slipped my mind. I enjoyed the Fray, but I am not upset that it is over.

The Holy Father declared this fight would be held at night, because the two full moons bring good luck.

More cheers sound from the rebuilt Arena and my brow furrows. I take off, already in a mood about my missing Dragon. I shove through the crowds that are streaming into the newly built Arena.

"TEAR ITS HEAD OFF!" someone screams.

~~I didn't miss this.~~

The thought hurts, so I ignore it.

"PUT 200 COINS ON THE WHITE ONE FOR ME!"

A horrible sort of *knowing* washes over me.

In the distant, far corners of my mind, someone screams.

*He wouldn't...no. He wouldn't do that.*

~~RUN.~~

My thoughts race. My heart pounds. Every denial runs through my head. I'm being sensitive. That's all. Yes. I'm being sensitive.

Or, there's another white Dragon. Yeah. *Yeah.* It's not like Anonyme is the only one.

Anxiety under control for the time being, I walk through the crowd and try to find a seat. Just as I'm about to sit down, something down below catches my eye.

Something *red.*

The Crimson Queen's daughter is bound in chains at one end of the Arena. Guards undo her muzzle and unravel the chains around her ankles. She cannot escape, but she can move. She can also attack and defend herself...from the Dragon laying in the sand across from her.

The *white* Dragon.

*My* Dragon. It's Anonyme.

Horror overtakes me and it's like something *numbs* it, drawing a blanket around me as the world around dims. Like the hands of another physically *move* me, my neck turns of its own volition.

Suddenly I'm not looking at the Dragons. I'm looking into the purple eyes of the Archmage.

*"Come down here, my child. Come watch the spectacle with me."*

I heed His call without hesitation. My body moves at His command.

Quickly weaving through the crowds as the blood within my body freezes, becoming a weight that fills my every step.

Closer and closer to Anonyme.

~~GET HER OUT.~~

The thought hurts but I don't ignore it. Not this time.

I approach the Archmage, who is closest to the Arena sand, having nothing to fear.

Sol Constantus protects Him from the Dragons, making Him more powerful than they are.

"Father," I greet Him with a neutral voice, going down on one knee with a bowed head, in the proper show of appreciation. I do not show the freezing anger that fills me.

"I thought your Dragon ought to finish what she started."

I blink and stand, glancing up and meeting his purple gaze. I shiver under the weight of his stare.

"Shouldn't we keep the Crimson Heir alive? For bait? The Asteroth girl will come for it. I guarantee it."

Pain shoots through my face at the hard *clap* of His palm hitting my cheek.

"You *dare* to question His will? This is all His design, Ireyna. His. Constantus is *all.*"

"Yes, sir," I force the words out as my cheek burns. I look down at my feet, unable to meet His gaze any longer.

"Stand there in *silence* and watch as your Dragon destroys the Heir. Or, perhaps, as the Heir destroys your Dragon. We will see." The Archmage smirks, as if this is all some *game* to Him.

~~It is. It IS just a game to him.~~

His hand touches my shoulder and the Archmage squeezes.

"None of that," the Archmage whispers, but I do not understand what He means.

The anger within me lessens, but deep down, I *question.*

*Is* this His will?

The crowd goes quiet as Anonyme's chains are dropped. She stands, extending her wings.

Both Dragons look so *young.*

*The red bitch deserves it*, a voice in my head whispers. *She tried to hurt your Dragon! Let Anonyme tear her to pieces.*

Yes. *Yes.*

The Crimson Heir tried to kill me and my Dragon. She doesn't *deserve* to live. How *dare* she think to challenge the Cult of Sol Constantus?

A new fury fills me. Not at the Archmage or at the situation, but at the red Dragon. At Amalia Asteroth. She stole *everything* from me. Os and I would have gotten back together if it weren't for her. I *know* we would have. Now, she and her red bitch want to steal my fucking Dragon.

"KILL HER!" I scream at Anonyme, who's head swivels to me. Our eyes meet and she blinks in shock.

I can sense her terror. But seeing me seems to fill her with confidence.

Yes. *Yes.* This is a good idea. It's time for *revenge.*

"Sit down," the Archmage hisses at me. "Or else you'll ruin the trap."

# CHAPTER 54
## AMALIA

Aanad and I made it to the valley above Castael Laryn in two and a half days. I'm nearly collapsed against Aanad when we finally make it to the Northern side of the Annag. My companion is equally exhausted. Sweat coats her black fur and she pants heavily. The suns are high in the sky, so we have to wait. At sundown, we'll meet up with Nyall.

Aanad heads straight for the nearest stream. I dismount, wincing at how sore and stiff my legs are, and squat. Quickly unlatching the girth, I get Aanad's saddle off so she can dry off and get a break.

We find a mossy spot and both lay down for the remainder of the day. Aanad curls around me, keeping me warm with her body heat. Despite the suns above, it's a chilly day and the breeze is cold.

Sleep comes quickly, and for once, I don't dream. When I open my eyes, the suns are just beginning to set. I get up and stretch, stiff and sore beyond belief.

Walking over to the stream again I crouch and cup water in my hands, splashing it on my face. The cold is shocking to my senses, and it wakes me fully.

Out of the corner of my eye, I spy some brown patches of grass.

*The entire Kingdom is slowly dying.*

As the suns dip lower in the sky, sundown quickly approaches. I make my way to the southern edge of the Aanag. Aanad follows, stopping at my right shoulder as we get to the edge of the forest.

*You know exactly what happens to Dragons in Ur Daoine. The longer you wait, the more pain she's in.*

"Thank you for your help, my friend." I whisper to Aanad, stroking her velvet neck. "But this is where our paths diverge. It's time for you to go back home."

She pins her ears and snorts, furious.

I sigh, "No, Aanad. This won't be safe for you."

She laid next to me all day, keeping close watch. She is better off far away from here.

Aanad paws the ground in defiance.

"I mean it," I tell her, standing in front of her so we're eye to eye. I wrap my arms around her face and press my forehead against hers. "It's much safer for you in the Ulster Wald. Go home, Aanad. *Please.* I have lost so much already—" my voice cracks. "I don't want to lose you too. Nor do I want Nyall to lose you. I know he's your friend."

Aanad calms slightly, her ears flicking up and forward upon hearing the name of her rider.

"Thank you," I press a kiss against her velvet snout. "I'll see you back at home, okay? You keep those wolves in line for me."

Aanad nickers and pushes her nose against my cheek before walking away.

I do the same, but my path is heading in the opposite direction.

I make my way on silent feet over to the eastern side of the wall of Castael Laryn. Exactly where Nyall said he would meet me.

I give it one hour before I give up.

*He'll be here. He promised.*

I can't wait for him any longer though. *Ryu* can't wait.

With a deep breath, I brace myself and enter the city, walking through the arched entryway.

Castael Laryn looks *almost* the same.

The sunlight quickly fades and the night sky becomes visible. It's a bright evening; our two moons are full and brilliant. They illuminate the entire city, which explains why it's so busy.

I enter the city and navigate through the crowds, attempting to behave normally. The glamour changes my coloring enough to make me blend in with the locals. To them, I'm just another Demis looking for a fighting job.

"Oy!" I whistle at a Demis dressed in something resembling fighting leathers. He has pointed ears and short red hair, accenting deep obsidian skin and golden eyes.

"The fuck's your problem?" he asks in a low, deadly voice.

I raise my hands innocently, "Woah, friend. I mean no harm, I was only hoping you could point me in the direction of the training yard."

The Demis crosses his arms and glares at me as people pass by us down the dirt walkway.

"I'm looking for work," I tell him.

"You and *everyone* else."

The sad resignation on my face is real.

With a nod, I turn to leave the Demis behind, when I hear a sigh.

"Check out the new Arena. I heard they're trying to restart the Fray," he grumbles. "Fucking idiots."

My heart sinks.

They rebuilt the Arena.

How the *hell* did they do that in such a short amount of time? I force a smile on my face as I thank the Demis and head down the city road in the direction of the old Arena.

I'm well aware this is a trap.

I just don't care.

Trap or no trap, I'm saving Ryu. She will not be their latest experiment. I *refuse* it.

A small tremor suddenly shakes the land, nearly knocking me over. I squat, bracing myself against the rapid movements. Others around me do the same.

Then they stop, and everyone goes about their evening like nothing happened.

*This is so wrong.*

Rocks and dirt crackle beneath my boots as I make my way through Castael Laryn. No one pays me a second glance.

A loud roar sounds in the distance. The sound makes my heart stop.

*I know that roar.*

*Ryu.* I'm sprinting before I can think of all of the reasons why I shouldn't.

None of them matter. *Nothing* matters outside of her.

My legs pound the dirt beneath me, every muscle in my body working as hard as it can to get to her as fast as possible.

All I can see as I approach it is the crowd of people.

*At night? The moons are bright, but what event would be held at night?*

Pushing through them, I elbow my way to the front. People curse at me and grunt as I push through the densely packed crowd, but I do not care.

Finally, *finally,* I make it to the edge of the in-ground Arena.

Ryu is fighting the white Dragon.

My heart pounds so hard I'm shocked it doesn't crack right through my ribcage.

I know this is a trap.

It was *always* going to be a trap.

A quick glance around shows Fae guards scattered throughout the stands.

The Archmage stands at the very edge of the flat, training area where the Dragons are battling it out.

There's a high-pitched shriek as Ryu evades the white Dragon, narrowly avoiding its sharp claws. Because of her bright red color, it's hard to tell what's blood and what isn't.

Then Ryu begins to limp.

Something is wrong with her foot. The claws on her front left foot are broken, as if the other Dragon's scales bent them backwards when Ryu tried to scratch it.

The white Dragon pounces, taking advantage of Ryu's moment of weakness.

A strange sense of Déjà vu hits me.

Last time I watched a red Dragon in a fight, I helped her...and then I watched her die.

I won't let that happen to Ryu.

*"Now, why do I get the feeling you're about to do something rash?"* Nyall's voice bursts into my head.

*"You're late."*

He laughs. *"Blame your wolf for that. But we will talk about that later. For now, save our Dragon. Time to spring the trap."*

There's an explosion so loud, it quiets the stadium and the Dragons.

Smoke and flames waft up into the air from the center of Castael Laryn. Screams of terror follow. I don't hesitate. As the guards run out of the Arena, I run down the steps, closing in on the flat sand beneath.

# CHAPTER 55
## RYU

*"NO! GET OUT OF HERE!"*

My scream goes unanswered. I can't reach Amalia's mind. The chains still around my ankles have weakened my magyk so much, I can't get to her.

*I have to warn her!*

She wears a glamour but the moment I spotted her, I saw right through it. Before I can do anything, the white Dragon slams into me. I hit the ground on my side with a hard thunk.

She bites at my neck, trying to get her jaws around me. The white Dragon is older, but I'm already as large as she is, if not bigger. Her jaws can't open wide enough, and I shove her off of me. I don't want to hurt another Dragon. It feels *wrong*.

*"SURVIVE!"* Os' words echo in my head.

Amalia draws her swords and sprints down towards me. She rips off a bracelet, revealing her true coloring, charcoal gray hair and bright blue eyes.

The crowd doesn't react to the sight of her, even as her blades go up in flames.

*The crowd...doesn't react?* That's strange.

Too strange. But I've lingered longer than I should, and the distraction costs me.

The white Dragon gets on top of me, scratching at my chest with her sharp claws.

*"You know what you must do, Ryu."* A voice echoes in my thoughts.

The voice in my head isn't my mother's. It's older, deeper, and more masculine. Every syllable drips with ancient magyk.

*Great Livyathin.*

"GET AWAY FROM HER!" Amalia is suddenly *beside* us in the sand.

*"No! Run, Ama. This is a trap!"* I scream at her, but she doesn't hear me. My magyk is too weak. The metal collar won't allow me to reach her.

"Oh good, I've been looking forward to a rematch," another voice calls.

The white Dragon's rider tackles Amalia just as she's about to stab it.

"I'm going to kill you," the white Dragon's rider taunts Amalia with a wicked smile. Never one to back down, Amalia charges her with a roar and a blast of Hellfyre, but the white Dragon's rider emerges unscathed.

Amalia hesitates for a moment, but that's all the rider needs.

The white Dragon's tail slaps me in the face, distracting me. Blood streams into my eyes. I can't keep track of where the pain is. *Everything* hurts.

Then I see it.

The white Dragon's rider twirls around Amalia in a dance of magyk and blades.

*Click.*

My eyes shoot to Amalia's wrist. The rider managed to cuff her. Amalia's blades turn back to normal as her Hellfyre ebbs. Panic and fury intertwine in her pale blue eyes. She looks towards me, fear plain on her face.

*"Survive,"* that ancient, eldritch voice whispers, echoing Os' earlier sentiment.

Survive.

With a deep breath, I pull on the memories of my ancestors. Not magyk, just genetics.

Their strength fills me, as does their knowledge of battle.

Blood dripping down my scales, I push up and face the white Dragon.

"RYU!" Amalia shouts, but the rider is there, a dagger in one hand and purple magyk around her other fist. The rider unleashes on Amalia with a scream.

**"NO."**

The rider and Amalia both freeze at hearing my voice aloud. It's muffled and the letters are difficult to pronounce, but the ground *shakes* in the wake of my words.

I face the white Dragon and bare my fangs, lifting my neck up and flaring my wings as to be at my full height.

**"NO MORE,"** I say to the white Dragon. She blinks, confused for a moment.

"KILL HER, ANONYME!" the Dragon's rider screams. "KILL THAT RED BITCH!"

"I don't need magyk to rip off your FUCKING HEAD." Amalia's words end in a harsh bellow as she attacks the rider with renewed vigor.

The rider is distracted, but her words worked. The white Dragon bares her fangs back at me as she gets ready to pounce.

**"STOP THIS,"** I tell it, but the Dragon does not listen.

A deep, sorrowful sense of resolve runs through my veins as the white Dragon rushes me.

*"Survive."*

That word repeats over and over through my thoughts as I slide to the right so that the white Dragon rushes *past* me. Just as her neck is parallel to my claws, I reach up and grab her face. She tries to fling me off, but I use my sharp talons to puncture her neck.

My roar is anger and pain and *survival* as I bring my jaws around her neck and *bite down.*

The hot, spicy taste of blood fills my mouth as her flesh crushes beneath my fangs.

The white Dragon—Anonyme—shrieks in pain, writhing and flailing in any attempt to get away from me. But my hold is too strong.

I might be younger, but I also have more to *lose.* I have a *family.* This Dragon only knows pain and manipulation.

*"I'm sorry,"* With the very last dregs of my magyk, I push the thought at Anonyme, hoping she hears me.

I will survive—and so will my family.

I will *ensure* it.

"NO! NO!" the Dragon's rider screams in the back, but Amalia tackles her, forcing her to the ground with a wicked kick.

My eyes meet Amalia's. Tears stream down her cheeks in an apology. I know this will break her heart.

It will break a part of mine.

Yet that does not stop me from ending Anonyme's life with a hard *crunch* as my fangs crush her bones, ripping her head from her body.

"NOOO!" Anonyme's rider screams in horror as the headless body beneath me crashes to the ground.

*"The sign of a true leader is being able to make the hard choices."* The memory of my Mother runs through my head. *"You did what you had to. You survived. Just like every Queen before you. You made the hard choice."*

*Queen.*

I have been aware of the consequences of my parentage. But I have avoided that word; avoided even *thinking* it. After all, how can I be the Queen to a place I've never been?

"I'm going to gut you alive," the Dragon's rider hisses at me before moving faster than I can track. Suddenly she's *behind* Amalia, instead of in front of her.

That's the only warning Amalia gets before the rider's dagger is shoved through her side.

*NO.*

Amalia gasps in pain as blood begins to stream from the wound.

"That's enough," a layered voice travels through the Arena.

A tall male with no hair and strange, glowing purple eyes walks down towards the sand. He is alone and dressed in fine robes.

I know this male from my mother's memories.

"You will get your revenge," the Archmage says to Ireyna, lifting his hand.

She immediately stops her attack of Amalia, withdrawing the dagger from her side. Blood falls harder.

The wound will heal, but with her magyk blocked, it will be a slow process. She needs to stop the bleeding or else she will bleed out.

I turn, facing the Archmage but he simply waves another hand. Chains explode out of the ground, twisting around me and pulling me against the sand until I'm down on my belly.

With a pained groan, I force my head to the side to see where Amalia is. She's covered in chains and on her stomach in the sand too.

*No.*

*I have to get to her!*

Clenching my jaw in pain, I pull against the chains as hard as I can. The metal groans and cracks as I try to crawl closer to Amalia.

Guards are suddenly on top of me, stabbing me with their prods and kicking me as they attach new chains to my legs and collar.

"GET. OFF. HER!" Amalia shouts in between gasps of pain.

The Archmage steps closer and claps his hands. The crowd in the Arena disappears, fading into mist on the wind, leaving the Arena completely empty, save a hundred or so guards and two people.

Being able to hold an illusion of that complexity for such a long period of time is *impossible.*

Or it should be.

*He's an Elf.* I remember, but it's not from my own memory. It's from my mother's.

The Archmage...is an Elf.

The knowledge hits me quickly as I run through the memories of my ancestors.

*Elves practice Dark Magyk.*

This...this is who took over after the Crimson Queen killed the High Councilor.

"You are *painfully* predictable." The Archmage smiles at Amalia.

"Happy to be of service," she groans. "I'd rather be predictable than a psychotic narcissist."

"Such big words for a girl from the woods." The Archmage's voice is saccharine and full of mockery.

Shouts from above us grab our attention. We both turn to look to see Nyall, cuffed and dressed in chains, as he's shoved down the stairs towards us by an armed escort of Fae guards.

"Really, I barely had to *try.* After all of this, I expected more of you," the Archmage turns to Nyall, "particularly you, my protégée."

Nyall gives the Archmage a wide, bloody smile. "It's cute that you think I was there to learn from you, you narcissistic cunt. Instead, I spent centuries learning *about* you. And now I'm going to use it to destroy you."

The Archmage sighs and claps his hands again. Chains burst from the sand once again, covering Nyall's body and sending him to his knees.

The rider is in front of Nyall a moment later, her fist shooting into his cheek. Something *cracks* as she punches him again.

The Archmage watches this all without a single emotion.

"Sol Constantus save you," Ireyna steps back, her fists bloody. She spits in Nyall's face. "Speak to the Holy Father like that again and I will flay Amalia's flesh from her back while you watch."

Nyall just winks at her. "Try it and I'll do more than threaten your precious Holy Father."

She goes to punch him again but a raised hand from the Archmage stops her.

"There will be plenty of time for that later. For now," he says, looking between Amalia and Nyall. "I'm so glad you're all here. We have much to discuss, the three of us."

Something hits me over the head. Pain explodes through my skull as the world fades to black against a symphony of Amalia and Nyall's screams.

# CHAPTER 56
## IREYNA

"I'm going to KILL HER!"

My screams echo throughout the chamber.

Guards scatter as I swipe my hands across the table, sending every dish and cup crashing to the floor. Glass is everywhere.

But I do not care.

"I'm going to rip off *her* fucking head!"

A hand on my shoulder stops me. I glance behind me and immediately bow my head.

"Your Holiness," I say.

"You will get your revenge," the Archmage croons in my ear. "But not yet. First...I need some information from them."

*NO. I NEED TO KILL THEM NOW!*

"Sh, sh, sh," He whispers. "Eventually, my child. Have patience."

I catch a flash of His purple magyk but ignore it. I have no right to question the Archmage's doings.

Instead, I remain in my head, furious beyond belief.

*THEY KILLED HER! THEY KILL—*

The thought stops and suddenly I can't remember why I was mad.

*Oh.*

*The Dragon.*

*Hmm. Yes, it's tragic. But I will get another.*

"Yes," the Archmage hisses. "It was disposable. There is always another. You will get your revenge, but not yet."

"Not yet," I repeat, agreeing with His Holiness.

He's always right.

# CHAPTER 57
## DYANA

I keep replaying my conversations with Vesimyr. About his stories and all of the answers he gave to my never-ending questions.

*Does it matter?*

That question replaces Embyrne's words.

Does it *matter* if Vesimyr is something else? I don't know what *else* he could possibly be.

The lie would matter, of course, but it would not change the fact that he is mine and I am his.

Vesimyr is my friend—and I...I think my friend is *lying*.

I walk down to the beach where we're all going to meet. The midday suns are burning brightly over our heads, turning the air warm and humid.

Mirielle waits by the water. She's in some sort of bathing suit but it covers her entire body, fitting like a glove against her soft curves.

I still find Mirielle beautiful. Terribly so.

Her red hair is longer and curlier thanks to the humidity and our time here, but the joy is gone from her face.

Now, as she meets my gaze, she's stony and cold.

"Thank you," I lift my chin and summon my courage, "for helping me in the Challenge. I know you didn't have to do that, and I appreciate it."

"You're welcome." She nods. Her pale green eyes go to the male walking towards us.

"And—thank you...for getting me here. For everything."

Mirielle blinks, her eyes widening.

"I never told you that, and I should have. I'm sorry."

She nods, looking dazed. "Of course."

Kairos approaches us. His dark locs are decorated with golden beads. He's dressed in a pair of skintight pants, baring his muscular upper body.

He's beautiful, but I feel no attraction to him, nor to any male at all.

"Ready?" He looks past me to Mirielle.

"Yeah."

"You're swimming there," I realize. "That's impressive."

And telling. Kairos has to be some sort of water shifter. Two mortal bodies can't swim all the way to Ur Daoine from here.

But something bigger could.

*Hmm.*

*"Have you ever heard of Sea Wyverns?"* Vesimyr asks in my head.

*"I have not."*

*"They were once known by another name: Ascidians."*

That name *feels* familiar, but I can't place how.

Vesimyr continues. *"I believe the smith is Ascidian."*

*"Wait, really? Would he be considered Beastkyn?"*

Vesimyr sighs in my head. *"Possibly. Their rules, their culture...it's very different from ours. We would call him Beastkyn, but he likely doesn't consider himself that."*

*Interesting.*

*"I will arrive at the beach shortly."* Vesimyr assures me, and I feel our connection go quiet as the silver Dragon leaves my mind.

"Where will you go?" I ask Mirielle quietly as Kairos situates bags made out of a similar material as their swimming clothes.

"I'm not sure—I need to find Nyall, first. Assuming he's still alive."

I wince. "I hope they both are."

"You'll look for Amalia, then?" Mirielle inquires.

"Yes. In the Ulster Wald, probably. That's where she would go."

"Then it seems our paths are finally diverging."

I stare at Mirielle. "Yes. It does seem so."

She gives me a half-smile. "Be well, Dyana Arkos. Be well and be happy."

"Same to you," I breathe.

Mirielle turns but...*what if this is the last time I ever see her?*

"Mirielle, wait—"

Vesimyr lands on the sand with a giant BOOM.

His magyk lances into my head and I wince. Mirielle grabs her ears and Kairos stands straighter.

Something's happened.

Something is *wrong.* I don't know how I know, but I do.

*"I've received word from Ur Daoine."*

My heart stops as Vesimyr turns his head to meet my eyes.

*"Amalia is alive. It's confirmed."*

I fall to my knees. Based on the reaction from the crowd of Dragons around us, Vesimyr is speaking to all of us.

*"The Drayven Prince, too,"* he adds for Mirielle's benefit. She gasps, relief flooding her face. *"And...the red hatchling. Kydis' hatchling."*

Vesimyr turns to address the dozens of Dragons landing next to us on the beach. Some remain in the air, hovering and listening. But all watch Vesimyr with fear and awe.

*"THE CRIMSON QUEEN'S DAUGHTER LIVES. THE HEIR OF ELYSIUM LIVES!"*

The Dragons gasp. Goosebumps break out along my arms, and I watch as *hope* spreads.

*"Say something,"* Vesimyr whispers in my head.

*"What the hell do you mean?"*

*"They won't agree to come with us until you ask them."*

*"What?!"* Even in my head, my screech echoes against my skull.

*"They don't trust me."* Vesimyr says. *"But you...for some reason, they seem to trust you, despite the fact that you scare them."*

*"I scare a Dragon?"* I gasp. *"That's silly."*

*"You are the unknown element. Something new. They don't know what to make of you, but this is your moment. Convince them to help us."*

I think back to his words.

Amalia is *alive.*

Nyall is *alive.*

"How do you know they're alive?" I ask aloud. The crowd looks between myself and the great silver Dragon before me.

Vesimyr takes a deep breath. *"Because I got word that all three of them have been captured by the Archmage. They're in Castael Laryn. In the—"* he hesitates, *"in the new Dragon Pit."*

The crowd breaks out in anxious whispers and gasps.

"Then that's where we go first."

The Dragons fall silent and their gazes all land on me.

How the *fuck* did I become the one in charge of rallying the troops?

I take a deep breath and raise my voice. "Amalia Asteroth and Nyall Drayven were willing to sacrifice themselves to save *YOU.*"

The crowd doesn't react, so I continue.

"Is there a chance that we will fail? Yes. Failure is always possible. But I will not let two people who gave up so much for *everyone* else rot at the hands of the Archmage."

A few Dragons nod.

"You know the Pit. All of you do. So let me ask you this: would you *damn* your saviors to that same fate?"

*"What about the Archmage?"* a voice I don't recognize asks.

With a single thought, I summon my light. It bursts through every pore, making several Dragons have to squint.

I twist the light, gathering it into a huge sword, and lift it to the sky.

"I *dare* him to challenge me!" I shout. "I will *burn* out his darkness with every ounce of power in me. His evil *filth* doesn't belong in our world."

*"He's so powerful,"* someone whispers.

"So help me take him *down!"* I respond.

I can tell they're nervous. I can *feel* it through the tension wavering in the air.

"I know you're afraid," I say, my voice breaking. "I'm scared too. Not for myself, but for my friends. Every single one of us knows the cruelty their captors are capable of. Every. Single. One of us. So I ask you: will you be brave, now? When the turn of the tides is upon us, will you look darkness in the face and *run?* Or will you show the world why the Dragons once ruled as GODS?"

The crowd is quiet for a moment, then a roar sounds from the back.

Then another, and *another,* until all of the Dragons gathered before us, both in the air and on the ground, *roar* their assent.

Vesimyr's snout nudges me from behind. *"You were made for this, Dyana."*

Embyrne joins us on the sand, a small bag at her side.

"That's all you're bringing?" I ask. "Are you leaving some things here?"

Her golden eyes inspect me. "This is all I was allowed to have."

My heart threatens to break at her words, but I hold it together.

"We'll fly faster, then."

She nods and together, we climb onto Vesimyr's back. He's large enough that there is plenty of room for the two of us, but Embyrne tucks herself close behind me.

Her hands tremble lightly but she clenches them into fists, trying to hide it.

I place my hand atop hers and she flinches before taking a deep breath.

The corner of her mouth twitches as she nods at me in a show of thanks. I smile back before securing my own bag against my side and attaching myself to Vesimyr's saddle.

We've never used one before, but he found one in the old armory earlier and suggested using it so that I can sleep during the flight.

It's less of a saddle and more like two wide strips of leather with hooks on them. They go around Vesimyr's neck and belly, weaving through his thick scales and sharp spinal spikes. Reins connect to it, more for emotional comfort than actual use.

I do not need reins to steer my Dragon. Nor do I need to do much of anything at all except *hold on.*

But the journey is long and arduous. Ensuring we all make it there in one piece is of the upmost importance.

*"Will we make the journey?"*

*"I'm scared."*

I catch a few stray thoughts from some of the Dragons around us.

I look over my shoulder at them and activate my light, gathering it within my hands.

*"I will heal you should any of you weaken,"* I offer.

Do I know how to do that?

No. But I sure will fucking try. Something tells me if I want my light to heal them, it will.

To my surprise, the Dragons look relieved at my words.

Mirielle and Kairos disappear into the water without another word. A flash of light catches my attention beneath the surface. A huge, dark gray shape appears, but it darts away so fast, I didn't make out much detail.

Embyrne is silent as we take to the air. Her gaze remains on the island as she says goodbye to the only home she's ever known.

As we ascend into the clouds, dozens of Dragons follow suit, decorating the sky in all of the colors of the rainbow.

Vesimyr points his body west as we take off for Ur Daoine.

*"Something is bothering you,"* he says in my mind. Not an accusation, but a concern.

*Shit.*

I cannot lie to my friend.

*"I have a question,"* I reply.

*"And I might have an answer."*

I bite my lip as the wind blasts my face and we pick up speed. Vesimyr flaps his two sets of wings, propelling us further away from the island.

*"When Embyrne borrowed your magyk, she said it felt strange."*

*"That is not a question,"* he notes.

*"Smart ass,"* I huff, before falling silent. *"Ves..."* I hesitate. *"You aren't a Drag-on...are you? Not really."*

Vesimyr lets out a sigh so heavy, it feels as if the weight of the world comes with it.

*"We have a long flight ahead of us, my young friend,"* Vesimyr says. *"I will answer your question, for the answer is neither short nor easy."*

A sliver of relief runs through me, woven together tightly with a thread of anxiety.

*He will tell me the truth, and for that I am glad.*

*But...he has been lying.*

So what exactly has he been lying about?

*"To answer your question, I need to go back to the beginning. To the very, beginning, when the world was wild and young."*

My heart skips a beat, and his next words make my mouth go dry.

*"In this young, newly made world, Gods walked amongst mortals—all but one. That God, he did not walk among the mortals...he ruled from the skies."*

# CHAPTER 58
## MIRIELLE

We shoot through the water so fast that I have to flatten myself against the saddle Kairos put on.

He designed it to easily slide over his head and neck.

Kairos' fins propel him forward so fast, it's hard to pay attention to the glowing undersea life around us.

We dart through giant schools of glimmering fish that tickle my cheeks. Sea turtles swim out of our path, not wanting to become a meal of the giant Sea Wyvern. The current appears up ahead, a huge, swirling tunnel of water that will take us all the way to Ur Daoine.

*"You are running out of time,"* a voice hisses in my head. Pain instantly throbs at my temple. *"Get to Castael Laryn before the Dragons. Do not let them kill the Archmage. Do not ruin my chances at freedom!"*

Kairos cranes his neck to the side, just enough to lock eyes with me.

*"Do whatever it takes. Nothing is more important than this."*

*"Yes, Great Lir."* Kairos and I respond in unison as our God withdraws from our heads and we enter the current.

*"Fail me at your own peril."*

I have many regrets in my life. Things I wish I had done or said differently. But this, I fear, I will regret most of all.

# CHAPTER 59
## AMALIA

I've been injured enough times in my 92 years of life that even half-asleep, I'm already analyzing my body and taking note of what is wrong with me.

My head throbs and there's a pinch of pain with each breath. *Concussion.*

My eyes hurt, but not so much that I want to scream. *Orbital sockets intact. Swelling is superficial.*

I can move, but it's like something heavy is on top of me, making it difficult. The weight is heaviest around my ankles and wrists.

*I'm bound, somehow. Not fully. Shackles around my wrists and ankles, most likely.*

*I'm bound...I'm a prisoner. That means I have to wake up.*

I try to open my eyes again, but they won't budge.

*Come on, wake up!* I scream at my body, but everything remains fuzzy and far away.

"Ama? Ama can you hear me?" A muffled voice calls, but it's like the voice is speaking underwater. I can barely hear it.

I try to open my eyes again—*nothing.* I can't move or wake up.

"She won't heal," another voice says.

"It's all of this fucking metal. They did something to it. It's suppressing all of us. If I could heal her—"

"You would have already," the other finishes. "We both know this."

Something hard thumps in the background.

"Please don't hurt yourself," one of the voices says quietly.

"I hate this. You should have stayed away!"

"No, we shouldn't have," one of the voices responds, sounding almost angry. "If we knew you were alive, we would have come sooner—."

"You should have left me. He *wants* Amalia. You've just handed him a weapon!"

There's a loud sigh. "He wants all of us, Os, for one reason or another. We're all tools for him to twist and use. And," the voice pauses, "if there is anything I've learned in the past two years…it's that no one uses Amalia Asteroth if she doesn't wish to be used. Not even the Archmage."

*He's right.*

Quiet descends.

"I will not apologize for coming here, Os, nor will she."

*That name. Why do I know that name?*

"Probably not," the lower voice sighs. "You're both stubborn shits."

"You're welcome," the other responds tartly. I feel the tension in the air lessen. They both fall silent again until the one who just spoke continues once more.

"At least, whatever is coming, we can face it together. There is no good doing *any* of this alone."

The realm of dreams wraps its hands around me and pulls me closer as consciousness fades away and darkness gathers. The conversation around me goes quiet as I drift slowly back to sleep.

"Rest," a distant voice says. "We're here, Blue. We're here."

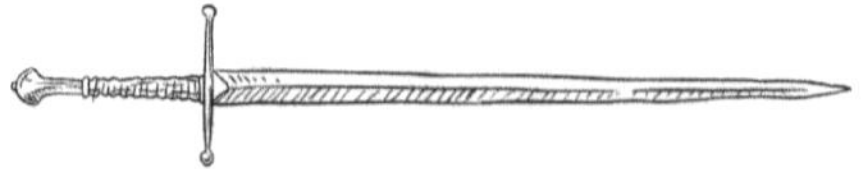

My dreams are full of blood and screams. I wake with a gasp, and it immediately turns into a harsh cough. Pain makes my face ache as I try to move it, but thick cuffs weigh down my feet and hands.

"You're awake."

*I know that voice.*

As if in a waking dream, I turn and meet the golden eyes of Remus Ostia in the metal cage next to me.

"Hello, *A gahrá.*"

His voice. Those words. I can't even respond. I can only reach a shaking hand out, fighting against the chains anchoring me to the floor. He stretches his own hand forward until our palms touch.

The heat of his hand *burns* and I gasp, but it turns into a choked, sob in my throat.

"You're *alive.*"

Remus smiles. All of his wavy black hair is gone, shorn tight to his scalp. His muscles and scars are more pronounced.

*Remus Ostia is alive.*

*My familiar is alive.*

"I'm here." Remus laces his fingers with mine as tears stream openly down my cheeks. "I'm here."

He's *alive. Oh my gods, he's alive.*

*"Thank you."* I send the prayer out in my head. There is no response, as always, but for the first time in a long time, I pray and give thanks.

"I thought I lost you," I sob. "I thought—"

"I know," he squeezes my hand. I never want to let him go. "I thought I was lost, too. But, as it turns out, I am much harder to kill than most."

"You were dead. I saw you die. You were dead."

The words tumble out as hard and fast as the tears falling down my cheeks.

Remus presses himself against the bars of the cage, scooting as close to me as possible. He lifts a trembling, bruised arm, and cups my face with one hand.

His touch *burns,* and it only makes me cry harder.

"I'm not dead, my brave, brave spark," he whispers. "I'm right here. Okay? I'm right here."

The grief *pours* out of me. The pain, the memories, the constant weight on my shoulders—it explodes from me like a geyser.

Remus never moves, never drops his hand. Not once.

"You're alive. Thank Gods, you're alive." I smile through the tears.

A pleased, masculine smirk appears on his luscious lips and if it weren't for the chains I would *dive* through the fucking bars and kiss him until I forgot my own godsdamn name.

The corner of his mouth twitches, as if he knows what I'm thinking. He wears chains similar to me, which is when I notice something behind him.

Something...*red.*

"Ryu!" My voice is hoarse as I shout at her, trying to get her attention. She's curled into a ball in the cage next to Remus. "Ryu! Are you okay? Tell me you're okay!"

The red Dragon lifts her head and gives me a nod. Her copper-and-silver eyes are full of pain, but something seems to relax within her as she looks at me.

"She was worried about you," Remus says quietly. "We all were."

"Can you shift?" I ask, already thinking about how we're going to get out of here. Or if it's even possible.

He shakes his head. "The day before Ryu arrived, the Fae brought me down here, forced me to shift and cuffed me. But the day before *you two* arrived, they made me shift back and blocked my Dragon form."

*Damnit.*

Ryu presses her snout against the metal bars of her cage as if to *push* her way to me.

"I'm so sorry, love." I whisper to her and only her. "I'm so, so sorry you had to do that."

It was a desperate hope that Ryu would never have to kill another of her own kind.

Ryu bows her head.

"She says that she would do anything to protect her family," Remus pauses and looks at me before his eyes glance behind me. "You both are her family. Ryu does not regret what she had to do, because she will always do what is necessary to ensure her family *survives.*"

My sobs return in full force.

"Sound familiar?" a voice asks.

Craning my neck to the other side, I meet the mismatched eyes of Nyall Drayven. His face is a miasma of purple and green bruises.

"You look like shit."

He cracks a smile at my greeting and stretches his arm between the bars, placing his palm on my arm and squeezing gently.

"We all look like shit," he snorts and then winces at the pain the action brings.

I smile, despite it all. Comfort and relaxation wash over me.

They're here. They're both *here.* We might be in a godsdamn dungeon, facing gods know what, but Nyall and Os are *here* and they're *alive.*

Ryu's tail thumps hard against the floor and she glares at Remus who snorts.

"Ryu also would like me to tell you that she missed you, even though you and Nyall are both, and I quote, 'Absolute idiots for walking into this trap just to save me', and," Remus pauses, sighing, "and someone named '*Old Fuzz-butt*' is going to hear about this. That is your wolf friend, I presume?"

Nyall laughs, "That's my girl." He winks at Ryu warmly.

"Get it in your scaled, stubborn head," I tell her, looking Ryu in the eyes. Then I smile, "*You* are my family. You are my *child.*"

"*Our* child," Nyall corrects. I glance back at him. His eyes are clear and earnest. There is no doubt or hesitation in him.

I look back at Ryu and smile again with a nod, "*Our* child. You are *ours,* and we are *yours.* There is no leaving you behind. I *refuse* it."

I half expect Remus to get upset at this, but to my surprise, he just smiles warmly.

No anger.

No sadness. Just...acceptance. Some fleeting feeling of being unworthy of such *pure* trust runs through me but the pain numbs it, *forcing* me to exist in the present.

I squeeze his hand again and sigh at the wonderful feeling of his warmth. *Dragonfire.*

"You do realize that she gets her stubbornness from you," Nyall sighs to my right.

Remus snorts in agreement.

"I'm not stubborn," I mutter, but there is no malice in my words.

"Mhm," Nyall clicks his tongue. "You keep telling yourself that, my dear."

I reach out, chain *clanking,* and slap his waiting hand. He laughs, eyes twinkling against the bruises decorating his face.

"You're far too cheerful. It's off-putting," I note with pursed lips.

"And annoying," Remus agrees, and I fight a smile.

"I was just thinking that *someone* needed to be positive around here since it's certainly not going to be either of you, Doom and Gloom."

I can't help but let out a scratchy laugh at the names. Even Os lets out a breathy snicker.

"Am I wrong?" Nyall chuckles.

"Thank the Gods for this cage, Nyall." Remus's words are meant to sound threatening, but there is no violence or offense.

It's a game. Not the words. Those are real. But this is a distraction.

That's all that can be done. We can barely move and are locked in magyk suppressing cages.

We could sit here and dissect our possible upcoming torture and/or death, or we could...talk.

About anything *else*. Even if it's pretending to argue.

Anything else is better.

Nyall winks at me before looking at Ryu, his tone turning serious. "There is no reality in which we leave you behind. None. Besides, this trap was unavoidable."

*Wait.*

"Nyall," I ask, with the sudden stunning realization that my Prince has been busier than I realized.

He shakes his head, looking around. "We can talk about many things, horse girl—" Nyall blinks twice and I realize my old nickname is a code. Horse Girl means someone is listening. "But that is not one of them."

*Only things that are common knowledge. No sensitive subjects, and especially, above all, no asking about possible other concurrent plans that rely on us not knowing them.*

I nod.

"Who's to say this is the only trap?" Nyall winks. "We just need to...be patient for a few days."

Suspicion brews, but I—I trust him.

"What are they going to do with us?" I ask.

"I don't know," Remus says. "They come once or twice a week to torture me and ask questions, but most of those questions were about *you.* "

Guilt threatens to consume me.

"Stop that," Remus hisses. "It's not your fault. But now that they have you...well, I don't know. I haven't overheard any plans."

*Shit.* That doesn't bode well.

"You've been out for two days," Nyall says. "They haven't been down here since they locked us up. I suspect they'll make some grand bullshit appearance soon."

"Where are we?" I ask, and Remus answers.

"The new Dragon Pit. What's left of it, at least."

*Lovely.*

"Oh good, you're *awake,*" the Archmage's voice calls from a distance. I try to scoot away from the front of the cage, giving myself as much distance as possible between us and him.

Remus snarls at him.

There is no more time to celebrate the fact that Remus is alive.

Guards open our cages and rush us, attaching more chains to our cuffs. They even grab Ryu, who snaps at them until they're forced to put a metal muzzle over her snout.

None of us say a word as we're dragged into an empty chamber. Four items are in the center of it. One covered by a velvet drape, and the other three are raw slabs of rock.

One by one, we're shoved onto our backs and chained to the rocks. The sharp points on the stone scratch painfully against my already raw skin.

I can barely move my neck, but a strained glance shows me that Remus is to my right and Nyall is to my left.

We watch as they attach Ryu's chains to hooks embedded into the dirt. The pressure forces her to her belly.

Once she's unable to move, the guards leave, and silence descends.

*Where is he? Where is the Archmage?*

As if he heard the call of his name in my thoughts, the Archmage steps out of the shadows. They curl around his robes, as if begging him to return, but he walks forward into the light.

"What a sight," he smiles and the sight of it makes my stomach turn. "The Beast, The Heretic Prince, and The Gray Wytch. It's an honor, truly."

*What the fuck is he on about?*

"He likes to hear himself talk," Nyall sighs.

Os snickers at the words. "Yes, I've learned that."

The smile on the Archmage's face drops and the air turns cold.

"Accept Sol Constantus as your one, true God, and this can be a pleasant conversation."

*Of course.*

"Belief does not come by force." Remus's voice is low and full of threats. "Belief comes from love and *respect*. Of which, for you, we hold *none.* "

The Archmage sighs. "You look but you do not see. Sol Constantus is *all*. There is no room for other Gods and nonbelievers."

It's the same shit the Fae have been spouting for the past 500 years.

"I'd rather choke," Nyall says pleasantly.

The Archmage's purple eyes land on me.

"What about you, Wytch? Is there anything left in your soul to save? He will forgive you, if you give yourself to Him."

"No thanks."

My words echo through the chamber. The Archmage's eyelashes twitch as he fights his anger.

A warm, pleased feeling settles in my belly.

The Archmage likes to stay in *control,* and I'm going to make him lose it.

Not right now, but soon. A plan begins to form in the back of my mind. I save it for later and prepare myself for the pain that is certain to be waiting for us.

"I see," the Archmage sighs and clasps his hands. "How *unfortunate.*" With the last word, his voice *changes.* It lowers, becoming inhuman and something terrifying.

"I have some questions for each of you." The Archmage walks over to the draped table. He pulls the fabric back to reveal a variety of large metal torture instruments.

It hits me with the force of a thousand suns.

"No," I say aloud. "Don't hurt her."

The Archmage clicks his tongue. "Accept Sol Constantus, and I will not."

*Fuck. FUCK!*

I meet Ryu's pained eyes. The red Dragon shakes her head. She can barely move and it strains the metal, but the message is clear, because I *know* her.

*Don't give him a single thing.*

I don't dare look at Remus or Nyall.

"Where is she?"

The question stops me.

"Who?" I ask, genuinely confused.

The Archmage picks up a big pair of pliers. "Don't play coy, Ms. Asteroth. *Morrigyn.* Where is she?"

I—what?

"I don't know what you're talking about."

The Archmage glances at me and sighs. "That is the wrong answer, Ms. Asteroth." He takes a few steps closer to Ryu and bends down to her claw. She tries to yank it away but the chains prevent her from moving. Ryu fights against the restraints but can't escape as the Archmage places the pliers around one of her long nails.

"You're doing this to piss me off," I tell him, trying to draw his attention. "If you want to piss me off, then come over here and leave the Dragon alone. Don't be a *coward* about it."

The Archmage doesn't react. He just yanks out Ryu's nail with a sick *crunch.*

The sound of Ryu's screams will haunt me to the afterlife.

Remus is furious and snarling beside me while Nyall hurls threat after threat.

None of us can look away.

Ryu's eyes remain on me, and I nod as if to say, *"I am here. You are not alone."*

Steaming tears fall from her copper and silver eyes as the dirt beneath her is soaked in blood.

The Archmage whirls to us and the ground begins to shake.

**"WHERE IS MORRIGYN BURIED? WHERE DID YOU HIDE HER BONES?"**

I risk a glance at Remus and Nyall; both look equally confused.

"You're insane," I tell him. "Morrigyn is a *God.* How would we know *anything* about where she is?"

"You're lying. You know where they are. I'll wring it out of you." The Archmage walks over to me and bends down, taking off my shoes with slow, creepy precision.

Remus's snarls get louder and Nyall's threats become more gruesome as the Archmage brings his large pliers around and reaches for my foot.

Nyall and Remus both call for me, but I don't look away from Ryu.

Our eyes never part, not even as the Archmage repeats his question.

"Where are her bones? Where is Morrigyn buried?"

"I don't know," I croak, telling the complete truth.

Ryu nods slightly at me.

As the Archmage tightens his pliers around my pinky toe and I jump into the dark void within the depths of my soul. I fall so far, I lose all feeling in my body. The world seems so far away.

Ryu is the string that keeps me tethered to this world. Her eyes ground me.

*"I am here. I'm am here."*

I take a deep breath.

The Archmage *yanks,* and then all I know is darkness and pain.

# CHAPTER 60
## RYU

I did not understand, before. But I understand now.

Something happens to you when you're forced to listen to the tortured screams of your loved ones for hours on end.

No, not hours. *Days.*

It's been four days since Amalia and Nyall were captured. Almost a week since I've been here, and yet it feels like a lifetime.

To think that my people, my *mother's* people spent centuries down here? It's unfathomable.

We're all covered in blood and bodily fluids, having no reprieve from the chains for even a second.

They started with Amalia, who lost three toes.

Then they moved to Nyall.

He lost multiple fingers.

But with Os...

First, they broke both his arms, then they broke his legs. The sound of his bones shattering, the sight of those white shards piercing through his skin...

I will never forget it. Never.

Finally, the Archmage ended with me. I passed out when he pulled out the second claw. The pain was too much.

Every day, the same routine repeated again. Healers came in during the night, dozens of them surrounding us, chanting while their strange purple magyk washed over our bodies.

In the morning, our bodies were healed.

Bones healed, fingers, toes, and claws all regrown. Amalia's hair is long again like it used to be. All of our ailments gone. Even Os' black hair has grown back.

Every day the Archmage shows up again, asks the same questions, and the dance repeats.

On the Fourth day, the Archmage gets too frustrated and leaves before he can rip my second claw out again.

"You're lying," he repeats, over and over, but they are telling the truth. "Tell me where the bones are and this all stops."

They do not know where Morrigyn is, or where her bones are buried, so they never answer.

Screams of pain follow shortly after.

There is nothing for them to tell him. They truly do not know anything about Morrigyn's bones or where they might be.

But... I think I do.

## THE EVENING BEFORE AMALIA & NYALL'S CAPTURE:

*"Try to get some sleep,"* Os says gently, brushing his claw against mine. "I can feel your exhaustion."

I sigh. *"I will try. Sleep is...difficult, here."*

Os nods. *"It is for me too, but you are not alone, Ryu. We have each other, now. I will look out for you while you sleep and wake you if I hear someone coming."*

A strange thread of relief unravels within me.

*"Thank you,"* I whisper. *"I will try to sleep."*

Os nods. *"Good. If you find your mind straying, try counting lambs."*

I blink. *"Count lambs?"*

He nods. *"It's what I taught my little sister when she was a hatchling. She always had a hard time sleeping. It sounds silly but think of counting a herd of lamb. Or some other delicious little creature. Think of flying above them and counting, one by one. And you keep counting until eventually you fade off."*

*"Does that work?"* I ask, bewildered.

*"It did for her and sometimes it does for me—but not always. It's worth a try, though."*

I nod and close my eyes, bringing up the picture of a herd of deer in my mind.

I do not know much about lambs and other farm animals, having grown up in the forest. But I do know about deer.

*Mmm. Deer.*

My stomach grumbles and I ignore it, focusing on the feeling of running behind a herd of deer. Not close enough to catch but enough to see their numbers.

Then I begin to count.

By deer 47, I feel sleep begin to wash over me.

The last deer I count is 58, when I finally fall soundly asleep.

*The terrain is steep, and I struggle to find a rock to hold onto as I climb up the mountain.*

*I have to get to the top. I don't know why though.*

*"What is this?" I ask, stopping and looking around. I feel the tug of need within my mind. Need to get to the top.*

*This is...a strange dream.*

*There's a heaviness to the air. A weight. I flick my tongue out and flare my nose, tasting the air for anything nearby.*

*Any sense of what this is.*

*Then it hits me, washing over the tip of my tongue.*

*Ethelen.*

*The drink of the Gods.*

*"You need to fly."*

*I turn and look to see my mother hovering in the sky. But she's not.*

*This only looks like my mother.*

*"Who are you?" I ask.*

*The being smiles. "I am Kydis."*

*"No, you are not." I say.*

*The being smiles. "Perhaps. But that does not matter. What matters is that you need to fly to get to the top."*

*"What is at the top?" I ask. "Why is it so important that I fly there when I can climb?"*

*"They need you to fly to the top. The God-Touched sisters and one that feels like water."*

*"Who are they?" God-Touched. I think that's Amalia. But is there another?*

*"You already know the answer, Ryu." the being says.*

*I already know...*

*No. I don't. But Kydis does. The real Kydis.*

*Which means the answer is in my mother's memories.*

*"Why do they need this?" I ask.*

*"The sisters—light and dark, sword and shield—they are mine. The water one is promised to the sea. But all must survive."*

*"How does this relate to my flying to the top of this mountain?" I snarl, losing patience with whatever this being is.*

*"The top of the mountain does not exist."*

*I glance up at the mountain, which does appear to very certainly exist—at least in this dream world—and look back to the being wearing my mother's body.*

*"Not truly," the being laughs. "The top of the mountain is not a place, young one. The top of the mountain is...balance."*

*I blink. "Balance?"*

*She nods. "Yes. Fly to the top, Ryu. Fly to the top and save them. Bring back the balance."*

*The being falls, slightly, growing blurry for a moment.*

*"I can't stay any longer. I am sorry to rush you, but you must fly."*

*Then the being rips me off the cliff and tosses me into the sky.*

*She whispers four final words in my ear before I hurtle towards the ground.*

*"Fly, daughter of Livyathin."*

*I try to flap my wings but they're weak from disuse.*

*I try harder but I'm falling too fast and crash into the ground.*

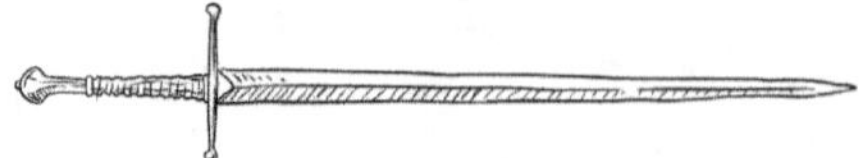

I wake up with a gasp, twitching.

*"Are you alright?"* Os asks.

I pant lightly as I reorient myself. My heart pounds in my chest.

*"It was just a bad dream,"* I tell him.

*"That happens to me as well. I am sorry it was a bad dream, Ryu. But you were not asleep long. Try and get some more rest. I will wake you in a few hours."*

I nod and settle my head back down on the ground, attempting to get comfortable.

But sleep does not come.

Instead, I keep thinking about the mountain, and the riddles spouted by a being wearing my mother's skin.

A being who, I'm quite sure, was a God. A *true* God. An *Eldritch* God.

And I think I know which God it was.

*Morrigyn.*

# CHAPTER 61
## AMALIA

Pain makes the days bleed together.

We might have been here for weeks. Maybe even months. Or only a couple of days. I do not know. The pain is so great that I can't concentrate long enough to think on it.

Consciousness drains from me as blurry healers stream into the room, ready to fix our bodies only so the Archmage can break us once more.

There's a muttered curse word and a low grunt to my side, but blackness takes me as I fade from the world, grateful for any reprieve from the suffering inflected upon us.

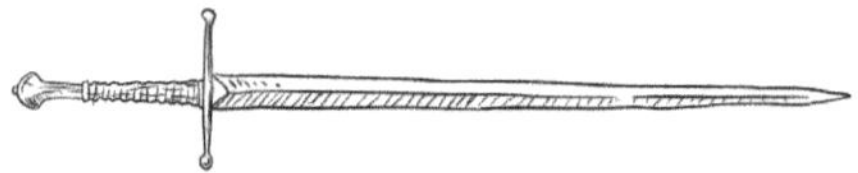

"Wake up, *A gahrá.*"

That voice.

That *voice.*

"Remus?" I croak, forcing my eyelids to open.

Golden eyes hover over me as my vision clears. Gold light swirls around the edge of Remus' being. Remus' hair has regrown, just like mine. His dark waves curl lightly around his ears, skimming the edge of his jaw.

He looks exactly the way he did the first time I saw him.

Trembling, I lift a hand to touch his face as tears begin to stream from my cheeks.

He smiles, his gold eyes softening.

"Is this real?" I breathe.

"No and yes." Nyall says, suddenly next to us. I glance to the side and find his mismatched eyes.

His words take a second to sink in.

*No and yes...*

"You're dreamweavyng," I realize and Nyall nods. "But, how?"

Remus looks at Nyall with a furrowed brow. "I too am curious."

Nyall smirks, the picture of pride. "I have many tricks up my sleeves."

Remus and I continue to stare and Nyall sighs. "Doom and Gloom is right. I've been *trying* to do this every night that we've been here. Our cuffs and the metal around us make it difficult. But not impossible."

One blink and Remus has his hand around Nyall's throat.

*Shit.*

I push up on my elbows, preparing to get in between them and stop whatever nonsense they're up to.

"What the *fuck* were you thinking?" Remus snarls, finally allowing his anger to release, and release it *does*. Like a breaking dam, the Beastkyn doesn't hold back. "Letting her come here! Do you want her to die, you fucking idiot? Why do you think they left me ALIVE, Nyall? They want her. It was never about me."

I knew this conversation would happen eventually, but I find myself not ready for it.

Nyall's face goes hard, but he looks at me and in his mismatched gaze, I only see trust.

"Stop, Remus." I yank him away from Nyall, leaning up on my knees until we're face to face. Pointing my finger into his chest, I'm suddenly so angry I could scream as my own dam breaks.

"How dare you," I snarl. "How *dare* you! You claimed you knew me and yet you *really* think I would leave you in here? That the second I found out you were alive, I wouldn't figure out a way to get to you? That I would, what, leave you to rot here? Fuck you!"

I shove at his chest, but he doesn't move. I'm a quivering mess of emotions but I can't stop now. Hot arms suddenly encircle me, pulling me tight against a scarred, muscular chest.

Then Remus' lips are on mine, and I *sob* into him.

I can't believe he's here. That he's alive.

"I thought you were dead," I whisper, my voice breaking. "You were dead. You were dead and it should have been *me.*"

I didn't mean to say that, but the truth spills out of me, and I am unable to stop it.

"Blue," Nyall sighs, looking at me with such emotion it makes my tears fall harder.

Remus doesn't move. He just holds me in his arms like he has all the time in the world.

"I don't care if this ends up killing us, Remus." My words are shaky as I confess to my Beast. With a trembling breath I look up, meeting his tear-filled gaze. My hand lifts to cup his cheek and I start crying in earnest again. "*Anything* to see you again. *Anything,* understand me?"

His large hand reaches up and cradles my cheek, and I sigh into his warm touch.

I don't care if this is a dream. The feelings are real.

*This* is real.

I nuzzle into Remus' neck, inhaling his delicious, sweet smokey scent for a moment, then pull back. Even a few centimeters of distance feels like a cavern of separation.

"Not to be a downer, but we do need to talk."

I turn around and face Nyall.

The male who watches me isn't the one I met two years ago. Nyall might look the same...but we have all changed.

Him, I think, most of all.

With a deep breath and a feeling in my heart akin to plunging off a cliff, I take a few short steps over to him and throw my arms around him. He pulls me tightly against his chest, one hand in my hair and the other around my waist.

Nyall lets out a relieved sigh.

"I would never let you do this alone, Blue," he whispers. "I told you before; I'm not leaving you again. Not ever."

"It seems that we have much to catch up on," Remus notes. Nyall and I slowly pull away, but my soul is screaming at me to keep a hand on both of them.

I don't want to let them go. Not even in a dream.

Nerves turn my stomach as I falter suddenly, not knowing what to say.

I never thought this moment would happen. That this conversation set before us was possible.

"I can feel your nervousness," Remus murmurs, stepping closer until he is at my right shoulder and Nyall is just at my left. Remus reaches up and caresses my cheek. "There is nothing you could say to upset me, my spark. You are my familiar. You are my other half."

I glance at Nyall, who looks equally nervous.

But, for different reasons, I think.

I pace to the wall, looking away from them with my hands on my hips as I try to draw in a breath.

I have to do this.

Not anymore.

Spinning, I meet Remus' confused gaze. "Nyall and I...are together. It's new. We...We thought you were gone."

Remus doesn't react, he just cocks his head.

"You are afraid I will be upset at this." Remus nods, not in confirmation but in understanding. "I see."

"Nyall isn't...he isn't what we thought."

I hear Nyall's sharp inhale.

For two years he has defended me...it's time I return the favor.

Because it is true.

Nyall *is* different. He is not who or what I thought he was.

I reach a handout, grabbing Nyall's and lacing my fingers with his. With a lifted chin, I face Remus.

"Nyall is good. He has protected me and Ryu. He is not like his father or the other Imperial Fae. He is everything they are not. We were wrong," I breathe. "We were so wrong about him."

Remus *hmms.* "I see. And you love him?"

I nearly choke on my own spit.

Remus flashes me a soft smile and then in a blink, is before me, cupping my face between his hands.

"I thought I might never see you again and yet, my familiar, my *love,* here you are. Within my arms once more. I don't care if you fucked his entire rebellion or if you're in love with a tree. You are safe. You are happy. You are alive. This does not change how I feel or what we are to each other."

My knees start to give out, but Nyall wraps his arms around my waist and catches me. Together, the three of us fall gently to the floor as my emotions explode.

"I don't deserve this," I whisper between quiet sobs. "I don't deserve you. Either of you."

"Respectfully, Blue," Nyall murmurs in my ear. "Shut the hell up. You deserve *everything.*"

"Nyall is right." Remus smiles before me. "I love you, Amalia Asteroth. That will never change, not as long as my heart beats within my chest and blood rushes through my veins."

"Romantic," Nyall quips and then suddenly Remus' arms have left me and he's slamming the Rebel Prince against the wall just next to me.

*Oh shit.*

"You love my familiar," Remus snarls. "She claims you are worthy of her, Prince. Is that true?"

Nyall smiles, but his eyes are wide and his pupils blown.

Remus *tsks.*

Then something...changes.

The hand that was around Nyall's neck loosens, turning into a gentle caress.

Nyall's breathing becomes ragged and his jaw drops.

"Do you think I didn't notice?" Remus asks, his voice low and full of dark promise. "Do you think I didn't notice how you look at me, how you *watch* me? You really think I'm that naive?"

Oh *fuck.*

Nyall's mouth opens in shock, "You...never said anything. I—"

Remus looks into the Rebel Prince's gaze. "I asked you to keep her safe, Nyall. *You*. Not anyone else."

*He—what?*

I look between them, suddenly confused.

Then it hits me.

"When?" I breathe. "When did you ask him to keep me safe?"

Remus glances back at me with a smile. "Just as the Crimson Queen hit the Arena floor. I knew my fate, and I knew yours was to *survive.* Who better to task with keeping you safe than the one already falling in love with you?"

Flabbergasted, I turn to Nyall. "You...felt that way? Even then?"

Nyall gives me a soft smile.

I turn to Remus, eyes wide. "You asked him to keep me safe?"

"How do you not see," Remus says gently, "how *precious* you are? You, who has sacrificed so much for everyone else. You, who would walk into a trap just to save me. How do you not see, my spark, that *we* would do just the same for you?"

My jaw drops and a tingling feeling swirls through me.

He...*they* love me.

It feels wrong. It feels *impossible.* Too good to be true.

And yet...here they are.

Remus takes my silence as acceptance and turns to Nyall. Slowly, so slowly I nearly catch on fire, Remus Ostia leans in and *kisses* Nyall Drayven.

I don't breathe. My heart does not beat.

There is nothing, *nothing* outside of this moment.

Nyall gasps into Remus' lips and my Beast swallows it, cupping his hand around Nyall's neck and sinking further against him.

Remus breaks the kiss and leans his forehead against Nyall's, both of them panting lightly.

"Thank you," Remus breathes. "Nyall...*thank you.*"

Nyall shudders, but it's Remus' next words that break him fully.

"I forgive you."

I do not understand what happened in their past, but I do know that whatever happened, these words crack Nyall's cool exterior.

Sobs overtake him as he leans against Remus, who wraps his arms around the other male.

I curl my body against Nyall's back.

Nyall shakes as his sobs go quiet.

"I'm...Os, I'm so sorry," he gasps.

"I know," Remus murmurs. "I know. In these evil times...survival is all that matters. You survived, and I suspect it is because of *you* that I was kept alive."

"You were right," Nyall cries. "You were right all along."

Remus sighs, "I wish I wasn't."

"I'm—I'm sorry too," I add, not wanting to take away from *them* and this moment. But the words are aching to be let out.

"Stop it," Remus says, but I put my hand on his arm.

"No, let me say this." I look around at the room we're in. It's similar to Remus' room in the old Dragon Pit, but the edges are blurry. "If there is any place safe enough to say this, it is within a dream."

I meet his golden gaze again. "Let me say this while I can, Beast."

He smirks at the nickname as Nyall's tears start to dry. I rub my hand against his back, desperate for contact.

"I'm sorry," I breathe. "About the lies...about the distrust, about everything. I'm sorry that I am the way that I am; so full of *hate* and fear. But you...*both* of you...you make me less afraid. You make me *see* what is real."

My own tears begin to fall harder as I tell Remus, "I'm sorry I ran."

I turn to Nyall and place a kiss on the back of his neck. "And I am sorry I didn't trust you."

The males before me blur, changing our arrangement so I'm now pressed between them, my legs wrapped around Remus' waist as Nyall curls himself against my back, his hands on Remus' shoulders.

"That's what they do," Nyall says, his voice full of resentment. "Their evil, their *greed,* their hate...the Fae did this. The *Archmage* did this. They taught us to fear and hate just the same."

Remus nods.

"If we are making apologies," the Beastkyn begins, "then I too have something to say."

I pull back and look into his eyes, leaning against Nyall's chest.

First, Remus meets my gaze. "I am sorry I didn't meet you sooner, and I am sorry to have not been there these past two years."

"You couldn't help it—" Remus stops me with kiss softer than the brush of a feather against my lips. By the time I can react, he's pulled back.

"I thought of you every day. Every single day."

My tears fall harder.

"Allow me this, my spark. I am *sorry* for the path we've been set on," Remus' eyes flick behind me to Nyall. "I am sorry for all of it."

Nyall clears his throat. "We're a sorry bunch, aren't we?"

I let out a gasping laugh despite the tears still falling in earnest. Remus chuckles too.

"Team Doom and Gloom."

I choke hearing Remus say those words.

"But Nyall?" I feel the male behind me still at the Beast's words. "You are hers, now," he pauses, reaching up to cup Nyall's cheek and pull him close. Their faces hover next to mine and I crane my neck to watch as Remus pulls Nyall in for another feather-soft kiss. Nyall moans but Remus is already pulling back. "You are hers, and you both are *mine.*"

The Beast bares his fangs as if to *dare* anyone to take us from his grasp.

This isn't Remus.

This is the Beast.

This is my *Dragon*.

Yes. *Yes.* I am theirs, and they are mine. A feeling of rightness settles within me. Distantly, in the far reaches of my mind, I feel a cord tighten between the three of us.

"How long do we have before…"

Nyall sighs, "Not long. An hour, maybe. Time works differently in here."

I nod and pull gently out of their arms, getting up to stand.

"What are you doing?"

"Get up." I order, and they both comply. A heady feeling comes over me at the *power* in knowing that they obey me.

"We have two choices right now."

They stare at me.

"Our first choice is to use the time we have left in here to make a plan."

"And the second choice?" Remus asks.

*This is just a dream,* I remind myself.

With a snap of my fingers my clothes disappear. Remus lets out a groan and puts his hand out to steady himself against Nyall, whose mismatched eyes roam greedily over my body.

"Option two," Nyall quickly responds, his gaze at the apex of my legs.

"Agreed."

I snap my fingers again and their clothes disappear.

"Whoops." I smile.

Remus looks at me and something *changes.*

I'm no longer staring down a male, but a *Dragon.*

An idea pops into my head, followed by an image so visceral it nearly sends me to my knees.

Appropriate, then.

I brush against Nyall's mind and send him the image in my head. He shudders, his eyes falling closed.

With a burst, they open, and he pivots, backing away from Remus to stand next to me. Already, Nyall's cock grows hard. The piercing at the tip glistens in the light of the dream.

My mouth waters just looking at it. But this is not about Nyall. This is about a *Dragon.*

"You've been alone for two years," I say, meeting Remus' burning gaze. "My poor Beast," I step forward and reach a hand up to trace my nail along his muscular chest, "tell me what you *need.*"

Remus' eyes close and he takes a sharp breath, shuddering.

"Tell *us,*" Nyall steps closer, one arm around my waist and the other twirling with Remus's hand.

I'm surprised I don't burst into Hellfyre.

I've never been so turned on in my life and it's just a *dream.*

*Stop thinking!* For once, I listen to my inner thoughts and just *be.*

So I get to my knees and take Remus' thick cock in my hands, and slip the tip into my mouth, sucking gently.

His back bows and his head falls back with a *hiss.* "You play with fire," he warns.

I *hum* around his cock and lick beneath the head, where it's most sensitive.

"I don't want to hurt you," he groans, panting lightly. "Either of you."

Nyall scoffs.

It used to be *them* telling me to stop holding back.

I want my Dragon *unleashed.*

I pull Remus' cock out of my mouth with a wet *pop.* "Stop holding back and *use me!*"

Nyall curses and then Remus is thrusting into my mouth, his cock hitting the back of my throat. A few thrusts and he pulls out, giving me a breath. Strands of spit connect us, and I gasp for breath but then he's back between my lips, fucking me with a feral snarl.

He pulls me off and turns slightly, his cock landing between Nyall's lips.

Nyall's mismatched eyes are on me and he smiles as he takes Remus all the way into his mouth.

My heart stops at the sight.

They're so gorgeous.

Who cares whether or not Gods are real.

These are my Gods, and I am *theirs.*

Together, we worship our Dragon, our lips tangling as we take turns until Remus explodes down the back of my throat with a mighty roar.

I'm panting and gasping for breath as I pull off his cock but then Nyall is there, his tongue sweeping into my mouth as he kisses me, searching for a taste.

I'm undone.

"Touch yourself," Remus suddenly orders, pulling me away from Nyall. I let out a pathetic whimper at the loss of contact but then there's a bed. I didn't even see it before, but I'm tossed onto the middle of it. Remus crawls up to lay on my right side and Nyall crawls up on my left.

The dynamic just changed.

"Her heart is racing again," Remus comments and Nyall nods.

They share an evil smile and suddenly I'm terrified...terrified and ready for more.

"Spread your legs and touch yourself, Amalia." Remus orders.

My chest rises and falls in a fast pattern, but my hand slides down my body before I have a chance to think about it.

Remus moves so he's kissing my collarbone while Nyall sucks on my neck.

"Reach your hand down and touch yourself, Amalia."

Remus' order makes me burn even harder. I slide my hand down, brushing my fingers through my folds.

"Gods, I've craved the taste of you every fucking day that we've been apart," Remus snarls and I moan, sliding one finger inside.

"Isn't she delicious?" Nyall purrs, and Remus makes a rough noise of agreement.

Remus has me add another finger, and then *another*.

*Oh fuck.*

A fourth finger and that's all it takes.

"Come for us, *A gahrá*. Ride your hand and come for us."

Nyall silences my screams with his mouth as I come, shouting their names into the ether of dreamland.

Then Remus is between my thighs, gently pulling my fingers out of me so he can replace it with his tongue.

A forked tongue slides inside of me and I gasp into Nyall's mouth. Nyall swallows every one moan and every cry as I explode again, coming all over Remus's face.

Then Remus is behind Nyall, tilting my mate's head back.

"Want a taste?" Remus asks, but Nyall doesn't have time to answer as the Dragon leans down and kisses him.

Nyall moans and it makes the Dragon smile.

Remus reaches down and grasps his hard cock. Nyall jerks and makes a strangled sound. Nyall's head falls back but Remus forces it up, looking at him with a single-minded intensity as the Dragon fucks the Rebel Prince with his hand.

"You are mine now," Remus purrs. "You are both. Fucking. MINE!"

Nyall explodes all over Remus's hand at the Dragon's unhinged roar.

The dream begins shaking and begins to fade.

"Shit, they're coming," Nyall says. "I'm sorry. We need to wake up."

"No, no, no. Please not yet," I cry out and Remus's head snaps towards me.

But they disappear as I slowly wake up to the sound of an alarm blaring above my head, back into the hell of my own making.

# CHAPTER 62
## AMALIA

I'm half-awake and already, I know that something is wrong. There's a sound far in the distance, but I can't make it out.

"That sounds like…" Remus stops, cocking his head which causes his chains to jingle. Behind him, Ryu lifts her head.

"I hear it too," Nyall groans. "Fucking *hell*, my head hurts."

I turn to the side, concerned, but the noise in the distance gets louder, holding my attention.

"Nyall?" Remus asks in a curious voice.

"Yes? Nyall asks, his voice pained.

"You mentioned multiple traps," Remus pauses. "Was getting *caught* another trap?"

Despite the pain, Nyall huffs a laugh. "Don't get your tail in a twist. It wasn't my idea, it was His. What better trap than one right under upturned noses?"

*His?*

The noise gets closer and I finally make it out.

*Footsteps.*

Footsteps…and the sound of *paws* thudding against the ground.

I let out a sob as Virgyl enters my line of sight. But worry follows close behind.

"You left the Ulster Wald," I say in way of a greeting.

He nods, unable to speak to me because of the cuffs we're in.

Then I see who is beside him.

"Mara?" Shock runs through me.

The blonde sighs. "Yes, well, I'm as surprised as you are. But...much has been revealed since you left."

Mara glances at the wolf with a pointed glance, her eyes wide and surprised. A few other wolves approach, a red and one I recognize from her white-tipped black fur. *Bea.*

"You keep many secrets, Amalia," Mara says, looking over our cages.

"Where are the guards and the Archmage? How did you get in here?" Remus asks quickly, not knowing Mara and not trusting her.

Virgyl's mouth opens, and his tongue falls out in a wolfy grin.

"They're currently preoccupied." Mara smirks and palms her short sword. Which is when I realize it's covered in blood.

"You're attacking Castael Laryn," I breathe. "You...you brought the rebel army."

Mara's royal blue eyes twinkle. "No more waiting. It's time to take the fight to *them.*"

"That's great and all," Nyall groans. "But let's focus on getting the fuck out of here."

Mara is in front of him a second later. "You're hurt."

"No shit," he coughs. "Don't worry about it. Just tell me you know how to get us out."

Mara looks at Virgyl who nods.

"Cover your ears," she says, sending a sympathetic look at Ryu, who is unable to do so. Our chains jangle as we lift our hands and cover our ears.

Even muffled, the sound of Virgyl's bark is *loud.*

So loud, it *bends* the bars of the cages.

The chains drop from the cuffs, and the metal around our ankles disappears. The metal around our wrists doesn't budge.

I can feel my magyk simmering beneath the surface, but it's far away.

I glance to Remus, "Can you shift?"

He closes his eyes for a moment and when they open, they're full of anger. "No. The cuffs are preventing it."

*Shit.*

We quickly get to our feet, but my first thought isn't Nyall or Remus.

It's Ryu.

I limp over to her cage, pain making every movement *ache*. But it's nothing compared to my worry for her.

I undo her muzzle, and large hands reach into my view as Remus works to loosen her chains.

Like us, the cuff around her neck remains, but she can move, finally.

*"Missed you,"* a voice says in my head. It's quiet, as if it was spoken from a great distance, but I know that voice.

Something like a sob and a laugh explodes out of me and I wrap my arms around the red Dragon, caressing her soft scales.

"I missed you too," I whisper, and place a kiss against her cheek. "Let's get the hell out of here."

**"We must move quickly,"** Virgyl's voice booms in our heads.

Nyall winces but Remus merely looks curious. As Ryu stands, Nyall does the same, but he wavers, grasping his head.

Remus is there a moment later, his arm going around Nyall's waist to keep him upright.

"Shit," Mara curses. "Can you make it out?"

"Yes," Nyall hisses.

"Then let's move," Mara nods and we follow.

"Where did they put our stuff? Where are my swords?" I ask, one hand still on Ryu as she walks beside me.

Mara glances back, already ahead of us.

"I'm sorry—I don't know."

Damnit.

"It's not your fault," I mutter, trying to pick up the pace.

"Can we trust them?" Remus asks Nyall. Not quietly, either.

"Yes," Nyall groans, but Remus merely nods, accepting the Prince's words as truth.

In a different situation, that show of trust would make me crumble, but there is no time for crumbling and breaking.

Only for escaping.

Bea walks by my side and the other wolf by Remus' as Mara and Virgyl lead us up to the surface.

# CHAPTER 63
## MARA

No one mentions the mauled bodies as we pass by them, or the dried blood covering the wolves' snouts.

I never thought there would be a time in my life when I would be *glad* to have the Gray Wytch by my side, or her pack of Dyre Wolves. But I am glad. Scared and glad. What Virgyl told us changes *everything*.

As we get close to the surface, the distant shouts of the city become audible.

"How much of the pack is here?" Amalia asks the Alpha wolf.

He glances back, his bright yellow eyes all-knowing.

***"All."***

Amalia inhales sharply. "Virgyl! The risk—"

He interrupts her, ***"The risk is far greater if we should do nothing."***

But I'm not sure Amalia understands the true risk.

"Tell her," I whisper to the wolf as we emerge into the light.

"Tell me *what?*" Amalia asks in a cutting voice.

Pandemonium greets us, distracting us all as we take in the destruction before our eyes.

Castael Laryn is burning.

Smoke rises towards the cloud, blanketing the air in darkness. Buildings and houses are on fire throughout the entire city. The screams of the citizens as they flee shake me to my core.

"Did you do this?" Nyall asks, horror in his voice.

I shake my head and Virgyl does the same. But to my surprise, he turns to *me*.

*He thinks we did this?*

"Nyall, I swear to you, this wasn't us. This was the Fae. They had already begun sacking the town before we even got here."

Amalia's eyes widen. "They're destroying their *own* city?"

Nyall curses. "They'll blame us for it. It's all a ploy."

"There's no time," I snap. "Soren and Fi are waiting at the outer walls of the city. Come, quickly. We need to get out of here!"

The large male with gold eyes picks up Nyall and tosses him over his shoulder. Nyall moans in pain at the motion but we can't afford to slow down.

***"Go!"*** Virgyl barks.

Breaking out into a sprint, we run through the burning city. It's chaos. Rebels and wolves attack those in armor. Citizens flee, screaming in terror as they run out of the city with only what they can carry.

**"BURN THE HERETICS!"** someone screams, and an explosion sounds to our right, blowing debris everywhere. Ryu spreads her great wings, shielding us from the onslaught.

I am thankful for her presence too.

*How quickly things change.*

A guard in armor sees us and shouts. "The traitors! They're escaping—"

His words cut off as I appear in front of him. In a single move, my hands go around his head and I *twist*.

With a sharp crack, his shouts fall silent as death grasps him. I let his body fall to the ground in a cloud of dust.

I glance back and meet Amalia's wide eyes. Then she nods her head in a sign of appreciation and respect.

Shock courses through me but my adrenaline is so high, I barely feel it.

"MOVE!" I shout, and we pick back into a sprint, making our way through the chaos.

Just as we're about to reach the edge of the city, another explosion sounds. Ryu steps over us and crouches, forcing us to do the same she protects us beneath her giant body.

When the coast is clear, we continue moving towards the wall, almost out of Castael Laryn.

*I never want to see this godsforsaken place again.*

Virgyl and I run through the walls, but the wolf comes to a screeching halt.

I don't see it at first, there's too much smoke obscuring my vision, which is why I run into the wolf. My hands go into his thick fur as those following us come to a halt.

Then the smoke clears.

*The Archmage.*

He stands in the middle just beyond the entrance to the city, the rider of the white Dragon from Matricia beside him.

"It seems I have another thanks to issue," he says with an eerie smile, flashing teeth an unnaturally bright shade of white.

I've never seen him up close before.

The male is bald, with eerie purple eyes that seem to glow. His skin is so pale, but there's almost a gray hue to it.

*This* is the Holy Father? *This* is the Archmage?

The Archmage looks at Virgyl, whose fur stands on end.

"Hello, *dog.*"

But this isn't the Archmage.

Not truly.

Now that I know the truth, I can't help but tremble in fear before the being in front of us.

"Tell me, where is that *bitch* you serve? Where did you hide that cunt's bones?

Virgyl snarls and the sound is so fierce, it causes a gust of wind to blow the Archmage and the rider back by nearly a meter, almost knocking them over completely.

**"You will *never* find Her."**

The words are not spoken in our heads, but aloud.

"Oh, but I will," the Archmage hisses. "I will find Her, and I will kill Her for good. Right after I kill all of you."

A low growl comes from the male with gold eyes.

*Os,* I think. The Beastkyn. But there has been no time for formal introductions.

He bares his teeth at the Archmage in open challenge. "I'd like to see you try."

"How sweet that you think you have any chance," the Archmage laughs and turns to the dark-haired rider beside him.

"This is fruitless, Os," the rider calls. "Accept Sol Constantus and see the light."

"You're insane," Os snarls.

"Insane? No," she shakes her head, "I see *clearly*. It is you who are ignoring the truth." The rider's dark gaze flicks to Amalia. "It's *her* corrupting you, isn't it? If the gray *bitch* hadn't come along, you would see the truth."

Amalia flashes a bloodthirsty smile and the sight of it gives me goose bumps. "I like that. Thank you, Ireyna. I needed a new nickname."

The rider—Ireyna—growls, her eyes flashing with purple magyk, but the Archmage holds up a hand and that purple magyk disappears.

"How ironic that you call Virgyl a dog," Amalia looks at Ireyna. "When the only *dog* here is you, rolling over and tucking your tail between your legs like the submissive little *bitch* you are."

Ireyna snarls, "I can't *wait* to kill you."

"Get in line." Amalia winks.

"Silence," the Archmage booms, looking at Virgyl. "Tell me where She is, or I will bleed it out of you. Your choice."

Virgyl lets out a chuff. ***"You will never find Her, intruder, because She is already dead."***

"Ah, but a God never dies," the Archmage smirks as the air grows tense. "Where did you bury Her, mutt? Where did you put Morrigyn's bones?"

*Morrigyn's bones?*

Virgyl told us much, but this, I know naught of. Virgyl bares his fangs again, saying no more to the Archmage.

"I see," the Archmage sighs. "How unfortunate."

"I told you; we don't know where they are," Amalia snarls, pushing to the front of the group and coming to stand at Virgyl's side.

"But you do, little wytch. You have Her power, after all. Some of it, at least."

Amalia doesn't react.

"God-touched," the Archmage whispers, a maniacal glint in his eyes. He steps forward, staring at Amalia. Virgyl growls at the closing distance between us. "*You* are proof that Morrigyn lives."

***"There is nothing of Morrigyn to be found. She is gone. Cease your search,"*** Virgyl warns.

"She's telling the truth, Father," the rider says, addressing the Archmage with his Holy titles. "But the wolf...his truth feels strange. It is the truth but it's also not."

Shit. The rider is a truth sayer.

I've only ever heard about them in stories whispered around the fire. It's an old power, one rarely seen.

But it means we cannot lie to her. She will feel it.

"Yes, I believe you are correct, my child." The Archmage sighs and then purple magyk *explodes* from his being, surrounding us all in a dome.

"Can you break this?" I whisper to Amalia.

She glances at the metal cuffs still around her wrists. "I don't know," she admits quietly. "But I will try."

*"Save your energy,"* Virgyl warns in our heads. *"Cover your ears."* We follow suit. With a loud bark, the purple magyk shatters, freeing us.

**"Let us go,"** Virgyl's low growl echoes through the valley behind us. **"Let us go and stop this madness!"**

The Archmage smiles. "What would be the fun in that, old friend? After all, I'm having such a lovely time with my niece."

My heart skips a beat.

*Niece?*

Then the Archmage looks squarely at Amalia and says, "Your Father resisted me too. But you both have...such a *weakness* for family."

"What the fuck did you just say?" Amalia asks in a voice so cold I'm surprised the air itself doesn't freeze.

With a snap of his fingers, magyk explodes from the Archmage once more. Not to surround us, though, but next to him. A tornado of power hovers in the air before dissipating and revealing a strange, older male with white, blonde hair and pale blue eyes. He's dressed in chains and rags.

Amalia makes a strangled sound. Virgyl leans into her, keeping her from falling to the ground.

*Who is this man?*

"That's not possible," she gasps. "This is an illusion."

Confusion runs through me. *What is happening?*

"Much of what you see is an illusion," the Archmage smiles. "I am the God of Illusions, after all."

My brain hurts trying to keep up with it all, but next to me, Amalia Asteroth *trembles.*

"You're lying," she breathes. "This isn't real."

The Archmage turns to the side, looking at the blonde man. He's dressed in dirty clothes and similar metal cuffs to what Amalia wears are around his wrists.

But his eyes.

I look to the side, searching Amalia's face.

They have the same *eyes.*

"Speak, brother," the Archmage orders the blonde man as purple magyk washes over him. "Speak to your daughter."

"What do you wish me to say?" The male's voice is monotone and emotionless, as if he's not really here.

There's a choked sound next to me as Amalia falls to her knees.

"Dad?"

# CHAPTER 64
## AMALIA

I can't think. Can't move. Can't make my body work other than to say one single word.

"Dad?" My voice breaks. "Dad, is that you?"

*This isn't real.*

*This can't be real. He's dead. I saw it. I saw his body.*

*This is another illusion. It has to be.*

Yet just the sight of him, just the sound of his *voice* has my heart grasping for the strings of hope.

"Hello, daughter. I see that you're alive." My dad cocks his head. "That is unfortunate for our plans."

It's like being stabbed through the heart with a sword. I would know that voice anywhere. My mind reels, moving so fast I can't focus on anything.

*Niece. Daughter. Dad.*

"I saw you die," I breathe.

The Archmage laughs. "You saw what I *wanted* you to see."

*It wasn't real?*

*It was a lie?*

I think back to the night that has haunted me for the past 82 years and replay the memory in my head.

**82 YEARS EARLIER (Year 420 PBM):**

*The howling wind shakes the small cabin. The old wood walls rattle and the roof groan, every worn shingle barely hanging on. The wind shrieks and moans, sounding like the screams of a thousand miserable, tormented souls in the depths of purgatory.*

*Suddenly, the wind stops, and the forest goes silent.*

*"Son of Shadow, did you think you could really escape? Did you think we wouldn't find out about the child?" Achan Drayven asks, everything about him evil even down to the sound of his voice.*

**No.**

**The voice changes.**

**It's not Achan.**

*I feel like a child, small and scared, as I watch through the small hole in the cupboard wall.*

*Father laughs, dark and emotionless.*

*"Did you really think I would let you anywhere near my child,* **brother?"** *he taunts. "There has never been a reality where you ended up with my daughter."*

**The memory shifts. I don't know what is the lie and what is real.**

*"You can't escape me, Asteroth. There's nowhere to run," Achan calls.*

"I love you, my darling," *Mother whispers into my mind.*

"You and your mother are the best things to ever happen to me. Never forget that little spark."

"I love you too. But what's going on, Daddy? You're coming back, right?" *I ask, but they don't respond. There is only silence and darkness. I squeeze closer to the hole in the wall, trying to see what's happening. Puff squeaks quietly in my ear, burrowing into my hair. Poor thing is trembling in fear—but I'm afraid his fear is justified.*

*The cabin begins to rumble and the floor wobbles. A tiny hole of light opens up from a can falling over.*

*My parents stand together, hands clasped, facing the* ~~horned fae~~ **GLOWING MALE.**

*"What the fuck do you think you're doing?"* **The Archmage** *snarls as they begin to glow.*

*One with shadow and one with light.*

**"MORRIGYN!" the Archmage shouts. "I KNOW YOU'RE HERE!"**

*They glow brighter, until I can barely watch.*

**"YOU WILL NEVER HAVE OUR DAUGHTER."**

*Then a huge BOOM sounds as a wave of energy explodes outward, and everything goes dark.*

*I have no idea how much time has passed; all I know is the ground is rough and something sharp is poking at my legs.*

*My eyes feel like sawdust as I pry them open.*

*Stars.*

*Why am I looking at the stars?*

*I push up and realize why.*

*The house no longer has walls.*

*The house fell in a perfect circle around me, but broken slats of wood line the circle's edge. I was too close to the outside of it and they started scratching me. I groan, pushing to standing, when something hits the floor.*

*It's a soft sound.*

*I cough at the ash falling in the air, looking down at my feet.*

*No.*

*No, no, please.*

*Puff's dead, crushed body sits at my feet, a blood trail beginning to form at his open mouth.*

*A scream builds in my chest, but another noise stops it.*

*A noise to the side of me. I turn slowly and stop when I see the source of this new noise.*

*My mother is on her knees, clutching her throat as* **the Archmage** *stands over her and laughs while she chokes on her own blood thanks to the dagger he has stabbed through the middle of her throat. He doesn't remove the dagger, he just stands there, smiling as she drowns, coughing up the blood now filling her lungs.*

*My father screams and jumps towards* **the Archmage, but he stops, freezing suddenly. He grabs his head in pain.**

*Something else roars then, too.*

*Something buried deep within me.*

*My mother is dead.*

**"COME HERE," the Archmage says, and in shock, I do.**

**"Daddy?" I whisper, coming up next to my father.**

**He doesn't respond.**

**"Such a rare little girl," the Archmage murmurs.**

*"Don't think of running. It's no use." He holds out his hand, a sinister smile on his face. "You belong to me, little girl."*

*I look at his hand for a moment.*

**"No," I breathe. Something inside me shifts. I move without thinking, pulling on magyk I didn't even know I had.**

*Everything goes black yet again as magyk surges out of me.*

*After a moment I look around and see a wave of fire so dark it's nearly black covering every surface.*

*Something falls on my head and I wipe my cheek, looking at the black staining my hand.*

*Ash.*

*Not snow, but ash.*

**"You are quite dangerous, niece," the Archmage whispers in my ear. I jump, startled at his sudden proximity.**

**I thought he was dead, but he's alive.**

**And...unharmed.**

**"So, Morrigyn chose you to inherit her powers. How interesting."**

**His hand reaches out and touches my forehead. "Sometime soon, you will learn the truth. It's inevitable. But not yet. Not now."**

**Then he disappears. The Arch**—a—*Achan disappears.*

*He fled.*

*He actually ran.*

*Beneath my brow, I watch as my hair burns like a coal ember, all of the white fading away.*

*Charred, half-frozen bodies lay around the entire clearing along with the broken trunks of ancient trees.*

*"Daddy?" I ask, voice trembling as I walk over to where my parents lay, now covered in flakes of ash. "Daddy? Please." I cry, falling to my knees at the sight of his cloudy eyes. "Wake up, Dad. Please, you have to wake up."*

**No.**

**This isn't real.**

**This isn't REAL.**

*The tears come, then. Sobs so loud, so violent that my entire body shakes. "Daddy, wake up."*

*He doesn't answer. His eyes don't open and his chest doesn't move. Air no longer fills his lungs.*

*"Mom? Please." I look over at the body of my mother, but there's no answer.*

*They're gone.*

*"Please don't leave me alone," I whisper, tears streaming down my face. The fire bursts from me again, surrounding me with a flame that is both hot and cold.*

*They're gone.*

*They're all gone.*

**THIS IS A LIE!**

*"Please don't leave me alone. Please come back," I beg. "Come back, Daddy. Please come back."*

*I don't know how long I sat there.*

*There is only them, and they are gone.*

*So I close my eyes, my hand around my mother's cold, limp palm, and my head against my father's chest, and go to sleep. Hoping never to wake up.*

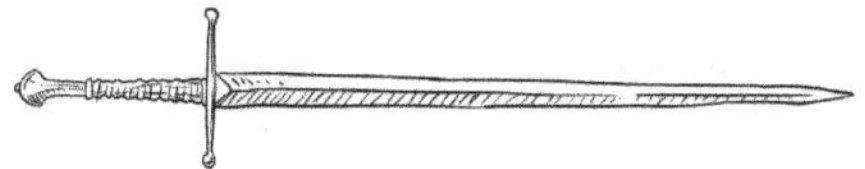

**NOW:**

The world pulls me back within its grasp. The memory was hard to fight through but now I see. Pain radiates through my temples, but I don't care.

I see everything—and we were so, *so* wrong.

*My father is alive.*

An anger like I've never felt before begins to burn deep within my being.

*My father is ALIVE.*

"How?" The word chokes within my throat, dying on the tip of my tongue.

How is this *possible?*

If I look at my father any longer, I will break into a thousand shattered pieces on the ground and never get back up again, so I look at the Archmage instead. My *uncle.*

*Why did I not know this?*

Virgyl steps forward, brushing against me as if to remind me that I'm not alone.

**"Are you going to keep lying, old friend? Or will you finally tell the truth?"**

The Archmage's eye twitches at Virgyl's words. "Ah, the truth," he whispers.

Then he snaps his fingers. "If you would like to talk about truths, *mutt,* then I am not the only one with something to share."

The scene around us disappears and the ground *swerves.* The city around us disappears, fading away as the Arena becomes clear.

Mara curses, looking around frantically.

She stops at the sight of me. Our eyes meet and for a moment, I see a flash of regret.

It's too much. I feel so much all at once and it's left me frozen.

**"But of course, the truth would change things...wouldn't it?"** Virgyl asks. **"I wonder if your followers would still pray to you if they found out the truth."**

"Of course they would," the Archmage snaps. "They would fling themselves at my feet and *beg* for mercy."

"Who are you?" I demand, that anger within me burning hotter and hotter by the second. A warm hand presses against my back.

*Remus.*

I am not alone.

*I am not alone.*

*I AM NOT ALONE!*

The Archmage smirks. "That is the wrong question, niece."

"I am not your fucking *niece,*" I snarl, spitting at his feet.

"But you are," he smiles, "the daughter of my youngest brother. I'm not surprised he never told you—they were always ashamed of me, my brothers. The family *stain.*"

"The question you should be asking," he continues, "is *what* am I?"

I blink.

**"Enough with these games, Constantyn. Enough!"**

I turn to look at Virgyl with wide eyes.

Constantyn. *Constantyn.*

*The Archmage is Constantyn.*

*The Archmage is a God.*

*The Archmage...is my uncle. My kin.*

*My uncle is a God.*

**"You have made your point. You're a God. You have achieved your goals. You have all the power you need! Now stop this madness! If you continue down this path, you will doom us all."**

~~The Archmage~~ Constantyn *smiles.*

A God.

He is a God. The Archmage isn't just Constantyn's disciple—he IS Constantyn.

It's too much. Goose bumps cover my entire body as the hair on my arms stands on end. I turn in slow-motion and look at the Archmage once more.

He brings his hand to the top of his forehead and then dips it away in some form of a greeting. "Lovely to formally meet you, *niece.*"

"How?" I breathe.

~~The Archmage~~ Constantyn sighs and purple light emanates from his being, then he begins to *change.*

His bald head grows hair, turning white, blonde. It's shorn short but the color is unmistakable. Purple eyes fade into a pale blue the exact same shade as mine.

This. *This* is Constantyn. The *real* Constantyn. The relation is obvious. He looks so much like the male at his side—my *father.*

Constantyn smiles at me.

"How? That is easy. I was once like your father. *Weak* and with relatively useless power."

Constantyn lifts his hand, and I watch in horror as shadows wrap around his wrist. Shadows exactly like mine.

"My brothers were content to be *weak,* but I wanted more. So, I found more."

**"You KILLED GODS!"** Virgyl barks and the sound hurts my ears. **"That power is *stolen.* It was never meant to be yours!"**

Constantyn bares his teeth. "It is mine now, and once I have Morrigyn's magyk, no being on *any* world can stop me."

"Hail Sol Constantus, the one true God," Ireyna intones, her pupils blown out.

Guards stream from the city, surrounding us, as they repeat Ireyna's words.

"HAIL SOL CONSTANTUS."

*Her pupils... Shit!* The realization hits me and I glance over to my father—oh gods, my *father.* Looking at him *hurts.*

Then I glance up into his eyes, the exact same shade as my own. His pupils are wide too. I get to my feet, that fury within me quickly turning into a blazing inferno.

"You're compelling them," I accuse. "You're forcing your will on them."

Constantyn smiles, lifting his hand to pat Ireyna's shoulder. "Sometimes, we need a *reminder* of what's really important. A little *push,* if you will. You're familiar with this, are you not?"

"What?" I lean back as if he slapped me.

"Ah, but you can. All Divine can compel. You are no different than me, niece."

No...no that cannot be true.

"Have you not *compelled* flesh to heal? In the final bout of the Gauntlet, you compelled that Crimson Bitch and the other one to fall asleep. You *forced* your will upon them, Amalia. We are one in the same."

Nausea churns my stomach. Bile rises in my throat, flooding my mouth with saliva.

"Did you compel Achan too?"

The question isn't mine, but Nyall's. I feel Nyall come up to my other side, wavering slightly but here.

The Arena around is empty, save for a large group of guards stationed around the top edge of the stands.

"Of course," Constantyn smiles as he looks at Nyall. "Achan was such a good little puppet. He didn't even fight it. He practically *begged* for it, but you—" he pauses, looking at Nyall with a proud smile. "You have exceeded my every expectation. Achan was a *fool* to think you were useless."

Guards begin to encircle us, trapping us with the Archmage.

Some of them have the eerie, glowing eyes of the Fae. But others...others have white hair just like Nyall.

*Elves.*

Nerves make my heart race. Ryu moves closer, her head hovering above our heads.

"Ah yes, the Heir. Your existence has been an...unplanned *annoyance*." Constantyn flicks his hand, and I expect guards to rush Ryu.

They don't move. I look around, a little confused, until I meet Nyall's gaze.

Nyall's blank, flat gaze. His pupils widen, consuming all color within his eyes.

*No. NO.* My heart sinks into my stomach.

Nyall takes a step closer to Constantyn and my hand flies out, grabbing onto his arm.

He pulls out of my grasp.

"I will kill you for this!" Remus flings vicious threats at Constantyn, but it changes nothing.

Nyall walks over to Constantyn's side, face blank.

"He was always my best pupil," Constantyn notes casually, patting Nyall on the shoulder. "But just like his father, his will is *weak*. It was so easy to break him."

"Did you really think your little Prince just *walked* into my city? That he just so *happened* to meet you?"

I'm going to throw up. Distantly, I'm aware of Remus snarling, but I can't look away from Nyall.

"No," I beg. "No. Don't do this."

"But I'm having so much *fun*." Constantyn smiles. "And we're only just getting started."

"Please," I beg. "Please, *uncle*. Don't do this."

*There has to be another way.*

Constantyn smirks and glances to the side at Ireyna.

"What do you think, my child? Does my niece deserve *mercy*?"

Ireyna's face is emotionless.

"No," she says flatly. "She does not."

"Then so be it," Constantyn claps his hands together, then looks at Nyall and *smiles.*

"Kill the Dragon and Amalia Asteroth."

# CHAPTER 65
## AMALIA

"Kill the Dragon and Amalia Asteroth."

**"No,"** Virgyl says aloud. **"You will not hurt her."**

"Then come here, *mutt,* and let's finish this."

With a mighty roar, Constantyn unleashes a wave of purple magyk at Virgyl, who avoids it with a sharp bark.

I pull at the cuffs around my wrists, frantic to get my magyk back, but they won't budge.

Mara screams and jumps out of the way as Constantyn sends another wave of magyk in our direction.

"Ryu!" I call to the Dragon behind us. "Can you access your fire?"

*"I cannot."* Her voice is so quiet in my head compared to usual.

"Shit," I hiss. "Remus, please tell me you can shift."

"I would love to tell you that," he lifts his hand and unleashes black claws. "But I can't get any farther than this."

"FUCK!" I scream, kicking the dirt.

There's a beat of silence.

"Move!" Remus shouts, but Nyall is already there, his magyk activated, light bands accentuating his arms.

Ireyna is next to him, blasting us with magyk. Some of it hits my hands and I can feel my skin begin to blister. It feels like being pricked by a hundred tiny needles.

"She's *mine,*" Remus snarls, all Dragon. "I'm going to rip out your fucking spine and feed it to you, you righteous cunt."

"You can try," Ireyna smirks. It's the mirror image of the face Constantyn makes.

Remus charges her with a roar so loud it makes the ground shake.

"Ireyna, keep the beast busy," Constantyn orders as he levels another attack at Virgyl. Howls echo from around the city as the wolves realize their Alpha is under attack.

Dyre Wolves begin to stream into the Arena.

They attack the guards, mauling them and ripping out their throats, but there are many shrieks and howls of pain. I watch as several wolves are gutted, their bodies thrown to the ground with heavy *thuds.*

I'll kill them. I'll fucking kill them.

*"No, allow* **me***,"* Ryu snarls in my head. She takes a step over me, heading towards the wolves, but a bolt of magyk hits her backside. She stumbles, crying out in pain.

There's no time to think as Nyall hurls another beam of magyk at me. I jump out of the way, my body groaning with every move. I hit the dirt hard, and sand gets in my eyes. Blinking away, I see my father watching me with a blank look in his eyes.

"I don't want to hurt you," I shout at Nyall. "Please, don't do this. I know you're in there."

A shadow covers me, and I look up to see Ryu's scaled belly.

*"Stop this!"* she orders Nyall, but he doesn't listen.

Instead, he blasts her with white magyk. Ryu flares her wings to protect me from it, shrieking as her wing membranes catch on fire.

In my mind, I *claw* at the spell keeping us from our magyk. But it's like the metal itself is magyk. Still, I kick and claw and scream at it.

A tiny sliver of my magyk slips through.

*YES!* I focus in on that small, miniscule tear and *yank.*

Shadows stream out of me, as if they're crawling out of my skin. With a roar I launch two whips of shadows in Nyall's direction, trying to yank his feet out from under him.

Remus curses behind me. I can't spare more than a second to glance back at him. Ireyna pummels him with purple magyk.

*Ireyna has magyk? What the fuck?* Before I can think any more of it, Nyall is there again, batting away my shadows and sending another bolt of white magyk towards us. I sidestep but it singes my outer right shoulder, drawing blood.

"Stop this!" I call to him, but Nyall does not respond.

We duel back and forth, my shadows and his white magyk. Hellfyre burns within me, but it won't emerge. The cuffs won't *let* it.

"Nyall, I know you're in there," I pant, sweat and dirt dripping into my eyes.

Nyall blurs, appearing before me and punches me in the face. His fist hits my cheek. Blood fills my mouth as pain bursts across my face. I spit at the sand, spraying it with blood.

I can't keep holding back. But I don't want to hurt him. With a scream I tackle him to the ground, leveling a wicked punch to his nose and clavicle. Something *crunches* and breaks, but Nyall doesn't stop.

He hits me in the side before tossing me to my back and crawling on top of me, his hands around my neck.

"Nyall—" I gasp, slapping his hands away, but he's too strong. "Nyall, stop!"

Black spots dance at the edge of my vision as my airway closes further, his hands squeezing the life out of me.

"I love you."

His hands falter.

"Nyall Drayven, *I love you.*" I repeat the words over and over again. His eyes twitch as the inner war begins. Nyall stumbles back and I stand, closing in on him. "Do you hear me, asshole? I love you. Even when you piss me off, even when you're always right, even when you *leave* me for godsdamn year!"

Nyall twitches as he fights the compulsion. I slap him across the face and send him to his knees.

"I love you," I repeat.

He looks up at me and for a moment, I see recognition.

"Blue," he pants. "Ki-Kill me. P-please."

I lean down and press my lips against his. We taste of sweat and dirt and blood and *love.*

"Never," I whisper. "Fight it, Nyall. Burn his compulsion out."

"I can't—" Nyall gasps. "It's t-too strong. I—"

Constantyn snarls in the background and sends a wave of purple magyk at us. It doesn't hit me, but it *enters* Nyall, soaking into his skin like a wet rain.

Then he's gone. Nyall's eyes go blank, and any recognition disappears.

Ryu roars, jolting me out of the moment. I turn and watch as she takes down each and every guard that challenges her.

If I wasn't so terrified, so overwhelmed and worn down, I would be beaming with pride.

"The Dragon will die first." Nyall murmurs in a monotone voice.

*No.*

He blurs, appearing before Ryu, as his magyk onslaught begins anew.

Ryu screams as his magyk *burns* through her scales, creating open wounds that gush with steaming blood.

*NO.*

I thought my nightmares were bad. This is worse than anything I could have ever dreamed of.

To my right, Remus and Ireyna duel with magyk and claws. He's covered in blood, and so is she, so I can't tell who is winning.

I glance past them and my heart stops as I watch Constantyn create a sword of purple magyk and *slice* into Virgyl.

The black Wolf lets out a pained shriek, trying to get away, but Constantyn is there, slicing into him once more. Blood streams down Virgyl's legs and he pants, clearly in pain.

To my left, Ryu lets out another cry of pain as she stumbles, falling to the dirt.

*I can't save them all.*

It's a living nightmare to experience this again.

To have to *choose* who to save...and who should die.

*"Please,"* I beg the Morrigyn, or whoever is out there to listen. *"Please, don't make me do this."*

There is no answer.

My eyes flick between the three fights, trying to follow all of them. My heart beats so hard I can feel it in my ears. Pain courses through my body but it is nothing compared to the pain I feel at hearing my loved ones *shrieks* of agony.

Ryu groans and tries to stand, but she stumbles in a pool of her own blood.

My father.

My protector.

My lover.

My familiar.

My daughter.

*I can't save them all.*

Forcing my body to stand, I watch as Nyall places his right hand on her snout. She cries out and tries to get away, but his hand doesn't move. White magyk swirls around them both, which is when I realize what's happening.

He's siphoning her.

*NO.*

With a roar, I let the anger and pain explode from my being. I jump to my feet and suddenly two swords are in my hands.

*Macha and Neiman.*

I don't know where they were or how they got here but I shove my magyk. This time, instead of Hellfyre, the black blades start to emit black shadows that slither up and down its length.

*"Please, please don't make me do this."*

Morrigyn doesn't answer. Nyall's past words ring clearly in my head. Once he begins siphoning and the spell activates...he can't stop.

I don't know what precisely can't *stop* means, but I don't want to find out.

*"Save us, I beg you. Don't doom us to this fate. Don't make me kill him."*

It is as silent as a grave as my prayers go unanswered yet again.

Then, in the quietest whisper, I feel a slight...*nudge.* It's like someone *moves* my eyes for me, and they land on Nyall's right arm. The one on Ryu's snout. The one currently siphoning off her magyk.

*He can't stop.*

I blur, racing towards him, not risking even a moment to stop and second myself. Tears streaming down my face, I launch myself at Nyall and bring my sword down, begging and praying to all of the Gods for forgiveness for what I'm about to do.

My cut is clean. For a moment, nothing happens. Then the magyk around Nyall stops, going quiet, as his severed arm falls to the ground.

Nyall screams, clutching the bloody stump that remains below his shoulder. The sound of his pained cries make me want to throw up.

"I'm so sorry," I cry. "I'm so sorry...but no one hurts our daughter."

Nyall falls to his knees as blood coats his body, pooling beneath him in the sand.

Nyall looks up at me, tears streaming down his face.

"I—" he gasps, "I love you too."

Then he passes out, falling limp to the ground. Already, his blood begins to clot.

Another agonized howl sounds from behind me and I turn in slow-motion, watching as Constantyn stabs my wolf in the side.

Remus hits the ground too, holding the flesh of his stomach. "It's not me that needs to see the truth, it's you," Remus snarls.

Charred skin sits behind his fingers.

She *burned* a Dragon.

If that's possible, then we're damned.

There is no way out.

No way to make it out of this alive.

My heartbeat gets louder, *THUMP-THUMP-THUMPING* in my ears like the beat of a drum.

*There's no way out.*

*There is no way out...*

I look up to the skies, and then back down to my father, who watches me without any shred of care or emotion.

"I'm sorry," I whisper to my father. "A long time ago, I made you a promise..." I run the palm of my hand across Macha's sharp edge, slicing my skin open. With a deep breath, I bend down and begin painting symbols frantically in the dirt. Looking up, I meet my father's pale blue gaze. "It's time to break that promise."

Just as I'm about to shove my magyk into the final sigil and unleash hell upon my own world, a noise sounds in the distance.

The fighting quiets down around me as we all strain to tell what it is.

The sky goes quiet. No birdsong, no wind.

Then a huge gust hits us and sand flies into my eyes. I cover them, trying frantically to see what's going on.

Ryu groans and crawls over to me, pulling me close to her body with her long neck. I crouch down against the wind as it gets stronger. Nyall is still unconscious next to me, but I place my hand on his body anyways.

Nothing, though, *nothing* could have prepared me for the sight of someone *plummeting* from the sky.

They land in the middle of the arena, creating a shockwave of dust.

Then something else lands.

Something *huge.*

I blink as the wind dies down and the sky turns quiet again. As the sand falls back to the ground and the air grows clear, the beings before us become clear...beings I *know.*

"Dyana?"

She sees me and a brilliant smile appears on her face.

"Sorry I'm late."

# CHAPTER 66
## DYANA

Amalia crumbles to her knees. Tears stream down her face at the sight of me.

"Hey, Ama," I smile at her. But that smile quickly dies as I zero in on the Archmage.

*Constantyn.*

Vesimyr told me everything. I thought I had an idea of what was going on, but now I realize how wrong I truly was.

"I was wondering when you were going to show up," Constantyn looks up at Vesimyr, completely ignoring me.

Good.

Ignore me.

*"Get to the wolf,"* Veismyr orders. *"I'll draw Constantyn away. We need the Shepard alive."*

*"Got it."* Silently, I step towards Amalia as Vesimyr stalks towards Constantyn.

Virgyl, wounded and bloody, lays in the dirt.

*Shit.*

I meet Amalia's gaze as I take a step closer, close enough that she can hear me.

"Let me heal him first," I say gently.

She blinks. The last time Amalia saw me, I was human. So much has changed, but there's no time to explain.

Eyes glossy, she nods. "It's your lead."

It's a punch to the heart. I've *dreamed* of hearing those words from her, but I never thought it would really be possible. I check the sky for the others. I told them to land outside of the city—there's no need for them to get hurt. But many of them protested, wanting a piece of the fight.

All are behind us. A few hours ago, Vesimyr felt a strange energy coming from Castael Laryn and said we were running out of time. I didn't realize he could fly so fast, but we raced against the wind towards the coast, leaving the others behind.

Embyrne didn't like it, but I had her do a midair shift to the back of a copper Dragon named Golan. I can't be the only one protecting the Dragons—I need her help to take care of the others. The ones who don't want to fight but are here because they have nowhere else to go.

With a deep breath, I slowly back towards Virgyl.

*"You've changed, little Dy."*

I hold back tears. Now is not the time for crying.

Now is the time for saving my fucking family.

*"A lot has changed. Now, this should work..."*

I would say I've never healed a God, but that would be a lie.

I just didn't *realize* it was a God.

I summon my light and it sinks into Virgyl's fur. Glimmering prisms full of every color on the spectrum hover above him. Picturing his body healed, I *push* the magyk into his wounds.

The wolf God gasps as his flesh begins to knit back together.

*"He gave you the other half,"* he laughs. *"We were wrong. Amalia isn't the right hand—you are."*

"I am," I nod. "And she is the left. So let's end this, *Shepherd.*"

I use his formal title, the one Vesimyr shared with me. Virgyl jerks to his feet, shaking his fur which is streaked with dried blood.

*"It's been many years since I was called that."*

The Shepherd. God of the Forest. Guardian of the Ulster Wald.

I thought my childhood was strange, growing up with a pack of Dyre Wolves. But it turns out, I was growing up with a God.

I think a part of me always knew.

Virgyl barks and Constantyn is tossed in the air.

*"This ends now,"* he says.

The wolf glances up at the silver Dragon.

**"Livyathin. It's been an age."**

**"Yes,"** the Dragon bows his head, **"yes, it has. It is time to finish what we started."**

Virgyl nods.

"Livyathin?" a voice asks.

I turn to see Mirielle and Kairos striding towards us, blades already wet with blood. A green Dragon follows, the one with the metal wing.

"Vesimyr is Livyathin?" Mirielle asks, her eyes sharp. "The Dragon God?"

I summon my light and form it into the shape of a blade. "Yes."

When he told me the truth, my first question was if he wanted to call him Livyathin. The great silver Dragon shook his head.

*"No,"* he said, his voice full of regret. *"That part of me died long ago. I was Livyathin, but now I am just Vesimyr."*

I promptly told him he was full of shit and that a God was a God. He will always be Great Livyathin to the Dragons, whether he liked it or not. He griped about how I'm a smart ass, but he and I both know the truth.

He *is* Great Livyathin. He is *also* Vesimyr. They are one in the same.

Mirielle's eye twitches. "That's...unfortunate."

*Um, okay?*

I lift my sword and point to Constantyn—though they will know him as the Archmage.

"He's a God too. His real name is Constantyn. The Archmage was a glamour." I tell them. "And Virgyl, the giant Dyre Wolf, is the Shepard of the Forest. Also known as Morrigyn's hound."

Mirielle's eyes close and she takes a deep breath.

"I see."

"You guys got here fast," I realize, then shrug. "All the better. Let's go kill a God."

Lifting my sword, I run headfirst towards Constantyn, assuming that Mirielle and Kairos are following behind.

Just as I approach the God of Illusions, something hard slaps against my chest, knocking the wind out of me and sending me smacking down to the ground.

*"Oof,"* I grunt.

Looking up, I expect to meet the eyes of Constantyn or that *bitch* Ireyna who I saw fighting Os. I even expect a Fae guard.

What I don't expect...is to meet eyes of pale green and curly red hair.

"What the fuck?" I snarl, not understanding the sight before me.

Mirielle winces, her eyes full of regret. "I can't let you do that, Dyana."

# CHAPTER 67
## MIRIELLE

Dyana reels back as if I slapped her.

Like carrion for vultures, I can feel myself slowly get eaten alive. Not by a creature, but by regret. For the past two years, I didn't allow myself to think about this moment, not even for a second. Because the moment I *did* think of it, I crumbled.

I hoped that maybe, *maybe* Dyana wouldn't find out. That she wouldn't be here to see as I betray everything, we've worked so hard for.

The first time I got into the water on the beach of Elysium two years ago, I heard a *voice*.

The voice of a *God*.

"What do you mean, 'I can't kill him?'" Dyana snaps. "What the fuck does that mean?"

I can't explain. Not with Constantyn hovering just beyond us. The fighting has come to a halt as everyone takes note of my staff pointed right at Dyana.

Basa approaches, coming to stand at my side. She bares her fangs at Dyana, who doesn't look afraid—she just looks shocked.

~~I hate this. I hate this. I HATE THIS.~~ I've had many years learning how to pretend. All for this.

Free Lir at any cost. That was the deal.

As soon as I submerged myself in the sea on the beaches of Elysium, he appeared like a phantom in the current.

I knew who it was the moment I saw him.

Dark blue hair, the color of the stormy seas, and eyes of pure black, like a shark on the prowl. His skin was covered in silver and blue scales of all shades, creating an intricate pattern almost like a tattoo. I only saw his upper half.

*"Mirielle Zenyth,"* he hissed, voice clear as day even beneath the surface. *"Free me, and I will give you what you need."*

He did give me what I needed.

Power—enough power to free me, and save my mother's soul...*if* I free him. Not then, not now, but soon. 5,000 years ago, Lir was exiled to the bottom of the Midheym Sea

I didn't know if Dyana would ever wake up. Without a hope or a plan, I agreed.

Without a plan or an idea in hell of how I was going to escape, let alone free the God of the Seas, I began to train, preparing to fight my way out.

Meeting Kairos was a gift. A Sea Wyvern able to transport me home, without ever needing the Dragons. Lir is not just the god of the Seas, though. He's also the God of Cycles. Including the cycle of *rebirth*. Lir knew exactly what to say to get me to agree to any of his demands.

*"I will ensure your mother's soul is reborn."*

I wasn't fully behind the idea of working with Lir, not until he put his final card on the table.

My *mother.*

She didn't pray to any of the Gods. My Father is the one who prayed to Lir, but Mother...she didn't believe. Only those who pray to Lir are reborn.

*"You can do that?"*

Lir smirked at my question. *"I am a God, Mirielle Zenyth. I can do anything I want."*

"Yes."

The words were out of my lips before I could think twice.

For my mother, for *Nyall,* for my father back in Sud Azyl...

For them, I will make this sacrifice.

*"Find the heretic Prince. Find the High Councilor's son. I have seen that he will start a movement to topple the Fae. Use him, and then kill his father. Kill Achan Drayven."* Lir ordered in a deep, accented voice. *"Leave the Archmage to me. He is the key to my freedom. He is not to be harmed. Do so, and I will sink your precious Eastlands and send everyone who lives there to the bottom of the Midheym."*

"Okay," I said, so shocked, it left me unable to reply with much else. Lir's image drew closer, until we were almost nose to nose. The phantom's image blurred, as if I was looking at him from above the surface of the water.

*"Swear it,"* he snarled. *"Swear that you will do this, and your mother will be reborn."*

"I swear it."

Magyk plunged into me, and I *felt* it winding around my body, trapping me within its confines.

*"The power of water is yours, Mirielle Zenyth."*

Then Lir was gone.

For months, I practiced, working on honing my magyk. Even while working at the forge, I would practice from the drops of sweat on my back, sucking the water away and manipulating it in the air. Preparing for when the time comes to free Lir and meet the Archmage.

But I had no idea the Archmage was *Constantyn.* That was kept from me.

A promise with a God cannot be broken unless death claims you before the promise is fulfilled.

I swallow my regret, my guilt and my heavy conscience, shoving it deep into the void within my soul as I lock it up and throw away the key.

"There will be no killing Constantyn today," I look at Dyana, who's eyes *burn* with a righteous fury at my betrayal. "You'll have to kill me first."

Basa growls, echoing the sentiment. A part of me wishes she wasn't here...another part of me is glad for her presence.

"You double-crossed us?" Dyana's eyes flash with unbridled fury.

I take a deep breath and send a quick prayer for forgiveness.

"Yes."

"What the fuck? Mirielle, you can't be serious. We're on the same side!"

I scoff, a very real and true anger rising to the surface. "The same side? The only side you're on, Dyana, is your own."

"Is this true?" A pained voice groans to my right.

*I know that voice.*

I turn my neck slowly and meet the glossy eyes of Nyall Drayven.

My friend. My *family.*

This is what I was regretting *most.*

The look on his face.

*"Do you want me to kill him?"* Basa asks calmly. I hide my flinch.

*"No! No. Do not kill any of them. Not yet."*

*"As you wish."* She steps back but stays close.

*"WAIT!"* I scream, realizing I need her help. *"I need you to break into the blonde Fae's mind. I need you to give him a message. Please, Basa."*

She nods and I give her the message.

Her eyes flick to Nyall and I watch as his face turns hard. She did it.

"It's true. Mirielle double crossed us." Nyall's voice is pained. A glance down has me realizing he's missing his right arm.

*YOU SHOULD HAVE SAVED THEM!* My conscience screams at me, but it's a lie. You can *never* save everyone. I learned that the hard way.

"If you won't tell me where her bones are," Constantyn sneers at Vesimyr—I mean, at *Livyathin*—and a large Dyre Wolf with black fur. "Then I will find them *myself.*"

His eyes begin to glow a deep, eerie purple and magyk shoots from the tips of his fingers down into the ground.

Constantyn looks at me with a wicked grin. "Keep them busy for me."

The floor beneath our feet *cracks* as glowing purple fissures explode around us.

Then the world begins to *shake.* He's...looking for something. But his search is going to doom us all. The quakes grow stronger and buildings in the distance begin to fall.

Keep them busy.

*"Lir, guide me."* I send out the frantic prayer as I cast my mind out, looking for the Abhaynn Gheal river nearby.

The water trembles with excitement as I connect with it. Goose bumps rise on my arms as my hair stands on end. I can *feel* the entire riverbed. The rocks that line the bottom, the branches that have fallen into the water.

I feel it *all.*

"Rise," I command it. *"Rise and flood the valley."*

I can feel the river stop rushing, changing course. It begins to flow *north,* pulling on the Midheym Sea where it meets the eastern coast.

"What the fuck are you doing?" a voice calls.

I'm glad Amalia is alive...I really am. But unfortunately, that means I have to kill her.

# CHAPTER 68
## AMALIA

**"CONSTANTYN!"** Livyathin roars. **"STOP THIS! You're going to kill us ALL!"**

Livyathin.

Vesimyr is the God Livyathin. Father of all Dragons.

I'm not surprised Virgyl is a God, but I thought he was the God of Wolves, or something akin to that.

God of the Forest, though...that fits. It makes so much sense, I'm mad at myself for not realizing sooner.

*The Shepherd.*

Virgyl *is* the Shepherd of the Ulster Wald.

He is the Father and the protector for all who dwell within it.

"No," Constantyn sneers at Livyathin. "I will survive. The rest of you, however..." he *tsks.* "You'll be buried beneath the sea with good old Lir."

Mirielle glances to the side, her eyes glowing blue. Something Constantyn just said upsets her. Water begins to *drip* into the Arena.

"Uh, anyone hear that?" Mara shouts and we fall silent.

A distant *rushing* sound grows as the water increases beneath our feet.

"She's flooding the Abhaynn Gheal," Remus calls. "She's flooding the valley!"

I glance at Mirielle in alarm.

Her face is set. She will not stop.

"We have to leave," I realize as the adrenaline hits. "VIRGYL! WE NEED TO LEAVE NOW!"

*"We'll have to fly."* Livyathin's voice booms in my head, causing sharp pain to blossom behind my temples.

"You can't hide Morrigyn's bones forever. I will find them. I will find them all, and then her power will be *mine."*

I stare at my father, who looks at nothing, his pupils wide and not a single emotion on his face.

I can't leave him behind.

But...it's him, or *all* of us.

"I will come back for you. I will save you from this, I swear." I tell him. "I will *come back,* Dad. Please hear me."

"I hear you," he says. "I just do not care. There is nothing to save me from. Sol Constantus is all."

I look at Constantyn, grabbing hold of my shadows and sending two whips of them his direction. The tips of them snap, scratching two lines of blood open on his cheeks.

"I will kill you. I don't care what it takes. I don't care what we destroy in the process. Your time is done."

Mirielle approaches, a new metal staff between her hands. "You can try."

I laugh and it's a bloody promise. "You do realize I *spared* you in the Gauntlet. I could have killed you so many times, but I didn't. Because I thought you were *good."* I step closer and slap her across the face before she can block me. I get into her face, hands clasping her tunic. A tall man approaches me.

"Put her down, or you will die," he says in a calm voice.

Remus curses. "AMALIA HE'S ASCIDIAN! RUN!"

*A Sea Wyvern.* They're supposed to be extinct.

Mirielle winks at me. "The only one who will be dying is you, you self-righteous, martyring *cunt.*"

*Martyr?* Interesting word choice.

"I won't hold back next time," I hiss. Dyana is at my side a second later, frantically pulling me away.

"Neither will I," she snarls at Mirielle. "I can't believe I ever trusted you, ever thought you were worthy of love. You deserve *nothing.*"

Ireyna approaches Constantyn's side, blood and sand covering her body. Her nose looks broken, and her arm is hanging at a strange angle.

A loud groan from my left shows Remus helping Nyall up. He practically has to carry the Fae Prince, but they begin piling on Livyathin's back.

**"HURRY!"** Vesimyr's shout nearly shatters my eardrums. **"I cannot carry all, though. You will need to fly, Your Highness."**

Ryu appears next to me.

**"I—I can't."**

Constantyn laughs. "I will see you soon, *niece.* Enjoy your home while it lasts."

The ground begins to shake beneath us as water streams in faster.

I put my hand on Dyana's arm. "Take Remus and Nyall."

I glance to the side, finding Mara. "You," I point with my free hand. "You're with me."

"What exactly does that—"

Mara lets out a shriek as Ryu's tail wraps around her midsection. Ryu carefully lifts Mara and places her on her back.

Good enough.

"Virgyl!" I whirl. "Get the wolves out of here!"

**"There's not enough time."** His voice is calm despite the chaos around us.

Livyathin bows his head, briefly closing his bright green eyes. **"I will carry you, my friend. I can carry three wolves…young Ryu will need to carry the rest."**

**"Carry my pups,"** Virgyl nods. **"I will wait with Amalia and Ryu."**

To my surprise, Ryu nods. I can see the fear in her eyes, but my brave Dragon doesn't show it.

"I'm not leaving you. Not again," Dyana says at my right. Tears fall down my cheeks as I lean my forehead against hers.

"I know," I whisper. "I will follow. I promise. But please…get them home."

Dyana blinks. "We have a lot to catch up on, apparently. I will keep them safe. And—I approve."

My jaw drops and Dyana flashes me a naughty wink before sprinting to her Dragon.

"LET'S GO!" she calls to Livyathin before making a vertical leap onto his back.

Virgyl howls and three wolves approach, Bea included. Livyathin jumps into the air, flapping his two sets of wings and hovering just above the sand. The wolves' tails go between their legs in fear and their ears go flat, but, even then, they walk towards Livyathin's claws, allowing him to gently pick them up and lift them into the air.

There's no time to ponder Dyana's new abilities. I turn to Ryu and place her snout in my hands.

"You can do this," I breathe. "You can do this. I know you can."

She nods, trembling lightly. *"Get on my back in front of Mara—and Virgyl, you come near my front claws."*

The wolf nods and gets close to her front left claw. I quickly crawl up and pull myself up onto her back. Mara leans to the side, allowing me to climb past. I slide in between two of Ryu's spinal spikes which are positioned perfectly as if they were meant to hold me in place.

There is, however, not very much to hold on to.

Ryu takes off in a fast gallop, Virgyl sprinting next to her, as we crawl out of the Arena. She stops at the top and I quickly see why.

There's a huge wave of water coming towards the city.

If we don't get in the air soon—we'll drown.

# CHAPTER 69
## RYU

"HURRY!" Remus calls from above as the giant wave grows closer. It reaches the outer edge of the city, taking down buildings and everything in its path.

*I can't do this.*

*I—I can't do this.*

*"Yes, you can, sweet one."* Kydis' voice is as clear as day in my head. *"You know what you need to do. Keep the balance."*

No.

Not Kydis—*Morrigyn.* I wouldn't believe it, but Great Livyathin, God of the Dragons, is just a few meters away.

*"Flap your wings,"* Virgyl orders. Then he takes off, running towards the burning city to grab any rebels left. *"Flap your wings and FLY!"*

*"Hold on,"* I warn my passengers.

I flap both wings, slowly at first. We teeter, hovering in the air as I begin to ascend.

*"What if I fall? What if I kill us?"* I whisper to Amalia, terrified of being her doom.

*"I trust you,"* she whispers, wrapping her warm arms around my neck. *"I trust you more than anyone. You can do this, sweetheart. I know you can."*

The human behind her makes a pitiful whimpering sound, but for some reason, that only makes me more determined.

She should feel *safe* on my back...they both should.

*Then show them there is nothing to fear.*

I take a deep breath and flap my wings harder, straining to gain enough height. It hurts. My muscles protest as pain shoots through my back.

*"Save them. Save them. Save them."* The words repeat over and over in my head until I'm not sure who they belong to anymore.

There is nothing except this.

*Save them.*

*Save the three.*

Suddenly, I hit a current. I fight it for a moment.

*"No! Don't fight it. Lean into it."*

I follow Livyathin's orders, even though I'm terrified, and stop fighting the current. It propels me forward. Amalia hangs on tightly, grunting as I struggle to find my balance.

Then everything calms. The air goes quiet as I glide down the current, allowing the wind to do the work.

Beneath us, we watch in silence as the wave hits Castael Laryn. Buildings collapse and anyone standing is swept away.

Beyond the city, patches of color show the Dyre Wolves racing to get out of the path of the wave. Each carry multiple rebels.

A bright flash of purple light comes from the Arena behind us, and we all glance back. Constantyn and his people leaving, probably. My tongue flicks out, tasting the air. I get a hint of sharp electricity—teleportation magyk.

They escaped.

*Was the city just a sacrifice to get to us? Who would do such a thing?*

Then it occurs to me that this entire time, I've been easily hovering in the air.

I—I'm *flying.*

*I'm FLYING!*

I let out a roar of pure joy and Livyathin roars back. A loud howl sounds from below. Then another, and another.

Suddenly the entire pack is howling, celebrating alongside me as I fly through the clouds above their heads.

Amalia lets out a half-laugh, half-sob as the suns set behind us and we fly North towards the Ulster Wald. In front of me, Dyana and Remus sit on Livyathin's mighty back, with Nyall draped in front of Remus.

*"You did it,"* Amalia laughs. *"Ryu, you did it. You're flying."*

*"**We** are flying,"* I correct her. *"I think we were meant to do this together. Alone...we falter. But together, we are strong."*

*"Together, we are strong,"* Amalia repeats with a joyous laugh. The world falls silent as we make our way to Eahmond.

As the town peeks through the clouds, my wings falter.

"Holy shit," Amalia gasps.

The Dragons...they came *back!*

*"There are so many of them!"* Amalia says with glee. *"I didn't—I didn't get to see them last time."*

*"It looks like almost all the Dragons who escaped have come back, but there are a few missing."*

*"You remember that?"* Amalia asks in shock.

*"No, but Kydis does."*

She *tsks. "That's right. Sorry, Ryu. Your magyk is so complex. I can't even...comprehend what it must be like to hear the voices of your ancestors in your head, to be able to see what they saw."*

*"Do not apologize. It is not for you to understand."*

She presses a kiss against my scales and sits up, eyeing the Dragons in the distance below. A few mortals stand with them. Rebels, as well as some I do not recognize.

My nerves get the better of me. *"Ama…why would they come back? After all they've endured here. Why would they return to the possibility of repeating their fates?"*

Livyathin slows and banks, pulling up beside us.

*"Not to eavesdrop, as Dyana would say, but Ryu—the Dragons came back for you. For their Queen."*

My wings falter once more at that word.

*Queen.* But…I don't want to be a Queen.

A voice pipes up from below. *"Not to rush you, but I would rather like to be back on the ground."*

"I agree with the Shepherd," Mara's voice trembles as she speaks up from her spot behind Amalia.

*"Sorry, fuzz-butt."*

Virgyl grunts at the nickname and lets out a sigh of relief as we make our way to Eahmond. The Ulster Wald looms in the background. I've missed the mountains. Missed the scent of the trees and the icy air on my snout.

When I look to the Ulster Wald, I don't see something wild and frightening. Instead, I look to the Ulster Wald and see *home.*

I land carefully, not wanting to jostle Amalia. My claw cramps as I let go of Virgyl.

Just as Amalia's feet touch the ground, the dirt beneath our feet begins to *shake.*

"Enjoy your home while it lasts," Amalia says quietly. Her head snaps up and she looks at the Ulster Wald in front of us. Her pale blue eyes go wide as all of the blood leaves her face.

Behind us, the mortals begin to panic. One of them—a tall female with deep amber skin and pale blonde hair cut short against her scalp—shouts at them to remain calm.

Usually the tremors only last for a few seconds, maybe a minute at a time. But this time, it doesn't stop.

It keeps going. The ground beneath our feet rumbles and shifts, as if the continent itself is breaking apart.

"Gods," Amalia suddenly gasps. "He—he's trying to bring down the mountain. Constantyn is trying to bring down the mountain. He must think Morrigyn's bones are buried *beneath* it."

Virgyl and the others nearby look at her, alarm in their gaze. The ground shakes harder and the Dragons squawk and groan, shifting around nervously. Some take to the skies. The mortals fully panic. Some begin to scream as buildings begin to collapse.

**"HE'S TRYING TO BRING DOWN THE MOUNTAIN!"** Amalia screams, projecting her voice.

# CHAPTER 70
## DYANA

Amalia's scream rings in my ears.

Mortals stream out of the town by the dozen. I don't recognize them, but most are armed.

*Is this the rebellion Vesimyr spoke of?*

**"Shepherd,"** Vesimyr calls, his voice so loud it shakes the nearby trees. **"There's too many to carry out."**

Virgyl bares his teeth.

**"Then it's up to us. I will need your power for this, old friend."**

Vesimyr blinks, a look of deep regret in his eyes. Then he nods.

**"It would be an honor,"** the Dragon's voice is quieter now, quieter than should be able. But knowing his true nature, nothing surprises me anymore when it comes to Vesimyr.

"What do you mean? What are you doing?" Amalia asks.

"I would like to know as well," I add with a pointed look at my Dragon God.

The ground beneath our feet begins to crack as the tremors get stronger. Many of the mortals behind us fall to the ground, unable to balance.

**"There's no time,"** Virgyl says. **"Come, Livyathin."**

Beneath me, Vesimyr follows Virgyl away from the town. They only walk for a few minutes. A glance behind me shows Amalia following, with Os and Nyall not far behind.

The wound on Nyall's right arm looks like it's finally started healing. The blood looks clotted and he's awake enough to walk, though Os has his arm around his waist.

Vesimyr and Virgyl come to a halt as the tremors increase. The cracks in the ground get wider.

Virgyl looks back at us and the world goes silent. I can't hear a thing. Amalia stops at my right, and I turn to her, pointing to my ears. She nods—Amalia can't hear either.

Virgyl lifts his head and howls. Even with whatever magyk is protecting our ears, I can *hear* it.

Vesimyr closes his eyes, and the air turns warm as gold shimmers above Virgyl. It settles into his fur.

The wolf looks back at us.

*"It was an honor to raise you,"* his voice rings clearly in our heads. *"Both of you."*

Virgyl turns around before we can respond, crouches, and pounces straight in the air. As his giant paws touch the ground again, it sends a shockwave through the land.

The tremors stop and our hearing returns. Then the sound of a giant *rip* comes from the south.

We watch in horror as a crack forms in the valley North of Castael Laryn. The crack crows larger and larger until it reaches the Abhaynn Gheal. There, the crack follows the path of the river. The Earth beneath us groans as Castael Laryn is made into an *island*. Water roars in, white tipped with foam as it churns into the crevice.

"Holy shit," I breathe.

Something *thumps* next to us, but for a moment, no one moves. We can't do anything but stare.

Virgyl tore the land apart.

Virgyl *saved* us.

I turn, looking for the wolf, when I see a large black lump on the ground.

A lump covered in *fur*.

# CHAPTER 71
## AMALIA

I can't believe it.

I can't believe that Virgyl just turned Castael Laryn into an island. Dust still flies around the air, making several behind us sneeze.

Light tremors can be felt, but they're distant.

The world is adjusting too. It didn't realize it was going to be ripped in two today.

Dyana's hand suddenly grasps mine. I look to the side, meeting her gaze, but her brown eyes are full of sadness.

"Ama..." She motions to something to our right and I turn, not understanding what she means.

Then I see him, and the world around me disappears.

"Virgyl?"

My voice is small and broken. No one responds.

My legs move without any thought as I sprint over to his body.

"Virgyl?" I place my hands on him, trying to figure out what's wrong. His breath comes slowly, in short pants. His eyes are cloudy, not the bright yellow usually burning within his wolfish gaze.

No. *Please* no. Not him.

I lay down on the ground next to him, caressing his cheek. "Virgyl? Let me heal you."

*"It won't work,"* Livyathin approaches. The great silver Dragon lowers his head, sniffing Virgyl. *"He's too far gone."*

*"Do—not w-worry,"* Virgyl says in my head, weary and tired. *"I saved m-my pack. I am h-happy to die for family."*

I want to scream. I want to rip my hair out and tear this world in two. Instead, all I do is cry.

"But I can heal you. Please let me try."

Virgyl shakes his head with a groan. *"No. Not this time, cub. For I am not injured. There is n-nothing to heal."*

*"He used the last of his divinity,"* Livyathin explains softly. *"I myself only have a small drop left after that."*

Tears stream down my face as I glance up at the Dragon, my hand still caressing Virgyl's cheek. My other is buried in his fur.

Dyana stands behind me, but she crouches down next to us.

*"I r-remember when the m-mountains were small,"* he gasps. *"I helped p-plant the trees. Do not be s-sad for me, cub. I have l-lived a f-full life."*

"But you have so much life left to live!" I protest. "Please don't leave me."

*"K-keep it safe,"* he pants. *"Keep the forest safe. I-it must remain a h-haven for all."*

"I will," I tell him. "I'll keep them all safe. But stay with me and help me do it. Please, Virgyl."

Virgyl leans forward, nudging my cheek with his wet nose.

*"I l-love you very m-much, cub. I am s-so p-proud of you."*

Dyana's hand caresses his forehead, and she leans in to place a long kiss there.

*"You too, D-Dyana. I a-am s-so glad you're a-alive. You g-girls need e-each other."*

"I love you too," she whispers, making me cry harder. "Thank you for taking care of me and giving me a home. The honor is ours, Virgyl, Shepherd of the Ulster Wald. The honor is *ours.*"

Then she leaves, giving me space to say goodbye.

*No. NO. This can't be goodbye.*

I feel like I'm breaking inside, and I'm scared there will be nothing left of me to put back together again.

There is no me without Virgyl. There is no happy life without him in it. He's been there from the beginning. He's been there longer than anyone else in my life. Through all of the lows, and the brief highs, it's been Virgyl curled up beside me.

A red snout enters my vision as Ryu lowers herself to the ground, curling around us, her snout near Virgyl's nose.

"T-take care of t-them, Ryu."

She nods, her copper-and-silver eyes full of sadness. *"I will. I promise. But know that I will miss you every single day...grandfather."*

A choked sound leaves me. I feel like I'm dying alongside him. I'm breaking apart.

Virgyl slowly moves his neck, his bright yellow eyes meeting mine. *"Y-you a-are my f-family—both of y-you. J-just as m-much as any w-wolf."*

"And you are our family," I whisper into his fur. "You're a God, Virgyl. Can't you choose to stay? Please. Please, stay."

*"None hold the power to live forever, not even the Gods. Nothing is truly infallible."* Livyathin says.

I want to scream at the stupid Dragon that this can't be true.

It can't be right.

There has to be a way to save him. He's a God!

*"He's not,"* Livyathin whispers in the back of my mind. *"Not anymore. He gave up the rest of his divine powers to save you. Now...he is mortal."*

FUCK!

The tears fall harder as I lay on the ground and clutch Virgyl in my arms.

"I can't do this without you," I cry. "I don't know how. I don't *want* to do this without you."

Virgyl sighs. *"I k-know, cub. But y-you m-must. The world n-needs you."*

"Fuck the world. I want my *family*." I sob. "I just want my family, Virgyl. Don't go. Don't leave me."

*"You w-will always h-have me. I will a-always be w-with you."*

"Please stay," I beg. "Please."

*"M-my t-time is n-near, cub. I c-can f-feel it."*

"No!" I cry. "No, no, no. Don't go. Please don't go."

*"M-my d-daughter..."* Sobs overtake me and I close my eyes, pressing my face against his as my tears stain his fur. *"Y-you have everything,"* he coughs, straining, *"e-everything you n-need. If you w-would just b-believe i-in y-yourself..."*

The voice fades.

"Virgyl?" I pull back, watching as his eyes look around wildly for a moment before going still. "Virgyl?"

Nothing.

"Virgyl, please," I sob.

No response.

"Come back," I whisper, shaking him lightly, but he's gone. "Please come back. I can't do this without you."

He—he's *gone.*

A wet snout touches my cheek, and I look up to see Bea.

"I'm so sorry," I sob.

Bea leans her head on my shoulder, laying down next to us. She sniffs Virgyl's body before letting out a small, sad whine.

Then another wolf approaches. And another. More whines explode from them as they confirm that their leader, their *patriarch,* is really gone.

Dozens of wolves surround us, silently mourning their leader.

Bea licks my wet cheek. *"This day was always coming. Be sad now, but do not hold onto it. Honor his memory."*

My eyes close and I curl into his fur.

*"Stand,"* Bea orders. Unable to make my thoughts stand still long enough to question it, I roll up and get to my feet, tears staining my face.

*"You are the Shepherd, now, Amalia. The forest needs you. We need you."*

"What do you mean?" My voice is hollow.

Bea looks down at Virgyl. *"The Ulster Wald—it's yours. Virgyl made you the new Shepard of the Forest."*

The great wolf bows and I gasp, a strange feeling coming over me. Not of magyk but of *knowing.*

*The Gray Wytch is dead,* I realize, or maybe this is what the Gray Wytch was really meant to be.

I nod, wiping my tears away, though they continue to freely fall.

Pain and numbness descend. This can't be real. I don't want it to be. I just want him back.

Bea presses her nose against my cheek. *"I know. But we will help you, Blue. But for now...we must take my Father. He needs to be buried as a wolf."*

"I will come," I croak, but Beatrice shakes her head.

*"No, Blue. You cannot. This is not for your eyes."*

I cry harder. "What are you going to do with him?"

Her green eyes are clear. *"When a Wolf in our pack dies...we consume them, so they are always with us."*

I nearly crumble to my knees.

*"Do not think of it,"* Beatrice warns. *"There is a reason mortals do not know our customs. It is not for them to understand—nor for you."*

I watch as the wolves around us gently grab hold of Virgyl's body with their teeth. Then they push their noses beneath him and hoist him onto their backs, walking in sync close together to carry him.

Their leader.

*Please come back.*

*Please don't be gone.*

*Please...don't leave me all alone.*

I stand there, silently crying, as the person who raised me is carried away. Bea nods at me and then follows them.

I close my eyes and let out a loud sob as my heart crumbles into pieces.

Arms surround me.

"I'm so sorry," Remus whispers. "I'm so sorry, A gahrá."

My tears fall harder at his kind words. I lean into him, eventually turning to hide my face in his chest.

We stand like that for a while.

Eventually, I pull back and Remus cups my face, wiping my tears away with his thumbs.

I nod and we walk towards the others as I shove my grief down.

So much has happened. I feel destroyed in a way I never have before.

"I can't believe Mirielle betrayed us," Remus mutters and I jerk, remembering the past few hours.

Someone clears their throat, and I pull away from Remus. Nyall approaches and lifts his hand to caress my cheek. His right arm has clotted and the bleeding has stopped, but looking at his wound makes my tears return.

"I-I'm s-sorry," I start but he wraps me in a one-armed hug.

"Shh," he whispers. "Don't apologize. You saved my life, Blue."

Still crying, I sniffle as he pulls away. I feel naked. Everyone is watching me break into pieces.

"And...Mirielle didn't betray us," Nyall says. "But it needed to look that way."

Dyana's eyes narrow, "Excuse me? What the hell are you talking about."

Nyall glances at her, "She didn't betray us. The green Dragon that was with her—Mirielle gave it a message. It was fast, but the Dragon *showed* me the truth."

"And what truth is that? Since Mirelle seems to be so good at everything *but* the truth." Dyana's voice is so cold, it could cut metal.

Nyall takes a deep breath. "Lir wants to get free, so Mirielle promised to help free him, but she never intended to finish the bargain."

"What do you mean?" I ask.

But Dyana steps forward, her eyes sharp.

"What am I not getting?"

"Nyall," Dyana says carefully. "I need you to explain what you mean. Right now."

"Mirielle is going to kill the Archmage. She's going to kill Constantyn. She isn't going to free Lir. Not truly."

Holy *shit.*

*"It's true,"* another voice calls in our minds. I watch as a green Dragon with a strange looking metal wing approaches. Its scales are a bright emerald that darkens around its neck, complete with eyes of pale silver.

"That's the Dragon who was with Mirielle. The one that carried the message."

Instantly my hackles rise.

"It followed us here," I snarl. I look around for a weapon but there is none.

**"Save your strength,"** the Green Dragon's voice is accented, and female. **"I mean you no harm. Mirielle bid me to follow you. I owe her my life. With this, my debt to her is paid."**

The green Dragon bows her head before addressing us aloud. **"Mirielle Zenyth is not a traitor. I would have sensed it. She told me some of her story, but I could feel there was more. Never evil, though. Just...*regret.*"**

Dyana rubs her temples. "Fucking hell. So many secrets. I don't know what's real and what's not."

"She's double-crossing them," I realize. "*Both* of them. Lir *and* Constantyn."

"Yes," Nyall sighs, and a pained look comes over him. "Mirielle is going to martyr herself. She doesn't plan on surviving this."

Dyana's jaw drops and her face goes pale.

Mirielle called me a martyr earlier. Was she trying to tell me the truth? Was that her way of apologizing?

Doubt ripples through me...but I believe Nyall. If he says she sent him a message, then I believe him. I'm just not sure I believe Mirielle Zenyth.

"What do we do?" Mara asks. "What happens now?"

"What do we do?" I gesture to the broken Kingdom in front of us. "This was just the beginning. The war for Ur Daoine has started," I look at my friends. My loves. My *family.* "Now, we plan. We prepare. We kill a *God.*"

"Sounds fun, when do we start?"

We all turn in unison at the feminine voice that answered. A tall woman I've never seen before approaches. She has deep amber skin and pale silver blonde hair cut short, and her eyes—her *eyes* are burning gold.

A *familiar* gold.

There's a gasp from my side as Remus takes a step forward. "Embyrne?"

The female's golden eyes look straight at my familiar and she flashes a brilliant smile full of sharp white fangs.

"Hello, *brother.*"

# THE END
# HAS BEGUN

"As once I loved you in my mortal flesh, without it now I love you still."

- Dante Alighieri, 1265-1321.
The Divine Comedy: Purgatory

xoxo, EAG

# EPILOGUE

<u>**MIRIELLE**</u>

The Black Citadel is just as awful as I remember it, but I school my face into an emotionless canvas.

Kairos spares a few glances at the monotone, stark decoration around us.

"Lovely," he mutters.

I snort.

Gods, I'm glad he's with me.

*"Free me,"* Lir's voice whispers in my head, and I will free him...if I live long enough to do so.

"You two," Ireyna snaps. "You'll stay here in the castle. Where I can keep my *eyes* on you."

My ex-trainer approaches, surveying me with a glare. "I don't trust you, Mirielle Zenyth. Nor do I trust your Ascidian friend."

"Your trust is inconsequential," I tell her. "I do not need it, nor do I care whether or not I have it. All I care about is freeing my God, and I need *your* God to do so."

Ireyna crosses her arms. "Make *any* wrong move, and I will slit your throats. Got it?"

I cross my arms, mimicking her.

"And if you so much as attempt to hurt any of us, I will drown you where you stand."

"There's no water around," Ireyna smirks. "so you can try."

*"Show her the power of the Ocean. Show her the meaning of fear."*

I smile and unleash my magyk, latching onto the water molecules in her blood.

I have never tried this, but for the past few weeks I've been debating how I might practice. Now, I know.

I will practice on *Ireyna.*

"Did you know," I muse, "that the body is mainly *water?*"

I *yank* and the water begins to stream out of her pores. Ireyna starts to choke as her organs dry up.

She falls to her knees, unable to breathe. I lean down and whisper in her ear, our cheeks nearly brushing.

"Keep pushing me and I won't hesitate."

With a snap of my fingers, the water re-enters her body and Ireyna gasps, coughing loudly.

"You're insane," she gasps.

I look down at her. "Haven't you realized? We're *all* insane."

"Enough," Constantyn walks into the room and Ireyna gets to her feet. He says nothing about what he saw, or that Ireyna and I were fighting.

"The Shepherd is dead," he announces.

I glance at Kairos who shrugs.

Constantyn sighs. "The wolf, Virgyl. Shepherd of the Ulster Wald. He's dead."

We all stare, unsure what to do with this information.

"What about his power?" Ireyna asks. "Can you take it?"

Constantyn frowns. "No. He used the rest of his power to break the land."

Castael Laryn is now an *island*.

"Livyathin is going to be a problem though."

The fact that Vesimyr is Great Livyathin still hurts my head.

"Then we will take them out. All of them and find Morrigyn's bones while we're at it."

Constantyn nods. "Yes, my thoughts exactly."

"What do you need, Father?"

Father...

*Father?*

"She's your daughter?" I ask, shocked.

Ireyna's head snaps towards me. "Insolent worm! I'll rip out your tongue for speaking to him that way."

Constantyn holds up a hand, "Calm, child. It is a fair question."

Ireyna glares at me but quiets down.

"She is my child as much as Nyall Drayven is."

Uh, what?

Seeing my confusion, Constantyn continues.

"Ireyna is Nyall Drayven's sister. Achan's second living child."

Nyall...has a *sister?*

# THE DRAGON QUEEN SERIES CONTINUES...

Pay the price. Become the weapon. Save the world.

## THE WICKED AND THE WORTHY

THE DRAGON QUEEN BOOK #3

*COMING 2026*

# GLOSSARY

**Abhaynn Gheal:** A large river just south of Castael Laryn, the capital city of Ur Daoine.

**Achan Drayven:** High Councilor and leader of all Fae. Age is unknown. Was present when the Fae arrived 600 years ago.

**A gahrá:** Means "my beloved" in the language of the Dragons. There is no true translation because Dragons have three vocal cords and their words are made up of sounds Os cannot make in human form.

**Amalia Roth:** The Gauntlet candidate from Twyn Fells. Human (supposedly), and in her late 20's. Died in the arena alongside the Dragon Kydis and Achan Drayven.

**Amalia Asteroth:** The true identity of Amalia Roth. Amalia Asteroth is an Arkaydian with will-based power. She wields Morrigyn's Hellfyre as well as Morrigyn's blades. Amalia Asteroth also goes by the name The Gray Wytch, which was given to her by the people of the North. She resides deep within the Ulster Wald alongside a pack of Dyre Wolves. 92 years old. Extremely dangerous.

**Amari:** Rebellion leader. General of the Westlands.

**The Annag:** A small forest to the West of Castael Laryn.

**The Archmage:** Previously High Councilor Achan Drayven's advisor, now the leader of Ur Daoine. An elf with immense power. Age, unknown.

**Arkaydia:** An ancient, magykal kingdom that has since disappeared.

**Arkaydian:** The race of beings that occupied Arkaydia. Arkaydians possessed great power related to the natural world. The Arkaydians were supposedly wiped out during the Great War, as the Fae viewed their power and connection to the land as dangerous.

**Ascidian:** Also known as Sea Wyverns. Huge, dangerous creatures that live in the water. They slightly resemble Dragons, but are more deadly. Dragons avoid the ocean for fear of being eaten by an Ascidian.

**Basa:** A green Dragon with a badly injured wing.

**Beastkyn:** Animals with the ability to turn into people. Not shifters, but true animals that just change shape. Very rare.

**The Black Citadel:** The High Council's fortress, in the center of Castael Laryn.

**Castael Laryn:** The capital city of Ur Daoine and seat of power of the Imperial Fae.

**The Cult of Sol Constantus:** The state religion of Ur Daoine, as implemented first by the Fae, and then by the Archmage. The Cult refers to those who follows the teachings and words of Sol Constantus; the God Constantyn.

**Dark Magyk:** A forgotten, evil type of magyk practice first created by the Elves thousands of years ago. The reason the Elves destroyed their homeland and went extinct. Dark Magyk users should be avoided at all costs.

**Davyn:** Rebellion leader. Nyall Drayven's right hand, manages the rebel camp. Demis mage.

**The Deceiver:** A nickname for the God Constantyn.

**Demis:** The offspring of a human or other Magyka breeding with a Fae. Demis simply means part Fae.

**Dragons:** Four and two-legged creatures widely regarded to be Gods. They're made of magyk. Dragons first originated in their homeland, Elysium, which lies to the far west, across the Midheym Sea.

**Dragonfear:** A biological phenomenon that occurs in lower beings such as humans, Demis, and Magyka when they lay eyes upon a Dragon. The more magyk a being possesses, the easier it is to shrug Dragonfear off. Dragonfear causes heart palpitations, high blood pressure, anxiety, and panic, as it instigates a fight or flight response.

**Dragonguard:** The personal Dragon Riders of the High Council. The Dragonguard is made up of a dozen or so tamed, lab-bred Dragons that have been domesticated. Only Imperial Fae have been able to ride Dragons, as the rest were eaten upon attempt. The Dragonguard patrols the borders and carries out assignments from the High Council, including the rounding up of Gauntlet candidates.

**Drystan:** Previous General of the Eastlands.

**Dyana Arkos:** Previously the human, adopted sister of Amalia Roth. 26 years old. Thought to be deceased but is actually trapped in Elysium after the Dragon Vesimyr used his magyk and blood to heal Dyana's wounds, and bring her back to life. New species and magyk: unknown.

**The Dragon Pit:** Previously a sprawling underground containment system, it was destroyed and has been haphazardly rebuilt.

**Dragon Song:** The language of the Dragons. The true name of the language is not known, but Dyana Arkos and those who are gifted the chance of hearing it have described the Dragon's language as sounding like layered notes of a song.

**Duke Haestan:** Leader of the Mercatus.

**The Eastlands:** The Eastern district of Ur Daoine. Known for being a big fruit and vegetable producer in the country.

**Eahmond:** A northland town, the closest down to Twyn Fells.

**Elves:** An extinct group of highly magykal beings who wielded dark magyk, a type of magyk that can suck the life out of anything living. There are rumors of some Elves that are still alive, but the ages of the Elves have centuries passed.

**Elysium:** The legendary kingdom of the Dragons. Thought to be a myth. Elysium is surrounded by a giant wall of clouds that hide the most complex, advanced ward that has ever been woven. This ward keeps everyone that isn't a Dragon out. Only a Dragon can grant passage to a lower being, but once you enter, the ward will never let you out.

**Elysian:** An ore native to the isle of Elysium—and the source of the island's name. Elysian can only be made near an active Volcano where Dragon eggs hatch. The science is unknown to all but the Dragons. Elysian is the strongest metal known in the world and can cut through anything, even Dragon scales.

**Embyrne:** Beastkyn. Remus 'Os' Ostia's sister. Has been imprisoned on Elysium for centuries due to her strange magyk; she's a mimic and can borrow the powers of others nearby.

**Ethelen:** The drink of the Gods. Not much is known about Ethelen, other than it can only be consumed by Divine beings.

**Fae:** A powerful race of supernaturals who appeared within a portal 600 years ago to take control of Arkaydia. After 100 years of war, they emerged victorious and now rule. Fae possesses heightened strength and hearing, and the royals hold magyk.

**The Father:** A version of Sol Constantus. A side sect of Sol Constantus believers pray to The Father. They believe that Sol Constantus and The Father are separate but equal.

**Fion:** New General of the Eastlands. Goes by Fi.

**The Fray:** A monthly tournament where the top fighters in the kingdom fight each other and Dragons, for the entertainment of the Fae.

**The Gauntlet:** A tournament to the death held every 25 years where 30 candidates, two humans from every town in the Kingdom, compete for a prize and the right to live.

**The Gray Wytch:** A legendary figure used to scare children into behaving. The Gray Wytch is thought to be dead, now, but she lived deep within the Ulster Wald with her pack of wolves, hunting down bad Fae and misbehaving children.

**Grimheim:** A town in the Northlands.

**The High Council:** The Imperial Fae rulers of Ur Daoine, made up of four councilors and a High Councilor. Highly skilled magyk users.

**The Holy Father:** Another name for the Archmage. Casually, especially in His circle, those who serve him sometimes refer to him as the Holy Father.

**Ignautius:** The Sene Skal, leader and ruler of Elysium.

**The Infinium Sands:** A large desert to the southwest of Ur Daoine.

**Ireyna:** Unknown species. Follower of Sol Constantus. The Archmage's right hand. Dragonguard rider.

**Kairos:** Blacksmith and forge leader on Elysium. He's an Ascidian—a sea wyvern, who are mortal enemies of the Dragons.

**Keave:** A town in the Northlands.

**Keres:** Rebel leader. Nyall Drayven's third. Head of training recruits. Demis mage.

**Kydis:** The Crimson Queen, a great red Dragon and the rightful ruler of Elysium. Sacrificed herself to kill Achan Drayven. Deceased.

**Lir:** The Arkaydian God of the Sea. Legend says that Morrigyn chained him to the bottom of the Midheym Sea. Believers of Lir live in the Eastlands. Few pray to Lir openly.

**Macha:** One of the two swords of Morrigyn, gifted to Arkaydia over two thousand years ago and hidden deep in the caves, only to be found by Remus Ostia five centuries ago. The pair to Neiman.

**Magyka:** Non-Fae magykal beings including shifters and vampires.

**Mara:** Rebel leader. Human. General of the Northlands.

**Matricia:** Army strong-hold of the Westlands. Home to the Mercatus.

**The Mercatus:** The black market. An event for illegal animal trade that happens a few times each year.

**Midheym Sea:** The sea to the west of Ur Daoine.

**Mirelle Zenyth:** Demis with an affinity for water. Previously in a relationship with Dyana Arkos. Escaped to Elysium with the Dragons.

**The Morrigyn:** One form of the Mother. The Arkaydian Goddess of War and Wisdom. Formerly had the world's largest temple devoted to Her. Few pray to her anymore.

**The Mother:** One form of the Morrigyn. The Arkaydian Goddess of Creation. She has two sides to represent the duality of being. For all light, there is dark. The Mother is the light, the Morrigyn is the dark.

**Neiman:** One of the two swords of Morrigyn, gifted to Arkaydia over two thousand years ago and hidden deep in the caves, only to be found by Remus Ostia five centuries ago. The pair to Macha.

**Nyall Drayven:** Crown Prince of Ur Daoine. Also called the Heretic Prince due to his refusal to pray to Sol Constantus. Half-elf, half-fae.

**The North:** The Northern Territory of Ur Daoine. The biggest land wise but the least populated due to the Ulster Wald.

**Oryx:** A rare breed of warhorse with a swirling black horn, eyes like rubies, and sharp fangs for teeth. Oryx are 25% bigger than a normal warhorse and have twice the speed and endurance. Oryx hasn't been seen in the Infinium Sands, their hibernation grounds, for centuries.

**Panormus:** The Army strong-hold of the Northlands. Home to a large base.

**Pass of Brón Mór:** A narrow and dangerous pass between the mountains of the Ulster Wald. Between the falling rocks, unstable ground, and cliffsides, it was extremely difficult to make the pass alive.

**Puggō:** A slur for humans.

**Remus Ostia:** Dragon Beastkyn. Previously the head trainer of the Gauntlet. Deceased.

**The Rulka Empire:** The continent South of Ur Daoine. Relations are unstable.

**The Sene Skal:** The title of the ruler of Elysium.

**Shifters:** People with the ability to turn into animals.

**Siphon:** A higher level magyk user with the ability to drain the lifeforce from any living being as well as the earth itself and transfer it to themselves or to another source. They can literally siphon and move magyk. Siphons are almost always of Elvish descent.

**Soren:** Rebel leader. General of the Southlands.

**The Southlands:** The Southern district of Ur Daoine, which includes the Infinium Sands.

**Sol Constantus:** The national religion of Ur Daoine, of which they pray to the Father, Constantus. It wasn't illegal to pray to one of the other Gods but only allowed in private.

**Sud Azyl:** A port town in the Eastlands, and a large supplier of food for Ur Daoine.

**Taran:** Originally the horse belonging to Mrs. Hunton's husband, Taran has been cared for by Amalia for years and now belongs to her. Taran is a large white horse with gray dapples and a black mane and tail. *Deceased.*

**Twyn Fells:** The Northernmost town in Ur Daoine.

**Ulster Wald:** A sprawling forest that takes up most of the Northern territory.

**Ur Daoine:** A large country ruled by the Fae. Ur Daoine is divided into four territories; The North (composed mainly of the massive Ulster Wald forest), The Westlands, The Southlands (with the Infinium Sands), and the Eastlands.

**The Westlands:** The smallest territory of Ur Daoine to the West of the Abhaynn Gheal and South of the Ulster Wald.

**Weaving:** A term used by some to describe magyk castings. Weavers use a combination of incantations and hand movement to pull visible magyk from the air. It's one of the few types of magyks that are always visible, outside of shifters.

**Windweed:** Dried bark from a particular type of tree in the Ulster Wald. When chewed, the bark produces a light sedative affect.

**Wytch:** Humans, fabled to have Fae-like powers.

# THANK YOU

I like to begin all of my acknowledgements with the animals who have changed my life. **Boomer, Luca, Flynn, Beau, Blue, Xena, Stanley, Tosh, Artemis, Sophie, Kid, Evie, Carmen, Jinx, Lady...** I could go on. I feel endlessly lucky to have met so many animals that have made resounding impacts on my life.

**Frankie;** thank you for being my best friend.

**Mom and Dad;** thank you for the endless support. I am so lucky that you are my parents; truly.

**Audrey and Katherine;** thank you for your constant support and love. You have given me the joy of feeling like I have siblings, which is such a gift for an only child. You both are so smart and so strong; thank you for pushing me to be a better person and make this world a better place for you.

The entire **Schaeffel, Wolski, and Garrett Clans;** thank you for making me feel like I'm not alone in this world.

To the friends who have become family; **Tiffany, Corrine, Becky (& DJ/Presley/Jackson/Jinx), Lyss, Beth, Rachel, Marilu, Lindsay, Reina, Jess, and Carley**. I love you all so much. It is your friendship and love that inspires me the most. Thank you for making long-distance friendship possible. Distance and time will never push us apart. I am so lucky to have you all in my life.

My writing group, **The Trash Bandits;** Writing with you all is such a joy and it keeps me going when I feel like throwing in the towel.

To my amazing editor **YarnWyvern**; infinite thanks and gratitude for your friendship, mentorship, and your keen eye. You improved this story so much, and I am so thankful.

To my **Alpha and Beta readers; Julia, Lindsay, Corrine, Becky, Maria Eugenia Gabi, Jasmine Alex.** Thank you for the honesty and thoughtfulness behind every opinion and answer. I am beyond grateful for all of you.

To my **Kickstarter backers;** You made me believe in myself, which is no easy feat. Thank you for taking a chance on me and showing me that my ideas are worthy. I'm still in shock at your generosity and am endlessly grateful. All of you have a permanent place at my table.

To the **University of Nevada, Reno, and the College of Liberal Arts;** You molded me into the person I am today. Liberal Arts degrees are incredible, and I hope to see more funding for Liberal Arts colleges in the future.

And you, dear reader. I would not be able to tell these stories if it weren't for your support. If you are reading this, I'm sending a big hug, because by doing so, you are making my dreams come true...and I'm just getting started.

**<u>REPUBLICA HELVETORUM</u>**
*gothic monster romance*
Here There Be Monsters
Here There Be Witches – *coming 2027*
There Are Monsters Beneath – *coming 2027/2028*

**<u>THE DRAGON QUEEN</u>**
*dark epic fantasy*
The Forgotten and The Feared
The Broken and The Brave
The Defiant and The Damned
TDQ3 – *coming 2027*

**<u>THE HOME FOR WAYWARD CREATURES</u>**
*paranormal romantic sci-fi*
Vol. 1
Vol. 2 – coming soon

**<u>SHORT STORIES & SERIALS</u>**
Rescue Me – *contemporary fiction*
FERN – *sci-fi horrormance*

EC Garrett is an Alaskan transplant now living in Kansas City, MO who writes fantasy/sci-fi speculative fiction. She received her Bachelor's Degree in English Literature with a focus in Early Modern and Medieval Literature and a minor in Medieval History from the University of Nevada, Reno in 2016.  ECG is currently attending the University of Missouri-Kansas City where she is working on her Masters in English literature. In her spare time, she's either reading or watching the latest fantasy releases, riding horses at the barn, spending time with her family, or playing with her very cute but extremely ornery dachshund mix, Frankie.

***She dreams of becoming a dragon rider.***

Follow ECG on social media to get all the latest updates.

www.authorecgarrett.com

Instagram: @authorecgarrett

Tiktok: @author.ecgarrett

Threads: @authorecgarrett

Facebook: @authorecgarrett

# Midnight Pages

indie publishing house + bookish candles

handmade in kansas city, mo

www.ingramcontent.com/pod-product-compliance
Lightning Source LLC
Chambersburg PA
CBHW070358310726
48977CB00003B/489